CROW INVESTIGATIONS

BOOKS 4-6

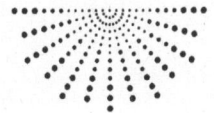

SARAH PAINTER

This is a work of fiction. Names, characters, organisations, places, events, and incidents are either products of the author's imagination or are used fictitiously. Any resemblance to actual persons, living or dead, or actual events, is purely coincidental.

The Pearl King Copyright © 2020 Sarah Painter

The Copper Heart Copyright © 2020 Sarah Painter

The Shadow Wing Copyright © 2021 Sarah Painter

All rights reserved.

No part of this book may be reproduced in any form or by any electronic or mechanical means, including information storage and retrieval systems, without written permission from the author, except for the use of brief quotations in a book review.

Published by Siskin Press Limited

ALSO BY SARAH PAINTER

The Language of Spells
The Secrets of Ghosts
The Garden of Magic

In The Light of What We See
Beneath The Water

The Lost Girls

The Crow Investigations Series
The Night Raven
The Silver Mark
The Fox's Curse
The Pearl King
The Copper Heart
The Shadow Wing
The Broken Cage
The Magpie Key

Crow Investigations (Omnibus Editions)
Books 1-3
Books 4-6

For my family

CHAPTER ONE

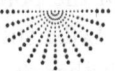

Lydia looked around the packed room of The Fork cafe. She did not know how to finish the story she had begun, or how the audience was taking the tale so far. Uncle Charlie had his arms crossed and his expression was unreadable. Lydia almost wished he would interrupt or start an argument, anything except the terrifying stillness of his face and body. She was glad he had his sleeves pulled down and that she couldn't see the tattoos which covered his forearms. They moved when he was angry or worried and Lydia wasn't sure whether that was something that everybody could see or whether it was another facet of her own abilities. She was so used to keeping those under wraps and secret from Uncle Charlie and the world, that it was just a habit now.

She hadn't slept in twenty-four hours and her eyes were gritty. She kept making eye contact as she spoke, though, and made sure her voice stayed strong and clear. She was a Crow. More than that, she was the daughter of Henry Crow, who was the rightful head of the Family. If she couldn't put on a good show, who knew what would happen next? She had been arrested, set up by the Fox Family, and if that didn't constitute a violation of the truce which had been in existence for eighty years, then Lydia didn't know what did.

It was all horrendously complicated, of course. She had been working for Paul Fox in good faith, developing a trust and a rapport that nobody in the room would believe or be pleased about. When she had been set-up for murder, one of Paul's brothers had given the police a false witness statement to bolster the case. Lydia still wasn't sure whether he was working alone, or whether she had been duped by Paul. All she knew was that she had to calm things down and make sure that nobody in the room went off on a revenge mission against another Family. Or the police.

She had to tell a good story and fast. 'In the story of the crow and the fox, the fox outsmarts the crow. He plays on her vanity and gets her to drop the food from her beak. I got close to a Fox,' Lydia looked around, daring them to judge her. 'You all know this. And I'm not ashamed. They are just people, good and bad to varying degrees like anybody else. The point is, though, that I have spent time with the Fox Family and I have learned something very important.' She paused for effect. 'Crows are smarter.' There were a few nods. Lydia ploughed on, putting every ounce of conviction she could muster into her voice. 'That means we've got to make the smart move now.'

'What's that, then?' Uncle John had his arms folded. He probably still saw Lydia as a tiny child and was anxious for the grown-ups to speak. Lydia fixed him with a stare and held it until he was forced to look away first. She wasn't afraid of silence. She wasn't afraid of her Family. She was afraid of being locked up in a tiny box, again, of hearing the cage door slam shut, but in this room, with these people, she felt strong.

. . .

An hour later, Lydia was beyond exhausted. She dragged herself up the stairs, feeling like every step was a mountain. Her mum and dad had said their goodbyes privately, waiting at the door leading to Lydia's flat while the crowd dispersed. Her mum had kissed her cheek and hugged her tightly, while her dad peered at her in confusion before giving her a formal handshake. 'Good to meet you,' he said, and the last of Lydia's emotional reserves drained away.

There was one last thing to do before she could pass out, though, and that was check on her flatmate. Jason was a deceased entity and her presence seemed to power him up, making him less ethereal and wispy and more able to make mugs of tea and, on occasion, save her life. He was sitting on the sofa in the room that Lydia used as both an office and a living room. Lydia could see the fabric of the sofa through Jason and she went and sat next to him. She was too tired to speak and was very grateful when Jason seemed to sense this and didn't ask her any questions. Perhaps he had been floating at the back of the crowd downstairs and had heard it all. Either way, he gave her a sympathetic grimace and put his hand on the chair next to Lydia, palm facing up. Lydia put her hand on top of his, feeling it become more solid by the second. It was exceedingly cold but Lydia squeezed it gently and let her head flop onto the back cushions of the sofa. She would just close her eyes for a moment. There was the smell of coffee and fried bacon, something which seemed to permeate the whole building from the cafe kitchen on the ground floor, and Jason's chilly hand was in hers. She was home.

The next day, Lydia got up early. She hoped that all had magically been sorted during the night but, of course, it had not. Lydia didn't live in a Disney movie and friendly woodland creatures hadn't appeared while she slept to sort out her problems.

Lydia made coffee and toast, slathering on a thick layer of butter and carrying it out to eat at her desk. Everything ostensibly was the same. The piles of paperwork she never got around to filing, her laptop and portable hard drive and the tangle of cables which seemed to breed in the night, and her Sherlock Holmes mug. But nothing felt the same. She didn't blame Fleet for doing his job, especially since he had tried to warn her, tried to give her time to do a runner, but those panicked few minutes before the arresting officers had arrived had thinned into something unreal. She couldn't hold onto the memory of Fleet's voice concerned and urging her to run, only the uniforms that followed. And the fact of his freedom while she had sat alone in a locked cell. Charlie had always warned her that they were from different worlds and now she couldn't stop replaying the moment when he had led her out of her flat, surrounded by his police crew. It made something shift inside. Something vital and delicate and very hard to replace.

As if sensing her thoughts, her phone buzzed with a text. It was Fleet.

Lydia finished her toast before reading it, and then went to make another two slices. She still felt empty inside, as if she would never be full again. One night in the slammer and she was utterly wrecked. She kept breaking out in shakes, remembering the feeling of being trapped. Caged.

Licking buttery crumbs from her fingers, she allowed herself to focus on Fleet's text.

Bridge? Midday? Please.

Lydia waited for the anger she expected. It didn't come. She pictured Fleet, his beautiful smile and warm eyes and waited for the usual mix of affection, longing, excitement and desire. That didn't come, either. Instead of being flooded by feel-good hormones or righteous fury, she felt blank. Nothing.

Hell Hawk. It would pass, she was almost sure, just a momentary lapse due to exhaustion and the after-effects of being arrested, but what was worrying was the feeling that she didn't want it to pass... She could feel her resentment solidifying. She knew that she was excellent at compartmentalising, keeping everything in her life separate. Some would argue she was a little too good at it. She could feel that mechanism kicking into gear, moving Fleet from the box marked 'significant other' to 'useful acquaintance'. That felt nice. Less painful.

IN BURGESS PARK Lydia approached the Bridge To Nowhere. She was early but Fleet was already there, waiting in the middle of the footbridge which spanned the grass. There had once been a canal here, back in the day, but it had been filled in years ago and the bridge was a souvenir. A reminder of how things used to be. Fleet wasn't in his work suit. He was wearing a smart long grey coat to protect against the cold but Lydia could see he had jeans and a jumper on underneath. She wondered if that had been a deliberate choice on his part, wanting to avoid reminding Lydia of his work persona. If so, it hadn't worked.

'All right?' she said, as he turned to greet her. He went to hug her and she took a step back.

He went still. 'You're angry.'

'Not with you,' Lydia said. But she felt the lie, bitter on her tongue.

'I'm so sorry,' Fleet said, his gazed fixed on her face, 'there wasn't anything I could do.'

'I know that,' Lydia said. 'And you warned me.'

He closed his eyes briefly. 'I can't believe-'

'Don't,' Lydia said, interrupting him. 'It's in the past.'

There was a pause and Lydia looked out across the park, unable to focus on Fleet for any length of time. She felt numb but knew it was a fragile protection, liable to crack at any moment. 'And I'm out now. It's done.' Lydia had accepted Charlie's offer to get her out of trouble which put her squarely in his debt. The price of his help had been entering the Crow Family business, something she had been at pains to avoid. To make matters worse, she had then been offered immediate release by a man she barely knew but suspected worked for the secret service. Desperate for freedom, she had shaken the man's hand. Now she owed him 'friendship', whatever that meant. A small part of her blamed Fleet for the mess, however unfair that was.

'I'm sorry I didn't come to see you,' Fleet's voice was quiet, earnest. 'I had to keep working the case.'

'My case.'

'Yes. Sorry. I had to keep working and I was worried it would make everything worse.'

'I understand,' Lydia said, although she didn't. Not entirely. There had been a sense of rejection, she realised, now. Fleet had always worked with her, always turned up and backed her up. In this case, she had felt abandoned. She hated how needy and vulnerable that realisation made her feel and consciously stuffed those feelings down as deeply as she could.

'What can I do to make it up to you?'

'There's nothing to make up,' Lydia said, forcing herself to look at Fleet. 'You had to do your job. I understand. I knew what I was getting myself into when I dated a copper.'

'That sounds horribly like past tense,' Fleet said, his eyes damp.

Lydia shrugged. 'We had a good run. Longer than I expected.'

'No.'

The pain was there, circling, but Lydia felt a calm, blankness at her centre. 'I think so. No hard feelings?'

'Stop it,' Fleet said, angry now. 'Stop talking like we've only just met. You can't just throw us away over this. We have a solid relationship, we can get through this. We just need to talk about it properly. I know you will need some time-'

'Honestly, I'm fine,' Lydia said.

'I'm not,' Fleet said. 'I'm not fine and I don't want us to be over.'

'I'm sorry,' Lydia said. 'But we are.'

CHAPTER TWO

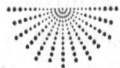

Lydia walked back to The Fork. Rain began to spit and she allowed herself a bleak smile. Of course it was raining. She had broken up with her boyfriend and now her hair was getting wet; she was a walking cliché. The feeble attempt at humour didn't help. She still felt wretched. That was the word. She knew she must be upset and in pain, but the dreadful numbness was still there. A blankness where feeling ought to be. Perhaps she was a sociopath?

A small girl was walking with an adult just in front of Lydia. The child stumbled on a piece of uneven pavement and fell. Her tear-streaked face was filled with pain and surprise, her mouth opening in a pitiful wail, and Lydia felt her own eyes fill in sympathy. Not a sociopath, then. Just a wreck.

Lydia knew she ought to reach out. To phone her best friend, Emma, or her mother, but she had never been good at opening up when she was in a bad way. She tended to forge on alone, and sort things out for herself. Independent, her mother said. Bloody stubborn, her Uncle Charlie called it.

Back at The Fork, she trailed up the stairs to her flat and

went straight to her bed to lie down. Just for a moment. She stretched out and counted the cracks on the ceiling, her mind carefully empty.

After a while she must have fallen asleep, because the next thing she knew, her left shoulder was freezing cold. She opened her eyes to see Jason next to her, his hand on her shoulder, shaking her gently.

'You were having a nightmare,' he said.

'Was I?' Lydia was still disorientated. A fragment of her dream was at the edge of her consciousness but when she examined it, it disappeared.

'You were shouting.' Jason looked worried. The familiar crease appeared between his eyebrows and Lydia wanted to reach out and smooth her finger over it, erasing it.

'I'm fine,' Lydia said, sitting up.

Jason moved away and while it was nice not to be flirting with frostbite in her shoulder, she missed the contact. He was looking at her warily. 'You look weird.'

'Charming.' Lydia scrubbed at her face with her hand, trying to wake herself up. Her eyes were gritty and filled with flakes of sleep and her cheeks were damp. She must have been crying in her sleep. Or drooling.

'Coffee? Toast?'

'I'm not hungry,' Lydia said. 'I ate half a loaf earlier. But thanks.'

Now Jason looked really concerned. 'What's happened? Are you having flashbacks?'

'Flashbacks? From what?'

'Being in jail?'

'No,' Lydia shook her head. 'Honestly, I'm fine.'

'You don't look fine,' Jason said. 'I'll make you a tea.'

'Coffee,' Lydia said.

'You need tea. With sugar. You don't look right.' He hesitated by the bedroom door. 'Is it from our trip?'

Lydia took a moment to realise what he was referring to.

So much had happened since Jason had hitched a ride in her body and they had gone to visit a ghost in the disused tunnels of the London Underground. It had been unsettling, and a physical challenge, but it paled in comparison to everything else. 'No,' she shook her head to add weight to her response. She took a breath, preparing to tell Jason about Fleet, but then realised that she couldn't say the words. Not yet.

LATER, after two mugs of disgustingly sweet tea, which she drank only to reassure Jason, Lydia sat at her desk, fully-dressed and ready for distraction. She couldn't bear to think about Fleet and, as if conjured into being by Jason's sweet concern, she kept having flashbacks to being trapped in the cell at the police station. Lydia's tried-and-tested approach for dealing with any sort of emotional upset was to throw herself wholeheartedly into something else. In the past this had resulted in a love affair with Paul Fox and a short-lived career as a pet-groomer. Now, it meant one thing - work. She pulled up her client list and scanned the case notes. She would dispense justice, she would ferret out truths, she would solve enigmas. And, if she buried herself with enough of them, perhaps she would begin to feel normal again.

Her files weren't very encouraging. There wasn't much in the way of enigmas, more a depressing list of infidelity cases, spousal uncertainty and background checks for companies doing due diligence on prospective employees. Those were the worst of all, in Lydia's opinion, entailing, as they did, a dull hour or two online and in databases and nothing else.

At that moment, Jason trailed in from the kitchen with a mug. 'No more tea,' Lydia said, as kindly as she could manage. 'Honestly, I'm fine.'

'It's coffee,' Jason said, putting it down on the desk. 'Are you sure you don't want anything else?'

'Actually,' Lydia looked up at him, a thought forming. 'How are you getting on with your laptop?'

Jason brightened. 'Great. I love it.'

'How do you feel about taking on a few clients? Just the background check ones. It's all computer work so it doesn't matter that you can't go out and about.'

'You'd trust me with that?' Jason's expression was radiant. It made Lydia feel bad that she was asking him for selfish reasons. He looked like she was giving him a gift.

'It's super-dull,' she warned him. 'Really routine. I'm passing them onto you because I hate doing them. You can say no.'

Jason made a grabby-hands gesture. 'Give them to me. And the log-ins so I can access the databases. Are they standard checks? Criminal, financial, and driving histories, right? Confirmation of identity?'

Lydia blinked. 'You've really been paying attention.'

Jason grinned. 'Yes, boss.'

LYDIA HAD SET up a proximity alarm for her flat. It was hidden underneath the carpet on the stairs so she would have warning when someone was approaching. Now she was wondering about getting her money back as someone was knocking on the glazed door to Crow Investigations without the alarm having been tripped.

She knew before she opened the door that it was the man who had sprung her from the police station. The one with the strange, unidentifiable power which made Lydia feel unwell.

'No parcel today?' This was in reference to the fact that he had been masquerading as a courier. In his line of work it was probably called 'deep cover'.

'Can we talk?'

Lydia stepped aside and gestured for him to enter. The hit off his power was as destabilising as always, but she was braced for it now, which helped. Plus, it was becoming familiar. She could separate its notes - the flash of canvas, whipping in the wind, the feel of rolling waves, and the glint of gold. It was a ship, she realised. That was probably why she had felt so sick the first few times she had encountered him. He made her seasick.

'You shouldn't be here,' Lydia said. 'If my Family see you...'

'I'll say I'm delivering something,' he said. 'But I take your point. I've got a safe house.'

'Of course you have,' Lydia said, trying not to be impressed.

'It's not *mine* mine,' he said, looking slightly abashed. 'It comes with the job.'

'And what is that exactly?'

He smiled, looking utterly assured again. 'I was thinking a regular check in would be best. Same time, same place. Then, if you don't make it, I know something has happened.'

'What if I'm just busy?'

'You won't be,' he said in a tone which spoke volumes.

'And what should I call you?' He had refused to give her his name in the police station, saying that whatever he said would have to be a lie and that he didn't want to lie to her. All very mysterious and quasi-noble, but not entirely practical.

'You choose,' he said.

'Living dangerously, there,' Lydia said. 'How do you feel about Cuddles? Or Mr PrettyBoy?'

He didn't rise to the bait, just smiled. 'You think I'm pretty? That's nice.'

'Mr Smith,' Lydia said. 'That's a good spook name. And I don't know you well enough for first names, anyway.'

'I hope that's going to change,' Mr Smith said.

He gave her an address in Vauxhall, not far from Kennington Park. Not a million miles away from the MI6 headquarters by Vauxhall Bridge, either. 'Close to your office, then,' she said. 'Handy for you. Or are you MI5?'

He looked blank, but that was likely the first thing you learned in spy school.

'Thursdays at eleven. Here's a key.'

'Seriously, though, what happens if I can't make it? Do I call you or-'

'No phones. No missing your appointments.'

'But my job,' Lydia began, appealing for him to be reasonable. 'I get caught up in stuff all the time. If I have to do surveillance for a client-'

'You'll manage,' he said. 'You are a resourceful woman.'

'Once a week is excessive,' Lydia tried another tack. 'Things just aren't that exciting around here. We'll have nothing to talk about.' She knew he wanted information on the Families and that she had agreed to give him some, that didn't mean she was going to make it easy.

'I'm sure we'll think of something,' he batted back and Lydia had the distinct impression that resistance was futile. Mr Smith wanted her to meet him every Thursday and that was exactly what was going to happen. At least until Lydia could figure out a way to get out of her obligation to him. On the plus side, she was as curious about him and his motives, as he was about her and her Family's. Part of her, the part which was always getting her into trouble, saw it as an opportunity.

'You had better be providing coffee and pastries.'

AFTER MR SMITH HAD GONE, Lydia poured herself a large whisky, figuring that she deserved it after that encounter. Every nerve was jangling and she didn't feel able to clear the mess off her desk, let alone face her client files or accounts. Passing on the outstanding background check work was a relief, but she still had a business to run.

As if eager to prove its worth, Lydia's proximity alarm beeped and, a moment later, there were footsteps on the landing. Lydia had a clear view from behind her desk to the front door, with its 'Crow Investigations' lettering and a tall shape appeared through the obscured glass.

She opened the door to a young Crow. Aiden was one of Lydia's many cousins. Or maybe nephews. She had never tried to keep track of her wide circle of relatives but supposed that would be something else she had to change, now. He looked older than she remembered, with a scruff of beard and wary eyes, which made her feel positively ancient. Lydia offered him a whisky, which he declined, and he took the client's seat by the desk, not the sofa, indicating that this wasn't a social visit.

Lydia sat down opposite and folded her hands. 'What can I do for you?'

Aiden was sitting forward on the chair, his spine straight. 'I want to know what you told the police.'

'I'm sorry?'

'You were arrested. And then you were let out.' Aiden paused, letting it grow as if he had asked a question.

'Yes?' Lydia said eventually. 'Your point?'

'What happened? Police don't just give up like that.'

'They do when they don't have a case,' Lydia said. 'And I didn't give them anything.'

Aiden shifted in his seat. 'That's not what people are saying. Everyone is nervous.'

'Well they shouldn't be. Everything is fine.' Lydia was trying to keep a lid on her sense of offence. The worst thing she could do would be to ramp up the tension in the room. She had to smooth the waters. Play nice. 'I already went over this,' she added, trying to sound calm.

'Yeah, but everyone knows you've been seeing a copper. You were with him, right? We've got a right to know what you've told him about the Family.'

Lydia was on her feet and around the desk before her mind caught up. She got her face up close to Aiden's and said, very quietly. 'Are you questioning my loyalty to my family? Think very carefully before you answer.'

Aiden swallowed. His eyes were flicking around, not meeting her stare. 'Course not.'

Lydia moved back a fraction. 'Good.'

'It's just... You've got to see... I mean, you can see why people are wondering. Crows don't get arrested. It just doesn't happen.'

'That's right,' Lydia said. 'They made a mistake. That's why I was out so quickly.'

'But-'

'Aiden,' Lydia said, leaning on the edge of her desk and crossing her arms. 'You've got two choices here. Either you decide that Lydia Crow, daughter of Henry Crow and endorsed by his brother, Charlie, head of the Family, is a trustworthy member of the Crows and you fly away now to tell everybody exactly that. Or-' Lydia waited a beat, watching Aiden squirm. 'Or you make an enemy.'

Aiden swallowed again, his Adam's apple bobbing.

'I'm waiting,' Lydia produced her coin and flipped it lazily in the air. She could make it spin slowly and with non-Family-members this was enough to put a little bit of 'push' behind whatever she was saying. She could make somebody answer a question truthfully or accede to her request. She didn't know if this was Crow magic or just their old reputation as fixers brought sharply into focus or a mix of the two, but she had never tried it on a fellow Crow before and was curious to see Aiden's reaction.

'I meant no offence,' Aiden said, his voice thin. 'I'm just passing on concerns. I said I would. And I have.' He was babbling, nerves overcoming the veneer of youthful cool that he had worn walking into Lydia's office.

'Pass on the good news,' Lydia said, smiling her own version of Charlie's shark smile. She had practised it in front of the mirror and was pretty proud of it. 'All is well in the Family. I am working closely with Charlie to ensure our continuing success and I am fully recovered after my wrongful arrest. We're all squared away with the other families and there is no call for retribution of any kind.'

'That's a separate issue,' Aiden said, rallying. He straightened in his seat. 'We can't let it stand-'

'I'm not letting anything stand,' Lydia cut across him. 'But the last thing we need right now is some idiot going off at the wrong person at the wrong time. Delicacy, strategy, negotiation.' She counted the words off on her fingers. 'Nobody is to make any kind of move against another Family. I thought I had already made that clear.'

Aiden's lips compressed into a thin line but he nodded.

'Good.' Lydia leaned back in her chair and tilted her head to indicate that the meeting was over. Another Charlie move.

She waited until Aiden was crossing from her office to the hall before adding. 'Spread the word.'

CHAPTER THREE

It was a cool morning and Lydia had Fleet's hoodie on over her unicorn-print pyjamas. The pyjamas had been a gift from her mum and they were fleecy and warm which, at this moment in time, trumped the fact that they were messing with her image. Jason was sitting at her desk in the main room, hunched over his laptop and tapping away on the keyboard. He had taken to the background checks like a duck to water and had powered through the backlog overnight. It was incredible. 'Fair warning,' he said without looking away from the screen. 'Your uncle is outside.'

'Outside?' Lydia had only just woken up and her synapses still weren't firing. 'Outside here?'

Jason nodded his head toward the roof terrace.

'How long?'

Jason shrugged, engrossed, again.

'Wait. How did he get in?' Lydia hadn't heard her alarm. More importantly, how had Charlie got into the flat and then out to the terrace? The connecting door was in Lydia's bedroom. She ran over her morning so far and realised that he must have strolled in while she was in the shower. Well that was creepy.

'Jason,' Lydia said, more sharply than she intended. She could taste the tang of Crow magic in the air, now, and was annoyed with herself for not picking up on it sooner.

He looked up. 'Sorry. Can't stop. I'm speaking to the head of mathematics at Harvard about code theory, he's only got twenty minutes before his next lecture,' he looked proud and incredulous. Like he had won the lottery. 'I bloody love the internet.'

Jason's face was glowing with pleasure and Lydia felt a rush of happiness for him, obliterating her irritation and fear and misery, just for a moment. It was nice to know that she was still capable. She held up her hands. 'I'll leave you two alone.'

Online contact, of course, was the ultimate equaliser. Nobody knew the colour of your skin or whether you were in a wheelchair. She looked at the ghost tapping away, his face lit by the blue light of the screen. Or whether you were even alive.

'You're a literal ghost in the machine,' she said out loud and, understandably, Jason ignored her.

After making a mug of coffee, more to warm her hands and to give her a little more time to gather her wits than any desire to drink it, she went out to the tiny roof terrace which looked out onto the narrow back street and found her uncle sitting and smoking. There was a folded newspaper on the small bistro table and an espresso cup which he must have brought up from the cafe downstairs.

'I see you've made yourself at home,' Lydia said. 'How did you get in?'

'I do own the place,' Charlie replied. He was wearing a mid-length black coat which looked like it was made of fine wool, maybe even cashmere, and had a grey scarf tucked around his neck. He looked perfectly comfortable while Lydia felt as if the cold had rushed straight through her clothes.

'I pay rent,' Lydia said, taking the seat opposite Charlie. The metal was icy against her legs and she twisted them together in an attempt to maintain body heat, hunching her shoulders inside her layers. 'I get that you'll have keys for emergencies, but you can't just let yourself in whenever you feel like it.'

'Not anymore.' Charlie clasped his hands.

'What?'

'I'm not taking rent payments from you. That's over.'

Lydia had started paying rent so that she wouldn't have to do jobs for Charlie. Now, of course, she had told him she would be 'all in'. That had been the deal in order for him to get her out of the police station where she had been held overnight. In the end, Mr Smith had offered her a deal, too, and she had taken it. The fear of being locked up for another second longer had been overwhelming. Lydia was ashamed of her terror and the way she had been unable to control it, but there was nothing she could do about that now. Except make damn sure she was never put in a cage.

'About that,' Lydia began, but Charlie held up a hand to stop her. He stood up and reached for the external light bolted onto the wall, fiddled for a moment, and then sat down again.

A second passed before Lydia realised what had just happened. 'You've got a camera out here?'

He shrugged. 'I told you I would keep you safe.'

'And you could keep an eye on me.'

Uncle Charlie nodded, utterly unembarrassed. 'Naturally.'

Lydia began to run through every conversation she had ever had on the terrace. She had spoken to Jason out here. What had Charlie seen? Her carrying out conversations with nobody? 'Listening, too?' She tried to make her voice casual, even while her whole body was vibrating with fury.

He shook his head slightly. 'That would be an invasion of privacy.'

Lydia widened her eyes, telegraphing disbelief.

'I don't lie to you.' He spread his hands. 'Lyds. You ask, I answer. It's not my fault if you never asked the question before.'

'I'm taking it down,' she said. 'While we're being honest.'

He shrugged and Lydia wondered how many other hidden surveillance devices he had hidden around the flat. 'I'm asking now. Do you have any other cameras or bugs in this flat?'

'No,' Charlie said. His eyes stayed fixed on hers and didn't flick away.

She was going to tear the place apart. Lydia took a moment to calm herself, to make sure that her voice wouldn't betray the tension in her body. She unclenched her jaw with an effort of will, helped by sheer stubbornness. Charlie wanted her rattled, on the back foot, and she didn't want to play his game. 'What did you want, anyway? I have to warn you, I'm not in the best of moods.'

'I heard,' Charlie said. 'Sorry to hear about your copper.'

'No, you're not,' Lydia said. She wasn't going to ask how he knew about her and Fleet. Wasn't going to give him the satisfaction.

'No,' he agreed. 'It's for the best.'

'So, what can I do for you this fine day?' She rubbed her hands together and blew on her fingers. Partly because she was freezing and partly to try to hurry Charlie along.

'I thought we should get started,' Charlie said. He leaned back in the chair, looking completely relaxed. 'Now you've joined the business, I thought I should bring you up to speed. I'm not saying you have to get involved practically,' he stressed the word. 'At least not immediately, but there's general background information you should know to start giving you a feel for the organisation.'

'Not a good idea,' Lydia said.

'How do you figure that?'

'You have to keep the business details away from me.'

Charlie tilted his head. 'What aren't you telling me?'

'Just that. Keeping me in the dark is for the good of the Family. I'm known to the police, now. Doesn't make sense to bring me into anything compromising. At least not right away.'

'I don't know if you remember our conversation. It was a few days ago. You were in Camberwell nick and I agreed to get you out. You told me you were 'in'. This doesn't feel a lot like 'in'. This feels a lot like evasion. Like going back on your word.'

Lydia flinched. She had been brought up outside the Family Business and protected from most of it but everybody knew that you didn't go back on your word with Charlie Crow. 'I know how it sounds,' she managed, skin prickling with a warning. 'I wasn't lying and I'm not going back on my word.'

Charlie was very still. His wool coat was hiding the tattoos on his forearms, but Lydia could imagine them writhing in displeasure. 'Explain,' he said, quietly.

'I'm in,' she said. 'But that means you have to listen to me and trust me when I tell you this is in the Family's best interests.'

'I'm going to need a little bit more than that,' Charlie said.

Lydia shook her head. 'Not now. But I would never do anything to hurt you or anybody in the Family. I'm trying to protect you.'

'Is this to do with your copper?' He said, after a long moment of silence.

'No,' Lydia said, honestly. Being in Mr Smith's pocket was nothing to do with Fleet.

He nodded. 'Right, then.'

'Are we okay?'

'For now,' Charlie said. Then he smiled.

It wasn't entirely reassuring.

AFTER CHARLIE HAD REFUSED to give her his spare key for the flat, refused to tell her how he had obtained the key after she had had the lock replaced when her new door was installed or how he had managed to get through her flat and onto her roof terrace without alerting her, just smiling in an enigmatic way and saying 'You have your secrets, Lyds, so I'm keeping mine', Lydia checked her bedroom for cameras and got dressed. She put on her standard work uniform. Jeans and a strappy black vest with a loose t-shirt layered over the top. She added a grey jumper and checked that the radiators were on before sitting at her desk and trying to get her head in the game.

Jason had moved over to the sofa and was instant messaging with his new maths friends like he had been born to it. The sound of his rapid tapping further underlined her lack of activity. Lydia got up and went through the flat, checking for cameras and bugs. She was as thorough as possible and she checked her own surveillance that she had installed on the outside doors downstairs.

Back at her desk, with the activity having removed most of the furious energy Charlie's visit had raised, Lydia finally felt ready to concentrate. She clicked on her client file folder and was instantly derailed by the buzzing of a phone call on her mobile.

'I need to see you tomorrow.'

Lydia hadn't intended to answer the phone to Paul Fox, but curiosity had got the better of her. In the story of the fox and the crow, it was pride, not curiosity, that was the crow's downfall. But either vice would do the trick, no doubt. She had to remain vigilant. She had thought he was on her side, that they were working together and that when he said he meant her no harm, he truly meant it. That was before. The fury and hurt came flying back, along with the taste of fur in the back of her throat.

'I don't think so,' Lydia said.

'I have something important to tell you,' Paul said. 'Face-to-face.'

'Whatever it is, you can tell me now. I'm hanging up in one minute, so you had better be quick.'

An exhalation. 'Little Bird, please.'

Paul Fox saying 'please'. Wonders would never cease. She opened her mouth to tell him to slink back to his den and die there quietly, when another thought occurred. She had her meeting with Mr Smith on Thursday. While she had no intention of telling spy-guy anything important about any of the Families, her first priority was protecting the Crows. If he really pushed her, having some little pieces of gold about the Fox Family might be handy in a tight spot. She didn't want to be a rat, but she would do whatever was necessary to protect her family. 'Fine,' she said. 'I'm not crossing the river for you, though. You have to come here.'

'Not Camberwell,' Paul said. 'Neutral ground. How about Potters Fields?'

The park was right next to the Thames, with a view of London Bridge. It was, technically, probably a bit closer to Whitechapel, but Paul would be the one crossing the river, so Lydia felt like it balanced out. She wondered if Uncle Charlie had to think like this all the time and whether he ever got tired of it. 'Okay,' she said. 'But it can't take long. I'm busy.'

'Tomorrow afternoon, then. I'll text you a time, I'm not sure when I'll-'

'I will text you a time,' Lydia corrected. 'Don't be late.'

CHAPTER FOUR

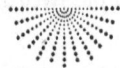

Lydia had gone to bed early, nursing a fresh bottle of whisky and the sweet quiet it afforded. She knew she wasn't coping brilliantly with her break up with Fleet, but she had no idea what coping well would even look like. She dragged herself out of bed in time for a shower and two strong coffees before it was time to leave for her appointment with Paul Fox.

The sky was clear blue, but there was an icy nip in the air. Autumn was over and winter had arrived so Lydia added a woolly scarf to her leather jacket and jeans and Dr Martens ensemble and stuffed a beanie hat into her pocket. She didn't pick up her bag, wanting to stay light on her feet if she had to run.

'I don't like it,' Jason said. He was in front of his computer, and hadn't moved from that position all night, as far as Lydia was aware. Could ghosts suffer from RSI? Lydia added it to the big list of things she didn't know.

'It'll be fine,' Lydia said, aware they had had this conversation before and that Jason had been proved right too many times for Lydia's liking.

Jason's attention was already being dragged back to his

screen. 'Am I interrupting something important?' She said, a tiny edge to her voice.

'Sorry,' Jason said, pulling his gaze back to her. 'I've done those checks you asked for. All the information is in the shared drive.'

'We have a shared drive?'

'Yes,' Jason said. 'And a password manager. Yours weren't secure enough.'

'How do you know my passwords?' Lydia said.

Jason raised an eyebrow. 'Please. Anyway, I've been practising a few things. Ways of getting into places we're not usually allowed. Databases. Staff records. Accounts.'

'That sounds useful,' Lydia said. 'And illegal.'

'Little bit,' Jason said cheerfully. 'But if we want to find out more about JRB, we're gonna need some moves. SkullFace310 has been telling me about rootkits, it's sick.'

'It's what? And who is SkullFace? That doesn't sound like the sort of person you should be chatting with,' Lydia stopped speaking, aware that she sounded like somebody's mother. Jason was a fully grown adult. Ghost. Whatever. And he appeared to have taught himself computer hacking in the time it took most people to work out how to do a mail merge. Besides, she had been investigating the shadowy organisation, JRB, all year without much success. 'Brilliant,' she finished. 'Carry on.'

Jason beamed at her and then turned back to the screen.

IT WAS mid-afternoon when Lydia arrived at Potters Fields. Too late for the lunchtime crowd and too early for the postwork rush. The cool morning had warmed, giving way to a bright winter's day. A couple of intrepid mothers with their assorted offspring were walking and chatting with takeaway coffees, while their small children ran in and out of the herbaceous borders shrieking. It wasn't a pleasant sound and Lydia could only imagine how much worse it would be in a confined space like a flat or coffee shop. How people did parenthood without losing their minds was beyond her. Perhaps it was a switch that was flipped when you got broody. A switch which turned down the dial on your hearing and up on your tolerance. Although, having said that, she had witnessed enough terrible parenting to believe the switch had to be faulty in many cases.

Tower Bridge looked especially fine against the blue sky and Lydia took a couple of deep breaths. London air, daylight, and a pleasant park to look at while she waited. She could still taste the panic she had felt when locked up in the cell at the police station, the sense of being trapped and having had her free will stripped away. The big sky was inviting and she felt as if she could rise up into it, the blue stretching all around, full of possibility.

The only thing that could spoil her afternoon was, at this moment, slinking into the park by the entrance nearest the Thames. Paul Fox looked gratifyingly tired, at least. There were lines of tension around his mouth and shadows under his eyes. Lydia had been sitting on a bench and she stood before he spotted her, wanting to be ready to move. Ready to run. Her hand slipped into her pocket and closed around her coin. She gripped it tightly and felt her spine straighten.

'Little Bird,' Paul said. He looked happy to see her and was radiating a relief which looked genuine. She didn't trust him, though. Not anymore. She had been so stupid to do so in the first place and that burned all the way down her throat and into her stomach.

She lifted her chin. 'Say your piece.'

'Can we walk?' Paul said, 'I've been travelling for the past twenty-four hours and need to stretch out.'

Lydia didn't answer, but they fell into step, walking along the path which led past a group of silver birches, their slender white trunks contrasting with some purple ground cover that Lydia couldn't name, and along to the more formal planting with low box hedges and a riot of autumnal reds and oranges, that was still clinging on even this late in the season. Global warming or possibly just the weird climate of the city.

'There has been a change,' Paul said. 'I know you don't trust me and won't believe anything I say, but I wanted you to hear it from me.'

'We're done,' Lydia said, 'you don't owe me anything and all I want is to keep far away from you and your siblings.'

'I understand,' Paul said, squinting at the sky. 'But we don't always get what we want and the word is that you are the new head of the Crow Family.'

'Not the head,' Lydia said. 'That's an exaggeration.'

'You have a significant role,' Paul said. 'You are Henry Crow's daughter.'

Lydia ignored that. She didn't know what she could say which wouldn't sound like she was protesting too much.

'You know we don't have a leader?' Paul continued.

'So you say,' Lydia said. 'But your dad-'

'I'm the new one.'

Lydia stopped walking. Paul took a couple of steps before he realised and then he stopped, too, and turned to face her.

'What do you mean?' There were bands around Lydia's chest stopping her from taking a proper breath.

'I told you I would find who was responsible for what happened to you. I told you I would make them pay.'

'I don't understand.'

'My father,' Paul said simply. 'He told the family that you needed to be protected from Maria Silver, as per my wishes, but that a little bit of rough-housing would be a good idea. To demonstrate, conclusively, that we were not allied.'

The little bit of rough-housing had been a moderate kicking, administered in broad daylight after Maria Silver had attempted to abduct Lydia. It had been the lesser of two evils, but still frightening and painful. Worse, though, had been the thought that Paul had actually been working to set her up on a murder charge.

As if reading her mind, Paul continued. 'And then there's the other matter. I had a frank conversation and he explained that setting you up for Marty's death had simply been an opportunity too good to miss.'

Lydia shook her head. 'You set me up.'

Paul closed his eyes briefly. When he opened them again and looked directly into her own, Lydia felt a bolt of electricity from her scalp to her toes. 'I did not.'

Lydia began walking again, needing the motion.

'This park has a bad reputation,' Paul said after a moment, his tone conversational.

Lydia gave him side-eye. She was still trying to process Paul as the head of the Fox Family, her mind spinning with what must have happened between him and Tristan for that to happen. Where was Tristan? He wouldn't take it lying down. She felt a spurt of fear for Paul's safety which was infuriating.

'People think it's called 'potter's field' because it was a pauper's graveyard, but it actually refers to potteries which used to work in the area. It's a funny phrase 'potter's field'. Do you know why it means common burial ground?'

'I have a feeling you're about to tell me.'

'It comes from the Aramaic meaning 'field of blood'.' Paul raised an eyebrow. 'I think that's why people don't like the name. But it's actually got a perfectly innocent history. Just people making bowls and mugs and all that. A case of mistaken identity.'

'I think people don't think about the name and if they do, they haven't the faintest idea of the Aramaic.'

Paul tutted. 'Don't underestimate human instinct. Right now, for example, the hairs on the back of your neck are raised. That's because I'm a Fox. I'm no threat to you, but your instincts keep warning you nonetheless.'

'Are you trying to tell me I can trust you or remind me that I shouldn't?' Lydia said. 'You need to work on your argument.'

Paul set off from the main path to the edge of the park and a line of lime trees which sheltered it from the buildings and road beyond. Lydia followed, wanting to hear what he had to say, despite everything, despite the warning she could feel in her skin.

'I'm not trying to do anything except be your friend,' Paul said, leaning his back against one of the tree trunks and looking down at Lydia. The light, filtered through the tree leaves made dappled patterns on the planes of his face. 'I'm being as honest as I know how and trusting that you will see the right path to take. You're clever, Little Bird, I know you'll work it out. I'm just saying that just because something has a bad name, doesn't mean it deserves it.'

Lydia tilted her head. 'Where is Tristan?'

'Japan.'

'Seriously,' Lydia said. 'Where is your father? You say he wanted to set me up or was happy to do so when the opportunity presented itself. Was it just his idea or did somebody suggest it?' Lydia didn't think it had been Paul, not in her heart, but it could have been one of the other Families or the Fox clan as a whole. She needed to know what she was up against and where the next attack was likely to spring from.

'My father is in Tokyo. At least, that is where I last saw him. He could be out in the countryside by now, or one of the other cities, Nagoya, perhaps, or Kyoto.'

'Does he even speak Japanese?' Lydia realised as soon as she spoke that this wasn't the most important question, but she was scrambling to keep her place in the conversation.

'You know, I forgot to ask. He'll manage. Foxes always do.'

'I don't understand what you are telling me.'

'My father put you in danger. His part in the violence against your person and the involvement of the Met in falsely accusing you was directly against my wishes. He knew this. I told him that I would not tolerate any act of aggression against you and I am a man of my word.' He flashed a lop-sided smile. 'Even if you don't believe that.'

'I still don't get Japan. You forced him to go on holiday?'

The trace of the smile vanished and Paul looked suddenly very dangerous. Lydia wanted to take a step back, but she forced herself not to move. It was getting easier with practice, this overriding of her fear with bravado. Maybe eventually she would bypass the fear altogether, become like Uncle Charlie. Or her dad.

'I banished him. Tristan Fox will not set foot in London for the rest of his natural life.'

'Banished?'

Paul smiled thinly. 'I gave him the choice. He could leave the country or he could die. He chose well.'

That made Lydia pause. 'You threatened to kill your own father?'

'I was pretty sure he would take the travel option, but yes.'

'He believed you, then?'

'I don't make threats unless I mean them. He knows me well enough.'

Lydia was still struggling to process this. 'You threatened Tristan Fox. And he was frightened enough to leave London.'

'Yes.'

She had always known that Paul was a powerful member of the Fox Family. The next in line after Tristan to take over, despite all his protestations about them not being a hierarchy or as organised as the other Families. But still. This was overwhelming. 'Why did you do that?'

'You know why, Little Bird.'

'I don't know what to say.'

'Just that you trust me.'

'I can't say that,' Lydia said. 'I'm sorry. I know this is a big gesture.'

Paul laughed and it was a harsh sound. 'I wouldn't call it a gesture. I would call it a stake in the ground. A marker. A line. Tristan's way is over. I'm head of the Family, now, and no harm will come to you.'

'I thought you didn't have a leader.'

'Things change,' Paul said.

'You're not wrong there,' Lydia replied. She blew out a breath of air. Paul was very close and Lydia could taste the tang of Fox and feel the physical pull he exerted. Despite everything, he still had a disturbing effect on her animal side. 'So, you sent him to Japan?'

'I took him to Tokyo,' Paul corrected. 'Twelve-hour flight each way. I just got back.'

Lydia frowned, but before she could ask the question, Paul answered it.

'You're wondering why I went on the plane? You don't just wave somebody off when you banish them. You have to root them somewhere new. Give them a new territory, sort of thing. Otherwise it's a death sentence.'

Lydia couldn't tell if Paul meant this metaphorically or literally. This was one of the many problems with the Families. Myth and hyperbole were part of the language, it was so difficult to know what was reality and what was a story from the old days.

'He's free to move wherever he likes within Japan, although Tokyo is his new den. He can travel, too, anywhere. Just not this island.'

'Britain?'

Paul nodded. 'Exactly. You never have to fear my father again.'

Lydia's automatic reaction was to say 'I never feared him in the first place', but Paul's revelations deserved respect and that meant not lying to his face. She nodded instead. 'That's... I don't know what to say.'

'Just say that you will consider an alliance between our Families.'

'I told you, I'm not the head of the Crows-'

'Still,' he shrugged. 'You are the person I want to hear it from.'

'Yes, then,' Lydia said. 'I will consider it.'

CHAPTER FIVE

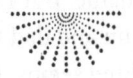

Lydia's landline rang while she was in the shower. It was eight forty-five which was a little early for a client. They often called at nine, the moment the day switched from personal to professional time. She could imagine them, waiting and watching the seconds tick by until they imagined her walking into her office or a receptionist donning a headset, ready to take their call. A lot of people rang first thing and Lydia understood it. The decision to contact a PI wasn't an easy one and was usually born from desperation. Once a person had made that leap, they were anxious to get on with it.

Whoever it was didn't leave a message which was, again, not unusual. When the same number called again, half an hour later, it was definitely not a run of the mill conversation.

'I need to speak to Lydia Crow.'

'Speaking,' Lydia said, opening a fresh notebook and picking up a pen.

'Are you a detective?'

'I am a licensed private investigator,' Lydia said. 'I offer a confidential service and the initial consultation is free.'

'You're a Crow, though? Or is that just a business name? Crow Investigations. I looked you up, but I wasn't sure-'

The voice on the line was deep and scratchy. He was speaking very quietly, too, which made it even harder to hear. Lydia pressed the phone tighter against her ear and covered her other. 'What? Sorry, can you say that again?'

'My name is not my name. But I can't remember my real one. I want to tell my mum and dad that I'm here, but I can't. Nothing is right. Everything seems different, it doesn't smell right. No, not smell. Not that exactly. But not right.' The voice got even lower. 'They might be imposters. I'm not sure if they're real.'

'Who are imposters?'

'Everyone. It just doesn't seem... Like things are right. I can't explain it. I need help to figure things out. I want to go home.'

A voice interrupted in the background and there was a muffled sound and then Lydia heard the man say, 'I asked if I could. They said I could.'

A moment later, the voice was back. 'My name's Ash. Not my real name, but the one they gave me. It'll do for now. You can find it out, you can help me remember it.'

'I'm sorry,' Lydia said. 'I don't understand what it is you need help with, can you-'

'You can reach me on this number or ask for ward fifteen at the Maudsley.'

'You're in hospital?'

'Just at the minute. That's why I need your help. I can't do this myself. We're allowed to use the computers in the room and I got your number from the world wide web. I found you on yell.com, it used to be a yellow book, I think, but they said you don't use those anymore. Just type it into the search bar and it comes back. I liked the thin pages, they felt nice when you leafed through them, like you were really getting something done. Do you remember the yellow book or is it something I made up?' Animation broke through his measured tone. 'They're being nice but I can't tell if they're real. They might not be real nurses and doctors. They might be them in disguise.'

Lydia didn't know what to say. She settled on a question. 'Who are you talking about? Are you afraid of someone?'

'Against the rules, but that's not the point. I think I'm back but nothing seems right. I might not be back at all.'

'I'm sorry, I'm not sure I can help you. If you're in hospital, the staff there will look after you. They are good people. You are safe.'

'I can pay. I'll be out of here soon enough, it's a seventy-two hour hold they said, and then I can go to the bank. I can pay you. I had a job at the newsagents. I was saving up all summer. It will still be there, the money, won't it?'

Lydia had her fair share of crank calls and time-wasters. This didn't feel like either, but it also didn't feel right. It sounded like a mental health issue. Plus, she was up to her neck in her own Family business and her investigation into JRB. 'I'm really sorry,' she said. 'I'm fully booked at the moment. And I don't think this is something an investigator should handle. If you decide you really want one, I can give you a number for another investigator. Really good guy, excellent work and very reliable.'

'No, no, no,' Ash said. Not distressed, just in a monotone. 'You're not listening. I need your help. This isn't normal. This isn't for just any one. This is for you. You're a Crow, you'll know what to do.'

'I'm sorry,' Lydia said, thoroughly rattled by that. 'I'm fully booked. I'm sorry I can't help.'

LYDIA THOUGHT that she had successfully put Charlie off for a few days at least, but he was the next phone call of the day, telling her to 'get herself downstairs pronto'.

'I'm working,' she tried, but Charlie was having none of it.

'Just a little outing with your uncle. I'll buy you lunch. You need feeding.'

It was smart to know when to choose your battles, so Lydia laced up her DMs and headed down to The Fork.

Seeing Uncle Charlie happy was a new experience for Lydia. Walking down Denmark Hill he seemed even taller than usual and when they got to their destination, an unpretentious pizzeria, he had barely stopped talking. 'African, Lebanese, Persian, fish and chips,' he was listing the restaurants as they passed. 'You can get anything here. And there's another pharmacy. And a Co-Op. It's a proper neighbourhood. A real place for people to live and thrive. You can get your clothes dry-cleaned, your haircut, visit the doc, place a bet, walk in the park, get a decent coffee.'

Lydia wanted to say 'you love Camberwell, I get it,' but there was no point poking the bear. She would let him enjoy his ebullience and bide her time. Eventually, he would tell her the real reason for their impromptu lunch.

Outside La Pietra Charlie paused. 'Quick stop,' he said, and led the way next door, into Aristotle's MiniMart. It was one of those shops which is packed from floor to ceiling and seems to sell everything from cigarettes and groceries to screwdrivers and haberdashery, plus an ever-changing stock of oddments which had clearly spent most of their lives on a slow cargo ship from China or Hong Kong. Small ceramic pigs painted with splotchy blue flowers, Japanese-style lucky cats, bumper packs of cocktail umbrellas and paper fans, and whatever was the latest craze amongst the tween crowd. Fidget spinners or loom bands or Pokémon cards.

'Mr Crow!' The man behind the counter was already half-way out to greet them. He was half Charlie's height and twice as wide, but he squeezed through the narrow aisles of the shop with practised grace. He was smiling and Lydia couldn't help but smile back.

'Tea? Lemonade?'

Charlie leaned down and hugged the man, clapping him on the back. 'We're not staying. Just wanted to introduce you to my niece, Lydia. Lydia, this is Ari.'

'Nice to meet you,' Lydia said. She knew that Charlie was teaching her something, but she hadn't worked out what, yet.

'Place looks great,' Charlie said, looking around. 'You can't even tell.'

'I know,' Ari was beaming. 'I can't thank you enough, Mr Crow-'

'Charlie, please,' Charlie said. 'And you don't have to thank me. That's what I'm here for.'

Ari ducked his head. 'Still,' he said.

Charlie nodded. He took Ari's hand in both of his for a moment and there was a moment of silent communication between them. Or benediction. Lydia spent the moment wondering how many £2.50 china pigs Ari had to sell in order to make the rent.

It was the same story at the restaurant. Wide smiles, manly hugs, and clasped hands. The chef came out to pay his respects to Charlie and the manager, a woman with enormous hoop earrings and perfect eyebrows, poured their table water herself. 'I will leave you in the capable hands of Mark,' the woman indicated a waiter who was hovering nervously to her left. It sounded like a question, not a statement, and Charlie nodded very slightly. 'I'm sure you are very busy.'

'The books,' the woman said, nervous energy pouring from her. 'You know how it is.'

'I do,' Charlie said. 'I have a guy, though. I could get him to swing by, help you out a bit.'

'No, no, no,' the woman said, taking a step back. 'I mean,

that's so kind. So kind. But I can manage them.' She gave a laugh which wasn't a laugh. 'I just need a few hours in my office and a strong coffee.'

Charlie nodded and the weird tension dissipated.

After Mark had given the menus and taken their drinks order, Lydia lowered her voice to ask: 'What was that about?'

Charlie hadn't opened his menu. 'You should have the sea bass. It's very good here. Or the Linguini.'

Lydia pointedly opened her menu and took her time perusing it. Annoyingly she did fancy the fish, but she chose a risotto instead, just to be contrary. She had already lost the battle to choose her own drink, as Charlie had ordered wine for them both.

He took a sip and nodded to Mark who was hovering. 'Run along, son.'

'The books,' Lydia prompted.

'You know we run a fund for the good of the community?'

Lydia nodded. She knew that if people needed money in Camberwell and they couldn't get it from the bank, they came to the Crow Family. Specifically Uncle Charlie. She also knew that every business, even those who hadn't been loaned their start-up money, owed an extra business tax. Some people might call it a protection racket and in the bad old days that might have been accurate, but now it was more like a non-optional Rotary Club. At least, that was Lydia's understanding. Her Dad had been light on the details of the business, having abdicated his position when she was born, choosing a life of safe normality in suburbia.

'Well, it's my responsibility is to make sure it's fair. It only works because everybody pays in their percentage. Everybody benefits, so everyone has to play their part.'

Lydia nodded to show she understood.

Charlie smiled as if she was endorsing the whole system.

'But sometimes I hear little whispers. Maybe this person is doing better than they are reporting. Maybe they are trying to keep their percentage amount as low as possible, so they are padding out their expenses, making it look like they're making less than they really are.'

'So you look at their books?'

'I don't,' Charlie said. 'I send someone.'

At that moment, Mark appeared with their meals. Lydia wasn't at all surprised when he put down two plates of sea bass. This entire day was a performance exercise. Charlie was setting out the new world order, one in which he said 'jump' and Lydia said 'how high?'.

'Really?' she said, indicating her plate.

'It's good for you,' Charlie said. 'Brain food.'

Lydia picked up her cutlery and began to separate fish from bone. 'What happens if you find out the whispers are true?'

Charlie stopped, a fork of sea bass halfway to his mouth. 'They don't do it again,' he said flatly.

CHAPTER SIX

It was a cold morning with the promise of rain as Lydia skirted Kennington Park. She had a coffee in a reusable takeaway cup, courtesy of Angel, and was wearing fingerless gloves and a gigantic scarf along with her usual leather jacket and jeans. It was late November and the shop windows were filled with decorations and every retailer was playing the Christmas Greatest Hits album. Lydia had retained a childlike love of Christmas but she didn't like to shout about it. It was unseemly for a hard-bitten private eye. She also knew that not everybody had the Crow Christmas memories. The burning log, candles filling the house for the special Christmas Eve dinner. If you went back far enough, Crows were Nordic and they still held onto the old Yul traditions. Light in the long darkness of winter was very important. That and strong alcohol.

The address was off Kennington Road, in a large red-brick Georgian terraced building with uniform rows of sash windows. It didn't have the feel of a residential building, more one which had long ago been subdivided into offices. There were plain blinds visible at some of the windows, no curtains, and Lydia glimpsed strip lighting. Letting herself in using the key, Lydia was not surprised to find herself in an anonymous entranceway with beige carpeted stairs leading up and a printed notice on the first door to her right which said 'Kennington Council Reception. Appointments Only.' To the best of Lydia's knowledge, there was no 'Kennington Council' as the area fell under the jurisdiction of Lambeth.

She took the stairs up and up again, arriving on the third floor and in front of an unmarked door with a Yale lock. Using the second key, she opened the door. Inside was a plainly furnished flat. Living room with a black leather sofa and matching armchair, kitchen-diner with a square beech-effect table and chairs which looked like they had been bought in IKEA ten years ago, and two bedrooms, both with twin beds. If it was a safe house, it would make sense that it would be set up to sleep the maximum number of people, Lydia supposed.

Having deliberately arrived an hour before her appointed time, Lydia spent the next forty minutes going over every inch of the flat. She looked in the drawers and cupboards, not really expecting to find clues to Mr Smith's employers, but knowing she had to try. Then she did a sweep of every light fitting, smoke alarm, plug-socket, and switch, looking for surveillance equipment. She didn't find anything. Of course, if Mr Smith was MI5 or MI6, the chances of them using the same level kit as Lydia has access to and would recognise, was slim, but Lydia felt more in control, anyway. She heard the key in the front door and straightened up from her position in the kitchen. She had just prised the baseboard off from under the built-in oven to check the space beneath the kitchen units, and she kicked it back into place before crossing the room to sit in one of the chairs and picking up her coffee. It was cold now, but she took a small sip as Mr Smith walked into the kitchen.

'You're early,' he said, his gaze roaming the room before settling back on Lydia.

'So are you,' Lydia put her coffee down but didn't move to stand up.

Mr Smith nodded and took the seat opposite her.

Lydia had braced herself for the effect of his strange signature and was pleased to find it definitely wasn't having as strong an effect as before. She was getting used to him. Or developing an immunity. A pleasant thought.

'I was hoping you could do me a favour?' Lydia said, having decided offence was the best defence. He might have dragged her to this meeting but she wasn't going to let him set the agenda.

His lips quirked into a smile. 'So much for the pleasantries.'

'This isn't social,' Lydia said. 'And you are putting me in danger by insisting on these meetings.'

'What danger?' He said forward. 'Have there been threats?'

Lydia glared at him. 'I was recently attacked by Maria Silver and her hired help, arrested on suspicion of murder after being set up by the Fox Family, and you have coerced me into passing on information, an activity which carries a health warning in my world. Trust is everything. This,' Lydia waved a hand. 'Could get me killed.'

Mr Smith smiled. 'I think you exaggerate. But please don't think I'm unaware of the sacrifice you are making.'

'Against my will,' Lydia said. 'You blackmailed me.'

'I offered a deal. You took it.'

Annoyingly, he wasn't wrong. Lydia glared at him, anyway. She had taken the deal to get out of the police cell. It didn't mean that she had to play nicely.

'If you follow simple rules, you will stay quite safe. I promise you. What favour?'

'I want to know what Alejandro Silver is up to.'

'What makes you think I know anything about this man? Other than the obvious. He runs Silver and Silver. He is a lawyer. He has extremely deep pockets.'

'The Silvers were looking after JRB. You told me you were working undercover for them both.'

'Oh, yes,' Mr Smith said. 'So I was.'

'You've stopped?' Lydia said. 'You're no longer pretending to be a courier?'

'I wasn't pretending,' Mr Smith said. 'I was an excellent courier.'

'You know what I mean.'

Mr Smith had a rucksack slung over one shoulder and he took it off and put it onto the table between them. 'You requested pastries,' he said, producing a bakery box from within. It was a little squashed, but the pastries inside were intact. Portuguese tarts, Lydia's favourite.

'Pasteis de Nata,' he said. 'Passionfruit and cocoa, blueberry, and classic.'

Lydia picked up the classic version. They were perfection already and didn't need any adornment or adulteration. She could smell the buttery pastry and vanilla custard, but she hesitated before taking a bite.

Mr Smith read her mind. 'Please. Why would I go to this much trouble to poison you? I could just pay Angel to slip something into your coffee.'

Lydia decided to ignore this disturbing idea. She took a large bite, savoured it, and then continued as if nothing had happened. 'I just want to keep an eye on what the Silver Family are up to and it's unwise for me to be seen to be keeping an eye. After the unpleasantness with Maria Silver, I need to let things settle down.'

'I'm more than happy to do you a favour, Lydia,' Mr Smith said. 'But it would be the third one. Are you sure you can pay your debt?'

'Third?'

He counted on his fingers. 'Getting you out of jail, reporting on the Silvers, and healing your wounds.'

'I didn't ask you for the last one. That doesn't count.'

He nodded. 'Quite right. My mistake.'

At least the man was going to be reasonable. Superficially, at any rate. She could tell he had been working closely with the Families as he seemed to know how to conduct himself. The modes of conversation were very familiar, which was alarmingly comforting. It was undoubtedly part of his training to emulate speech patterns to put his subject at ease. Knowing that didn't stop it being effective, though, which was irritating.

'Are you going to ask your questions, then?' Lydia said. 'Collect your debt.'

'There's no rush,' Mr Smith said. 'This is a long-term indenture, you will return your obligation in small pieces, once a week. I thought I had made that clear?'

Lydia finished the pastry instead of replying. She chased it down with some coffee, forgetting that it had gone cold, and stood up. 'Great. See you next time, then.'

Mr Smith sat down and selected a blueberry pastry. 'You've been very busy with Charlie Crow this week. How is your training going?'

'Training?'

'For the Family Business. Or has he started to test you in other ways?'

Lydia gritted her teeth. It went against everything she had ever known. You didn't reveal anything about your Family to an outsider, not even something innocuous. You never knew the importance of the smallest detail, so it was safest to just keep your mouth shut.

'I have accompanied my uncle on visits to local businesses, he likes to keep an eye on people in the community and helps them out when there is trouble.'

'How did it make you feel?'

'What relevance does that have?'

'Indulge me.'

Lydia disliked talking about her feelings almost as much as she hated talking about her Family, but at least it wasn't expressly forbidden. 'I felt proud.' Lydia had selected one of the feelings from the complicated mass. It wasn't a lie, but it wasn't the whole story. Seeing Charlie's reception first-hand had been impressive and unsettling. People were clearly grateful to him, but frightened, too.

Mr Smith smiled, as if guessing the words she was leaving out. He held his hand out to shake. 'Thank you, Lydia. Until next time.'

She clasped his hand and shook it briefly. She was braced for the power surge, but it still made her stumble. Material whipping in the wind, salt on her lips, and the creaking of wood. Gold flashing in the sun, blinding her. Lydia closed her eyes and breathed through her nose until the smell of the sea retreated and she no longer felt as if she was rocking.

'We're going to have so much fun.' Mr Smith looked positively gleeful and Lydia turned away, using all of her energy not to stagger as she made it to the door.

Hell Hawk.

LATER THAT DAY, Lydia was watching the husband of a client. It was her only remaining open case, aside from the background checks, not that she would admit as much to Charlie. She was grateful for the well-placed cafe and its generous window, but her backside was numb from the high stool she had been perched upon for longer than it was designed for. She understood the market and didn't begrudge the cafe their choice of uncomfortable seats which didn't encourage the punter to linger past their welcome, but it was hard on an honest P.I. going about her business.

Outside, the rain had slowed to a drizzle. Lydia had drained her coffee long ago and was just wondering whether to add a sandwich to her next refill, when she caught a familiar gleam. She gripped the table edge and watched Fleet's reflection in the window as he slipped onto the stool next to hers.

'Can we talk?'

'I'm working,' Lydia kept her gaze on the shop opposite. It was just for show, though. Purple elephants could have come tap-dancing out of the front door and she wouldn't have seen them. 'Speaking of, how did I not see you coming?'

'There's an entrance at the back.'

'Thought I would do a runner?'

'Something like that, maybe.'

She caught the flash of his smile in the glass and it was too much. The pain was circling above and she knew it would land at any moment. 'How did you find me?'

'You told me about this place,' Fleet jerked his chin across the road. 'Ongoing job, right?'

Well that was another reason not to be in a relationship. All that caring and sharing was unbecoming to a P.I. 'I'm not ready for this.'

'For what?'

'Friendly chit chat. It's too soon.'

'That's the thing,' Fleet said. 'I'm not either. I don't want to be your friend.'

Lydia pushed her cup away and pulled her jacket from where it was bundled up by the window. She wanted to say 'well, that's all that's on offer' but, suddenly, couldn't trust herself to speak. She slipped from the stool, turning away.

'Lyds,' Fleet's hand was on her arm and the heat of it was startling. There was the sound of rushing water in her ears.

'No,' Lydia said. Her feet were stuck, her entire body frozen in place. She had to leave, but she couldn't move.

'Look at me,' Fleet said. 'I messed up. I know that. I should have handled things differently. I don't know how... I don't know what, but I know I should have done something. But I'm on your side. I'm always on your side.'

'I can't do this,' Lydia managed. Fleet was on his feet, now, he was pulling her arm, pulling her towards him. For a moment she let herself go, let his arms go around her and her body rest against his. She closed her eyes and tilted her chin upward. It was sheer muscle memory, blind habit, but part of her wanted to do it anyway. It would be so easy to kiss him and for all the thinking to stop.

'What can I do to make it up to you?' His breath was on her face.

She opened her eyes and looked into his, so close and so beautiful. The thinking was loud and insistent. Lydia knew she couldn't trust herself for a moment longer. She moved back a step and his hands released her instantly. He would never try to restrain her against her will. Not unless it was part of his job.

With that thought, the bitterness was back, acrid in her mouth and mind. 'You can't,' she said flatly.

'I can leave my job.'

The words hung in the air between them. Lydia could see that he was serious and that shocked her into silence for a long moment. 'I'm not asking you to do that.'

'I know. But you feel like I chose my job, my position, over you.'

'Because you did.'

'It's not that clear cut and you know it.' Fleet reached for her hand, pulling her back to him. 'I will do it, though. I choose you.'

Lydia was shaking her head before she realised she was saying 'no'. 'You love your work. You can't give up your career for me. It's too much pressure, it would break us.'

'But you're saying we're broken, anyway, so–'

'So it's impossible. Some things can't be fixed. That's just how it is.' Lydia pulled her hand back and turned to leave. Her eyes were prickling with tears and she needed to get away. Blinking, she wrenched the front door open, but Fleet was behind her. 'You're working,' he said. 'I'll leave.'

She didn't trust herself to say anything else, so just nodded and returned to her position by the window. Which gave her the perfect view of DCI Fleet walking away.

CHAPTER SEVEN

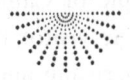

Another day, another cafe. On the Saturday, Lydia found herself sitting in the window of a Costa, waiting for Jayne Davies to leave her position behind the counter at 'Jayne's Floral Delights', the florist opposite. She was discovering that surveillance on behalf of somebody else was nowhere near as satisfying as when she was carrying out work for her own business. The past hour had dragged by, not helped by the fact that she kept half-expecting, half-hoping, Fleet to walk in and try to talk to her, again. She both yearned for it and dreaded it.

She dragged her attention back to the view of the street, people streaming past, intent on their phones. Charlie had indicated that Jayne's contribution to the local welfare fund was way down and he wanted to confirm her story about falling profits. All she needed was a moment alone with Dylan, Jayne Davies' step-son and Saturday helper. Although she hadn't seen anybody walk into the florist in the time she had been watching, which suggested they were telling the truth about hard times in the flower-selling business.

Lydia didn't feel good about doing this job, but she had

to show willing in some capacity. This was the tip of the iceberg when it came to the Family business, she knew, and it seemed like a small ask. Besides, it was this or letting him know more about her Crow powers and that was a can of worms she would like to leave closed tight for as long as humanly possible. Plus, the welfare fund was a genuinely good thing for the people of Camberwell, and Lydia was probably a more welcome visitor than Uncle Charlie. She took a hit from her Americano and pushed down the bad feelings. Her situation contained more rocks and hard places than ever before and working out a path between them was giving her a permanent tension headache. She took a flask from the inside pocket of her jacket and added a generous glug to the coffee. That was better.

Finally, Jayne Davies appeared out the front of the shop. She walked down the road at a purposeful pace and Lydia assumed she was going for her usual lunchtime routine - a browse in the Italian deli followed by a filled ciabatta at one of their tiny tables in the back. She watched as Jayne walked past the greengrocers with its inviting displays outside on the pavement. Lydia had gone into the place once, drawn in almost against her will by the Pearl mojo inside. She had avoided that stretch of pavement ever since and she wondered, now, whether Charlie had included the Pearls in his community programme.

Lydia stepped into the florist, past a huge display of funereal wreaths and up to the counter where a bored-looking boy-man was slouching over his phone. 'Dylan?' Lydia said, making it a question, even though she knew the answer.

'Yeah?' He dragged his eyes from his phone briefly, clocked that Lydia wasn't anybody he knew, and returned his gaze to the screen.

'How's business?' The place was empty on a Saturday lunchtime, so bets were on that it wasn't good, and that

Jayne hadn't been lying, but still. Good to be thorough. A good result here might get Charlie off her back for a few days. Maybe.

Dylan took his own sweet time before dragging his attention back to her. Lydia's fingers itched to produce her coin. She would enjoy seeing Dylan's eyes widen in fear as he realised who he was casually ignoring, but she also knew the punishment was too great for the crime. With great power comes great responsibility as Sun Tzu said. Or was it Spiderman?

'What?' He said eventually, a small frown creasing his dozy features. 'Do I know you?'

'No,' Lydia said, forcing a pretend smile. 'Just making conversation. I'm in the market for a wreath. Or a bunch of flowers. I haven't decided.'

'Example wreaths are over there,' Dylan indicated the display, 'or we can create a seasonal spray. What's the occasion?'

'Retirement,' Lydia said. 'And it's a rush job, I need it for Monday morning.'

Dylan shook his head. 'Not likely. We're slammed.'

Lydia looked around at the empty shop. 'Is that a fact?'

'Yeah,' Dylan turned his phone toward Lydia and she saw that he hadn't been chatting with friends or browsing Insta, as she had assumed, but he was looking at a customer management database. He only flashed the screen in her direction so Lydia didn't have time to take in any details. 'Online orders, innit?'

'Right,' Lydia said.

'We could get something for later in the week. Maybe Wednesday?'

'What?' Lydia had momentarily forgotten that she was meant to be in the market for flowers. 'No, that's okay. That'll be too late. I'll pick some up in the supermarket.'

Dylan was already engrossed in his phone again.

'Can I ask you something?'

Dylan looked up, eyes still blank. If his was the face of a criminal mastermind Lydia would be extremely surprised.

'Can you recommend a good accountant? I run my own business and mine is crap.'

'We use Weston's. They're okay, I think.'

Lydia knew the firm, they were on Camberwell Grove. She had run surveillance on one of their staff for a separate case a while back. A personal matter, though, nothing to do with the professionalism of the accountancy practice. She thanked Dylan, who had already dropped his chin, his face bathed in the blue light from his phone.

BACK AT HER FLAT, Lydia was feeling optimistic. She could do this. She could learn small parts of the Family Business, nothing too serious or very illegal. She could make nice with her Uncle Charlie. She could cope with him ordering her food and she could smile and look attentive. Maybe not all the time and she would have to drink plenty of whisky, but she would manage.

Sitting at her desk, Lydia unscrewed the brand-new bottle of whisky and poured until her Sherlock Holmes mug was more than half full. Then she tipped the bottle again until it was up to the rim. It was medicinal, she told herself. It was cold in the room, the high ceilings working against the single radiator which was clanking and hissing underneath the window. It had been cold in her bed, too. She missed Fleet and she hated that she missed him. She drank from her mug, letting the alcohol warm where her thoughts could not. She would survive this, she knew. She just had to keep her business going, focus on work, keep Mr Smith happy without letting anything important slip, and keep Charlie happy without losing her soul. Simple.

She looked up Jayne's Floral Delights and browsed the

website for a few minutes. It certainly offered online ordering and seemed slick enough to be successful. The photographs of the bouquets were modern and arty and looked entirely different to the style of floristry she had seen in the shop. It was no guarantee they were selling, of course, but it might mean Charlie would want further investigation. She made some notes for Charlie, trying not to think about the implications. What if she did confirm that they were doing good business? Would that mean that Jayne was lying to Charlie about her profits? And if so, what would the repercussions be? It couldn't be really bad, surely. This wasn't the Bad Old Days. The Crows were legit, now.

When she had been training in Aberdeen, her mentor had told her that she couldn't think too much about the knock-on effects of her investigations. 'We're paid to do a job and as long as we do it well, we get to sleep at night.' Lydia had never found it that simple, though. She was meddling in lives, she knew, unpicking knots that sometimes would be better left tangled.

Next, she tapped a message to her best friend, Emma, apologising for not being around. She cited work and said she hoped Emma was well. Part of Lydia longed to pitch up at her friend's house, to sit on her comfy sofa and unburden herself. But old habits die hard. Lydia was not the touchy-feely sharing type and never had been. She preferred distraction and pushing those squashy icky emotions down deep inside until they couldn't make her feel anything.

Lydia clicked around in her files, willing herself to get dragged into busy-ness. Anything to stop thoughts of Fleet and everything she had lost. She ought to take on some new clients, phone back some of the possibilities which had come in via email or had left telephone messages, but her mind kept jumping around the Families and the events of the last few months. After a few more minutes, she pushed her chair back from the desk and tilted her head back, shutting her eyes and looking inward. There was a tightness in her chest and she wanted, more than anything in this particular moment, to drain the whisky bottle and crawl back to bed. Instead, she made herself take several counted breaths and then turned her mind to the facts. Tristan Fox had seen an opportunity to set her up and had jumped at it. Was that just his dislike of her being friendly with Paul? An old-world concern about mixing their Family blood? Basic prejudice? Or had he been encouraged by somebody else? The old alliance between Crows and Silvers was on shaky ground, Maria Silver's actions had seen to that, and maybe somebody saw that as an opportunity. Break up alliances one by one, isolate each Family... But why? To weaken them? To break the truce? Lydia shivered at the thought.

Despite herself she felt a surge of gratitude toward Paul Fox. She might not be able to trust him, again, but he appeared to be trying to mend their shaky alliance and that had to count for something. She still couldn't quite believe he had sent Tristan to another continent, though. She allowed herself to imagine it was true, just for a moment, and the surge of relief was overwhelming. She hadn't realised how frightened she still was of Tristan and, by extension, Paul's brothers. She ought to include Paul in that group, but the part of her who had fallen for him all those years ago persisted and he was separate in her heart and mind. Which was a different kind of terror.

There was something else on her mind, something which had occurred to her while she had waited for Mr Smith. She went to see her flatmate to discuss the matter.

'How are you doing?' Lydia leaned on the door frame, watching Jason's hands fly over the laptop keyboard. He was completely absorbed and took a moment before he looked at her.

'I'm learning about encryption and rootkits.'

'You look happier,' Lydia said, choosing not to engage

with the tech-speak. The subject she wanted to discuss was a delicate one and she didn't know how best to raise it. Jason had been so content since she had passed on her old laptop, it felt cruel to drag things up.

Jason smiled. 'I am.'

She took a breath. 'I'm sorry I didn't find out about your last day. And about Amy. I told you I would look into it and I didn't get very far.'

'It's okay,' Jason said, his face clouding. 'I appreciate you trying.'

'Thing is,' Lydia crossed the carpet and sat on the bed next to Jason. 'I asked Fleet for help with it before, but I've got a new contact, now. One who works higher up in intelligence. He might be able to find something out for us. If you still want to know.'

Jason's outline was shimmering, very slightly, and Lydia put a hand on his forearm to still him.

'I don't know,' he said after a moment. 'I'm kind of scared. And we've found a way to get me out of the flat, now. With you.'

'That's kind of what I thought,' Lydia said. 'But I just wanted to check. I didn't want you to think I'd forgotten about it.'

He nodded his thanks. 'I'll let you know if I change my mind, but right now it's nice to live in the moment. I can feel a future for the first time since I died.' He laughed. 'That's a weird sentence.'

'It's a wonderful sentence,' Lydia said, meaning every word. 'I'm so happy you are happy.'

And it didn't hurt that he was doing all of her corporate background checks. Money was rolling into the business bank account like never before as she had always limited the number of cases she took like that as they made her want to cry with boredom. 'And I'm so glad we are working together,' she added. 'You are a brilliant partner.'

Jason's smile got even wider and she patted his arm before leaving him to it. Time was money, after all.

BACK IN HER OFFICE, Lydia stood next to the radiator for a moment trying to warm up. She eyed the whisky bottle which was, unaccountably, already half-empty. She hadn't yet eaten lunch but she didn't feel remotely buzzed. Her tolerance for alcohol had always been extremely high, but this was ridiculous. Perhaps it was something she should keep an eye on. Immediately, Lydia dismissed the thought. Bigger fish. Besides, if she never got drunk, she couldn't have a problem. That was the rule, right?

She went into her bedroom to get another pair of socks, hoping that warm feet would make the rest of her feel less icy. The door to the terrace had a thin curtain that was pulled half across. The slice of the outside world was unappealing. Sleety rain was coming down heavily and Lydia grimaced at the thought of leaving the flat for supplies. Since Charlie had revealed his surveillance, Lydia hadn't felt the same way about her outdoor space. It had been bad enough that a hit man had attempted to throw her off the roof, but now she had Charlie and his covert cameras. It didn't matter that she had removed it and checked over the terrace carefully. It felt sullied. Bloody Charlie.

Paul Fox was on her mind. Having admitted to herself that she wanted to believe him, even after everything that had happened, she knew she had to be smart. Animal charm had always gone a long way in the Paul and Lydia show and she had to make sure he wasn't playing her. First off, she could check his facts. She counted back the hours from their meeting and searched for flight times to Tokyo out of London. Having narrowed down the list of most-likely flights, she thought about asking Jason whether his hacker skills were up to accessing the airline's passenger information before realising there was a simpler solution. She made a call to Karen, her old boss in Aberdeen, the woman who had trained her as an investigator. Karen had been in business for over twenty years and had a vast network of useful contacts. For a reasonable fee she could find out most things, and Lydia knew she had helpful friends in every transport sector. You often had to know if someone was doing a flit, especially when a lot of your work involved infidelity, custody battles and acrimonious divorce. One of Lydia's proudest moments as a trainee had been when she had stopped a man from taking his three small children to Central America during his monthly contact-visit. She could still see the pure relief on the mother's face.

In less than an hour, Karen called her back. 'Paul and Tristan Fox were on the passenger manifest for flight 2102 from Heathrow to Tokyo on Tuesday. They both had the chicken.'

'What about the return journey? Did you manage to find that?'

'Of course,' Karen said. 'Just Paul, as you expected. He had the chicken again.'

'Thank you,' Lydia said. 'Invoice me.'

'Nae bother, hen,' Karen said. 'Anytime.'

LYDIA MET Charlie downstairs in The Fork to give her report on Jayne's Floral Delights. He was in his favourite seat and she slid onto the chair opposite. 'Shop was dead on Saturday.' Lydia didn't know what made her omit her online research, the fancy website with its high-end arrangements, but obeying her instincts was a reflex she hadn't broken. Besides, it might make Charlie think badly of the business without proper proof.

'All right,' Charlie said. 'Check it again next weekend, just to be sure.'

'I have clients I have to get back to, a business to run.'

Charlie sighed. 'Do I have to remind you of our agreement?'

'That Pearl fruit shop seems to be doing a good trade,' Lydia said, keen to change topic. 'As you would expect.'

'What about it?' Charlie sounded defensive.

'Just that it's odd. Right in the heart of Camberwell.'

'High streets are dying, hadn't you noticed? Some nice little business want to move into Camberwell, we're not going to block them.'

'We?'

Charlie frowned. 'Have you heard of the Camberwell Regeneration Plan? Miles Bunyan has been pushing for it.'

Lydia shook her head and said, 'No'.

'Part of the deal, which has subsidies and tax breaks to encourage development in this area, involves encouraging small businesses. I can't go around running people out of Camberwell for being born into a particular Family.'

Put like that and Lydia was shocked. 'That's not what I meant, I'm not trying to keep people out, I just wondered. I didn't know where we stood with the Pearls these days. As a Family, I mean.'

Charlie shrugged. 'Pearls have always been quiet. Useful for supplying you what you need from their nice little stalls and shops, but not too bright.'

'Don't be prejudiced,' Lydia said.

'I misspoke,' Charlie waved a hand. 'I meant not too powerful. They never bothered to conserve their energy, keep it close. They diluted their power all over London and beyond.'

'Now you definitely sound prejudiced. I heard in biology lessons that nature prefers a wide gene pool. Makes for strong babies. Just look at the Royal Family, we want to watch we don't end up with weak chins.'

'Biology,' Charlie smiled indulgently. 'I'm not talking about that. I'm talking about Family Power. Different rules.'

Lydia wanted to argue further, but she recognised that it was pointless. Charlie was set in his ways and it would take more than a lively debate to shift him out of them. A lot more.

CHAPTER EIGHT

A single magpie was sitting on the wall of Uncle Charlie's house. Lydia greeted it as she entered and it hopped along the path in front of her, as if leading the way. 'I've been here before, you know,' she told the bird and then felt faintly ridiculous when it flew away.

Charlie opened the door in a black tracksuit with a white towel around his neck. 'I didn't think you meant literal training,' Lydia said. 'I'm not dressed for the gym.' And will never set foot in one, she added silently.

'Come and get a coffee,' Charlie was striding back through his house, heading to the kitchen. The energy was flowing off him and Lydia realised something; he was excited. The knot in her stomach tightened. This was not going to be an easy conversation. She accepted a small cup of espresso and a bottle of cold water from the fridge. 'Caffeine and hydration, hot and cold, it's the best combination to really wake you up. And we need to be fully awake today.'

'Right,' Lydia wasn't fully listening as her brain was busy with trying to formulate the right words. 'I need to talk to you about something,' she managed.

'Fire away,' Charlie said. 'This way.'

'It's about the business side of things,' Lydia spoke to his back as she followed Charlie up the stairs. He was showing no signs of pausing for a chat and Lydia had to get this out. 'I'm not sure I'm a good fit.'

Charlie didn't pause on the stairs but he stopped at the top and turned around to face Lydia. He always towered over her, but with the height advantage of the stairs, he was like a mountain. Lydia curbed the urge to shade her eyes as she looked up. 'You said you were 'in'. You made a deal.'

'I'm still 'in', that's not the issue,' Lydia said. 'I just don't think I've got an aptitude for the business side. And I've got my own business to run. I think it's better left in your capable hands.'

Charlie's eyes narrowed. 'There's something else.'

'I think you should keep the details of the business side quiet. Don't involve me. It's safer if I don't know the nitty gritty.'

'What do you mean 'safer'?'

'I'm 'in'. I would never do anything to harm you or the Family or the business. I need you to trust me when I say it's better if I don't know certain things.' What she didn't know, she couldn't pass onto Mr Smith in a moment of weakness. Or through coercion. He was being very gentlemanly at the moment, but who knew how long that would last?

'Have you got back together with that copper? Is that the problem?'

'I'm not with Fleet.' Lydia swallowed past the sudden lump in her throat. 'That's not the point, anyway. I just think it makes sense. If I'm not running the business side, why tell me about it in detail? The fewer people know about our business the better, right? That includes me. Loose lips and all that.'

Charlie shook his head. 'This sounds a lot like you going back on your word. I want you in the business. Getting to grips with it at every level. Running the books, everything. I won't be around forever.'

'Crows will be lining up for the honour. Pick someone.'

'I already have,' Charlie said, but Lydia could tell he was weakening. Maybe she wasn't his first choice, after all. Maybe he had just wanted her on side as a sign of loyalty to his big brother or for the look of things. Succession had always been important and she was the rightful next in line. Maybe he just had to be seen to be following the line and would be grateful of a way out of working with her.

'I don't think it's where my skills lie,' Lydia said, truthfully enough.

'Drink up,' Charlie said. His voice was neutral and he turned away too quickly for Lydia to get a read on his expression. They were on the third floor of his house. Lydia expected a home office, maybe a spare bedroom, instead Charlie opened the door on a large empty space which spanned the entire footprint of the house. There was a single pillar about a third of the way across the space which must have been put in to replace a load-bearing wall when the rooms were knocked through. The floor was oak, the walls white and winter light streamed through the large windows which lined the front and back walls. If she didn't know Charlie better, she would have said it was a dance studio.

She walked into the middle and turned slowly, taking it in. This amount of unused space was probably one of the biggest luxuries in London. 'What do you do in here?' There was no gym equipment, no mirror, no plants, furniture, or storage. Nothing. She felt a breeze on her cheek and turned her head, looking for the source.

Charlie was watching her and she stopped. The hairs on the back of her neck lifted and she thought, for a second, that somebody was standing just out of her field of vision.

Someone in the corner of her eye. And then they were gone.

'This was where I trained your cousin.'

Maddie.

'She was making great progress until...' He stopped.

Until she had gone off the rails, almost killed a man, crashed a car, run away, hidden with Paul Fox's help. When Lydia had found her (at Charlie's request), Jason had had to save Lydia's life. Then Maddie had invited Lydia to join her in her mad rampaging world, before disappearing. She was the Night Raven in Lydia's mind. A spirit who visited her dreams and reminded her that the myths of her Family were alive and kicking.

'Why are you showing me this?'

'If you're not going to get involved in the Family Business, there are other ways you can demonstrate your loyalty. Other ways you can be useful.' Charlie tilted his head. 'We all have to play our part, Lyds, you know that.'

'I don't have any skills,' Lydia said. 'Except investigating. I'm quite good at that and getting better all the time. Crow Investigations is at your service.'

'Don't insult me,' Charlie said. 'You are Henry Crow's daughter. You have our coin. Show me.'

Lydia felt her coin appear at her fingertips and she folded it into her palm. Not fast enough to evade Charlie's gaze, though, and he nodded at her closed fist. 'You're the rightful heir, don't you want to find out what that means?'

For her whole life, Lydia's parents had told her to stay away from Uncle Charlie, to hide what she could do and that if he so much as sniffed opportunity, he would use her without thinking twice. Given that she felt essentially powerless, her only ability to sense the power in others, it had never seemed like much of an issue. Of course, nothing had seemed like an issue when she was growing up. The Crow Family stories were just that, stories. Her mum and dad had protected her well. Now she had to protect them. She thought fast and said: 'You know what I can do. You think I can refine that? Learn to read my senses better or have a bigger range? That could be overwhelming in a place like London. If I'm sensing people's Family power from further away, I'll get too many at once, they might all just blend together.'

Charlie shook his head. 'That's just the start. Maddie couldn't lift a paperclip when we began, she was able to drive a car after a while.'

'She was able to crash a car,' Lydia amended. 'And I'm not interested in driving with my mind.'

Charlie spread his hands in a gesture which told her he didn't really care what she was interested in and said: 'Why don't we just get started. Sooner we start, sooner we finish. And if you're not going to be hands-on with the business administration...'

'Fine.'

'Close your eyes.'

Lydia did as she was told. Instantly, she felt vulnerable. She was standing alone in the middle of a vast room. Charlie was near the wall by the door and he was her uncle. She was safe, she told herself, but her body didn't agree and felt her heart rate kick up.

'You can feel your coin in your hand. Hold your arm out straight and open your hand so that your coin is lying flat on your palm. You've flipped your coin a million times, but now you're going to float it. Just have it lift up from your palm and hold it in the air a few inches above your hand.'

Lydia obeyed the instruction. She could feel her coin, the slight weight of it and the edges against the shallow cup of her stretched palm. 'I don't see-'

'Concentrate,' Charlie said and his voice brooked no argument.

Lydia realised that she wasn't getting out of the room

anytime soon unless she showed willing. She scrunched up her forehead to show she was concentrating.

'Picture your coin floating six inches about your hand. Just steady in the air.'

Lydia didn't bother to picture anything, she just concentrated on looking like she was trying to do something. She tensed her muscles and scrunched her eyes. After what felt like a decent amount of 'effort' she put her arm down and opened her eyes. 'Sorry-' The words died. Her coin was hanging in mid-air, directly level with her eye line and an arm-span away. It wasn't spinning, just sitting in the air perfectly level as if held by an invisible shelf.

'Good,' Charlie said. His face was flushed and Lydia grabbed her coin, pocketing it. 'Next, we'll try a neutral object.'

'I'm tired,' Lydia said, trying to inject exhaustion into her voice. She let her body slump a little. 'I feel woozy. Like I'm going to faint.'

Charlie crossed the room quickly and put a concerned hand on her forehead. 'You do look a little pale,' he said. 'Don't worry, you'll get stronger with practice. It will get easier.'

All Lydia could think about was getting out of that room and away from Charlie's house. There was a fizzing in her body, like something was going to explode. She didn't think she was going to throw up, it didn't feel like nausea, but it wasn't beyond the realms of possibility.

'Good work, today,' Charlie was saying as he followed her from the room and back down the stairs. 'Get some rest. Get Angel to give you dinner. I've told her to feed you.'

Lydia managed to thank him and get out of the door. There were five magpies on the path and she nodded to acknowledge them, not trusting herself to speak.

Halfway home, Lydia couldn't keep speed-walking and she crouched down on the pavement to take a few breaths.

She hung her head low, trying to get oxygen back into her system and to stop the ringing in her ears. Her coin was safely back in her pocket, she knew that, but somehow it was in her hand at the same time. And, when she opened her eyes, it was also hanging in the air about six inches from her nose. That wasn't possible. That wasn't right. Her coin was part of her, like her thumb. It appeared when she wanted it and disappeared when she didn't. She could flip it in the air, make it spin a little more slowly. She had never made it hang in the air like that before, it had never occurred to her that such a thing was possible. And now there were three. But that wasn't right. There was only one, she knew that, as surely as she knew she had two feet. So why could she feel one in her palm and see one in front of her? How was that possible?

'No,' Lydia said, and the coin in her line of sight disappeared. She straightened up and checked her pocket. Nothing. Just one coin, again, heavy and reassuring in the centre of her palm.

CHAPTER NINE

Waking up alone, starfished across a cold bed in a room that felt as if Jason must be somewhere close, leaching the warmth from the air, Lydia's head pounded. It took her a moment to orientate herself. She had dreamed of Maddie but, unlike the run of nightmares she had experienced in the past, Maddie was just a distant figure, silently standing at the edge of her dream activities, not interacting with Lydia, not warning her. It was as if Maddie had given up.

Lydia focused on the almost-empty bottle of whisky which was on the nightstand. She wanted to drink it and, at the same time, registered that this was not a good impulse. The bottle was at her lips and the liquid burning down her throat before she thought any further. Slumped against her pillows, Lydia waited for her head to clear. Booze had always been good at sharpening her up, counter to what most people seemed to experience and, these days, it felt like the only way she could function. All of her senses were screaming that working for Charlie was a bad idea, that meeting Mr Smith was a bad idea, let alone the giant chasm of miserable need which had opened up inside since she had left Fleet. It was too much.

Enough. Lydia had finished her permitted ten-minute pity-party and now she forced herself up and into the shower. As she scrubbed at her scalp and lathered the shampoo, her mind wandered back over her dreams. She had been somewhere dark and filled with dense foliage. Trees creaked and an owl hooted. It had been a fairy tale landscape that she only half-remembered from childhood stories, filled with dangers she couldn't quite see. And Maddie. Somewhere in the dark, just off the twisting path. Watching Lydia fuck up from a safe distance.

JASON WAS IN THE KITCHEN, making tea. He eyed the empty whisky bottles on the counter and then glanced at Lydia.

'Don't say a word,' Lydia said. 'I'm not in the mood.'

Jason held up his hands. 'No judgement. You're missing Fleet. I get it. It's grief.'

'He's not dead,' Lydia said and then regretted it. 'Sorry.'

'That's all right,' Jason said. 'You're grieving for the loss of the relationship. There are five stages-'

'Feathers, don't tell me that,' Lydia tried to smile. 'I can do one. Maybe two stages of this. No more.'

'Seriously,' Jason said. 'If you need to talk…'

'I'm fine,' Lydia lied.

'Drowning your sorrows isn't a long-term solution.'

'Really, I'm fine,' Lydia lied again. 'Let's talk work. If I stay busy, I'll be even better. Honestly.'

'All right,' Jason held up his hands. 'Talk to me about your cases.'

Lydia felt her shoulders sag. 'Not much to say. I'm on my last cheater and I'm not in the mood to take any more. Charlie has got me running over town at his beck and call and now he's added training into the mix.'

'Training?'

'Don't be pleased, I can't bear it. Be on my side.'

'I am on your side. What training? Like kick-boxing? Circuits?'

Lydia picked up the tea that Jason had made and wrapped her hands around the mug, warming them. 'Crow power stuff.'

Jason's eyes widened. 'Holy shit.'

'Yep.'

Jason stretched past Lydia in the small space and picked up the kettle, refilling it at the sink and hitting the switch. Then he got a stack of bowls from the cupboard and began pouring cereal. He compulsively made breakfast food and hot drinks when he was thinking, or upset or concerned which meant, in practice, that they went through a lot of cornflakes and teabags. 'It's okay,' Lydia tried. She put a hand on his arm. 'Jason.'

When he looked at her, his eyes were shining. 'Aren't you a bit excited? To see what you will be able to do? To find out more?'

Jason had always been curious about Lydia's Crow power, but Lydia had been brought up to hide it, minimise it, stay normal and stay safe. It was a tough habit to shake. Plus, she had never felt powerful. Her Crow whammy amounted to sensing power in others which had only increased her sense of inadequacy. All of these magical Family members strolling around London and Lydia just able to know they were there. It wasn't exactly the stuff of legend.

'I mean, you power me up, right? What if you could access that ability to power yourself? Or do other things? You must have wondered about it.'

'Maybe,' Lydia said. 'I don't like being forced into it, though. I don't trust Charlie.' Saying the words out loud made everything seem worse. Lydia took a sip of her tea and swiped a bowl of cereal. To change the subject, she updated Jason on her surveillance of the florist. 'The website looks slick, but there's no way to know if it's actually doing good business.'

'Oh, there definitely is,' Jason said.

'What?'

'Hack into their site, look around and see if there's a way to access their customer management database. They probably use a separate secure payment system, but the emails with order confirmations should be pretty easy to get into. You want me to try?'

'Could you look without anybody knowing?'

'Yeah,' Jason said. 'I wouldn't change anything and I wouldn't do anything bad. Just look.'

It wasn't ethical, but if it put them in the clear with Charlie it would definitely be in Jayne Davies' best interests. And if it didn't put her in the clear? Well, Lydia would worry about that when it happened. One problem at a time. She gave Jason the go-ahead to try and he instantly abandoned the cereal in favour of his laptop. Small mercies.

Jason was sitting on the sofa, tapping away, and Lydia made some buttered toast. By the time she carried it through and joined Jason, he was scrolling through an email account. 'This is the email account which handles the customer orders,' he angled the laptop to show Lydia. 'There are lots.' He clicked into one message and Lydia scanned the order confirmation. It was for a hand-tied winter bouquet, delivered to an address in Camberwell, and the customer had apparently paid almost £200. 'Feathers, that must be quite the bouquet.'

Jason resumed scrolling through the messages while Lydia ate her toast.

'Looks like they took around twenty grand in orders last month. I will have to go further, take a look at their accounts to see profit and loss to get a net figure.'

'That's all right,' Lydia said. 'That's enough to let Charlie know they haven't been entirely honest with him.'

Before she could second guess herself, she rang Charlie and gave him an update. She had been commissioned to do a job, just like any other, and she had to see it through. Besides, if she didn't, he would find out another way. There was little that got past Charlie Crow and, for all Lydia knew, this job might have been a test of her loyalty. She was on thin ice in that area already and couldn't afford to fail it.

A COUPLE of days later and Lydia hadn't heard anything else from Charlie. She allowed herself to hope that he was getting bored of using her as his pet project. Perhaps her lack of enthusiasm for either the Crow Family business or the training had paid off and he was going to back off. Leave her to run her investigative firm. It wasn't likely, but a few minutes of hope with her morning whisky was the closest thing to happiness she had felt in a while.

The relaxation was short lived as it was Thursday again. Lydia kept a sharp lookout for a tail on her way to her meeting with Mr Smith. She didn't like having a pattern of behaviour and she especially didn't like having one she hadn't chosen. All it would take was for one suspicious Crow, Aiden perhaps, to catch wind of her connection to Mr Smith and all hell would break loose.

Lydia was trying to be just enough of a disappointment for Uncle Charlie to lose interest. She knew that clinging to the hope that everything could go back to the way it was before was probably not realistic, but she wasn't ready to let it go, just yet. If she worked hard enough at being ordinary, perhaps she could make it so. It was like childhood all over again.

That thought reminded her that she hadn't spoken to Emma for a few weeks. She pulled out her phone and pressed the call button. Emma had coped extremely well with the discovery that Lydia lived with a ghost and Lydia had intended, as always, to be a more consistent friend, but her job and her life conspired against her. And, of course, Emma had her own busy life. Two small children, a husband, family of her own, and a job. While Lydia no longer had to pretend to be normal around her best friend, which was a relief, it was also another thing that had changed, another new world order to navigate. After a few minutes of catching up on Emma's news, Emma asked how work was going for Lydia. 'Fine,' Lydia said, approaching the safe-house building. She walked past it, toward the park, doing a loop back to flush out anybody following.

'I know what that means,' Emma said. 'You sound stressed.'

Lydia rolled her shoulders. She was a Crow. Crows didn't feel stress. 'Nah, I'm all right. Just got a few things going on, you know how it is?'

'I know how you are,' Emma said. 'You don't have to pretend with me.'

'Honestly,' Lydia said. 'I'm not loving working with Charlie, but it's a necessary evil. It won't last forever.'

'You think?' Emma wasn't being unkind. She was honest and straightforward, just two of her excellent qualities.

'It better bloody not,' Lydia said lightly. 'Or we'll end up killing each other.'

'Don't even joke,' Emma said.

As ALWAYS, Lydia had arrived early for her meeting. She swept the flat each time, looking for surveillance equipment but also for anything that might have been left carelessly around, any clue as to the activities of Mr Smith's department. Lydia didn't expect to find anything, but it felt like a small measure of control. Besides, that was par for the course in investigative work. You sifted through a whole lot of nothing in return for the occasional win. It wasn't a profession for the impatient.

Mr Smith, for example, wouldn't have made a good P.I. Not based on his current demeanour. They had spent twenty minutes playing 'Mr Smith asks Lydia a question and Lydia side-steps it', when a tell-tale muscle began jumping in his smooth jawline.

'You don't seem to understand the terms of our deal.' Frustration finally broke through. 'I did you a favour and now you are returning it by giving me updates from your life.'

'You're not asking me about my life,' Lydia said. 'You're asking about my uncle and my father and they are both off limits.'

'You can't answer every question with a question of your own,' Mr Smith said. He was visibly trying to restrain himself and Lydia felt a click of understanding. He wasn't really angry. He was playing it as another gambit. Pretending to lose a little bit of control in order to make Lydia feel powerful. If she felt powerful, she might make a mistake. She couldn't help but admire the man. And maybe she could learn a technique or two. Free training from the spy guy.

'Are you MI5 or MI6? You never clarified.'

Mr Smith flashed a smile, all traces of frustration and tension instantly gone. 'I told you, that's not how this works.'

'We didn't really hammer out the details,' Lydia said. 'You never expressly forbade questions. Anyway, I'm just making conversation. If I've got to be here, we may as well be friendly.'

'You want to be friends?' His expression was suddenly serious. 'I would like that very much. But I don't think you mean it.'

'What if I did?' Lydia pushed the box of pastries across the table toward Mr Smith. 'You know I've lost my police connection. I need another one.'

'I'm not police.'

'Not exactly, but that doesn't make you useless.'

His lips twitched. 'Thanks. My department works with both security services, but isn't a formal part of either.'

Lydia suppressed a shiver. A department that was too secret to be a formal part of MI5 or MI6. That sounded dangerous. 'So, it would help me to help you if I knew the kind of thing you are interested in. What is your department investigating? Is it the organised crime angle or the weird stuff?'

'Both,' he said, picking up his cardboard coffee cup. 'Which you already know.'

Lydia nodded, trying to hide her discomfort. 'And do they know about you?'

A slight hesitation. 'No. They don't have your ability.'

'My ability?'

'You sense it, right? Power in others?'

It was Lydia's turn to hesitate.

'Don't bother denying it,' Mr Smith said. 'Can we keep the lies between us to a bare minimum. I know you're a Crow. Why quibble on the details.'

He was being disingenuous, details were everything. Still, Lydia made herself smile and made it look easy and relaxed. She forced the tension from her muscles. 'Fine, let's not quibble. What's the end game? What are you hoping to achieve?'

Mr Smith shrugged. 'I'm on a task force. It's very new and very quiet. The stated objective is information only. Observation. Like documentary makers, we're not supposed to interact or affect our subjects. That will change, but I don't know when. Higher ups probably don't even know. It gets political at the top.'

'And you're all right with that?'

'Information is power. And I have a personal interest.'

'Because of your-' Lydia waved her hand. 'Stuff. Have you always been able to heal people?'

'Yes.'

'Tell me about your first time.'

He shook his head. 'I don't think so. We're not friendly enough for that.'

'Okay, tell me about your department. What do they think is going on with the Families? Do they believe the stories?'

'They're not big on belief,' Mr Smith said. 'They're into facts. Science.'

It was interesting that he referred to his department as 'them'. Either he wasn't strongly affiliated, which might work to Lydia's advantage, or he was pretending not to be in order to ingratiate himself. 'I'm not going to be a lab rat,' Lydia said.

Mr Smith shook his head. 'They don't cart people away and do illegal tests. This isn't the seventies.'

'How do they do their science, then?'

'Volunteers.'

'I find that very hard to believe.'

'Aren't you curious? Don't you want to know if there is something in your DNA or a new enzyme or a part of your brain that you are using in a different way to normal people?'

'I am normal,' Lydia lied. 'I grew up in Beckenham. I had a guinea pig. I watched TV on a Saturday morning and had swimming lessons in the afternoon.'

He shook his head. 'You know what I mean.'

'I hope you're not looking for a new volunteer, because that's never going to happen.' She had no intention of becoming somebody's experiment.

Mr Smith held up his hands. 'I want to be your friend, that's all.'

'And for me to inform on the Families,' Lydia said baldly.

He winced delicately as if she had made a faux pas at a tea party. 'I wouldn't put it quite like that.'

'I would,' Lydia said. She stood up. 'And now I'm leaving.'

'You'll come round.'

'I will not,' Lydia said, as she grabbed her jacket from the back of the chair. She was at the door, grabbing the handle when Mr Smith spoke again. She didn't break stride, didn't look around, but the words landed nonetheless.

'You're as curious as I am.'

CHAPTER TEN

Lydia had gone to bed early. She felt tired in a way that wasn't related to exertion. Tired in her soul. She had dozed for an hour and, around midnight, woken stark awake and lay there, looking at the familiar shapes and shadows of her room, lit by the dim glow of streetlights seeping through her curtains. She heard Jason walk down the hall and assumed he was heading for his bedroom, but then he knocked on her door, lightly.

'Come in,' she said, sitting up. The air was cool and she pulled the duvet up, knowing it was about to get even colder.

'You need to see something,' Jason said, hurrying over with his laptop.

'You're glued to that thing,' Lydia said. 'Don't work too hard.'

'I love it,' Jason said, instinctively hugging the computer close. 'But look.' He sat on the bed next to Lydia and opened the screen. 'After I catalogued the order emails, I had a poke around. This is a business email, so not much personal stuff, but I found messages from the online bookkeeping site they use which led me into their accounts.'

'Led you into?' Lydia said, raising an eyebrow.

'Well,' Jason shrugged. 'I went looking. But in there I found a strange pattern of payments. Look.'

Lydia peered at the screen. It showed a list of incoming and outgoing transactions, labelled neatly for the end of year accounts. Lydia used a similar system for her own business. She was just about to ask Jason what was unusual when she saw it. A payment for three thousand pounds from JRB Inc two days ago.

'I couldn't find a corresponding order,' Jason said. 'And there's no payment reference, no invoice in the accounts or the sent folder of the email address.'

'What the hell has a florist in Camberwell got to do with JRB?'

'Yeah,' Jason said. 'I mean, first I thought that an order was made in person and somebody forgot to put all the details into the system. But it's odd they forgot. I mean, that's a lot of flowers.'

'Or the payment was for something else entirely.'

'Several somethings, actually,' Jason said. 'There are matching payments made on same day for the last four months. The first has a note in the 'reference' section, which says 'address withheld as per customer instruction', so I'm guessing it's a recurring payment for a regular order to an address that has been recorded somewhere else.'

'Who on earth are JRB sending three grand's worth of flowers to every month? And why wouldn't they want the address put into a database? That's pretty paranoid behaviour…' Lydia trailed off as she realised that they were, at that moment, mining the florist's private accounts for information. 'Can you get more on JRB from these transactions? Is there the digital equivalent of a paper trail?'

'I don't know,' Jason said. 'I will ask the collective and see what they advise.'

'The collective?' Lydia couldn't help but ask.

Jason was tapping away, but he nodded. 'They might need payment. Is that okay?'

'Sure,' Lydia said. 'We can pay them for their time. That's fair. I wonder what the going rate is for hacking. I guess it's too much to hope that they're all ghosts, too.'

WATCHING the florist on the following Saturday, Lydia observed the same lack of visible commerce. Again, she waited for Jayne to take her lunch break and paid Dylan a return visit. Once again, he was engrossed in his phone, and he didn't look up as she browsed the shop.

Stepping up to the counter, he dragged his gaze from the screen. Lydia didn't see any recognition in his eyes. 'Do you do deliveries?'

'Sure,' Dylan said. He pulled a hardback notebook from underneath the counter and flipped it open. The page was marked with a tatty ribbon and Lydia saw some scrawled writing and a few doodles of robots. 'What do you want?'

'I'm not sure, yet,' Lydia said. 'I just wanted to check the charges.'

'Free delivery with orders over fifty quid. Within London.'

'Okay,' Lydia nodded. She could see an open door behind Dylan which, she assumed led to the stock room and the place where the bouquets were made. If she knew more about flowers, she might be able to get him to go out there for a moment.

Dylan returned to his phone, saying. 'Retirement, right?'

'Sorry?'

'You were after a wreath. Last week? Sorry we couldn't help.'

'That's okay,' Lydia said. 'I got a bunch from M and S. This order is big, though. And I don't need it until next month.'

'How big?'

'I don't know, what can I get for five hundred?'

Dylan perked up. 'We've got lots of examples on our website. Browse the gallery there.'

'I want to know what they smell like, though. What have you got that smells good? Really strong.' Yep, flower-talk was not Lydia's strong-suit.

'Roses have a scent,' Dylan indicated a bunch of yellow flowers in a bucket to her left.

Lydia shook her head. 'I need something stronger.'

'Hang on,' Dylan said, 'I think we've got some Gardenia in the back.'

The moment he disappeared through the door, Lydia leaned over the counter to get a closer look at the notebook. Figures, messages to 'call Beth' and a prosaic 'to do' list. Lydia took out her phone and flipped the pages, photographing each one. She registered that there were occasional name and address with order numbers and, sometimes, prices, but she didn't try to read anything, just worked as quickly as she could.

She had only done six when she heard Dylan return and she had to flip the pages over and stand back.

Dylan was empty-handed. 'We don't have any out the back, but I'll make a note to get some in, if you want to come back?' He picked up a pen and hovered over the notebook. 'Can I take your name?'

'Shaw,' Lydia said. 'Rebecca Shaw.' She gave him the number of one of her burner phones and thanked him.

BACK AT HER DESK, Lydia went through the pictures. There weren't many addresses, especially given the amount of income Jason had found. Lydia's guess was that only telephone or in-person details were taken in this way and the rest were recorded by the online payment system used by the florist's website.

The addresses were all in affluent areas, which made sense until you stopped to wonder why folk would travel to Camberwell to order a bouquet of flowers when they lived on the other side of the river. Perhaps they were laundering money for JRB and part of the agreement involved sending flowers to JRB's friends? Assuming JRB had any. Could shell corporations have friends?

Lydia hated this type of investigation almost as much as she hated the background checks for corporations and recruitment agencies. It was so bloodless, so technical. Whether it was money laundering or tax evasion or insider trading, you could easily forget that there were real people suffering, somewhere along the line. And the people truly responsible were never the ones who got punished for it. At least, hardly ever.

Lydia didn't like to admit the other reason she was in a bad mood about it. The Crow Family had been involved in schemes not a million miles away from this kind of thing back in the day. Protection rackets, money laundering, and feathers-knew what else. It made her shudder. The Bad Old Days.

On the final page she had managed to capture, there was only one address. It was surrounded with flowers and vines, like someone had been doodling while on the phone, but had decided to take a break from the comical robot which appeared on the other pages. The address was near Hampstead Heath. Lydia recognised it because it had been in the news for being one of the most expensive addresses in London. What really made Lydia's heart race, though, was the name above the address. No first name or title, just the surname. Pearl.

Next to the address, almost obliterated by the doodled foliage was a date and the word 'paid'. Lydia went back to the florist's accounts and found the most recent payments for three grand. The date matched.

THE HOUSES in this part of London were not for ordinary mortals. The street that Lydia was driving down was known as billionaires' row and the address she had been given was on a gated street with a private security guard in a small wooden cabin. Lydia pretended to consult the clipboard she had brought with some mocked-up paperwork to give him the address and explained that she was making a delivery on behalf of Jayne's Floral Delights. She had hired a white van for the day and was hoping that the guard didn't ask to look in the back, as it was entirely empty.

'Where's the usual guy?'

'Sick bug,' Lydia said.

The road led to a row of detached mansions. Each had to be no more than five or ten years old, but they dripped with white columns, leaded windows, mullions and topiary and fountains, like miniature stately homes. They were all similar, clearly built by the same developer, but some were even larger than others. The address on Lydia's phone led her the biggest of all. It had a carriage driveway which swept past the house, and neatly clipped box hedges enclosing an ornamental garden. The heavy wooden gates at the entrance swung inwards as Lydia approached and she could see security cameras on the gateposts pointing both outward and in toward the house. Lydia couldn't see any signs of life, just large leaded windows reflecting the weak January light and an impressive doorway, flanked by white columns.

As she drove around the curving driveway, the front door opened and a small girl with tangled blonde hair adorned with a plastic tiara, muddy jeans, and a checked shirt which reached her knees hopped down the steps and stood, watching.

Lydia got out of the van, trying to smile in a non-threatening manner.

'You're not from the flower shop,' the girl said, tilting her head. Her voice was surprisingly mature. It was the voice of a small child, but the intonation was more adult. It was unsettling.

'I'm Lydia,' Lydia said. 'And I wanted a word with the head of the Pearl Family.'

'You're Lydia Crow,' the girl said. 'And you must mind your tone. Our king doesn't meet with any bird that flutters by.'

'I apologise,' Lydia said. 'May I meet with the king? I would very much like to make his acquaintance.'

'Not his,' the girl said. Baby lips pursed while she thought.

After a moment she turned and opened the door fully, leading Lydia into a huge square entrance hall. Open doorways led off in all directions and a staircase led up to an open gallery which ran across three sides of the hall. The floor was shiny marble, which Lydia imagined came as standard in these homes. What was almost certainly not standard, was the tree growing up through the middle of the room. It had a twisted trunk which looked like several trunks plaited together and the spreading branches reached the gallery railing above, twisting and twining with the wooden railing of the gallery.

Lydia followed the girl through an arched doorway which led to a set of stairs leading down. These stairs were less opulent than the main staircase, but the walls and thick carpet were immaculately clean and glowed with subtle mood lighting. It felt more like a five-star hotel than a private residence and there was the slightest scent of chlorine. 'There's a pool down here?'

The girl didn't answer.

The stairs turned a corner and, at the bottom, there was

a space with a console table, small armchair and two closed doors. One was plain oak or another hardwood, polished to a high shine to bring out the woodgrain, the other looked like nothing else in the house so far. It was lacquered black and embedded with hundreds of tiny pieces of mother-of-pearl, like the lid of a jewellery box. There was the faint thump of a bassline through the door, a sound which was suddenly amplified when the girl opened it.

Lydia stepped into a room which could only be described one way, even if that way seemed faintly ridiculous in the twenty-first century. It was a throne room and the person lounging on the throne was both beautiful and sharp like a piece of broken glass. Music pulsed from hidden speakers, coloured lights danced, and throughout the large space, bodies were moving rhythmically. It was a small nightclub underneath a house, the mirrored walls making it difficult to assess its size.

The girl tugged on Lydia's arm until she bent down to the girl's height. 'You may approach,' her companion whispered, her breath hot in Lydia's ear. 'But you may not linger. Make your point quickly.'

'The king,' Lydia whispered back. 'Are they a he or she or should I stick with 'they'?"

The child shot her look of confused offence. 'You say 'your majesty'.'

'Of course,' Lydia said, trying to look reassuringly contrite. The child was frowning, as if rethinking this introduction. Feeling as if she was taking part in a play and a hot sense of self-consciousness creeping up her neck, Lydia stepped forward toward the purple velvet armchair. It had an enormously tall back and shiny-black scrollwork on the frame, stylised and cartoonish like something out of a Disney film. The king wasn't looking at Lydia, they were watching the dancers with half-closed eyes. One hand, draped across the arm rest twirled in lazy circles at the wrist, as if conducting the revelry through a drug-haze.

Lydia didn't know if she should bow or clear her throat or say 'greetings, your majesty' but it was a moot point as, suddenly, she didn't feel as if she was able to do anything at all. A strange sense of being rooted to the spot, along with a sludgy feeling in her veins, like everything had just slowed down. She could hear her heartbeat in her ears, which seemed impossible given the loudness of the music, but there it was, thumping slowly, slower than she expected.

The king was looking at her, now. Out of the corner of their eyes, their head very slightly tilted in her direction. She had never seen any person so beautiful before, Lydia realised. Not in real life. It was overwhelming. Somebody was at her side. It wasn't the child who had led her into this place, it was an older girl. She could have been twelve or twenty, it was difficult to say with the elaborate face paint. A line of sparkling crystals curved along each cheekbone and she had a bright rainbow of eyeshadow and thick black eyelashes and liner. It ought to have looked ridiculous, but somehow (probably because she was young and very beautiful), it didn't. 'The king is too busy to see you today,' the girl said. 'You must follow me.'

Lydia wanted to say that the king didn't look all that busy, but she felt herself unrooted from the floor and had enough sense to follow the girl meekly, after bowing her head in what she hoped was a respectful manner in the direction of the throne.

The teenager led her back up the stairs to the entrance hall. It was shadowed and dark, the enormous tree mysterious and vaguely menacing in the darkness. Lydia blinked, wondering if her eyes were taking time to adjust, the flashing lights from downstairs were still exploding in her vision. Then she realised that the elaborate window coverings had been drawn against the daylight.

'Goodbye,' Lydia said to the teenager who was already walking away. She didn't reply. When Lydia turned back, wondering whether she could get away with a quick look around the rest of the house, she jumped in surprise. The small girl who, Lydia would have sworn couldn't have beaten her upstairs without being seen, was standing at the front door, twisting a strand of blonde hair around her fingers while she waited.

'You made me jump,' Lydia said, hoping that acknowledging it out loud would ease her discomfort. It didn't.

Back outside, Lydia was surprised to find that night had fallen. The street lights were lit and the temperature had dropped another couple of degrees. If pushed she would have said she had been in the house for twenty minutes, tops, but her phone told her it had been closer to two hours.

'You bored us today,' the little girl said. Her voice was far older than her face. Or perhaps that was the confidence in her tone. 'The king says that if you decide to visit again, you must bring two gifts. One to make up for today and one for the visit itself.'

Lydia didn't bother asking how the girl knew what the king thought, even though she hadn't seen them converse. Instead she tried to make her voice deferential, which didn't come naturally. 'What sort of gift?'

The girl shook her head. She inserted a finger into her mouth and tugged on the nail.

'What does the king like?'

The girl had already turned away, and was halfway through the open front door of the house.

'Ah, come on,' Lydia said. 'Just a little hint. If you tell me what you like, I could bring you a gift, too.'

The girl stopped. She turned slowly back to face Lydia. 'Lydia Crow is offering me a gift of her own free will?'

Lydia swallowed. What had she walked into? 'Yes,' she

said. She thought quickly. 'A gift that I choose, but given freely.'

The girl nodded. 'That is a very good offer and well put.' She smiled and Lydia felt herself lean forward, wanting to be closer. That was the Pearl she supposed. The girl could have lifted her foot and Lydia would have kissed it.

'I like colourful things. And glitter.' The girl turned back and moved a few more steps. At the door, just when Lydia thought she was going inside, she looked back over her shoulder. 'The king likes dead things.'

CHAPTER ELEVEN

Lydia tried to keep her pace even, not allow herself to speed up as she walked back to the van and got inside. She itched to move faster, to run, to fly. The sound of beating wings was deafening as she turned the key in the ignition. She forced herself to drive beneath the speed limit on the way home. She was too late to return the van for the daily rental rate and would have to deal with it the following morning. An irritation which barely registered above the pounding in her chest.

Lydia's heart rate didn't slow down until she was safely behind the locked door of her flat. Jason was in his customary position on the sofa, laptop open. He looked up when she walked in and closed the lid immediately. 'What happened? You were ages.'

Lydia sat next to Jason and told him about the Pearls' house, the strange girl and the king. She left her request until last. 'They are big on gifts and the king won't speak to me without a good one.'

'I take it you're not thinking of a bottle of wine,' Jason said. 'What about some money? You said Pearls like that.'

Lydia sat next to Jason on the sofa. 'You can say no,' she began.

'What?'

'The kid said that the king likes dead things.'

'Well that's not creepy at all.' Jason was trying to smile but it didn't reach his eyes.

Lydia touched his cold arm. 'You don't have to decide now, think about it. But you do fit the bill. And we know we can get you out of the flat, now.'

'You need to find out what the Pearls are up to,' Jason said, after a moment. 'You think they're working with JRB?'

'Maybe. Or they might know something about them. If they've been messed around by JRB, they might consider an alliance with us. That would be pretty handy right about now.'

'Since you pissed off the Silvers.'

'Yes,' Lydia said. 'There is that. But it's completely fine if you don't want to do it. It's a big ask.'

'You think an alliance with the Pearls would be a good idea? For the Crows? For you?' Jason wasn't vibrating but he was looking slightly-more-dead than usual. He was always pale, but his face had a grey-ish pallor. 'There could be safety in numbers.'

'I don't know,' Lydia leaned back, resting her head on the back of the sofa. 'It just feels like the ground is pretty shaky at the moment. Like one more little mistake could snap the truce into pieces. And then feathers-knows what would happen.'

'Maybe nothing,' Jason said, hopefully. 'Maybe it's just all stories. Stuff from history and none of it matters any more. Maybe the truce isn't needed anymore.'

Lydia looked at him. 'You believe that?'

'Sadly, no.' Jason leaned back next to Lydia, his body signalling defeat.

'Me neither.'

A couple of days later, Lydia was due at Charlie's house for another training session but she called to put it off. His demands in that area had been increasing and it was harder and harder to keep control. Part of Lydia was elated that she wasn't as powerless as she had always assumed, but most of her was frightened by it. She didn't like not knowing what was going to happen or what she might inadvertently reveal to Charlie. Every training session was an exhausting charade. 'I'm not feeling well.'

'Is that a fact?'

'Stomach issues,' Lydia said. 'You don't want the details. Trust me.'

'That's a shame.' Charlie managed to make the phrase sound like a threat. 'Feel better soon.'

The light on Lydia's answer machine was flashing and she listened to her messages. A prospective client left a number, but no details. She sounded angry and Lydia guessed it was another infidelity case. Not that it mattered. While juggling Charlie and Mr Smith, Lydia couldn't see how she could effectively do her job. A fact which made her furious. And thirsty. She looked at the whisky and then forced herself to make a mug of coffee, instead.

While she was in the kitchen, the phone rang and she let the machine pick it up.

The voice was agitated and the sentences disjointed. The caller was speaking very fast, but Lydia recognised it as the man who had called a couple of weeks earlier. She crossed back into her office, teaspoon in hand to listen. 'This is Ash. Uh, I've called before. Please call me back. I need help. They extended my hold and I know they mean well, but they can't help. They've got a certain perspective. A medical perspective. I need someone to find out what's really going on. I'm older than I...I'm not... I still don't have the right...' Then something unintelligible. 'I can pay. Call me back.'

Lydia looked at the blinking red light for a moment and

then went back to make her coffee. She felt sorry for the man, but she had enough problems.

CHAPTER TWELVE

Christmas Eve was always a big deal in the Crow Family and Henry had kept the traditions he had grown up with. Vikings always counted the new day as beginning when the sun went down on the old one, so Christmas officially began once darkness fell on Christmas Eve. That was when feasting and gift-opening and drinking began in earnest. Christmas Day was for visiting family but, in deference to her mother's wishes and for Lydia's general protection, they had ducked out of the Crow Family Christmas Day gathering, seeing Charlie on Boxing Day when he arrived in the suburbs, hungover and quiet, ready to watch sport with Henry while Lydia played with her new toys.

The insurance money for Lydia's stolen Volvo had come through and, with the money she had saved from Paul's apology-cash, she had just enough to replace the ancient banger with a new rust-bucket. What she hadn't had, though, was the time or energy to do so. Lydia booked an Uber and packed a wheelie case and rucksack with hastily wrapped gifts. Then she checked on Jason. He was reclining on a pile of pillows on his bed, laptop resting on his knees. 'Is it okay if I stay overnight?'

'Course,' Jason said easily. 'My charge seems to last a good twenty-four-hours these days.'

'Still chatting with your hacker pals? Will they go offline for Christmas?'

Jason glanced up, a single eyebrow raised to show her just how stupid a question that was.

'But it's Christmas!' Lydia said, playing on her ignorance. She could see how much Jason enjoyed having an area of expertise. One that was current and not a result of his status as a ghost. It was good for him and he seemed more alive than ever. 'Even SkullFace has to celebrate Christmas!'

Jason shook his head, with a mock-withering look.

'Your present is on my desk. It's not much.' A book of fiendish math and logic problems, set by GCHQ, and a large notebook with squared paper. Lydia had hesitated over the packs of Sharpies, but she didn't want to encourage Jason to start writing on the walls again.

'I haven't got you anything, I'm afraid.'

'You're doing all the background checks for me, that's gift enough.'

'Aren't you giving me a salary?' Jason asked, his face serious. He held it for a couple of seconds, long enough for sweat to break out on the back of Lydia's neck, before grinning. 'Gotcha.'

'Hilarious,' Lydia said. 'Have a good night.'

THE SUN WAS low in the sky as Lydia travelled to the suburbs where she had grown up. The Uber driver was playing Last Christmas on a loop and Lydia didn't even mind. Christmas Eve had come at a good time, she needed away from Camberwell and Charlie's constant presence. She felt hemmed in, by him and by Mr Smith and by the Families.

She had promised to be 'in' and she would keep her word, but that didn't mean she liked it. When her mum opened the door wearing a Santa hat, Lydia felt prickling in her eyes. She couldn't afford to be weak, but this was the one place she ought to be able to let her guard down.

As she followed her mum through to the living room, she vowed to open up about her feelings. Emma was always telling her that she wasn't alone and that she had to stop acting as if that was the case. 'Tea?' Her mum said over her shoulder. 'Say hello to Dad and then come and help me make it.'

Lydia stopped in the middle of the room. Henry Crow was hunched in his favourite chair. The snooker was on the television, but he wasn't looking at it, he was staring down at his lap. A line of drool poured from his slack lower lip. Lydia was stunned with the horror of it, but her mum swooped in with a fresh Kleenex, wiping up the dribble. There was a child's plastic sippy cup on the coffee table, next to the pillar candles and foliage her mother always put out in December.

She turned horrified eyes onto her mother, who was hovering, uncertainly. 'It's okay, darling. Let's make tea.' She scooped the cup off the table and said, in a loud and bright voice, 'Cup of tea, Henry?'

Her dad didn't respond.

In the small kitchen, Lydia could almost imagine everything was as it should be. It looked exactly the same as it always had. There was the blue vase in the window, the souvenir magnets on the fridge, the metal pan rest on the counter and the beige toaster with the faded dial which her parents had had since the early eighties and refused to replace even though it burned one side of the bread.

'Why didn't you tell me?' As soon as the words were out, Lydia knew why. Because she would have come to the house and her presence made her dad worse. Her power-up ability seemed to strengthen whatever was ailing her dad and his Alzheimer's-like symptoms got more intense whenever she was around.

'I didn't want to worry you,' her mum said, turning away to fill the kettle. 'You've had more than enough on your plate. And I don't suppose that's changed now.'

'I had to go in,' Lydia said switching subjects. The thing that had once seemed unthinkable had happened, but it paled into insignificance next to what was happening in this house, right now. 'I made a deal with Charlie when I was in jail. It seemed like the best option at the time. Now, I don't know...'

'I'm proud of you,' her mum said. Lydia was getting the milk from the fridge and she was glad they weren't looking straight at each other. She didn't have to see the conflict and pain in her mother's face, and could pretend that she was okay with her only daughter choosing to go all in with the Crow Family after she had given up her career and spent twenty-five years in the suburbs in order to keep her away from it.

'Don't let him push you around, though.'

Lydia knew she meant Uncle Charlie. 'I won't.' There was the sound of feathers fluttering in her ear and she forced herself not to flinch. 'What is wrong with Dad? Has he been to the doctor?'

'They say vascular dementia. Tiny strokes destroying his brain.'

Lydia sagged against the counter. 'Hell Hawk.'

Susan shrugged. 'I'm not convinced. I've asked for a second opinion, so we're just waiting on the appointment. I don't want them looking at his age and jumping to conclusions.'

Lydia wanted to say 'we both know what's wrong with him' but she wasn't sure whether her mum was ready to hear it. That Henry Crow was ill because he had been repressing his magic, his Crow nature, keeping it under wraps for the sake of his wife, who wanted to give their daughter a normal upbringing. 'When did it get this bad?' Her last coherent conversation with her dad had been when he had used a charm to sharpen his mind. A relic from Grandpa Crow. Had using it done this?

'He had a fit last week,' her mum said, dumping teabags into the food recycling. 'He's not been right since, but it's just a matter of time. He'll be better again, I'm sure of it.'

'Is there anything I can do?' The moment the words were out of her mouth, Lydia regretted them. She knew the best thing she could do was to stay away, her presence always seemed to make her dad worse.'

Her mum put a hand onto her arm and gave a gentle squeeze. 'I don't think so, darling. You spend as much time with him as you want.'

She didn't say 'while you can' but Lydia heard it loud and clear.

WAKING up on Christmas Day in her childhood bedroom, Lydia wanted to have a drink. It was still early, though, and she didn't know if her mum kept whisky in the house. She wanted to take the edge off the world so badly it made her hands shake.

Her mother was in the kitchen, wiping down already-spotless counters and stirring a pot of porridge on the stove. 'You want croissants? I've got some in the freezer I can put in? Or there's toast. I know you won't want any of this,' she indicated the pan of oaty gloop.

'Just a coffee, thanks,' Lydia kissed her mother on the cheek. 'How's Dad?'

'Still asleep,' she replied. 'He won't be up until after lunch, I'm afraid.'

'I have to go to Charlie's,' Lydia said. 'Sorry.'

'That's okay, thank you for coming.'

They were being weirdly formal with each other.

'Are you seeing Emma today? I've got gifts for her little ones.'

And there was the urge to cry, again. This normal world of gifts and her normal best friend and semi-detached houses, where the worst thing was the possibility of hateful porridge. There was a thumping noise from upstairs and her mother hurried up. Lydia stirred the oats. Not the worst thing. Not by a long shot.

LYDIA DROPPED off the gifts at Emma's house on her way back to Camberwell, walking the distance to Emma's house and booking another Uber to get to Charlie's. First on her list after the holiday had to be getting a car.

It was a family day and she didn't want to intrude, but the half an hour of watching Archie and Maisie hyperactively bouncing around the living room while Tom and Emma laughed with each other was the single most precious thing Lydia could imagine. Maisie was so enamoured with the gift she had opened moments before Lydia's arrival that Emma couldn't coax her into opening Lydia's gifts. 'I'm sorry,' Emma said.

'No worries,' Lydia said. 'It's nice that she's enjoying herself.'

When it was time to leave, she hugged Emma tightly and felt the power of friendship flow between them. It wasn't Crow magic, but it was real and solid.

Emma pulled back and looked into her eyes. 'You doing okay? Really?'

Lydia gave her a rare full smile. 'Today was lovely. Thank you.'

Emma accepted the side-step, possibly because Maisie had just come out of the living room and into the hallway.

She barrelled into Lydia's legs and wrapped her arms around her knees. 'Not go.'

Lydia couldn't kneel down with Maisie gripping her so she patted Maisie's curly head and promised a trip to the local soft play centre in the near future.

When she looked up, Emma had her eyebrow raised. 'You have to stick to that, you know. Maisie won't forget.'

'I know,' Lydia said, a touch defensively.

'Blimey,' Emma shook her head. 'You are full of Christmas spirit.

CHARLIE'S HOUSE had two topiary trees in enormous stone planters on either side of his front door. His nod to the season was that they were tastefully lit with white lights and inside the house was ablaze with white candles in pewter holders. He might have looked like a thug in a suit, but Charlie had taste.

Lydia hadn't seen this many Crows in one place since the meeting in The Fork and it was overwhelming. Feathers, claws, and the beating of wings, plus the occasional uncanny sense that she was soaring high above the city, the feeling of a warm thermal current buoying her up as the horizon tilted. If she was completely honest with herself, it was a rush. The way she imagined drugs would feel.

Her Aunt Daisy had been the one to open the door to Lydia. Her face was flushed and Lydia guessed that the alcohol had been flowing for several hours. After they exchanged season's greetings and a slightly stiff hug, Daisy led the way down the hall to the big kitchen diner. Happy chatter, party hats, people wearing tinsel and Christmas jumpers, Bing Crosby on the discreet audio system; everything was the same as no doubt every other house in the street. Except for the real candles flickering on the tree in defiance of the London fire prevention service's best advice and the life-size straw goat which Lydia knew would be waiting outside on the patio, ready to be lit when darkness fell.

'What would you like?' Daisy had led the way to the bar, a table covered in white linen and booze bottles of every kind.

'Whisky,' Lydia said, already reaching for the blessed amber liquid.

'Charlie's in the living room,' Daisy was saying as Lydia poured herself a full tumbler. 'And John's here, somewhere,' she looked around. Without warning she leaned in close, gripping Lydia's arm hard enough to hurt. 'Have you heard from her?'

Never mind Mr Yul Goat, you could have lit Daisy's breath. She shook her head. 'Sorry.'

Daisy's eyes narrowed. 'Don't lie to me.'

Lydia pulled away. 'I've got to pay my respects.'

'Yes.' Daisy said, her voice loud and a little slurred. 'Yes, you do.'

Lydia wove through the crowd, nodding and exchanging greetings as she went. She needed to be seen by as many as possible, be visible and smiling for a half an hour or so and then she could slip away. Go back to her flat and drink one of her Christmas presents with Jason and his hacker collective for company. She felt bad about side-stepping Daisy, for telling a half-truth, but she could hardly tell her the full version. That she saw Maddie in her dreams. That sometimes she felt she was hovering just to the left of her shoulder, but when she turned, she was nowhere to be seen. That sometimes, when she was walking down the street or sitting at the metal table on her roof terrace or conducting surveillance in her old Volvo, she felt eyes upon her and would have laid money that Maddie was somewhere nearby, watching.

In between the large kitchen diner, there was what had

been a dining room when the house had first been built and was now a kind of entertainment space. Low leather sofas, a wall of books, and a flat screen fixed above the fireplace. Aiden was slumped on one of the sofas, squished with a couple of similarly-aged, similarly-boneless-looking Crows. They all wore loose woolly hats and low-ride skinny jeans, and Lydia stood in front of them just long enough for them to notice her. 'Aiden,' she said, keeping her voice chilled. 'Good Yule.' After a moment, the youths struggled to their feet and offered handshakes and season's greetings.

In the living room, which had an impressive bay window shielded with both white blinds and wooden shutters, an enormous log was burning in the fireplace, kicking out more heat than was necessary with the press of bodies.

Charlie was standing in front of the fireplace, holding court to a circle of Crows. When he spotted Lydia, he threw his arms wide and shouted her name in a booming voice. Everybody stopped talking and looked, which was exactly the point. Charlie loved a bit of theatre and this was his moment. The prodigal child had returned to the fold and Charlie was going to make sure everybody knew where the credit should lie. It was also no mistake that she was now approaching him in his palace, like an acolyte hoping for benevolence. She walked into his embrace, the whisky she had just downed helping her to smile at the crowd once Charlie had released her from his hug and slung an arm around her shoulders. She looked around at the Crow Family and felt the smile begin to hurt the muscles of her face. It was going to be a long afternoon.

CHAPTER THIRTEEN

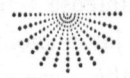

Lydia had downed another two tumblers and was ready to leave. She had paid her respects and, more importantly, had been seen to do so. 'I'm heading off,' Lydia said quietly to Charlie. 'Need an early night.'

'Nonsense,' Charlie said. 'You've got to stay for the goat.'

When Lydia had been small, she had dreamed of being at Charlie's famous Christmas party, of getting to watch the Yule goat, a life-size straw animal adorned with red ribbons, go up in flames. Now, standing in Charlie's house with her wider family all around and her mother's blessing to be there, she only wanted to run away. Fast.

'You'll stay,' Charlie was saying, now, certainty in his voice.

Then another cousin or great-uncle or somebody-removed, joined them, red-faced and grinning. 'Game's starting. You two in?'

Charlie shook his head and the man opened his mouth, maybe about to cajole or tease and then clearly thought better of it. He dipped his head at them both, suddenly deferent.

'What game?' Lydia said, feeling sorry for him.

'Poker. In the kitchen. Low stakes, just for fun.'

'Maybe,' she said. 'I'll be through in a minute.'

After the man had moved away, Charlie spoke mildly. 'I wouldn't. Not unless you're very good. Philip will rob you blind.'

Lydia had been thinking she could join a hand or two to shake Charlie and his intense tete-a-tete and then melt away. She wanted to tell Jason about her dad. Never having been much of a sharer, there was something about Jason's undead status which seemed to loosen her natural reticence. Some of the time, anyway. Maybe it was because he was a ghost, maybe it was because it was Christmas or maybe it was the sixth tumbler of whisky, but she felt like some caring-sharing time in her PJs.

'Besides,' Charlie said. 'We've got some business to attend to.'

'Today?' Lydia asked, surprised.

She followed Charlie through the packed house, hoping he didn't mean a bit of training. With everything swirling around inside, she felt like it wouldn't take much to bring up her lunch. He led the way out of the front door and onto the street. The cold was a slap in the face and Lydia felt her nausea clear. 'Where are we going?'

Charlie opened the passenger door and waited while she got inside before walking around and getting into the driving seat.

'Won't take long,' he said, flashing her his shark smile. 'Then it's goat-burning time.'

'Home-time for me,' Lydia said. 'You can drop me off. I told you, I'm knackered.'

Charlie ignored this and pulled out into the quiet street. Camberwell was subdued, but there were still plenty of people around. London didn't stop, not even for Christmas Day. As they approached the Thames, the roads got even busier, although there was definitely less crawling and waiting than usual.

Charlie chatted as he drove, talking about different people at the party and anecdotes from parties past. Lydia recognised it for what it was – a wall of conversation to stop her from asking questions. She settled into the leather seat and looked out of the window, biding her time.

A hotel carpark sign came into view and Charlie steered down into it. After they had parked, he led the way to a door marked 'reception' which opened into a stairwell and lift. He punched the button for the top floor and stood very still and quiet, arms crossed like a bouncer. Lydia sensed him putting on a cloak and she tensed herself, wondering what the hell was so important that Charlie would revert to work-mode in the middle of his Christmas. Having promised herself she wouldn't beg Charlie for information, reasoning that if he wanted her to know where they were going, he would have told her, she could feel her resolve weakening. Before it broke, the lift doors dinged and slid open and Lydia was hit by a wave of Silver.

It was a party. Lydia heard elegant background music – something classical. Men in black tie and women in jewel-coloured gowns and high heels were drinking from champagne flutes, standing in little groups and talking and laughing. Picture windows filled one wall, with the lights of the city twinkling and a view of the river.

Charlie's hand was on the small of her back, steering her forward, when every part of Lydia wanted to fly away. 'What in the name of…' she began.

'This way,' Charlie said. 'And play nicely.'

A few people nearest the lift doors looked at them curiously as they passed, but there had been too much drink taken to raise anything other than a few eyebrows. Lydia expected screaming and, perhaps, violence, glasses thrown and the cry of 'intruders!' but they moved through the throng with minimum fuss. Charlie seemed to know exactly where he was going and, before Lydia had managed to get her breathing under control or adjust to the sense-overwhelm of so many Silvers in one place, they were through the main room and out into a short corridor before the door to a hotel suite was opened for them by a woman in a hotel uniform. 'Would you like anything to drink?' The employee asked. Lydia saw that she wasn't in hotel uniform, after all. The clothes were too expensive, even for a nice gaff like this. The white blouse was silk and she was wearing spike heels with red soles under perfectly-cut narrow black trousers. And she was a Silver. Lydia hadn't realised immediately because everything tasted of the cool sharp metal.

'No thanks, love,' Charlie was saying. He walked over to the window and looked out. 'Nice view.'

Lydia was looking around. They were in a living room area twice the size of The Fork and when an inner door opened, she caught sight of a bedroom with a bed that looked like two king-size divans put together. A bed that could sleep a football team.

Alejandro Silver was wearing a suit which looked more casual than the sea of tuxedos in the main room, but still managed to look sharper and smarter than all of them put together. That was bespoke tailoring, Lydia assumed, with a good helping of excellent genetics. And natural power.

'Charlie,' Alejandro said, shaking his hand and barely glancing at Lydia. 'Thank you for coming.'

'Best to get this sorted,' Charlie said. 'You're looking well.'

'And you,' Alejandro said. 'I trust the holiday season has been good to you?'

Charlie nodded. 'And to you.' He nodded in the direction of the party. 'Celebrating a good year for the firm?'

'The firm and the Family,' Alejandro said. He spread his arms. 'We've been blessed.'

'Glad to hear it,' Charlie said. 'Now, the matter of the children.'

Alejandro nodded. The woman who had let them into the suite, went to another door and opened it, producing from within the unwelcome sight of Maria Silver. She was wearing a blood-red floor-length gown and a silver tiara that made her look like royalty.

'What's going on?' Lydia asked Charlie, who looked completely unperturbed. She felt her hands curl into fists, nails digging into palms. She forced herself to unclench. Produced her coin instead and held it there, secret and comforting.

'Maria, my dear,' Charlie stepped forward.

Maria's expression might have appeared neutral to a casual glance, but Lydia could see the suppressed fury in her eyes. She was feeling the same and a bolt of unexpected kinship shot through her. They were both here under duress, she realised, wayward children dragged to account by disappointed elders.

'Mr Crow,' Maria said, leaning in to air kiss Charlie on each side.

'Charlie,' Charlie said. 'I am such an old friend of your father.'

Maria's eyes half-closed and Lydia could see a muscle jumping in her cheek. There was a pained silence before Maria managed to say 'Charlie'.

Alejandro and Charlie nodded in unison. Satisfied.

'You don't have a drink,' Alejandro said. 'Were you offered one?'

It wasn't a serious question, Lydia could see. Alejandro knew the woman who had let them in, whoever she was, hadn't forgotten her duty. It was something else. A reminder that he was the host? That they were visitors in his world? What had it taken to bring Charlie Crow to the Silvers on Christmas day? Lydia screwing up, she supposed. Big time.

But she was the wronged party. She was the woman who had been set up by the police. Yes, she had put Maria in jail a few months earlier, but that had been different. Maria had been guilty of murder.

The murderess herself was staring at the floor like she wanted to die herself.

'I think we should get this sorted,' Charlie said. 'It's always good to see you, of course, but we need to get back.'

'Of course,' Alejandro said. 'Maria will be your point of contact from now on.' He didn't glance at his daughter as he spoke. It was like she wasn't there.

'You'll be busy with your parliamentary duties. Congratulations.'

Alejandro held up his hands, mock humble. 'Too soon to say, but I am daring to hope. Yes.'

Charlie snapped his fingers at Lydia and she wondered what he wanted her to do. Beg? Roll over? Fetch a newspaper?

'It will be a great honour to serve the city I love and its people,' Alejandro continued. He sounded like a politician, that was for sure. Duck to water.

'We wish you every success,' Charlie said. 'You have the support of the Crow Family.'

The Silvers had had people killed. Maria had attempted to kidnap Lydia to do Feathers-knew-what, but Lydia could see the logic in Charlie's move. The truce had to hold. It was good sense to make nice with the Silver Family and to keep the alliances strong. Especially if Alejandro was going to add political power to his arsenal. Still. It didn't mean she had to like it. Or that she hated Charlie for blindsiding her with this meeting, rather than talking to her about it first. He was treating her like a naughty child dragged in front of the grown-ups to apologise. Sod that.

She stepped forward to Maria, hand out. 'Congratulations on your new position as head of the firm. They are lucky to have you.'

Maria blinked. Then she touched Lydia's hand in the briefest, weakest handshake the world had ever seen.

The bolt of Silver travelled up Lydia's arm but she plastered on a smile and offered her hand to Alejandro next. 'To new beginnings.'

THE DRIVE back to Camberwell was quiet. Lydia could sense that Charlie wasn't finished, so she wasn't entirely surprised when he refused to drop her at The Fork. 'Day's not over, Lyds,' he said. 'Duty calls.'

She wasn't going to give him the satisfaction of complaining about the surprise meeting, wasn't going to act like the shamed teenager even if he was treating her that way. Head up, game face on and don't show them you care. Advice from Henry Crow when Lydia started secondary school. Lydia looked into her own reflection in the window, staring into her eyes until they felt like a stranger's. A stranger who didn't care about anything.

Back at Charlie's house, the party was continuing as if they hadn't been away. Lydia plastered on a festive smile and knocked back a whisky at her earliest opportunity. She had been given the perfect chance to tell Charlie about finding the Pearl King while they were alone in the car, but the Silver meeting had thrown her. Lydia had always known that Charlie had very rigid views on how things ought to be done, but she was beginning to realise exactly what that meant.

A red-faced couple stumbled past Lydia in the hall as she headed to the kitchen. She was just pouring another drink when a ripple of excitement went through the party. She heard somebody say 'it's time!' and the phrase was taken up, repeated.

Charlie appeared, carrying a bundle of twigs, bound into a torch. There were cheers and hoots, people stamping and clapping and pulling on outer layers. Charlie led the way out of the glass doors and into the garden. The burning of the straw yule goat was one of the oldest Crow traditions, brought over from Scandinavia when they first landed on the British shores. 'As you all know, it is a great honour to light the midwinter fire. We burn the old year to usher in the new and we cleanse our world of our enemies.'

More cheers, glasses raised and clinked together, applause. Lydia was near the back of the throng and, being on the short side, didn't have a good view.

'This year, I am pleased to announce that my niece, Henry Crow's very own Lydia, is to have that honour. Step forward, Lydia.'

The crowd parted and Lydia could see Charlie, the torch now lit and held aloft in front of him. The fire was bright in the darkness and she blinked, trying to clear her vision. The faces of her family were strangely lit, glowing from below as many people had picked up candles on their way out of the house. She walked through the crowd, which was now eerily quiet. Halfway to Charlie, she realised something important about the straw shape. It wasn't the usual Yule Goat. It was a creature with pointed ears and a long brush tail. Its face was comically elongated making it look both more ridiculous and menacing at once. A fox.

'Nobody messes with this family.' Charlie's voice carried clear and strong. 'And we will show no mercy to those that dare.'

He passed the torch to Lydia, the heat coming from it was fierce and she had to blink away sudden tears from the smoke. He nodded at her. 'Go on.'

Lydia knew what he was doing. A final bit of theatre for the Family. He was in control, he was the leader and he had brought Lydia in from the cold. Now she had to show the

Family where her loyalties lay by burning an effigy which represented Paul Fox and his Family. Show him and everybody else that she wasn't stepping out of line, that the old ways and the old alliances were holding firm and that she, Lydia Crow, was ready to follow them.

She was a Crow and Crows didn't flinch.

Hating Charlie in that moment, she stepped forward and thrust the torch into the body of the fox. It caught instantly, the fire ripping through the straw, consuming the body and the head of the creature almost immediately.

Lydia barely registered the whoops and cheers. She watched the blazing figure and tried not to feel as if her freedom was burning up along with it.

CHAPTER FOURTEEN

Once Lydia was finally released from Charlie's house, she walked home. She needed the air and movement to clear her head and to release some of the tension which had built up. Her thoughts chased each other, looping in circles with no resolution. Perhaps she should have told Charlie about her contact with the Pearls, her suspicions that they might be working with JRB. His little performance had put her out of the sharing mood, but it was more than that. He was clearly still all-in with the Silvers and that didn't sit right in Lydia's gut. She thought he was making a mistake.

Jason was watching The Princess Bride on his laptop, and there were several mugs lined up across Lydia's desk. 'Merry Christmas,' he said, hitting pause on the film.

'It's Boxing Day, officially,' Lydia said, flopping next to him on the sofa. 'Sorry I'm so late. Charlie was in a weird mood.'

'I forgot you weren't here,' Jason said, indicating the mugs. 'I was working.'

'Christmas, Jason,' Lydia said, mock-scolding him. 'All work and no play…'

He shrugged. 'It's not my favourite time of year.'

Lydia instantly felt awful. Of course it wasn't a fun day for the bereaved ghost. 'Sorry.'

'I like my book, thanks.'

Lydia accepted the change of subject. 'Shall we finish the film?' She went and got herself a drink and a blanket from her bedroom and curled up next to Jason to watch Westley and Buttercup and to try, very hard, not to think about Fleet.

A COUPLE OF DAYS LATER, and Lydia found herself making an odd decision. She didn't know if it was because Charlie had not-so-subtly forbidden fraternisation with the Fox Family and it had ignited her inner rebel, or whether she was just being diligent and thorough because it made sense to investigate who had been whispering in Tristan Fox's ear, suggesting that he set Lydia up for murder. Either way, she called the most recent mobile number she had for Paul Fox, the one he had used to call her, and was both disappointed and a little disgusted at her weakness when it was out of service.

It made sense that Paul would have ditched his phone, but it did mean that Lydia had to head over to the Foxes' den to find him. A thought that made her skin break out in goosepimples, but strengthened her resolve. She couldn't walk around jumping at Fox-shaped shadows. She couldn't do her job or live her life if she was afraid. So, she wouldn't be afraid. She produced her coin and made it spin in mid-air about six inches above her outstretched palm. Watching it was like a meditation and, within minutes, the fear had drained away. She could do this.

Still. There was no point being foolhardy. She might be willing to believe that Paul didn't want her dead, but that didn't account for the rest of his Family. She wrote a note and called her preferred bike courier, arranging for immediate pick-up. She met the courier at a Turkish cafe a couple of streets away, having given a false address as her office. She wasn't paranoid enough to believe that every courier in London was a front for the secret services, but there was no need to let everybody know her business. She had an account with the company under the business name 'Magpie Holdings'. Couriers were only human and the temptation might be too strong to take a peek at the correspondence of a P.I. Curiosity was a powerful motivator, after all, and there was always the chance of a little opportunist thievery.

The courier, who had no idea of Lydia's suspicious ruminations, removed her bike helmet before walking into the cafe, revealing highlighted blonde hair in beach-girl waves and a tan which must have come from a bottle, unless being a bike courier paid better than Lydia imagined. She took the sealed jiffy bag and Lydia signed with a fingertip squiggle on the proffered screen. 'Guaranteed within two hours, right?'

The courier nodded. 'Your receipt will be emailed.'

AN HOUR AND A HALF LATER, during which Lydia had read a book borrowed from the stack of Angel's cast offs, which she had taken to leaving on a free library shelf at the back of the cafe, and eaten a plate of crispy fried potato rosti and eggs, Lydia's phone rang with the number of the phone she had sent to Paul.

'Very cloak and dagger,' Paul said, approvingly. 'What are you wearing?'

'Excuse me?'

'I'm imagining a trench coat and a monocle. Maybe one of those old-fashioned hats. Trilby?'

'Sorry to disappoint you,' Lydia said.

'Never,' Paul's Fox charm was effective even at this

distance and Lydia concentrated on breathing evenly and telling her weak physical body not to respond to him. It wasn't entirely successful.

'Stop it,' she said, irritation breaking through. 'This was just a courtesy. To let you know that I formally acknowledge the great sacrifice made by your Family in banishing Tristan Fox. I didn't appear entirely trusting when you told me and I wanted to make sure it had been properly...' Lydia paused for a moment, the correct word evading her. Finally, she finished with 'noted'. Which wasn't really impressive enough, but would have to do.

'You checked it out, then.' Paul said.

Lydia kept quiet.

'We should meet,' he said, after a moment. 'To celebrate our continued alliance. Swap notes in these troubled times.'

'I don't think that's necessary,' Lydia said, ignoring the spurt of excitement. She did not need to see Paul Fox.

'I might have important information.'

'Do you?'

'I will tell you when we meet.'

'I'm too busy for games,' Lydia said.

'We both know that's not true,' Paul said. 'See you in an hour.'

After he hung up, a text came through with the words Imperial War Museum. Lydia hoped it wasn't a sign.

It was too cold to be standing around and Lydia circled the green space in front of the museum while she waited for Paul. She couldn't help thinking about the first time she had met him after returning to London, in this same place. Realising that she had reached the exit back onto the street, she turned back and saw Paul on the path behind her. The full force of 'fox' hit her and she realised that she must have been truly preoccupied not to sense it before she had turned. Sloppy. She truly had decided to trust him again, that much was clear. That much was alarming. Her heart leapt a little at the sight of him, too. It was an old reflex from when they had been an item. Which was history. Ancient history.

In a concession to the cold weather, Paul was wearing a black beanie hat and a khaki green bomber jacket over his standard uniform of close-fitting black t-shirt and jeans. It was something of a relief to see that he had a small amount of human weakness.

'Little bird,' he said, stopping a respectable distance. 'You don't look well.'

'I'm fine,' Lydia said. As soon as the words were out she could taste the lie. She felt shaky. And she wanted to sip at the flask that was stashed inside her jacket.

Paul tilted his head. 'Gotta look after yourself. I didn't just banish my father to have you drop down dead of your own accord.'

'Was that a joke? Are we joking about this already?'

Paul smiled. 'Just trying to ease the tension. I want you to relax.'

Lydia shook her head. 'Not going to happen. Not now, not ever. What information did you want to share? I assume it doesn't come free?'

'I spoke to Jack and the rest of them. They said that Tristan was very unhappy about us reconnecting.'

Lydia was going to ask why but she wasn't sure she wanted to hear the answer. Besides, this was old news. If Paul had dragged her across town to hear the same apology, the same explanation, she was going to lose it. She didn't have time for games or powerplays from Paul, she had her hands full with Charlie and her own personal spy master.

'Then, some Russian told him that the Crows were planning to move against our Family.'

'I remember. And I've already told you that wasn't true.'

'As far as you know,' Paul said. 'Don't know how forthcoming your uncle is with you.'

'Very,' Lydia said. She felt her coin in her hand and gripped it tightly. 'Especially now. I'm his right-hand.'

'And do you know what the left hand is doing?'

'Of course,' Lydia said.

Paul waved a hand. 'But I've been looking into the Russian and have found out something interesting. He picks up payments in cash from an office off Chancery Lane. It's registered to-'

'JRB,' Lydia interrupted. '*Feathers.*'

BACK IN CAMBERWELL and on foot, Lydia was trying to walk off the nervous energy which was fizzing through her. Seeing Paul was always a little disturbing. He reminded her of her past lust and their ill-advised relationship. She was in no state to deal with it, not with the aching emptiness Fleet had left in her middle. Her phone was in her hand and her fingertip hovering over his number, before she was conscious of the movement. She forced herself to switch the device off and put it back in her pocket.

As Lydia approached Well Street, a black cloud of smoke appeared above the roofline and there was a smell of burned plastic. Turning the corner, she sped up automatically, ready to step into the road to avoid the Pearl-owned grocers, when something made her stop moving altogether. The space which had held the sickly-pastel frontage of Jayne's Floral Delights was no longer there. Or, more accurately, the space was there, but it now held a burned-out shell, illuminated by the flashing lights from a police car and fire engine. The emergency services looked like they were packing up.

Lydia turned and moved down the nearest side street.

Her phone was in her hand and she called Charlie. 'What the hell?'

'Not on the phone,' Charlie said and cut the connection.

Lydia headed for Grove Lane and Charlie's house. The front garden was filled with birds, mainly corvids, and Lydia greeted them as she marched up to the front door. She banged on the wood with the side of her fist, trying to release some of the adrenaline. She had to play this right. Be calm. Not antagonise Charlie. Get answers.

Her uncle opened the door, eyebrows raised. 'You're in a hurry.'

Lydia pushed past him and into the house. 'What did you do?'

Charlie's brow furrowed in an excellent impression of gentle confusion. 'What are you talking about?'

'The florist. Jayne Davies' place. It's been torched.'

Charlie shook his head. 'Very unfortunate. Such a shame they weren't up to date on their business insurance payments.'

'You did this.'

'We did this,' Charlie said, all pretence at gentility gone. 'You can't run Camberwell without being firm. Otherwise we couldn't keep control. If I let one business screw with me, what's to stop everybody else doing the same? You have to toughen up, Lyds. This is the real world.'

Lydia didn't answer him for a moment. She allowed herself a beat to modulate her breath and to let the first flurry of possible replies run through her mind.

'I know it seems harsh,' Charlie said, his voice a little softer. 'But I made sure there wasn't anybody in the building. They are closed this week for Christmas.'

Lydia felt her insides liquify. It hadn't even occurred to her that somebody might have been hurt. It was a place of business, but that didn't guarantee nobody had been inside when the fire was started. She forced herself to nod. 'Okay. Good.'

'Late night start, checked the place out thoroughly in case of surprises. It could have been so much worse.'

'Good,' Lydia said. 'Smart.' She didn't even really know what she was saying, just that every particle in her body wanted to be out of the house and away from the man standing in the hallway. He looked like the uncle Charlie she had known her whole life, but he wasn't the same man. That man was someone who ran a family with a dodgy past, someone who commanded respect and kept the worst of the drug gangs out of Camberwell, but someone who was part of the modern world. The man stood in front of her at this moment was something else. He wasn't acknowledging the past or honouring their traditions, he had one foot planted firmly in the 'bad old days'. No, more than that. The bad old days were the bad current days.

'I'm glad you popped round, as it happens. Here,' Charlie said, reaching behind Lydia to a small console table just inside the front door. 'Your payment.'

'I don't want payment,' Lydia said. She wanted to get out before she threw up. Karen might have insisted that they couldn't think about the consequences when they did their job, but Lydia didn't agree. Besides, she had known something bad would happen. She had known and she had told Charlie about Jayne Davies' business anyway. The guilt was a hammer to her stomach and it took her breath away.

'Take it,' Charlie pressed a set of car keys into her hand and then closed her fingers over them, using both of his hands. He held them like that for a moment, looking her dead in the eye with his shark's gaze. 'You're with us, now, Lyds. And you need a motor.'

CHAPTER FIFTEEN

Charlie waited, watching as Lydia walked down the path to the main road. Lydia pressed the key fob and a gunmetal grey Audi which was parked directly outside the house responded. Lydia glanced back and Charlie raised a hand before retreating behind his door. The satisfied expression on his face made her stomach hurt. The car wasn't a flashy or brand-new model, but it was in excellent condition and far beyond anything she could have afforded to buy with her insurance pay out. Inside it had been expertly valeted and there was a branded air freshener hanging from the rear-view mirror. She drove it back to The Fork, finding her usual parking space a street away. Lydia tried not to admire how perfect the vehicle was for her needs and how quiet the engine, how deft the handling and definite the brakes. Any trace of enjoyment in the car felt like a betrayal of her independence and her moral code. Charlie had burned down a business like it was just another day at the office.

She had barely set foot inside her flat when her phone rang. She stared at the screen, frozen. She had been expecting an unknown number, which would be Paul calling from his new phone. Maybe to tell her again that she didn't know what her own flesh and blood was up to. Which, unfortunately, had just been proven to be perfectly accurate. But instead it was DCI Fleet and it took every ounce of her willpower not to slide the green icon to the side to hear his voice. He had respected her request to stay out of her life up until now and she wondered if there was an emergency. Something really important. As she wrestled with her emotions, the seconds ticked away until the phone stopped ringing. It had gone to voicemail and she waited to see if he would leave a message.

He didn't.

The disappointment was a punch to her stomach. Lydia tried to get back to work, but her concentration was shattered. She kept looking at her phone as if willing it to ring again, even as she was aware that she still wouldn't allow herself to answer. She couldn't speak to him, couldn't trust herself to stay strong and separate.

After ten minutes of torture, she picked up her jacket from the sofa and left the flat. She would go for a brisk walk, do some food shopping for dinner and maybe some comfort food for right now. Outside the air was like a slap in the face. London never usually got that cold, especially in comparison to Aberdeen, but this winter was the exception. Or Lydia was less robust than usual. She zipped up her jacket and stuffed her hands into her pockets.

Lydia turned left outside The Fork but had only taken a couple of steps when a familiar car pulled up alongside the kerb. Fleet got out, his hand resting on the roof. 'Can we talk?'

Lydia couldn't answer for a second. The sight of Fleet, tall and beautiful and wearing one of his delicious suits with the familiar grey wool coat over the top was too much to take in all at once. He was both known and unknown, this man. She knew every inch of his naked skin, had whispered and laughed with him in the dark, had spent hours staring into his eyes, and now those same eyes were roving around the scene, skittering from her feet to her shoulders to her face and then bouncing away, as if burned. Lydia thought she had prepared herself for the pain of seeing Fleet as a separate person, no longer her better half, but she had not.

'Just for a few minutes?' He said. 'In the car, if you like, it's freezing today.'

'Okay,' Lydia managed. She opened the passenger side door and got into the car, moving on autopilot. She could do this. The moment Fleet closed his door, she realised her error. They were too close and in an enclosed space. She could smell the Fleet bouquet and she was lost, hurtling backward in time to his bed, to her bed, to her sofa, desk, kitchen worktop and every floor in the flat.

'What do you need?' She was proud of that. It was business-like. Calm and contained. Efficient.

Fleet still couldn't meet her eye. He looked out of the windscreen as he spoke. 'A case that might be your kind of thing.' Then he described the man who had telephoned Lydia from the Maudsley hospital a few weeks earlier.

For a moment Lydia regrouped. She had been expecting Fleet to ask her about the arson attack on the florist, that he must have somehow subliminally divined that a Crow was involved. 'He's an in-patient in the psychiatric unit, right? He requested my services and I told him 'no'.'

'He said. He keeps phoning the station, though, and there's nothing we can do. I thought you might reconsider.'

'To stop him bothering you?'

Fleet flashed a sheepish smile. 'Partly. But mainly I think it's your kind of thing. It sounds a bit-'

'Odd?' Lydia supplied. 'Weird? Unreal?' She stopped herself before she said 'magic'. She wasn't with Fleet. Which meant she had to make sure those walls went back up. She remembered the feeling of being in the police cell. How had he not come to see her, there? Not reassured her? He said he had been trying to help her and, logically, she believed him and understood the difficult situation he had been in. Illogically, though, her body was tensed for flight and there was a bitter taste in her mouth.

'You know what I mean. I can't help him, but maybe you can.' Fleet shrugged. 'I feel sorry for the guy. He sounds really distressed. And we're really stretched at the moment.'

Lydia narrowed her eyes. She felt manipulated. And she had enough of that from Charlie. 'Isn't it below your pay grade? Why do you know about a random phone call to the station?'

'He told the sergeant that he had tried to engage your services so it got passed to me. Now I'm trying to pass it back.' He gave a small, regretful smile. 'Thought I would try, anyway. I'm slammed at the moment.'

Lydia ignored the fact that Fleet still had anything related to her passed straight to him. She thought, instead, about asking him about his current cases, but she stopped herself. She wasn't his girlfriend, his support, his confidante. 'I'm too busy. I told him that.'

'Fair enough,' Fleet said. 'Sorry to have bothered you.'

Lydia reached for the door handle, ready to leave. What had been so weird that Fleet would contact her, though? She ran over the story from when Ash had telephoned. It hadn't struck her as out of the ordinary in a magical sense. She turned back. 'What was weird? I get that the man is unwell, but he's being looked after by mental health professionals. If he has been wrongfully sectioned, then that's a civil matter surely? Something for a solicitor.'

Fleet looked at her, then, a deep crease across his brow. 'Ash believes that he has lost his true identity due to amnesia, and he wants help tracking down the details of his life.

He wants help to track down his parents so that they can clear up the mix-up and bring him home.'

'He said his name wasn't his real name,' Lydia said. 'When he called me, he said that the people around him were imposters and that they had given him a false name or something. It definitely sounds like a mental health issue, so he's in the right place getting help from trained professionals. I don't see how me getting involved is going to help him. It might make him worse, confirm his delusions.'

Fleet nodded. 'Makes sense. Sorry. I got taken in. He sounded quite reasonable.'

Lydia was battling her senses. Not just her normal animal ones, the ones which were twisting her guts in a mix of anguish and desire, but her Crow sense. The one which told her when a person was packing power. She had caught an unusual gleam from Fleet in the past, but had become used to it with repeated exposure. It had been just part of him, the general 'Fleet' feeling. Now, having had no contact for almost a month, it was more distinct. It wasn't recognisable as Crow, Fox, Pearl or Silver. It was closer, if anything, to the flavour she got from Mr Smith. Which was disturbing.

'There's something else,' Fleet was saying.

'What?'

'I'm worried about you.'

'Don't,' Lydia said. 'My welfare is not your concern.'

'You're in touch with Paul Fox. After everything. You can't trust him.'

'And how would you know that? Am I under police surveillance, officer?'

Fleet winced. 'It's not like that.'

'If you are watching me in your own time, that's called stalking. So, which is it? Professional or personal invasion of privacy?'

Fleet's face went blank. 'Just be careful,' he said. 'Please.'

Lydia opened the door and got out of the car as quickly as she could. It had been a mistake to get into it in the first place. Standing on the pavement, sucking in lungfuls of Fleet-free air, she knew that she couldn't make that mistake again. She wasn't strong enough.

CHAPTER SIXTEEN

Despite the fact that it was the week between Christmas and New Year, traditionally a time for lounging about in PJs or taking it extremely easy while pretending to work and eating the leftover chocolate, Lydia knew that Mr Smith would still expect her to keep their standing appointment. On the plus side, Lydia had something she wanted to ask him.

Lydia knew that she shouldn't confirm Mr Smith's suspicions about her own power, but she also knew that she had to show willing in some way, soften him up. Since going home she hadn't been able to stop thinking about her dad and what would come next. Her mum would look after him at home as long as possible but, at some point, it would end with Henry Crow in a care home or hospice. Sitting in a chair or bed, staring into the distance and seeing nothing. It was the kind of thing you knew might happen to your parents one day. One day far in the future. But now, all Lydia could see was his face and the horrible blankness where his eyes used to be.

She pushed the pastry box away, the association with these enforced meetings spoiling her enjoyment forever more, and took a long sip of her coffee. She itched to add a nip from her hip flask, but resisted the urge. She needed a clear head. 'I've been thinking about you.'

Mr Smith licked sugar from his fingers and then wiped his hands on a paper napkin. 'That's nice.'

Lydia took a deep breath. 'You have an unusual signature.'

Mr Smith looked interested for the first time. 'Is that so?'

'How did you heal me?'

His expression closed down immediately. 'We're not here to talk about me.'

'I wondered if it was something you could do again. On somebody else. And whether it would work on a brain condition.'

Mr Smith tilted his head, appraising. 'Who are we talking about?'

This was a big disclosure. Henry Crow was officially out, but he was still the rightful head of the Crow Family and weakness of any kind was not something the Crows advertised. Still. If there was a chance Mr Smith could fix her dad, it was a risk she had to take. 'My father,' she said, her throat closing up as she spoke. 'He's got Alzheimer's or something similar.' She didn't add that it might be a magical disease, brought on by suppressing his own power. Firstly, that was just a guess on her part and secondly, the habit to disclose the bare minimum in any given situation ran deep.

'I don't wish to cause offence,' Mr Smith said, 'but the Crow Family are not considered to be generally a good thing. You must be aware that the NCA have been investigating them for years for organised crime. Making Henry Crow stronger isn't high up our list of priorities.'

Lydia didn't betray her surprise. Her understanding was that the Crows had been borderline legit for years, and that Charlie's recent foray into arson had been an aberration. She had assumed that the National Crime Agency would have lost interest decades ago. Either Mr Smith was lying or she was seriously naïve when it came to her family's activities. She had a horrible feeling it was the latter. Pushing that aside, she leaned forward, planting her elbows on the table. 'I'm Crow Family,' Lydia said. 'You healed me.'

'You're different.'

Lydia looked Mr Smith square in the eye. 'I'm also difficult to motivate.'

After a moment, he nodded. 'It might be possible. And I suppose I could leave it out of my report. I can't promise it will work, though.'

'Noted.'

'And I would need a gesture of goodwill. And payment up front.'

'I am happy to demonstrate my motivation, and I can do a part-payment first, but full payment only after my father is cured.'

'Not cured. After I've attempted a full cure.'

'No. Part payment for the attempt. Full for the cure.'

'But I might not be able to do it, why should I even try if I won't get the full payment?'

Lydia thought for a moment. She had to be sure that he was going to give it his full effort. She had seen the drained look on his face after he had healed her of a few bruises and a broken rib. He was playing her for all he could, doing his job, but it was possible there was more to it. If she had learned one thing from her father and Uncle Charlie's attempts at training it was that magic was tricksy. It never gave without taking away. 'Fine,' she said. 'Full payment for full effort, regardless of results. But how will I know you are giving your full effort?'

'I give you my word,' Mr Smith said.

Lydia was about to tell him that she wasn't a small child and that she would need more, when she realised he meant it. 'We would shake on it?'

He nodded. 'Coin to coin. Binding.'

Lydia remembered the chink sound of metal on metal when she had shaken his hand in the police station. Was she really about to make another deal with the mystery man? She thought of her father's slackened face and the line of drool hanging from his mouth and held out her hand.

After they had shaken, Mr Smith sat back in his chair. 'Now, that gesture of goodwill.'

'What do you want?'

'I want to hear about your life. How is working for your uncle going? Have you had any further trouble from the Silvers?'

'No more trouble,' Lydia said, ignoring the question about her uncle. She thought for a few seconds, calculating the least-worst piece of information she could give Mr Smith. He would need breadcrumbs if she was going to lead him toward healing her father.

'I've got something for you,' Lydia said.

Mr Smith inclined his head, but didn't say anything.

'You're familiar with the truce, I assume?'

'Set in 1943, when the four Families agreed to put an end to the fighting in light of the losses incurred.'

'Good,' Lydia said, glad she didn't have to give a history lesson. 'Well, someone has been trying to break it.'

'Who?'

'I don't know, but every lead points to your old pals, JRB. You know they were clients of the Silver Family, maybe still are, but finding information on them has been difficult.'

'This sounds like the lead up to another request for my help, rather than you offering me something of value. Your debt is growing.'

'I've found evidence that JRB are linked to the Pearl Family. They might even be one and the same, I don't know. That means the Pearls are in some way complicit, if not active, in trying to destabilise the Families.'

'Not necessarily,' Mr Smith said. 'How strong is this link you've found?'

'What do you know about the Pearls? I thought they were quiet shopkeepers, not very powerful, not very interested in politics and power-play.'

'Unlike the Crows and the Silvers.'

'Yes,' Lydia said impatiently, 'which is why our alliance with the Silvers was always so important. If we were on the same side, we were less likely to tear each other apart in the race to the top. At least, that was the theory. And it's all dust now as far as I'm concerned.'

He raised an eyebrow.

'Maria Silver has been named the new head of the Silver Family. And she's not my biggest fan.'

Mr Smith nodded. 'This is a reaction to Alejandro setting his sights on politics, I assume?'

Of course he knew about that. 'So, the Pearls?'

He leaned back in his chair and regarded Lydia for a long moment. When he spoke, it was in the tones of someone recounting an often-told story. 'Once upon a time, a woman went through a door in a chalk hillside and married a prince. When she came back, three hundred years had passed, and all of her human family were long dead. She wasn't alone, though. Growing inside her belly was a child. Half-fae, half-mortal, and that baby girl was the first Pearl.'

'I don't believe in fairies,' Lydia said.

'Nobody sane does,' Mr Smith said. 'That doesn't mean they don't exist.'

ON NEW YEAR'S DAY, Lydia woke up late, a foul taste in her mouth. She had finished another bottle of whisky the night before and the evidence was on her nightstand. She had slumped down, shoving her laptop to the bottom of the bed, sometime after two. She retrieved it, and pushed her pillows up against the headboard. Once she was sitting up and had swilled her mouth out with a stale can of cola, Lydia felt her mind clearing.

She fired up the computer and checked her email. Jason had sent her a neat list of work completed with a hyperlink to their new shared folder. Feeling ridiculous, she emailed the ghost back to say 'thank you'.

Fleet had reminded Lydia about the phone call and with the need to do something which felt like a positive act, she called the Maudsley and asked for the ward that Ash had given. 'This is going to sound a bit odd,' Lydia said, 'but I received a call from one of your patients. He said his name was Ash. No surname. And that might be a nickname. He didn't seem completely sure.'

'How can I help?' The nurse on the line sounded genuinely sympathetic and Lydia wondered what it took to do that job and still be gracious to randoms interrupting your busy work day.

'He sounded distressed and, I don't know, I felt like I should check on him. Or alert you or something. I don't know...'

'This ward is for inpatients receiving psychiatric treatment. Unfortunately, many of our clients are often distressed. You're not family?'

'No,' Lydia said. 'I don't know him at all. I know you can't give me details and I'm not asking for any information, I just wanted to pass on what he told me in case it's medically relevant, I guess. If just felt wrong to completely ignore it.'

'I understand,' the nurse said. 'I'll make a note. When did he call?'

Lydia gave the details she could remember.

'And what did Ash say to you? Did he give a reason for contacting you?'

'He wanted to book me. I'm an investigator, and he wanted me to find his parents. He said his name wasn't his real name and that everything had changed. He said there were imposters everywhere, that nothing was real.'

'I see,' the nurse said. 'That sounds distressing. I'm sorry.'

'No, it's fine,' Lydia said. 'I was just thinking about it and I felt bad that I hadn't tried to help him, I guess. Can you just tell him that I called to check up on him?'

'Of course. May I take your name?'

'Lydia Crow.'

There was a pause. 'That's interesting,' the nurse said. 'I'm looking at his file right now and you are down as his emergency contact and on his approved list of visitors.'

'How is that possible? I've never met him.'

'He gave us those details, actually. We haven't been able to track down his family. We've actually passed his details onto the police in case he comes up on the missing person database.'

'Wait. He was right? His name isn't Ash? You don't have his actual identity?'

'It might be. We haven't been able to confirm that. He had no ID on him when he arrived. He was transferred from A and E to us for emergency assessment.'

'So you haven't been in touch with his family?'

'Unfortunately not.'

'Can I speak to him, now?'

'I'm afraid he's in group at the moment. I will tell him you called, though, and you can always visit. Open visits are allowed between two and four every day and ten until twelve on Saturdays. You will need to bring some ID and there is a list of items you may not bring with you or gift to a patient on our website.'

After hanging up, Lydia spent a few seconds hoping that she hadn't inadvertently got Ash into any kind of trouble or contravened her own rules for privacy for clients. He wasn't a client, of course, but he had come to her for help. She had the feeling she had done the wrong thing, but couldn't work out what the right action would be and, after a minute more of fretting, she let it go.

THE FORK HAD BEEN CLOSED over Christmas and New Year, but it opened on the third of January and seemed as busy as normal. Life in London never paused for long. Lydia had ordered a coffee and a bacon roll and, as a nod to health, a glass of orange juice. Angel wasn't serving, she was leaning on the counter scrolling through her phone while a new employee fumbled with the coffee machine. He had a slight build, light brown hair, and an intensely worried expression, but that was probably because he was new. Lydia didn't imagine that Angel was a very patient teacher.

'Thanks,' Lydia paid the new guy and took a sip of her coffee while he went into the kitchen to retrieve her breakfast.

'You seen this?' Angel straightened up.

'What?'

She passed her phone to Lydia, clicking her tongue on the roof of her mouth as she did so. 'Aren't you supposed to be a detective?'

'Investigator,' Lydia corrected. 'For hire. Doesn't mean I spend my days scanning the news for jobs.' She trailed off as her attention was caught by the video playing. It was from the BBC website and Angel had subtitles on. A high-ranking police officer was giving a press briefing in front of a cordoned-area, her face serious, but Lydia wasn't reading the words. She had caught sight of a familiar figure behind the yellow tape, amongst the crowd of people. Fleet.

'It's local, though,' Angel was saying and Lydia forced herself to focus on the words being spoken by the reporter. The fifteen-year-old daughter of local councillor Miles Bunyan had been missing for three days and police were appealing for witnesses. Lydia knew that meant the team were scraping the barrel for leads, and would now have to contend with a stream of time-wasting phone calls, most innocent, some intentional, and some downright psychotic.

She squinted at the screen, trying to work out where the film had been shot and what the cordon was protecting but the clip ended and another one started, a climate change report this time. Rolling news. An onslaught of misery and fear.

'Bunyan,' she said out loud. 'That name rings a bell.'

'Head of Southwark Council,' Angel said, sniffing. 'Always banging on about the Camberwell Regeneration Plan.'

Lydia didn't reply, she was replaying the glimpse of Fleet, waiting for the spike of adrenaline to fade. Had he looked tired? Happy? Worried? It was pointless to speculate and it was, she reminded herself, none of her business, but the thoughts kept looping.

Her breakfast appeared and she took it to a table in the window. Her appetite had gone, but she forced herself to eat, scrolling on her own phone while she chewed. She found the news story and followed the various reports. There wasn't much information, but that didn't mean much. Fleet's team would be careful about what they released to the press, especially when launching an appeal. The more they kept quiet, the easier it would be to spot the genuine tips. She put her phone face down. She felt bad that a girl was missing, but it wasn't her job. The name Bunyan was very familiar, though. Then she realised why – Charlie had mentioned him. He counted Bunyan as an ally in the continual fight to keep Camberwell afloat.

Draining her orange juice like the glass of medicine it was, Lydia stood up to leave. There was something else tickling at the back of her mind. Something important. It wasn't until she had walked back upstairs to her flat and sat at her desk for ten minutes that the thought finally sidled out from the shadows and into the light.

She leaned back and examined it for a few moments, cross that it hadn't struck her before. It had been when Angel had handed her the phone, it had reminded her of when Angel had pointed out the man hanging from Blackfriars Bridge. Kicking herself, she went downstairs to confront a certain dreadlocked person.

Angel was sitting at one of the cafe tables, reading a paperback while the new kid swept the floor.

'Give us a minute,' Lydia said to him. He looked at Angel who nodded.

Lydia stood by Angel's table, trying to marshal her thoughts. Charlie hadn't just been watching her through his camera or turning up to ask her things. He had been pushing her around without her even knowing it.

'You work for Charlie,' Lydia said flatly.

'Yeah,' Angel put the book face down on the Formica. 'What of it?'

'You showed me that news article. The hanged guy on Blackfriars Bridge.'

Angel shrugged. 'You would have seen it, anyway. The story was everywhere.'

'You've been reporting to Charlie, I assume?' Lydia forced herself to unclench her fists, to let her arms hang by her sides and her face to relax. Angel was an unknown quantity and she moved quickly. Lydia had seen her wielding a giant cast iron pan over a burner and had no desire for things to get physical.

Angel shrugged. 'He pays my wages. He asks, I answer.'

'Did he tell you to nudge me toward certain jobs?'

Angel sighed, looking bored rather than anything else. 'Sometimes. He seemed to think that the direct approach wouldn't be most effective.'

'Why does he want me to look into this?' Lydia tapped

the phone screen to reawaken it, revealing a picture of Miles Bunyan and his wife looking tearful.

'I think you're misunderstanding the nature of our agreement. He asks, I answer. Not the other way around.'

'And that's okay with you?'

'He's Charlie Crow. And I work at The Fork.' This was spoken like Lydia was a functional idiot.

She smiled, producing her coin and spinning it in the air. She had been trying not to use her mojo on people, not wanting to walk too far down the path of coercive control, but Angel was pissing her off. 'I'm Lydia Crow,' she said. 'And I think we should have a little agreement of our own.'

Angel gave her a look which was both vaguely annoyed and very tired. 'You gonna pay?'

'I'm going to let you keep your job,' Lydia said. 'Which is pretty reasonable from where I'm standing.'

BACK UPSTAIRS, Lydia sat at her desk and poured the last of the whisky into her mug. She didn't know why she was so thrown by the news from Angel. She had been aware that Charlie had been trying to control her from the moment she stepped foot back in London, but it was unsettling that she hadn't suspected Angel. It made her wonder what else she was missing.

CHAPTER SEVENTEEN

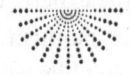

Lydia paced her floor until Jason asked her to stop because she was making him nervous, and then called her uncle. 'Are you near the cafe? I need to speak to you.'

'And a happy new year to you, too, Lyds.'

Lydia didn't reply. After a moment, Charlie said. 'I could go for some more breakfast.'

Angel looked alarmed when Lydia arrived back downstairs and even more worried when Charlie pushed open the door.

'Coffee,' Lydia said. 'Make that two.'

She steered Charlie to their usual table.

'I might want to eat,' he said.

'No time,' Lydia said. 'I saw the news.'

She watched Charlie's eyes, expecting him to flick toward Angel. They didn't and, once again, Lydia marvelled at how good her uncle was at concealment. He was wasted in Camberwell. 'Did you ever think about joining the secret service?' Lydia said.

'What?'

'Nothing,' Lydia sipped her coffee. 'Shame about that missing girl.'

Charlie lifted his cup. 'I wanted to talk to you about that, as it happens.'

'Oh, right?' Lydia kept her voice light.

'It's something we should get involved with. See what we can dig up.'

'By "we" I assume you mean "me".'

He shrugged. 'You're the expert. You found Maddie.'

'I'm a bit busy at the moment,' Lydia said. What she didn't say was that she didn't like being manipulated and she *really* didn't like casual arson. If she investigated something on Charlie's behalf, what would the repercussions be this time?

'Not too busy for this,' Charlie said and his eyes were flat. He flashed his shark's smile and his eyes didn't change. It was a warning and Lydia didn't even need to glance down to know that the tattoos just visible beneath the folded cuffs of his black shirt were writhing.

'Why do you care so much?'

'Miles Bunyan is an old friend. He has been very good to this area.'

'The Camberwell Regeneration Plan?'

'Amongst other things,' Charlie waved a hand. 'Miles Bunyan has cared about Camberwell when his colleagues would happily see all funds diverted to Bermondsey.'

'Is he a good father, too?'

Charlie paused. 'What are you insinuating? That he's the reason Lucy has run off? He has done everything for that girl. He has been mother as well as father ever since Caroline passed, held down his job, been head of the council, active with charity work-'

'Okay, okay,' Lydia held up her hands. 'Got it. Father of the year.'

'It'll be that boy of hers. Unsuitable outside influence. Happens all the time, some good-looking kid turns a young girl's head, makes her forget her sense.'

Lydia decided to pretend that Charlie wasn't having a go at her. Tensions were already high between them and didn't need any more stress applied. 'I'll see what I can do,' Lydia said, placating. Then, because she couldn't help herself, she added 'it would help if I was still friendly with Fleet.'

Charlie bared his teeth. 'You don't have to be friendly to get information.'

'I can't promise anything,' Lydia said. She made to leave and Charlie stopped her with a hand on her arm.

'Not yet. We need to pay our respects.'

MILES BUNYAN WAS SITTING on the brown leather sofa in the narrow living room of his Victorian end terrace. It wasn't a big room, but there were the original sashes in the bay window and the house was close to Burgess Park. Lydia wondered how much council leaders got paid.

'It's good of you to come,' Miles was saying. 'I don't... I don't know what I'm doing at the moment.' He started to stand up. 'Would you like tea?'

'Lydia will make some,' Charlie said.

Lydia was glad to escape to the kitchen, away from the heavy sadness in the living room. She found mugs and teabags and filled the kettle, then took the opportunity to have a good look around the room. It had a dining area which led to doors and out to the garden. The conversion was nicely done and fairly new-looking. There were a few takeaway menus pinned to the fridge with magnets and a pile of post on the counter.

She went upstairs and found Lucy's room. The last time she had been snooping in a missing girl's bedroom it had been Maddie, her cousin, who was missing. Maddie had turned out to be alive and well, well enough to attempt to kill Lydia, in fact. Lydia hoped that history would only half-repeat itself in this instance. The room was very clean and tidy and looked like the 'after' in a Marie Kondo clip. Either Lucy had been that way, or her father had taken the opportunity of her absence to have a clear out. There was a white desk with an angle-poise lamp and a single succulent in a teal pot. Before Lydia could get started on the bedside drawers, she heard the living room door open and Miles's voice. She slipped out of the room and into the bathroom across the landing. She flushed, washed her hands and headed back down the stairs, smiling at Miles who was standing at the bottom, looking lost.

'I thought you might need... A hand. Directions.'

'I'm fine,' Lydia said. 'You can help me carry, though.'

In the kitchen, Lydia concentrated on finishing making the tea. Miles stood stock still, like a clockwork toy that needed winding. 'We are really close. She wouldn't go off without telling me. She knows how worried I would be. How worried I am. She would never... I know what you think. What the police think, but you're wrong. She was happy. She had no reason to leave.'

And then, the awful sound of him crying.

Lydia turned, a mug in each hand. She ought to put them down, comfort the broken man, but she didn't know him and was trespassing on his grief and fear.

He wiped his face with his hands. 'Sorry. Sorry, it's just... I can't help think something bad has happened. Otherwise she would be in touch.'

'Not necessarily,' Lydia said, hating herself for offering hope when it might not be warranted. 'She's fifteen. She might not be thinking straight or be worried that she's in trouble with you.'

'No,' Miles shook his head violently. 'We are more like friends. And she's very sensible. Very grown-up. She just wouldn't.'

'Okay,' Lydia put the mugs down on the counter and squared her shoulders. 'What have the police said?'

'They asked a lot about Josh. That's her boyfriend,' Miles's lip curled. 'He was with her on the night she went missing. He's a bit older than her, just passed his driving test although I won't let her get in the car with him. Too risky. Statistics show...' Miles trailed off. He wiped his face, again. 'You do everything you can to protect them, you know? Everything. And then... This.'

'What is he like?'

'Joshua?' Miles shrugged. 'Seventeen-year-old boy. Polite, at least. Speaks to me which is more than I can say about the last one. He was bad news. I told the police, I told them they should be looking at her ex. They keep saying they are following all enquiries, standard language.'

Lydia nodded. 'They will be, though. They will do everything possible. What does Josh say about Lucy? I assume they've asked him about that night?'

'He's claiming amnesia. Says he doesn't remember anything before he was found wandering around Highgate the next morning. He must have taken something. Drugs. What if he gave Lucy something? She could be ill... Lying somewhere.'

Miles moved suddenly, picked up a mug and turned away. There was a deeply snotty noise as he cleared his throat. Lydia followed him back to the living room but he paused right outside the door, speaking quietly and quickly. 'They suspect me. I know they do. I don't mind, I understand, I know it's usually,' his voice caught and he took a ragged breath, 'it's usually someone they know, I know that. But I don't want them to waste their time. I want them to find her.'

SITTING in Charlie's car afterward, Lydia recounted the conversation. Charlie nodded. 'That's pretty much what he's been saying to me. I told him we will do everything we can. He has been good to us, good to Camberwell, we owe him.'

'What happened to Lucy's mother?'

'Cancer,' Charlie said. 'When Lucy was three. It's been her and Miles ever since. He's not so much as looked at another woman. His daughter and his work are his world.'

'What is his work?'

'Apart from leader of the council? He's got a directorship, I believe.' Charlie looked away and Lydia didn't know if he was being evasive or whether he was embarrassed by not having more specific information.

'You want me to use my contacts? See if I can get an update on the investigation?'

Charlie nodded, not looking at her.

'You could have just asked me, you know,' Lydia said. 'You don't need to go the long way round.' She wondered if he would acknowledge his use of Angel.

Charlie started the engine and checked his wing mirror before pulling out into the traffic. He didn't answer and Lydia could see the tattoos on his forearms writhing. She added another piece of information about her uncle Charlie. He didn't like being confronted.

When they arrived at The Fork, Charlie stopped outside and made no move to get out of the car. 'Right then,' Lydia said. 'Thanks for the lift. I'll be in touch.'

Charlie didn't look at her when he spoke. 'This is bad, Lyds.'

'I know, she's just a kid.'

He shook his head sharply. 'Everyone knows Miles is a friend of mine. He should be protected.'

'You can't be held responsible for everything,' Lydia said, wondering if Charlie had always been this cavalier about other lives. *There was a kid missing.*

He glanced at her then and Lydia saw that his eyes were bloodshot. 'I'm the head of the Crow Family. If people think

I can't protect my close friends, what are they going to say about my ability to protect the community? Their families? Livelihoods?'

TAKING A DEEP BREATH, Lydia texted Fleet. She headed it 'work enquiry' to head off any suggestion that this was a personal request. The mug on her desk had the dregs of whisky in the bottom and she swirled it out in the sink before adding a fresh shot. Her phone rang five minutes later.

'What can I do for you?' His tone was calm and professional, and Lydia could hear phones ringing and other office sounds. The sound of his voice still punched her in the gut, though. A spike of longing so strong it made her hunch over in her chair.

'Lucy Bunyan. I was hoping you could talk to me about it.'

'Why?'

'Family connection,' Lydia said, standing up and pacing the floor. She had to let out the excess energy coursing through her body or she would crack open like an egg. 'Charlie is pals with Miles Bunyan. He asked me to help. If I could.'

'I can't tell you anything that hasn't been given to the press. This is a sensitive operation with a high profile.'

'You getting pressure?'

'Nothing I can't handle,' Fleet said, there was the sound of a door closing and the office sounds disappeared. 'I can't do this.'

'Fair enough,' Lydia said. 'I said I would try and I've tried.'

'No,' Fleet said. 'Not on the phone. You want to talk, meet me for a drink tonight.'

. . .

LYDIA HESITATED OUTSIDE THE HARE. She cursed Charlie and his demands and the world at large for putting kids in danger. There wasn't anything she could do that an entire police department couldn't, but now that she had met Miles Bunyan and could put a grieving, frightened father to the story, she couldn't help but try. Damn Charlie and his intuition. He had known the best way to get Lydia onside.

Fleet was at the bar, waiting for his pint. He nodded at Lydia. 'Usual?'

'Red wine,' Lydia said. 'What? It's bloody freezing.'

Sitting in the corner of the pub with her back to the wall and a large glass of red within grasping distance, Lydia reminded herself to breathe. She might not be romantically involved with Fleet now, but he was a good person. She could trust him. Not the way she had, perhaps, but enough for this particular job.

'I'm going for a slash,' Fleet slid out from his seat almost as soon as he had sat down.

It took Lydia a moment to realise what he had done on his way - unlock his iPad and leave it on the table. She didn't hesitate, scrolling through the images.

When he returned, she didn't put it down and angled it to show him exactly what she was looking at. She had enough spy-shit mind games with Mr Smith. 'CCTV places her and her boyfriend partying in Highgate Cemetery.'

Fleet nodded. 'We've had a witness come forward to say that they saw a couple matching their description heading into the woods just after half eleven.'

'Highgate Woods? Which entrance?'

'The one nearest Highgate tube station. Gypsy Gate.'

'Credible witness?'

'Yes.'

'And what is this?' Lydia pointed at the evidence photograph. It showed a blazer jacket which was either old and originally black, or new and dark grey.

'Boyfriend's jacket. Complete with blood stains. Also belonging to boyfriend.'

'How much blood?'

'More than a shaving cut, less than an arterial bleed.'

'Lovely. Does that mean he isn't a suspect anymore?'

'Could have been defence wounds, if he was attacking her, but no. No other blood found and we haven't found any motive. By all accounts they were a golden couple. We're looking into her ex, apparently he was the jealous sort.'

'Good,' Lydia said. 'Miles mentioned the ex.'

Lydia tapped for the next image. The previous image had shown the jacket laid out on a table in the forensics department, but this was it in situ, where it had been found by an officer during the mass search of the woods.

'It was off the path, but otherwise not hidden. Just sitting there,' Fleet said. The jacket was on top of a large tree stump, folded, as if its owner had intended to come back for it.

'It must have been freezing that night. Why would he take a layer off?'

'Teenage love keeping him warm?'

Lydia nodded to concede the point. 'And alcohol. They were partying in the cemetery, right? Just drinks?'

'CCTV shows them drinking from cans of Marks and Spencer's ready-mixed gin and tonic before things get a bit heated. Then they move out of shot. There are only cameras around Karl Marx's grave because of the vandalism there. And those were only installed relatively recently. We're lucky we got anything.'

'Gin and tonic?' Lydia screwed up her face. 'What the hell is going on with today's teens?'

'Swiped from home, most likely. Opportunity rather than taste. Although, who knows? People can surprise you.'

'He's seventeen. Can't he buy whatever he wants? Or does he look young?'

'Maybe he's not a big drinker. Maybe they thought it was romantic. When I said they were getting heated, I didn't mean they were arguing...'

'Got it. Has the search finished?'

'Yes, last night. Nothing else found, sorry.'

'Better than finding something,' Lydia said, thinking about decomposing remains and shallow graves in the frozen mulch. She could hear birds calling as they wheeled high in the sky and shook her head to clear it.

Fleet was looking at her and Lydia could practically hear him thinking.

'What?' She said, her patience snapping.

'There's something else. We're keeping it out of the press.'

'My lips are sealed,' Lydia said.

'We've interviewed the boyfriend. He was found by a dog walker early on the first. He was confused and hypothermic and still seems to have total amnesia for the whole evening.'

'Seems to,' Lydia repeated. 'What does the hospital say?'

Fleet shrugged. 'Just that it's perfectly possible and that there's no way to tell if its genuine or not. He says that the last thing he remembers is heading out to meet Lucy just after seven on the thirty-first. He claims he was at home until then, sleeping in until midday and then revising in the afternoon. He's doing A Levels at Peckham College, which is where he and Lucy Bunyan met, and they've got mocks next week.'

'You believe him?'

'About the amnesia or his claim that he was studying?'

'Any of it.'

'Amnesia is convenient, but he doesn't have anything resembling defence wounds. If anything, he looks like a victim. And he appears genuinely distressed that Lucy is missing.'

'What do you reckon?'

Fleet paused. 'That he's telling the truth. He seems like a traumatised kid. You want to see for yourself?'

'Is that allowed?'

Fleet shook his head. 'When has that stopped me? Besides, I value your opinion.' He slid his iPad across the table and Lydia took her ear buds from her pocket and put them in. The video of Joshua's initial interview was queued up and she hit the arrow to start it playing.

Fleet was right, Lucy Bunyan's boyfriend looked like a frightened child. Yes, he had scruffy sideburns and a proto-goatee which he had probably been proudly growing for months and the muscles of a sporty young man, but the expression behind his eyes was that of a nine-year-old lost in a crowd. Lydia had the urge to comfort him. His right leg bounced up and down throughout the questions and he kept rubbing his eyes like a tired toddler. As well as his female legal representative, there was a man from social services there for safe-guarding. At seventeen, Joshua didn't fall under the rules for children, but he wasn't legally an adult either. The two police officers interviewing him did an excellent job of radiating calm concern for his welfare, while also subtly questioning every aspect of his story. Just as Fleet had said, there wasn't much of a story. Joshua didn't remember anything from the time he left his house to meet Lucy.

'Joshua's father has confirmed that he was home all afternoon, in his room.' Fleet said.

One of the officers on the video was asking Joshua about his A 'Levels, trying to put him at ease. Then, the other one chimed in with a different question. 'Do you remember where you were going to meet Lucy?'

'I don't know,' his hands were fists, rubbing at his eyes.

'What do you usually do when you meet up with Lucy? Do you have favourite hang outs, activities?'

'Depends. Sometimes we go to each other's houses. Or

we do something, go to Nando's or whatever. I don't remember what we did that day. We'd talked about doing something for New Year's Eve, but I'm not sure we'd chosen. Some mates were having a house party, maybe we went there?' When he moved his hands away, the skin around his eyes was red from the repeated action. He blinked back tears. 'I swear I don't remember. Did anybody else see me? They can tell you what we did.'

'Your dad hasn't seen you since you left the house on the thirty-first. He agrees that you had plans to see Lucy.'

Joshua's shoulders sagged. 'You see, I'm telling the truth. I'm trying to help, I swear. I don't know why I can't remember. Do you know where she is? How long has it been? I want her to be okay. She's got to be okay. She's my... She's...' He struggled for breath, doubling over.

'Can we take a break?' The legal rep said.

'No,' Joshua sat up. 'I'm okay. I want to help. You've got to find her. I love her.'

The simple way he said the last words had the ring of truth. Lydia could feel it in her teeth, her blood. This kid wasn't lying.

'All right, Joshua. Let's skip to the woods. You were found walking in Queen's Woods. Do you remember how you got there?'

He shook his head. 'No.'

'What is the last thing you remember?'

'I was really cold. I think I had been asleep. But I wasn't lying down. I was just walking. There were loads of trees and my throat hurt. Like I'd been shouting or I'd smoked a lot. It still hurts.'

'That's really good,' the officer nodded, encouraging him. 'Do you remember seeing anyone?'

'The lady with the dog. She was walking her dog and she asked if I was all right.'

'That's the last thing? What about just before you met the dogwalker? Can you think back?'

He closed his eyes, was silent. After a minute, he opened his eyes and shook his head. 'No. Sorry. I can't. I don't know why. I don't think I hit my head or anything. Why can't I remember?'

'Why do you say you didn't hit your head?'

'It doesn't hurt,' he said, running his hands over his skull. 'It would hurt if I had, wouldn't it? Wouldn't I have a lump or something? My chest hurts, though. And my arms.' He stretched them out and stared at the bandages. 'What happened?'

'You had a series of superficial wounds. Not serious but there were a lot of them and they were quite open. They put antibiotic spray and then covered them over to keep them clean while they heal. Do you remember that.'

He nodded. 'Yeah. I forgot. I just thought it was something else for a moment.'

'I think we should leave it there.'

The recording stopped and Lydia took her ear buds out. 'What were the injuries on his arms?'

'Little cuts. Done with something sharp.'

'Razor blade?' Lydia said, immediately thinking of self-harm. 'Does he have a history of hurting himself?'

'Not as far as we know. And he says he didn't do it.'

'How does he know? He says he can't remember anything.'

'There is that,' Fleet said, acceding the point. 'He says he didn't intend to hurt himself and wasn't carrying a blade of any kind, to the best of his memory.'

'Do you have pictures?'

Fleet tapped the screen and turned the iPad back to Lydia. The cuts chased any thoughts of self-harm straight out of Lydia's mind. They were intricate patterns, visible despite the blood which was seeping, even though Lydia knew the picture would have been taken immediately after the wounds had been cleaned. Her stomach turned over. Someone had taken care when carving these images into the boy's arms. She couldn't imagine anybody managing to do this to themselves, particularly with no prior experience. It had to have hurt like hell. And then there was the clincher – the design spanned the tops of each arm up and reached well above the elbow onto the biceps, each arm matching and equally neat. The kid would have to be an ambidextrous contortionist to have done it to himself.

'What do you think?' Fleet asked, watching Lydia carefully.

'That it's all a bit weird.'

Fleet nodded.

'I believe the kid, though,' Lydia said, indicating the iPad. 'What's your gut say?'

'I'm trying not to go with that so much these days.'

Lydia felt like she had been slapped, although she wasn't sure exactly why. She was probably being sensitive. Fleet was talking about work, that was all. He ruined that theory by softening his gaze and leaning a little closer.

'How are you doing?'

Lydia picked up her wine and drained half the glass before answering. 'This isn't a social visit.'

'I'm doing badly.' Fleet picked up his pint and then put it down without drinking. 'Very badly.'

Lydia avoided his eye and pretended that her heart wasn't trying to leap out of her chest. 'Any other lines of enquiry? Will you let me know if there are any developments?'

'I shouldn't,' Fleet said. 'But I will. Because I choose you. I choose you every time.'

'Not every time,' Lydia said, feeling suddenly heavy. She stood up to leave.

Fleet leaned back in his chair, looking up at Lydia with his steady brown eyes. 'You want me to show you where the jacket was found?'

Lydia had picked up her own jacket but she hesitated. *Feathers*. 'Yes. Let's go.'

CHAPTER EIGHTEEN

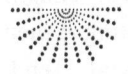

Lydia agreed to go in Fleet's car for simplicity. Plus, he had immunity to parking fines. They were cutting it close time-wise as the park shut at sunset and at this time of year that would be half four. The sky was a flat grey, cloud covering the low sun. 'We can always jump the gate if we get locked in,' Fleet said.

Lydia kept her window open a crack, letting in a steady stream of cold air. She scrolled through her phone and tried to pretend that the silence between them wasn't awkward. Fleet got the last space in the small car park behind Highgate Underground. There was a disused train station above the tube line and two exits. They took the most direct route to Muswell Hill Road, assuming that the kids would have done the same. They passed The Woodman pub on the corner and up the road running between Highgate Woods and Queen's Woods. It was unsettling to see this many trees in London, it was even worse than the suburbs where she had grown up.

Fleet voiced the same thought. 'Feels different around here, doesn't it?'

'It's not Camberwell,' Lydia agreed. And it was about to

get worse. They took the Gypsy Gate into the woodland, with its information maps and green metal sign, Fleet leading the way. They hadn't walked for very long when the trees became more dense and the sounds of the traffic faded away. There were bare branches, mixed in with the shiny dark green of the holly and some of the big trees still had brown-ish looking leaves clinging on. 'Is that climate change?' Lydia said, pointing at them.

'Hornbeams,' Fleets said. 'Tend to keep their leaves in winter, apparently.'

'Mr Nature,' Lydia said. 'I had no idea.'

Fleet gave her a brief smile. 'I read up on the woods. You never know what will turn out to be significant.'

Lydia was about to launch into some weapons-grade teasing about the likelihood of tree knowledge pertaining to a crime investigation, but then she stopped herself. She had to remember that this wasn't social and that laughing together was no longer on the cards. One day, maybe, but not yet. It was too soon. Would they ever be actual, real 'just friends'? She had no idea. Taking covert glances at him was like sips of water after a week crossing a desert. Both unbelievably sweet and nowhere close to quenching her thirst.

The trees were getting closer and a few minutes later, the sky disappeared behind a ceiling of branches. 'I think it's this way,' Fleet said.

'You think?' Lydia replied, stepping over a tree root. They had left the wide main path almost immediately, and the well-trodden informal trail they had taken seemed to have disappeared, too. Now, they were walking over the dry mulch of fallen wood and bark and leaves. Drifts of brown leaves which remained from autumn, rotting down and hiding who-knew-what. Lydia shivered. *Feathers*. It was cold.

They kept moving, not speaking. Lydia no longer felt the silence between them was awkward, it felt like a held breath.

Like they were both listening to the creak of the trees, the rustle of dry leaves. Then Lydia realised what she wasn't hearing. Birds. She stopped moving and thought. She had heard calls when they had started out. Blackbirds definitely, and something trilling and small, maybe a chaffinch. Now there was nothing.

Fleet was a few feet away, looking down at the ground. Lydia wanted to say something, get him to walk back to her, but she didn't know what and, suddenly, she felt her throat close up. It was fear. Primeval fear. She was on the balls of her feet, ready to lift, and could feel the muscles of her back and shoulders flex, as if they could sprout wings. There was a rushing in her ears and Lydia felt time slow as she scanned the trees, trying to find the danger.

There was a movement in the distance, hard to say how far as the closely packed trunks and undergrowth formed an optical illusion. Lydia tracked it, keeping perfectly still and waiting for the figure to reveal itself. A flash of red-brown caught the breath in Lydia's throat. For a moment she thought it was a fox, but it was too high up. Something much larger. A deer? It didn't seem likely.

Fleet wasn't looking at the ground, now, he was staring in the same direction. 'You see that?'

The sound of his voice released Lydia's feet and she moved toward him, not taking her gaze away from the animal, whatever it was. When she was in touching distance of Fleet she said 'what is it?' very quietly.

'Something doesn't feel...' Fleet began, but stopped. His words were falling on dead air, like it was muffled. It was more than just the effect of the woods; it was aggressively deadened. A creepy, unnatural effect that made Lydia feel as if they had walked into a trap box with invisible walls. And now something was happening to the trees. They were growing. Quickly and smoothly, branches extended, twigs appeared, and leaves uncurled. Green leaves in every shade from pale grey to deep emerald, red, white and shining black berries, sprays of white blossom, every possible state of every tree and bush burst into life. Lydia would have doubted her eyes, but the silence was broken by the sounds of cracking wood and the rustling friction of leaves, the damp sound of berries ripening all at once.

'What the -?' Fleet had grabbed her hand, pulled her against his side.

'I don't know,' Lydia's throat was dry. She squeezed his hand. 'We should move.'

The ground was shifting, the drifts of brown leaves whipped by a wind Lydia couldn't feel. She could taste green in her mouth, pollen and leaves, and her nose and eyes were itching. *Children holding hands in the dark wood.* That wasn't a helpful thought and she pushed it away. She had to think. She had to work out how to get them out.

She couldn't see which way to go, but instinctively turned around, pulling Fleet by the hand. They could go back the way they had come. Toward the main path and sanity. Fleet swore as a branch crashed to the ground, just to their left. The wind was stronger, now, and the air was filled with small twigs, leaves, and bark. Something heavy landed on Lydia's lip and she brushed it away with instinctive revulsion. It was a large beetle, which had presumably been minding its own business underneath the leaf mould until a few seconds ago.

And then, as quickly as it had begun, the wind died. The vegetation which had been whipping around their faces, poking their eyes and invading their mouths, dropped back to the forest floor. A shaft of sunlight pierced the tree canopy and illuminated the scene. Lydia was shaking, adrenaline coursing through her system. The greenery had gone and the trees were back to their winter state. Bark on the hornbeams glinted silver in the sunlight and the oak trees stood solid and still, as if they would never dream of shaking their branches.

'Did that just happen?' Fleet was looking around, dazed.

'Has it stopped?' Lydia said.

'Yeah,' Fleet pulled Lydia into a quick hug which she didn't resist. He dipped his head. 'You okay?'

His face was too close, the movements felt too natural. Lydia stepped away, swallowing hard. 'Fine. That was weird, though.'

'Understatement,' Fleet said, straightening up.

His expression was hard to read and Lydia wondered why he wasn't more freaked out. The truth of this hit her like a blow. He had always been exceedingly calm with weirdness. Too calm. Was it linked to the strange gleam he carried? And if so, what did he know about that? What hadn't he told her?

'Look,' Fleet was moving away, his attention focused back on the ground.

The eerie, muffled silence had dissipated and Fleet's steps sounded normal. Small twigs were snapping under his feet and, somewhere up above, there was the sound of birds calling. 'Someone was here.'

Next to the thick trunk of an oak tree there was an area of compressed undergrowth. It was flattened in a shape that would suggests a body had sat there. Plus, there was a pile of cigarette butts. At least ten, maybe more. In addition to those physical signs, Lydia's senses were giving her further information. She closed her eyes to better identify the signature. Pearl. Very faint, just the residue, but unmistakable.

Fleet was snapping on gloves and Lydia did the same. He took photographs of the area, the remains of the cigarettes and the flattened patch of ground before picking up two of the cigarette ends and sealing them in a plastic evidence bag.

Lydia crouched down next to the tree, scanning the

ground carefully. She worked methodically, breaking up the ground into quadrants and studying each section left to right, like reading lines on a page. Once she had done the first area, she moved out a little way and repeated the exercise, ignoring the crick in her neck.

'I'll call it into the team, they will get SOC out here and go over the area. We should leave.'

'In a minute,' Lydia said. The greys and browns and greens of the ground had revealed themselves in all their variation. The decaying leaves, fraying pieces of bark, tiny white fungi peeking from between patches of rich green moss. Even in December, there was life, if you were prepared to look hard enough. The smudge was tiny. A little iridescent turquoise glitter on a well-preserved oak leaf. She bagged it.

'What's that?'

Lydia straightened up and gave him the bag. 'Could be make up, or a fleck from clothing. What was Lucy wearing?'

'Nothing sparkly, but I don't know about accessories, make up. Can we get out of here, now? This place gives me the creeps.'

'Too many trees,' Lydia agreed. 'It's not natural.'

CHAPTER NINETEEN

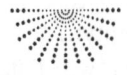

Back in the car with Fleet, Lydia was thinking hard. Fleet stayed quiet, driving back to Camberwell. 'That wasn't normal,' Lydia said, breaking the silence. 'You saw it.'

'Yes.'

Just one word, but a huge admission. 'Does that happen often to you? Seeing things which aren't normal?'

Fleet kept his eyes on the road and Lydia did, too. It was easier to talk about something like this side-by-side. 'Not often. Something out of the corner of my eye, sometimes. A gut feeling which feels stronger than normal.' After a pause he said, 'I saw a man at your flat once. Just standing there.'

'What did he look like?'

Fleet glanced at her, then, a frown creasing his forehead. 'A weird loose suit with the sleeves rolled up.'

Lydia realised something about being finished with Fleet. Her worst fear had come true, already, so it didn't matter if she was open with him. She couldn't break the relationship because that had already happened. What difference could it possibly make if he decided she was a lunatic or a freak? 'That's Jason,' she said. 'He's a ghost. He died in the eighties, that's why he's dressed like that.'

A beat. 'If ghosts exist, why is this my first?'

'Good question. I think I power people up. Any latent ability gets stronger when you are in contact with me. Which explains why your most intense experiences of seeing unusual things have been when we're together.'

'Makes sense.'

'Does it? That's good.'

'And when you say ability...'

'Magic.' Lydia said the word flatly. 'Or Crow power. I don't know what to call it. An extra sense?'

'Could be a brain wiring thing. Like people who smell colours or have ADHD. Neurodiversity.'

'Or you could be having a psychotic break and I'm enabling you.'

'No,' Fleet said. 'I don't think that. I have never thought that. And if I accept that you have different abilities, I must also accept that they are a possibility in other people. Even me.'

The seriousness of his tone made tears spring to Lydia's eyes. Hell Hawk. She was a mess and she needed to get her mind back on the case. 'Which hospital is Joshua Williams in?'

'He's at home, now,' Fleet said. 'Why? You planning to visit?'

'I want to see if he has remembered anything else from that night.'

'He hasn't said so far. We've got a FLO staying with the family and he says Joshua hasn't been chatty on the subject.'

'Can I have his address?'

'His mother won't let you in to question her traumatised son,' Fleet said. 'Even if I were to give you the address which I absolutely should not.'

'Let's go together, then,' Lydia said. 'You want to speak to him again, anyway, don't you? Just let me tag along. I won't say a word.'

Fleet let out a short laugh. It seemed to surprise him. He glanced at her and sighed. 'I can't say no to you, Lydia Crow.'

'Good to know,' Lydia said. She ignored the traitorous flutter in her heart and looked out of the window.

JOSHUA WILLIAMS LIVED with his parents in the 1930s modernist Ruskin Park House, which had well-tended gardens, and three five-storey blocks with an art deco feel to its curved lines. They made their way up a remarkably clean stairwell with pale yellow tiles on the walls to a second-floor apartment. The FLO opened the door and, after checking Fleet's ID card carefully, invited them in for tea.

Joshua was sitting on the sofa in the small, neat living room, eyes fixed on the television screen where a first-person shooter PlayStation game was displayed. He was gripping the controller so hard that his knuckles were white, but Lydia didn't know if that was his usual intensity when shooting digital zombies in the head. It was warm in the flat and he was wearing a grey T-shirt, the bandages on his arms reaching from his wrist and disappearing up inside the sleeves. Lydia had seen it on the video but Fleet was absolutely right – there was no way Joshua had inflicted those wounds by himself.

Fleet introduced himself and Lydia.

'Hi.' Joshua didn't look away from the screen or pause in his movements.

'How are you feeling?'

'Have you found Lucy yet?'

'No,' Fleet said. 'We will tell you as soon as we have any news.'

'Right,' his eyes flicked at them, just once. 'Sure.'

'I'm not police,' Lydia said, deliberately not looking at Fleet. 'When DCI Fleet introduced me just now, he didn't mention my rank and that's because I don't have one. I'm a private investigator and I'm going to do everything I can to find Lucy.'

Joshua looked at her for a longer moment. 'Why? Did my dad hire you?'

Before Lydia could ask him why he thought his father might be so keen to find Lucy Bunyan, he elaborated. 'He's worried I'm going to be taken in again for questioning, that you will keep me as a suspect unless Lucy comes home and explains to everybody that I didn't do anything to her, that I could never hurt her.'

'Yeah, they kind of jumped on you, didn't they? Don't take it personally. You were the last person to see her and you're romantically-involved. It's just statistics.'

Joshua widened his eyes, then looked at Fleet.

'I'll go help with the tea,' Fleet said, and headed out of the room

'Can I sit?' Lydia moved toward the sofa. It was a four-seater and Joshua was at one end, leaving plenty of space.

'Okay,' Joshua stabbed a button and froze the action on screen.

'No,' Lydia said, glancing at the door, 'leave it playing.'

Joshua frowned.

'Privacy,' Lydia said quietly, cutting her eyes at the living room door, which Fleet had left ajar.

Joshua nodded and turned his body toward her.

'I've just been at the woods.'

Joshua visibly flinched.

'And I know you have nothing to do with Lucy's disappearance. You are as much a victim as she is and I'm really sorry this has happened to you.'

He blinked. 'Thank you.'

'This is going to sound weird, but I don't have much time,' Lydia glanced, again, at the door, estimating how fast she would have to cut to the chase. 'There is something not right in those woods. I could feel it. And then the trees changed. They sprouted leaves and berries all at once, but it wasn't pretty, it was really sinister.' Lydia fixed him with a long look. 'Believe me, I don't scare easily and I couldn't wait to get away.'

'That's... I don't know why you're saying that.'

'Yes you do,' Lydia leaned forward a little. 'Because you and Lucy saw the same thing.' That was a guess, of course. She produced her coin and gripped it in her right hand, for luck.

Joshua was shaking his head but his eyes were wide. 'It wasn't like that. It was really dark. I didn't realise it would be that dark and we were using our phones to see so we didn't trip over.'

'You were pointing it at the ground? Looking down?'

'There were leaves and roots and little mounds of, like, moss. We were well off the path and Lucy was going really fast. She had my hand and was pulling on it, trying to make me go faster, but it didn't feel right. It was like there was someone watching us and that was freaking me out. I thought maybe there was a pervert around or that we were about to disturb a drug deal or something.'

Ah, growing up in London.

'Then it started moving.'

'What did?'

'The ground. It was writhing like it had come alive. Like there were tentacles or snakes or something.'

'What did you do?'

'Shouted to Lucy, tried to get her to stop, but she let go of my hand. She ran off.'

'Which direction?'

'I don't know, she had switched off her phone flashlight. I was looking at the floor, trying to move out the way of that stuff, whatever it was, trying not to fall over, and when I looked up, I couldn't see her.'

'She had disappeared?'

'No, I could hear her running. It was really quiet, like there was no other sound at all, not even traffic, so I could hear her really clearly. Getting quieter though as she got further away... I called out to her, I told her to stop messing around and to come back, but she didn't.'

'Did you try to go after her?'

'I couldn't. The stuff on the ground was up around my legs and I couldn't move. Then there was this feeling like something was running over my body.' Joshua shuddered. 'That's it. I can't... I don't remember anything else.'

'Thank you for telling me,' Lydia said. 'That's really helpful.'

'Really?' Joshua shook his head. 'You're going to have me committed.'

'No I'm not,' Lydia said, keeping eye contact. 'You're not crazy. That really happened. Something bad took your girlfriend and cut your arms and I'm going to find out what and how and, if I can, bring Lucy home safely.'

Joshua put his hands over his face and his shoulders shook. Lydia didn't know if she ought to pat his arm or say something comforting. She could hear Fleet's voice, chatting to the FLO and, a moment later, they appeared in the room. Fleet was carrying a tray filled with mugs. He looked from Joshua's shaking form to Lydia, an eyebrow raised.

Joshua sniffed deeply and dropped his hands. 'One other thing,' he said, ignoring Fleet and the FLO completely. 'Lucy was laughing as she ran.'

'Manic or genuinely happy, do you think?' Lydia asked quickly.

'The happiest I have ever heard her.'

OUTSIDE JOSHUA'S HOUSE, Lydia leaned against Fleet's car rather than getting in. She crossed her arms to try to stay warm. Two children walked into a dark wood… Only one came out. Lydia shook her head to clear it. She didn't need more bedtime stories, she needed to focus on the facts. 'You haven't found her phone, I assume?'

'Nothing from the scene. Just Joshua's jacket. And we've checked her number and her phone has been switched off or out of action since just past midnight. Triangulation with the towers shows Lucy's last known location was the woods. It corroborates Joshua's story, but doesn't give us any further information.'

'Are you going to tell me what Joshua said to you?' Fleet had his hands in his coat pockets. 'Or shall we get going? It's cold out here.'

'I'll walk home from here,' Lydia said. 'Thanks, anyway.'

Fleet held her gaze, not saying anything. At one time, Lydia had felt that she could tell what he was thinking. Now she wasn't so sure. 'He saw the tree roots moving. And he said he felt like something was crawling over him. He might have taken his jacket off then, if he felt like something had got inside.'

Fleet nodded. 'Okay.'

'Thanks for today,' Lydia said, pushing away from the car, ready to leave.

'That's it?'

'What do you mean?'

Fleet looked away, his jaw tensed. 'I thought we were being honest with each other? You told me things you haven't said before. I'm glad you're being open with me. It will put us in a stronger position this time.'

Lydia stepped back, her heart racing. 'That's not what I meant… I'm sorry. I think I'm finally able to be honest with you about my… stuff,' she indicated herself, 'because we're not together anymore.'

'I don't understand,' Fleet said, his brow creasing. 'That makes no sense.'

'I was always so worried about getting too close, showing you too much of my life and the Crow stuff. Now it doesn't matter.'

'What doesn't matter? You're not making any sense.'

Lydia took a breath. 'What you think of me. It doesn't matter anymore.'

Fleet looked like she had punched him.

Lydia could feel tears gathering and she wanted to get away before they fell. She turned and walked toward Denmark Hill.

CHAPTER TWENTY

Lydia's route from Ruskin Park House to Camberwell took her past the Maudsley Hospital. It had a handsome red-brick and stuccoed façade with creamy white columns and an engraved stone pedestal above the entrance. She checked her watch. It was past visiting hours, but she could try.

The reception area was bleak. Not because it was dirty or bare, although the wire mesh screen and safety glass which separated the staff from the rest of the room didn't inspire warm feelings, but because of something in the air. Something beyond the institutional bouquet of pine disinfectant with a whiff of cooked cabbage. After a few minutes waiting, Lydia realised what she could sense. Despair. Terror. Confusion.

The woman behind the screen smiled and her tone was friendly. Lydia explained that she knew she was out with the regular visiting hours but that she had been passing and wondered if she could see Ash.

'Let me see what I can do.'

Lydia waited, scrolling through her phone and making a few notes.

When the woman returned, she was smiling. 'He hasn't had any visitors before, so we're making an exception. This way.'

While Lydia wanted nothing less than to walk into yet another institution, she followed obediently through doors which clicked locked behind her and down bland corridors. 'I'm glad you're here. Ash is a lovely guy and it breaks my heart that he hasn't had any visitors. He's very gentle, very calm, but I can sit in on the meeting if you would be more comfortable?'

'No, that's fine,' Lydia said as they arrived at a plain door. Unlike some of the others they had passed, this was ordinary ply and didn't have a keypad next to it or a viewing panel. The woman fiddled with the lanyard around her neck and lowered her voice. 'Honestly, I'm not sure how much longer Ash will be with us. He would have been treated as an outpatient by now if we had somewhere stable for him to go. Few more days and we'll probably have to turf him.'

'To sheltered housing?'

'Eventually. Probably a hostel first. His key worker has been doing his best to find something suitable, but,' the woman shrugged. 'We're stretched.'

She opened the door to reveal a small square sitting room. There was a varnished pine coffee table and four armchairs with wipe-clean fabric. Two bland art prints of boats were on one wall, off-set by the laminated no-smoking sign.

A man wearing grey joggers and a black hoodie got up from one of the chairs when they walked in. He was somewhere in his early thirties and was exceptionally good-looking. Lydia knew it was exceptional because he was attractive despite the harsh fluorescent lighting, the ill-fitting clothes and the dark circles under his eyes.

'Ash?'

'Nice to meet you,' Ash said holding out his hand.

'I'll leave you to it,' the woman said. To Ash she said, 'Twenty minutes, okay?' He nodded, not taking his eyes off Lydia's face, his hand was in mid-air and Lydia reached out and shook it over the scuffed table. A powerful shot of Pearl magic ran up her arm and through her body and it took every ounce of Lydia's self-possession not to gasp out loud. As soon as their contact was broken, the sensation disappeared.

'Shall we sit?' Ash was gesturing to the chair nearest Lydia and waited until she had sat down until he did. Polite. Part of Lydia's brain was dissecting what had just happened. She hadn't sensed Pearl at all walking into the room, which was seriously odd. The Pearl signature which had run off Ash didn't feel quite right, either. It wasn't something natural and easy, sitting on him like the colour of his eyes. It was borrowed. Or maybe left. The remains of something left where it had no business being in the first place.

'I'm glad you're here,' Ash said, clasping his hands loosely between his knees.

'How are you doing?' Lydia was leaning forward, trying to get a sense of the Pearl magic, again. There was nothing. If she hadn't felt that single bolt of magic, she would have laid money on him having entirely Family-free blood.

'I've been trying to get my head around what has happened. The computers they have here, the phones. It's all new. Like something from the future.'

'The hospital passed on your details to the police. They will check through the missing person's database and, with a bit of luck, you'll be on there. You have to trust that they will do their job and just concentrate on getting better.'

'I thought you might've changed your mind. About taking my case.'

'No,' Lydia said. 'But I will chase up that police enquiry with my contact. Make sure it's at the top of somebody's to do list.'

There was a pause. 'I can pay.'

'You're not my client which means I'm not billing you. Don't get your hopes up, I really don't think there's much I can do.' Lydia took out her phone. 'Do you mind if I take your picture, though? It might help.'

'Okay.'

Lydia held up her phone and snapped a few shots. He had the sharp cheekbones and wide, shapely mouth of a model. The kind of person who wouldn't need Pearl magic to make people fall in love, want to be with him. 'It might be helpful if you can tell me what you remember about your old life. Before this happened and everything seemed wrong. I'm guessing your name and address hasn't popped back into your mind, by any chance?'

'You think I'm lying?' Ash looked thunderstruck.

'No,' Lydia said. 'I was making a joke. Sorry.'

He shook his head. 'That's okay. People don't joke much in here. I'm a bit out of practice.'

Lydia blinked. Ash no longer sounded unhinged. He sounded sad and very lost. She wanted to ask him if the name 'Pearl' meant anything to him, but had the vague idea that she might plant ideas in his mind. Wasn't there something called 'false memory' syndrome? What if she put back his recovery in her eagerness?

Ash closed his eyes. 'Millennium playing on the radio, everyone worrying about the Y2K bug. That's what I remember. I guess that wasn't a problem, after all.'

'That's a long bout of amnesia,' Lydia said.

'That's what my doctor says.' Ash opened his eyes and looked directly at Lydia. 'I've accepted that the world is real. I don't think everyone is lying anymore. I've used Google. I've looked in a mirror. It would be too elaborate a charade. It must all be real. Which means I've travelled in time. I was sixteen years old and now I'm clearly not. Which is also insane. I do know that. I'm not so crazy that I don't know that.'

'Do you remember anything at all from the last few years?'

'Partying,' Ash said. 'I've been at a party. Lots of music and dancing and drugs. Or I assume drugs, because it's been like I've been tripping, seeing things. Impossible things.'

'What sort of things.'

'I can't say,' Ash said, suddenly sounding panicky, more like he did in their first conversation. He pushed the sleeves of his over-size hoodie up his arms and Lydia caught sight of pale scars, swirling over his skin. 'I'm not allowed. I know that much. They wouldn't like me talking about them.'

'Okay, forget that. What's the last thing you remember before the party?'

There was a pause so long that Lydia started to think that Ash had gone catatonic. He was entirely motionless, staring at his clasped hands. Lydia was just wondering what she ought to do, when he spoke.

'I was meeting my mates, I think. I was excited about New Year's Eve. Everyone had big plans.'

'Right. And this was 1999?'

'Yes. We were too young to get into the clubs, so we went somewhere. We had our own party planned...' Ash trailed off. 'I wish I could remember. We definitely had something special planned. Not at someone's house or anything.'

'It's all right,' Lydia said. 'That's really good. You can call me if you remember anything else.'

'The woods,' Ash said suddenly. 'We were going to party in the woods.'

CHAPTER TWENTY-ONE

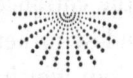

Lydia slept heavily, her dreams filled with twisting trees and strange wet, black foliage, which threatened to suffocate. Once she surfaced, fighting the imaginary branches which turned into the twists of her duvet, she showered to slough off the night sweat and went downstairs to the cafe to get a late breakfast. If there was one advantage to discovering that Angel had been working for Charlie, steering her towards cases and reporting back to her uncle, it was that now she felt no compunction whatsoever over cadging food. Angel was clearing tables after the morning rush. 'Where's the new kid?' Lydia said, surprised.

'Scrubbing. He burned my favourite pan.'

'I didn't think he did any cooking,' Lydia said.

'And he won't be again,' Angel said. 'That's what I get for trying a bit of training.'

Lydia stood in front of the counter and contemplated the menu. 'I'll have the full breakfast with toast. And hash browns.'

Angel raised an eyebrow. 'Is that a fact?'

Lydia smiled. 'Quick as you like, I'm starving.'

Angel's expression went nuclear, which was fun. 'Anything else for her ladyship?'

Lydia widened her smile. 'Just some tea. And orange juice. Thanks, Angel. You're the best.' Then. Before Angel could launch across the counter and smack her, Lydia retreated to her favourite seat. It was in the back corner, facing the counter and the entrance with her back against the wall and the big window to her right. Best sight lines, and quick access to the door which led back up to her flat. The food helped to wake Lydia up, but it was still hard to shake the dregs of her dream. Seeing Ash in the hospital had been unnerving. He wasn't crazy and something very odd had clearly happened. It was also weird that the last thing he remembered involved woodland. Lydia didn't believe in coincidences, and she was planning to search the news reports from 1999 for a missing sixteen-year-old, when something else happened to push all thoughts of Ash from her mind.

Charlie was outside on the street, heading for the cafe, but there was something in his gait. He was moving very quickly and Lydia felt her heart rate kick up. Having hesitated too long to get upstairs and avoid him, she watched as he headed to her table with a dark feeling of foreboding. He hadn't so much as nodded at Angel, which meant something serious was definitely up. You could say a lot of things about Charlie Crow, but he was extremely courteous. Lydia put down her cutlery and pushed her plate away. 'What's wrong? Have they found Lucy Bunyan?' She tried to push away the sudden image of a dead girl, hidden under a pile of rotting leaves.

Charlie sat next to Lydia, not opposite her the way he usually did. He put a hand on her arm. 'Your Uncle Terrence is dead.'

Lydia frowned, trying to place the name.

Charlie glowered, removing his hand. 'Don't tell me

you don't know Terrence. What was Henry thinking? Feathers, we're your family. You should know their names at least.'

'There are a lot of Crows,' Lydia said defensively. Henry had told her plenty of stories and she hadn't been separated from the family at large. She had been to parties for naming days, Christmas, and New Year. She didn't remember an Uncle Terrence.

'Terrence is banged up in Wandsworth,' he paused. 'Was. He was found dead in his cell yesterday morning. I only just heard.' Charlie looked outraged at this, as if the delay in communication was the worst of it.

Lydia didn't know which question to start with. Who was Terrence and why was he in prison? How did he die? Luckily, Charlie ploughed on. He scanned the cafe as he spoke, seemingly unable or unwilling to look at her. 'You know the old days? Doing time was something of an occupational hazard. It's not like that now, of course, but our old-timers are still doing their stretches. We look after them as best we can, executive cells, cushty jobs, plenty of money flowing in for sundries, all that.'

Lydia nodded as if Charlie hadn't just started speaking a completely different language. Not for the first time, Lydia appreciated why her parents had warned her against Charlie and the Family business. 'What happened?'

'He was seventy-five,' Charlie said. 'Found with a noose. You don't do that at seventy-five. He'd been inside for over thirty years. They're making out he couldn't hack it. Why would he do thirty years and then decide to check out? Makes no sense. Someone did for him.'

Charlie's phone buzzed and he pulled it from his pocket, glancing at the screen. He answered it, still not looking at Lydia. She had never seen him so agitated. His mood worsened over the course of the short call. 'No,' he said, flatly at one point. His entire body had gone dangerously still and

Lydia pushed her plate further to the other side of the table, her appetite truly gone.

'What?' She said, once he had put his phone facedown on the Formica.

'Terrence's friend, Richard, has gone, too. Shanked. He was in intensive care overnight and he just passed.'

'Is Richard one of us?'

Charlie nodded. 'He was on his toes back in the seventies but he came home when we had a spot of bother with the law. Took the stretch to protect the rest of us. He's a bloody hero. Him and Terrence were the last from that era. They sacrificed their lives so that we could fly free.'

'I can't imagine,' Lydia began, the terror of being locked up still very fresh. She couldn't imagine the strength it took to choose that.

'Yeah, not really your style.' Charlie was angry and Lydia could see she was just the nearest target. She compressed her lips to make sure she didn't retaliate.

Charlie blew air out of his nose, closing his eyes for a moment. When he opened them again, he twisted to face Lydia. 'You don't know what it was like, then. I'm guessing Henry didn't include any of it in your bedtime stories. Police had been bought off for years, everything was in harmony. They knew that we were keeping order in Camberwell, that things could be so much worse. It left them free to allocate resources to Peckham. If things weren't strictly legit, they knew we had a code and that there was a fairness to our operation. We were getting paid, but nobody works for free, right?'

Lydia nodded.

'Then there were changes. New blood in at the top, but mainly political reform. A spotlight got turned on police corruption, pressure was applied and, all the time, the drug problems were multiplying, homelessness, overcrowding, racist attacks. Some bright spark decided that some serious crime arrests, a nice package for the organised crime hard-ons, would smooth the way.' Charlie shook his head. 'Probably someone was looking to climb the greasy pole, thought it would look good on their CV. That's all it takes, you know?' He eyeballed her. 'You think individuals don't have power in something like the police, but they do. That's why I was so against you getting friendly with your copper. An avalanche can start with one little rock.'

'I get it,' Lydia said. 'Really.'

'I don't think you do,' Charlie said, but he sounded calmer. 'Lyds, you're just a kid, still. You're brand new to all this and I'm sorry it's not a better time. I wanted to hand you the keys to a palace, you've got to believe that.'

Lydia nodded to show she did, even though she wasn't entirely sure what he was talking about.

'Anyhow, Terrence and Richard and a couple of old boys, long since passed, swallowed all the charges. And that was that. We went back to business, nice and quiet, the regime changed a few more times at the Met and the political focus shifted to immigration and, eventually, the war on terror.'

'And business changed, too, right?' Lydia said. 'It's not like it used to be.'

'Right, right,' Charlie said. 'We're very professional these days. Everything looks neat and tidy.'

That wasn't exactly reassuring.

'The Silvers have helped us with that over the years. Which is a worrying loose end.'

'They'll keep quiet,' Lydia said. 'They've got as much to lose as we have. Especially now Alejandro is in Westminster.'

'I think you're underestimating how much you pissed off Maria Silver. And now she's in charge-'

'I know, I know,' Lydia closed her own eyes. Just for a few seconds. When she opened them, she didn't want to ask the obvious question. She lowered her voice. 'Do we know who did it?'

Charlie shook his head. 'But I'm going to find out.'

CHARLIE TOLD her he was handling it, but Lydia knew she had to help. Partly because it was what she did, but also because it was important that the Family saw her take action. Lydia wasn't naïve enough to think that only Aiden had his doubts about her loyalty. Finally, if it turned out that another Family was responsible for the deaths of two Crows, then it would be better if she found out before Charlie. Hopefully it was a random in prison, some internal squabble over the in-jail pecking order. Not a sign of something bigger. And definitely not something triggered by her nosing around the Pearl residence. Or Maria taking the reins of the Silver Family.

Getting access was not going to be easy. She did have a card to play, but it wasn't one she wanted to flip. Every time she thought she was closing the door on Fleet, it swung open again. Still. Two Crows were dead and so there was no real choice. She dialled the number. When Fleet answered she just said, 'I need a favour.'

WALKING into Wandsworth Prison was like stepping back in time. The building was Victorian and the ambience in the reception room was straight out of the seventies. Lydia wouldn't have been surprised to see a Playboy calendar on the wall. Fleet spoke to the prison officers and Lydia kept her mouth shut. After they signed the paperwork which had carbon copies – the officer passed across the yellow portion to Fleet – they were given a thorough pat down which was, according to Fleet, the bare minimum security, and then they were led through an innocuous door and down a short corridor to a set of bars with a locked gate. Instantly, the atmosphere changed and Lydia could feel the ceiling pressing down on her head. There were shouts and screams, echoing off the walls, and a rhythmic banging sound. Part of Lydia was curious to see the main prison. Fleet had described the landings filled with cells, radiating from a central area, but mostly she was just relieved that they were heading to a different place. Once through the first set of bars, they took a side door and crossed a small open yard and into a separate building.

'Visitor suite,' Fleet whispered.

'Suite' was entirely the wrong word. The room the officer led them into was covered in fag burns and paint was peeling from the top of the walls, revealing swathes of damp. A table was bolted to the floor and there were a few mismatched chairs. It smelled of disinfectant and something far worse; the remains of whatever the disinfectant was meant to clean up.

'This is the visiting room?' Lydia was trying to imagine more than a dozen prisoners and their families in the room. Even that small number would be a squeeze and there were nowhere near enough places for them to sit or have any measure of privacy.

'No, miss,' the officer said. 'This is for private meetings. Legal counsel, police interviews,' he nodded at Fleet as he said this. 'General visits are in the main block.'

'Right,' Lydia felt stupid and vowed to keep her mouth shut and just take it all in. Her senses were buzzing but not with any particular 'Family' or power sense, more just a heightened feeling of danger. All those bars between her and freedom. All the badness – and misery – of the incarcerated. She tried, again, to imagine the loyalty it had taken to voluntarily walk into a place like this, knowing you were signing away the rest of your life to it.

Fleet had warned Lydia that their contact was unlikely to

talk to them. He was serving eight years for aggravated assault, possession with intent to supply, and three breaking and entering charges. It seemed like a long sentence to Lydia but Fleet said he would 'only serve four'. Besides, when he walked in, Lydia saw that he was also paying the skin tax. Black offenders routinely got handed longer sentences than their white comrades.

'Got any burn, bruv?' Azi strutted to the table and sprawled onto the chair, legs wide and one hand on his inner thigh, practically cupping himself. 'What's up, sweet thing?' He jerked his head up in Lydia's direction, giving her a smouldering look.

Lydia had expected incarceration to humble or beat down a person and that had to be the case for many. It didn't seem to have affected Azi that way, however. Unless his confidence levels pre-prison had been truly stratospheric and she was witnessing him at fifty-per cent ego.

'Don't smoke, sorry,' Fleet said.

Azi ignored him, keeping his gaze on Lydia. His tongue darted out and licked dry lips.

'We're here to talk to you about Terrence.'

Azi looked at Fleet, then. 'What's that to you? Nobody cares in here, innit? He was buzzing all day.'

'Buzzing?' Fleet said. 'He was on something?'

'Nah, bruv. Red light, you get me?'

'He was in bang up?' Fleet asked, understanding dawning in his eyes.

Lydia was still having difficulty following the conversation. 'He was locked in his cell?' She clarified. 'Or isolation?'

Azi shifted his gaze again, taking his time to lick his lips suggestively and move his hand to slip inside his baggy prison-issue joggers. Lydia held his gaze, willing herself not to blush or look away.

'We're banged up all day, innit. Not enough staff to let us out for our rehab classes. I'm supposed to be learning how to dry wall.' The officer by the door shifted. 'You should write *that* down.'

'Terrence was using his emergency bell before he died? Was that unusual? For him, I mean?' Fleet had his notebook out and Azi looked at it hungrily. 'You give me one of them, fam. I tell you what you want to know.'

'You want a notebook?' Fleet raised an eyebrow. 'Give over, Azi. You can't write for shit.'

Lydia hid her shock, but Azi let out a barking laugh. It was the most genuine sound she had heard from him so far.

He nodded at Fleet. 'He hardly never used that bell. Had no need. Was hardly in bang up. He was executive, you get me? Big pad on the ones with a PlayStation and all that.'

Fleet had explained to Lydia that white-collar criminals often held positions of responsibility in the prison and the nicer cells on the ground floor were perks of the jobs they did for the prison staff. High-ups like Terrence walked straight into the best prison jobs and cells, running complex systems of barter and favours with inmates and staff alike, using their skills and power from the outside world and transferring it to the inside.

'How was he before? Did you speak to him? Did he seem his usual self?'

Azi flicked a look at the officer and said. 'He won at snap. Same as.'

Fleet nodded as if this cryptic phrase made perfect sense.

'No problems with anyone recently? Nothing brewing?'

Azi shook his head.

'I find that hard to believe,' Fleet said. 'There's always trouble. And Terrence is dead.'

Azi shrugged.

Lydia produced her coin, flipping it over the knuckles of her hand. She didn't care that Fleet would see, was past that. He had showed her the scope of his commitment to his job and she wasn't going to hide hers. She was a Crow. She was all in. And it wasn't any of his damn business, any more.

'Look at me,' she said. 'You know who Terrence was?'

Azi flicked his eyes in Lydia's direction and they widened, just a small amount. He was hard, but he wasn't impervious.

'Gangster, innit.'

'That's right,' Lydia said, making her tone the sing-song of a nursery school teacher speaking to a recalcitrant toddler. 'But he wasn't just any good old boy, he was a Crow.'

'I know his name,' Azi said, after a moment. He was watching the coin, no longer looking at Lydia's face.

'Terrence was my blood,' Lydia said. 'I'm keen to find out who is responsible for his death.'

'I dunno,' Azi said. 'He wasn't no bother. You would have to be cracked to take a pop...' He trailed off before suddenly leaning forward, elbows on knees, and whispering. 'Unless it was a screw.'

'That's not going to fly,' Lydia shook her head briskly. 'One of the inmates did this, probably under orders from somebody outside. I need a name.'

'I dunno,' Azi said again. His eyes went to the guard at the door.

'I'm not going after the man who pulled the trigger, I want the person who pointed the gun.'

Azi's eyes flickered with confusion and Lydia wondered if she should rephrase the question.

Fleet stood up and went to speak to the officer at the door. Lydia didn't know if he was going to try to talk him into leaving them for a few minutes or just to ask for a cup of tea, but she took the opportunity to lean in closely to Azi. She could smell body odour, cigarette smoke, and a strange sweet chemical top note. Her senses picked up fear and she flipped her coin, suspending it right in front of Azi's face. She knew he wanted to rear back, to get away, and his eyes were all white, but she wouldn't let him. She put a hand on his knee and stared into his eyes, pushing a little harder than she had ever tried on a person before. She only had a few seconds. 'Who stabbed Richard?'

'Malc.' Azi looked confused that the words had popped out.

'And did he do Terrence, too?'

Azi started to shrug, but it didn't quite take. 'I swear I dunno. Could be. Or one of the same crew.'

'Best guess?'

'I can't,' Azi said, and Lydia saw tears in his eyes. 'They'll kill me.'

'Just tell me who leads the crew. Who pointed Malc at Terrence and Richard?'

Fleet was back, standing behind Lydia's chair, blocking the guard's view. 'Thank you for your cooperation, Azi,' he said loudly. 'You've been very helpful.'

'I haven't!' Azi said, pure panic now. All traces of swagger had drained away and his skin was ashy and damp with sweat.

'This has been so productive, DCI Fleet,' Lydia said. 'I reckon we should stay awhile. Make this a nice long chat. Forget speaking to anybody else on our list, waste of time when we've got Azi, here.'

He looked confused. 'I'm not saying anything.'

'It's been very illuminating,' Fleet said. 'The police would like to recognise your cooperation. I wonder if there is something we can do? Officially.'

'You can't,' Azi whispered. 'You can't do that.'

'I can do whatever I like, son.'

'Malc did it.' Azi said. 'He's the one. Just got the idea on his own. Just did it.'

'And how has Malc been recently?' Lydia said.

'What do you mean?'

'Happy? Depressed? Worried? Anything unusual? Has he come into money?'

'Been living it large? Had more spice and burn than usual? Buying in bulk from the commissary?'

Azi's eyes were rolling, now, he was close to passing out from fear. Lydia pushed away her concern and empathy. There was a job to do and they had to do it. 'Answer the DCI,' she said, shoving a little more Crow into her voice.

Azi licked his lips. 'He's been flush. Like he got a payday.'

'Since Terrance and Richard died?' Fleet confirmed.

Azi nodded, mute.

WALKING AWAY FROM WANDSWORTH, Lydia had to stop herself from running. The urge to fly was running through every bone in her body. All of those doors and locks and bars. They made something primeval in her brain go blank with panic, same as when she had been locked in the Camberwell nick. Crows did not like cages.

She got into the car with Fleet and accepted a lift back to Camberwell. It was going to be hard to be in the enclosed space with Fleet, but the rain was cold and falling with enough force to bounce up off the ground. Besides, she still had some questions.

'So, Malc took a contract in return for cash or favours.'

'Looks that way,' Fleet was watching the road which meant Lydia could watch him. The line of his jaw, the creases around his eyes, the scar on his chin from when he came off a swing set as a kid.

'But how did the order get in? Don't they monitor correspondence?'

'Yeah, all calls are recorded and written communications are read, whether emails or letters. Plus, inmates aren't supposed to have mobiles.'

Lydia didn't miss the phrasing. 'But they do?'

'Yup.'

'Your standard gang-banger pay-as-you-go untraceable phone is another form of currency inside. Payments are made to and from outside payment systems, bank accounts of friends or family members, all sorts of things. You can't have a load of cash change hands or money wired into the inmates prison account, naturally, so the big deals are all done via a third party.'

'So unless we have the burner in question, we can't trace the person who gave the order.'

'Correct,' Fleet said. 'Which is why we're going to have his cell tossed. If he's smart, he doesn't keep it there, but you know most of the boys in there aren't criminal masterminds. We might get lucky.'

GOOD AS HIS WORD, Fleet used his police clout and got Malc's cell searched that afternoon. He called Lydia straight after. 'Text with Terrence and Richard's names came through last week. Idiot didn't even delete it.'

'Number?'

'Switched off. Probably already been dumped.'

Lydia blew out a sigh of frustration. 'Why can't they all be stupid?'

'I've turned phone over to tech bods and they'll see what else they can find. Don't hold your breath, though.'

'Right. Thank you.' Lydia was sitting in her office chair, facing her overflowing desk. From this vantage point she could see her laptop half-buried in papers, three old coffee mugs and two empty whisky bottles. She really ought to tidy up before she had a client in here.

'You still there?' Fleet said.

'Yes,' Lydia straightened up. 'Sorry. Just tired. What will happen to Malc? Can we talk to him?'

Fleet paused. 'I will push for a conviction, but I have to warn you the chances are low.'

'Azi named him,' Lydia said.

'Yeah, but he won't do that again. Not in an official capacity. Put that kid in front of a judge and he'll forget his own name let alone anyone else's.'

Lydia knew that she had used her Crow whammy on Azi to make him talk. And she knew he would be in fear of his life if he gave evidence in court against another prisoner. Still. It seemed unlikely that it was that easy to get away with murder when you were already a convicted criminal and in a closed unit like Wandsworth. 'Won't the guards have seen something? Be able to coordinate evidence and with the mobile phone, too-'

'It's not in their interests,' Fleet said. 'Management will want an outcome that doesn't point to negligence on their watch. It looks bad if people can order hits within a highly secure prison.'

Lydia swore quietly.

'I'm sorry. I know they were your family.'

'I never knew them,' Lydia shrugged off his sympathy. 'It's not that. I'm angry.' And worried. If the law was going to let them down, what would Charlie do in retaliation? 'Can you get me in to interview Malc?'

'I'll see what I can do.'

'Thanks.' Lydia was still distracted, rehearsing the conversation with Charlie, wondering if there was any way she could keep this bit of information from him, for Malc's safety. It wasn't like Charlie was just going to drop the matter, decide not to bother to look into it. If Lydia didn't get results, he would get them another way.

Fleet broke into her thoughts, echoing them exactly. 'I guess you're going to tell your uncle about Malc?'

Lydia nodded. 'No choice.'

'I get that,' Fleet said. 'I will warn the prison to put him into protective custody. If they've got the resources.'

Lydia couldn't feel much sympathy for the man who had murdered a couple of old-age-pensioners, even knowing that Terrence and Richard Crow had undoubtedly been no angels. 'You do what you have to do.'

CHAPTER TWENTY-TWO

Charlie texted Lydia, demanding an update. She drove to Grove Lane, trying not to think about what Charlie was going to arrange once she had given him Malc's name. There was no way out of it, though. It wasn't as if Charlie was just going to drop the matter. And if she didn't tell him, somebody else would. Eventually. And then he might guess that she had held out on him.

When Charlie opened the door, he looked drawn. His olive-toned skin was yellow-ish and the lines on his face were deeper than usual. He ushered Lydia inside. 'Quickly,' he said. 'We're not safe.'

'Has something else happened?' Lydia said, feeling sick.

'No. No. Not yet. Only a matter of time. Getting you arrested was a warning shot. This is the real deal. If our alliance with Alejandro is over-' He shook his head. 'I don't even want to think about it.'

It had certainly occurred to Lydia that if JRB were intent on destabilising the Families into breaking the truce, then killing a couple of Crows would be an excellent way to do so. They would have to pin the murders on one of the other

Families, though. 'It's not necessarily the Silvers.' She told him about her visit to Azi and the person he named.

Charlie went still. 'That's good work, Lyds.'

'I'll find the person who ordered the attack. That's who we want.'

Charlie nodded, his mind clearly working.

'We shouldn't do anything rash. Not until we've got all the information.' Lydia was watching Charlie carefully. He had gone dangerously still.

'Naturally,' Charlie said. He clapped his hands together, the action loud and sudden after the quiet pause which had come before. He turned on a humourless smile. 'You need to train.'

'I was going to work my contacts, find out who ordered the hit.'

'Training isn't optional,' Charlie said. 'Especially now. You need to be strong. For your own safety.'

Lydia could recognise when it wasn't worth arguing with Charlie so she followed him upstairs to the training room.

It was a grey day but what little light was available streamed through the large windows, illuminating the room. Charlie was in a strange mood. Intense and distracted and Lydia spent the next hour regulating herself, making sure that nothing unexpected happened. She spun her coin, held it in mid-air and produced multiple coins, just ephemeral copies but they looked real enough, and sent them clattering to the floor in a shower of flashing metal. It was tiring, but Lydia felt like the true exhaustion came from continually holding onto her self-control, trying to make sure that only a little happened. She could feel a larger power, hovering, just above her as she obeyed Charlie's instructions. The thing was, it was drawn from somewhere. She was a battery, powering up other people, at least that was her working theory. But that powering-up had to be drawn from somewhere else. She didn't understand it, which meant she didn't like it.

'Okay, that'll do,' Charlie said. 'I can see you're tired.'

'Thanks,' Lydia said, injecting exhaustion into her voice.

'Unless,' Charlie had been leaning against the far wall and he straightened up, now. 'You're putting it on.'

'Sorry?' Lydia tensed.

Charlie was staring intently, his small eyes flat and unreadable and Lydia felt a prickle of fear. She pushed it down. He didn't know. He couldn't know.

'I just wonder if you're trying hard enough,' Charlie said. He glanced away, though, his body seeming to relax.

Lydia felt her own fear slip down a notch and she forced herself to walk near him, to pick up her water bottle and take a casual swig.

The bottle fell from her hand as Charlie looped an arm around her neck, pulling her back so that she was off balance. His forearm was hard against her neck, compressing her windpipe and making it impossible to breathe, and she scrambled for her footing, feeling Charlie behind her like a solid wall. She grabbed his arm, trying to pull it away, dragged her foot down and stamped on his instep as hard as she could, but he was too big and too strong.

Her mind was white with panic. A man had grabbed her like this on the street, tried to bundle her into a van, seconds before the Fox brothers had shown up. She had been strangled by Maddie, too, and Jason had saved her life. Jason wasn't here, though. And the chances of the Fox brothers arriving to save the day and then beat her to a pulp, were slim. Little black speckles were all over the whiteness, now, and Lydia knew she was going to pass out very soon. She had done self-defence training back in Aberdeen and knew that she should have stepped back and to the side, ducking and twisting out of the lock but she had missed the moment in her shock and Charlie had her up against his body, with no room to manoeuvre.

'Come on,' she heard Charlie's voice. 'Fight back.'

Lydia couldn't feel her body anymore. She had retreated to the place on the knife edge of consciousness. Any second and she would be gone. Killed by her own uncle. She supposed it would be handy for him. He had always said he wanted her in the Family, proper, but she had proved a disappointment. And she was a loose cannon, fraternising with Foxes, baiting the Silvers, not showing him the deference he felt he deserved.

A wave of tiredness washed over Lydia and she thought about going to sleep. She was exhausted by it all. 'Oh, for fuck's sake.' It was a woman's voice. Familiar. Not overly welcome. It took Lydia what felt like a long time, but must have been a split second, to realise who had spoken. It was Maddie. Maddie wasn't here, so it had to be a delusion. She had a lot of those. And she was passing out. Or passed out and on her way to being dead.

That did it. She didn't want to be dead. Especially not at the hands of Uncle Charlie. Her mother had warned her to watch out for him and she didn't want her to say 'I told you so'. Teenage petulance wasn't the most noble reason for fighting, but it was better than nothing. Lydia pulled the power which had been waiting in the wings onto centre stage. It felt difficult, like every thought was slow, but she pictured her coin and that helped. She couldn't feel it, couldn't see anything except flashes and speckles and was pretty sure her eyes were rolled up back in her head, but picturing it helped her to focus.

She pulled the power around her, like a cloak. It was warm and comforting and with that comfort came a little more mental clarity. Her coin was in her mind's eye, clear and bright. She saw the room she was in, Charlie behind her, the grey winter light casting pale shapes on the wooden floor, her water bottle rolling away. Her coin in front of her was more real than reality. In that moment, Lydia knew it came from somewhere else. Or it belonged in a slice of reality that was different to the water bottle and the floor and her own body. All she had to do was to join it. At once, she was outside of her body, looking down. She could see her own face, pale and desperate, Charlie's meaty arm across her neck, his tattoos moving. His tattoos had a touch of the hyperreal, too, but they were nowhere near as crisp as her coin. This vantage point should have been scary, the last moments of hallucination before death, but Lydia no longer felt afraid. She took her time, looking around the room, ignoring her own struggling form below, and seeing the vaguest outline of a second Lydia suspended in mid-air reflected in the multiple mirrors. She looked a bit like Jason when he was at his most insubstantial, a thought which made her smile. She reached out a ghostly hand and passed it over Charlie's arm, feeling a tingling in physical body as she did so.

Instantly the pressure on her neck disappeared and she sucked in lungfuls of painful air. She was back in her body, doubled over and dragging in ragged breaths while every part of her screamed with sensation. She had forgotten, even in those small moments of being incorporeal just how much *activity* a body experienced. She could feel blood moving in veins, muscles stretching and contracting, air moving over tiny hairs in her middle ear, the squeezing of peristalsis in her guts, and the electric crackle of her neurons firing. As her oxygen levels improved with several more breaths, the intense awareness faded and she was able to think about other things. Like the slumped form of her uncle, who was leaning against the wall, hands on his knees.

His breathing was coming in gasps, too, like he had been sprinting.

She moved toward the door, keeping her eyes on Charlie in case he made a miraculous recovery and sprang for her. Out of the corner of her eye, she thought she saw a black shape moving. She whipped her head around to see, but the corner of the room was empty. For a second, she thought she saw a black winged shape reflected in the mirrors, but she blinked and it disappeared. It was probably the after-effects of the oxygen deprivation or the adrenaline that was still coursing through her body, making time move differently and colours appear saturated. She couldn't trust her own eyes or her senses. She needed to get away and rest somewhere dark and safe.

'What the feathers was that?' Charlie managed, bringing his head up to look at Lydia.

She felt a spurt of confused anger. 'You tried to kill me.'

'No!' Charlie's voice was different, but Lydia couldn't work out how.

She backed up a few more steps, getting closer to the door while keeping her eyes on Charlie.

'I was,' he paused to suck in some more air. 'Training.'

It didn't bloody feel like it, Lydia thought. Charlie was still bent over and was showing no signs of moving, but Lydia didn't want to wait for him to recover his strength. She was at the door and ready to turn and open it, to flee down the stairs and out of the house. She didn't know what to do after that point and realised that she had to make sure Charlie wasn't coming for her. Otherwise she would have to leave London altogether. She hesitated. 'And did I pass your little test?'

Charlie's shark eyes were moist, like he was actually going to cry. 'What did you do?'

'I don't...' Lydia stopped. Tried again. 'You shouldn't have done that. You really scared me.'

'I got that,' Charlie said, a spark of his old self igniting.

Lydia took another step back, her hand on the door. And that's when she saw what was different about Charlie. His tattoos weren't moving.

CHAPTER TWENTY-THREE

Lydia knew she couldn't go back to The Fork, not at that moment. She would have to eventually, she had to collect Jason or see him to make sure he didn't start fading, but right at that moment she had to get away. Somewhere safe. Somewhere Charlie wouldn't think to look. She drove while she thought, putting distance between her and Charlie. He had attacked her. That had just happened.

Lydia arrived at her destination without fully acknowledging to herself that she had decided to go there. She dialled the number before she could lose her will. 'Are you home?'

Fleet had answered the phone after the second ring. 'What's wrong?'

'I'm fine,' Lydia said, aware that the last time she had called about his flat, she had just taken a beating. 'I can't go home right now, though.'

'I'm on my way there. I'll meet you outside.'

Lydia stayed in the car on the quiet street, counting breaths in and out. She saw Fleet's car in her rear-view mirror and watched him park. He unfolded himself from the driving seat and she felt herself sag with relief.

Inside the flat looked exactly the same. Extremely neat, warm and comfortable. 'Tea?'

'Thanks,' Lydia said. She sat on the sofa and stared at the wall, trying to gather her wits. She had tried in the car on the way over, but the panic had still been keeping them on a loop. Now that she was off the street and hidden, she made more progress. Charlie didn't know this place. He didn't think she was with Fleet and if he decided to check, he would have to find Fleet's home address which wasn't easy. Not impossible, though. Not for a man like Charlie Crow. The fear gripped her, again, and she was on her feet.

'I need to go,' she called. 'Sorry.' This had been a mistake. She should keep moving.

'Wait,' Fleet came out of the kitchen and crossed the room. He put his hands onto Lydia's shoulders and dipped his head to look into her eyes. 'What's happened. Talk to me.'

'Can't,' Lydia said. 'I need to hide out.' Her mind flashed to Maddie, hiding on the narrow boat courtesy of Paul Fox. She had thought Maddie was the bad one, the wild card, but now she had a glimpse as to why she had wanted to run away. Had Charlie trained her in the same way? Maybe Maddie hadn't started out as sociopathic. Maybe Charlie had created that particular monster.

'Lyds, you're shaking. I've never seen you like this. And when I first met you, someone had just tried to kill you.' He tried a small smile. 'You're alarming me.'

Lydia focused on Fleet's eyes. Warm, steady, and full of genuine concern. Hell Hawk, she was not going to cry. She refused. She dug her finger nails into her palms and straightened her spine. 'Charlie. He attacked me.'

Fleet frowned. 'What do you mean?'

'Just that,' Lydia broke from his grasp, it was too intense to look into his face for a second longer. She sat back on the sofa and let her head fall back. The tiredness was lapping at the edges, threatening to pull her under.

'Are you hurt?'

Lydia shook her head. 'A few bruises, that's all. He scared me though.'

'I'll kill him,' Fleet's jaw was clenched. 'Say the word.'

'It was training,' she said. 'It wasn't... He said it was for my own good. Well, not my own good specifically, the good of the Family.'

'Training?'

Lydia let her eyes drift closed. 'You know what I am. Crows can do certain things. Apparently those abilities can be trained to make them stronger, more effective. It's Charlie's obsession. He says we need to be strong, that a war is coming. He doesn't think the treaty is going to hold for much longer. Not now somebody is having Crows killed in prison.'

'Is that why Alejandro has left?'

Lydia's eyes opened and she straightened to look at Fleet. 'What do you know about the Silvers?'

'Just that Maria is the new head of the Family.'

'Is that official intelligence or copper gossip?'

Fleet shrugged. 'You know how it is. Half the people don't believe in the Families and the other half tell tall tales just to make themselves sound interesting. My great aunt was married to a Fox and we all had to give teeth as a wedding present, that kind of thing.'

'Well, it's not wrong. Alejandro is following his political ambitions.'

'That's ominous,' Fleet said.

'I'm not sure it's relevant, though. Charlie is fixated on the Families because he knows them, but JRB are the Silvers' clients and they seem to have connections to the Pearls, too.'

'The prison killings could be more random than you

think. We can't jump to conclusions. A list of people pissed off with your family would be handy, though.'

Lydia tilted her head. 'How long have you got?'

Fleet smiled sadly. 'And now Charlie has lost his mind. You want to press charges?'

Lydia almost laughed. 'No, thank you.'

'This is serious.'

The urge to laugh disappeared. 'I know. He's freaking out about the murders. It's a warning. No, more than a warning, it's an act of war. And I'm not strong. He wants me to be strong.' As Lydia spoke, she could feel her thoughts swirling and looping, circling to find an order that made sense.

'You're not defending him?' Fleet said.

'I don't know. I need to think.' Lydia pulled out her phone and texted Paul. She told him she had gone to Fleet's flat and asked if he needed the address.

No need. On my way.

'Paul Fox is coming here. He won't be long. I just need to speak to him and I don't want to do it on the phone.'

'I don't understand, why him? Why now?'

'I can meet him outside if you want.'

'No, that's not what I'm saying.'

'I need to see him. I need all the help I can get.' Lydia was acting on instinct. Something had ignited when Charlie had grabbed her. She had never trusted her uncle and she had been proved right. Maybe the old lines of Family weren't set in stone, maybe there was a better way of deciding who was a friend and who was a foe. Maybe it didn't have to start and end with blood.

Fleet went out to the kitchen to finish making tea and Lydia paced the room, looking out of the window every few minutes.

Paul Fox must have broken the speed limit, unless he had been fortuitously close to Camberwell. He also managed to park and get to the flats without Lydia seeing him from the window. She buzzed him upstairs and opened the door.

'What's happened, Little Bird?' Paul's look of concern was genuine and Lydia realised something as Paul walked into Fleet's flat. The tang of Fox was no longer a warning.

'Trouble at home,' Lydia said shortly. 'I might need to hide.'

Paul nodded. 'Easy.'

'Come to the station,' Fleet said, walking into the room. 'We can protect you.'

'No,' Lydia said. 'I will not willingly set foot in that place as long as I draw breath in this city.'

Fleet's eyes widened and he nodded. 'Fair enough. I can provide police protection, though. Short-term at least. And I've got some holiday accrued. I could take that and be your own personal guard.'

'Don't need it, mate,' Paul said. 'Got all the man-power we need.' To Lydia he said, 'We've got this. Nobody will get near you.'

'You're trusting him, now?' Fleet said. 'This is the man who sold you out. That police station you hate? He's the man who put you there.'

'I seem to remember you were there, too,' Lydia said mildly. 'And Paul didn't set me up.'

'I suppose he told you that?'

Lydia's patience snapped. 'Don't question my judgement on who I trust or I will reassess all of my connections, starting with you. If you want to help me, you're going to have to accept that Paul is on my side. I need your help. I need both your help. But I can't spend all my time refereeing. I'm tired and I'm scared and I need all my attention on fixing this. Are you in or are you out? Decide now.'

'I'm in,' Fleet said immediately.

Paul nodded, his lips tight.

'Good.' Lydia wanted to sit down. Truthfully, she wanted

to lie down and sleep for twelve hours straight, but above the exhaustion was terror. And that made her jumpy with adrenaline. She paced up and down, trying to think. 'Charlie doesn't know this place so I'm safe here for the time being. Long term, I don't know. I don't know what to do.'

'You want us to move on him?' Paul said.

'No. Don't do anything. I just need to work out how to play this.' Lydia took a breath. 'Malcolm Ferris, goes by "Malc". Know him?'

'Nope.'

Paul was an excellent liar, Lydia had no doubt, but she also thought he looked genuinely blank. She was studying him for any flicker of recognition and caught none. 'Someone commissioned him to kill a couple of Crows,' Lydia said, deciding to just come out with it. 'They were all in the same block in Wandsworth. Emphasis on the word 'were'.'

'I'm sorry,' Paul said. 'That was not a sensible move.'

Lydia caught something else in his tone. Relief. 'What did you think I was going to say? You sound almost happy.'

'No, no. It's just...' He took an audible breath. 'I'm glad my father is in Japan. Otherwise I would have put him top of the list of suspects and that would cause more problems for you and me.'

Lydia ignored the romantic connotations of 'you and me', deciding he intended the phrase to indicate professional friendship. Family alliance. Wholesome stuff. 'Can you ask around?'

'I can send people out and about, see what we can dig up. There might be some whispers.'

'Thank you,' Lydia said.

'Take this,' Paul reached inside his jacket and produced a burner phone. 'Use this if you need me. I can hide you.'

'I seem to remember Lydia found Maddie when you

were hiding her,' Fleet said. 'What makes you so sure Lydia will be safe with you?'

Paul flashed Fleet a dead-eye look. 'I wasn't trying to hide Maddie. I wanted shot of the psycho.'

'Did Maddie know that?' Fleet asked pointedly.

'Stop it,' Lydia said. 'Charlie Crow is unstable and my neck hurts and I need you both to stop bickering.'

Paul and Fleet called a halt to their staring match and Paul looked, instead, at Lydia's neck. 'I'll kill him,' he said. 'Say the word.'

'I'm trying to avoid war, not set it off,' Lydia said. 'But I appreciate the offer. What I really need is information. Charlie isn't wrong to be worried. Someone is gunning for us.'

Paul nodded. 'I'll do the rounds. Someone has got to know who commissioned the hits.'

'Thank you,' Lydia said, opening the door.

When Lydia turned back to Fleet, his face had a strained look and she knew he was trying, very hard, not to comment. After a moment more of silent struggle, he offered to run her a bath.

'Shower would be great, actually,' Lydia said, suddenly viscerally wanting to sluice the last few hours from her skin. And to have some privacy.

LYDIA HAD a long hot shower in which she allowed herself a good cry. She could still feel Charlie's hands grasping, his breath on her neck, and she lathered and scrubbed her skin. When she emerged from the warm steam, wrapped in one of Fleet's soft and fresh-smelling towels, she felt halfway human again.

Fleet had made pasta and poured two large glasses of red wine. The smell of garlic and basil made her mouth water instantly and Lydia realised that she hadn't eaten all day.

Fleet sat at his table, work spread out around him. He had passed Lydia the remote control and a bowl of pasta and left her to consume carbohydrate and some mindless television. Lydia was grateful for his understanding. She wasn't up to any more talking and definitely not big questions.

When it got late, Fleet began to set up a makeshift bed on the sofa. 'You take my room,' he said. 'I've put clean sheets on the bed.'

Lydia hovered in the doorway. 'I know it's a lot to ask, but can we put pause on our personal situation and be friends? Just for tonight.'

Fleet stopped moving. He abandoned the sheets and straightened to look at her. 'What does that involve?'

Lydia thought he was making a comment on the fact that he had already given her a place of safety and fed her dinner. She tried to explain. 'This distance between us. I asked for it and I know it's the right thing in the long run, but tonight... I can't...' She took a breath. 'I need you with me.'

Fleet crossed the room and folded her into a hug. Lydia leaned against his chest, breathing in the smell of Fleet, which had always meant safety and, as she did so, she realised that it still did. Something small and hard she had been holding onto dissolved and she wrapped her arms around Fleet's back, letting one hand drift up to the nape of his neck.

He looked down just as Lydia looked up, their mouths meeting in an easy movement. The relief to be kissing Fleet again was like the first taste of whisky and, despite everything, her heavy heart soared.

When they broke for a moment, breathing heavily, hands everywhere, and Fleet's bed miraculously closer than before, having stumbled their way into the bedroom, Fleet smiled and the sweet joy in it almost made Lydia cry. He had his hands on his T-shirt, ready to rip it over his head, when he hesitated. 'I thought maybe you and Paul...'

'Paul?' Lydia tried to shake the emotion and lust from her head long enough to formulate a proper response. Instead she opted to peel off her jeans and socks and step forward to help Fleet with his clothes-removal. 'No,' she said and kissed him. 'Just you.'

CHAPTER TWENTY-FOUR

The next day, Lydia woke up in Fleet's comfortable bed. Fleet was asleep on his front, his head turned to one side on the pillow. She looked at his beautiful face for a moment before quietly getting up. He stirred as she was putting her jeans on.

'Don't get up,' Lydia said. 'It's still early.'

Fleet blinked and rolled over, pushing himself up on one elbow. 'You're leaving?'

'I'm going home,' Lydia said, ignoring the sudden spurt of fear. 'I was wrong last night. I can't run away from Charlie. And I won't run away from my home.' Or desert Jason.

'What if he attacks you again?'

Lydia shrugged, feigning nonchalance. 'He can try. He won't catch me off guard again.'

Fleet pressed his lips together and Lydia could tell he was trying, very hard, not to say something.

'What?' Lydia sat on the bed to lace up her boots.

'I'm just worried.'

'Look. He's still my uncle. He crossed a line yesterday but I'm sure he regrets it. He's under a lot of stress.' As she heard the words, Lydia felt sick. They were the kinds of excuses abused spouses made.

'What can I do?'

Lydia leaned over and kissed him lightly on the lips. 'I'll check in with you every few hours. And I'll call if there's trouble.'

'What if you can't speak?'

'If I say everything is 'hunky dory' then you know I'm in trouble.'

'I'm being serious,' Fleet said.

'I'll leave the GPS working on my phone, and if I go more than six hours without texting or phoning, you can call the cavalry.'

'Four hours.'

'Five. And you text first.'

STEPPING BACK INTO THE FORK, Lydia half-expected Charlie to be waiting for her and was both relieved and a little disappointed to find that he wasn't. She was tensed and ready for a confrontation and it felt like a waste of adrenaline to not see him right away. And, if she was honest, there was a small part of her that had hoped he might be waiting for her to apologise in person. It would make things so much easier if he was contrite. The whole incident could be put away in a box marked 'one off' and they could both pretend it had never happened at all.

It wouldn't work, of course. Charlie Crow would find it difficult to pull off contrite convincingly, and nothing could erase the image of the real man that Lydia had glimpsed. She just wanted to know what the next move would be. In his mind, Charlie was undoubtedly the injured party, and she was the ungrateful child. The only question was, how was he going to deal with her insubordination? And did he still view her as a potential weapon that he could control or a personal threat?

When Lydia had finished updating Jason on the previous day's activity, she finished by asking him if there was a way of finding the person who had sent the text instructing Malc to murder Terrence and Richard. She didn't have any particular hope, but since Jason's new hacking skills seemed close to magic she thought it was worth asking.

'Not without the other phone,' Jason said. 'I don't think, anyway. I will ask around, though, see if we're missing something.'

'Thank you,' Lydia said.

'But what are you going to do about Charlie? That's... Bad. I can't believe he attacked you.'

'He probably thought it was for my own good,' Lydia said, keeping her voice steady with a force of will. 'But, yes. It's a problem.'

'Stop downplaying it,' Jason was shimmering a little at the edges. 'You don't have to pretend to be okay. What if he does it again? And what does it mean that his tattoos stopped moving? Did you hurt him?'

'Sorry,' Lydia said, blinking away tears. 'I can't think about it too much. It's too much. I'm just carrying on like it didn't happen because I can't afford to do otherwise. I can't fall apart.'

'You shouldn't be here,' Jason said, wrapping his arms around himself. 'It's not safe.'

'Crows don't run,' Lydia said, looking him dead in the eye. 'And this is my home.'

Jason shook his head, his outline rippling. 'It's because of me, isn't it?'

Lydia forced a smile. 'Don't be daft.'

'You've come back for me.' Jason took a step toward Lydia and she felt the air cool around her.

'Well don't make a big deal out of it,' Lydia said. 'It's a

good flat, too. Now, please can we get back to work. Distract me.'

Jason hesitated, and Lydia could see that he was torn between his desire to hug her or carry on arguing.

'Please,' she said. 'Help me to keep going.'

He nodded and picked up his laptop. 'You got the phone number?'

'Yep,' Lydia had written it into her little flip notebook and she opened the relevant page and read it out.

Jason's fingers flew over the keyboard. 'Numbers are linked to specific phones and every phone has a serial number. An ID. I reckon police can probably get phone records from relevant network. They'll be able to find out where it was bought, too. And when.'

'Any way to find out where it is now?'

'Not if it's switched off. If it's on, it pings the nearest mobile tower, gives a general location. The phone records will show which tower it was near when the text was sent. I think.' He carried on reading for a few seconds and then looked up. 'Unless they've left the GPS on, then we'd get a much more accurate location.'

'Don't think we'll get that lucky,' Lydia said.

'Yeah, if they know enough to use a burner...'

Jason was hunched over the computer, his body curved toward the screen. Lydia touched him lightly on the shoulder. 'How do you know so much about this already?'

He didn't look away and his fingers didn't slow. 'Google.'

LYDIA PUT on her jacket and hat and ventured out onto the roof terrace. It was a flat grey day with a bite to the air. A siren wailed somewhere in the distance and Lydia could feel dampness on her skin within seconds of being outside. She called Emma, trying not to think about how the records could still be found. No wonder Paul and Charlie were so hot on meeting in person.

'Sorry I haven't been in touch.' Lydia wondered how many times she had said that in the course of their friendship.

'What's wrong?'

'Nothing. I'm fine.'

Emma blew out a sigh. 'Don't phone me to lie at me.'

'I'm not-' Lydia began before stopping herself. 'Sorry. I'm sorry.' She felt tears in her eyes and told herself it was the cold air. 'Things are bad, here. Charlie has lost the plot.'

'What did he do?'

Lydia told Emma as briefly and unemotionally as she could. 'I discovered I have a couple of aged relatives in jail. Or, I did. They were killed.'

'Oh God,' Emma said. 'That's awful. Are you coming home?'

When Emma said 'home' she meant the suburbs they had grown up in together. For a second Lydia felt its pull but then remembered that her childhood home now housed the shell of her father. And that her presence made his condition worse. She was a curse. 'I can't.'

'You need to get out of London, then. Put some distance between you and this mess. It doesn't sound safe.'

'I'm not running away,' Lydia said. 'I'm a Crow.'

'Come and stay with us, then.'

'Thank you, but no.' The idea of Charlie anywhere near Emma and her family made Lydia go cold all over.

'You're doing what you always do,' Emma was saying. 'Isolating yourself in the mistaken belief that it makes you stronger.'

'I don't think it makes me stronger,' Lydia replied. 'But I don't want anybody getting hurt on my account. I can't stand the thought that I will hurt people without even trying.'

'And there's the irony,' Emma said, her voice tight. 'The further you push us away the more hurt we get. Everybody loses.'

'You get to stay alive, though,' Lydia said.

Lydia made toasted cheese sandwiches, tidied her desk, and watched Jason work while trying to concentrate on a novel. She had checked the locks and stacked tins from the kitchen behind the front door, balancing a variety of utensils on top. It wouldn't stop Charlie from getting inside the flat, but it would make a hell of a noise. And inside her bedroom, she had dragged a chest of drawers in front of the door which led to the roof terrace. Her eyes kept straying to the hallway and the makeshift intruder-alert, a visual reminder that things were not okay. The words in the novel kept jumping around and her eyes felt gritty, so she went to bed, piling blankets on the bed and drinking a whisky nightcap to ward against the chill. The room was even colder when she woke up several hours later.

'I've made some progress.'

Lydia opened her eyes to find a ghost hovering next to the bed. 'Boundaries, Jason,' she said, rubbing her eyes and sitting up. He knocked over an empty whisky bottle from next to the bed as he came closer, and Lydia shifted so that he could sit down. 'What time is it?' She was rubbing sleep out of her eyes and trying to focus.

'Dunno. Early. It's not important.'

'Not to you,' Lydia said. 'You don't need to sleep.'

'You need to stop downing a bottle of whisky as a night cap.'

'It's been a stressful time,' Lydia said. 'Did you not even bring me a coffee?'

Jason put his laptop down between them. 'Will you listen?'

'Sorry,' Lydia knew that Jason wouldn't have woken her up without good reason. He looked tense and excited in the blue wash of the screen. 'I'm awake. I'm listening. Is it Malc's phone records?'

'No, nothing on those, yet. I went back to JRB.'

'Oh. That's good. Thank you.' Having an assistant that didn't need sleep was proving to be a real bonus.

'You know JRB is a shell company?'

'Yeah. I think so. I don't really understand how it all works.'

'Basically, it's registered as a business services company, but not in this country. The offices that you found are more like a PO Box, they evade all the UK listings and regulations by not being registered here. Anything that needs UK registration to operate, like trading, uses a subsidiary company which is owned by JRB.'

'Okay,' Lydia said, still not sure she fully understood. 'You said something about following the money?'

'I did,' Jason said. 'And I got a bit of help.'

'From SkullFace?'

'And others,' Jason nodded. 'There is a lot of money. It goes to offshore accounts for tax avoidance, as you would imagine. Everything is neatly squared away. But they weren't quite as slick when they first started.'

'When did they start?'

'A company called J.R.B. and Sons Ltd was registered with Companies House in 1887. Original registered address was a shop in Peckham and company director was a member of the Coster Guild.'

Lydia was awake, now. 'That sounds like Pearl business. They've always been more open to outside influences, though. Mixing up their Family. Dad used to say it was because they had always moved all over London as street traders, and dealt with people from around the world at the docks. Less parochial and closed than the Crows or Silvers or Foxes.'

'That sounds healthy,' Jason said. 'In-breeding is not a good look.'

'I agree,' Lydia said, 'but historically that hasn't been our official position...'

'And look where it's got you all.'

'I said I agree,' Lydia snapped, irritated. She was allowed to criticise her family, but nobody else could. That was the rule.

Jason moved the trackpad to wake up the laptop screen. He had a notes app open with a bullet-point list, which he read from. 'Founder and director is John Roland Bunyan, and it looks like the company passed from son to son for generations until it was wound up in 2001 which was when the new, off-shore company, JRB Inc, no full-stops, was formed.'

'Bunyan?' Lydia stared at Jason open-mouthed. 'And you're sure they're same company?'

'Not completely sure, I suppose.' Jason had a funny look on his face. 'Just internal memos confirming the fact. Accounting notes which reference trading done at J.R.B and Sons in the opening accounts of JRB Inc.'

'How on earth did you get those?'

'Any piece of information that is kept on a server is accessible if you know how to look for it.'

'Aren't things locked up?'

'Yeah, you have to know how to open certain digital doors.'

'And you know that stuff now?'

Jason grinned. 'It's amazing what you can learn when you don't need to sleep and you have no social life.'

'This is brilliant. Really well done.'

'It's helpful?' Jason said, looking hopeful.

'Definitely.' Lydia leaned close to read his list of notes,

ignoring the chill of his skin. 'I take it, this information gathering wasn't strictly legal?'

'Not remotely,' Jason said cheerfully.

'We'll make a Crow of you, yet,' Lydia said, putting her head on his shoulder.

After a pause, in which Lydia felt the cold seep from Jason's shoulder into the bones of her cheek, Jason said. 'If JRB are linked to the Pearls, what does that mean?'

Lydia lifted her head to look at him. 'I think it means I need to pay another visit.'

'With a gift?' Jason's expression was terrified and Lydia felt like hell.

'If you can face it, yes.'

AFTER SPEAKING TO JASON, she burrowed back under the warm covers and dozed for a couple of hours. It was still early when she gave up on sleep. Light was coming through the thin curtain which covered the door to the roof terrace, cut off by the chest of drawers. She felt the sick fear in her stomach and wondered, for the millionth time, what Charlie was going to do. He had attacked her but she had won. He might decide she was more valuable than ever, a weapon to hone and control. Or he might have decided that she was a threat. Which would be very bad news. Lydia reached automatically for a fresh bottle of whisky, but realised as she began to twist the cap that she didn't actually want a drink. She got dressed and cleared the laundry off her floor, then moved into the bathroom, spraying cleaner around the sink and bath and scrubbing while she thought. There was so much going on, and she had to make a decision about what to deal with first. The Pearls were linked to JRB and JRB had been founded by someone with the Bunyan name. That couldn't be a coincidence. Lydia knew that she ought to focus on making nice with Charlie or on solving the murders of her Family members, but a fifteen-year-old girl was missing. As she used the shower attachment to hose down the bath, Lydia realised that it wasn't a difficult decision at all.

She found Jason in the kitchen. 'The Pearls might know something about Lucy Bunyan.'

'I don't want to do it,' Jason said immediately.

'I know, I'm sorry to ask. But she's only fifteen and the police haven't got anything.'

'You don't want me to do it, either. Hitch a ride, I mean.' Jason was making his fourth bowl of cereal. He had moved on from pouring cereal as a comfort activity, by and large, but things were clearly stressful enough to send him backward. 'You hated it.'

'I didn't hate it,' Lydia said, feeling the lie burn her tongue. 'Not all of it,' she amended. Mostly she had just been scared. Carrying the ghost inside was like swallowing death.

He folded the cardboard flaps of the cereal box back down and put the box into the cabinet. 'You want milk on this one?'

Lydia didn't want any of the cereal, full stop, but she nodded. If Jason found making the breakfast of his childhood calming, she wasn't going to spoil his fun. After he had taken the seal from a new two-pint bottle and splashed milk onto the cornflakes, sprinkled sugar over the top and added a spoon, he wasn't vibrating anymore. He didn't take deep breaths, as he didn't need to breathe, but sometimes his shoulders raised and lowered, like he was emulating one, and Lydia knew he had come to a decision.

'I know it's important to get closer to the Pearls and if you think this is the best way, then I'll do it.'

Lydia started to say 'thank you', but Jason hadn't finished.

'You can't leave me there forever,' he said tightly.

'I wouldn't,' Lydia said, shocked. 'It will be ten minutes, maybe twenty.'

'Wait. What? I thought I was a gift,' Jason said. 'You usually give those. As in, for keeps.'

'Feathers, no,' Lydia couldn't believe how stupid she had been. She hadn't explained this right at all. 'I would never give you away. I couldn't, I don't own you in the first place. The gift is getting to meet you. That's the gift I'm bringing.'

Jason's face cleared instantly and he smiled with pure relief. 'That's fine, then. No problem. I mean,' he said. 'Some problem. I'm still scared and I won't like it, but that's okay.'

'You thought I was asking you to leave your home and go and be the plaything or companion or whatever of some complete stranger for the rest of your... For eternity? And you were thinking about it?' Lydia was flabbergasted.

Jason gave a tiny shrug. 'You wouldn't ask unless it was really important.'

Lydia put her arms around Jason and hugged him tightly, ignoring the cold which flowed into her.

'Gerroff,' Jason said, after hugging her back for a moment. 'You need to eat your breakfast.' He looked at the line of cereal bowls. 'It's going to take a while.'

CHAPTER TWENTY-FIVE

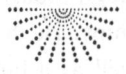

Standing outside The Fork with a shimmering, fading, panicking Jason felt like deja vu. 'Quick,' Lydia said. 'Hop on.'

Having done it before, Lydia thought this time would be easier. She was wrong. It was just as unpleasant and alarming. The cold flowed through her body, highlighting every vein and capillary with traces of icy fire.

Lydia wasn't sure whether she would be able to drive while carrying a ghost, so she took a practice spin in the Audi. If she ordered an Uber, she would probably be safer during the journey, but might be left without a quick getaway at the other end. Time had behaved oddly on her last visit and Lydia wasn't confident that an Uber driver could be paid to wait for an undefined period. The journey to the north end of Hampstead Heath took forty long minutes. She could feel Jason's presence inside her mind, keeping politely and quietly to the edge, but undeniably there. And he was there in every movement, her body feeling both heavier than usual and also strangely untethered with a sense of fluttery panic. Every particle of her being wanted to push the interloper from the nest and fly high, high into the air. She controlled her instincts but it was exhausting and by the time they arrived at the gatehouse, Lydia felt as if she had run a marathon.

She wound down her window as the guard approached and arranged her face into what she hoped was a winning smile. 'I'm here to visit a friend.'

'No cars allowed through today, miss,' the guard hoisted his belt higher on his hips. He had a walkie talkie in a holster on the belt as well as a bulky flashlight and what could have been a multi-tool or an illegal taser, Lydia couldn't tell. 'Private event.'

'That seems extreme,' Lydia said.

The guard shrugged. 'Private road. Their rules.'

'I can walk along to see my friend, though?'

'Name?'

'Lucinda Pearl,' Lydia said, plucking the name from the air, and adding the address of the Pearl house. 'I'm Lydia Crow. I've got a gift.'

'Wait a moment, please'. The guard stepped away, reaching for the walkie talkie.

Lydia tried to look unconcerned as he carried out a conversation. She kept the engine of the car running, the stick in reverse and her foot poised over the accelerator. Just in case.

The guard was frowning when he walked back and Lydia almost slammed out of there, but it was regret. 'You'll have to leave your car here and walk, I'm afraid.'

Lydia forced a sigh.

The guard indicated a parking space marked out on the street. There was a sign which said 'No Parking – Drop Off Zone'. Lydia could feel the drag of carrying Jason as she exited the vehicle and made her way past the guard's cabin and on the pavement of the private road. Seen on foot, the houses were no less grand, but there was even less to see. High hedges and walls, gated driveways, and security cameras, the street was a testament to the privacy that wealth could afford.

As Lydia approached the Pearl residence, she saw a couple of kids standing outside the closed gates, looking pinched and pale in the cold. They were dressed in grubby, oddly-matched clothes, and had thin faces and sharp eyes, and looked more feral than residents of billionaires' row. Lydia gripped her coin for strength and straightened her spine. She had to hide any trace of tiredness and was glad she had thought to apply some red lipstick on the journey, rubbing a little into her cheeks to give the illusion of vitality. As she got closer, Lydia recognised the girl who had led the way last time, she was talking to her companion, a boy, in a low tone. The boy gave Lydia a blank look and then ran off in the opposite direction, his enormous hoodie flapping.

'I've got a gift for the king,' Lydia said.

The girl looked through her as if they had never met before. Lydia had hoped not to go through the whole production, again. She could feel Jason inside her body, the cold and brain fog and fear, and it wasn't improving her mood. 'I might have got you something, too,' she said. 'But only if you get me inside quick. It's cold out here and I'm a busy woman.'

The girl tilted her head, appraising Lydia with those unnaturally pale eyes. They were rimmed with red and Lydia felt a tug of concern and the urge to comfort the child, to hug her. A second later she recognised the impulse. Pearl magic.

'Is it sparkly?' The girl asked.

Lydia stared her down for a moment. Sympathy aside, you never showed your hand too early in a negotiation. She might not have been at Uncle Charlie's level, but she was a Crow through to her core.

After a few moments of staring right back – Lydia admired the girl's spirit – she turned and the gates opened.

She walked up the driveway to the house and Lydia followed. She checked behind her, just once, and the gates were swinging smoothly shut.

Inside the house, Lydia recognised the giant tree growing through the centre of the entrance hall, but she could have sworn they were going a different route to the basement. Either the house was even bigger than Lydia had appreciated, or its interior had been changed since her last visit. Or it was all an illusion and they were in an entirely different construction. Anything seemed possible in that place. The air was thick with Pearl magic and Lydia could feel it reflecting and refracting off every shining surface. The walls of this stairwell were lined with black mirrors, pieces of shell, plates of metal. A hodgepodge collage of reflective surfaces which deceived the eye and clouded Lydia's senses until she felt like she was walking through treacle with every step. At a wall that didn't look like it contained a door, the girl stopped and held out her hand. After thinking for a split second that the girl intended Lydia to hold it, she realised that the girl was demanding payment.

'It's through there?' Lydia indicated the wall. It was shining black ebony or painted wood, hard to tell in the dim light, and inlaid with thousands of tiny pieces of mother of pearl. It was as if the jewellery-box door she had gone through last time had morphed and grown, the pearl-encrusted-surface spreading through the house like a living thing.

The girl nodded.

'How do I open the door? There's no handle.'

The girl looked pointedly down at her outstretched hand, her lips compressed into a thin line so that they almost disappeared.

'Feathers,' Lydia said. 'You have trust issues, did you know that?' She reached into the inside pocket of her leather jacket and produced the heart-shaped locket she had bought in Ari's shop. It had an iridescent rainbow chain and a sparkly hologram picture on the front of the locket which changed from a cartoon kitten to a smiling rainbow when you tilted it. It was cheap, plasticky, kitsch and very, very glittery. Lydia had looked for something she and Emma would have gone nuts for aged eight and crossed her fingers that this girl wasn't so different.

The girl's eyes lit up and her hand darted out as if to grab the necklace. She stopped short, though, her fingers close to the jewellery without touching. Lydia pressed it into her hand. 'A gift from me to you, freely given.'

The girl put the necklace on immediately, tucking it safely inside her thin sweatshirt. 'This way,' she said, turning back to the black wall and putting both hands onto it, palms flat. She pushed and Lydia thought she heard a click. Or maybe she imagined it as a door appeared, swinging outward on well-oiled hinges. The girl caught the edge and opened it wide enough for them to pass through.

It might have been a different entrance, but the room Lydia arrived in was the same. This time, however, it was quiet. There was no music or dancing, just strobing lights reflected on the mirrored walls. And a crowd of good-looking people, wearing what Lydia assumed was high fashion as it was expensive-looking and a bit weird. A young woman to her left was wearing a white body con dress with a deep V-neck, exposing a bony sternum and shoulder pads which extended far past her own body, like fins. She hissed as Lydia walked past and it should have been comical, but it wasn't.

Walking through the crowd of almost-silent, eerily still bodies, was more menacing than Lydia would have imagined. She could feel Jason inside her, too, stirring uneasily through his own misgivings or because he was picking up on hers. She forced herself to breathe evenly and slipped a hand into her pocket to hold her coin. She could do this.

'Your Majesty,' Lydia said, bowing her head. She thought that she was prepared for the king's beauty this time, thought that she had remembered it from the last time and that it would make less of a toe-curling, mind-warping, sweat-inducing impact. That was not the case. The androgynous figure lounging on the throne-like chair was, if anything, more beautiful and perfect than last time. More disturbing still, they were looking straight at Lydia this time, not merely giving her side-eye. The almond shaped eyes, edged in black with silver-painted lids and glowing skin and cheekbones; each feature was attractive and perfect. All together it was like looking at the sun.

'You again.' The king's voice was soft and mid-range. It was as gender-neutral as the rest of them. Not gender neutral, Lydia corrected herself. Gender-insignificant. Gender new. From where she was standing, gender perfect. Why be one or the other? Why not be this perfect blend of two, making so much more than the sum of two halves? Her mind was cloudy, she knew. Her hands were out of her pockets and her coin was nowhere. She could feel Jason, and thought that he might be trying to tell her something, to speak, but she couldn't hear his words. She just wanted to look upon the magnificence of the majesty.

Lydia.

Someone was saying her name. With a force of will, Lydia dragged her attention from the king's ethereal face. 'What?' She spoke out loud and the moment she did, the spell was broken. Her coin was in her hand, Jason was on board, she was standing in a night club in the middle of the day and the head of the Pearl Family was sitting six feet away, smiling at her like she was a performing monkey who was about to juggle.

'I have brought you a gift,' Lydia said. She flipped her

coin over her knuckles, using it to keep her anchored in the moment. The Pearl magic had always pulled people in, made them want, made them need until they would be willing to part with any amount of cash in order to satiate that vast emptiness. This, however, was different. The rumours were true. Mr Smith hadn't been lying when he said the Pearls had evolved.

The king straightened a little, eyes lighting with interest. 'A gift from a Crow. What an unexpected pleasure.'

Ninety percent of Lydia wanted to throw herself down at the king's feet and beg to be permitted to stay within their perfect presence for all eternity, but the rest, helped by Jason, was keeping a watchful eye on the crowd, seeing who was circling behind her to block the exit. 'My gift is a show. A temporary performance, made all the more special by its fleeting nature.'

An incremental shift of a perfect eyebrow.

'If your friends are allowed to enjoy the gift, they need to be here,' Lydia indicated the space in front of her, 'in order to appreciate it.'

The king inclined their head and the crowd which had formed behind her, moved back to nearby, in front of Lydia. She took a step backward, toward the exit, trying to appear casual. 'Right, then.' She licked her lips and wished she had something to moisten her dry throat. 'I am pleased to introduce Jason Montefort. A man who died in 1985.'

There was a little ripple throughout the room, as people craned their necks and whispered to their neighbour.

'Okay,' she said quietly. 'You can come out, now.'

Feeling Jason leave her body wasn't quite as weird as feeling it enter, but it came close. She took several long slow breaths to get oxygen to her brain and make sure she didn't pass out or throw up. The latter would probably be tantamount to treason in the king's presence.

His form was thin and Lydia could see the king through

his torso. She smiled at him reassuringly and took his hand. 'Ready?'

Jason nodded, his outline shimmering in the disco lights.

Lydia gripped her coin in her other hand and concentrated on focusing her energy. The training with Charlie had taught her that she wasn't a cup of magic that could quickly be drained, she was more like a dynamo, converting her human electrical energy into Crow force. She didn't know if it had an end or whether she could keep replenishing the fire, so to speak, forever. Charlie had said she could be limitless and maybe that was true. All she knew in this moment was that she could hear wings beating and feel wind on her face like she was flying, part of her was high above this building, in the clouds with the city spread out below. Once Jason was fully solid and stable, she pushed her energy out further, in a wave. She didn't know if this would work or for how long, but felt a core of confidence. It would work. She would push until it worked.

There was a gasp from the assembled crowd and, through her sweat-stinging eyes, Lydia saw Jason standing in front of the crowd. She could hear his voice and, from the reactions of the king and courtiers, they could, too.

'I'm honoured to meet you,' Jason was saying.

Very polite. Very proper. Good man. Lydia pushed a little harder, making sure that every person in the room could see and hear Jason. She could feel it like a net she had thrown out across the room, or a thin piece of fabric like a veil. She could see it loosely covering every person's head and draping down at the edges of the crowd.

The king clapped their hands, delighted. 'This is a very fine gift, very fine.' They beamed at Jason and then at Lydia and she felt, again, the Pearl-pull, the urge to throw herself at the king's feet and kiss their toes. Bleurgh.

'You may approach,' the king said.

Jason glanced at Lydia and she nodded encouragingly.

The crowd had got closer, people shifting forward, those at the back wanting to see better and their murmuring voices combined in a single, entranced song. Lydia was checking out the vast room, while simultaneously trying to pretend that she wasn't. There was a bar area along one wall with glittering glass bottles housed in a beautiful art nouveau cabinet and a row of stools in front of a polished slab of wood. The stools had carved wooden bases, shaped like twisted tree trunks and polished to a deep shine. Without the strobing lights, which had given the impression of a night club, Lydia could now see that the interior was far finer than your average dance pit. And it had to have cost a fortune.

The crowd were leaning in, their faces avid, and Lydia was checking that the veil she had cast was covering every member, when she spotted a figure who remained outside the circle. A female figure, young-looking and half-hidden in the shadows behind the king's fancy chair. Even in her mind, Lydia refused to say 'throne'. The figure wasn't looking at Jason, as he held out his hand for the king to shake, but was gazing instead at the king as if they were the most beautiful, mesmerising creature they had ever laid eyes upon. Even with her face made-up with rainbow glitter and wearing a prom dress, Lydia recognised the girl. Lucy Bunyan.

CHAPTER TWENTY-SIX

The king reached out and attempted to touch Jason's outstretched hand, but theirs passed through it. They laughed, thrilled. 'Very, very good. Thank you for visiting. I hope you will do so again.'

Lydia spoke before Jason could say something unwise like 'not on your life, mate'. 'We are very glad to have pleased,' she stopped short of saying 'your majesty' but dipped her head respectfully.

'And what is it you wish to request? Speak quickly, before I tire.' The king smirked as if aware they were speaking in a parody of royalty, but there was a haughtiness around the eyes which was entirely genuine.

Lydia swallowed. She couldn't ask the question she had planned upon. Not with the object of that enquiry currently making moon-eyes from the back of the room. She flipped to her other area of interest and hoped that the king would deem it sufficiently important not to guess that Lydia had actually come for another purpose. 'I would respectfully ask about the collective known as JRB. I am an investigator, a business which is based on information, and that is an area where my knowledge falls away.'

The king regarded Lydia for a long moment. 'JRB is an incorporated company. It is registered with the proper authorities.'

Lydia's heart sank. She had started with the wrong question. And she needed more time. Extracting Lucy Bunyan was not going to be easy when she was so drastically outnumbered, but she was hoping to reassure the girl, at least. Lydia forced herself not to glance around.

'They are also a family, of sorts.'

Lydia looked up at the king, holding her breath, and momentarily distracted from Lucy.

'They keep us.'

Lydia waited, not wanting to interrupt. After the silence stretched on, though, she asked. 'Keep you?'

The king waved a hand. 'Pearls have always had a weakness for money and the pretty things it can buy. We would sew mother-of-pearl to our jackets to catch the light, pick a silver piece from a midden, fill our carts with polished tin and sell it for ten times its value.'

Lydia compressed her lips, stopping the urge to interrupt. She didn't want a history lesson or more stories but if it kept them talking, it bought her time.

The king smiled. 'You want the truth? The unvarnished reality, not this,' they waved a hand, indicating the large room, the beautiful people. 'The truth is this; JRB offered us a great deal of money and we took it. Now we are here. In this jewel box.'

'You're trapped?' The question was out before Lydia could stop it.

'I am a king,' they spoke in icy tones. 'And everybody is trapped in one way or another.'

Which wasn't a real answer. The king was looking increasingly impatient, however, and the crowd was shifting.

'Jason,' Lydia said, quietly. 'Come here. Walk backwards.'

Jason obeyed, backing away from the throne with small steps.

'We thank you for your time,' Lydia said. 'You have been most gracious and patient. I hope this can be the start of a friendship between our two Families.'

The king smiled with their mouth only. 'You wish an alliance? That will require a far larger gift. The coin you hold concealed in your hand, perhaps. Or this toy.'

For a second Lydia didn't realize the king meant Jason. 'I do not have the authority, sadly,' Lydia said. 'I will carry your message back to the head of the Crow Family.'

The king wagged a finger. 'You must not tell lies, Lydia Crow. I have a mind to teach you a lesson. I shall keep your gift, I think.'

With a speed and fluidity which surprised Lydia, the king was off their throne and in front of Jason, hands plunged into his chest.

He looked over his shoulder at Lydia, eyes wide and terrified.

'No!' Lydia said firmly. In her mind she added 'bad king' which was probably the product of fear, but it made her smile, which reminded her of an important fact. She wasn't powerless. She had always assumed that she was, had always felt like the spare part, the damp squib, the disappointment. But that wasn't true. It had never been true, she just hadn't known it.

She reached for Jason's hand and took it firmly in her own. It was solid and real under her touch and, as always, very cold. At the same time, she whipped away the veil she had cast over the crowd, removing their sight so that they could no longer see Jason. The king hissed displeasure, but she ignored them. She pulled Jason back and he stumbled against her. For a second he almost overbalanced her with his weight and in the next second he was insubstantial as a puff of air. Air she breathed in, gathering him inside for the trip home.

'That was very rude,' she said. 'You should not take things which do not belong to you.' Lydia let her gaze fall on Lucy Bunyan who was still gazing adoringly at the king with exactly zero comprehension on her face. 'There will be consequences.'

The king flicked a glance at Lucy before looking back at Lydia. 'You presume to threaten me, Crow?'

'I very much do,' Lydia said. 'And now I'm leaving.'

'Unlikely,' the king said, turning beautiful and terrible eyes upon her.

Lydia turned and realised that the crowd had encircled her. They no longer looked like a group of glamorous partygoers, their faces were twisted with anger and ugliness showed in every line. A split second more and Lydia realised something else. It wasn't just anger transforming their faces, it was age. Wrinkled skin sitting loosely over bone, milky-eyes, and gnarled fingers reaching. The king wasn't immune. They flickered between the perfection of youth and a well-preserved sixty-ish, black hair turning grey and then back again. A truth occurred to her. The Pearl court wasn't composed of newly evolved Pearls or the watered-down versions which she had encountered out and about in London, but of the old guard. The original, most powerful members of the Family. 'I see you,' Lydia said. 'And I am not afraid.'

The king laughed, but Lydia caught the flicker of uncertainty in their eyes.

'You will return what you have taken and I will forgive your transgressions. There is no need for the truce between our Families to be broken.' Lydia drew herself up to her full height. It wasn't very impressive, she would be the first to admit, and she could feel Jason's panic inside her mind, lapping at the edges and frilling her thoughts with sharp anxiety. The fear was good. When Charlie had attacked her, she had reacted instinctively, the terror of being choked had unleashed something wild and unknown. Now that she recognised the feeling, the shape of that something, she knew she could reach for it. Like the different powers she sensed in others, it had a signature. It was wings beating, it was the cushion of warm air lifting from below, it was sleek feathers shining in a noonday sun, and a sharp beak ripping into flesh. Not just one beak or two wings, though, hundreds. Thousands. A multitude of beating hearts. Lydia raised her arms, stretching them wide. She didn't stop looking at the king, keeping eye contact as she pushed the feeling out.

The crowd took a collective step back. Lydia could see the way out of the party basement. The door had a mirror attached and would have blended completely into the wall, becoming invisible, but Lydia had noted its position when she had come into the room and left it partially open. She backed toward it, keeping the Pearls in sight. They were frowning, uncertain as to why they hadn't rushed Lydia, as their king so clearly required.

Lydia didn't know how long this mass-whammy was going to work or how long it would hold if they all decided to push back. The basement club was covered in reflective surfaces and it made it seem as if the crowd were ten times larger than it really was. There were ten Pearls there, maybe fifteen, but their expressions were replicated and fractured in the multiple mirrors, polished wood, and mother-of-pearl inlay which formed the walls. With the lights, there were so many surfaces glinting and refracting light, so many areas shining, it was hard to keep your bearings, keep your thoughts on track.

Lydia.

That was Jason. Lydia tried to concentrate above the

rhythmic beating of wings. The expressions in the crowd no longer looked angry, they looked excited.

Lydia realised that she had stopped moving toward the door. She didn't know when that had happened. She hadn't meant to, but she was rooted where she stood. She tried to move her feet, but they were planted. Was that the sound of wind in trees? How could she hear that? The music was too loud. And they were in a basement. A fancy basement, sure, but a basement. There was no wind.

Lydia! Money!

Yes. Good point, Jason. Good man. Excellent assistant. Lydia reached into her pocket and found her coin. She held it between finger and thumb, arm stretched out in front of her body. All eyes in the room snapped to it. Lydia could see hunger. Faces that had seemed beautiful, now looked knotted and creased like old bark. For once, the assembled Pearls looked their age.

Lydia forced the power she had felt, those thousands of tiny pulsing hearts, those beating wings, and fractured the coin into hundreds of gold Crow coins. Then she flung the lot high into the air so that they clattered down on the Pearls. And then she turned and ran.

THERE WAS a roaring sound from behind, but Lydia ran up the stairs and into the grand entrance with the tree. Up here, Lydia could hear cracking and a low rumble, like something was moving deep under the ground. The floor began to shudder and the tree was shaking as if blown by an invisible gale. Lydia dived for the front door, yanking it open and throwing herself out, and running down the driveway to the closed wooden gates. She almost fell as the ground moved. Earthquake, Lydia thought, even as her mind told her that it was no such thing. Just ahead, a tree root broke through the stone chipping of the driveway and

Lydia ran into air that was suddenly filled with earth and vegetation, and this time she did fall, catching herself on her hands and knees, the jolt of the impact traveling through her joints. Ignoring the pain, she forced herself back up and ran around the tree roots which were bursting through the ground, one four feet in the air and whipping around like the tentacle of a mythological sea monster.

The gates were closed but Lydia was pretty sure she would be able to climb over. There was a decorative lattice in the top half which ought to provide hand and footholds and, besides that, she had no choice. A moment later another tree root burst through the ground underneath one of the gateposts, spraying chippings and spitting earth, Lydia instinctively threw her arms in front of her face and felt sharp pains on the backs of her hands. The gate was splintered and sagging on one side and Lydia didn't break pace, pushing through the gap and stepping over the raw jagged edges of the broken wooden boards.

Lungs burning, skin stinging, and her breath coming in harsh rasps, Lydia forced herself to keep running as she emerged onto the street. She ran diagonally, putting as much distance between herself and the exploding grounds around the house as possible. Lydia felt as though she was still sprinting as she reached the end of the private road but, truthfully, she slowed by the time she made it to the gatehouse with its road barrier. She was dragging one foot in front of the other as every part of her screamed for rest, the weight and cold of Jason dragging her to the ground, but she ducked under the barrier and kept moving.

Lydia didn't want to be grateful to Uncle Charlie, but right at the moment, she was extremely glad to see her new car, parked where she had left it. Once she was in the driving seat, all doors locked and shaking hands gripping the steering wheel, Lydia allowed herself a moment. Just a moment to take some deep, shuddering breaths.

The ground felt stable, now, which was a relief, but she could feel the ghost inside her and the strain of keeping him contained and stable. The beating of wings had receded and Lydia knew that whatever that power was it had turned down, like the volume on a television. She started the engine and kept her eyes on the rear-view mirror, ready to floor the accelerator if she saw even a single Pearl. She dialled Fleet and put the phone on speaker.

When Fleet answered she gave him the essential details. The address of the house he would find Lucy Bunyan. 'It's the Pearls,' she said. 'And they are pissed.'

'With you?'

Lydia could almost hear him resisting the urge to say something sarcastic. 'Yes. If you get here quick, you'll catch them on the hop. I doubt they'll expect me to call the police, they seem quite old fashioned.'

'Where are you now? Are you safe?'

'I'm at the bottom of their road in my car.'

'Well get moving. I'll call you when we have Lucy.'

'I want to help.' Even as she said the words, Lydia knew she didn't have a good follow up. She had barely got herself out of the house. 'They're strong.'

'An armed response is on its way,' Fleet said. 'Ten minutes.'

Lydia gripped the steering wheel. She should move. Get away. But what if the Pearls moved Lucy? If they were going to leave, she needed to see. Get a direction or a number plate. Something.

The minutes crawled past and Lydia's rear-view mirror remained devoid of action. She could feel the weight of Jason and wasn't sure how much longer she could hold onto him. Lydia didn't know what would happen if they separated in her car, but she knew one thing for certain; if the Pearls decided to come for her, she wouldn't be able to protect herself or Jason. She was exhausted.

At minute eleven, Lydia saw the first blue-and-yellow police cars. The guard didn't approach, just waved from his little cabin and raised the barrier. Three marked cars and two police vans headed up the private road and Lydia peeled away. She was still a little nervous of the police as an official entity and couldn't afford to get stuck giving a witness statement, not with a ghost onboard.

She drove carefully back to Camberwell, grateful that Jason was staying quiet, and, as soon as she had one foot through the door of The Fork, she pushed him out of her body. Lydia was glad that it was almost closing time and the place was deserted, but she honestly couldn't have waited for another second and would have ejected Jason even if the place had been packed in a midday rush.

'We made it,' Jason said, shimmering just in front of Lydia, his feet not bothering to connect with the floor. 'You look like crap.'

'I'm... Okay.' It was an effort to speak.

Angel pushed through the door from the kitchen, a mop bucket in hand, and stopped when she saw Lydia doubled over. 'You all right?'

'Fine.' Lydia managed. 'Stitch.'

'Well, that's running for you. Terrible idea.'

Lydia made her way upstairs. Jason had disappeared and she hoped it wouldn't be for long. She knew how much he hated blinking out of existence. She didn't need to worry as he was waiting for her in the office and his stoic silence in the car had given way to verbiage.

'I can't believe they... I don't think they were going to let us go. And how did the king do that? Put their hands in me. That was horrible, I felt them grabbing.' Jason shook his head. 'I never want that sensation again. Do you want some tea? I need to make tea.'

Lydia sucked in another breath. Every part of her body wanted to be asleep but she forced herself to breathe, to stay with the conversation. Another moment and she would go to bed. Or just pass out on the floor. That sounded nice.

Jason had been talking rapidly, expending nervous energy and Lydia understood the need. After he wound down, he took a step closer and asked: 'Did you really just give them your coin?'

Lydia straightened up. If Jason hadn't been a ghost she would have said he looked pale. Since he was, it felt like a redundant observation. He looked more dead than usual, though.

'No,' she produced her coin, after a moment of effort. Her finger tips burned as she held it, as if her coin was angry. 'I tricked them.'

Jason looked gratifyingly impressed and Lydia quickly pocketed the coin again. She sagged against her desk, exhaustion sweeping through her body.

'So, that was the Pearls.' Jason was trying for jokey, but his feet were still hovering an inch above the floor. 'Not sure I'm a fan.'

'I don't suppose we're on their Christmas list, either.'

'They all looked about a hundred and fifty years old. It was creepy.'

'That's how I spotted Lucy.'

Jason frowned. 'Lucy Bunyan was there?'

'You didn't see her? At the back? She was behind the king's ridiculous chair.'

'You're refusing to say 'throne' aren't you?'

'Damn straight,' Lydia forced a smile. 'Didn't you hear me call it in? That's why I was waiting for the police.'

Jason shook his head. 'Everything is dark after we got upstairs. We were running. I mean, you were running. And there was this noise like the earth was breaking apart and I just, sort of, blacked out.' He looked embarrassed. 'I'm a wuss.'

Lydia checked her phone. Fleet would call as soon as it was safe.

'So, the police arrived?' Jason was speaking hesitantly. 'They're going in, now, and they will rescue Lucy?'

'That's the idea.' Lydia wished she had been able to grab Lucy herself, like an action hero from a film. If she was a big dude with a gun, she could have thrown Lucy Bunyan over one shoulder and muscled her way out. Of course, there had been the Pearl magic which would have rooted her in place, stopped her gun hand from moving, and then she and Jason would be deader than dead.

'What do we do?' Jason blinked at her, his feet still hovering above the floor and his edges shimmering in distress.

Lydia swallowed. 'We wait and we hope.'

CHAPTER TWENTY-SEVEN

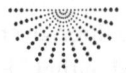

If Lydia had been smart she would have gone back to the Pearls and given them fair warning that Fleet and an armed response unit were going to burst through their front door and rescue Lucy Bunyan. She could have given them the chance to release Lucy, to maybe amend her memories and have her turn up somewhere neutral. In return for this favour, the king might have agreed an alliance between the Crows and the Pearls. It would have been, how would Charlie put it, 'a real world' solution. And one which would have elevated the Crows' power and position, secured their future.

Lydia wasn't clever. At least, not in the way Charlie wanted. She wasn't going to risk harm to Lucy Bunyan in order to curry favour with the Pearls. Not when a kidnapping charge was up for grabs. What if the king decided to dispose of the evidence by spiriting Lucy away or putting her six feet under? Charlie might believe that collateral damage was an acceptable cost of business, but Lydia did not.

Lydia paced the floor, gripping her phone in one hand and her coin the other. Like it was a charm that could ensure Lucy's safe return. What if the king had heard Lydia's threat and decided to do something violent, just to spite Lydia? To teach her a lesson. Lydia had fully convinced herself that she had signed the girl's death warrant when Fleet rang.

'We've got her,' he said. 'She's fine. Unharmed, thank God.'

Lydia crumpled to the floor, overwhelmed with relief.

'Nobody hurt our end, either.' Fleet sounded elated and Lydia knew that this moment was the culmination of many long days and sleepless nights for him. She knew how relieved he would be that Lucy was alive, because he was a good person, but also because the pressure from his boss would have been pushing down with unbearable weight. This was a result.

'Her dad's on his way to the hospital. She's being checked out, just a precaution. But she really does seem healthy. Bit confused, but physically well.'

'That's great,' Lydia said. She straightened up from her crouching position. 'Happy ending.'

'Thanks to you,' Fleet said.

There was a pause, and Lydia heard the background sounds quieten. He had moved away from whoever he was standing near. When he spoke again, his voice was quiet. 'You want me to keep your name out of this?'

'That would be best.' Lydia's mind was whirling, now. Had the Pearl King released Lucy Bunyan because of Lydia's visit? Had they been that impressed by Lydia's show of power?

'You won't want to give a statement.'

It wasn't a question and Lydia didn't answer.

'Will do,' Fleet said, raising his voice, his tone turning clipped and professional.

Lydia was about to end the call, but Fleet continued, his voice quiet. 'Bit odd, though. The place was just like you described, except there was nobody there. We bust through the door and searched the whole place. Found Lucy in an upstairs bedroom fast asleep and not another soul in the building.'

'Did you see the tree? In the hallway?'

'I saw a lot of rubble. Nice place, but looks like it's in the middle of a major refurb.'

Lydia swallowed. 'You went down to the basement?'

'I saw the swimming pool and the gym. And a bloody great hole in the wall. They must be planning an extension down there.'

'What about the party room? The private nightclub place?'

'Funny thing about that, Lyds,' Fleet said. 'There wasn't one.'

THE NEXT DAY, Lydia went downstairs to find some free breakfast. Angel came out from behind the counter, looking unusually anxious. 'Have you seen Charlie?'

'Not today,' Lydia replied. 'Why?'

'He's not answering his phone,' Angel said. She pulled her dreads back into a ponytail as she spoke, wrapping an elastic tie to secure it.

'What do you need?'

'Nothing.' Angel's eyes slid left. 'Just wanted to ask him about opening hours.'

'Uh-huh. I thought he left operating matters to you.'

'He does, I just…'

'Angel,' Lydia said, tiredness eroding her patience. Her eyes ached. 'Just tell me.'

'I'm supposed to check in with him every day and he always answers.'

'You deliver him a report on me every day,' Lydia said, just for the sake of clarity and, if she was honest, to let Angel know that she was done pretending that everything was fine.

Angel's face went blank and Lydia produced her coin. 'It's unusual for him not to answer then?'

Angel nodded.

'But there's more to it. You're worried about Charlie because you've noticed he's become a bit erratic.' That was an understatement.

Angel looked like she didn't want to answer but she glanced at the coin held up between Lydia's thumb and forefinger and nodded again.

'What else?'

'Aiden was here,' Angel said, sounding aggrieved rather than worried. 'Said he had to pick something up for Charlie and then he took some of my good knives.'

Lydia's scalp tingled. 'What else?'

Angel really did not want to answer. Lydia felt her resistance and pushed it away like it weighted nothing at all. In a previous life, this would have pleased Lydia. It was evidence that she was stronger, her Crow abilities becoming more finely honed, but in this life it made her feel grubby.

'I heard him on the phone,' Angel said. 'As he was leaving. I think he was talking to Charlie and it didn't sound good.'

'Charlie's in trouble?'

Angel shook her head. 'Someone else is.'

'Connected with the Crow murders in Wandsworth?'

Angel winced. 'I reckon.'

'Hell Hawk,' Lydia swore under her breath. She still felt exhausted from her encounter with the Pearl King, but Charlie's behaviour was spiralling with no concern for her need for rest and recuperation.

'Where?'

'I don't know,' Angel said, her eyes sliding left.

'I won't ask again,' Lydia said, spinning her coin in the air and watching Angel's eyes widen in fear.

'He mentioned the arches.' Angel looked like she was trying not to cry and Lydia felt like hell.

'Close the cafe and go home,' Lydia said. 'Better yet, take a holiday out of London.'

'I can't-'

Lydia cut across her. 'Charlie is off the rails. We both know it. If you wait to see just how far off, it might be too late. I'll let you know when it's safe to come back.'

LYDIA LEFT Angel blinking and a little dazed and headed to the railway arches on Camberwell Station Road. By some miracle, she squeezed the Audi into a space right outside the row of shuttered arches underneath the railway line. There was a lot of graffiti, mostly gang tags, and a few arches had brown metal shutters and rusted padlocks that looked as if they hadn't been touched in a decade or two. There was a place with fresh blue metal shutters and a poorly-painted sign advertising auto repairs and another one, further down the row, with a corrugated red garage door and no sign. Lydia walked back up the street, reaching out for 'Crow' with her senses. Every impression – the pavement under her feet, the pinkish sky as the sun set above the railway, the smell of cooking oil and diesel – were sharp and distinct. There it was. As she neared the blue auto shop again, the taste of feathers in the back of her throat. Crows.

The door had a brand new, high-end padlock, the kind that was a bastard to pick and not easy to saw through. It wasn't securing the door at the moment, though, which added to Lydia's assumption that whoever owned the unit was already inside. Lydia banged on the door with the side of her fist. It made a hollow booming sound. Nobody came to the door and she pressed her ear up against it, trying to listen. Nothing. She thumped again.

Lydia was just debating whether to try the handle,

weighing up the advisability of surprising Charlie and whoever else was inside, against the possibility that she would be left standing on the frozen pavement indefinitely, when the door swung inward. Lydia had been expecting Charlie and it took her a moment to react properly to the sight of Aiden. He looked younger than when she had last seen him, and his skin was pale, his eyes wide and anxious.

'All right, Aiden?' Lydia said, keeping her voice light and friendly. The kid looked unwell, like he was going to throw up at any moment.

'You're not invited,' Aiden said. Then he looked over his shoulder.

Lydia took the opportunity to push past him. Immediately her nostrils were assaulted by the smell. Someone had recently voided their bowels. If Lydia had to bet, it was probably the man who was tied to a chair in the middle of the lock-up.

'What's all this?' Lydia spoke to the man in charge, her dear old Uncle Charlie who was crossing the cement floor to meet her. His bulk obliterated her view of the man in the chair and all she could see were his flat eyes.

'Head on home, Lyds,' Charlie said. 'This doesn't concern you.'

'I think it does,' Lydia said, squeezing her coin tightly in one hand, drawing strength and focus. 'Who's that?'

'Let's go outside a minute, yeah?'

Charlie hustled Lydia out of the room, half-closing the metal door behind him. 'It's necessary, Lyds. You know we're under attack.'

Lydia took a deep breath of fresh air and tried to order her thoughts. She kept flashing on the image of the man in the chair. His face was bruised and bloody, his nose clearly broken. More than the injuries, though, it was the expression in his eyes which stayed with Lydia. The naked fear. 'Who is that?' Lydia indicated the lock-up.

'Big Neil,' Charlie said after a moment's hesitation. 'He's part of a crew I've had my eye on for a while and he just went to the top of my list.'

'He's Camberwell?'

'Peckham,' Charlie said.

'But the burner used to contact Malc was bought in Camden.'

Charlie shrugged. 'Originally, yeah, but it could have been sold on. How many phones were bought at the same time?'

'Ten,' Lydia said, conceding the point. 'And whoever bought it could have deliberately gone to a different area to do so.'

'Exactly,' Charlie formed a finger gun and pointed it at Lydia. 'Whereas my boy in there,' he jerked his head at the closed door. 'Is a little shit. Been mouthing off against us for months.'

'People talk,' Lydia said. 'It doesn't mean anything.'

'Doesn't mean nothing, either,' Charlie shot back. 'Everyone knows he's friendly with the Fox Family, too. Doesn't stack up well.'

Lydia felt a shiver of dread and the hairs on the back of her neck raised. 'What do you mean? Being friendly with the wrong person is a crime now?'

Charlie shrugged. 'Dangerous times. If you're friends with an enemy of the Crows, then you're an enemy of the Crows. You should think on that, Lyds, get your head straight.'

Lydia forced herself not to look away. It was an overt threat and she wasn't going to bother trying to argue that Paul Fox wasn't an enemy of the Crow Family. That he had banished Tristan, his own father, for moving against them. Instead she asked: 'What are you doing to do?'

'Find out what he knows.'

Lydia glanced at the closed door, ice in her stomach.

'This isn't right. I will find out who ordered the killings, you don't need to do this.'

Charlie turned flat, dead eyes onto her. 'Don't tell me my business, Lyds.'

'I'm not,' Lydia said. 'I just want a bit of time. I can sort this. No blood spilled. If we retaliate like this,' she indicated the door. 'It will escalate. I'm right, aren't I?'

Charlie's shoulders lifted very slightly. 'Ever since you strolled back into Camberwell you've been telling me you don't want to be a part of Family business. Well, congratulations, you're out. Now off you fuck.'

BACK IN HER CAR, Lydia did the only thing she could think of and called Fleet. There was being a lone wolf and an independent woman and then there was good sense.

'I'm a bit tied up at the moment,' Fleet said. Lydia could hear voices in the background.

'The Bunyan case? How is Lucy doing?'

'Yeah,' Fleet's voice dipped and she heard a door close. When he spoke next, his voice was echoey like he had stepped into a stairwell. 'She's okay. Her dad has been praising us to the higher ups, so that's nice. They'll forget it by the next budget meeting, but still.'

'Things are a bit sticky here. I really need to find the person who sent the text into Wandsworth. I know it's not high up the list for the CPS and the case will probably get dropped, but I need-'

'You don't have to explain,' Fleet said. 'I get it.'

'Is there anything you can do?' Lydia was grateful that Fleet didn't ask her for details. She couldn't tell him that Charlie had a man tied to a chair in a lock-up. He was on her side, but he was still a copper.

'We didn't get anything else off the burner from Malc's cell. We've applied to get the records for the phone number which sent the text from the mobile provider, but it'll take a day or two.'

Lydia swore. Big Neil didn't have a day or two.

LYDIA PULLED on her jacket and wrapped a thick scarf around her neck. She was in the unusual position of actively wanting to speak to Mr Smith. She wished it was Thursday or that he had given her a burner, that would make things a little easier. Instead, she walked to Kennington Road. As always, she walked a slightly different route, doubling back on one of the side streets, and kept a sharp lookout for a tail, stopping once to window shop and once to pretend to tie her shoelace. Over the last few weeks she hadn't seen a single repeated figure, nothing to suggest surveillance was following her to her meetings with Mr Smith, but she wasn't about to get sloppy.

At the anonymous beige reception area, Lydia looked above the doors, in the corners of the room and the stairwell until she found the camera. It was small and higher-spec than you would expect in a council office building, but not hidden. Lydia stood in the middle of the reception area and waved. Then she pulled the piece of paper she had prepared before leaving the flat and held it up so that the words faced the camera and then sat on the bottom step to wait. She wondered whether there was another meeting going on in the flat upstairs with another source being hounded for information. More likely they used different flats for different operations. She wondered what was on her file and whether Mr Smith referred to her with a case code name, like the Met did for complicated operations.

Ten minutes later a telephone began ringing. Putting her ear to the door marked 'Kennington Council, Appointments Only' made the ringing louder. Lydia expected the door to be locked so was surprised when it opened easily. It was an office complete with box files, filing cabinets, standard furniture and a thirsty-looking spider plant. Lydia picked up the phone receiver. 'Hello?'

A woman's voice delivered four words and then there was a click.

'Vauxhall Bridge. Five minutes.'

Lydia was about halfway to the river, heading down Kennington Lane when a Mercedes saloon with tinted rear windows pulled up alongside. A large man in a suit was out of the car and taking Lydia by the elbow before she had time to react. 'This way, please, Ms Crow.' It wasn't a request.

Within seconds, Lydia was in the quiet, leather interior, the heavy thump of the door cutting off the sounds of the traffic. If Lydia had ever wondered what money could buy when it came to automobiles, now she had her answer.

'You wanted to see me?' Mr Smith was wearing a suit and he looked more intimidating than usual. Or perhaps that was the car and the staff sat up front.

'Is this bullet proof?' Lydia tapped the side window. 'And don't the tinted windows attract more attention than they deflect?'

'I assume it's important?'

Lydia was fiddling with the door, looking for the handle, and she didn't bother to reply. She wasn't frightened of Mr Smith, but she liked to know she could leave whenever she chose. 'Two Crows have been killed in Wandsworth nick.'

Mr Smith didn't reply.

'Police have got a burner phone used to order the hits, but it will take forty-eight hours to get the records from the mobile company.'

'You summoned me for another favour.' Mr Smith's tone was flat, his face unreadable.

'I'm not asking you for anything, just sharing information.'

'I see.'

'JRB. You know about them. More than you've told me. And I'm wondering if they might be stupid enough to kill a couple of Crows?'

Mr Smith tilted his head but didn't speak.

'They were founded by a Bunyan back in the nineteenth century, but that company was dissolved in 2001. My understanding is that they had a special relationship with the Pearls. Something that has since gone a bit sour.'

'You've been busy,' Mr Smith said. 'And now you're wondering if JRB are in the market for some new friends?'

'It occurred to me that if they had fallen out of love with the Pearls, they might be keen to destabilise the truce. If the Families feel off-balance, they're more likely to partner with an outsider. At least, that's what JRB might think.'

'You think they're wrong?'

'I think they're underestimating the way the Families feel about blood. The Pearls have always been more open.'

Mr Smith nodded. 'Well done on finding Lucy Bunyan, by the way.'

'I had nothing to do with that,' Lydia said. 'It was DCI Fleet and his team.'

'Modesty is overrated.'

'Discretion is not,' Lydia countered. The Pearls hadn't vanished into thin air. There were thousands of Londoners with a little bit of Pearl in their blood and Lydia, like Charlie, had assumed that they represented what was left of the Family. They had been wrong. There was still a strong core to the Family. The powerful ancestors of the Pearl Family were, impossibly, still alive, and that alone had to take a lot of juice. They had to have moved somewhere and Lydia would find them. She didn't know if her aim was to make friends or burn their court to the ground, but she assumed she would figure it out along the way. In the meantime, Lydia had absolutely no compunction over using them as a bargaining chip with

Mr Smith. 'Interesting thing about the Pearls, though. They are able to manipulate time. Or time behaves differently around them. Or something. I bet your boffins would be interested.'

'They would indeed,' Mr Smith said. 'I don't suppose you have an address for them?'

'As I'm sure you already know, they have cleared out.' Lydia tilted her head. 'Lucy Bunyan might be able to give some more information, though, once she's recovered.'

'She doesn't seem overly distressed,' Mr Smith said. 'Seems to think she was at a lovely party.'

'That's good, I guess. I might know someone who spent a little more time with them, though.'

Mr Smith went still. It was as much of a reaction as she ever got and Lydia mentally high-fived herself. 'It's another quid pro quo situation.'

'Of course it is.'

'I want you to find out who ordered the hits on Terrence and Richard Crow. And quickly.'

'And in return you will introduce me to your mysterious friend?'

'Well, there's a little more legwork on your part, but yes.'

'Deal.' Mr Smith's lips twitched in a smile. 'What have you got?'

'He went missing on New Year's Eve 1999.' Lydia took out her phone, navigated to the image she had taken in the Maudsley and passed it to Mr Smith. 'If you can find his identity, contact his family, and arrange some kind of financial recompense for twenty years lost time, he will tell you everything he remembers about his time with the Pearls.'

Mr Smith paused. 'How do you know he was with them? What proof do you have?'

'I can feel it,' Lydia said. She glanced at the figures in the front of the car and then raised her eyebrows at Mr Smith. He nodded. 'You know I can sense power in other people?

Well I can tell which Family they belong to. With this guy, I know he isn't a Pearl, but their signature is all over him.'

He frowned. 'Like residue? Magic dust?'

'I guess,' Lydia said. 'And his entire body is covered in scars, just like the ones Joshua Williams will have when the cuts on his arms heal. Some of the partying evidently included writing on his body with a blade.'

'Interesting.' Mr Smith took out his own phone and took a picture of Lydia's screen. Then he reached forward and tapped the driver on the shoulder.

The car stopped and Lydia heard the mechanism unlock her door.

'You'll look into the hits? I'm on a tight schedule.'

'JRB,' Mr Smith said. 'I'd lay money.'

'Not the Silvers?'

Mr Smith pulled a face. 'They're not there, yet. And you're right. JRB are in the market for a new alliance. That means they want the four Families at each other's throats.'

'I'm going to need a name,' Lydia said. Charlie wouldn't just take her word and she couldn't even tell him about her connection to Mr Smith. She could imagine how well the news that she had been chatting to the secret service would go down.

'I'll see what I can do,' Mr Smith said. 'See you Thursday.'

LYDIA DIDN'T HAVE a name for Charlie, but she did have the strong suspicion that the hits taken out on Terrence and Richard would be the work of JRB, working to destabilise the Families. Or, also a possibility, the work of the Pearl King. In revenge for Lydia taking away their new toy.

Either way, it wasn't something she would expect Big Neil to have any knowledge of and that had to be enough to stop Charlie doing whatever he was doing. Lydia felt a lurch of nausea and she pushed away the thoughts and images her mind had readily supplied. Beating a man tied to a chair. Torture.

Swallowing hard, Lydia texted Charlie. 'On my way. Don't start until I get there.'

Lydia was driving to the lock-up when her phone buzzed with a return text. With a massive effort of will, she waited until she had parked on the street to check it.

Party over.

Well that wasn't good. Lydia's stomach was rolling as she made her way to the lock-up. She banged on the door but nobody answered. She swore at the metal door and the newly-installed lock and at her obstinate, terrifying uncle. It didn't help.

She texted Charlie back:

We need to talk. Where are you?

She waited for a reply and then, out of ideas, Lydia trailed back to The Fork. She parked as close as possible and, squared her shoulders, before heading inside. Maybe the text message didn't mean what she thought it meant. She had to keep an open mind, not jump to conclusions. And, most importantly, she had to keep her cards close to her chest. Whatever Charlie said, she would hide her feelings.

The cafe had the closed sign flipped when Lydia arrived and there was no sign of Angel. Lydia hoped she had taken her advice in full and was on her way out of town.

Lydia walked the empty cafe, checking the kitchen, the storage cupboard and the alley which ran behind the building. She had expected Charlie to be waiting for her, ready to issue some more orders or justify his actions. She had a cold feeling in her stomach that something was very, very wrong, but could not believe that he had meant she was cut out of family business altogether.

Her phone buzzed with an incoming text.

Home.

A ONE-WORD ANSWER. Well, that didn't bode well. Lydia locked the front door of the cafe and drove over to Charlie's house, trying to ignore her gut which was telling her not to visit Charlie on his home turf. Sitting outside the house, Lydia texted Fleet to let him know what she was doing. She finished with the words 'I will check in with you in one hour.' She didn't add 'if I don't, send help', didn't have to spell it out.

Despite Charlie's violence, the way he had spoken to her earlier, and the warning in her gut, Lydia still couldn't quite believe she was in real danger. It was Uncle Charlie. Her dad's brother. He was on edge, but Lydia couldn't help but feel that fences could be mended. There had to be a way to fix this. She knew he had crossed a line with Big Neil, but she still held out hope that he was redeemable. That it wasn't as bad as she imagined.

The path leading up to Charlie's front door was the first sign that things were not right. It was usually lined with corvids, but today it was deserted. The garden was silent, too, not even a breath of wind moving the shrubbery.

Charlie opened the door before she knocked. He must have been watching her approach from one of the front windows. 'Inside,' he said, and turned away.

Lydia followed Charlie into his living room. The fireplace still held the remains of the yule log and its ashes and the room didn't look like it had been cleaned properly since the party. There were piles of papers and books stacked on the sofa and chairs, mugs and glasses and dishes on the coffee table and sticky patches on the wooden floor where drinks had been spilled. It was cold and smelled of cigarette smoke and Crow.

Charlie leaned against the mantle and lit up, narrowing his eyes through the smoke.

Lydia couldn't remember seeing him smoke before and it didn't seem like a good sign. He was wearing a coat so she couldn't see his tattoos. She wondered whether they were moving or whether whatever she had done to him was permanent.

'It wasn't random,' Lydia said. 'But I don't think it's one of the Families. And I'm pretty certain it's nothing to do with Big Neil. When you said 'party over' what did you mean? What happened with Neil? Where is he?'

Charlie ignored her. 'I don't know why you're here, Lyds. I told you to keep out. You've wanted to be out of all this and now you are. Only thing I want from you is the keys to The Fork because you're pissing off back to Scotland.'

'There's a company, JRB. They're a client of the Silvers, but are effectively a shell company in the UK. Very dodgy. I've been investigating them for a while and it looks like they've been trying to make trouble between the Families. I think they want to destabilise the truce. Big Neil has nothing to do with them, no connection.' Lydia was going to tell Charlie more, but his face was weirdly blank and he looked as if he wasn't even listening.

'It doesn't matter.' Charlie dropped the butt onto the stone hearth and ground it out with his shoe. 'But, yeah, Big Neil is off the hook,' he said, finally.

'Good,' Lydia felt the knot in her stomach loosen. 'Do we need to smooth things over with Big Neil's crew?' Beating up Neil was bad, but it was salvageable. Lydia could walk things back. With the wider community and with Charlie.

Charlie shook his head. 'He's not going to run and tell tales.'

Lydia shivered as cold premonition rolled over her. She didn't want to say the words out loud, but she had to be sure. 'When you said the party was over… What did you mean?'

'Big Neil is no longer in attendance,' Charlie said. 'He's taken up permanent residence in a housing development in Brixton. Basement flat.'

It took Lydia a second to comprehend Charlie's words. Then she realised. Big Neil had been added to the concrete foundations of a new build, somewhere Charlie presumably had contacts.

'No windows,' Charlie was saying, 'but he's not in a position to argue.'

'I get it,' Lydia said. The nausea she had been feeling disappeared as she gripped her coin tightly in a closed fist. 'You murdered him.'

Charlie's face twisted into sudden anger. 'Don't you dare judge me. You've been in Camberwell for a year, I've been here my whole life. I've been keeping this family on top, keeping us safe, keeping us solvent. You have no idea what it takes.'

'I'm starting to,' Lydia countered. 'But I don't agree with your definition of essential action. You didn't have to end his life. He hadn't done anything to us.'

'You think he was nice guy, Lyds? Trust me, no one will be crying at his funeral.'

'That isn't the point,' Lydia spat. 'That doesn't justify-'

Charlie laughed. A short, humourless bark which would have made Lydia jump if she hadn't been gripping her coin in her palm so tightly it hurt. 'The ends always justify the means. Always. You think that's the hardest thing I've ever done? You think finishing that idiot ranks in my top five? It doesn't even register, Lyds. It's just business. I had to check out a lead because, in case you forgot, someone *murdered*,' he emphasised the word, throwing it back into Lydia's face like a weapon, 'two members of our family.'

'And if you'd knocked seven shades of hell out of the person responsible, I'd understand, but you knew Big Neil wasn't a big player, that he wouldn't have given the order even if he was linked in some way. What about a bit of restraint?'

Charlie went very still. 'A bit of restraint? You don't

think I'm in control? I measure every single fucking action every single fucking time. It's not easy and you've got no idea what I deal with every day, Lyds. No clue.'

Lydia opened her mouth to argue, but Charlie was in full flow.

'When hard decisions have to be made, when certain things have to be done, I do them. That's what being a leader means. I learned that from my father and so did your dad, so don't think for a second that he's some sort of perfect angel. You do what you have to do. And I'm good at it. That's what makes me a leader, that's why I was trusted to take over when Henry retired early.'

'You were next in line,' Lydia said, fury overtaking her sense of self preservation. 'This Family is all about lineage, about blood. You were next in line and that's why. It wasn't some divine decree.'

'Like you would know anything about that time,' Charlie said. 'And I bet your dad hasn't filled you in, either. Not while he was busy protecting his precious baby girl, keeping her safe from us big bad Crows, all the nastiness he decided wasn't good enough for his princess.'

'Don't expect me to feel bad for you,' Lydia said. 'You love it. You were just telling me you're the natural leader of the Family. You can't have it both ways.'

Charlie's voice dropped low and it got dangerously calm. 'You need to watch your tone. What about a little bit of respect? I am the leader of this Family, something you seem to keep forgetting. Or is there more?'

'What do you mean?'

'You gunning for me, Lyds? Is that what this little performance is all about? You think you've got what it takes to lead the Family?' His eyes were flat and cold and Lydia wasn't sure she even recognised him anymore. 'You trying to take me down? Want to take your father's place?'

'That's not–'

'You've not got it. It's not just about Crow power, it's about balls.'

'Is that a fact?' Lydia could feel her anger returning, pushing the fear to the corners.

'Family wouldn't accept your authority. That is a fact. And neither would Alejandro.'

'What have the Silvers got to do with anything?'

'Allies are important.' Charlie seemed to catch himself. 'The right allies. Running around with your teenage dream crush doesn't count. Alejandro and I are bonded. You push me out, you'll have problems there, too.'

Lydia already had problems with the Silvers. And Maria had taken over as the head of the Silver Family, a fact that Charlie seemed to be ignoring.

'I don't think the Silvers are going to be our allies for much longer, anyway. Maria...'

Charlie waved a hand, dismissive. 'Alejandro is still in charge. Don't let that little PR stunt fool you. And he trusts me. He knows I will do whatever is necessary for the greater good. We go way back. You've got none of that. None of the history. He will never trust you the way he trusts me. We're bonded in a way you'll never match, because you won't make the hard decisions. I don't flinch and Alejandro knows that. When his father needed a problem sorting, he came to me. A Crow. And not your Grandpa, either, not Henry – me.'

'What problem?' Despite herself, Lydia was diverted. There was something tugging at the back of her mind.

'His own niece, Alejandro's little cousin, was stepping out with someone outside the Family. He left it run, hoping Amelia was just acting out, bit of young rebellion, but when they got engaged,' Charlie shrugged. 'He called me.'

Lydia felt as if a bucket of ice water had been thrown over her head. 'There was a Silver wedding at The Fork. Back in the eighties.'

'Amelia's wedding breakfast,' Charlie nodded, caught up in his own recollection. 'It had to be off Silver turf, make it easy for the cops to file it as natural causes. I had nothing against the guy, but I did the job. That's what I mean, Lyds. You have to be willing to do the unthinkable. The ends justify the means, even when the means are pretty bloody harsh.'

'You killed them? On their wedding day? The Silvers are that hung up on their bloodline that they ordered a hit?'

'Old Man Silver waited until they had actually got married, when it was definitely too late for Amelia to come to her senses and call it off. He gave the kid a chance.'

'How kind of him,' Lydia said, trying to keep a lid on her fury. She couldn't think about Jason, not now, it would make that rage boil over.

'But why kill Amelia, too? Please don't tell me it was some sort of honour killing.'

'No,' Charlie said, a flash of regret crossing his face for the first time. 'It was an accident. That was a shame. When her new husband had his heart attack, Amelia went mental. She went for her father in front of everyone. It wasn't discreet. Alejandro pulled her off him and into the kitchen, away from the crowd, to calm her down. I tried, too, but she wasn't having it. She went for me, then, and I pushed her back. Bit too hard, as it happens,' his face clouded. 'That was an accident. I do feel bad about that one. She went back, slipped on the floor and cracked her head going down.'

'How did you do it? Kill...' she almost said, 'Jason' but caught herself, and finished with 'him?'. She felt physically sick.

Charlie rolled his shoulders, like she was asking him out of admiration. 'Now that was a neat bit of work. I stopped his heart.'

'Just like that?'

Charlie tilted his head. 'I have my moments.'

Lydia was trying very hard not to picture Jason and Amy on their wedding day. Jason young and vital and alive on what should have been one of the happiest of his life. The start of his marriage to his beloved. All of that happiness, all of that potential, snuffed out in an instant because Charlie wanted to make powerful friends. Charlie had made a calculation and carried out a professional hit on an innocent man. He had murdered Jason in cold blood. Lydia had been trying to convince herself that Charlie was under stress and acting poorly because of the hits in Wandsworth, but this changed everything. Charlie had been dangerous for a very long time. At once, Lydia's nausea had disappeared. It was replaced with a cold, clear mind and one thought. Charlie had to be stopped.

CHAPTER TWENTY-EIGHT

It was one thing to realise that your uncle was a murderer and that he had to be stopped and quite another to take action. He was Family. More than that, he was 'family' with a small 'f'. He had swung her up high in his arms when she was five, taught her card games at seven, and slipped her £20 notes when her parents weren't looking when she was a teen. Lydia had been brought up away from the Crow Family and their business, but Uncle Charlie had visited his big brother every couple of months and those visits had always been memorable.

Back at the flat, Lydia brought Jason up to speed on what had happened with Big Neil. She didn't know how to tell him about Amelia. Amy. How did you tell a person that a member of your own family had murdered them and then accidentally killed your new wife? There wasn't a handbook for that conversation.

Jason was remarkably calm about the news that Charlie had tortured and killed Neil, though.

'You don't seem surprised,' Lydia said. 'Why aren't you more shocked?'

Jason shrugged. 'Sorry. It kind of fits with my idea of

Crows.' Seeing Lydia's face, he apologised again. 'Just the rumours I heard. The stories. I thought they were just stories, but then I met your uncle and they didn't seem so far-fetched.'

'Hell Hawk,' Lydia sank on to the sofa and put her hands over her face. She wanted to block out the truth. She couldn't continue as a member of the Crow Family with Charlie in place. Which left her with two options. Leaving or taking over. She was tingling with nervous energy and could feel her Crow power, too, beating wings and the taste of feathers. She pulled her shoulder blades back. Could she forge a real alliance with the Fox Family? Or perhaps they could go quiet? If Charlie agreed to retire to the countryside, somewhere far from London, maybe she could wind down his businesses and just run Crow Investigations, quiet and legit. No big centre of power, nothing to threaten anybody else.

Even as her mind ran down these possibilities, she knew it was futile. Nobody would believe that the Crows were stepping away. They would be seen as weak and somebody, a Family or JRB or an unknown threat, would attack. People believed in Crow power and that meant that people feared it. Fear made people strike out, to seek to destroy.

She removed her hands and found Jason hovering uncertainly in front of her. 'I was just trying to come up with an exit strategy.' She couldn't even bring herself to tell Jason the thoughts of a moment ago. Maria Silver wanted Lydia dead and buried. Putting Paul Fox to one side, the rest of the Fox Family weren't her biggest fans, and she had just pissed off the Pearls by taking away their latest toy.

Her head was spinning and she had several calls from Fleet on her mobile. She texted to tell him that she was fine. 'I'm going to sort this,' she told Jason, hoping that sounding confident out loud would magically translate into certainty within.

'I know,' Jason said. 'But if you can't, I'll run with you.'

Lydia paused. The Fork was Jason's home. More than that, it was the place he was tied because it was where he died. She felt tears pricking her eyes and she hugged Jason in a quick, chilly embrace.

Lydia placed her phone in the middle of her desk and looked at it for a long moment. There was a full bottle of whisky on her bookshelves and she looked at that for a moment, too. A calmness filled her centre and, instead of pouring a drink, she walked out onto the roof terrace and lifted her face to the sky. The city lights and a full moon meant that the winter sky was navy blue, not black, and the clouds silvery grey where they met the lunar glow. Lydia reached inside and felt the edges of her power. She produced her coin and made it spin out beyond the railing, holding it suspended high above the street below. Then she made more and more coins appear, dotting them around the terrace, above the street, and up, up into the air until they were sprinkled up as high as she could see, catching the light and shining like stars.

LYDIA WENT DOWNSTAIRS and headed out the back exit and along the alley which ran behind the building, joining the main street away from The Fork. She called Paul's burner.

'I haven't got anything,' he said. 'Nobody is talking about Malcolm Ferris or the move against the Crows. I'm sorry, Little Bird.'

'Not on the phone,' she said. 'I'm heading in your direction.'

'Potters Fields?'

BEING BACK in the park and spotting Paul waiting for her at the entrance, brought home to Lydia how much her loyalties had shifted. She was done with following her Family blindly, just because they shared her blood. And she was done being pulled along in their wake.

'What's happened?'

Lydia checked that nobody was within earshot and filled him in. The loose plan she had been formulating coalesced as she spoke. She wasn't going to run, which meant Charlie was going to have to take a holiday.

'He's not going to go lightly,' Paul said. 'You might have to consider a permanent solution.'

This was not news to Lydia, who had barely been able to think about anything else since the death of Big Neil. She felt her stomach turn over again. 'I can't hurt him.' She had been going to say 'I can't kill him' but she couldn't even form the words. She couldn't murder anybody. She wasn't a killer. 'And we don't have banishment in our Family.'

'Don't you?' Paul said.

'What do you mean?'

'There is a place which has always contained Crows. Not many of you, admittedly, but it's not unheard of.'

The penny dropped. 'I can't have him locked up.' She heard the slam of the door in the police cell, the wave of sheer panic which had rolled over her. Crows didn't belong in cages.

Paul shrugged. 'He's been running an OCG his whole life. Gotta have considered it an occupational hazard. And it's not like he would be powerless inside. No one would touch Charlie Crow.' Paul's eyes widened as he appeared to remember recent events. 'Sorry. That was stupid. I just mean-'

'I know,' Lydia said. 'And you're not wrong.' Especially if she sorted out whoever had attacked Terrance and Richard. And there might be an alternative to a place like Wandsworth. Somewhere more secure from ordered hits. 'I just need to know that the head of the Fox Family would formally recognise Lydia Crow as the head of the Crow Family.'

Paul's lips twitched into a smile. 'The kids are taking over,' he said. 'I approve.'

BACK AT THE FLAT, Lydia knew she couldn't put it off any longer. No matter what else was going on, she owed it to Jason to be honest with him. Lydia found Jason in his bedroom, typing on his laptop. He was absorbed, content. Should she break that peace? Barge into his world with information that would bring pain? Worse still, pain without the hope of resolution.

'Do you believe in what I do?' Lydia sat on the bed cross-legged.

Jason looked up. He must have seen something in her expression as he shut the lid of the laptop and pushed it to one side. 'Investigating?'

'Yeah, my business. Do you think it's a good thing?'

'Where is this coming from?'

'Spending all this time with Charlie,' Lydia said. 'I don't like a lot of what he does, what the Crow Family business looks like, and it's made me wonder about my own business. Am I any better? I cause people pain all the time.'

Jason shook his head. 'You don't cause the pain. You give information. You solve things. You give closure to people or details about their relationships which help them to make decisions about their lives.'

Lydia twisted her fingers together. 'You make it sound like a public service. I snoop for money.'

He smiled. 'Yeah, but you've got a free-loading house-mate who gets through a lot of cereal, you've got to make bank.'

'Make bank?' Lydia raised an eyebrow. 'You're really picking up the lingo. Is that your online friends?'

'Don't do air quotes,' Jason said. 'They are my friends.'

'I'm teasing,' Lydia said. 'I'm happy for you.'

There was a short pause, while Lydia wrestled with her conscience. Then she said, 'do you think the truth is always better than not knowing? For our clients, I mean.'

'Yes.' Jason spoke without hesitation.

'I've got something to ask you, but it's about your life. You've seemed much happier and I don't want to rake up things up if it's going to upset you.'

Jason went very still. Usually, when he was upset he vibrated slightly and, if he got very emotional, he became less and less 'alive-looking' and more and more 'definitely ghost'. Right now, however, he was sitting very still and looking very solid and holding her gaze. 'I am much happier but I still want answers. Even if they aren't very nice.'

'Right-'

'I mean,' he smiled suddenly. 'I'm dead. My wife is dead. I already know it wasn't a happy ending.'

Lydia reached out and took his cold hand. 'You told me before that you didn't know Amy's parents very well. That you hadn't spent much time together.'

He nodded. 'They were always nice to me, though.'

'Were they?'

'I told you before, they seemed fine. Amy said they left her alone, had done ever since she was a teenager and they realised that if they tried to control her it would just make her more rebellious.'

'Smart move,' Lydia said.

'Exactly. And they were. Really smart. Really clever, I mean. So was Amy. She was incredible, could have done anything she wanted.'

'They were at your wedding?'

He frowned. 'Of course.'

'And at the party, here?'

'What are you getting at?'

'You still don't remember anything about that day?'

'No,' Jason was vibrating, now, and Lydia squeezed his hand tighter, hoping to anchor him. If he got very upset, he might just disappear. It had barely happened over the past few weeks, since discovering programming and hacking and an online social life, but it had used to happen with alarming regularity. He would disappear and when he returned, hours later, he had no memory of where he had been. It was something out of his control and Lydia knew it frightened him.

'I think Amy's parents made a deal with Charlie.'

'What sort of deal?'

'Alejandro is like Tristan Fox in one regard, he doesn't believe in diluting the Family's bloodline. And his father was just the same.' Lydia took a deep breath. 'Amy was Alejandro's cousin. Her uncle was the head of the Silver Family.'

'No, they were fine with us,' Jason said. 'I told you.'

'I know,' Lydia said. 'I'm sorry. This is hard to hear, but I don't think they were as accepting as they pretended.'

Jason held up his hand. 'You've found something out?'

'Yes,' Lydia said. She was about to say 'from Charlie'.

'Don't tell me.'

'Are you sure?'

'What if it gives me closure or something and I disappear? I'm happy. I have a life.' He tried a smile which didn't quite work. 'I mean, I have a kind of life. I don't want to lose it.'

'Okay,' Lydia said. 'Let me know if you change your mind.'

'Have you worked out what you're going to do about Charlie?'

For a split second Lydia thought she might have accidentally told Jason about his murder, anyway, but then she realised that Jason was just trying to change the subject from his untimely death. 'I think so. It involves asking for a favour, though.'

'Well that should go well,' Jason said, deadpan. 'You're really good at asking for help.'

'Hilarious,' Lydia said, pushing him lightly on the shoulder.

LYDIA IGNORED a call from Charlie as she walked over to Miles Bunyan's house. The pressing issue of her homicidal uncle aside, she knew she had to speak to Miles. Besides, it was a bright, crisp day and she wanted to enjoy London in the winter sunshine. Walking usually helped to calm her mind, but today her thoughts kept going churning, searching endlessly for a new way out of the problem. She couldn't work with Charlie and she couldn't let him carry on as the head of her Family, not after the things he had done, but she didn't know if she was willing to step up and take his place. Charlie was wrong about a lot of things, but he was right there.

The Bunyans' Victorian terrace looked the same as on Lydia's previous visit, but the atmosphere inside was entirely different. It was light and happy and Lydia wondered if that was something anybody would be able to sense, or whether it was her Crow power. Since the confrontation with the Pearl King, Lydia had been wondering just how different her abilities made her, and how far they might go. It was a novelty after years of ignoring, denying or being embarrassed by them.

She followed Miles down the hallway and into the kitchen, as he explained that Lucy was napping but that she was welcome to stop for tea. 'If she wakes up, you can see her, but I'd rather not disturb her.'

'That's fine,' Lydia said. 'It was you I wanted to speak to, really.'

'Is that so?' Miles was bustling around the kitchen,

getting mugs and opening a packet of biscuits. He shot her an astute look. 'No Charlie today?'

'No Charlie,' Lydia said. 'I'm following up on something.'

'I thought he would be here, wanting to collect his dues.'

Lydia frowned. 'You were paying him to investigate?'

'No, no. Nothing like that.' Miles shook his head. 'He likes to receive thanks in person, that's all. Not that I'm not grateful,' he added hurriedly. 'Tell him I'm very grateful. Eternally grateful. I assume he pulled some strings with the police…'

Lydia forced a smile. 'I'm really not here on Charlie's behalf. There's something I wanted to ask you.'

'Sugar? Milk?'

'Just milk,' Lydia said. 'It's about a company called JRB.'

Miles had been taking a teabag out of a mug and his hand jerked, splashing tea across the counter.

'You've heard of them?'

Miles looked at her, then. 'Is this about Lucy?'

'Why would JRB have anything to do with your daughter?'

'No.' Miles shook his head. 'This is ridiculous. It's just a story.'

'What is just a story?'

Miles turned back to the tea. He put his hand on the milk carton but didn't lift it to pour. He was thinking and his jaw was tight. Lydia guessed that he was about to ask her to leave. She spoke quickly. 'I just want to make sure that you and Lucy stay safe. I know who took her and I think I know why they gave her back, but I want to be sure it doesn't happen again. The house where she was found, the people there have a link to JRB, a company that used to bear your family name. This is just between us. It's not for the police or the press, it won't go any further than this room.'

'Nobody would believe you, anyway,' Miles said. 'It's completely mad.'

'J.R.B and Sons was started by John Bunyan. Relative of yours?'

'It's nothing to do with me,' Miles said. 'I was never on the board. My father was a director, but the company was dissolved twenty years ago. It doesn't exist.'

'What happened?'

'My father passed away ten years ago. He would be the one to ask. I don't know anything about it.' Miles was getting increasingly agitated.

'What was 'mad'?'

'Sorry?'

'About the company.'

'There was a disagreement, I think,' Miles said. 'With their business partners. Or fellow directors, I'm not sure which. A big blow up, though. The company had always been very successful and I know that it would have been better for dad to stay and for it to keep going, so it must have been over something pretty serious. He came out with money, of course, but he always said it was a shame it had ended. He had wanted me to join at one time, but I had other ambitions and, well, you don't always want to just follow in your parents' footsteps, do you?'

Lydia kept quiet.

'So they wound it up and that was that.' Miles dropped the teaspoon into the sink.

'What aren't you telling me?'

'I told you, it's nonsense. Dad got quite confused at the end. He didn't know what he was saying.'

Lydia crossed her arms and leaned against the counter, indicating that she was willing to wait.

'He said there were some weird terms. Some of the people involved had taken the split very personally, very badly. Dad said they made a joke document but it wasn't very funny. It was full of these pretend terms which were supposed to apply as a result of dissolving the company.'

'Can I see it?'

Miles frowned. 'No. I've got absolutely no idea where it is. Probably lost. Or it might be in the attic. Or it might have been shredded when we cleared dad's house.'

'You read it, though?'

Miles shook his head. 'Dad said it was a spoof. Made out to look like a legal document but full of daft fairy tale things.'

'Such as?'

'Oh, I don't know, I can't remember.'

'Try,' Lydia said, squeezing her coin in her palm.

Miles closed his eyes. 'Floral bounty. Freedom below. Your first-born girl.' His eyes flew open. 'My father didn't have a girl.'

'No, but you did,' Lydia said. 'If I were you, I would find that document and burn it.'

CHAPTER TWENTY-NINE

The next day was Thursday and Lydia made her way to her meeting with Mr Smith. She stopped on the way and bought takeaway coffees and two large slices of chocolate fudge cake. She didn't bother to arrive early to sweep the flat for bugs, having accepted that it was futile. Mr Smith belonged to a world with far greater resources and tech than she did.

He was already in the kitchen, the bakery box of Pasteis de Nata on the table.

Lydia put down her cardboard tray. 'I brought a farewell gift. Cake.'

'But we're just getting started,' Mr Smith said. 'This will cheer you up. I found your friend's family and the reunion went very well. I filmed it on my phone, if you want your heart-warmed.'

'He's leaving the hospital?'

Mr Smith nodded. 'Discharged and on his way to his parents' home. I can give you the address. FYI, his name isn't Ash. It's Simon.'

Lydia lifted the lid on her coffee and blew on the liquid

inside. 'I'll take his details. And I'll follow up to make sure he stays safe and well.'

'I don't know what you're implying,' Mr Smith said. 'But he has volunteered to speak to us about his experiences. And he will be well compensated for his time.'

Lydia used the shark smile she had been practising. 'You're giving me your word?'

A small crease appeared between his eyebrows. 'Has something happened? You seem a little...'

Lydia took a sip of her coffee and pushed the tray toward Mr Smith. 'Have some cake. It's not poisoned.'

'You said 'farewell gift'. You know that's not how this works, right?'

LYDIA PUT HER COFFEE DOWN. 'What would you say if I said I could deliver my uncle into police hands with enough evidence to put him away?'

'I would be surprised,' Mr Smith said. 'Can you?'

'There's a bigger problem. Two Crows were killed in Wandsworth. I don't think prison is safe.'

'Agreed. Your uncle must have many enemies.'

'Your department,' Lydia said. 'Do you detain people?'

'Sometimes,' Mr Smith said. 'Are you suggesting that my department would handle the incarceration of Charlie Crow. Keep him safe while he's locked up?'

'I don't know,' Lydia said. 'Is there a deal to be made? One which protects Charlie and gives him more freedom than prison, but still...'

'Removes his civil liberties?'

'That's not exactly what I... Something like that.'

'No halfway house on that, I'm afraid,' Mr Smith said. 'We could give him comfortable accommodation, treat him with dignity and respect, only include experiments with his full consent, allow him visitation rights and communication tools, but a locked door is a locked door.'

Lydia closed her eyes. The mutilated body of Big Neil filled her mind, snapping into horrific focus. 'If I delivered Charlie to you, would you heal my father?'

Mr Smith inclined his head. 'I assume he wouldn't be coming willingly? He may not cooperate with our research?'

'Not willingly or knowingly. He won't walk into prison quietly. As for research, I don't know. He's curious about the Crow powers, too, so he might cooperate if you offer to share results. I honestly don't know.' She clasped her hands together. 'You would do things without his consent, wouldn't you?'

'Absolutely not,' Mr Smith said. 'We have a code of conduct, same as any branch of the civil service.'

'But we're talking dark ops and without seeing a copy of that code, that doesn't mean very much.'

Mr Smith nodded. 'True.' He didn't elaborate.

Lydia had turned over this in her mind ever since it had occurred to her, sometime after she had finished throwing up. Big Neil had not been a good person, but he hadn't deserved to die in fear and pain. And Lydia could not belong to a Family which acted in that way. She had to do something. She had to change the rules and that was never going to happen with Charlie in charge. Even if she took over from him, he would continue to pull the strings, to order people around. He had been doing it for longer. He knew how the game was played and Lydia barely knew what the game was. 'I'll bring you the evidence you need. You'll have to act fast, though. He can't see you coming. And in return, you will heal my father. If you can't do that, the deal is off.'

'I can do it,' Mr Smith said.

'You said before that you would only be able to try, that you couldn't guarantee it would work. What's changed?'

'You have sufficiently motivated me. Good job.'

'How do I know I can trust you? If you lied about that...'

'I didn't lie. When I heal somebody, it takes something from me. It's not something I do lightly. I said I would try, but I was keeping the proviso that it might not work or work completely so that I could stop the process if I felt it was taking too much from me.'

Lydia nodded. That actually made sense and Lydia found that she believed him. It was possible that Mr Smith's powers or the prize he offered was interfering with her judgement, but Lydia didn't think she had a choice. She had to believe him. Believing him meant that she might be able to save Henry Crow. 'We have a deal, then.'

'Are you really going to do this? Swap your uncle's freedom for your father's life?'

Lydia swallowed. 'I think so.'

'Better get more sure than that,' Mr Smith said, his voice gentle.

SAYING the word and meaning it were two different things. Standing outside in the cold air, tasting car exhaust, Lydia knew that she had to be absolutely certain. There would be no going back from an action of this magnitude against Charlie Crow. And she had to make sure everything was tied up before she pulled the trigger. There was a chance things would go poorly, even allowing for the mighty power of the secret service. She used the contact details from Mr Smith and called Simon's home phone number. A woman answered and Lydia asked for Simon.

'Are you a journalist?'

'No, a friend.' Lydia felt a stab of guilt. She had no right to that label. 'Lydia Crow.'

'Simon? There's someone on the...' The woman's voice became muffled as she put a hand over the receiver. A moment later, Simon's voice said 'hello'.

'I just wanted to check in on you. See how you're doing.'

'I'm okay,' he said. There was a pause as if he was waiting for something and Lydia could imagine his anxious mother retreating to another room, Simon watching her go. 'I mean, it's weird,' he said, finally. 'They're old. I still feel, I dunno, pretty much the same. I don't know why I expected everything to be the same. It's not like I hadn't seen my own face in the mirror. I knew time had passed, but I still... It's stupid.'

'I'm sorry,' Lydia said, feeling helpless.

'Don't be. I'm glad you called, I wanted to say thank you.'

Lydia physically flinched. 'Don't-'

'That guy, the one who found my parents. He's giving me money and he said that you...'

'It's nothing. Don't thank me.' Lydia took a deep breath and crossed her free arm around her middle, hugging herself. 'I'm sorry. I should have helped you sooner. I was caught up in my own stuff and I thought you were...' She broke off before she could say 'delusional'.

'I saw something on the news,' Simon said. 'A girl went missing in Highgate but she's been found.'

'Yeah,' Lydia said. 'That's right.'

'I was in Highgate.'

'What?'

'I'm remembering a little more. Just pieces. But it was Highgate Woods we went to on New Year's Eve. I drank a lot of Mad Dog and some vodka, I was pretty out of it, but I remembered something else.'

'What?'

'There was this little kid. A girl. She was holding my hand, I think. I got lost from my mates and it was really cold and I was drunk, but like, not so drunk that I didn't know I was seriously freezing and that I might end up with hypothermia or something. And then there was this little kid and she said she knew a really good party. It was weird, because she wasn't old enough to be out at that time. Or partying.'

Lydia thought of the Pearl girl outside the house.

'She said something really old fashioned about me going of my own free will. And I think we went underground.'

'Underground? Where was that?'

'The woods. I don't remember going anywhere else. Everything after was underground. Different rooms, different places, but no windows.'

'Do you remember any of the people at the party? Anything else about what happened?'

'I'm not allowed,' Simon said, his voice cracking a little. 'I mustn't. I know that. But I was thinking about that girl. Not the little girl, the one in the news. If she went missing same place as me, maybe the same people took her. And that means maybe they've done it before or will do it again.'

'Maybe,' Lydia said, squeezing her coin in her palm. 'I wouldn't think about it. Just concentrate on getting better. I mean, you've got your life back.'

'What's left of it,' Simon sounded angry, now, and Lydia couldn't blame him. 'I've lost twenty years.'

'It's not fair,' Lydia said. 'I'm sorry.'

'It's not your fault. It's them. The people who kept me. They can bend time or wipe memories, because I can't remember much, but I know I feel like I was only with them for, like, months. A year tops. They can't get away with it. They've stolen years of my life.'

'You can't look for them. Best thing you can do is to forget about it.' Lydia felt the uselessness of that statement and wasn't surprised when Simon laughed.

'I'm going to find out who they are and stop them from ever doing this again.'

'That's a very bad idea.' Lydia pushed a little bit of Crow whammy into her words. The poor guy had been manipulated enough by magic, but this was definitely for his own good. The Pearl King and their court were extremely dangerous and, thanks to Lydia, extremely pissed off. Simon needed to stay well away. To her surprise, her power seemed to bounce right off him.

'I'm serious,' Simon was saying. 'I need something to live for and getting back at the bastards who stole my life is as good as anything. Do you know I can't sleep? And I can't get used to my name. I mean, I kind of remember that I was called Simon, but it doesn't feel right.' He lowered his voice. 'Every time they use it, mum and dad, it makes me flinch. I miss the name 'Ash'. That's insane, right? I hate the people who gave me the name and I miss it at the same time. If I don't do something I'm going to lose my mind.'

'Let me help you,' Lydia said. 'Let me look into things.'

A pause. 'You'd do that?'

'I told you, I should have helped you before. This is my atonement.'

'I can pay.'

'No pay,' Lydia said. 'Just promise me you'll sit tight until I can do some digging.'

There was a short pause and then Simon agreed. 'How long will it take?'

'I've got an urgent matter to attend to today, but I'll get started as soon as possible. And I'll keep in touch. Don't do anything until you've spoken to me first.' Lydia stared across the street for a moment after hanging up, not really seeing anything. She had let Simon down and had to make it right but, more than that, the man had a point. How many others had the Pearls abducted over the years? How many little playthings had the king taken? And had Simon just been unlucky, a case of wrong place at the wrong time, or had he been chosen?

. . .

LYDIA KNEW that she was teetering on the edge of a cliff, and before she jumped off, there was one final thing she had to do. She rang the buzzer on Fleet's building and waited for the door to unlock. When Fleet opened the door to his flat, he was in shirt sleeves, his tie loose. 'You can use your key,' he said.

'I didn't want to presume,' Lydia said. 'We're still...' She had been going to say 'broken up' but the words got stuck.

Fleet nodded and turned away. 'Can I get you something to drink?'

'I'm fine, thanks.'

He turned back. 'Is everything all right? Did something happen with Charlie?'

Lydia didn't know how to explain and she felt her eyes aching with unshed tears. She shook her head. 'He's not going to be in charge anymore.'

'You quit?' Fleet said, one eyebrow raised. 'How did that go down?'

'That's not really...' Lydia stepped into Fleet, trusting that he would hold her, and let her head rest on his chest for a few precious seconds. She had been so angry and hurt, had felt that Fleet had let her down. He had chosen his job, his position as a copper over Lydia and, when she as in custody in Camberwell nick, she felt he had sided with his profession. Deserted her in her hour of need. Now, she had seen the true meaning of betrayal. Betrayal not just of Lydia, but of everything she had thought a person was capable of. It really put things into perspective.

'What's happened?' Fleet was rubbing small circles on Lydia's lower back. 'What's wrong?'

She looked into Fleet's steady brown eyes and read the love and concern which lived inside. 'I'm going to take over as the new head of the Crow Family.'

His frown deepened. 'What does Charlie think about that? Is he going to go after you?'

'He won't be in the picture,' Lydia said. 'I'm calling in a favour from MI5. Turns out,' she smiled a little, 'the official channels have their uses.'

Fleet was searching her face, his frown still very much in evidence. 'There will be repercussions. Charlie isn't going to take this quietly.'

Lydia shook her head lightly. 'You're not listening. I'll be the head of the Crow Family. I'll be the new Charlie. Nobody is going to move against me.'

Fleet opened his mouth to argue but Lydia ploughed on. 'That's not why I'm here, though. I'm not asking your advice or your permission. This is my work, my Family, and I don't think I've got a choice.'

'Okay, but-'

'I wanted to ask you something. It's the final thing I need to work out before I go ahead.'

'What's that?'

Lydia took a deep breath. 'Would a London copper consider a steady romantic relationship with the head of the infamous Crow Family?'

Fleet's frown smoothed away and a smile like sunshine appeared. 'This one would.'

LYDIA SAT at her favourite table in The Fork. It was one at the back, giving her a good view of the whole cafe, and the wall behind meant that nobody could approach without her knowing about it.

She hadn't turned on the overheads, so the room was lit with the glow of the streetlights and the headlights of passing cars. Lydia flipped her coin over the back of her knuckles and waited. The cafe had been called The Fork after a fork in the road. A place where two diverging paths met. Charlie had given so many people stark choices in this room, often two terrible options. He wouldn't have hesitated. And, if Lydia knew her uncle, he wouldn't have lost sleep about them afterward. She wasn't her uncle, but she was a Crow. And Crows don't flinch.

Lydia felt the brush of a wing on the back of her hand just before a noise from the kitchen alerted her that she was no longer alone. The door behind the counter opened slowly and there was a pause before Charlie walked in. Lydia imagined he had been peering out through the gap, assessing the situation, probably wondering if she was stupid enough to meet him alone.

'It's just us,' Lydia said. 'For now.'

Charlie moved through the dark cafe like a shark cutting through water. Everything about him that Lydia had once found terrifying - his certainty, obvious power and those dead eyes – were still very much in evidence. Lydia felt the urge to run away or to bend to his will, and shoved it down.

Charlie sat opposite her and leaned back in his chair, assessing. 'Not very bright, Lyds. You can't summon me.'

'Clearly, I can,' Lydia said.

Charlie's expression didn't betray anything but Lydia felt the tension in the air increase. 'This isn't a pissing competition,' she said. 'I'm not trying to score points or disrespect you. I'm just telling you that you need to step down from your position and head out of town. I don't care where you go as long as it's far away from London and you keep very, very quiet.'

Charlie smiled then. He gave a little head shake, like she was a pet that had learned an amusing trick. 'You're giving me an ultimatum? This is...' He waved a hand while pretending to think. 'What? A threat?'

'Not a threat,' Lydia said. 'A chance. I wasn't going to give you one. You've crossed too many lines and I'm having you removed. I made a deal with the secret service. Agents are at your house right now. If you hadn't come to this meeting, you would already be in their custody.

They've got a room in a secure facility with your name on the door.'

'What are you talking about?' Charlie was going for bluster, but there was something moving behind his eyes. Something which suggested that the penny had dropped.

'That was the plan, honestly. I've given them the lock up and Neil's whereabouts and they exhumed his corpse a couple of hours ago, gathered the DNA evidence required from your torture party. Not that the secret service need much in the way of evidence.'

Charlie was on his feet, looking around as if he expected soldiers to rappel down from the ceiling.

'But I decided to give you one final chance. Turns out I'm not as cold as you. It's not as easy as I thought it would be to sell out a family member, even when they're a killer. So you've got a tiny window of time. Get out now, go far away. It's your only chance.'

Charlie narrowed his eyes. 'You're lying.'

'Look at me,' Lydia said.

Charlie's eyes bored into hers. After a moment he swore.

Lydia glanced at her phone, which was face up on the table. 'You don't have long to decide. When they don't find you at your place, this is the next place they'll look.'

Charlie lunged for her without warning. His hands thudded down onto her shoulders, his thumbs digging into her windpipe, squeezing. Lydia jerked back instinctively, smacking the back of her head against the wall. She tried to stand up, but Charlie was pressing down with his whole weight and Lydia knew that she would never win in a strength contest.

'I don't know what you're playing at, Lyds, but it's not clever to threaten me.' Charlie's voice was completely calm. 'I'm not going anywhere.'

Little bursts of light were appearing across Lydia's darkening vision. The instinctive panic, pain and lack of oxygen, working together terrifyingly fast to cloud Lydia's thoughts. Luckily, she didn't have to think about producing her coin. It was just there. A comforting shape in the palm of her hand, anchoring her to consciousness. Her head pulsed with pain, in time with her hammering heart, but she ignored that and reached out instead to feel for the nearest Crow heart that didn't belong to her. It was thudding pretty fast, too. Adrenaline. Excitement. Exertion. Whatever the cause, it made it even easier to find in the dark than Lydia expected. She reached out and held it. The edges of her coin dug into the flesh of her palm as she closed her power around Charlie's heart and squeezed.

The pressure on her neck released instantly as Charlie clutched his chest. He crumpled to the floor, his face drained of colour and lips rapidly turning blue. Lydia let go of his heart, feeling it fluttering back to life as she tipped her head back and dragged ragged breaths through her bruised airway.

Her head cleared as the oxygen flooded back, and the pain of her throat began to make itself known. She touched the back of her head gingerly and found a lump. She should probably get checked out in hospital, but Lydia felt a fistful of painkillers and a lie down in a dark room would do the trick. Charlie was unconscious on the floor. Lydia eased herself into a crouching position until she could press her fingers to his neck and feel for pulse. The movement made her head swim and her headache intensify. After checking that he was breathing, she pulled Charlie over into the recovery position.

The stairs to the flat felt like a mountain, and Lydia had almost made it to the top when she heard a thump from the floor below. It was a quiet thump. Discreet. But was followed by the sound of a door crashing open, thudding feet, and shouted orders. She had left the front door unlocked, deliberately, and hoped Smith's retrieval team would collect Charlie without smashing the cafe up too much. Considering she had knocked him out cold, she had provided them with the easiest possible job. The least they could do would be not to make a mess.

Lydia made it inside her flat and she locked the door. Halfway along the hall, her limbs were barely moving, but she forced herself onward. Just a few more steps. The pounding in her head had amplified to a continuous all-encompassing globe of pain. She hoped it was a mild concussion and not a sign that she had pushed her power too far too quickly.

In her bedroom, Jason's form appeared in her narrowing vision. His icy touch was like a balm and she felt him support her weight, helping her to the bed. Her phone buzzed as she lowered herself to the pillow, its cool softness almost making her weep. She held the phone in front of her face and forced her eyes open just enough to see the text message. Unknown number, of course. 'It's done.' And then she let go of the phone, closed her eyes and let the waters of sleep close over her aching head.

When Lydia woke up the next day, she felt remarkably well. Her throat and head both still hurt, but they were perfectly manageable and some more painkillers and a pint of water helped. After showering and getting dressed, Lydia accepted a mug of tea from Jason. As she sipped it and contemplated breakfast, she realised what had changed. She was free. Not of dealing with her family, of course, but of dealing with Charlie. She probably ought to feel more conflicted about his fate with Mr Smith, but it was difficult. Charlie had made the choice and there was no doubt in Lydia's mind that he had intended to kill her last night. That really helped with the guilt.

Her phone rang with her parents' number and she snatched it up.

'Lydia?' There's a man here. He says you sent him.'

'What's he look like?'

'Young, very short hair,' her mother said. Then she lowered her voice. 'Handsome.'

'Mr Smith?'

'Yes! You know him? I assumed it was a made-up name. It sounds like a joke.'

Lydia decided not to explain. 'No, he's fine. He's visiting dad.'

'That's what he said. I told him I would check.'

'You did the right thing. Sorry. I didn't know he would be with you so quickly. I would have warned you. I'm on my way.'

'You don't have to if you're busy…'

'I'll be as fast as I can.'

LYDIA PULLED up outside her childhood home just in time to see the front door opening and Mr Smith leaving. She got out of the car and met him as he approached his own car. The Mercedes with the tinted windows. Lydia waved at the suited man in the driving seat who ignored her.

'Did you do it?'

'And good morning to you, too, Lydia Crow.' Mr Smith's skin was ashy and he had dark circles under his eyes. He looked at least ten years older.

'My dad?' Lydia hated the raw hope in her voice.

'I did my best,' he said. 'You're hurt.' He was looking at her neck.

Lydia stepped back. 'I'm fine.' The last thing she wanted was another favour from Smith. 'So, you and I are done.'

Mr Smith nodded. He was clearly exhausted, swaying slightly on his feet. 'Until next time.'

'There won't be a next time,' Lydia said. 'It's over.'

'As you wish.'

She expected a little more resistance, but perhaps her spook was as knackered as he seemed. Lydia watched as Mr Smith got into the car and it peeled away.

She took two steps toward the house and then doubled back to her own car, rummaging on the back seat for a scarf. Once she had arranged the material around her neck, hiding the bruises, she went inside.

The front door hadn't been closed properly and Lydia walked into the empty hall.

Her mother appeared at the top of the stairs. 'Come on up, he's asleep.'

Lydia couldn't remember the last time she had been inside her parents' bedroom. It looked and smelled the same. Floral curtains, dark furniture, the mix of her mum's perfume and her dad's aftershave. In the double bed, lying perfectly still, was Henry Crow. He had a bit of grey stubble which was rough on Lydia's lips as she kissed his cheek.

'Who was that man?' Her mum was whispering and her eyes were bright with unshed tears. 'He just sat here. On the bed. And held your dad's hand. Was it something religious?'

Lydia shook her head. 'Nothing like that. Just someone I thought might be able to help. Did dad wake up at all?'

'No. He's been sleeping a lot recently.' She tried a wan smile. 'I think it means he's more relaxed, more comfortable.'

Lydia noticed the things in the room which were different. The line of medication on her mum's dressing table. A plastic cup of thick pink liquid with a straw. Something that looked suspiciously like a commode in one corner. It was the bedroom of a very ill person.

'I'm sorry I haven't been helping,' Lydia said.

Her mum sat next to her on the bed and put an arm around her. 'It's all right, love. We've been fine.'

Lydia rested her head on her mum's shoulder for a moment and blinked to make sure she didn't start crying. That wasn't going to help. She felt the disappointment settle in her stomach like a dead weight. Mr Smith hadn't promised he would be able to cure her father, but Lydia had still hoped.

Her mum stood up. 'Tea?'

'Thanks,' Lydia turned back to her dad. His breathing was so shallow she could barely see his chest move. 'I'll sit here a while longer, if that's okay.'

Henry's hands were outside of the covers, lying neatly on top of the duvet. Lydia adjusted her position so that she was a little more comfortable and then picked up his nearest hand and held it. Maybe there would be an improvement. Mr Smith had looked like hell, so perhaps he had managed some kind of cure. Lydia felt the hope and the fear and the urge to cry got stronger. Give me a sign, Dad, she said silently. Please wake up.

Henry Crow opened his eyes. He blinked and then turned his head on the pillow until he was looking at Lydia. She formed a smile, squeezing his hand at the same time. She would not hope. She would not cry.

Henry Crow frowned a little as if surprised to see her and then he said: 'Hello, Lydia, love. It's been a while.'

THE END

ACKNOWLEDGMENTS

Some books are trickier than others and this one put up a bit of a fight. My eternal gratitude to Dave, Holly and James for putting up with me while I wrestled it into submission.

I love writing books (even the tricksy ones!), and I am deeply grateful to my lovely readers for enabling me to do my dream job.

As ever, thank you to my brilliant author pals; Clodagh Murphy, Hannah Ellis, Keris Stainton, Nadine Kirtzinger, and Sally Calder. Thank you for the support, camaraderie and understanding.

This book was largely written during the Covid-19 pandemic and ensuing lockdown. Like everyone, I've been anxious and discombobulated for much of the time and, more than ever, I want to thank my friends and family for their love and support.

On that note, special thanks must go to the internet. Thank you for the video chats, streaming content, and the ability to carry on working.

Thank you to my editor, cover designer, early readers, and wonderful ARC team. You are all wonderful.

In particular, thanks to Beth Farrar, Karen Heenan, Melanie Leavey, Jenni Gudgeon, Geraldyne Greenwood, Ann Martin, Caroline Nicklin, Judy Grivas, Paula Searle, Deborah Forrester, and David Wood.

And, as always, love and thanks to my Dave.

CROW INVESTIGATIONS:
Book Five

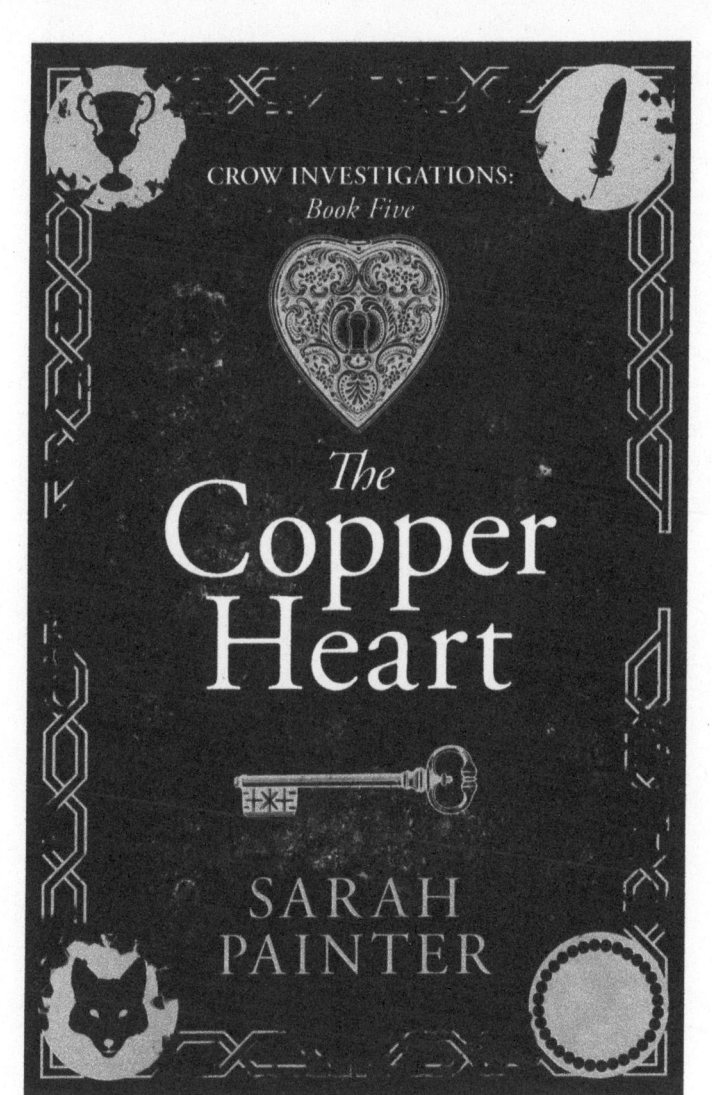

The Copper Heart

SARAH PAINTER

For my wonderful readers,
thank you for taking Lydia Crow under your wing

CHAPTER ONE

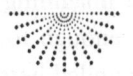

It was a typical spring day in central London. A dense grey sky crouched over the city and the air was damp with threatening rain. Lydia was clinging to the cold metal of a steel cylinder, her feet braced against more steel, and she was trying, very hard, not to think about the thirty floors below her. One hundred metres of empty air ending with solid tarmac.

The Shard, London's tallest building, was a tapering pyramid of glass panels held together by a steel cage and, according to the website Lydia had looked at, a concrete core. The metal struts were accessible on the four corners of the pyramid and the evenly spaced horizontal pieces looked invitingly like a narrow ladder. From the ground, at least. Close up, the rungs were too far apart, and the upright beam too wide to comfortably grasp. Lydia had a pouch of chalk and was wearing grippy climber's shoes, but she still felt she could slip at any moment.

Ignoring the trembling in her muscles, she hauled herself up another rung. The spring breeze was stronger at this height and a gust blew bits of hair into her face. She hugged the pole for a while, taking a mini-rest and spitting the strands from her mouth. Lydia had scraped her hair back into a ponytail but it evidently wasn't enough. She should have worn a swimming cap.

Lydia focused on the smooth metal inches from her face. She didn't want to look up, to see how much more towering skyscraper she still had to climb. And she definitely didn't want to look down. Just imagining the tiny people on that hard, hard ground, was enough to make her stomach flip. She was a Crow, she reminded herself. She wasn't afraid of heights.

Being a Crow, of course, was exactly the problem. It was the reason she was clinging to one of the most iconic buildings in London, breaking the injunction against trespassing the owners had been forced to institute to stop people from doing, well, exactly what she was attempting.

The sun broke through the cloud at that moment, early light reflecting on the glass and shining steel and almost blinding Lydia. Clinging where she was, muscles burning and shaking, was not a tenable position. She knew this so she forced herself to start moving again. One foot up onto the next rung, then sliding her hands up the pole, wrapping them around for a better grip and then, with increasing effort, the second foot up. The fear was circling. Every time she moved upward there was a moment when her body was too far away from the building for comfort, when she had to trust muscle and grip and momentum. The test was to get as far up as possible, which required careful calculation as well as guts. If she climbed until her energy was completely gone, she wouldn't be able to descend safely. There was no rope, no harness, no giant bouncy pillow. Nothing to stop her from breaking every bone on the unyielding ground far below.

That was it. She was going back down. For a second, just the thought of descending made her body go liquid with relief. Lydia began reversing her movements, at first finding them even worse than climbing up. Each time she moved a foot down, it was reaching blindly for the rung below. The urge to just stop and cling to her position, both feet firmly on a metal strut, both hands gripping, was almost overwhelming, but she knew that if she gave into the urge, she would die. Her muscles, already exhausted, would quickly tire and she would fall. There was nobody coming to help, so she had to keep moving. She moved her hands, bent her legs and sent another foot downward.

The sounds of the city began to flood back as she descended. Traffic, car horns, a pneumatic drill, and intermittent sirens. It gave her a jolt of adrenaline. The ordeal was almost over. Lydia took a deep breath and forced herself to keep moving steadily and safely. This was no time to rush. She was still twenty floors up when a voice by her ear made her jump in surprise. She adjusted her grip, making sure it was firm while looking around. The voice had said her name. Just once, but very clearly. There was nobody there. Only glass and steel and a glimpse of grey sky and other buildings, an unwelcome reminder that she was way too far off the ground. Of course there was nobody there. She was experiencing an auditory hallucination because she was exhausted. It would be something to do with the build-up of lactic acid in her muscles. Something like that. 'Sod off,' she said, anyway. Just in case. Living with a ghost had taught her that there were all sorts of people in the world and some of them were non-corporeal.

'Lydia,' the voice said, again. It sounded human, if that human had an extremely sore throat. And had smoked approximately three thousand cigarettes.

Lydia wanted to close her eyes. She touched her forehead to the metal pole, increasing her grip as best she could. Her fingers were numb and she was frightened the strength in her hands was ebbing away. What would happen then? She saw, in horrible technicolour, her fingers uncurling and slipping, her body leaning away from the metal scaffolding, her arms pinwheeling uselessly in the empty air as she fell backwards and down, down, down.

There was a crow perched on the metal frame of one of the sheets of glass, its head cocked. Lydia blinked, expecting to dispel the image, but no. It remained. Chunky body, powerful black beak, black feathers and a single, shiny black eye fixed upon her, as if waiting.

'What?' Lydia knew she sounded rude, but it was hard to modulate her tone. She was, in all likelihood, about to slip and fall to her death. 'I could do without an audience,' she said. 'I'm not having the best day.'

The crow shifted its feet and a small shiver ran along its body, ruffling its feathers.

'Yes, you're very beautiful,' Lydia said. 'And you can fly, you smug bastard.'

There was something about seeing the crow which had cheered her up a little. She wasn't alone. And she was a Crow. A rush of energy ran through her body and she continued climbing down, her pace steadier.

ONCE SHE GOT to the last few feet, Lydia was dismayed to see that there were plenty of people on the pavement. She had started before dawn and the area around The Shard had been almost deserted. She hadn't been that long, but already commuters and street cleaners had filled the thoroughfare. Hell Hawk. That was London for you.

Aiden was waiting where she had left him. He had his phone in his hand and was still filming. 'You can stop, now,' Lydia said, holding her hand up.

'Not bad,' Aiden said.

'Feel free to head on up there yourself,' Lydia said, drily. Her limbs were like jelly and her heart was thudding. She was managing to resist the urge to drop down and kiss the ground, but only just.

Aiden flashed a smile. He looked better these days, a bit of colour in his cheeks and a body that was young-skinny, rather than malnourished. When Lydia had taken over the Family from her uncle Charlie, she had inherited Aiden as a right-hand man. He was one of her many cousins, and only twenty years old, but he had worn the haunted expression of a much-older man. 'Nah, you're all right,' he said, easily.

'You get it all?' Lydia said, falling into step with Aiden as they joined the crowds milling around the London Bridge station. 'Because I'm not doing that again.'

'Unless someone challenges you,' Aiden said.

'What?' Lydia had thought that climbing the highest building in the city was an induction thing. Like a hazing. 'I thought it was one and done.'

Aiden shrugged. 'Only if you'd reached the top. You've left it that someone can challenge you by climbing higher.'

'You're kidding?'

'No one's going to do that,' Aiden said. 'It would be... Disrespectful to challenge the head of the Family.'

'Damn right,' Lydia said, smiling to show she wasn't offended, while inside she swore. Feathers. Another tradition to worry about.

BACK AT THE FORK, Lydia sat at her favourite table and waited for Angel to bring her breakfast. There were perks to usurping Charlie Crow and one of them involved a full English, gratis, and brought to her with the bare minimum of scowling. 'What's happening with Charlie's house?' Angel surprised her by asking.

'What do you mean?'

'If you're not moving in there, is it being sold? Seems like a waste.'

Lydia knew that it seemed odd, ignoring a massive house in favour of her little flat above the cafe, but she had no intention of leaving Jason. He could leave the building if he hitched a ride inside her body, which was exactly as weird and uncomfortable as it sounded, but otherwise was confined to quarters. 'What's it to you?'

Angel's expression closed down and Lydia mentally kicked herself. She hadn't meant to be so blunt, but every day since stepping into her role as the head of the Crow Family had been a barrage of questions. People looking to her for decisions and her having to pretend she knew what she was doing. Not easy when every day brought fresh horror as the full extent of Charlie's business practices came to light. Lydia was dismantling the criminal side to the Crow Family business while, simultaneously, trying to keep the members of the family happy. Or happy enough that they didn't mount a rebellion. It was exhausting.

Her phone buzzed with a text from Aiden.

Everyone is very impressed. Good job, boss.

Lydia wondered if he learned this style of handling from dealing with Charlie. Lydia found it risible, but there was a part of her that liked it. A part that she would have to watch.

Upstairs in her office-slash-living room, the landline rang. 'Hi Mum, everything okay?'

'Everything is perfect. Your dad sends his love.'

In the few weeks after Mr Smith had used his healing mojo to restore her father's mental capacities and stop the series of small strokes which were eroding him further, Lydia had spoken to him on the phone regularly. It had seemed, in the past, that her presence made Henry Crow worse and she didn't know whether Mr Smith's cure would extend to keeping him well or whether she still needed to stay away. There was only one way to test it, and she didn't want to risk making him ill again. Her parents agreed, without them ever needing to have a frank discussion on the subject. They had been on a six-week cruise, returning the week before and Lydia guessed things would return to normal with Lydia mainly speaking to her mum and visiting rarely.

'He's sorry to miss you, now,' her mum was saying. 'He's just catching up after our trip.'

'Snooker?'

'Table tennis,' her mum replied and Lydia could hear the smile in her voice. 'He played on the ship and now he's talking about joining the local league. He used to play with Charlie, back when they were kids, I think. But, yes, the telly's been on twelve hours a day while he catches up on everything he missed.'

Lydia winced at the mention of her Uncle Charlie. She tried to imagine him wielding a ping pong bat and failed. Lydia hadn't told her parents that she had traded Charlie's freedom for a mystical cure of her dad's illness. She told them, instead, that he was out of control and had tried to kill her. Both true, but she still hadn't done it lightly and she felt sick when she thought of Charlie incarcerated in a secret government facility. Then she remembered that he was the man who had murdered Jason and she stopped feeling bad.

LYDIA LET herself into Charlie's house. He had been very careful and there hadn't been much in the way of incriminating evidence to clear from his study, but in visiting the house to look it over, Lydia had started a habit that she wasn't ready to break. She checked in on the place every few days and viewed the video from the security cameras, which were set to record only when triggered by movement. This meant scrolling through carrier bags blown in the wind and post deliveries. Luckily, the local canvassers were well-trained to avoid the house and Lydia didn't have to watch random charity-collectors ringing the doorbell. She also got confirmation that her Crow power was stronger than it used to be. She ought to be caught on the video approaching and leaving the front door, but the footage went fuzzy with white snow. She had known that Charlie had that effect on video recording, whether consciously or as a side effect of being a powerful pure blood Crow, and now it seemed Lydia did, too. Occasionally, Lydia's surveillance would be rewarded in other ways. An old contact of Charlie's would appear, a baseball cap pulled down low in automatic-camera-avoidance. Sometimes they shoved cryptic notes through the letterbox. 'Call K'. 'H sends regards.' Stuff like that, usually scrawled on the outside of a piece of junk mail. Today, there was a neatly-folded note on the polished wooden floor. Lydia pulled on a pair of nitrile gloves and picked it up.

It's later than you think.

With the note safely sealed in a plastic bag, labelled with the time, date, and location, Lydia moved through the rest of the house. She checked the doors and windows for signs of forced entry, just in case the cameras had glitched, then, when she was satisfied that nothing was out of place, she went up to the training room.

It ought to be a place of bad memories. She had hated being forced to train by Charlie and had spent the entire time trying to keep her power in check, to moderate how much of it she allowed Charlie to see. She knew that he had pushed her cousin, Maddie, beyond breaking point, causing the mental instability and psychotic rage Lydia had experienced first-hand. Lydia had tried to keep herself safe, holding the warnings she had grown up with firmly in her mind. She had no wish to be used as a tool or weapon by Charlie Crow. Not to mention the time he had attacked her, trying to provoke a bigger, stronger reaction. Well, he'd got what he'd wanted. Lydia had discovered that she wasn't the weak link she had always believed. And she also wasn't just a battery, powering up those around her. In that moment of terror, maybe as a result of all the training that Charlie had forced, she had discovered a new facility. She had accessed a well of power that seemed both within and without herself. She had reached out and found a thousand wings beating, a thousand hearts beating, every single one giving her strength.

It had been almost three months since Charlie had been taken by Mr Smith and his government department. Spring sunshine poured through the tall windows, reflecting off the wall of mirrors and turning the sprung wooden flooring yellow-gold. Lydia stood in the middle of the room and closed her eyes. Her coin was in her hand and she extended her arm, placing the coin in mid-air. In her mind's eye she saw it suspended there and then made it spin, first clockwise and then counter clockwise, before adding coins, one by one, and holding them in different points around the room. Making them spin in unison, or randomly. It was a warm-up or a meditation, this routine, and Lydia found it calming. The sun was welcoming on her upturned face and she felt her power humming both within her and in that liminal space beyond. The place where wings spread in the high blue sky.

Her phone was ringing. Lydia opened her eyes, wondering how long it had been before she had noticed. For one second the room was still full of gently turning coins, and in the next second, they were gone.

Her phone was on top of her hoodie and she felt something as she bent to pick it up. A wash of dark feeling. A premonition.

'Sorry,' Fleet's voice sounded strained. 'I know you're training.'

'What's wrong?'

'Alejandro Silver is dead.'

CHAPTER TWO

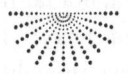

Lydia walked to St Thomas' Hospital by Westminster Bridge. The day had developed from the unpromising grey start to a pleasant late afternoon, with a blue sky and fluffy white clouds. The iconic sights of Big Ben, the London Eye and the Houses of Parliament looked like a tourist postcard in the sunshine, but Lydia's mind was distracted. How could Alejandro Silver be dead?

St Thomas' sat on the opposite bank to parliament and Lydia imagined the ambulance that would have rushed across the bridge, siren blaring, hours earlier, carrying the stricken head of the Silver Family. That was how she still thought of him. Alejandro might have told Charlie that his daughter, Maria, was the new head of the family now that he was heading into politics, but nobody had believed it. Least of all Lydia.

Fleet was waiting for Lydia at the main entrance of the hospital. He led the way to the north wing and down to the lower ground floor, filling her in on the details as they walked. 'He collapsed in the street, that's all we've got so far. It seems as if he was en-route to the house for a vote on a new clause on a finance bill. Didn't sound especially significant, but we're looking into it.'

'Was he attacked?'

'Not that I have heard,' Fleet didn't look at her, was scanning the list of departments on the wall.

'Where did it happen, exactly?'

'Victoria Embankment, not far from that floating pub.'

'The decommissioned ferry?' Lydia was momentarily distracted. She had always thought it was odd that people would choose to go to eat and drink on the water without going anywhere. It seemed like all the downsides of being on a boat with none of the benefits. It was something different, though, something novel. For tourists and corporate events, presumably.

'Yeah, that's the one. Concerned passer-by called an ambulance then stayed with him until paramedics arrived. It took six minutes, which is good going, but by the time they got him to the hospital, he was gone.'

They took a right out of the lift and, finally, saw the discreet sign for the mortuary. Hospitals never shouted about this department and Lydia couldn't blame them. It was evidence of their failure. The limits of their power. Nobody liked to be reminded of that.

'Did he speak to the good Samaritan?' If Alejandro had been conscious, perhaps he would have handily explained exactly what had happened before he expired.

'I'll find out,' Fleet said.

'Is Maria here?' Lydia wasn't looking forward to a reunion with Alejandro's daughter. They had history and none of it was good.

'I don't think so. I'm not even sure if she knows, yet. She's in court.' He looked at his watch. 'They'll finish soon, though. Judges don't work late.'

'Don't they need to wait for her to see him before the post-mortem? Isn't this a bit fast?'

'I don't know.' Fleet looked uncomfortable. 'These things usually take a little longer, but I'm assuming it suits the CPS to fast track it through. I mean, it's high profile and there is a good chance it wasn't natural.'

Something was definitely off about Fleet's manner. 'What's wrong?'

He still didn't meet her gaze. 'I'm not on this. Officially. A friend told me because they know I'm connected to you.'

'Right…'

'I've asked to be assigned, but they haven't returned my call.'

There was clearly something else going on there, something that was bothering Fleet, but there wasn't time to get into it.

Inside the first door to the mortuary was a small waiting area and another door, this one with a keypad and an intercom. Fleet pressed the button and identified himself. There was a buzz and they were inside a short corridor with several closed doors leading off and double doors at the end with another keypad lock. Lydia steeled herself for the mortuary itself, remembering the clinical whiteness and horrifying steel tables from her last visit to one. She could smell bleach, formaldehyde and other things that she didn't want to think about too closely.

A man wearing a surgical cap and gown and carrying a mask, pushed through the double doors. 'What can I do for you DCI?'

'We're here to observe the Silver post-mortem.'

'I don't think so,' he said shortly. 'I'm the lead pathologist and this is the first I'm hearing about it.'

Fleet had already got his credentials out and he flashed them at the doctor who looked unimpressed. 'I've not had notice that you were coming,' he repeated.

'Why is it an issue? I just want to get your initial impressions ahead of the formal report. I won't quote you anywhere, but I'm sure you know this is a high-priority case.'

'He's high profile, I am aware. We've had to shuffle the schedule to accommodate the requested turnaround time.' He looked at his watch in a meaningful manner. 'I really need to get started.'

'I'm not going to hold you up,' Fleet said. He paused. 'But I'm not going anywhere. I can wait while you phone my gaffer. It's up to you.'

Lydia watched the doctor wrestle with his desire to pull rank over Fleet and the equally pressing desire to get moving and get home in time for dinner. The second urge seemed to win out.

'I'm about to start,' he said. 'You can go into the viewing room, but nowhere else. I may be able to spare a few minutes after, depending on how long it takes. And I will put this interruption into my notes, too. This isn't a bloody circus.'

'I appreciate your cooperation, sir,' Fleet said smoothly.

The doctor opened a single door, revealing a square room with what passed for comfortable seating in an NHS hospital and a large window in one wall with sliding shutters which were currently open. There was a table in one corner holding a vase of plastic flowers and someone had gone to town with a lemon-scented air freshener.

'I wonder if they have done the formal identification yet.'

Lydia made a non-committal sound in reply. Truthfully, she wasn't paying close attention to Fleet. The pathologist had appeared through the double doors which she now saw led into the examination room she was looking at through the glass viewing window. He looped his mask around his ears and approached the table in the middle of the room.

'You okay?' Fleet touched her arm, but she couldn't look away from the viewing window. The body of Alejandro Silver was lying on the metal table. His dark hair was swept back from a lightly lined forehead, his short beard was neatly clipped and there were a few silver-grey hairs at his temples. In life, he had looked young and vigorous for his age. In death, he looked... dead. That was the nature of it. There was something unmistakable and alien about a person once their spark had gone out. What did they used to call it? Soul case? Alejandro's soul case was unmarked, at least from where Lydia was standing. And he had a white sheet covering his lower half.

Lydia reached out her senses, but they felt choked by the artificial lemon scent. She thought she could taste a little hint of Silver magic, but it was an after-image. Nothing like the raw power she had felt from Alejandro in life. In fact, it was so faint it could almost be her imagination, something she expected to feel. She closed her eyes and produced her Crow Family coin, gripping it to help her focus. The sense of Silver remained elusive, seeming to disappear the harder she tried to grasp it. Lydia wondered if it was because there was a solid wall and double-glazed glass between them. Or, perhaps, Alejandro's 'Silver' essence had dissipated now that he was dead. She had sensed 'Fox' from the deceased Marty, but his ghost had been in attendance. She had a good look around the room, just in case Alejandro's spirit was hanging about, watching the proceedings, but didn't really expect to see anything. If Alejandro's spirit had been present, Lydia was pretty sure she would be tasting Silver at the back of her throat.

A door on the far wall opened and a small figure, also gowned, walked in. His mask was pulled down around his neck and he looked surprised to see visitors through the window.

The pathologist walked to the wall and a speaker set in the corner crackled into life. 'This is my technician,' the pathologist said, through the speaker system. 'And he's late.'

'Sorry,' the technician muttered. 'There was a queue at Pret.'

Lydia's stomach turned over at the thought of food.

The pathologist turned away from the window and got to work. He switched on a recording device and began to examine the skin surface from the head down, making his observations out loud. There was no bruising or broken skin, no signs of trauma. Lydia was conducting her own examination, reaching out her senses for Alejandro's ghost, trying to see if there was any kind of supernatural signature. Once she was sure there wasn't anything she could detect, she touched Fleet's sleeve and shook her head. 'I'm going to wait outside.'

AN HOUR LATER, Fleet met Lydia on Westminster Bridge, next to one of the ornate Gothic triple-lanterned lampposts. 'When you said "outside" you really meant it.'

'Hospitals,' Lydia shrugged. Given the choice, who in their right mind would sit inside a linoleum palace of pain, when they could be outside, looking at the slow water of the river, instead? The sky was tinged with lavender and a few lights had flickered into life, but Lydia couldn't see the sinking sun. It was hidden behind clouds and pollution. 'What's the verdict?'

'Inconclusive,' Fleet replied. 'Pathologist didn't find any evidence of trauma and preliminary exam shows cause of death as heart failure. Which is usually a coroner's way of saying "I don't know, yet. Go away officer and let me finish my job in peace." He'll finish up tomorrow, but we'll be waiting a bit longer for lab results.'

Lydia was leaning on the green-painted iron balustrade, keeping her gaze on the wide expanse of the Thames. She had been mulling over the ramifications of Alejandro's death ever since she heard the news, and was no closer to working out what she needed to do. Two Crows had been killed in Wandsworth prison and now this, the head of the Silver Family. She had suspected that representatives from a mysterious company, JRB, were intent on causing rifts between the four magical Families of London, which would put them – whoever they were – at the top of the list of suspects for this latest outrage. If that was the case, Lydia needed to know their endgame. 'Who would benefit from a war between the Families?'

'It's not necessarily murder,' Fleet said. 'No signs of trauma, no defensive wounds. It could be natural causes. He wasn't *old* old, and was in good shape, but it's not unheard of.'

'Please,' Lydia said, impatiently. 'Alejandro Silver was hale and hearty. Alarmingly so.'

'You were frightened of him?'

'I had a healthy respect for his power,' Lydia said witheringly.

'Well, I'm glad. I sometimes wonder if you have a realistic view of the danger you keep courting.'

'I don't court danger,' Lydia said. 'All I want is a quiet life.'

Fleet pulled a 'yeah, right' face and Lydia went up on tiptoes to kiss him. Cool air on her skin, the sounds of the city all around, and Fleet's warm lips on hers. For a few seconds she could forget that she was supposed to be in charge of the Crow Family business or that Maria Silver was probably, at this very moment, sharpening a sword ready to plunge it directly into Lydia's soft parts at the next available opportunity. Probably one of her Family heirlooms. The Silvers were the kind of people who had antique weaponry on their office walls.

Lydia blinked and realised that Fleet was no longer kissing her. His face was still close, though, and his gaze was searching. 'I lost you, there. Do I need to brush up on my technique?'

Lydia smiled. 'Sorry. No. Your technique is on point, as always.'

'Glad to hear it.'

'Maria Silver is going to blame me for Alejandro's death.'

'I know.'

'I need to find out who did this, and fast. I need to be able to prove to Maria that it wasn't the Crows.'

'Any point in me telling you that you don't need to get involved, that the police will investigate?'

'None at all.'

Fleet nodded. 'Thought as much.'

BACK AT THE FORK, Lydia found Jason sitting on the sofa with his laptop. She ignored the whisky bottle and got a beer from the fridge, instead.

Jason raised an eyebrow. 'Still on that health kick?'

'My body is a temple,' Lydia said, popping the cap and taking a long swig.

He was still looking at her and his expression was unnervingly sympathetic. 'What?'

'You might want something stronger.'

'I know about Alejandro, I've just come from the mortuary.'

'Wait. What?' Jason frowned. 'What about Alejandro?'

'He's dead.' Too late, Lydia remembered that Jason's wife (of one day) had been a member of the Silver Family. Back in the 1980s, but still. 'Sorry for your loss,' she said. 'He collapsed by the Thames this morning. I assumed you'd seen it on the news or...' Lydia trailed off, realising that he clearly hadn't. Couldn't have, in fact, as it hadn't been reported, yet. 'Never mind. What's your thing?'

'It's nothing,' Jason shook his head. 'The broadband is down. Alejandro Silver died?'

'Yeah,' Lydia sat next to him on the sofa. 'It's a problem.'

Jason's eyes were wide and he was vibrating slightly. 'Maria is going to blame you. She's going to flip... I mean, she's going to –'

Go on a Crow-killing spree. Lydia straightened her spine. 'We'll find out who did it. Deliver their head on a plate. Easy.'

'Or prove it was natural causes. Could it have been natural?'

Lydia shrugged. 'Anything's possible, I suppose.' Alejandro had looked peaceful in death, something she didn't associate with the man. She had expected him to go down swinging and coldly furious, even while suffering a heart attack. His cool, measured voice rang in her mind as she imagined him telling a myocardial infarction that it didn't have an appointment. 'There wasn't anything obvious in the post-mortem. Nothing obvious the pathologist shared, anyway, and I'm no expert. I just had to stop myself from throwing up. Now we have to wait for the blood and tissue tests.'

'You saw him?'

Lydia grimaced. 'He looked fine. I mean, he looked dead, but wasn't cut up or covered in bruises.'

'Poisoning, then, maybe. Like those Russians in Salisbury.'

'I hope not,' Lydia said. If it was a nerve agent like Novichok she had just been exposed to it. 'Although you're right. They do love their poisonings.' Had he pissed off the Russians? Or maybe he had been an agent or a double agent all along. Lydia shook her head gently. The business with her overly friendly spook, Mr Smith, had put spy nonsense into her mind. This was more likely to be a political move. Or something to do with his role as head of the Silvers. A bit of good old English corruption.

'He's only just left the law firm. Could it be a disgruntled ex-prisoner? Someone he helped to put away?'

'That's a good shout,' Lydia said. 'He was a criminal barrister, I think. Before he stepped into corporate law. It was a while ago, but that would give time for somebody dangerous to have served their time.'

'And if they've been nursing a grudge...' Jason turned his palm upwards.

Lydia was quiet, thinking it over.

'Do you need me to ask him?'

She grasped his offer immediately. 'I didn't see his spirit at the hospital, but I could go to where he collapsed. See if there's anything hanging around. Although,' a thought occurred. 'I think he died in the ambulance. Could his spirit have got caught in that?'

Jason shrugged. 'Well, if you get a whiff of Silver, I'm happy to hitch a ride and play twenty questions. I mean, it could be the quickest way to solve his murder.

CHAPTER THREE

Fleet had arrived at The Fork later that night and was gone at dawn. He kissed her before he left. 'Sorry. Don't wake up.'

'Too late.' Lydia had kissed him back, half-hoping to delay him for a more thorough awakening and half-wanting him to head out the door so that she could get on with her own day. She needed to hunt for Alejandro's spirit and should really have got started the previous evening, but had been exhausted; her muscles complaining about their early-morning free-climb. Even the prospect of Maria Silver hadn't been enough to make her get the tube to the embankment.

'Stay safe today, okay?' Fleet said, one hand on her bedroom door.

'You, too,' Lydia said.

He hesitated. 'I'll let you know as soon as the coroner's full report comes in.'

'Great. Thanks.'

Fleet was clearly working up to saying something else. 'What?' Lydia prompted.

'It's not just Maria you need to worry about,' Fleet said.

'Until we know who hit Alejandro, we can't be sure they aren't going after all the major players. That includes you, now.'

Well that was a cheery thought.

The embankment was lined with tour coaches and people thronged the pavement. It was a sunny spring day and the great white wheel of the London Eye was just across the Thames, turning slowly. Like the floating restaurant, Lydia didn't see why anybody would voluntarily sign up for an hour inside the Eye. Heights were bad enough, even without being locked up inside a glass bubble with a group of farting, sweating, *talking* tourists.

Lydia wasn't sure of the exact spot where Alejandro had collapsed and there was no handy crime-scene tape marking out the area, so she just walked slowly up and down the stretch. At one point she ended up at Cleopatra's Needle and realised she had gone too far, walking back she could see Big Ben in the distance and the Whitehall Gardens on her right. On her left, the river flowed slowly, unchanged and unconcerned. It had seen more death and destruction than Lydia could even imagine, and held the secrets of countless unlucky Londoners in its murky depths. A couple were standing next to one of the orange lifebuoys for a picture.

As she approached the staid green arches of Westminster Bridge, Lydia stopped. She sat on a bench so as not to look too conspicuous and closed her eyes, reaching out with her senses. There was exhaust fumes from the traffic, a waft of spicy fried food which made her stomach rumble, and the scent of perfume. Something very strong with jasmine and patchouli. And then, just when Lydia had decided that she was wasting her time, she got a hit of Family magic. Unfortunately, it wasn't the clean bright tang of Silver, but a woody musk. Fox.

'Enjoying the sun, Little Bird?'

Lydia opened her eyes. Her head was already tilted, giving her a full and uncluttered view of Paul Fox. He was wearing his standard uniform of black jeans and a fitted black T-shirt, emphasising his narrow waist and wide shoulders. They had worked together off and on for long enough now, that she had become inured to the animal magnetism which was bundled into the Fox signature. She was still human, though, and the view was pretty magnetic all on its own. 'Working.'

'I heard.'

'And you decided to just hang out here on the off chance I would show up?'

Paul smiled. 'Close enough.'

They might have an active truce and a decent working relationship, but Paul Fox still couldn't answer a straight question with a straight answer.

He sat next to Lydia on the bench. 'Should you be out and about?'

'It's fine,' Lydia said, waving at the crowded street. 'Maria isn't going to kill me with this many witnesses.'

Paul gave her a long look. 'Somebody took Alejandro out with exactly this audience.'

The man had a point. Not that Lydia was going to concede it. Although how he knew the details so quickly was an interesting question. She was going to ask Paul if the story had hit the news sites, already, but she decided to save her breath.

When it became apparent that Lydia wasn't going to elaborate, Paul shook his head. 'Please tell me you're not staying at The Fork, at least.'

'Crows don't run,' Lydia said. 'And I'm the head of the Family, now. I can't bail.'

'You need a new HQ. Somewhere with better security.

Or with more privacy. Too many people know about your current location.'

'Because it's my place of business,' Lydia said. 'I'm not closing Crow Investigations.'

'But why not? You've got enough to do. I've been watching and you haven't drawn breath since Charlie disappeared. You can't do it all. Not forever. And it's not like you need the work, now.'

Lydia decided to ignore the 'I've been watching' part, to assume he meant it figuratively. 'Since when did you start doling out life advice? I'm fine. And I like my work.'

Paul held up his hands. 'Just saying.'

It didn't matter how much trust had built between her and Paul Fox, she wasn't about to start sharing and caring. This wasn't a sleepover and Paul didn't have enough hair to braid. A memory of running her hand over his buzz cut, the way it felt on her skin, jumped into the front of her mind and she felt colour in her cheeks. *Hell Hawk.*

'So, what's the plan, Little Bird? And please don't tell me you're going to visit Maria with your condolences. You're too soft-hearted for your own good.'

Lydia glared at him. 'Classified.'

'I'm asking around,' Paul said. 'Seeing if anybody knows who might have the balls to take on Alejandro. I can share the whispers with you,' he paused. 'If you want.'

Lydia forced herself to stop glaring. 'That would be helpful.' She needed to give him something back. She might not want to start sharing and caring, but she had to do a bit of the former, at least. It was the price of doing business, she told herself. Just business. 'You know I told you about how Marty died? That he had been frightened to death by something he thought was the ghost of his ex-girlfriend?'

Paul nodded. 'I remember.'

'I found out by speaking to Marty's spirit.' Lydia decided to leave out the part involving Jason. Or the fact that she could sense Family magic. One revelation at a time. 'I came here on the off-chance that Alejandro's would be hanging around.'

Paul looked at her for a beat. Then he said, 'That's a very useful party trick for a detective.'

Lydia shrugged. 'I have my skills.'

'Yes, you do.'

Lydia broke eye contact and ignored the way her stomach was flipping. She scanned the view, instead, without any real hope. 'He's not here, though.'

Paul stood up. 'I'll go and speak to my live and kicking contacts, then. See what I can dig up.'

'Thank you,' Lydia said.

'And if you change your mind about moving out, you know where to find me.'

'You're offering me a place to stay? Don't think your family would be too pleased if I turned up with my toothbrush.'

Paul's stance shifted and he became something feral, dangerous. 'I've told you before,' he said, voice low. 'I'm the leader, now. It's my den, my rules.'

The frequency of his voice set off a fluttering in her stomach. Lydia took a steadying breath and told herself that it was just a primal fight or flight reaction, nothing more. She forced a nod and then watched him walk away. Within a few steps he seemed to melt into the crowd, disappearing from view. The after-image of something red, moving through dark green undergrowth, flashed across her mind. Being this close to the most powerful Fox in London was possibly not the best idea she had ever had. Still, better the devil you know. And with the Silvers probably amassing contract killers as she sat, it was better to keep her alliance with the Fox Family. However confusing she found it.

. . .

Before heading home, Lydia spoke to the people running the booths next to the Westminster Pier. There was one selling tickets for tourist boat trips and another offering dodgy-looking burgers and ice cream cones. It was busy enough that they didn't want to get into a long conversation, but Lydia thought they were telling the truth when they each denied seeing anything. Lydia was walking away when a skinny young guy with bleached blond hair and a neat black beard, caught up. 'I saw the ambulance,' he said. 'Just up there,' he indicated back along the wide pavement, away from the bridge.

Lydia confirmed that the time matched Alejandro's collapse. 'Were there a lot of people around?' Lydia gestured around. 'Was it this busy or quieter?'

'About the same,' he said.

'Do you know if he was on his own? Did you see him speaking to anyone before he collapsed?'

He shook his head. 'I didn't really see him. Just the ambo.'

'You work here often?'

'Every day,' he said.

Lydia gave him her card and a twenty-pound note, and told him to call if he remembered anything else. He might not have seen anything useful this time, but another pair of eyes was always handy.

Aiden was waiting back at The Fork, a cup of coffee on the table. Lydia slid into the seat opposite him and tried to keep the irritation out of her voice. 'What now?'

He looked offended. 'Charlie liked to be kept up-to-date on everything. I had to keep him informed. We all did.'

'I told you, just keep everything going. I gave you my rules, but everything else you can use your own initiative.'

Aiden opened his mouth to argue and then seemed to think better of it. He nodded, tight lipped.

Lydia sighed. 'What?'

'It's not that simple. People know Charlie isn't around. If you let people get away with stuff, word is going to spread.'

Lydia resisted the urge to rub her forehead. 'What stuff?'

Aiden went quiet. After a moment he reached for his coffee and Lydia stopped him with a look. 'Don't make me ask again.'

'People want to speak to you. They need to see you around, too. Not all the time and not everyone. But there's a hierarchy. Those at the top need to feel they've got special access, special consideration, or they start to wonder if they really are.'

'Are what?'

'At the top.'

Lydia hadn't banked on spending her time massaging egos. She had a new understanding of why Fleet was so stressed and unhappy at his work these days. He had mentioned that managing teams of people sounded important and powerful, and that he would be able to delegate all the dull grunt work and be left with the pick of the tasks, but the reality was that he spent his time at his desk or in interminable meetings, putting out fires. 'I wish that wasn't metaphorical,' he had said. 'At least I'd be more active.' Looking at Aiden and considering the prospect of meeting and greeting the crème of Camberwell in order to keep the peace, Lydia felt closer to Fleet than ever. She too would prefer a nice old-fashioned burning building right about now.

UPSTAIRS, Lydia let herself into her flat and headed out onto the roof terrace. She sat on one of the metal bistro chairs and got her phone out ready to make a list. There was nothing like a nice neat 'to-do' list to make her feel more in control. And to put off actually doing any of the tasks. Jason materialised in the middle of the terrace, almost making her drop the phone. 'Feathers!'

'Sorry,' Jason said.

'That's okay.' Lydia felt bad for swearing. Jason couldn't always control where and when he appeared.

'I didn't know you were out here.'

'Don't suppose you'd agree to wear a bell?'

Understandably, Jason ignored that. 'Any luck at the embankment?'

Lydia shook her head. 'Nothing. Not even a hint of Silver.'

'It was a long shot,' Jason said. 'You're in one piece, though, so that's a result.'

'I don't know why everyone is so worried about me. I'm the head of the Crow Family. I'm basically untouchable.' Lydia didn't like everyone being so nervous. It was making her jumpy. 'Besides, Maria must know I wouldn't make a move on Alejandro. She might front up for the look of it, but she won't think I'd be that stupid. Maybe I should just go and see her, clear the air.'

'What? You're just going to stroll into her office and explain that you didn't kill her father. Yeah, that's a wonderful idea.'

'There's no need for sarcasm.' Everyone's a critic, Lydia thought. First Fleet, then Paul, and now Jason.

'I'm just saying,' Jason said. 'Maybe Fleet should do it. She's not going to kill a cop.'

'I'm not sending Fleet to do my job. I can't look weak.'

'Better than looking dead.'

338

CHAPTER FOUR

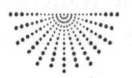

Since he had banished his father, Tristan, Paul Fox was the head of the Fox Family, Maria had stepped into Alejandro's place as the head of the Silvers and, now, Lydia was the head of the Crows. The Family had adjusted pretty quickly, all things considered. Lydia had expected more resistance, but it seemed that her status as Henry Crow's daughter had gone a long way. Of course, the tricky matter of where, exactly, Charlie had gone, and why he hadn't said goodbye still had to be resolved. Most, though, seemed to decide that it wasn't their business. If Charlie had left Lydia in charge and gone into retirement, as per Lydia's story, then all was well. And if Lydia had killed Charlie in order to take his position, it was probably better not to ask questions.

John, Maddie's father, had been one of the few exceptions to put up a bit of a fight. He had cornered Lydia at a pot luck dinner, and asked a few searching questions. 'What did Charlie say? Why didn't he talk to anybody else? Why doesn't he want anybody to get in touch?'

Lydia had shrugged and done the whole 'you-know-Charlie-law-unto-himself' act, but John hadn't been derailed. He had taken Lydia's arm and moved them to quiet corner. 'Are you in trouble?'

'Not at all.'

'Where is he? I know you know.'

Eyes wide. 'I know as much as you, Uncle John.'

Then, John losing his temper, and forgetting his tone. 'Stop it. We need to know. If there are going to be repercussions. Will the police be involved? Is he dead? I need – we need – to know.'

Lydia had snapped into her new role. 'Pull yourself together, John. Charlie has retired. It's lovely news after his long years of faithful service to the Family.'

'But…' John had begun to argue, but Lydia hadn't let him continue.

She fixed the old man with a firm stare, pushing a bit of Crow behind it. John had sagged back against the wall, defiance draining from him in an instant.

'He's got what he deserves,' Lydia had said. 'And I don't want to hear any more about it.'

Now, looking at her coffee and thinking about Alejandro's body in the mortuary and Maria Silver somewhere in the city, no doubt plotting her revenge on the world, Lydia experienced a confusing mix of sympathy and anger. She also knew she couldn't afford to make a mistake. She was the head of the Crow Family and if she didn't act like it, someone would challenge her for the position. And those kinds of challenges often were the 'last woman standing' variety. Apart from the possible-death aspect, passing on the reins to a willing successor wasn't so bad in theory, but only if that successor was up to the job and not batshit crazy. Lydia might not have dreamed of being the head of the Crows as a little girl, but she was damned if she was going to lead her Family into madness and ruin.

She needed to act like a leader. And, whatever Paul, Jason or Fleet might think, that meant showing no fear. Lydia called the Silver and Silver office and asked for Maria.

'Ms Silver is in court today, can I take a message?'

'Are you expecting her in the office later today?'

'It's possible,' the assistant replied. 'But there are no available appointments.'

'That's all right,' Lydia said. 'It's not urgent. What's the case?'

Having obtained the name, Lydia opened the case list on the Old Bailey website. The name belonged to a Bulgarian HGV driver accused of manslaughter when twelve female immigrants were found suffocated in the back of his lorry, due to a lack of oxygen and space. It was being held in court five and this was the third day of the trial. Lydia guessed that the law didn't allow for grief and that Maria would have to postpone her feelings until it was completed. Unless she was allowed to sub in a different barrister and it was just her own professional pride that was keeping her working. Maria was a Silver-hearted murderous witch, but on this point Lydia could relate. The show must go on.

Lydia decided to catch Maria on her way out of court. Outside the Old Bailey had to be one of the safer places for a chat. It wasn't private enough, but Lydia didn't have a death wish. No matter what the men in her life seemed to think. Court five was in the new building so Lydia waited outside the Warwick Passage entrance, hoping that the barristers didn't have a secret exit that wasn't listed on the visitor guide.

It was easy to see when the court let out, with a sudden stream of people coming from the public gallery. Once this had petered out, Lydia adjusted her stance against the soot-stained façade of the building and waited thirty minutes until staff members began leaving. There weren't any in the distinctive barrister's robes which either meant they were changing inside before leaving for the night, or she was waiting at the wrong place. Not for the first time, Lydia realised the limitations of being a one-woman-band. She added 'take on an assistant' to her mental to-do list. There ought to be a line of young Crows looking to be helpful, and money was no longer the pressing concern it had once been. Aiden had made it clear that her new role came with a generous stipend. She had yet to access it, but there would come a time when her hand would be forced. She wasn't taking on as many paying clients as her time had been swallowed by her new duties.

Giving up for the evening, Lydia walked to Blackfriars station and caught an over ground train to Denmark Hill to head home. Minutes into the journey and she felt a compulsion for a different destination, so she got off at London Bridge and changed trains to one heading to Honor Oak Park.

WHEN LYDIA HAD BEEN a child and had yet to realise the extent to which her family was not the same as the other families in their street in Beckenham, her father had taken her to visit her ancestors. As always, he spoke to her as if she was an adult, which meant that she felt valued and respected, if occasionally confused. 'Not all of them, unfortunately, burial grounds get squeezed around here. Remains are moved. Still. It's good to pay our respects.'

Henry Crow had explained that the Camberwell Old Cemetery which was, in fact a couple of miles away from Camberwell proper and closer to East Dulwich, had only been built when St Giles church ran out of room in its graveyard. 'Too many bodies. The curse of modern life.'

'They moved Grandma?'

'No, lovey. This was years and years ago. And, luckily

enough, it didn't really matter to us. Crows aren't buried in churches, anyway.'

'We're atheists?' Lydia had asked, having just learned the meaning of the word and utterly thrilled to get the chance to use it so quickly.

'I wouldn't say that, no. Just not very Christian.'

'But we're here?' Lydia remembered the ironwork gates of the cemetery seeming extremely tall, and the word 'Camberwell' picked out in black against a white sky. It was winter in her memory and the metal was freezing to touch.

They walked past fallen gravestones and up a hill, which felt to Lydia very steep and very long. At the top there was a copse of trees and, on the other side and covered with dark green ivy, a structure which looked, more than anything, like a stone Wendy house. It was only when Lydia got closer, that she realised that the peaked roof of the house was formed from carved gravestones with ancient, crumbling inscriptions, and what she had thought were little windows were recesses for more engraving. The lettering in these was better preserved, as it was protected a little from the elements. She began sounding out the chiselled letters, trying to find words she could read, but when she turned to ask her father a question, she found him standing between two trees, looking in the opposite direction. 'Over here,' he said. Lydia held his hand, her finger bones like a tiny bird in his giant palm. Down the slope, beyond granite grave markers and green hedges, the distinctive London skyline hung pale grey, like a ghost of itself, or a mirage in a black-and-white world. 'Crows' final roosting, somewhere up high, where we can see the city.'

Walking up the hill now, it seemed like a gentle slope. The trees around the tomb were still wild and overgrown, but there were far fewer than Lydia remembered, and when she approached the edge of the rise to look out at the view, the suburban sprawl seemed closer and larger than in her memory. The view of the city was still there, though, and she fixed her sights on it, ignoring everything else. This was a good thinking place. And, with her increased knowledge of her own powers, or perhaps her relationship with a deceased person, she felt the presence of the Crows who had gone before. It was faint, though. She didn't think the spirits of the Crow Family stayed anchored here in the earth, however pleasant the view. We're up there, she thought, tilting her neck to look at the blue expanse of sky. She heard beating wings and felt air running over her feathers, like a caress. Comforting and exhilarating all at once. Home.

She patted the stonework as she passed, looking for the sundial that she liked as a child. It was blue-weathered bronze and on the southern side of the tomb. The old-fashioned lettering which had confounded her as a small person, now leapt out. 'Life is but a passing shadow, the shadow of a bird on the wing.'

LYDIA WALKED BACK to The Fork from the cemetery. It took almost an hour, but pounding the pavement had always been good for her thought processes. Besides, it put off the moment when she had to walk back into the building which no longer felt like her refuge and home.

It was late in the evening and the cafe was shut. Angel should have been long-gone but the lights were on downstairs. Lydia recognised Aiden's outline through the window and steeled herself for another unwelcome surprise, or another piece of Crow business she would instantly wish she didn't know.

'Hang on,' she said to Aiden, crossing to the counter to make a strong coffee. The ritual was soothing, but it was really a delaying tactic. It didn't put off the inevitable for long, though. Sipping the bitter liquid, Lydia was trying not to think about how much she was relying on Aiden to act as the conduit between herself and the rest of the Crows. He had worked closely with Charlie and everybody seemed to like and trust him, so it made sense. But the fact that he had worked closely with Charlie meant that Lydia didn't know how loyal he still was to his old boss. Aiden was running through various issues, most of which he had already sorted out, and he seemed in his element. But how much could she trust him?

He had been one of the most pragmatic in the Family after Charlie's disappearance, but Lydia wasn't stupid enough to take people at face value. Especially not Crows. She loved her family, of course, but they were known to consider every angle. To work every possible advantage and to think several steps ahead. Lydia realised that Aiden had stopped speaking and was looking at her expectantly. If the niggles and petty rivalries and minor theft had been sorted out, why was he telling her about them? Oh yes, Lydia realised, so that she would know he had sorted them out. Aiden was looking for a pat on the head. Management didn't come easily, but Lydia forced a smile. 'Good work.'

Aiden looked momentarily confused, then his cheeks pinked a little. 'Everyone is satisfied with your climb.'

'Good,' Lydia said. She sensed there was more, though. 'What? Is it Alejandro? Has the news got out?' She made a mental note to check online. If it was out, there would be questions and concern. A lot of concern.

'It's not that.'

'Really. I'm monitoring the situation and will update everyone as soon as I have solid information.'

'People are still whispering. About Charlie.' Aiden hesitated. 'Some people have wondered why you aren't looking for him.'

'He doesn't want to be found,' Lydia said smoothly. 'And if people want to talk to me about it, they can do so.

Anytime. It's not like they don't know where to find me.' She gestured around the cafe.

Aiden stood up. 'Right. Right, I'll tell them.'

'You do that,' Lydia fixed him with her best Charlie-stare. Dead-eyed. 'Let them know I'm not a fan of whispers.'

LYDIA WAS CLIMBING THE SHARD, but this time the wind was whipping at her face and hands like it wanted to rip her from the building. Her muscles were trembling and her fingers were numb from the cold. She flexed them tighter, willing herself to hold on. Eyes watering, she forced herself to reach for the next rung. The sound of giant wings beating, dangerously close, made her heart hammer faster. She was sweating with fear and exertion and she wanted to close her eyes, to pretend it wasn't happening. This is a dream, she realised. She was reliving her climb. If she looked over, she would see the crow. The dream state continued with that immersive, cold dread. The premonition that if she looked, she would see something terrible and unforgettable. Lydia wasn't going to give into fear, not even when asleep, so she turned her face and looked. It was her cousin, Maddie. She was bruised and broken and had blood running down her face. Her eyes were beseeching. When she opened her mouth to speak, her mouth was a graveyard of broken teeth. 'Why don't you fly?' With that, Lydia felt her hands slip and, with an awful weightlessness, she was falling backwards and down, the air suddenly rushing past her ears.

Lydia woke up in a tangle of duvet, her face and neck clammy with cold sweat. She thought she had been woken up by the nightmare but then realised that her mobile was ringing. It was an unknown number and Lydia's befuddled brain just had time to process that it might be the burger van guy she had given her card, before the theory was smashed by Simon's voice.

'It's Ash,' he said.

Lydia sat up, her brain firing, now. Simon had been taken by the Pearls at the age of sixteen and had spent three years partying with them against his will. They had rechristened him 'Ash', although that was likely to be the least worst of the liberties they had taken. Time had run faster outside of the Pearls underground home and twenty years had passed by the time he was released.

'I can't get used to Simon,' Ash said. 'I'm just going with Ash. I know it's probably Stockholm Syndrome or something, and I should stick with the therapy, but I feel like Ash, now, so...'

'Lots of people change their name,' Lydia said. 'It's your choice.'

'Yeah,' Ash said, sounding a little brighter.

'I don't want to be unsympathetic,' Lydia began, squinting at her phone screen. 'But it's three-thirty.'

'Shit. Sorry. I lost track.'

'What's up?'

'I think I found it.' Ash's voice went up in excitement.

'Found what?'

'Their lair. The entrance to it.'

'Please tell me you're at home.' The audio quality sounded like he was outside, but perhaps he was standing in his parents' back garden, enjoying the air.

'Highgate,' he said.

Lydia focused on the grey shapes in her room, letting her eyes adjust to the gloom. 'Go home. Please. I told you I would find them for you.'

'But you haven't,' Ash said. 'I'm not complaining, I know you're busy, but I need closure.'

That was the therapy talking, Lydia supposed. Was closure a real thing? Something human beings actually got? It sounded like things had to stop changing, to Lydia. And that meant death. 'Closure is overrated,' she said. 'Breathing free air is pretty great. Why don't you focus on enjoying that instead?'

'I can't.' Ash's voice had faded, like he had moved his mouth away from his phone. Then he said: 'Gotta go. I think I see something.'

'I'll come to meet you,' Lydia said. 'Don't do anything until I get there.'

A pause. Lydia heard a siren in the background, then Ash's voice. Frightened, now. 'Back up would be good.'

CHAPTER FIVE

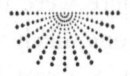

It didn't take Lydia long to dress and head across the river to Highgate. She took her car, counting on reasonable traffic given the unreasonable hour, and arrived at Queenswood Road half an hour later. The road cut through the middle of Queen's Wood, which was Highgate Woods' lesser-known neighbour. There were spaces marked along the side of the road and, praise be, plenty free for parking. The trees reached their limbs across the thoroughfare, forming a tunnel of branches and foliage. It was eerily quiet, traffic noise from the main roads curiously muffled. The last time Lydia had set foot in some London woodland, she had felt like she'd taken an acid trip. Or, at least, how she assumed one would feel. Lydia had bypassed the drugs-as-rebellion stage, figuring 'forbidden relations with Paul Fox' was bad enough.

She checked her phone for updates and, not seeing any, used the flashlight to head into the wood at the next proper path. It looked like people had cut into the woods at different points, wearing unofficial paths up the sloped bank and into the woodland, but Lydia wasn't straying today. It was dark enough to conceal all kinds of threats, even if the Pearls weren't up to their old tricks.

She heard Ash before she saw him. A dull thump followed by an exhalation, surprisingly soft. The first sound had been a punch, Lydia realised, as she turned the corner. Ash was doubled-over, his arms wrapped protectively around his stomach. There were five figures surrounding him at a distance with one, likely the puncher, closer. He was wearing a baseball cap and baggy jogging trousers which looked cheap but had a logo on the back, so might have been expensive. One of the others saw Lydia first and shouted at her to 'just fuck off'.

Lydia stopped and sized up the situation. They were very outnumbered and that was even assuming Ash was fit and able to hold his own. But the faces turned to her looked young, barely in their teens. 'Police' she slipped her ID from her jacket pocket and flipped it open, holding it up briefly. 'Unless you want a trip to the station, you lot can do one.'

The group didn't move and Lydia jerked her chin up in the international signal of 'get on with it'.

After another moment of bravado, with nobody moving a centimetre, the leader gave Lydia a long look up and down and shrugged. 'Boring here, innit.' And they moved off, a pack of kids who ought to have been safely tucked up at home, killing things on their PlayStations.

Lydia watched them move up the path until they disappeared into the trees, taking one of the unofficial paths off the main route. There was a chance they would double-back for a re-run and, kids or not, things could get tricky. Especially if they were carrying blades. Lydia grabbed Ash's arm. 'Come on,' she marched him back the way she had come.

'I've got to show-' Ash began.

'Shut up,' Lydia said.

He didn't try to speak again until they were out of the woods and at the road. 'You can let go of my arm, now.'

'Can I?' Lydia said, but she dropped her grip and stood in front of him, arms folded.

'You're angry,' Ash said.

'You're an idiot.'

'I didn't ask you to rescue me,' Ash said. 'I would have been fine.'

'You called me,' Lydia said.

'Oh, yeah,' Ash passed a hand over his face. He looked tired. His face was washed yellow by the streetlamp, dark shadows under his eyes and cheekbones. 'I wanted to show you what I found. A doorway. I think it's them.'

Lydia was pretty sure the Pearl court had a way to enter their underground home in Highgate Woods, but she was also certain that it wouldn't be findable unless they wanted it found. Fleet and his team hadn't seen anything when combing the area for Lucy Bunyan earlier in the year and the sense that Lydia had got was of very old, very strong magic. That sounded ridiculous and it wasn't something she was in a hurry to say out loud, but there was no other word for it. The Pearl Family had appeared to be diluted and weak, their family members scattered throughout London, running shops and stalls and working as hotel receptionists or accountants, their Pearl ability a shadow of what it had once been, but Lydia had recently learned that there was a core section of the Pearl Family which was extremely powerful. They looked young and beautiful but Lydia had glimpsed their true faces, and seen that they were very old indeed. Possibly even the original Pearls. At once, the fairy stories of how the Pearls had come into existence had seemed entirely plausible. Once upon a time, a fae and a mortal had a baby girl... 'Look,' Lydia forced herself to speak gently. 'You can't keep looking for them like this,' she indicated the deserted street and the woods beyond. 'It's the middle of the night and you're alone. And what was your plan if they popped up in a clearing for a chat, anyway?'

Ash pulled a knife from inside his black bomber jacket. It was very shiny and had an intricately-decorated handle. 'It's iron,' he said. 'I've been reading up on the lore and they don't like iron.'

Looking at the blade, Lydia decided she wasn't a huge fan, either. Several possible responses ran through her mind, but she settled on the mildest of them. 'Put that away before you hurt yourself.'

Ash's expression hardened, but he obeyed. 'I'm not playing,' he said. 'They stole my life. They might have done it again. They could have a new hostage down there. I can't just get on with my life and forget it happened.'

'Let's go for breakfast,' Lydia said. 'My treat.'

As they crossed the river, Ash yawned so wide his jaw cracked. 'You want me to drop you home, instead?'

'It doesn't feel like home.'

Lydia took that as a no.

'Don't you want to know what I found?' Ash said, his face turned to the window.

'I can guess,' Lydia said. 'A place in the woods which felt odd. It went really quiet and the air felt funny, electric like there was about to be a storm. Maybe you saw the trees moving like they were growing.' She didn't take her eyes off the road, but could feel Ash staring at her.

'How did you know that?'

'Finding the entrance isn't the problem,' Lydia said. 'It's getting in without an invitation.' And getting out alive, she added silently.

It was almost five when they arrived at The Fork and the sky was lightening. Lydia left Ash prowling around the cafe, looking at the framed pictures on the walls, and went into the kitchen to forage breakfast. Angel wouldn't be thrilled, but she wouldn't say anything. Not now. Lydia cracked eggs into hot oil, and put bread into the toaster. The cooking gave her a little more time to think. It was true that she had dropped the ball on Ash's investigation. She could argue that she had been very busy and that would be accurate, but it still wasn't a satisfactory excuse. Lydia had offered to help Ash because she felt guilty about letting him down before, not investigating his case quickly enough when she thought his concerns were down to poor mental health. She seemed to be repeating her past mistake, rather than atoning for it.

She piled everything onto a tray and carried it out to the cafe. Ash was sitting at one of the central tables, lining up the little packets of sugar. He swept them into his hand when he saw Lydia.

'Eat,' she said, putting the tray down on an adjacent table and unloading it. She put a plate with fried eggs and bacon and buttered toast and a mug of tea in front of him. It wasn't up to Angel's standards, but Lydia wolfed her portion down, realising as she ate that she had forgotten to have dinner the night before. She was going to have to watch that. She had cut down on her whisky, after realising that her powers were much stronger when she wasn't drinking a bottle or so a day, but the unstable hours of a private eye weren't conducive to a healthy lifestyle.

'Why did you say you were police?' Ash said, after a few minutes of picking at his food. 'You could have told them your name and they would have run away.'

Lydia was pleased he thought so. 'That would be like using a machete to give a hair cut.' And she didn't want to advertise her presence in the Pearls' manor. They seemed to have a penchant for using kids as scouts and there was a small chance word would have been passed on. Lydia thought about her own network of informants around the city. It was still pretty small, but growing steadily. One day, she would be like her old boss and be able to find out anything at all with a well-placed phone call or a couple of site visits with some crisp twenties in her pocket. 'You can't put yourself in danger like that,' Lydia said. 'I'm sorry progress has been slow—'

Ash opened his mouth to speak and Lydia held up her hand. 'You're right to be impatient. I've been distracted. I haven't given it my full attention and I'm sorry. But I will from now on, okay? But you've got to promise me that you'll stop hunting them on your own. I can't do my job if I'm worrying about baby-sitting you at the same time.'

'I want to be involved. I can't stop thinking about them and I need to be a part of it. I can't just…'

'And you will be. But we go together. With a plan.'

Eventually, Ash nodded.

Lydia mopped up the last of her egg with a crust of toast and smiled at him. 'Trust me.'

CHAPTER SIX

'Brain aneurysm,' Fleet said.

'Good morning,' Lydia managed. She wiped drool off the side of her face and sat back in her chair, the bones of her spine cracking. It was almost ten and the sun was pouring through the window. She had driven Ash home just after six and had intended to forgo sleep, sitting her arse in her desk chair and beginning to work through the notes from Aiden. Instead she must have fallen instantly asleep. At least it had been dreamless.

'Lydia?'

'Yep. I'm here. Just processing.'

'It's being marked as natural causes. No criminal investigation necessary.'

Hell Hawk. That wasn't good.

Fleet sounded relieved. 'It's not murder, that means there's nobody to blame.'

Lydia heard the subtext. *Natural causes means Maria can't blame you.* Shame he was wrong. 'Has Maria been informed?'

'Officers are on their way to her now. They thought it would be better in person. Top brass want it handled with the utmost sensitivity. He was an MP, after all. And the rest.'

Yes, the rest. Alejandro Silver, until recently, had run the most successful law firm in the city. Plus, there were still people in London who believed the old stories about the magical Families and had a little dose of extra respect for the head of the Silvers. 'It doesn't make sense, though,' Lydia said. 'He was very fit.'

'Hidden killer, apparently. Unlucky bastard.' Fleet paused. 'At least it was quick.'

'I thought he died in the ambulance?'

'Fairly quick,' Fleet amended. 'Doc said that he wouldn't have known, wouldn't have been conscious.'

'She's not going to believe it was bad luck. And she's definitely not going to be satisfied with no investigation.' Lydia felt a spurt of empathy for Maria. She would feel the same in the circumstances. Brain aneurysm or not, a lack of police investigation would feel like a smack in the face. Disrespect to her father and her whole family.

A pause. Then Fleet's voice, trying to be reassuring. 'You don't know that.'

Something was bothering Lydia, but she wasn't sure how to identify it from all the things that were troublesome. 'You watched the autopsy, right?'

'Some of it,' Fleet said. 'Why?'

'I don't know. Probably nothing.'

'Am I seeing you later?'

'I hope so,' Lydia said. 'Will you let me know if you hear anything else?'

'Of course. Will you stay away from Maria Silver?'

Lydia couldn't promise that, so she didn't answer. 'Have a good day. See you later.'

AIDEN HAD TOLD Lydia that she had to make herself available to the community and her solution had been to set a kind of open house in The Fork on a Tuesday. She had thought that by providing set hours, she could contain the business-side of being the new Charlie, and keep the rest of her time free. Of course, investigation work didn't sit well with a regular schedule of any kind and it was, invariably, awkward timing. Sadly, today was the day and she had missed the last two, so she had a quick shower and dragged herself downstairs. She poked her head into Jason's bedroom on her way to say 'hello and goodbye'.

He looked up from the large pad of paper he had propped on his knees. 'Going to dispense your wisdom? People lining up to kiss your ring?'

'What?'

'The Godfather, you know. Marlon Brando.'

'Never seen it,' Lydia said. She was about to say 'before my time' but didn't. She was trying to be a better person and that included not reminding Jason that he was a ghost living out of his natural timeline, having died in the mid-eighties.

'It's a classic. We should have a film night.'

DOWNSTAIRS IN THE CAFE, Angel was behind the counter. She nodded at Lydia and turned to pour her a coffee without being asked.

There were a few punters at tables, tucking into fried breakfasts, but Lydia spotted a man sitting on his own, nursing a mug of tea and looking worried. She took her favourite seat at the back of the room and waited. Once Angel had delivered her coffee, the man got up and walked nervously to her table.

'Ms Crow?'

'Lydia,' Lydia said. 'Have a seat.' She indicated the chair opposite and the man sat down. He was in his fifties with a grey beard and a mostly bald head. 'What can I do for you?'

'I have a problem,' he began and Lydia dug her fingernails into her palm to stop herself from snapping 'obviously'.

People didn't come to her with good news. People didn't line up to share a joke or be friendly. When all was well, she might as well have been invisible. In a flash, she felt a moment of sympathy for Charlie. This was what he had been dealing with his whole life. Decades of it.

Lydia flipped her notebook open. 'Name?'

'Mark Kendal. Sorry. Why are you writing that down?'

Lydia looked at him for a beat before replying. 'I always write case notes.'

'But, won't that be... I dunno. Evidence? Charlie never wrote anything.'

Mark Kendal had gone from nervous to terrified. Lydia closed the notebook. 'Tell me what's on your mind, Mark.'

'I run a phone place on Southampton Way, by the barbers.'

Lydia didn't know it, but she nodded as if she did.

'I heard that the nail place over the road is going to start selling phone cases.' Outrage overtook the fear in Mark's voice. 'I sell phone cases. That's half my business.'

'Right,' Lydia said. 'That's a shame.'

He spread his hands. 'This is my livelihood. I can't take a pay cut right now. My eldest is at university and it's crippling me. Can you stop them? Have a word?'

Lydia paused. Could she? Should she? Wasn't a free market good for the consumer? Competition giving choice and all that. Stopping price fixing. But did Charlie control who sold what in Camberwell? Was this part of the service? Lydia wished he had left a handbook. Or that she had bothered to learn the business before having him taken away. She could ask Aiden, but didn't want to go to him for everything. It looked weak. Besides, she was the new Charlie. Which meant she could do things her way. Which, in this case, meant stalling. She kept her voice even and told him she would 'look into it.'

The gratitude was embarrassing. Mark Kendal grasped

her hand and seemed ready to kiss the back, before Lydia pulled away. Maybe she should watch The Godfather sooner rather than later. Maybe it would give her some pointers.

AFTER MARK HAD DEPARTED, Lydia motioned to Angel for a fresh coffee. There was a woman in a headscarf clutching her handbag and looking like she was working up the courage to approach and Lydia needed another shot of caffeine first.

Lydia had talked to her dad about The Fork. She was keeping away from him, but they had spoken a few times on the phone and she hadn't wasted the opportunity with small talk. Henry had told her that when he had been working in the business the cafe had been neutral ground. Somewhere people could come to sort out their differences without resorting to violence. Once Charlie had taken over as head of the Family, he had adopted it, making it no longer available for folk to sort out their issues amongst themselves, but instead a place where he took troublemakers and gave them a choice. 'You're at a fork in the road, my friend,' he would tell them. And then he would lay out their choices. 'He wouldn't force anybody to do anything,' Henry had explained, but they always ended up doing the thing that Charlie wanted. 'Well, almost always.' His voice had gone very quiet.

The woman in the headscarf approached. She looked vaguely familiar, but Lydia couldn't place her. She was wearing expensive-looking yoga-pants and a drapey batwing-sleeved top in dark grey. Her face was unlined and she had perfectly threaded eyebrows and expertly applied make-up. At once, her name dropped into Lydia's mind. They had met during one of Charlie's meet-and-greets around the community, when he had been intent on showing Lydia what a big man around town he was. Sorry, when he had been training Lydia in the Crow Family business. 'Chunni,' she said. 'What can I do for you?'

Chunni dipped her chin, a blush rising to her cheeks.

More details were swimming up to the surface of Lydia's mind. Chunni ran a Pilates studio. It was an exclusive little establishment in a renovated mews property near the library, kitted out with those weird Pilates machines, the ones that look like medieval torture racks. Chunni had said that she only took three clients at a time and Lydia had wondered how much she charged the punters to make the finances work.

'I'm not sure I'm in the right place,' Chunni began. She glanced toward the door which led to both the customer toilets and the stairs to Lydia's flat. 'Are you still doing that work?'

'I'm still an investigator,' Lydia said. 'I'm not taking many clients at the moment, but I prioritise locals.' There was a vulnerable vibe coming off Chunni which Lydia definitely hadn't got the last time they had met. It was making her skin prickle with foreboding. Something was very wrong. 'Do you want to go upstairs? Talk more privately?' Over Chunni's shoulder, Lydia could see that another couple of people were waiting to speak to her. Ducking out early was not going to be a popular decision. 'One moment,' she said and rang Aiden. 'I need you at the cafe.'

HAVING ASKED Angel to tell people that Aiden Crow was on his way and would be taking notes on Lydia's behalf, she took Chunni upstairs. It was a feeling of escape, which really didn't bode well for her prospects as the new Charlie. She was going to have to come up with a new system, a new way of handling the business, as pure avoidance wasn't going to work long term. There was enough residual respect and fear to keep things on the rails for a while, but that would run out. People's memories were irritatingly short.

Lydia made plenty of noise unlocking the front door and inviting Chunni into the flat, just in case Jason had moved from his bedroom and needed time to get out of the living room with his laptop. Chunni wouldn't be able to see him, of course, but a floating computer might raise an eyebrow.

The coast was clear and Lydia settled Chunni in the client's chair and took her place opposite. She took a pen from the mug on her desk and prepared to take notes. 'Fire away.'

Chunni was holding her handbag on her lap, she put it onto the desk and there was something about the gesture, the way the bag was angled which caught Lydia's attention. The movement hadn't seemed entirely natural.

'I'm being sued.' Chunni said. 'At least, I think I am. They haven't sent formal letters or anything, nothing from a lawyer. They say they're going to, though, and I'm worried.'

'Sued for what?'

'This man. Sean Ryan. He says he damaged his shoulder because the machine wasn't calibrated properly. He says he's in constant pain and can't do his work, so he's suing for loss of earnings and stress caused.'

It didn't seem like something that needed privacy, but perhaps Chunni was worried about word getting out that she injured her clients. To be fair, that would be bad for business. 'Has he approached you in person?'

'On the phone,' Chunni said. 'And an email.'

'May I see?'

'I will forward it to you,' Chunni said, suddenly guarded. 'I didn't bring my phone.'

Unlikely, Lydia thought. Which was curious. The 'off' feeling was growing. She would have been tempted to chalk it up to run-of-the-mill paranoia, but given recent events,

Lydia thought she should pay attention. 'This sounds like something a lawyer would deal with for you.'

'But I didn't injure him. I thought you could prove that for me. Make him stop this. Follow him and record him or...' Chunni trailed off.

'You want me to scare him off?'

Chunni shrugged. 'If he sees I'm not an easy target...'

There was logic to that. And it was the sort of thing she would usually take. There was just this nagging sense of 'wrong'. And the tricky matter of payment. 'Are you asking me to do this in exchange for a favour, or are you commissioning me as an investigator. If it's the latter, here are my rates. I need a part-payment to get started.' She scribbled down some figures and pushed it across the desk.

'Payment is fine,' Chunni said. 'I don't know what kind of favour I could offer.'

'Okay,' Lydia said, expecting Chunni to take the piece of paper and leave. Instead, she stared at Lydia for a few moments longer, as if waiting for something else.

'Is it true that Mr Crow isn't coming back?'

'Yes,' Lydia said, hoping she was right.

AFTER CHUNNI HAD GONE, Lydia went to find Jason. He was lying on his bed with his arms crossed behind his head, eyes closed. 'I think my new client just recorded our first meeting.'

'That's weird,' he opened his eyes, blinking a couple of times like he was waking up.

'You okay?'

'Just resting,' Jason said. 'And thinking.'

'Anything I can help with?'

Jason shot her an amused look. 'I was mulling over the twin prime conjecture.'

The creepy twin girls from The Shining jumped into

Lydia's head but then she remembered who she was speaking to. 'Maths?'

'Maths.' Jason confirmed. 'Are you sure? About the recording?'

'No,' Lydia shook her head. 'Just a hunch.'

LYDIA KNEW she still needed to pay a visit to Maria. Having failed to accost her outside the court, she might have to take the more dangerous step of visiting her office or home. It would be the respectful thing to do, as the head of the Crow Family and in deference to their long alliance. There was the small chance that Maria would try to kill her, of course, but hopefully that bad feeling had been put to rest. Or, at least, Maria's practical side would prevail. Lydia was the head of the Crows, now. And Maria was the head of the Silvers. They both had to act like it.

What Lydia really wanted to do was see her dad. Knowing that Alejandro was lying in cold storage in the mortuary, had shaken her more than she could understand and she wanted the comfort of her living, breathing father.

However, Lydia was rationing her contact with her dad. Mr Smith had healed him, brought back his mind from the brink of destruction. But that deterioration might not have been run-of-the-mill Alzheimer's. Her presence had always made him worse, and she and Jason had developed a theory. That her power worked like a battery, charging-up those nearby. Anybody with an ounce of magical energy, found themselves more powerful near to Lydia. Which was why Jason had become corporeal in her presence and why her father, who had spent Lydia's life suppressing and denying his Crow magic in an attempt to give her a normal life, had almost been broken by the effort. Lydia had written to him, outlining her theory. She had hoped that he would say that he would no longer try to suppress his nature. She was an adult, now. And part of the Family. He had written back, explaining that he couldn't do that to Lydia's mother. He had made a choice to live a normal life for her sake, and he wasn't going to go back on that promise. And that now that Lydia had stepped up to Charlie, there was no going back for her.

As instructed, Lydia had burned his letter, but she could still remember the last lines, word-for-word.

I'm an old man and not just in years. My time is spent and I have not spent it flying. You are the head of the Family, now. There can only be one. I would be a distraction, an encouragement to dissent, a confusion. With a murder there can only be one winner. Burn this.

LYDIA DIDN'T KNOW if her father believed she had killed his brother, or whether he was referring to the collective noun for a group of crows. Either way, the message was clear: 'You've made your bed, now lie in it. Alone.'

At once, the walls seemed too close and Lydia had to get out of the flat. She headed out into the cool evening, striding quickly in an effort to mute her tangled feelings. She arrived at Burgess Park without consciously deciding on a destination and proceeded to walk aimlessly along the tarmac paths. She had thought that with Charlie gone she would feel a sense of freedom. Instead, she felt more trapped than ever. Wings beating against bars. Claws scrabbling on a metal floor. Caged.

Her dark thoughts were interrupted by the realisation that she was being followed.

CHAPTER SEVEN

A split-second later, Lydia felt the pull of Pearl magic. When she turned she wasn't entirely surprised to see the girl from the Pearl King's court standing by a sycamore tree, watching. She decided to take the initiative. 'Hello, again. What's your name?'

The girl still had dirty blonde hair and torn jeans, and several necklaces slung around her birdlike neck, including the one Lydia had given her on their last meeting. She picked up the lightest sense of Pearl from the girl. Just a dusting. A sheen. But the girl didn't say anything, simply kept on staring with those unnervingly light eyes. After a minute or so, Lydia turned away and continued her walk.

The girl stayed on the grass next to the path, maintaining her distance from Lydia but clearly keeping pace. They were approaching the lime kiln. It was another relic from when the area had been a hive of industry, fed by the Grand Surrey Canal. Boats had brought lime from other parts of the country, ready to be fired into quicklime before being taken to the London factories. Now it was an odd, flat-topped octagonal structure marooned in a sea of municipal parkland. Lydia stopped, as if studying the kiln. She spoke without looking at the girl. 'I thought you lot had cleared out.'

Still nothing.

'It would be better if you had,' Lydia glanced at her. 'I'm not a fan of the kidnapping.'

The girl smiled. She was missing a front tooth and a couple more were askew. When she spoke, her voice made the hairs on Lydia's neck stand up. 'You're in so much trouble.'

Lydia tilted her head. 'Is that right?'

The girl smiled wider, but didn't speak again.

After another minute of staring, Lydia had had enough. She stepped up to the girl and grasped her arm. Her hand wrapped easily around her narrow biceps and the girl turned shocked blue eyes upward. 'I think you should come with me,' Lydia said. 'Let's find you somewhere safe and warm to sleep tonight. Make sure you get a decent meal.'

The girl began to struggle like a wild animal, bucking and clawing. Lydia got her arms wrapped around her from behind and lifted her off the ground. Her legs were kicking wildly and one of them connected painfully with Lydia's knee. 'Enough,' she said, pushing a bit of Crow behind the word.

The girl stopped kicking, went limp. 'Don't take me,' she said, her voice plaintive. 'Please.'

Lydia lowered her to the ground, keeping hold of one arm. 'Why are you following me?'

The girl glared at her from underneath tangled hair. 'Was told to.'

'You're reporting back on my movements? To the king?'

The girl shrugged as if that was obvious.

'Why?'

The girl wrenched her arm out of Lydia's grip and ran. She disappeared behind the lime kiln and Lydia followed, not even sure what she was going to do when she caught the girl. Could she really force her back to The Fork for a meal? Should she? She peered into the first opening of the kiln, expecting to see the girl hiding in a corner, but it was empty. The same thing was repeated in the next couple and then Lydia was back where she started. She looked around the park. There was no way the girl could have run away from the kiln without being seen, there simply wasn't enough cover nearby. And yet, she had disappeared. To underline the fact, Lydia couldn't feel even the slightest wisp of Pearl. The girl had most definitely vanished.

FLEET CALLED. 'I've pulled the CCTV from Westminster Pier. You bring the popcorn.'

Lydia had settled into a routine with Fleet. On the nights they were both off work, she would go to his preternaturally neat flat. Fleet often cooked, or they got Pad Thai from the takeaway, and they had head-banging sex. If they had fallen into a rut, Lydia didn't mind.

She pressed the bell for his flat and waited to be buzzed inside. 'You can use your key, you know. That's why I gave it to you.'

Lydia didn't bother to argue that the key was for emergencies only. And that had been the basis upon which she had accepted it. She deflected him with a kiss, reaching up on tiptoes and holding the back of his neck and head, feeling the tight curls of hair under her fingers as she pulled him closer.

Fleet looked slightly dazed, which was gratifying. His particular gleam, something a little bit magical, but not one of the four Families Lydia could identify, sparked a little brighter. It always hit her during the first few moments of being with Fleet and then it faded to the background as she adjusted. It wasn't alarming. Just part of Fleet. Along with the sunshine and salt scent of his skin, and his elusive smile.

'Are you hungry?' he asked, 'I can put the pasta on whenever you're ready.'

Lydia bent to unlace her boots, stepping out of them as quickly as possible. Then she towed Fleet to the bedroom. The pasta could wait.

LATER, Fleet dished up bowls of amatriciana and Lydia poured red wine. They sat on the sofa and prepared to scroll through the camera footage. There were two angles showing the street, giving good coverage of the stretch where Alejandro collapsed. The pavement was really wide at that part of the embankment, with steps down from one section to another path directly alongside the river. With the numerous benches, leafy trees and the view of the London Eye, it was a popular rest stop and there were groups of tourists and office-workers grabbing a lunchtime sandwich in the sunshine. Lydia had her notebook open next to her on the sofa, ready to jot down questions. The first one was 'why was he walking?'. It was a nice day, sure, but he was a busy man with a car service. Or, was this his habit? If so, somebody could have scoped out his schedule in order to accost him at an opportune moment. But if they knew his routine, wouldn't there have been a less public place to stage an attack?

They had the timing so didn't have to wait long before Alejandro appeared in frame. He was wearing a three-piece-suit and carrying a cane with a silver top. Anybody else would look dandyish, theatrical or old-fashioned. Alejandro looked armed. He was walking with purpose and a determined expression, not glancing around at the scenery or ambling in the sunshine. Perhaps he was considering the vote he was walking toward, or his day's business. Or, perhaps, he was aware, somehow, that he was entering the final minutes of his life.

The pavement was busy and, for a few seconds, Alejandro was swallowed by a group of people walking in the opposite direction. When he emerged, his head was down, his face hidden. Lydia couldn't see if pain or knowledge passed across it in the split second everything went wrong. It was as if he had been shot. Alejandro collapsed to the ground. Lydia replayed the moment. Alejandro didn't clutch his chest or arm or any part of his body. He just collapsed. Like his brain had stopped sending the messages to his limbs to stay strong and keep moving.

'If I was a betting man, I'd say that was a brain aneurysm.' Fleet waved his fork at the screen.

He wasn't wrong, but Lydia couldn't help think that they were seeing what they expected to see. She skipped back and watched the moment again. And again. 'That group. The ones who surround him just before. Have they been interviewed?'

Fleet shook his head, swallowing a mouthful of pasta before speaking. 'It's not considered suspicious. No need.'

'Could someone have attacked him? In that moment when we don't get a good look. I mean, he's surrounded just before he collapses, isn't that suspicious?'

'I would have bet on poisoning before the post mortem,' Fleet said. 'But there's no evidence of that. There's evidence of a-'

'Aneurysm,' Lydia finished. 'I know.'

Fleet put his empty dish onto the coffee table and picked up his wine. 'You seem angry.'

'It's Alejandro Silver,' Lydia said. 'He can't just die. Not like that. Not for no reason.' She felt a lump in her throat and picked up her own glass. Chugging wine so fast it burned.

'Sometimes people die,' Fleet said gently. 'It was too soon, of course, but he wasn't young. It happens. I'm more concerned about you.'

'I'm fine,' Lydia said automatically. 'How much more is there?'

Fleet gave her a final, worried look, and then turned back to the screen, pressing play. A stream of people walked past Alejandro on the ground, and then two women in hijabs stopped. One crouched down next to Alejandro and Lydia could see her speaking, reaching out to touch his shoulder. Then the angle was obscured by a tour bus and, when that had passed, another group of people standing gawking on the street.

'What about the citizen who called the ambulance?'

'I knew you were going to ask and I asked around. No official statement was taken, but the call was recorded.' He produced his phone and scrolled for a moment. 'It was a woman. Aysha Hussain. The dispatcher talked her through CPR while she waited for the ambulance. I've put in a request for the audio file.'

'Don't we see her on here?' Lydia clicked to play the video again.

'I don't think so. That group doesn't move.'

Lydia shot him a look. 'You watched this already?'

'Just a quick scroll through. I wanted to check it was the right file and that it wouldn't be a complete waste of time.'

'Well, I appreciate you getting it for me.'

'So formal,' Fleet said, his mouth quirking into a smile. 'Is that an official thank you from the leader of the Crows?'

Lydia felt the weight of his words like a binding spell. She stiffened her spine and looked him dead in the eye. 'Is that what you want?'

Fleet's smile fell away in an instant. 'Jesus, Lyds. I was joking.'

Lydia forced her muscles to relax and she stood up, taking her plate to the kitchen and dumping it on the side. She looked in the fridge, more for something to do than in expectation. There was a cheesecake plated up and a punnet of strawberries. She felt her stomach turn over at the thought of more food.

'Come and sit down,' Fleet said.

'I'm going to head home,' Lydia said. 'Do some work.'

'Don't leave,' Fleet stood up. 'Let's talk about it. I'm sorry I joked about your family.'

He was picking his words, clearly at a loss as to her response to his joke. It was probably an over-reaction, Lydia knew, but she hadn't realised how much she needed to keep the worlds separate. She couldn't be the head of the Crow Family when she was lying in bed with Fleet or enjoying post-coital pasta. She just couldn't.

'It's fine,' she said, reaching up on tiptoe to kiss him. 'I just want to think about all this,' she indicated the screen.

Fleet boxed up dessert while Lydia laced her boots, handing it to her at the door, with a final, thorough kiss which made her toes curl and her mind reconsider whether she really wanted to leave.

'You're not planning to speak to Maria, are you?'

'No,' Lydia lied, busying herself with the container of cheesecake to avoid looking him in the eye. There was no point in worrying Fleet more.

'You need to be careful.'

'I always am.'

CHAPTER EIGHT

At lunchtime the next day, Lydia was sitting at her table in The Fork destroying Angel's signature lasagne when Aiden walked in looking worried. 'I need a word.'

She put down her fork with some regret. 'Of course you do. What's up?'

'Mr Kendal is unhappy. He says he came to you about a business issue and you haven't done anything about it.'

'The phone case guy? It's a free world.'

Aiden winced. 'He pays us to look after him.'

Lydia indicated that Aiden should sit in the chair opposite. She could do without his lanky form looming over her, blocking the sunshine streaming through the windows of the cafe. 'What do you mean he pays us? I didn't think we did that anymore.' She lowered her voice. 'The protection game.'

'No, no you're right. We don't,' Aiden said. He was about as convincing as a nun in a strip club. 'But we do have a select few special relationships.'

Lydia pushed her plate to one side. 'What sort of relationships?'

'They pay us to help them stay ahead of the competition.'

'What exactly do you mean?'

Aiden hesitated. 'The last place that moved in nearby and started selling phone accessories closed after two weeks.'

Lydia held her hand palm-out in a 'stop' gesture. 'That's enough.'

'We closed them.'

'I got it,' Lydia said. She glanced around at the half-full cafe. 'Let's walk.'

Once they were outside, walking along a quiet side street, Lydia resumed the conversation. 'Why do we look after Mark Kendal and his pisspot little phone shop?'

Aiden shot her a guarded look. 'He supplies burners.'

'Okay,' Lydia said. 'What else?'

'That's not nothing,' Aiden said. 'You get a phone from Mark, you know you haven't been caught on some mook's CCTV, you know there's no receipt in the till showing when you bought it.'

'I'm an investigator,' Lydia said, 'I know why that's important. What else?'

'You really want to know?'

Lydia resisted the urge to stop walking and kick Aiden. Instead she nodded. 'Tell me.'

He rubbed a hand over the scruff of beard on his chin, gazing at the pavement like it contained the secret of life. When he looked up, his expression was a mixture of fear and defiance. 'It's one of our legit businesses.'

Lydia stopped walking and stared at him.

Aiden shrugged, unable to meet her eye.

'Explain,' Lydia said eventually.

'We need places to wash funny money, so we're good friends with a few businesses in Camberwell. They use the dodgy cash, we look after them, do favours and that, and we get nice clean money in return.'

It wasn't the most important part of the story, but Lydia

found her brain had snagged on the cash. 'I thought everything was digital, now. Cards and online banking.'

Aiden shrugged. 'Charlie was old fashioned.'

'You know who else likes cash? Dealers.'

Aiden shook his head. 'No drugs. Charlie made sure of that.'

'I know he wasn't a fan,' Lydia said. Although, as she spoke, she realised that he hadn't been keen on drug gangs moving into Camberwell from Peckham and Brixton. That didn't mean he wasn't running his own operation. At this point, nothing would surprise her.

They resumed walking. 'Tell me who else washes for us.'

After Aiden had listed the businesses and Lydia had asked a couple more follow-up questions, they looped around and began heading back to The Fork.

'I thought we were going somewhere,' Aiden said, as they crossed to Camberwell Grove.

'I just wanted to talk in the open air,' Lydia said. 'Less chance of being recorded or overheard.'

Aiden frowned. 'You don't think The Fork is safe? No one would dare...'

'I don't trust anything anymore,' Lydia said. 'And neither should you.'

CHARLIE CROW HAD BEEN VERY careful with the details of his business. He had rarely spoken about it on the phone and Lydia had never seen him write anything down or use a computer. Now that he was out of the picture, cooling his heels in a government facility, Lydia had checked through the house to ensure there were no nasty surprises and nothing to incriminate any of the Family, should the police come knocking. After the news from Aiden and the realisation that the criminal side to the Crow Family business was very much a going concern, Lydia let herself into the house with a fresh perspective. She was going to be more thorough this time. It was a further invasion of privacy, but she had already done far worse.

She worked systematically, room by room, using the training from her PI mentor, and the details she had picked up through experience. She had come prepared with a crow bar and chisel and she prised every dado rail and skirting away from the walls to check behind. Searching was easy when you didn't have to worry about leaving things exactly as they had been before. She emptied every drawer from every piece of furniture and kitchen unit, checking the backs and underneath.

The living room fireplace was cleanly swept, the remains of the yule log and its ash properly cleared away after the winter holiday. The fire was important. The log had to stay alight for the twelve days, or there would be bad luck. Burning the old year to make way for the new, as well as providing light at the darkest time. Lydia paused by the enormous mantelpiece, struck by the memory of Charlie leaning there, lord of all he surveyed. She could still smell wood smoke in the dead air of the unused room. Charlie had followed the traditions, but that hadn't saved him from Mr Smith and his secret department of the British government. Lydia spent her waking hours avoiding thinking about her uncle and what he was experiencing now. The guilt was too great. He had tried to kill her, but still. Family was Family.

Truthfully, Lydia had expected a greater backlash from the Crows. Certainly, she had expected more questions. It seemed, however, that Charlie had trained them not to show curiosity, to trust the leadership of the Family. She was the rightful leader, the direct descendent of Henry Crow, and the Family appeared happy to accept it. Of course, that could all be a ruse. Any one of her relatives could be biding their time, lulling her into a false sense of security before launching a coup.

Lydia ran her hands along the mantelpiece, checking for switches. There wasn't likely to be a concealed compartment or a false wall which would swing out, revealing a secret room – this was London after all and there wasn't the space – but it wasn't impossible. Upstairs, Lydia hesitated outside Charlie's bedroom door. But only for a moment. It was neat inside, with crisp white bedding like a hotel and blinds at the window. An enormous arty light fitting hovered in the middle of the room, an alien spacecraft visiting planet earth. The bedroom furniture was a dark, polished wood and Lydia checked the matching nightstands. Books, tissues, reading glasses she had never seen Charlie wear, and a small packet of photos. Lydia shook them onto the bed. There was her dad, his arm slung around another young man's shoulders. He was smiling at whoever held the camera, handsome and young with a grin that promised adventure. The other man, Lydia assumed it was Charlie, was looking off to the side, as if his attention had just been caught by something out of frame. Lydia studied the one visible eye and eyebrow, the edge of his mouth. Yes. That could be a young Charlie. There was something determined and cold in that eye. Or she was projecting.

The next photo was definitely Charlie. It was a few years later and he had filled out. He was a solid wall of muscle wearing a fitted white t-shirt and jeans and an unreadable expression in those shark eyes that Lydia knew all too well. A girl with black hair and pale skin had both arms wrapped around his narrow waist and was beaming like she had just won the lottery. She looked familiar, but Lydia didn't know why. Growing up, she had never seen her uncle with a woman. He had been married to his job. The embodiment of the road her father hadn't taken.

Lydia looked under the bed, ran her hands under the

mattress and pulled the drawers out of the nightstands, checking the backs and underneath. Then she went through the storage in the dressing room, rifling through Charlie's neatly folded clothes. If he had a laptop or notebook, it would be somewhere handy so that he could use it regularly. She had been sure it would be here, in his inner sanctum. The en-suite didn't yield results, only the discovery that Charlie used herbal toothpaste, which smelled of liquorice.

Pacing the room, Lydia heard the floorboard creak as she crossed the middle of the floor. She went back over the spot, covered with a red Persian rug, taking careful steps and adjusting her weighting until she heard the creak again. It was very quiet, but there was a tiny difference in the floor, the smallest amount of flex. Rolling the rug away, Lydia scanned the polished boards. They looked neatly dovetailed, but she pulled out a pocket knife and began testing the seams of the boards. One came up. Inside was a cavity. Reaching inside, her fingers touched something soft. A cloth bag. She pulled it out and found a small notebook and a rectangular metal tin. Packed inside were bundles of money. A couple of rolls of fifties and a roll of ten-shilling notes. Spreading one out, Lydia studied its front and back a couple of times each to check she wasn't losing her mind. It was, as far as she could tell, an authentic, used ten-shilling note from the nineteen fifties.

The notebook was about the size of her hand with a hardcover and black elastic holding it shut. Inside were columns of numbers and notes which were not written in anything resembling English. Shorthand, possibly, but a quick google showed that it wasn't the official version. A code of Charlie's own devising?

Lydia sat down and went through the pages carefully, looking for anything which might refer to familiar names or businesses in Camberwell. An entry marked MKM had a string of numbers in different pens, written presumably at different times. MKM could easily be Mark Kendal mobiles. But it could be a thousand other things, as well.

Lydia packed it all back into the cloth bag for easy transportation and put the floorboard back into place. She locked the house up carefully, wondering what other surprises it still held.

LYDIA DIDN'T KNOW if it was seeing the old photographs of Charlie and her dad, but she told Aiden she wasn't available the next day and called Emma to see if she was free. By happy coincidence, Emma had a trip planned to the National Gallery and agreed to meet Lydia afterwards for a walk along the embankment.

The following afternoon, the sky was pale blue and spring sunshine made the river sparkle. It reflected off Emma's sunglasses, and the can of lager that somebody had left on a low wall, and made dappled patterns on the ground beneath the trees which lined the embankment.

They had caught up on the essentials of life and Lydia had been reassured that Archie and Maisie were thriving and that Tom, Emma's husband, was doing much better health-wise. In turn, she had filled Emma in on the last few months with the broadest of strokes.

'When you say Charlie has 'gone'. Is that a euphemism?'

'No.' Lydia took a deep breath. 'At least, I don't think so. As far as I'm aware, he's alive.'

'And you've got his job?'

'Yes. Kind of. I've delegated most of it to other people in the family. But I'm the last word. Theoretically, at least.'

'Bloody hell,' Emma said. 'That's major.'

'I'm sorry I haven't been around,' Lydia said it quickly, like ripping off a plaster. She wondered how many more times she would say these exact words to Emma and how many more times she would be forgiven before her oldest friend cut her losses.

'I need a drink,' Emma said.

'Pub?' Lydia perked up.

'Coffee.' Emma was making a beeline for a nearby booth. Standing in front of Lava Java, she glanced at the menu. 'Maisie has been waking up all week. Nothing serious, night terrors, but I'm bloody knackered.'

Night terrors sounded extremely serious. Lydia was struck, all over again, by Emma's calm competence in the face of astounding horror. Whatever depravity or danger Lydia's job revealed, the intricacies and responsibilities of parenting never ceased to impress and alarm her.

Large coffees in hand, they resumed their stroll. 'What's it like?'

'Sorry?'

'Being in charge.'

'Exhausting,' Lydia said. 'And scary. I don't know what I'm doing.'

Emma pulled a sympathetic face. 'I guess he didn't leave a handy guidebook?'

Lydia shook her head. 'Plus, I don't really want to do things the way he did. At least, not everything. He was...' She lifted the lid on her coffee cup and blew on the liquid to cool it down.

'I've heard the rumours,' Emma said.

'Exactly.'

'I don't mind you being busy,' Emma said. 'I understand. You know I've always understood your hours are weird and long and you have to disappear into cases sometimes to get them done. I get all that.'

'I know, but it's still rubbish for you. I want to be a better friend. More steady. You deserve a better friend.'

Emma pulled a wry face. 'I've got plenty of friends. I'm not sitting by the phone waiting for you to call.'

'I didn't mean that,' Lydia said. 'I know that. I just feel bad.'

'Well don't,' Emma said briskly. 'I've told you a million times. You don't need to worry about me.'

Lydia tried her coffee. Still too hot.

'I think it's more than busyness though.' Emma was watching her with a wary expression.

'What?'

'I think that sometimes, like maybe recently, you keep away from me deliberately. You lost your uncle and I know you two were close. You can talk to me, you know. You don't have to push me away.'

Emma was right, she had been close to Charlie Crow, and there was a confused soup of emotions regarding his absence. But she didn't deserve a caring, sharing session, with the sympathy and understanding she knew Emma would provide. She felt guilty and that was only right. She had betrayed Charlie. More than that, she had done the very worst thing she could do to a Crow. Worse even than killing him, she had put him in a cage.

'Do you want to talk about it now?'

'It's fine,' Lydia said. 'I'm fine. And I'm sorry I've been distant. You're right, some of it has been deliberate. I was waiting to see how things settled down. I didn't want you caught in... Anything.' Lydia kept Emma separate from the Crows, but it wouldn't take a genius to work out that she still kept in touch with her friend from school. A single unguarded conversation with her mum would do it. And if someone came looking for leverage or retribution... It didn't bear thinking about.

'You're doing your usual thing,' Emma said, annoyance clear.

'What thing?'

'Pushing everybody around you away. I don't know why

you think you have to do everything on your own. It's not weak to need people.'

Well that was blatantly untrue. And not the point. 'I need to keep you safe.' She didn't add 'and your children' because she couldn't even form the words. The idea that she could be the cause of any harm coming to Maisie or Archie was, quite literally, unspeakable.

Emma regarded Lydia over her coffee cup for a long moment. 'You don't, though. I'm a grown woman. I make my own choices.'

Lydia opened her mouth to explain that it wasn't about choices or adulthood, but life and death. She encountered some very bad people in her line of work and now she was walking around with a bullseye drawn on her back. Emma, however, hadn't finished.

'And you can't seem to see the irony. The more you push everybody away, the more you keep secrets and tell half-truths, the worse off we all are. I don't expect you to be available, but I do need you to stop hiding.'

'I'm sorry,' Lydia said. She wanted to tell Emma it was for her own protection, but she also didn't want to frighten her friend. And she was afraid it would sound like a bullshit excuse, anyway.

'Don't be sorry,' Emma touched her arm. 'Talk to me.'

'I'll try,' Lydia forced a small smile. 'Old habits.'

Emma nodded. 'Good. Now, I've got to run.' She checked the time on her phone. 'School pick-up awaits.'

After hugging Emma goodbye, Lydia stopped by the booths at Westminster Pier. She recognised the man with bleached-blond hair that she had spoken to before and waited for the queue of people to clear before approaching. 'Do you remember me?'

He nodded fast. 'I was going to call.'

Lydia had just intended to check in, to keep her request fresh in the man's mind. She hadn't expected any actual information. That was the thing about investigative work. You shook a lot of trees before getting hit on the head with an apple. 'Why were you going to call? What's happened?'

'There was a woman asking about that day. Like you were.'

'A woman asked you about the day Alejandro Silver collapsed over there,' Lydia gestured to the spot, making herself absolutely clear. That was another thing she had learned over time. Don't be ambiguous when questioning a source.

He nodded eagerly. 'Yeah, yeah. She asked all about it. What he looked like. Who was with him. All that.'

'What did she look like?'

'I dunno. Dark hair?'

'When was this?'

'Monday. I was off yesterday.'

'You remember anything else about her? How was she dressed?'

'Smart. Black.'

'She was black?'

'No. Definitely white. She was wearing a black suit or something. Businessy. But nice.' There was a bit of leer as he recollected the woman. This was the kind of man who showed every single thought on his face. His eyes probably turned into the shape of chicken drumsticks when he was hungry.

'And she spoke posh.'

'Got it,' Lydia said. She gave the man another twenty. 'Next time, call me right away. Okay?'

CHAPTER NINE

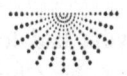

On the way through Camberwell, Lydia couldn't shake the feeling that she was being followed. She took evasive action, stopping to pretend to look in shop windows while checking out the pedestrians and traffic in the reflections, walking in and quickly out of a deli and through a cafe she knew had two different street entrances. She didn't see anybody following, but kept up the looping walk, avoiding her usual route and doubling back at random times in the hopes of either catching sight of the surveillance or forcing them to stop. She expected to catch sight of the Pearl girl or, perhaps, someone from Mr Smith's department. She wasn't naïve enough to believe that just because she had told him she wasn't working with him any longer, that he would simply accept it. Eventually she got close enough to The Fork to walk past her dark grey Audi and she considered getting in and going for a drive. The feeling of being watched had gone, though, and she hadn't seen anything suspicious. She was being paranoid.

She could go home, now, but somehow she kept on walking, looping around and around Camberwell like a caged animal pacing the confines of its environment. Everything was different without Charlie at the helm. People spoke to her differently, people looked at her differently and everything was suddenly *her* problem. The investigator part of Lydia loved the insider information and the sense of seeing beneath the veil. But at the same time, she felt like her jacket was too tight and she couldn't take a proper breath.

Without realising, Lydia had looped around and back and was now passing St Giles Church on the main street. Not knowing why, she ducked through the entrance and into the quiet garden behind the church. Lydia wasn't religious, but she had a soft spot for this particular church and the saint it was named after. St Giles, the patron saint of the poor, destitute and the crooked. The last being the physically deformed, rather than criminal. Plus, they held a weekly jazz club in the crypt below the church with live music and a licensed bar. That was the kind of church activity Lydia could get behind.

The headstones were against the brick walls surrounding the garden and Lydia found herself walking slowly past each one, trying to read the worn inscriptions, like it was a pilgrimage to the past. This wasn't an important place to the Crows. She knew that, but still she felt something here. Something tugging at her senses, dragging her through the public garden and along the wall of memorials, looking for an unknown destination.

Most of the graves had been moved to the Camberwell cemetery, and the remaining space remade into a garden, with grass and trees and benches, but there were still a handful of memorial stones against one boundary wall and the occasional tomb dotted on the grass. Two children, around Archie and Maisie's ages were playing on top of one. She caught the lines of a nursery rhythm being chanted in victory. 'I'm the king of the castle'. It was a good mix, Lydia thought, the reminder of death in the midst of life.

And with that thought, the hairs raised on the back of Lydia's neck and she felt the unmistakable sensation of being watched. Turning slowly, Lydia cast a casual look around. The young father with the two small children wasn't looking in her direction. He was standing with one hand in his jeans pocket, head bent over his phone. There was nobody else there.

Turning back, Lydia pretended to be focused on the gravestones. She was reading the words without really meaning to when a phrase jumped out: 'Sacred in memory of Alice Elizabeth wife of John Crow of this parish who departed this life on the 14th April 1846.' She wondered how that grave had been missed in the mass exodus to the Family tomb in Camberwell Cemetery. Had this Alice Crow done something to piss off the rest of the Family? It would have to be something pretty bad to have her left out of the Family resting place for all of eternity. Or it was just a sign of how little stock the Crows put into churches and graves. The earthly remains of Crows could be anywhere, their spirits would still be high in the sky. Lydia closed her eyes and gripped her coin until she could feel them, mingling with live Crows, borrowing their sight, feeling the air riffling through feathers and senses sharp.

Pearl. Just a trace, but Lydia felt it and it pulled her down from the freedom of the sky and back to the green earth. She turned around to scan the park again and saw Ash step from behind a tree close by. 'Feathers, Ash,' she said. 'You scared me.'

His expression didn't change for a moment and the blankness reminded her of the Pearl girl who had followed her in Burgess Park. It crossed her mind that she should perhaps be a little more careful. She was clearly too easy to find. Lydia instantly rejected the notion. She wasn't going to let anything curb her enjoyment of her city. Besides, if somebody took a hit out on her, avoiding the park wasn't going to keep her safe. They could turn up at any one of her known haunts. Or, as someone had chillingly told her once, they could just poison her food. 'What's up?'

'I've found it,' Ash said, becoming animated.

'What?'

'They've done it before.'

Lydia knew that the Pearl Family, or the core members of the family, known as the court, had taken a girl. Her name was Lucy Bunyan and one of her ancestors had signed a contract with a company which had stated they had the rights to a first-born daughter. It was creepy and definitely not legally binding, but that hadn't stopped the Pearl King from plucking the sixteen year old from Highgate Woods and keeping her prisoner until Lydia had disrupted the party. Months earlier, unbeknown to Lydia at the time, Ash had been released by the Pearls after spending twenty years in their company. Ash knew about Lucy, but she gently reminded him.

'No. Not just her,' Ash shook his head, bouncing lightly on the balls of his feet. He was still just as thin as when he had first re-entered the world, the sharp planes of his face showing that he wasn't eating enough. Or that the effects of twenty years of not eating enough were difficult to eradicate in a few months. Lydia felt a spurt of anger toward the Pearls and was relieved that she was still capable of caring. Ever since she had allowed Mr Smith to take her uncle away, she had been battling a growing numbness.

'Let's walk.' Lydia didn't want to draw unnecessary attention and she thought the motion might keep Ash calm. Instead he began pacing up and down in front of the gravestones, waving his arms as he spoke. 'I found it. I found the pattern.'

'What pattern?'

'It's been going back decades. I went to the newspaper archive in the British Library. I know everything is supposed to be online, now, but I wanted to be sure, and I found them. Kids go missing. I only searched for sixteen year olds, but there might be loads more. Different ages, I mean.'

'What makes you think it's them?'

'Every twenty years a sixteen year old goes missing from Highgate Woods.'

Lydia paused. 'All from the same place?'

Ash nodded. 'There was one, in nineteen twenty one which was Hampstead Heath and another where they didn't have a last known location, but the age and timing was right. And they were never found. None of them were ever found. Apart from Lucy.'

'And you,' Lydia said. 'You need to stay away from Highgate.'

'I told you, I've been at the library.'

Lydia thought about the girl. 'Have you seen any Pearls? They use kids. Have you been followed?'

Ash looked at Lydia with a mixture of confusion and anger. 'You think I'm weak. I'm not stupid. This happened to me. You think I wouldn't notice if I saw one of them?'

'I don't think you're stupid,' Lydia tried to placate him. She didn't want to say 'you're traumatised and are clearly not thinking clearly or looking after yourself' so she settled on 'I'm just worried about you. I want you to stay safe.'

'I'm being careful,' Ash said. 'But I won't stop. I can't.'

BACK AT THE FORK, Lydia picked up a mug of coffee from Angel and headed upstairs to work. She found Jason meditatively making a hot chocolate. He had branched out from cereal and tea and Lydia wasn't sorry. She opened the fridge and passed him the canister of whipped cream. It felt a little light, but there were three more lined up on the shelf and a catering-size bag of marshmallows she had stolen from the cafe kitchen on the countertop. In her continuing effort to stop drinking hard liquor all day every day, hot chocolate with all the trimmings was a helpful distraction.

She told him about the mysterious woman who had been asking about Alejandro at Westminster Pier.

'Maria?' Jason said.

'Sounds like it,' Lydia said. 'And something else occurred to me this afternoon.'

'Oh, right?' Jason shook the can and applied a towering spiral of cream to the mug.

'Maria has a decent motive to off Alejandro. He made her head of the Family but it's possible people weren't really treating her like the new boss. She might have figured that he needed to be out of the picture for the world to really see her as the new power. And I assume she's the heir to all his cash, too.'

Jason raised an eyebrow. 'You think she would kill her own flesh and blood?'

'I did worse.'

Jason was silent as he added mini marshmallows to the cream. Lydia didn't blame him, there was no argument. She had consigned her father's little brother to a fate worse than death. Caged. Experimented on. Tortured, maybe. Who knew what horrors he was enduring? Jason slid open a drawer and removed a packet of chocolate flakes, sticking one into the mound of cream and sugar. 'Enjoy,' he said, pushing the mug toward Lydia.

TAPPING A PENCIL ON HER NOTEBOOK, she tried to marshal her thoughts. The woman asking questions at Westminster Pier certainly sounded like Maria. The question was, did this make it more or less likely that she had offed Alejandro herself?

Lydia put herself in Maria's shoes. It was an uncomfortable fit and didn't really help. Maria might investigate if she believed someone had hurt her father, but she might also ask questions if she had done the deed. Either to check that she had adequately covered her tracks and that there were no pesky witnesses who might need incentivising to keep quiet, or to give the impression of investigating Alejandro's death in order to appear innocent and clueless. Lydia opened her eyes, startled into laughter by the idea of an innocent Maria Silver. The woman had been born with a black shrivelled heart.

Jason had appeared while her eyes were shut and was sitting on the sofa, quietly tapping away on his ever-present laptop. He glanced at her. 'You're in a good mood.'

'I saw Emma,' Lydia said, deciding not to explain her attempts to get inside the mind of Maria Silver.

'That's good,' Jason nodded. 'You don't want to get too isolated. It's lonely at the top.'

'So I am discovering,' Lydia replied.

If Maria had killed her own father, she would definitely need it to look like natural causes. Not only to keep herself out of prison, but to stop retribution from other Family members. The more Lydia thought about it, the more convinced she became. Maria had shown homicidal tendencies in the past, had tried to have Lydia kidnapped and, most likely, killed. She had certainly threatened to end Lydia on more than one occasion. She was more than capable.

Lydia called Fleet and asked him to meet her in the pub. 'Crazy day, here,' Fleet replied. 'Is seven all right?'

When he walked in, Lydia was waiting at her favourite table in the corner, a pint of Fleet's preferred beer and a bag of salted peanuts in his place.

'Uh-oh,' Fleet said, after kissing her hello and sitting down.

'What?'

He gestured to the drink and snack. 'You want something.'

'I always want something when you're around.' Lydia was attempting a flirtatious tone but Fleet just frowned at her in confusion. So much for using her womanly wiles. 'If I wanted to kill somebody and make it look natural, would a brain aneurysm be a good cover?'

Fleet had his glass halfway to his mouth and he raised it in a small salute. 'There it is.'

Lydia clinked her glass against his, but refused to be distracted. 'Is there a poison that would cause an aneurysm?'

'An undetectable poison?' Fleet said, after taking a sip of his pint. 'No. Not that I have heard of, anyway. We did think of that before marking it as a non-suspicious death, you know? At the Met we pride ourselves on that kind of due diligence.'

Lydia ignored the sarcasm. 'How well do you know the pathologist? Could he have been convinced to provide a false report?'

'I don't really know him, but that would be difficult to do. It's not one person's word, there are lab techs and an assistant pathologist involved.'

'Not impossible, though?'

Fleet shrugged. 'Chain of evidence is a big deal for a reason. Mistakes happen, but less often when every stage is documented.'

'But it's hypothetically possible?'

'Very hypothetically.'

'I guess you would need access? Or the ability to bribe somebody with access?'

'At the very least.' Fleet put his glass on the table. 'First principles. Maybe the most likely explanation is the truth. Alejandro died, sadly, before his time. A previously-undiagnosed weakness leading to an aneurysm. I know you think you all have some kind of extra-special power which protects you, but it has its limits.'

'Don't lump me in with the Silvers,' Lydia said sharply.

'But you take my point,' Fleet said.

Lydia drained half her glass to avoid answering.

Another beat. 'Do you want to speak to the pathologist?'

'Yes, please. I was going to rock up to the mortuary, but I thought an official intro would be more successful. I'm sorry to ask…'

'Don't be,' Fleet said. 'I know you're sick of me saying this, but I'm on your side. Whatever you need, you can come to me.'

'I'm not sick of you saying it. Not at all.' Lydia leaned in and kissed him. Partly because she wanted to and partly because she wanted to avoid continuing the conversation. She wasn't sick of Fleet telling her that she could trust him. She just wished she could believe it.

CHAPTER TEN

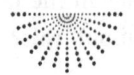

Alejandro's funeral must have taken a team of people and deep pockets to organise, but no matter the planning and money which had been thrown at the event, they hadn't been able to control the weather. The day dawned warm and bright, the meteorological version of a massive 'fuck you' to what ought to have been black and raining.

'Are you sure about this?' Fleet was wearing a black suit and tie and Lydia was hit by how inappropriately attractive he was, even in funeral garb. It was distracting. She was wearing the basic black dress she put on when pretending to work in an office or posh hotel, which sat below the knee. She had a less-basic black version which sat far higher for those occasions when she needed to pick someone up. It had been a long time since she'd done honey-pot work and was glad that hadn't been off the hanger in a while. Lydia twisted her hair at the nape of her neck and fixed it with pins, matching a sensible hairstyle to the outfit. She wasn't going to have anybody saying that Crows weren't showing proper respect to the occasion.

'She suspects it wasn't natural causes and that means she probably suspects my Family. All the more reason to follow tradition. I can't be seen to snub the Silvers by not attending the funeral. And I need to speak to Maria, let her know I'm investigating and I'm her best chance of getting justice for her father. That way, she might not try to kill me.' Lydia tugged at the dress, checking that she looked properly sombre and demure.

Fleet was watching her in the mirror. 'That's not what I meant. Are you sure about this?' He gestured to them, framed together.

The boring dress was good. It might help to balance out the fact that she was walking in on the arm of DCI Fleet. Could risk be balanced that way? 'I'm sure,' she said out loud. 'I'm not hiding.'

'And that's fine,' Fleet said evenly. 'I agree, you know I do. But is this the best occasion to step out together officially?'

'Step out?' Lydia paused in the act of searching for her black court shoes. 'How old are you, again?'

He flashed a smile which made her stomach flip. 'You want to come here and say that?'

'Not if we're going to make the funeral on time,' Lydia said, not without regret. 'And that probably would start a war.'

THE TRAFFIC on Chancery Lane was halted by leather-clad motorcycle riders, parking across the busy lanes and crossing their arms, ignoring the cacophony of horns – a blaring sound which cut off abruptly as people caught sight of the funeral procession. It was led by a shining black carriage, its windows etched with silver filigree, pulled by four black horses with silver plumes and livery. The coachman had matching black and silver clothes and a top hat and the top of the carriage was covered in white flowers. Lydia wasn't one for pomp, but she had to admit it was quite beautiful.

Crawling behind the carriage were several Rolls Royce limousines in black and grey and behind those, more flashy cars including a Maserati and two Bentleys. 'Bloody hell,' Fleet said, indicating one of the cars. 'That goes for quarter of a million.'

The procession was heading to the distinctive round structure of Temple Church, which was intrinsically linked to the legal profession. It had been built by the Knights Templar, the original bankers, but the Inns of Court had moved in during the fifteen hundreds and it had been the lawyers' local one-stop for births, deaths and marriages ever since.

Having been able to duck down side streets, Lydia and Fleet arrived ahead of the procession. Once they stepped away from the bustle of Fleet Street, the courtyards and chambers of the temple area swallowed them. There were lots of people arriving at the church for the service, clad in smart black clothes and looking suitably solemn. Several people were in their justice robes or barristers' outfits, clearly fitting in the service in the midst of a busy day lawyering.

Fleet slipped his arm from around Lydia's waist and gave her a serious look. 'Last chance to back out. You don't need to prove anything to me.'

'I know that,' Lydia said. She felt a stab of uncertainty. 'Would you rather we kept things quiet? Are you worried about who will see us here?'

'Not in the slightest,' Fleet said, taking her hand.

'That's all right, then-,' Lydia broke off as she spotted a familiar face in the crowd milling outside the church. 'Wait. Is that-?'

'Chief of the Met? Yep.'

'Feathers,' Lydia breathed. She tried to slip her hand out of Fleet's and take a step to the side. There was expecting Fleet to go public and then there was making him parade his relationship with the head of the Crow Family in front of the boss of all his bosses.

Fleet squeezed her hand. 'I'm not hiding.'

They walked up to the crowd, past a couple of barristers in black court robes with bright white collars, who were carrying briefcases and navy bags with embroidered initials which looked like PE bags from primary school. Fleet spotted somebody he knew and they made small talk for a few minutes before going inside. He introduced Lydia by her first name and his acquaintance as 'Nathan from five-a-side', as if Lydia ought to know who he was talking about. She made a mental note to pay better attention to Fleet's life. They were in a committed relationship now, and she should act a bit more like a proper girlfriend. Probably.

Black marble columns reaching up to the vaulted ceiling, wooden pews lining the central aisle and a magnificent stained-glass window at the far end. So far, so-churchy, but the stone effigies on the floor of the round part of the church, like knights had decided to take a nap and then been ossified where they lay, added an eerie quality.

Neat lines of choristers dressed in white robes waited while the mourners took their seats before opening their mouths and releasing the kind of pure sound which makes every hair on the body lift. Lydia could understand why the church went in for that kind of thing. It was close to magic, and in the days before movies and the internet or even electronically amplified music, those clear voices echoing in the great vaulted space must have seemed other-worldly.

Alejandro's coffin was carried down the centre aisle on the shoulders of Silver Family members. Lydia had prepared herself for being around so many and she took shallow breaths through her nose, tasting the clean tang of metal in the back of her throat. Maria let the coffin reach its destination before making her entrance. She walked down the aisle alone wearing a sharp black dress with a pencil skirt and long sleeves, and high heels. She had swapped the enormous black sunglasses Lydia had seen her wearing as she got out of the car for an antique-looking black lace shawl which was draped over her head in the traditional Spanish style.

The church was packed, with many people standing in the round part of the structure, unable to find a seat. Lydia scanned the mourners, looking for any surprises. She found herself subconsciously looking for Charlie, as if Mr Smith and his department would have released him for the occasion. As the choir's singing and the sound of suppressed sobbing worked on her emotions, Lydia found herself blinking back tears of her own. She wouldn't allow them to fall. They weren't for Alejandro or his daughter so it would be disrespectful, but she had to produce her coin discreetly in one hand and squeeze it tightly, her other hand held in Fleet's.

Filing out into the sunshine, Fleet asked if they were going to the wake. It was in a hotel just behind the church and the mourners were streaming through the narrow streets and courts, no doubt anticipating a rejuvenating beverage and, for some, the chance to conduct a little business, cement some important relationships. A man was dead, but it would take more than that to stop the wheels of commerce and law from turning.

Lydia knew she had no right to the moral high ground on that front. She was still conducting her business, after all. Was only in attendance as she had to be. She represented the Crow Family and respect had to be given and, just as importantly, be *seen* to be given. The hotel restaurant had been booked out and there were many good-looking waiting staff weaving through the crowd with trays of drinks and canapés. There was a great deal of pale marble, gold mirrors and glittering chandeliers, as well as teal velvet seating. If you ignored all the sombre clothing, it could have been a PR event or a wedding reception. A line of well-wishers waited to pay their respects to Maria, who was still veiled in black lace and flanked by men in suits with earpieces. Lydia had to hand it to Maria, she knew how to play her part.

'Come on,' she said to Fleet, who had just picked up two glasses of whisky from a tray and was holding one out. She knocked back the drink. 'I think we've done our duty.'

'Excuse me.' A man who was twice the width of Fleet and looked stuffed into his suit was suddenly barring Lydia's way. 'Ms Silver would like a word.'

More performance. Lydia would play along. She put her glass down on the nearest table and then she and Fleet walked past the line of people waiting to pay their respects, following the man mountain.

'We are sorry for your loss,' Fleet said when they arrived in front of the bereaved.

Maria nodded. She held out her hand to Fleet. 'DCI Fleet. Have you tried the canapés? They are divine.'

On cue, a security guard led Fleet away. Up close, Maria's eyes were hollow. Lydia felt a clutch of sympathy, while keeping her eyes on the security still standing nearby. Large men who looked like they were barely containing their urge to stomp Lydia out of existence. Lydia wondered where Maria had hired them. You could pay for violence easily enough, but not emotion. 'I'm sorry for your loss,' Lydia said.

Maria tilted her head. There was a loaded silence before she asked: 'Are you?'

The question sounded genuine and Lydia paused to give it the consideration it was due. 'I'm sorry your father is no longer with us. I preferred dealing with him.'

Maria's smile was like a skull. All teeth. 'Pretending to be candid. Is that your new thing? I should have you beaten to death.'

Her intonation didn't change for the threat and it was all the more chilling. Maria wasn't bluffing. Lydia didn't break eye contact. 'I am here to pay my respects on behalf of the Crow Family. In recognition of the old alliance which existed between our families. And on a personal level, for the courtesy always extended to me by your father. Courtesy which seems sadly lacking today.' Lydia spread her hands, palm up. 'Which is, of course, perfectly understandable given the depth of your grief.'

At that moment Maria didn't look upset. Just furious. Which didn't mean she wasn't grieving in her own way. Lydia could relate. When she thought she had lost her own father she had wanted to burn the entire world.

'You think this,' she waved a hand, 'makes you look trustworthy? You think I don't know that you have been plotting against me and my Family?'

'That isn't true,' Lydia said.

'Do you know how my father died?'

Lydia nodded. 'Brain aneurysm.'

'That's what they say.'

'You don't believe it?'

Maria held her gaze. 'Do you?'

Lydia didn't answer. She could see the lines of tension around Maria's mouth and a flash of sadness broke through the anger in her eyes, making her seem more human than usual. One of her security staff stepped up and whispered in Maria's ear. Her gaze flicked behind Lydia and she nodded once. 'Bring him next.'

Lydia wasn't sure if she was being dismissed, as Maria was still staring over her shoulder.

'Look at them all lining up,' Maria said eventually. 'Everyone wants a favour, now. I've been head of the firm for months, nobody said shit, but now... Now they want me.'

'Change can be slow,' Lydia said. 'And people can be very old fashioned.'

'That's true,' Maria said, snapping her eyes to Lydia and

seeming to collect herself. 'A lot of these old men didn't believe I was in charge. They have no choice, now. He's gone.'

Lydia nodded. She had another unexpected clutch of empathy. She felt the wind whipping around her face as she climbed The Shard, playing the stupid games to prove she was a worthy successor to Charlie.

'I think our Families should continue to work together,' Maria said. 'Whatever my personal feelings, I must acknowledge that, historically, there has been a mutually beneficial relationship.'

Maria was definitely a lawyer. Fifty words where five would suffice. 'I'm pleased to hear it,' Lydia said. 'For my part, I vow that I will find out the truth of your father's death.'

Maria's eyes widened a little.

'I will prove that I had nothing to do with it. That no Crow had anything to do with it. And, if you require, I will help you to exact justice on the person or persons responsible.' Wordiness was catching. Lydia took a deep breath and forced herself to stop speaking.

Maria's eyes had narrowed, again. She tilted her head back a fraction. 'You will bring me your findings first.' It wasn't a question.

'If I can,' Lydia said, after a moment of hesitation.

'What about your pet policeman?' Maria indicated Fleet who was watching them intently, flanked by yet more security.

'This has nothing to do with Fleet or the Met,' Lydia said. 'This is Family business.'

CHAPTER ELEVEN

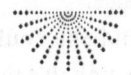

The day after the funeral was a Friday and Fleet called Lydia. 'Shall we go out to eat? Or I could cook, if you're happy to come to mine.'

'Not tonight,' Lydia said. She wanted to dig into Alejandro's life for the last few months, maybe see if Jason could use his computer wizardry to dig up any secrets. 'You can come here later, though. If you want?'

'Sure.' Fleet paused. 'It would be nice to go out sometime, though.'

'Like a proper couple,' Lydia said. 'You old romantic.'

'Less of the old. Nothing wrong with a proper date. There's a Caribbean place in Vauxhall that's supposed to be good.'

'Next week, maybe. Or when things are more settled.'

Fleet paused. 'I hear what you're saying, but I think we should go tonight or this weekend. If we wait for our lives to be more settled, we're never going to go.'

Lydia found a hot chocolate on the counter, the whipped cream deflated and congealed on the brown surface. She poured it down the sink. 'Are you annoyed?'

'Not at all. But I would rather we accepted that this is

how our lives are and prioritise each other now, rather than waiting for it to get easy.'

The man made a lot of sense. But Lydia didn't hold the best track record in making time for normal life. 'You know what you signed up for,' she said, keeping it light. 'I'm more about the late-night stakeouts, takeaway, sex and an unhealthy work-life balance.'

'I know,' Fleet said and she could hear the smile in his voice. 'Think about it, though. It's not like I'm asking you to take a holiday. It's just an evening out.'

'If I say yes and you book something I might have to cancel at the last minute.'

'So might I, still not a reason to not even try.'

'Well, if you're going to be all reasonable about it...' Lydia hoped that she sounded faux-annoyed rather than proper-annoyed. She felt proper-annoyed but knew she had no right to the emotion and that fact was enough to make the irritation worse. She felt as if there were pulls on her time and attention all the damn time and now Fleet was asking for more.

'Just wait until you taste the salted fish, it's supposed to be amazing with the curried goat.'

'You had better be joking.' Lydia was more of a pizza-and-a-beer kind of a girl, as Fleet well knew.

'Chicken.'

THAT EVENING FLEET arrived with a thin crust pizza and a bottle of red wine and hadn't argued when Lydia had said she still had a bit of work to do. She nibbled at a slice of margherita while she read yet another puff piece article about the wunderkind Alejandro Silver and his wildly successful career. Fleet was working at the other side of her desk, slumped in the client's chair with his long legs stretched out to the side. At least, Lydia assumed Fleet was working. He might have been playing Candy Crush on his phone for all she knew. She had been researching Alejandro online, going over the last few months of his life and making notes. Which were mostly just questions and blank spaces. She wasn't going to panic. All cases began like this, with random pieces floating in a big sea of 'what the hell?'. If she followed the process, she would find more pieces and, eventually, fit them all together. What was clear to her after his funeral, though, was that Maria was no longer Lydia's prime suspect. Not off the hook for his death, but no longer top of Lydia's list. She was a Silver and naturally extremely convincing, but Lydia had seen real grief in her eyes.

Alejandro had decided to enter politics the year before and, within months, had become the MP for Holborn. She broke the companionable silence to say as much to Fleet. 'How did he manage that so quickly?'

Fleet looked up from his phone. 'I have no idea.'

Lydia opened her laptop and began researching. The parliamentary seat had opened up in February when the existing MP had keeled over. Which was interesting. A Silver had got the very thing they wanted as a result of a timely death. The MP had been approaching seventy but there were pictures of her completing a five kilometre fun run the week before she died. It wasn't conclusive, of course, but it suggested a certain level of health.

A little further down the page, Lydia got her answer. It wasn't age or health related. The MP, Nadine Gormley, had been hit by a car while holidaying with her family in Greece. It was a hit and run and the case remained open.

Fleet stood up and walked to her side of the desk, leaning down to read over her shoulder. 'That's convenient.'

'That's what I was just thinking,' Lydia said. 'Don't suppose you've got a handy contact in the Greek police?'

'I can ask around. Nothing official, but someone might

chat as a favour. Interpol are probably involved, too. It's an MP, after all, not-'

'A nobody,' Lydia finished.

'I wasn't going to say that,' Fleet said. 'Of course, it could be something else, something entirely unrelated to Alejandro's political career.'

'He worked criminal law,' Lydia said, echoing what Jason had suggested. 'Could be a bad guy from his past, freshly out of jail and looking for revenge.'

'I'll look at his old cases and see if anybody has been recently released.'

'I know the bill he was going to vote on that day didn't look controversial, but was there anything else scheduled that someone might want Alejandro to miss?' She was on the parliamentary website which listed all the public bills currently going through the houses. 'What are private bills?'

Fleet scanned the page. 'Things that relate to private companies, I think. They're not secret.'

Nothing jumped out to Lydia, but then anything could conceivably be enough to kill a person over. Everything important enough to make it to parliament had ramifications, even if you couldn't see them right away. Ripples spreading outward from a pebble thrown into a pool.

Fleet straightened up. 'Maybe there isn't a motive.'

Lydia was still skimming the list of bills. 'Mmm?'

'Because maybe it isn't a murder. Maybe the pathologist is right and it was a brain aneurysm.'

'I can't go back to Maria and say that. It's not going to fly.'

'Even if it's the truth?'

Lydia kept quiet. She didn't believe it was the truth. No, more than that, she *knew* it wasn't the truth. It was down there in her gut, a certainty that only grew with every piece of so-called evidence to the contrary. Alejandro Silver did not drop dead of a brain aneurysm from some undiagnosed condition. He did not. If she told Fleet, he would say that she didn't want to believe it. Or he would be defensive of the system he had dedicated his professional life to, the system he believed in. He would say that Lydia was mistrustful of his work, and that she had an inflated sense of the power of the Families. He wouldn't go so far as to say she was letting emotions cloud her judgement – the man wasn't a fool – but he might think it.

Fleet stood up and cleared their plates, then went and made coffee. When he came back, he opened his work laptop and Lydia felt a small release of tension. He might not agree with her hunch, but he would do the work. He was a good copper.

'So, motive,' Fleet said after a few minutes. 'I pulled recent releases who might have a grudge against Alejandro and there was nothing obvious. One man got out in December but he was in for white collar crime and I can't see him turning violent. Only other possibility was released the week before Alejandro died. He just served twenty-three years for killing his wife with a hammer. Found God inside, apparently.'

Lydia made a disbelieving noise.

'Quite,' Fleet said. 'But even if his piety wouldn't stop him from going after Alejandro, there are more obvious targets first. Like the brother-in-law who gave evidence. And I don't see him as the mastermind type who could organise something as controlled as this. I looked at his file and he's twice as thick as he is nasty, and has all the impulse-control problems associated with his crimes. I mean, if Alejandro had been bludgeoned in a pub then we'd have a suspect...'

'Got it,' Lydia said. 'You know I was keen on Maria for it?'

'You've changed your mind?'

Lydia decided not to reveal her moment of empathy with

Maria and stuck instead to the facts. 'I haven't found anything. She was in court on the day he died and alibis don't get much better than a full room at the Old Bailey.'

'So we're back to an undetectable poison,' Fleet said.

Lydia liked the 'we' in the sentence. 'Or something less prosaic.'

'What do you mean?'

Lydia didn't want to say the word 'magic' out loud and she tried to think of an alternative. 'I was thinking about the Families,' she began. 'JRB have been trying to stir up trouble between us. This would be an excellent way to turn up the heat. Maybe I'm supposed to suspect Maria and she's supposed to go for me and, before you know it, there's a full-on war.'

'What about the Foxes? Couldn't it be one of them?'

It was no secret that Fleet didn't like or trust Paul Fox and Lydia didn't blame him. 'I doubt it, the Foxes tend to keep out of this kind of thing. And I don't see Paul trying to start a war. Too much work.'

'You're blind when it comes to him,' Fleet said. 'Your history…'

'I see perfectly well,' Lydia said. 'You don't know him the way I do.'

'Well, that's true.'

'Let's not fight,' Lydia said. 'Bigger fish.'

'So. JRB. How close did you get to a contact there?'

'Not close at all,' Lydia said. 'Shell corporations within shell corporations like a bloody Russian Doll. Best lead was the link to the Pearls.'

'You're not going there, again.' It was a statement not a question.

'Not unless I have to.'

. . .

STEPPING into the barbershop which hid the entrance to the Foxes' favourite drinking establishment was out of Lydia's comfort zone. It was nowhere near as scary as the first time she had done it, though. Things were very different now. Paul Fox was the head of the Fox Family and, crucially, Lydia was the head of the Crows. Still, her pulse speeded up as she pushed open the door, nodded to the barber and headed down the stairs which led to the concealed door.

One of Paul's brothers was sitting at the bar and Lydia battled the urge to walk straight out again. She had last seen him kicking her while she lay on the ground, so her second urge was to go over and stab him somewhere soft and painful.

Luckily, Paul appeared from the gloom, and wrapped his arms around her. Lydia wasn't a big hugger and Paul hadn't greeted her that way since they were an item, but she figured it was part of the show. He was marking territory with his Family and making it clear that Lydia was welcome, so she went with it. She had prepared herself for the onslaught of 'Fox' but the added proximity to his skin unleashed an extra set of pheromones into the mix. It felt like the hug went on for longer than was strictly necessary, but the sensation of being pressed up against Paul's hard chest wasn't unpleasant. Once he released her, he gazed into her eyes. 'It's good to see you here'.

She smiled her shark smile and planned a cold shower for when she got home. 'Drink?'

'Of course,' Paul signalled to somebody behind Lydia and led her to a table to sit down.

Moments later, two glasses and a bottle of Macallan arrived, courtesy of the brother Lydia had seen when she walked in. He didn't look thrilled at waiting on Lydia Crow and he would probably have preferred Paul beat him up again. After Lydia had been set upon, Paul had arranged, or more likely administered, a beating of each of the perpetrators, matching their injuries to Lydia's. And then he had banished his own father for his part in the proceedings. As apologies went, it had been pretty comprehensive. Still, the Fox sibling by the table bowed his head as if expecting further retribution.

Paul flicked his eyes and he moved away. Lydia let out her breath. She knew that she wasn't in physical danger and that the guy had been following orders from his own father, but she had no desire to chat about the weather. Or, for that matter, to have a big heart-to-heart. The past was done. He couldn't take it back and she wouldn't forget.

'I've got a proposition for you,' Paul said, uncorking the bottle and pouring two fingers into each glass. 'An alliance.'

Lydia had guessed what he was going to say, but sitting in the Den with a glass of whisky in her hand, it suddenly became very real. Could she forge a formal alliance with the Fox Family on behalf of the Crows? Should she? It was one thing to be friendly with Paul but quite another to make it official. And the Crows didn't trust the Foxes. Nobody did.

'I know our reputation,' Paul said. 'And I know we haven't been on the Crows' Christmas list for a very long time, but things have changed. We're the new generation. We don't have to be bound by the past. We can work out a new way of doing things.'

It sounded fine, but the past was still there. Was that why she kept being led to graveyards? Were her ancestors trying to remind her of her duties? That was a crazy thought. The pressure of leadership making her unstable. Already. 'I'm here because Alejandro Silver has been murdered and that is bad for all of us.'

Paul nodded approvingly. 'You're not taken in by the coroner's verdict, then?'

Lydia raised an eyebrow. 'Please. The Silvers aren't going to believe it, either. They will still be looking for retribution. I think it's important to present a united front, at least until we find enough evidence so that Maria Silver accepts the police's verdict or we find those responsible. It is also a gesture of goodwill and trust between our Families that is the first step toward a more generous and peaceful existence.'

Lydia clinked her glass against Paul's and they both drank.

'You sound different,' Paul said, head tilted back. 'You been giving lots of speeches?'

Lydia allowed herself a small, honest smile. 'It's exhausting.'

'How was the funeral?'

'Fancy,' Lydia said. 'And a bit creepy. Have you been inside Temple Church?'

He shook his head. 'I know it's where the Silvers conduct all their significant events. Christenings, memorials, weddings. Rumour has it, the main bloodline Silvers are interred underneath the church.'

'Does your Family have a church?'

Paul snorted. 'No. Not really our thing. You know the Silvers aren't really believers? The Temple Church connection was purely business.'

Lydia did know. As well as bedtime stories about the Crows, Henry had told her tales from the other Families. At the end of the sixteenth century, the Inns of Court were using the Temple Church and its environs and had invested in architecture and so on. Being men of law, and having learned from the decline of the Knights Templar who were buried deep under the church, they knew the value of a good contract and they wanted to protect their position. They petitioned King James for a charter that would ensure they could use the Temple in perpetuity and King James, being no more immune to legal persuasion than anybody else, agreed. In gratitude they gave him a gold cup which got lost years later by a broke Charles I. What wasn't in the history books, is that the Silver Family had arrived from their travels in the New World with a large cache of gold and silver and an uncanny ability to persuade others to see their point of view. They found their perfect match in the Inns of Court and quickly ingratiated themselves into the profession. Nobody knew how, but within five years of the original charter being agreed with King James, the Silvers had added an amendment; they also had use of the church in perpetuity with a special dispensation to build a Family crypt under the chancel. And there, nestled between the cherub-cheeked choristers above ground and the bones of the Knights Templars deep below, the Silver Family had interred their most important ancestors ever since.

'What most people don't know,' Henry had explained. 'Is that they liked the gold cup that the Inns of Court had used, so they made a silver one for their amendment. But, being the Silvers, they didn't just give it to King James as a souvenir to be lost among Royal baubles. They made a big ceremony, where the King and the head of the Silver Family drank wine from the cup in recognition of their fealty. And then they convinced King James that the cup should remain with the Silvers, in their Family crypt as a sign of their devotion to the crown. Which meant, of course, that it was forgotten by the Crown as soon as King James passed on and the Silvers got to give a gift while never losing anything at all.'

Lydia wasn't in the habit of revealing her own knowledge, much better to find out what other people knew first, so she just said, 'I know the Inns of Court used to use the church to do their lawyer stuff back in olden times.'

Paul's expression had turned serious. He put his glass down and folded his hands. If Lydia had been dealing with anybody else she would have said he seemed suddenly nervous.

'I don't want to talk about the Silvers anymore.'

'Okay.'

He tilted his head. 'There's another way to unite our Families. Fast-track it.'

'Is that a fact?' The whisky was really good and Lydia finished her glass and poured another. She had missed the burn of it. The feeling of warmth and wellbeing. She had always had an exceedingly high tolerance and never seemed to get drunk, but four or five drinks had the pleasant effect of muting some of the buzzing in her mind and body, buzzing that she was barely aware of until the volume was turned down and a little bit of quiet space opened up.

'We should be together.'

Lydia managed not to choke on her whisky, but it was a close-run thing. 'What?'

'You heard,' Paul said calmly. 'And don't pretend to be surprised.'

'I don't think... I'm with Fleet. You know that.' There was a great deal more that Lydia could say, but invoking her prior commitment seemed the politest option.

Paul shrugged. 'It's not like you're married. And he's police.'

'I am aware,' Lydia said drily.

He sat forward suddenly, hands clasped together on the table. Lydia felt the increase in animal magnetism and the answering tension in the pit of her stomach. She wondered if he was consciously able to control it, like she could with her Crow power. Charlie had thought that the Crows had the most power and were the only ones able to train it, to harness it. He had peddled the accepted view that the other Families were vastly diluted, their powers dimmed over the decades to an echo of what they had once been. But maybe he had been wrong.

'I want you. I know you want me. I've proved that I'm loyal. What else is there?'

'You're being serious?'

'The DCI is from a different world. You must know it's not going to work out.'

'You're not in a position to comment on my relationship.' Lydia pushed herself back in her chair. She had been leaning forward, toward Paul, and that had to stop.

'I think I am. I know you.'

'You knew me, once. A long time ago.'

'Not that long. You can't trust him. And I don't want you to get hurt.'

'Funnily enough, he says exactly the same thing about you.'

CHAPTER TWELVE

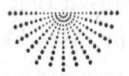

Lydia hated the feeling that she was dancing to the Family's tune, but it seemed that smoothing things over with Mark Kendal would be the quickest way to appease John and, by association, the rest of the old guard. She had always thought that being at the top meant you didn't have to worry about what those below you thought or felt, but it didn't seem to be the case. And if she didn't want a revolt on her hands, she was going to have to work on her diplomacy skills.

She walked into Mark's phone shop, the door setting off a loud buzzer. Racks of phone cases hung from the walls and a metal grill was across a glass case behind the cash desk, protecting the high cost items - the iPhones and laptops – from a quick theft. She had expected to find Mark himself standing behind that desk, but he was nowhere to be seen.

'Hello?' Lydia looked around a second time, just to be sure, but the shop really wasn't big enough to hide a person. The cash desk was another glass case, this one without a grill, filled with boxes of phones and bling-tastic accessories. A multi-coloured LED sign loomed over the set-up and a desk fan turned semi-circles, making the hanging cases quiver in the draft. She waited for another minute, but Mark didn't pop up from behind the desk or walk through the front door, carrying a takeaway coffee.

There wasn't an obvious door to a backroom, but after letting her eyes adjust to the rows and rows of brightly coloured cases, Lydia realised that there was an exit in the corner. It was covered in cases like the wall, rendering it almost invisible. There was a recessed handle halfway up and Lydia pulled, expecting it to be locked. Consequently, it swung open faster than she had intended and a few cases fell to the floor. Stepping over the mess, Lydia entered a room cluttered with cardboard boxes. She had to squeeze through a narrow path between towering stacks of boxes labelled with Apple, Samsung, and brands she didn't recognise. 'Mr Kendal?'

The boxes wobbled dangerously as she moved. The guy should really tidy up his store room, it was a health and safety nightmare. Turning a corner, Lydia stopped thinking. Mark Kendal was lying on the floor in a pool of dark sticky blood. His head was caved in on one side, so thoroughly and deeply that yellowish matter was visible amongst the gore. Brain, Lydia's mind supplied. That's probably a bit of Mark's brain.

Bile was in her mouth and she turned away to take a couple of breaths. She contained the urge to spit the foul taste onto the floor, it was a crime scene after all, and fished for a tissue instead. She pulled on nitrile gloves and approached the body, careful not to step in the blood. He was definitely dead, but she felt she ought to feel for a pulse, anyway. Mark Kendal's neck was cold and the flesh, as she pressed it, had a strange texture. She was no pathologist, but he had been dead for a while.

Lydia straightened up, thinking fast. Her phone was in her hand and she knew that she ought to phone the police.

Instead, she took photos of the scene, working systematically around the body and the room. The urge to vomit passed as soon as she began analysing, which was a bonus. The injury was on the side of the head, not the back. That didn't rule out somebody surprising him from behind, but it made it less likely. To Lydia's untrained eye, it looked like a single, forceful blow. The murderer was either very strong or they used something very heavy. Lydia looked at the space and tried to judge whether a largish person would have had the room to get a decent arm swing. Next she tried to judge whether it had happened in this room, or whether the body had been moved after the event. The blood spread out from the head, with no drag marks or blood trail.

She crouched down and patted the body down, checking pockets and the hands for defensive wounds. The hands looked undamaged and although the fingernails were grubby, it looked like everyday dirt rather than blood. Mark's wallet was in his front jeans pocket with a couple of credit cards, a donor card, and over a hundred in cash. Folded behind the donor card was another bank note. A ten-shilling note like the ones she had found in Charlie's bedroom. It was soft and well creased, clearly folded and refolded many times. Without thinking too much about it, Lydia pocketed the ten-shilling note, and put the rest back. Mark was lying face down and Lydia slid his wallet into the back pocket of his jeans to avoid having to reach underneath again. Once had been bad enough.

LYDIA EMERGED from the back room cautiously, but the shop was still deserted. She closed the door and wiped it down with her sleeve. There was a CCTV camera pointed at the cash desk, but a closer look showed that it had been sprayed with black paint. Whoever had been here first had already disabled it. There wasn't a back door out of the shop so

Lydia had no choice but to emerge from the front, onto the street. She moved quickly and mentally crossed her fingers that nobody was paying attention.

In one hand she could feel her coin, solid and reassuring, and in the other she held her phone. Her first thought had been to phone Fleet, but her second and third thoughts had followed fast. Mark had come to her for help and now he was dead. This was connected to her family. Her first duty had to be to protect them. Besides, Mark was past helping, now. What would Charlie do?

Pushing that unhelpful thought aside, Lydia moved through Camberwell as fast as she could without running.

BACK AT THE FORK, Lydia went straight upstairs to find Jason, but the flat was empty. She sat on his bed for a few minutes, in case her presence would make him appear, but the room remained stubbornly empty. She still wanted to speak to Fleet, but before that she needed Family help. She called Aiden.

He must have been nearby, as he arrived in ten minutes. He was wearing shiny jogging trousers and a hoodie, his hair damp with sweat. 'Sorry,' he said, gesturing to himself. 'Football.'

There was something to be said for clicking your fingers and having people drop everything to obey. Especially in an emergency. Out on the terrace and with the radio playing, Lydia ran through the details.

'We need to clean it up,' Aiden said.

'I wiped everything down,' Lydia said. 'And the camera was blacked-out.'

'The body is still there, though.'

'Does that matter?' Lydia was thinking about the police investigation. They hadn't done this and she hadn't left any evidence of finding the body, so now the Met could take over. That was fine.

Aiden was frowning at her. 'You just found him?'

It hit her. Aiden thought 'found him' had been a euphemism. 'Yes! Why would I have hurt him?'

'Not my place to speculate,' Aiden said quickly.

'If I had, we have a way to clean up?'

'Well, yeah.' Aiden must have caught something in her expression, because he added, 'Emergency use only.'

Lydia paced the terrace, thinking. After turning over the issue in her mind, she realised something important. 'We should clean up, anyway.'

'Right you are,' Aiden already had his phone out. 'I'll speak to John.'

'Uncle John?' Lydia said, boggling.

'Yeah, he's got a friend of a friend. That's who we use.' He paused. 'Can I ask why? I mean, if it wasn't us?'

'It wasn't me,' Lydia said, 'but that doesn't mean it wasn't us. I still don't know what is going on with every part of the Family. I don't even know if you're telling me the truth half the time.'

Aiden opened his mouth to argue.

'Don't take it personally,' Lydia said, 'I'm not a group hugger, I don't trust easily, and most of the stuff I've found out over the last few months I don't like. Which means I'm always waiting for the next horrible surprise.'

'It wouldn't be one of us,' Aiden insisted, 'not unless you ordered it.'

He sounded certain, but he was very young and a natural follower. Lydia wasn't convinced every single Crow acted with the loyalty and unity Aiden seemed to believe. And there was a more worrying possibility. 'Okay, let's assume an outsider did this, we have a different problem. Someone murdered a local businessman with ties to us, someone of importance who was under our protection. That cannot stand.'

'Yeah,' Aiden nodded enthusiastically. 'We've gotta pay those mother-'

Lydia held up a hand and he fell silent. 'It's two problems, really. First,' she held up a finger. 'If there are whispers in the Family that I'm not a worthy leader, this isn't exactly going to make them go quiet. He wasn't a Crow, but he was supposedly under our protection. That's going to make the Family nervous. And second,' she held up another finger. 'If this was a deliberate act of aggression from outside the Family, we must assume they are looking for a reaction.'

'And they're gonna get one,' Aiden said. 'They'll see they can't fu-'

'No,' Lydia cut him off. 'If we clean it up, put the rumour out that Mr Kendal has gone on holiday or something, we stall a murder investigation and buy ourselves some time to find out who we're dealing with. And we starve them of the instant gratification. If they're watching and hoping for a public embarrassment, they'll be disappointed. And that might make them show themselves.'

'Shouldn't we be paying them back straight away? Showing that we're not to be messed with?'

'That's exactly the reaction they are looking for. It's got to be, unless it was a random robbery gone wrong from someone out of town or terminally stupid. And it didn't look that way.'

'You think they'll just call up and confess?'

'I think people are fundamentally impatient. And winning often just means being willing to wait longer than the other side.' Lydia was excellent at waiting. It was the very first thing you learned to do as a PI.

'If they want a reaction and don't get one, what if they decide to try something else?'

Lydia smiled at him. 'That's what I'm counting on.'

. . .

'WE HAVE A PROBLEM,' Aiden said, sliding into the seat opposite Lydia.

'This is getting to be a habit,' Lydia said. 'We need to be more careful.'

'Cleaning service couldn't operate. There were visitors in attendance'

'Police?'

Aiden nodded.

'Well, that's that,' Lydia leaned back in her seat. 'It's probably for the best.' She should probably keep the lying and criminality to a bare minimum. Especially given that her boyfriend was a DCI in the Met. That was a strange thought. Fleet and 'boyfriend' in the same sentence. It didn't feel right. He wasn't a boy, that was for sure.

Aiden was fidgeting, rubbing at the scruff of beard on his jaw.

'Spit it out.'

'We can't look weak.'

'You mean I can't look weak.'

Aiden swallowed. 'I've been doing your bidding. You know I'm loyal, I just think…'

'Not your job,' Lydia said. 'Leave that part to me. Speaking of which. We need to take a walk.'

Outside, Lydia waited until they were seated on a bench in Brunswick Park before continuing the conversation. She knew she was probably being paranoid, but she couldn't shake the feeling that Mr Smith was still watching her, waiting to gather fresh leverage. She was grateful to him for healing her father and always would be, but that didn't mean she wanted to jump back into his pocket. Especially now she could do real damage to her Family. She knew too much, now, to risk getting caught and that was a sobering thought.

Aiden was looking spooked, too. He rubbed at his goatee and kept putting his beanie hat on and off, as if unable to decide whether to wear it or not. His hand floated toward it for the third time. 'Touch the hat and I'll burn it,' Lydia said, and he snatched his hand away.

She waited until a couple holding greasy bags from a fast food restaurant had passed by and turned to Aiden. 'I asked you why Mark Kendal was important.'

Aiden looked down. 'I told you.'

'You said he supplied burners. But I found this.' Lydia produced the ten-shilling note and held it in front of Aiden's face. She wanted to see how much more lying Aiden was going to do.

'Old money. That's weird.'

'Yeah,' Lydia put it on the bench between them, keeping one finger resting lightly on the paper to stop it blowing away. 'You seen one of these before?'

'No,' Aiden said, and his eyes slid left. 'Why would he have that? Maybe he was into history.'

Lydia slid the note across the bench toward Aiden. 'Pick it up.'

'No!' Aiden's reaction was sudden and loud. At once he looked terrified. 'I'm sorry. Please don't.'

Lydia frowned. 'Don't what? Give you an old bank note? Tell me what the feathers is going on. Right now. I found a roll of these hidden in Charlie's house.'

Aiden's shoulders slumped. 'They're like a black spot.'

'I'm not following.'

'You know. When pirates are cursed, they have a black spot on their palm. It means they're marked for death. Or if you look into the face of the night raven, it means you'll die. Maybe not straight away, but you're marked. No escape.'

'Charlie used these to mark people?'

Aiden blinked slowly. He looked tired, but instead of making him look older, it emphasised the youth in his features. Lydia felt a lurch of sympathy. But she couldn't let up. 'I'm waiting, Aiden.'

He nodded. Resigned. 'Let's say someone had got on his bad side. Done something against the Family. Or against Charlie. You'd have a meeting with him, explain your case. And then you'd go home and find it in your pockets. Then you knew you hadn't been successful.'

'And that's it? A bit of theatre so that people knew he was going to pop round and stab them in their sleep?' Lydia felt anger at Charlie and it was a relief. The guilt she felt about handing him over to Mr Smith was never far from the surface and she craved validation that it had been justified.

'Mostly,' Aiden said, staring at the note like it was going to jump off the bench and bite him. 'If he booked a removal, he had the operator leave one. Not always, but if he wanted to send a message.'

'A removal?'

'Renovations for non-permanent work, removals for permanent.'

'Gotcha.' Bloody crime bosses and their slang. 'Why a ten-shilling note?'

'He said the Crows had always used coins but joked that it was because of inflation.' Aiden shrugged. 'I don't know. He didn't tell me everything.'

Well that was certainly true.

CHAPTER THIRTEEN

That evening, when Lydia arrived at his flat, Fleet was in a foul mood. She got two beers from the fridge and passed him one. 'Bad day?'

He put it straight onto the counter and crossed his arms. Not a good sign.

'When were you going to tell me?'

'Tell you what?'

Fleet breathed deeply, like he was trying to hold onto his temper. 'Camberwell is my manor. Did you think I wouldn't find out?'

'Give me a clue,' Lydia said, playing for time.

He stuffed his hands into his pockets and held Lydia's gaze with a look which could have stripped paint off a car.

'Is this about Mark Kendal?'

'I am practically on probation at my work. Didn't you think to give me a heads up on this one?'

'I only just heard,' Lydia said. 'What makes you think I had prior warning? And what do you mean probation? You just got a promotion.'

Fleet didn't answer for a moment. He still looked frustrated but there was a weariness, too, like he couldn't be bothered to hold onto his anger. 'Not really. It was a sideways move,' he said eventually. 'The kind that buries me in meetings and keeps me behind a desk. I need to keep my nose clean and suck up to the brass or I'm never getting a decent case ever again.'

Lydia was stunned. 'But, why? You're brilliant at your job.'

A quick smile escaped. 'Thank you. But I'm in my boss's bad-books. Or her boss. Or both of them. It's fine, they'll get over it. I'm serving my time until they forget about punishing me or something else distracts them. But in the meantime, it would be nice to look halfway competent.'

'It's because of me, isn't it?'

Fleet's shoulders went down a notch. 'It'll be fine. Don't give it another thought.'

'You should tell them it's over. We'll go back to keeping it secret.' Lydia tried a smile. 'It'll be like old times. All that sexy sneaking around.'

'Don't try to distract me, I'm interrogating you.'

'Are you indeed?' Lydia put her hands on her hips. 'How's that going?'

Fleet sighed. 'About as well as usual.' He paused. 'Is there anything I should know?'

Lydia widened her eyes. 'About Mark Kendal? I don't know anything about it. I just heard about it from Aiden.'

'Fascinating,' Fleet said, definitely trying not to smile, now. 'And how did Aiden know?'

'It's his job to keep me informed on the local news. I don't ask about his methods.' Lydia said primly. 'Do you want to speak to him?'

Fleet looked at her for another beat before, thankfully, shaking his head. 'Did he tell you how Mr Kendal died?'

'No,' Lydia said, working hard to keep her expression neutral. 'I assumed burglary gone wrong.'

'He was bludgeoned with a heavy object. His skull was entirely compressed on the right side.'

'Oh,' Lydia's mouth went dry. At once she could smell the blood, see the brain matter exposed and tangling with his matted hair.

'Nothing was taken. And the scene looked clean, SOCO is still there, though. If anything was left, we'll find it.'

Fleet was eyeballing her in a meaningful way. He left a space and Lydia knew he was waiting for her to fill it. 'Of course you will,' she said reassuringly. She had always been so comfortable withholding details from Fleet, from everybody, really, it was as natural as breathing. This time felt different. Her stomach was cramping with guilt, but she pushed down the urge to tell him the truth. 'Shall we eat?'

Lydia woke up to the sound of Fleet yelling, his voice hoarse as if he had been shouting for hours, not seconds. The light was filtering around the edges of his thick blackout curtains and she realised it was morning. Almost time for the alarm to go off. He was having a nightmare, that was clear, but Lydia hesitated. There was something more than inarticulate fear pouring from his rigid body. Light. Or something her brain was interpreting as light. The strange gleam that she had sensed from Fleet the first time she had met him, the gleam which said that somebody, maybe way back in his ancestry, had some power, but one she couldn't identify, had ignited from a gleam to a glow. No, she had seen it sparked into a glow before. This had intensified from a glow to a radiance.

Lydia didn't know what to do. Sweat was pouring down Fleet's face and his body was contorted, tendons standing out in his neck as he strained against some invisible force. She called his name, shook him by the shoulder and, in desperation, pinched his ear. Hard. When none of that woke him and he was still hoarsely shouting, the garbled sound forming into a single word 'no', she grabbed the half-full glass of water from her side of the bed and dumped it over his head.

It wasn't instant, but over the next few seconds, Fleet's yells quietened and he became conscious. His eyes focused on her face and he swallowed hard, rubbing his face with both hands and then looking at them. 'I'm wet.'

'My fault,' Lydia said. 'Sorry. Are you all right?'

'Just a bad dream.' Fleet didn't smile much but, when he did, it was like the sun coming out. The one he managed, now, was small and insincere. It was meant to reassure Lydia but all it did was give her a stomach ache.

'That wasn't a nightmare,' Lydia said.

Fleet was already getting out of bed. 'I'm going to shower.'

'What happened?' She was speaking to his back. 'That's not the first time, is it?'

'Don't worry about it,' Fleet didn't turn around, just headed into the en-suite and closed the door.

Lydia got dressed and considered stripping the bed. Then she decided that she had no desire to set a precedent for housework so she went and messed with Fleet's expensive coffee machine until it gave up the good stuff.

Fleet took his time and Lydia was wondering whether she ought to break down the door and check on him, when she heard the water shut off. She sat on the sofa and sipped her coffee, giving him space. She didn't want to admit it, but part of her was afraid. Fleet was usually unshakeable.

He emerged from the bedroom fully-dressed in a suit and tie. 'Gotta get going,' he said, kissing the top of her head and picking up the coffee for a quick sip.

'We should talk,' Lydia said.

'It's fine,' Fleet replied, pulling on his coat and patting the pockets for his keys.

Lydia had an indication of how annoying it was being in a relationship with her. Being avoidant and saying 'I'm fine' when things were clearly far from it was not helpful. She stood and walked over to Fleet, put her hand on his chest and reached out with her Crow senses. All the practice was paying off and she got a string of impressions.

'Don't,' Fleet took a step back.

'You can feel it,' Lydia said. 'Something is changing. You know I seem to power people up? People like me. I think...'

'Don't,' Fleet said, again, his face stony. 'I've got to go.'

As Lydia had thought many times before, nowhere did pubs like London. She had several favourites. None of them pretentious, although one was edging that way and was saved only by its incredible twice-fried skin-on chips and comfortable seats. This pub, however, was as far from the places Lydia preferred as it was possible to get without it being an entirely different species.

Linoleum covered the floor, scratched and burned and with so much ground-in dirt the original colour was impossible to discern, and the bar was plywood, recently remodelled after the latest brawl. Figures sat alone, drinking with the grim determination of the terminally alcoholic, while a small group of old men sucked their teeth over a game of dominoes. One table was covered in glasses half-filled with beer and whisky, but nobody was sitting down. A cigarette burned in an ashtray, abandoned. This wasn't a place that cared about the indoor smoking rules.

The woman behind the bar was very thin and very tanned and had a halo of platinum curls that looked like it had been bought in a fancy-dress store. She took a last drag of her own cigarette and put the end into a mug which said 'World's Best Grandma' which had clearly been used for the purpose many times before. 'You're not welcome in here, Crow.'

'Don't be rude,' Lydia said, producing her coin and making it spin in the air. 'I'm looking for Jimmy.'

'He's not here,' the woman said, her eyes crossing as she stared at the coin as it turned lazily inches from her face.

'When did you last see him?'

'This morn-,' she broke off. 'Dunno.'

'Is there a back room?'

'Yeah. Wait... What?' The woman's eyes were glassy.

Lydia heard the scrape of a chair and knew that at least one of the drinkers was thinking about getting involved. She spoke without looking around, just raising her voice a little. 'I wouldn't if I were you.'

She plucked her coin from the air and gave the woman a wide smile. 'Thanks for your help. Is it this way?' Lydia kept moving toward the door she had spotted and ignored the movement to her right. She knew nobody would be stupid enough to take a swing at the head of the Crow Family in this shit-show little dive bar. And if she believed that wholeheartedly, she would make it true. You had to commit. If she had learned one thing, it was that.

Lydia made it to the backroom without incident and discovered another space which both time and hope had forgotten. Nicotine-stained walls, mismatched furniture and a television on one wall playing sport. The room was dominated by a pool table and three men with shaved heads and tattoos. Two of the men were in the middle of a game and the third was sitting in the corner, his feet up on a chair.

One of the pool-players gave Lydia a full up-and-down look with a leer that suggested his thought processes went on somewhere far south of his brain. 'You lost, girl?'

Lydia ignored him, fixing her attention on the man in the corner. He raised his gaze to meet hers and she felt a jolt. Not of Family power, there was no Pearl, Silver, Crow or

Fox in the room, but power nonetheless. The power which came from being the biggest badass on the street and everybody knowing it. The power of being the smartest person in the room and the one with the vision. The man everybody looked to for direction, for a plan, for the big score and the smart play. In his own piss-poor small-time way, this man was a leader and Lydia could feel it. She smiled her shark smile. 'I've got a proposition for you, Jimmy.'

Jimmy Brodie, also known as The Hammer, tipped his head back a fraction, as if wanting to get a better view. He had prison tattoos on his neck and hands, faded green with age, and a thickset body which suggested bulky muscle which wasn't used quite as much as it used to be. 'Just a business deal,' Lydia said. 'Cash in exchange for an introduction.'

She knew the leering pool player had moved behind her and wasn't surprised when he spoke. 'You walk in here carrying cash? You're asking to lose it.'

'I'm not losing anything,' Lydia said, holding the boss man's gaze. 'Just looking for a certain service and happy to pay the fee.' She was working on the principle that if someone had paid a professional to take out Mr Kendal, it had to be somebody unconnected to any of the Families or, at least, someone who didn't care about the politics of the Families. Her second thought was that it was likely a local who had paid for the hit, which meant they would have sourced it locally, too. People tended to ask for recommendations for this kind of thing. It wasn't the kind of service you Googled, which meant they had probably started in the sketchiest non-Family pub in the area. Lydia reasoned that if she followed their footsteps, she ought to find the same contractor. 'So, if a girl was in the market for a reliable contractor to carry out a bit of work, who should she see?'

Jimmy's eyes had started out small and mean-looking, they had narrowed further giving the impression that he was peering through smoke. Lydia knew it was supposed to make him look even-more intimidating, but it had the opposite effect. She gave him a friendly smile and pushed a little bit of Crow into her voice. 'Quick as you like.'

'Renovation or removals?' Jimmy looked surprised after the words spilled out, as if he hadn't intended to speak.

'Removals,' Lydia said. 'And I'm crunched for time, so they need to be available to start immediately.' Whoever had killed Mr Kendal had been in the area very recently and Lydia was hoping that would further narrow down the pool of local professionals.

Jimmy nodded slowly, his eyes very slightly glazed. Lydia could hear the men behind her shifting and could feel the atmosphere in the room tighten. They were waiting for the signal from Jimmy and didn't understand why he hadn't given it yet. Lydia wondered if they had enough self-control to carry on waiting. 'Happy days,' Jimmy said, after another beat. 'He's right here. Felix, don't be shy.'

Lydia didn't look away from Jimmy and one of the men who had been playing pool moved into her field of vision. It wasn't the leering man, but his companion. A man Lydia had categorised as the least dangerous in the room, which just went to show that you could always learn something new. He had a short, neatly-trimmed beard which was just one step up from stubble, dark hair and eyes. If he didn't take plenty of holidays in the sun, he had Mediterranean heritage somewhere in his gene pool, and he had a slim-build which, now that Lydia was paying attention, could suggest martial arts. Or a reliance on long-range weapons.

'I can help you,' Felix said. 'But I must warn you, my rates are high.'

'They really are,' Jimmy said, seeming to not want to lose control of the conversation.

The leering man was sitting on the edge of the pool table, now, tapping a cigarette from a packet. The sense that she was about to be beaten up, or worse, had dissipated and Lydia wondered what secret signal she had missed. 'Can we speak in private?'

Felix looked instinctively toward Jimmy and then shrugged. 'Sure.'

He led the way down a short corridor which led not, as Lydia had been hoping, to a back yard with the good clean air of Camberwell, but to the toilet. Walking into a confined space with a hitman wasn't the most reckless thing Lydia had ever done, but it might make the top ten. She kept herself close to the door and squeezed her coin in her palm for strength.

Felix glanced at the filthy urinal, wrinkling his nose against the pungent smell, before facing Lydia. 'I know who you are.'

'Good.'

'I'm happy to do contract work, but I'm not looking for a permanent position.'

Lydia was momentarily surprised. 'That something you've been offered before?'

'Your predecessor. He liked the idea of full control over my schedule.'

That sounded like Charlie. Lydia felt cold as the full implication dawned. Charlie had been dropping enough bodies to warrant a hitman on retainer.

She pushed the thought away and straightened her spine. 'I'm after something else. A name.'

Felix's expression closed down. 'You know I can't do that.'

'I'll give you one, first,' Lydia said. 'Mark Kendal.'

Felix's face didn't so much as flicker.

'I need to know who ordered the job.'

'I don't know this name,' Felix said. 'I can't help.'

Lydia flipped her coin high into the air, making it spin slowly. Felix watched it, seemingly against his will. 'You left evidence at the scene. If you don't tell me who commissioned the job, I will make sure that evidence reaches the police.'

Felix dragged his gaze from the coin to find Lydia's face. 'I don't leave *anything*.' His lip was curled in disgust, his eyes alight with pride.

Lydia pushed more Crow behind her words. 'Who hired you to kill Mark Kendal?'

Felix didn't want to speak, but she was dragging the words out one at a time. 'Not. Me.'

There was something there. Something in the spaces between the words that were unwillingly passing his lips. He was grimacing, now, like he was in pain, and Lydia knew that the second she relaxed her hold, he was going to lunge for her, wrap his hands around her throat and squeeze.

'Who, then? Is there another operator in town?'

Felix laughed then. 'How the fuck should I know? We're not a bloody club.'

He was lying. Not about the club aspect, but about not knowing. Lydia had other concerns, though, she could feel her hold slipping.

A sudden electronic beeping sounded. Felix pulled a phone from his pocket and frowned at the screen.

Lydia was already moving for the door, taking the moment of distraction to get out. She flew down the short corridor and shoved the bar on the fire exit at the end, praying for a back street and not a dead-end. With a rush of relief, she felt the door yield and she slammed it shut behind her. She was in a backyard with old beer barrels, wheelie bins, sodden cardboard and a collection of pint glasses on the ground overflowing with cigarette butts. It was contained by a wall with no gate, but the back windows were mercifully blind, bricked in or covered with plywood. Lydia didn't hesitate, scrambling onto a metal keg and grabbing the top of the wall to pull herself up, feet scrabbling on the brickwork. Her arms screamed in protest, but the adrenalin gave her strength and she managed to get up and over the top. She heard the fire door slam open and a furious male voice, but she was dropping down on the other side and flying far away, fast.

CHAPTER FOURTEEN

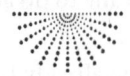

Back at the flat, Lydia was sitting at her desk. She had also been eyeing up the almost-full whisky bottle on top of her filing cabinet which had been making 'come hither' eyes at her for the last hour. It had been that kind of a day.

Her phone buzzed. Aiden. 'People are asking for a meeting.'

'When you say people...'

'John, mostly. But some others.'

Lydia got up and moved to the kitchen. She filled the kettle while Aiden spoke, realising as she did so that she wasn't thirsty for anything except alcohol. She got a beer instead and popped the cap. 'They aren't happy about...'

'Not on the phone,' Lydia warned.

'I know. I'm on my way.'

Lydia's motion sensor went off a second later and she heard Aiden's heavy footsteps in the hall. She opened the door before he could knock and led the way to the roof terrace.

With the radio playing she indicated for Aiden to speak by gesturing with her beer.

'It doesn't look good.'

'I'm aware.'

'The community knows that we were friendly with Mark. And now he's dead. That makes us look weak.' Aiden winced, as if expecting Lydia to throw something at him. 'Sorry.'

'What does John want me to do about it?'

'He wants a meeting...'

'Don't give me that. He already knows what he wants me to do and he'll have been shooting his mouth off to anyone who will listen.'

Aiden looked at the floor. 'He wants a proportionate response.'

'An eye for an eye?' Lydia sighed. That sounded right. John was nothing if not traditional. Especially since he never had to get his hands dirty. He and aunt Daisy lived in their comfortable house and enjoyed the reputation and financial safety net of the Crows without getting into the messy details. An eye for an eye sounded pretty good when you didn't have to gouge it out yourself. 'So, it's just face-saving? Not personal?'

'How do you mean?'

'Was anybody close personal friends with Mark Kendal? If someone is going to do something silly, I need to know.'

'Not that I know about,' Aiden said. 'But I'll ask around.'

FLEET CALLED on his way to the gym in a not-wonderful mood. Lydia thought she might leave some of her activities out of the 'how was your day, honey?' conversation. Pissing off a professional killer, for example.

Lydia had eaten earlier, but she offered Fleet leftover pizza, if he wanted to come round. 'I ate at the office,' Fleet said. 'And I'm heading home to crash. I wouldn't be good company tonight. Sorry.'

'No worries,' Lydia said. 'Bad day?'

'Yeah, I guess. Long, anyway. Meetings. And I've been kicked off the Mason case. Sorry, not kicked off. Reassigned.'

'To what?'

'Cross Pollination and Synergy Leveraging Solutions.' Fleet's disgusted tone let Lydia know that this was a whole new level of corporate bullshit.

Fleet seemed to find all the management and meetings far more stressful than the more-obviously dangerous parts of his job. Lydia could relate. Then a horrible thought crossed her mind. 'They're punishing you.'

'I don't think so-'

'For being with me. It's a message.'

Fleet's voice was cut out by the sound of a siren passing. Then, 'It's just the job. You get promoted and, after a while, it's all desk duty and meetings. It's not personal.'

He didn't sound totally convinced, though. 'I spoke to a captain in the Hellenic police, and she said there were no leads on the hit and run. It was a fairly busy location, not that far from the hotel where the MP was staying, but there were no witnesses.'

'None?'

'Alex Papoutsis, she's the captain, said that she had one witness originally, who said he saw a van travelling at high speed away from the area, but he recanted his statement. Said he had the wrong day.'

'Someone got to him?'

'Definitely a possibility. Although, she was telling me that hit and runs are a major problem in Greece. And they're currently classed as a misdemeanour, so there isn't a lot of budget spent on following up. If it isn't an easy solve, they usually get buried. In her experience, anyway.'

'There would have been heat on this one, though,' Lydia said. 'From the UK. Did Interpol get involved?'

'She said not really. Said it was more a case of sending on the report. Information-sharing in the spirit of inter-departmental global collaboration.'

Lydia could hear the air quotes in Fleet's voice. 'You think it was just a box-ticking exercise?'

'Exactly. I guess Interpol is as stretched as the rest of us.'

So, there was a possibility that somebody close to the MP Nadine Gormley would have a motive to kill Alejandro. If he had been involved with the hit and run in Greece and if that person knew, or suspected, him of that involvement. An image of Maria, her face obscured by black lace, her high heels and sharp skirt like weapons, jumped to the front of Lydia's mind. She saw people lining up to offer their condolences, to kiss her hand. If Alejandro had arranged a hit on an MP in order to free up a political position, how much had Maria known about his plans? How involved had she been in her father's meteoric rise? She said at the funeral that people hadn't taken her seriously before and Lydia wondered what she would have been willing to do to be seen as the rightful leader of the Silvers.

HAVING DRAINED her beer and poured a large whisky, Lydia was sitting at her desk in the growing darkness and cradled the glass. Jason was in his room, Fleet was home, and the cafe was shut up for the night. Her mobile rang with an unknown number and she answered, expecting a new prospective client or a sales call.

Mr Smith's measured tone sent a bolt of adrenaline through her body. Her first thought was that he was calling to tell her that Charlie was dead. But her second was that he wouldn't do that. Charlie would die alone and un-mourned and the Family would never even know he had passed. That was part of the punishment she had doled out. One of the many decisions in her life which had led to her sitting alone in a dark room drinking whisky. 'What do you want?'

'To help you,' Mr Smith replied. His voice set off an echo of his signature and Lydia held onto the desk to steady herself.

'How kind,' she said. 'I'm fine.'

Mr Smith made a tutting noise. 'Mr Kendal isn't fine. And I'm guessing your family isn't too pleased about his murder, either. It doesn't look good, does it?'

'I don't know what you're talking about,' Lydia said. If Mr Smith thought he could trap her into talking about protection rackets on the phone, he was delusional.

'You're out of your depth,' Mr Smith went on. 'I'm offering to throw you a rope. Let me help you. I've got the resources. I could find the person responsible for Mr Kendal's death, effect a quick resolution. Then you can go back to your family and claim all the glory. Get them back onside.'

Lydia wanted to ask him why he thought her family weren't supporting her as their leader, what rumours he had heard, but that would involve admitting that she was concerned about it. 'Why are you offering to help? Just feeling charitable? Bit of community service?'

'Maybe there's an element of that,' Mr Smith said. 'You know I'm very fond of you, but the fact is you're not cut out for this. You're an investigator. A freelancer. You're not Charlie and everybody knows it. That's dangerous. If people don't have the proper respect, there will be casualties. Poor Mr Kendal is just the start.'

Lydia's throat had gone dry. She knocked back some whisky, but when she spoke her voice still came out a little cracked. 'What would you suggest? That I retire?'

'That you let me help you. It will be our secret. I can help you hold onto your Family and hold onto your power and I won't ask anything of you that you won't be happy to give.'

'Let me think about it,' Lydia said, playing for time.

'You can reach me on this number. I suggest you do so sooner rather than later. Serius est quam cogitas.'

It was almost eight o'clock and the Pilates studio was shut. The window at the front was screened by a jungle of house plants, but there were no electric lights showing beyond, and the front door was locked. Lydia had assumed they would stay open in the evening. Surely people had to fit in workouts after office hours? And with such a small space, they could hardly cram in enough business to stay afloat without working all the hours of the day.

Lydia rapped on the glass of the front door. She was about to call Chunni when a door at the back of the studio opened, spilling light across the polished wooden floor. Chunni crossed the studio and unlocked the front door. She apologised for keeping Lydia waiting.

'I was catching up on emails. Come in.'

As soon as Lydia crossed the threshold, she felt it.

'My office is out back,' Chunni was weaving through the machines to the doorway. 'It's a bit small, I'm afraid, but you know London rent.'

'You live here?' Lydia asked.

'Would you like tea?' Chunni began listing types of fruit and herbal tea and Lydia tuned out, concentrating instead on her other senses.

The back room stretched the definition. When Chunni had said 'a bit small' she meant 'a cupboard with a kettle'. There was a single upright chair which had a closed laptop on the seat. Lydia stood in the doorway watching Chunni fussing with little paper sachets, then she moved away to walk around the studio. 'Where do your clients change?'

'On the right.'

Lydia set off, not asking for permission. A plain door led

to a flight of stairs. On the first landing there was a door to a toilet and a changing room. Looking inside there was a single stall and basin. The changing room had a light wooden bench and a row of hooks on the wall. It smelled of feet, despite the reed diffuser in the corner. The feeling was stronger on the stairs and weaker in the changing room. Carrying on up to the next floor, Lydia knew she was getting closer. The building reminded her of The Fork but instead of a half-glass door inscribed with 'Crow Investigations', she was met with a plain door, swinging hastily shut, and the smell of cooking food.

Chunni was coming up the stairs behind her and Lydia raised her voice to ask, 'Who is up here?'

She knocked on the door and then opened it. There was resistance, but Lydia shoved and it yielded.

An extremely petite woman with a waterfall of fine pale blonde hair was turning to run and Lydia caught her arm.

'Don't!' Chunni was there, grabbing at Lydia from behind. 'Leave her alone!'

Lydia let go of the blonde's arm. She suddenly realised that both women were frightened. Of her. Which was a strange feeling. 'I'm not going to hurt you,' she said, raising her hands in a gesture of peace. 'I just want to talk.'

'We haven't done anything,' the blonde woman said and, if Lydia had been in any doubt, the sound of her voice clinched it. She was Pearl.

'You came to me,' Lydia looked at Chunni over her shoulder. 'I'm here to help because you asked me to.' The blonde woman took the opportunity to retreat into the single-purpose room. It had the exposed brick walls and industrial light fittings of the studio downstairs, but with an unfolded sofa bed in front of the television and a sleek fitted kitchen against one wall. 'Why don't we sit down and you can tell me what's going on. Why are you so frightened?'

Chunni let go of Lydia and crossed to meet the blonde woman, taking her hand. 'This is my wife, Heather.'

'Okay.' Lydia concentrated on making herself look as friendly and non-threatening as possible. It wasn't something she had ever had to work at before and it felt bizarre. She was a short woman with moderate fighting skills, which had only ever been used in self-defence. She had no language or experience for reassuring women that she wasn't going to hurt them. In a flash she realised this was how good men must feel all the time. 'Let me help.'

Chunni and Heather exchanged a glance.

'Is it the case you brought to me?' Lydia tried, when nothing was forthcoming. Still nothing.

'I'm sorry,' Chunni said, her voice very small.

The penny dropped. 'There is nobody suing you, is there? You just wanted to speak to me.'

A hesitation. Then an imperceptible nod.

'Why?'

Another shared glance. Heather was so pale she looked as if she might vomit. Lydia felt sympathy but a surge of impatience was there, too. She considered pushing a little. A bit of Crow whammy to move things along. She was busy. And Chunni had lied to her. 'I'm waiting,' Lydia said, mildly enough.

'We heard you had taken over,' Chunni said hesitantly. 'And Charlie hadn't been bothered about me and Heather, but we didn't know if you would be different. I wanted to meet you. To see what you were like.'

For a split second, Lydia thought Chunni meant 'to check if you were homophobic' but then she realised the more obvious concern. 'You thought I might not approve of a Pearl-owned business in Camberwell?'

A quick nod. 'Charlie didn't care. He said business was business.'

'Why do you think I would feel differently?'

'My mum said it used to be a rule,' Heather said. Her voice was quiet but with a beautiful tone. Lydia could feel the pull of the Pearl, the urge to lean in and listen closer, and she consciously stiffened her muscles to hold herself in check. 'She said it wasn't allowed and that if Jack Crow was still alive, he'd have strung us up outside The Old Hermit and nobody would have said a word.'

Lydia had only the vaguest memories of her grandfather, but she could see why that rumour had taken hold. She remembered glittering black eyes and a hooked nose below a sweep of white hair. In that moment, another memory chased behind the image. Her father, looking very tired and very scared, speaking quietly and quickly in the kitchen on the old corded phone which had hung on the wall. Her angle was sharp, as if Lydia were down on the floor. 'No, I can't,' her father was saying. A deep breath. Then: 'I won't.' Why had that memory surfaced? Had he been speaking to her grandfather? Lydia brought herself back to the present. 'Is that why you recorded me?'

Pure terror flashed across Chunni's face.

'It's all right,' Lydia said briskly, trying not to enjoy her reaction. 'I just want you to delete the footage. And never do it again, obviously.' She didn't want people waltzing into her office and taking clandestine recordings. Chunni *should* be sorry for that. She fixed them both with a hard stare. 'I help people. Especially those that live in Camberwell. But you don't need to lie to me.' She waited a beat before adding: 'It's a bad idea.'

'I'm sorry,' Heather whispered. 'We're sorry.'

'It's already deleted,' Chunni was saying. 'I swear.'

Lydia looked at the women. They seemed cowed, but how much of that was an act to get them off the hook and out of trouble? Suddenly it felt very important to Lydia to be sure these women wouldn't cross her again. She needed to make an example of them, something which could act as a warning to others. She hated the idea that Mr Smith might have had a point. She was Lydia Crow and she couldn't have ordinary people disrespecting her. Not without repercussions. Aiden had been warning her that she had to show strength or people wouldn't maintain the proper respect for the Family and now this. Lydia didn't want to be like Charlie, but she wondered what he would do. An image of Big Neil tied to a chair in the lock-up, beaten and bloody flashed into her mind.

Chunni and Heather must have seen something cross her face as they began babbling further apologies. Lydia held up her hand to silence them. She produced her coin and spun it in the air, drawing their attention. 'Lydia Crow knew that you had betrayed her trust and she came to your home and she hurt you both in ways that you can't even think about without feeling sick.'

The colour drained from Chunni and Heather's faces, leaving dark hollows around their eyes. 'You will tell anybody who will listen not to cross Lydia Crow. That she knows when you are lying. And that her little sparrows are everywhere. Seeing everything.' A tiny moan escaped from Heather's lips.

Lydia waited a beat to make sure the message had sunk in and then plucked her coin from the air. 'I'll see myself out.'

CHAPTER FIFTEEN

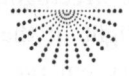

'What time is it?' Fleet's voice, thick with sleep. Lydia opened her eyes and met darkness. Her eyes adjusted slowly as her brain kicked into gear. Her phone was ringing. She rolled over and retrieved it from the floor, stabbing at the answer button. 'Yes?'

There was heavy breathing, the rumble of traffic. 'It's me. I just wanted to say 'goodbye'. I wanted to say-'

'Ash? Where are you?' Lydia was sitting up, now, the phone pressed against her ear. 'Are you okay?'

'Thank you for everything.'

'Feathers!'

Fleet was sitting up, too, and he rubbed a hand over his face, stubble rasping in the sudden quiet. 'What's up?'

'He said 'goodbye'.' Lydia got up and began to pull on her clothes. 'Hell Hawk. What is he doing, now?'

Fleet swung his legs from under the duvet.

'It's okay,' Lydia said. 'You go back to sleep. I'm pretty sure I know where Ash will be.' She was using her phone to access Ash's mobile GPS as she spoke. Jason had installed the software and she wasn't sure if it was entirely legal, so she didn't elaborate further.

447

'I'll come with you,' Fleet said, clicking on his bedside light. 'Give me a second.'

IT WAS ALMOST five as Lydia drove to Highgate, Fleet yawning extravagantly in the passenger seat. Sunrise wasn't for another hour and the streetlights were still lit, but there was the suggestion of light in the sky. Dew covered the parked cars and colours emerged murkily in the early morning twilight.

'You think he'll be here?'

'Where else?' Lydia took the Archway Gate into the woods.

'Is this a good idea?' Fleet caught her hand, stopping her. 'Should we try calling?'

Lydia understood his reticence. She didn't particularly want to go wandering among the half-lit trees, either. The sense of Pearl was suffusing her mind, pulling her into the darkest part of the forest. It was an inducement and a warning. 'He's vulnerable,' Lydia said. 'I can't leave him.'

Fleet tilted his head back, as if the sky would give him an alternative answer. When it didn't, he sighed and resumed walking. Their feet crunched on the ground and Lydia stopped every few paces to listen. She wanted to call out to Ash, but it felt foolhardy. She knew where he would be anyway, so she picked her way back to the place where Lucy Bunyan had disappeared.

The small clearing held the still shape of Ash as if it was built for him. He was on the ground, hands scrabbling in the dirt and a stream of low guttural noises coming from his throat, like an animal. He looked up as they approached and Lydia caught the flash of wild eyes. His stringy hair hung like foliage around a face which gleamed white in the dim light. He was even thinner than the last time she had seen him and his bony wrists protruded sharply from filthy shirt cuffs. His hands looked black and Lydia realised that they were caked with dirt and blood. He shook his head, as if denying their existence, and then turned back to his self-imposed task of digging in the earth with his bare hands.

'Ash,' Lydia began, keeping her voice low and calm. 'We're here to help.'

He didn't stop his frenzied action or even appear to hear Lydia.

'All right there, mate,' Fleet tried. 'Come along now, let's get you somewhere warm. Get something to eat and drink.' It was his copper voice. Soothing and authoritative all in one go and Lydia was impressed at Ash's ability to completely ignore it.

She took a step closer and a twig broke under her Dr Marten with a loud crack. Ash looked up at that, his nose lifted to the air as if he needed to use senses other than sight. Lydia could relate. The stink of Pearl was strong in the clearing, but the trees were behaving so far. The sense of Pearl was like perfume hanging in an empty room, but Lydia wanted to get them all far away before the Pearls returned. 'Come on, Ash. It's not safe for us here.' She put a hand on his shoulder and he reared back as if burned.

'It's okay.'

Ash seemed to focus on Lydia's face for the first time. Sweat was pouring down his forehead and he blinked hard. 'Lydia?'

'That's right, it's me.' She held out a hand. 'Come with me, now. I'll get you sorted out. You can stay at my place, get some rest.'

Ash's eyes cleared for a fraction of a second and he sat back on his heels. Then a keening sound reverberated around the clearing. For a moment Lydia wasn't sure if it was the wind in the trees or a small animal caught in the jaws of a trap. Then she realised it was coming from Ash.

Tears sheeted down his face and his mouth widened as the high keening became a howl.

'Shush, shush,' Lydia couldn't stop herself, she put a hand over his mouth. 'Ash. Quiet. You've got to be quiet.'

He spoke against her hand. 'I want them to come.'

'No, you don't.'

'I do. I want them to take me back. Why won't they take me back?' He fell back to the ground, fingers scraping desperately through the dirt. 'I'm here. Let me in. I want to come home. Let me in.'

Ash moved into the air. Fleet had his arms wrapped around his body and was hoisting him from the ground. 'We've got to go,' he said to Lydia over Ash's bucking shoulder. He had his arms pinned and Lydia caught hold of his flailing legs. They managed to get out of the clearing and Ash stopped struggling. Fleet stopped and readjusted his hold so that Ash was half-walking, one arm around Fleet's neck. 'Your place or mine?'

Ash was Lydia's problem. 'Mine.'

ONCE ASH WAS prone on her sofa and Fleet had left for work, Lydia asked Jason to keep watch so that she could get some sleep. After an hour's nap which felt like falling down a deep hole, she sat at her desk and poured caffeine down her throat until she felt halfway awake. She watched Ash's chest rise and fall as he slept, his face pale and hollow and somehow still tense, even in the depths of sleep. Jason had gone into the kitchen, but she couldn't hear the sounds of breakfast. It was possible that he had disappeared. She tried to remember if that was happening more often these days and realised that she wouldn't know. She hadn't been home enough. And she had been distracted.

Lydia leaned back in her chair and fought the desire to go

back to sleep. There was a tiredness that wasn't just physical. She missed her client work. Or, more accurately, she missed the feeling that her life was her own. She had more power than she had ever had in her life, but the strings attached had wrapped around her life and her soul and they were getting tighter every day. Ash keening in the forest felt like an omen. A visitation from another realm. And a warning of what would happen if her spirit got any more twisted.

He woke up at midday and Lydia coaxed him to drink some soup. Ash had refused anything except water, babbling about keeping his body 'pure and clear' and Lydia had been forced to use a little Crow persuasion. 'You've got to eat,' she said, as he sipped from a mug, eyes anguished as if she was making him drink poison.

After he had drained the mug, she gave him the choice of juice, milk, hot chocolate or lemonade. Anything with calories, basically.

'Water.'

'Feathers, Ash. You're wasting away.'

'I can't,' he said. 'Just water. Please. They won't take me back if I'm not pure.'

Lydia swore loudly. 'You weren't exactly treating your body like a temple when they took you before. Weren't you drunk?'

'I was young,' Ash said, sadly. 'That counts for a lot.'

'But why do you want to go back? I thought you wanted revenge? I thought you wanted to make sure they didn't take anybody else?'

Ash started crying silently, which was worse in the domestic quiet of the flat than it had been in the woods. The pain radiating from him was infecting the air, making tears prick behind Lydia's eyelids and a lump form in her throat. 'I can't help it,' he managed after a while. 'I miss it. I miss them. I don't belong here anymore. I ache all over and the longing is like a pit I can't fill. I have no appetite, human food tastes like filth. Like dead things.'

'Go vegetarian. Be a vegan. Clean eating and all that,' Lydia tried.

'Plants die when they are picked. Fruit spoils from the moment it breaks from the tree. I can taste it. The rot.' He heaved suddenly and the tomato soup so carefully sipped came gushing out, over his shirt and jeans, splashing onto the carpet.

When Fleet arrived after work that night, he was bearing gifts. Takeaway noodles, wonton soup and a bottle of red. Lydia wasn't long back from dropping Ash at his childhood home and she filled Fleet in on the day while he poured two large glasses and she fetched cutlery and kitchen roll.

'I feel like I should have gone in and spoken to his parents but he's a grown up.'

'You're not responsible for him.'

Lydia pointed her fork at him. 'You can't talk. What about that guy from that refugee case? You still check up on him.'

'That's different,' Fleet said. 'And it's not like I keep tabs on every single person I arrest.' He took a swig of wine. 'And this isn't your fault. You helped him get out of hospital. You gave him answers. You believed his story when nobody else would.'

Lydia wasn't going to let herself off that easily. 'I let him down.'

They ate in silence for a few minutes. Fleet wasn't attacking his food with his usual gusto and he finished his glass of wine quickly, pouring himself another glass and topping up Lydia's before she had taken more than a couple of sips. 'I need to tell you something.'

Hell Hawk. Lydia put down her fork. 'What's wrong?'

'I've been given an official warning at work. They talked about suspension, so I should be grateful, really.'

It took Lydia a beat to realise that, for once, Fleet's trouble wasn't her fault. 'What do you mean? Why?'

'I got into an argument.'

'That's not...'

'And I lamped Butler.'

Lydia knew the name. Fleet had complained about his laziness and general incompetence many times. 'He probably deserved it. It's not like you to get violent, though. Must have been a bad argument.'

'He was being a dick,' Fleet said. 'And I've been a bit tense recently. Part of me was waiting for a reason.'

Lydia wanted to say she had noticed, but it felt like kicking a man when he was down. She settled on: 'You've been unhappy at work, I know.'

'Well, I'm off my only remaining cases, now.' He forced a smile. 'I'll be able to take it easy for a few weeks.'

'Was it really enough to get a formal reprimand?'

Fleet shrugged. 'Maybe not in usual circumstances. Butler was pushing me first so it wasn't one-sided, but I'm under a cloud at the moment.'

Lydia was horrified. 'Because you're with me?'

Fleet flashed a wry smile. 'Probably. They'll get over it, though.'

'We should go covert again.' Lydia attempted a leer. 'I don't mind being your dirty little secret.'

'No,' Fleet reached and cupped her cheek. 'I told you. I'm all in. I'm not fucking this up again.'

She leaned into his hand. The warmth of his skin and feel of his strong fingers against her face sent feelings to other parts of her body and she moved closer, as Fleet did the same. Their lips met and his hand slipped to the back of her neck, tangling in her hair. Her brain momentarily shorting out in the most enjoyable way.

'Stop distracting me,' Lydia broke from the kiss, mock severe. 'And I'm serious. I don't want to ruin your career. You don't have to choose.'

'I do,' Fleet said, his face still close, eyes warm. 'And I choose us.'

She could smell the fresh ozone of the sea and feel sunshine on her skin as she leaned closer.

AFTER A PLEASANT HOUR of choosing each other, Lydia stretched on the bed, feeling the deep relaxation in her muscles.

'Shall I warm up the food?'

'There's ice cream,' Lydia said. 'Get two spoons.'

She watched Fleet pull on boxer shorts and enjoyed the view as he crossed the room. There was a scar on his right shoulder blade and she made a mental note to ask him about it. They should know everything about each other, now. No secrets. Lydia felt a spurt of fear. She had no idea if such a thing was possible, but she knew she wanted to try.

When he returned with the ice cream and cutlery, she was sitting up against pillows. 'Tell me what happened at work.'

'I already did,' Fleet peeled the lid open and passed the carton and a spoon.

'You hit a colleague in the office. That's very much not like you.'

'I hit him in the face,' Fleet said, trying to keep things light.

'DCI Ignatius Fleet,' Lydia waved her spoon threateningly, 'tell me what happened.'

'He has been asking for it for weeks, making little comments. Insults. And it's been worse since Alejandro... He's been indicating that you will be next.'

'What the hell?'

'It's my fault for reacting. He's like a child and I gave him attention. He's the needy sort.'

'So he's been saying things about me?' Now the pieces clicked into place. Someone had insulted Lydia and Fleet had defended her honour. 'I don't care about that and neither should you.' Lydia stopped. It wasn't like Fleet to care about the opinions of an idiot. He was the most evolved, controlled, *grown-up* man she had ever known. 'What aren't you telling me?'

Fleet took the carton and excavated a spoonful of ice cream. 'I don't want to talk about it. I'm embarrassed by my behaviour.'

Lydia took the carton back and set it on the bedside table. She took one of Fleet's hands in her own and waited for him to elaborate.

After a moment he let out a sigh which seemed to come from deep within. 'It wasn't just about you. He suggested that my career progression wasn't down to ability.'

Lydia inhaled sharply.

Fleet smiled at her expression. 'Not affirmative action, although I think he meant that, too. More that I was playing both sides of the law and that gave me information. An edge. He suggested that the reason I made so many collars was because I was responsible for half the crimes. Or that I knew the people responsible.'

Lydia swore. 'He was asking to be smacked, then.'

Fleet shook his head. 'I played into his hands. He accused me of being a criminal and I committed assault. Not my smartest comeback.'

CHAPTER SIXTEEN

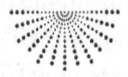

Lydia was on her roof terrace, enjoying the weak morning sunshine on her face. It had rained in the night and the air was still damp and chilly, but jeans, boots and a thick hoodie were keeping her comfortable and the mug of strong coffee was sparking her synapses. Jason had been near the railing, looking down into the street but then had shimmered for a moment and disappeared. Lydia was waiting to see if he was going to reappear. That sometimes happened, especially if he had disappeared on purpose, and she was determined not to jump if it did.

'Boo!' A voice right next to her ear. Lydia jolted but managed not to yell out.

'You're not funny,' she said, twisting to glare at the ghost.

'I'm bored.' Jason shoved at the rolled sleeves on his baggy grey suit. 'I can't seem to settle to anything.'

Lydia knew he was restless. Leaving the building might not have been fun for either of them, but it had opened a door in Jason's world. A door that seemed to taunt him.

'What are you doing, anyway? You've been staring into space for twenty minutes.'

'Trying to think,' Lydia said, taking a sip of her coffee. 'Trying and failing.'

'About what? Alejandro?'

Lydia nodded. 'I feel like he was involved in the hit on Nadine Gormley, but there's no evidence to link him to it. And how did he pay for it? He's the head of the Silvers, though, maybe he took it from the firm?'

'Why would he have an MP killed?' Jason asked. 'Just to open up a vacancy? That seems extreme.'

'Yeah, but it's a one-in, one-out kind of a job. And he was in a hurry.'

'Jesus,' Jason shuddered. 'I had no idea they could be that ruthless.'

Lydia skipped over that. Jason hadn't wanted to know the details of his own murder, which had occurred on the day of his wedding to Amy Silver. A match which had been distinctly unpopular with the rest of the Family. And she was going to respect his wishes and keep her mouth shut, unless he expressly requested the information. Sometimes ignorance was, well not exactly bliss, but survival. She distracted him. 'And that's probably expensive, right? I don't know the going rate for a hit, but it can't be cheap. But you know the firm. The size of the offices, the amount of money that place must generate. I thought the whole Family was richer than God.'

Jason frowned, thinking. 'It depends on where the bulk of the accessible cash is, though. If his private wealth is tied up in assets like property, he wouldn't have loads on hand. And he couldn't just take it out of the business, that would leave a trail. More likely he borrowed it or was being bankrolled by an invested third party.'

'But he must have a ton of money in his personal accounts. Or under his mattress.'

'I don't know,' Jason said. 'The hit might only have been

part of it. He went from nothing to MP really fast. Is that normal?'

Lydia's grasp of politics was minimal. 'No idea.'

'Me neither, but it seems possible that some bribery was involved. Maybe the costs mounted up. Or maybe it wasn't just cash that was needed.'

'Favours?' Lydia understood back-scratching. A lot of the Crow empire had been built on it. 'Someone wanted him in in power so that he could do bigger, better favours.' It niggled, though. Who was powerful enough to manipulate the head of the Silvers? Who would dare?

They went indoors and Jason drifted to the sofa to pick up his laptop.

The alarm on the pressure pad she had under the carpet in the hallway sounded. 'That'll be Fleet. Better make yourself scarce.'

'Because you're going to get naked in here?'

Lydia tried very hard to pretend he hadn't just said that. Having a sex life in a haunted building was entirely contingent on her ability to conveniently forget that she lived with a ghost who could appear in any room at any time.

'No JOY with getting hold of the pathologist, he's on holiday,' Fleet said, after kissing Lydia 'hello'. He took off his coat and threw it onto the sofa so recently vacated by Jason and his computer.

'Hell Hawk.'

'Yep. See, other professionals take time off.'

'Hilarious,' Lydia replied. 'When is he back?'

'A month.'

'That's a long holiday.'

'He made an extremely thorough report before he left,' Fleet said patiently. 'You've seen the extremely thorough report. Is it really that important to speak to him?'

'Something doesn't feel right.' Lydia had been going back over the day in the hospital mortuary; the smell of chemicals and death, the bright lighting. She hadn't been in the viewing room for very long, but she had seen Alejandro on the table. His hair had been swept back off his face and his features had looked waxy and weird, both familiar and completely wrong. All impressions completely in-line with seeing a dead body. It wasn't her first, after all.

She closed her eyes. What else? His arms had been by his sides, palms facing up. A sheet covering most of his body. The pathologist in his gown, looping his mask around his ears and talking to Fleet, barely glancing in her direction. The technician had come in, then. He had been late. Lydia could see the scene in her mind's eye and remember her revulsion. She wondered if she would ever get used to the smell of mortuaries. There hadn't been the tang of Silver and she had put that down to being in the other room, separated from Alejandro by a wall and thick glass.

'My boss had a word.' Fleet sounded tense and Lydia opened her eyes to look at him.

'About the case?'

'About me trying to get hold of the pathologist, yes. I don't know who told her, but she wasn't best pleased.'

'Because it isn't your case?'

'That. And the fact that it isn't a case at all.'

'Right,' Lydia turned away. It wasn't her concern that the Met seemed hell-bent on filing this as unsuspicious. Good for their stats, she supposed.

'That's odd, though,' Fleet said. 'I mean, I'm in the dog house, but it still seems weirdly petty. Not something she would usually get bothered about.'

'What are you saying?'

Fleet held her gaze. 'I'm starting to come around to your way of thinking. Maybe this wasn't natural. Or even if it was, there is something going on. Something is definitely not right.'

AS THE DOORS closed on Michael Corleone and the credits began to roll, Lydia glanced at Fleet. His head was back on the sofa and his chest rose and fell gently. Jason was sitting on the floor on her other side, his back against the sofa.

'I'm not sure that helped,' Lydia said. 'He killed the heads of the other families at the end. I'm not sure mass murder is entirely practical.'

'Don't rule it out,' Jason said, glancing over his shoulder.

'You think I'm too weak?'

'No, definitely not.'

'But?'

'I think there's a different lesson. About teamwork.'

Lydia wasn't a team player, she knew that. That's why she had settled on PI as her career of choice. It meant working alone almost all of the time. Long hours sitting alone for surveillance. Not speaking to another human being for days at a time. Watching from the outside and not having to join in. Bliss. 'You think I should get closer to Aiden and the rest?'

'I don't know,' Jason said, his voice serious. 'But did you notice the heads of the family at the end when they got whacked? They got them when they were alone.'

'You really know how to ruin film night, you know?' Lydia reached down and kissed the top of Jason's cool head. 'I'm going to bed.'

'Lightweight,' Jason said, and pressed the remote to start The Godfather Part Two.

THE NEXT DAY Fleet left early for work. Lydia was still in bed when he called. 'Meet me at the park.'

Burgess Park was their place and Lydia knew she would find Fleet at the Bridge to Nowhere. What she didn't know was why he had a face like thunder. 'I thought we should speak outside,' he said, not moving to kiss her 'hello'.

'Sounds serious,' Lydia.

'Mark Kendal,' Fleet said.

Lydia waited, wondering what was coming next.

'Jesus, Lydia, you were there and you didn't even tell me.'

Ah. 'What makes you say that?'

'I asked you straight and you lied to my face.'

'What are you talking about?'

'CCTV on the street covers the front. We reviewed the footage from the day he died and will be tracing all the customers in and out that day.'

Hell Hawk. 'Am I going to be brought in?'

Fleet waited a beat, watching her. Then shook his head. 'So it was you. I wasn't sure.'

'I didn't kill him.'

'Well that's something.' Fleet rubbed a hand over his face. 'It was a quiet afternoon. Not many customers and nobody at all after four.'

Lydia had been preparing to explain why she hadn't told Fleet about finding the body, but his words derailed her. 'You thought I did it?'

'The CCTV is council-owned and we got it quickly. I watched the lot and there were a couple of weird outages. The screen goes fuzzy for a minute at four forty-six and again eight minutes later.'

'And you assumed that was me?'

'Well, I remember something similar happening to the CCTV when that Russian hitman who threatened you died in hospital. I was following a hunch that it was a Crow thing and that made me think of you... A hunch that you just confirmed.'

'Right,' Lydia said, stalling for time. 'Very smart. You really do have excellent investigative instincts.'

Fleet raised an eyebrow in a way that meant flattery was not going to help. 'That time with the Russian, I'm assuming that was your Uncle Charlie? And I figured you would have told me if it could possibly be... Wait. Is your uncle back?'

'No. Of course not.' Lydia tasted feathers at the back of her throat and felt a shiver run up her back, cold talons tapping on bone. She hoped it was just the thought of it and not a premonition.

'Right. Well that's what I thought. So, if it's not Charlie, it had to be the other powerful Crow I know.'

'You thought I might have killed that man?'

Fleet shrugged. 'If he attacked you, maybe. Or you had a really good reason. Or you'd just popped by for a friendly chat. I don't know.'

Lydia didn't know whether to be horrified or flattered. It was one thing for the good folk of Camberwell to have a healthy respect for her authority as the head of the Crows and quite another for Fleet to be so casual about her ability to murder another human being. Suspected ability. Whatever.

'Don't take it the wrong way,' Fleet said. 'I just meant that I trust your judgement. If things got violent, there was a good reason.'

'But you know that I didn't do it? You believe me?'

'Of course I believe you,' Fleet said, but his eyes slid left. Another moment. 'Would you tell me if you had? Do you trust me?'

'Of course,' Lydia said, but she wasn't sure if she was telling the truth.

CHAPTER SEVENTEEN

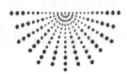

Accessing the Silver Family's final resting place definitely fell under the heading 'poor taste'. Worse than that, it was the kind of action that could start a war between the families. Or, at the very least, give Maria a reason to kill Lydia. Of course, Maria already seemed keen on that idea, so it probably wasn't going to make things any worse than they already were.

Lydia needed a wingman, someone to cause a distraction so that she could slip downstairs in the Temple Church. She had been going to ask Aiden, but she wasn't sure of his abilities. Or whether she was ready to trust him. Fleet was out for two reasons. First off, if he used his badge to gain access, it might get back to his bosses and she didn't want to make his work life any more difficult than it already was. And secondly, she was pretty sure he was still angry about the Mark Kendal lying incident. It didn't seem like the right time to ask for a dodgy favour.

The Silver Family crypt was underneath the main church, but that was all she had been able to find out online. It wasn't like they advertised how to access it.

Paul Fox was waiting outside the side entrance to the

church and he greeted her with his customary, 'Hello, Little Bird.'

Lydia nodded 'hello', not even bothering to tell Paul not to call her 'Little Bird'. She wasn't looking forward to going underground and didn't have the bandwidth for anything else. 'I don't know what to expect in there. You might need to distract the priest. Minister? Whatever. I was thinking you could ask about having a wedding and that should get him talking.'

'Is this your way of saying you've been reconsidering my proposal?' Paul's tone was teasing, but his eyes were serious.

'No,' Lydia said quickly. 'I think our alliance should remain purely platonic.'

'I don't think you mean that,' Paul said. 'You're lying to yourself.'

'I've changed my mind. I don't need your help, thank you.'

Paul held up his hands. 'Truce. I won't mention it again. Not today, anyway.'

Lydia hesitated. Now they were here, it seemed a shame not to go in together. She pushed her emotions to the side. This was business. And she didn't want Paul to have the satisfaction of thinking that he had rattled her. 'Fine. You distract whoever needs distracting and I'll find the crypt.'

'I think I should come with you,' Paul said. 'You might need a hand.'

'I don't see how we can both sneak backstage.' Lydia stopped. 'Is it called backstage in a church? That doesn't sound right.'

'You're nervous,' Paul said.

'Obviously,' Lydia said. She could feel the sharp tang of Silver just standing this close to the church. Residue from the sheer number of Silver Family gatherings on the premises, or the effect of the bodies in the crypt below her feet. Which was creepy. Lydia didn't scare easily, but the prospect of opening a coffin to look at a recently deceased Alejandro Silver was a little daunting. 'If I don't need you to run interference, I will welcome your help in the crypt. Happy?'

Paul nodded. 'Ecstatic.' He slung an arm around her shoulders as they walked through the door.

Lydia was going to object, but she guessed it would look natural if they were posing as an engaged couple. She tried her best to ignore the warmth of his body against hers, the Fox magic clouding her mind and igniting her nerve-endings.

Sunlight danced through the stained-glass windows and lit up dust motes in the air. Lydia took shallow breaths and concentrated on the incense and wood polish notes. There were a few visitors sitting in separate, silent contemplation, and a group of tourists in the round section of the church, gawping at the Templar effigies on the floor.

There was a white-robed figure at the chancel end of the building and to his left, a thick wooden door set in an arched doorway. 'Ready?' Lydia broke away from Paul and walked up the aisle, looking around as if admiring the architecture. Paul followed her and took her hand. 'Follow me,' he whispered close to her ear, his warm breath making her shiver.

Lydia had planned for Paul to approach the minister and engage him in conversation while she slipped through the door, but he seemed hellbent on ignoring that perfectly good set-up. He pulled her straight up the aisle to the chancel. They were close enough that Lydia could see the priest's white hair and thin-rimmed reading glasses. He was bent over a large book, The Bible, presumably, and didn't look up as they approached. Paul pulled her by the hand to the doorway and within a matter of seconds they were on the other side. Lydia held her breath, expecting shouting or for it to be yanked open and an irate priest to ask them what the bloody hell they thought they were playing at. Paul was moving through the chamber, which seemed to be a kind of dressing room with old hymnals piled in one corner and a rack of robes.

'How-?'

Paul shook his head. They passed through another door and found a short stone passage. At the end was a thick external-looking door and to the left was a narrow opening with a stone arch and steps leading down. It looked like something from a castle and at the same time too prosaic and accessible a route to lead to a crypt, but it was definitely the right direction so Lydia started down, holding the rough stone wall to keep her balance as the steps wound tightly downward. As they descended, Lydia felt the air getting cooler, although the chill of the stone beneath her fingertips cooled her blood further.

At the bottom of the stairs another opening led into a small stone room. An incongruously modern door was set into the far wall along with several red and white health and safety notices which warned of everything from toxic fumes to uneven flooring. A channel ran along the stone floor and disappeared under the innocuous pine door.

'How did you do that? He didn't seem to see us.'

Paul was examining the lock on the door and he looked sideways at Lydia. 'Foxes are good at not being noticed if we don't want to be.'

Lydia reached for her small roll of picks from her inside jacket pocket, but Paul already had a pick and a bump key and was working on the mechanism with an impressive focused calm. Again, she hadn't seen him move. One moment he had been studying the lock and the next he was halfway to springing it. At once, Lydia appreciated that the Fox's reputation for stealth wasn't just a way of avoiding the more overtly prejudiced term of 'sly'. The man had skills.

Behind the modern door there were more steps down

and then a short passage with a low barrel ceiling and a black iron gate. It had a lock but was hanging very slightly open which was somehow immensely creepy, like an unseen presence had just gone through. Behind this was a short flight of stone steps which then opened out into a wide vaulted passage. The air was noticeably cooler and drier down here and there was a stillness that came from being in the presence of the dead. Or it was the psychic residue of grief and religion. Lydia could taste Silver in the back of her throat and in her nasal passages and its cold, clean odour made her shiver.

They moved forward, alert and ready for the sight of tombs or shelves of coffins or whatever it was you found in ancient creepy crypts. The space was impossible to calculate, the short pillars, shadowy recesses which could lead to a new section or passage or just a dead end, confusing the eye. It looked like the start of a labyrinth, a place you could wander for days, lost. The low ceiling was a reminder of the weight of the earth above and Lydia took a deep breath to steady herself.

Paul whistled quietly. 'Is that what I think it is?'

Ahead, Lydia saw something gleaming in the semi-dark. The Silver Family cup was placed in a recess in the stone. Lydia reflexively grabbed Paul's arm, bracing herself for the onslaught of Silver she had experienced the last time she had encountered the relic. That had been in Alejandro's office when he had deliberately exposed her to the cup to gauge her reaction. She had lost her lunch on his office carpet.

Strangely, nothing happened. The base level hum of Silver remained constant, even as she moved cautiously closer.

'Sneaky bastards,' Paul said. 'I suppose they swapped it for a replica.' The Families placed their relics into the British Museum as part of the 1943 truce. The Crow Family had kept their real coins back, so they couldn't really cast stones.

'This is one, too,' Lydia said, close enough, now, to reach out a finger and touch the intricately moulded surface of the cup. 'It's a fake.'

Paul shot her a calculating look. 'How do you know?'

'I've met the real deal before,' Lydia said. 'And this is not it.'

They moved further into the crypt, finding a room with large, sealed tombs with ancient engravings, which dated back to the sixteen-hundreds. Down here, away from the elements, they were well preserved and perfectly readable. Another chamber had shelves carved into bare rock, each holding smaller sealed stone caskets. A warehouse of the important dead.

'Here,' Paul said from another section. He was temporarily obscured by a pillar. 'This is the more recent stuff. I've found Alejandro's great-grandparents.'

Lydia joined Paul next to an array of stone tombs. Each was topped with a smooth marble top, the engraving crisp and new. The last two were blank, presumably waiting for their residents to move in. Paul was leaning over another. 'Here he is,' Paul said. 'Alejandro.'

'What about Maria's mother?'

'Not here,' Paul said. 'Not that I've seen. Perhaps you have to be main bloodline to make it down here. Or she wasn't considered important enough?'

Lydia shrugged. 'I blame the patriarchy.'

The tomb was recently sealed with a line of caulking visible underneath the slight overhang of the marble top. Paul produced a chisel and a small hammer from inside his jacket and Lydia eyed him as he got onto the floor to study the seal. 'Have you done this before?'

'He'll be embalmed so there shouldn't be much odour,' Paul said. 'You ready?'

'Wait,' Lydia put a hand on his shoulder. Grave desecration. It was a big step. And seeing the fake Silver cup had given her a better idea. She put her hands onto the marble surface and closed her eyes. Nothing.

'What are you doing?'

'Feeling for him. I can sense the Family powers.'

Paul seemed to take this information in his stride. 'Even when we're dead?'

'It's much fainter, but, yeah. Especially if it was strong in life. Alejandro gave off quite the signal.'

Paul leered up at her from his reclined position on the stone floor. 'Why do I suddenly feel jealous?'

'Because you're a weirdo.' Lydia moved over to another of the caskets and placed her hands on the marble. Instantly, the background level of 'Silver' increased, like she had turned the dial on a radio. It was clear and sharp.

As an experiment, she went back to one of the oldest tombs and placed her hands on the stone. It took a few seconds of concentration, but then she felt it. A metallic taste on her tongue. She closed her eyes and felt the Silver sense intensify. She saw the warm glow of a flickering candle, reflected in the polished surface of a silver plate. There was roast meat, spilling its juices across the burnished surface, and the anticipation of a hot meal. A warm fur wrapped around her shoulders. The sound of a crackling fire.

Lydia opened her eyes and returned to the cold chamber. She felt wetness on her face and realised she was crying. She had been warm and safe and she wanted to go back to that place. It took an effort to move her hands from the stone but she managed it. Paul was behind her, his arms encircling her and she allowed herself to lean back, drawing warmth and strength from his presence. The sadness ebbed away as she came fully back to herself and the present. She was leaning back against Paul Fox, his body warm and solid against hers.

She shifted, suddenly embarrassed, and scrubbed at her cheeks with her hands. When she could trust herself to speak she said: 'Definitely Silvers in there. Doesn't matter that they've been dead for centuries, I can still feel them.'

She walked back to Alejandro's resting place and tried again. Even with her palms pressed firmly against the marble surface and her eyes shut against distractions and every part of her reaching out in the dark, all she got was a vast emptiness where Silver ought to be. There was nothing. She opened her eyes and found Paul regarding her, his eyes unreadable in the dim light. 'I would lay money that the body inside here is not a member of the Silver Family.'

Paul tilted his chin up. 'Fair bet it's not Alejandro, then?'

'I would say the chances are absolutely zero.'

CHAPTER EIGHTEEN

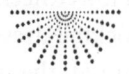

The restaurant was a modern European place just off Carnaby Street in Soho. Fleet said that a proper date ought to be somewhere different to their usual haunts and Lydia didn't disagree. Eating out in Camberwell was no longer a private affair and she could just imagine the bowing and scraping from whichever pub or restaurant she chose. Charlie had loved all of that, but it made Lydia shrink inside her skin.

Lydia had arrived on time, which was something of a miracle, but Fleet had texted to say he was running late. She crunched a breadstick, admired the colourful op-art mural which took up the entire side wall of the restaurant and tried to get herself into a date frame of mind. Which made her wonder if she had ever been on a proper date. She had had hook-ups and relationships, but never done the romantic date thing. Was that normal for the times or utterly tragic? Lydia couldn't decide.

At that moment, Paul Fox slid into the seat opposite. It was as if she had conjured her ex just by thinking about her relationship history. She was facing the main body of the restaurant but he had managed to get this close without her seeing his approach. Not for the first time, she wondered about the extent of the Fox Family powers.

'You look very nice tonight,' Paul said, getting an eyeful. 'Special occasion?'

Lydia was wearing her standard uniform of jeans, Dr Martens and a black top, although the top was thinner and silkier than usual, with a lower neckline than she wore day-to-day. It was hardly a cocktail dress. She gave him her best dead-eye stare and ignored the warm feeling that had ignited low in her stomach. It was just pheromones. Animal lust. Biology. It meant nothing.

'Sorry to crash the party,' Paul leaned back in his chair, not even pretending to look regretful.

'What do you want?'

'Straight to business, is it? No soft soap, no little dance? Not even a drink?'

Lydia waited, not speaking. She resisted the urge to look around to see if Fleet had arrived. She didn't want to show any weakness.

'He's not here,' Paul said, as irritatingly able to read her mind as ever. 'Loverboy is late. I do hope that isn't a bad sign. Are things cooling off between the two of you?'

'Leave Fleet out of it,' Lydia said. 'Do you have news for me?'

'As it happens, I do. People like to talk, and I've been doing the rounds. I heard that Alejandro Silver was in the market for a bit of credit. He needed the kind of cash you don't get from a bank.'

'I know about that,' Lydia said, relieved and disappointed in equal measure, 'but I appreciate you coming to me with it. Anything else?'

Paul smiled. 'I take it you also know about Operation Bergamot?'

Lydia kept her features neutral.

'I mean, I'm sure you do. Alejandro was observed having

cosy chats with a high-ranking officer on three occasions. It took quite a bit of persuasion and no small cost to find out he was the focus of a police operation. You'll know all about it, already, of course. It's a big deal for the Met and you've got a direct line to the police. At least, I assume that's the appeal of the DCI. Not that he isn't tall and handsome.'

Paul's gaze flicked over her shoulder. 'Speak of the devil.'

Fleet was wearing a dark wool coat with a three-piece suit underneath. He looked like a grown-up with a proper job and a pension plan. Which Lydia found extremely hot. Next to Fleet, Paul looked even more like a thug from the wrong side of the tracks. Which Lydia also found extremely hot. Both men were sizing each other up like they wanted to get physical. Which was complicated. And, right now, she was battling the urge to throw her drink at Fleet. Also complicated.

She stood up and kissed Fleet on the cheek, refusing to give Paul Fox the satisfaction of seeing that he had her rattled. 'Paul was just leaving. He brought us some information about Alejandro so we're very grateful.' To Paul she said: 'Thank you. I owe you one.'

He didn't take the hint to leave, watching Fleet carefully instead as he spoke. 'I was just telling Lydia about Operation Bergamot. I was surprised she didn't already know about it.'

Fleet visibly flinched and Lydia felt it like a blow to the stomach.

'Yeah, I thought as much. Makes me wonder how much she can trust you.' Paul leaned into Lydia and spoke close to her ear. 'Watch out for him.'

'Have a nice evening,' Lydia said. 'Give my regards to your brothers. I hope they're keeping the aggravated assaults to a bare minimum.'

Paul bared his teeth. 'We've paid for that.'

'Thank you for stopping by,' Fleet said, slinging a protective arm around Lydia's shoulders. She moved away and took her seat. When she chanced a look at Paul, he was back in laconic mode, a smile playing on his lips. She hated to think what conclusions he was busy drawing behind that relaxed exterior.

'Well, good night, kids. Don't stay up too late. You're both out of your territory, here.'

'Is that a threat?' Fleet was still standing and Lydia could see tension written into every muscle.

'Of course not, DCI Fleet,' Paul said, emphasis on the DCI. 'But you might want to think about being more honest with your girlfriend. She's too smart to stay with a liar for long.' Paul didn't look at Lydia again, just stared at Fleet for a beat. When Fleet didn't respond, he nodded like it was exactly the response he expected and he was perfectly satisfied, then turned on his heel and left.

Fleet sat down, shooting the cuffs of his shirt and folding his hands on the table. 'You want to tell me why Paul Fox is joining our dates, now?'

'Really?' Lydia dug her fingernails into her palm to stop herself from raising her voice. 'That's what you want to lead with?'

'What?' Fleet's brows lowered.

'Operation Bergamot.'

He had the decency to look abashed. 'I was going to tell you about that tonight.'

'Before or after dinner?'

'After, ideally. This is supposed to be us having a normal evening like a normal couple.'

'We're not a normal couple,' Lydia said, standing up. 'I'm not normal.'

'Don't be like that.' Fleet was frowning in earnest, now, and he wasn't able to keep the frustration out of his voice.

'I'm going home,' Lydia said. 'I'm not hungry, anyway.'

. . .

THE NEXT MORNING Lydia found herself wide awake before six, watching the patterns of light on her bedroom ceiling. She got up and dressed in stretchy clothes on the basis that walking wasn't going to be enough to release the tension she felt and she was going to have to try running. The situation was truly drastic.

Outside The Fork the street was deserted. The line of parked cars were damp with dew and Lydia stretched before setting off at a brisk walk, arms swinging to warm up. She was so intent on moving that it was a second before her conscious mind caught up with an anomaly that her unconscious instincts had logged. One of the cars wasn't covered in condensation. Which mean that it was warm.

She didn't break stride, continuing to the corner at the end of the street without looking around. Once around the corner, she stopped and waited. A moment later a man appeared. He flicked a glance at Lydia and then continued past. He was wearing a suit and Lydia got the very slightest feeling of motion sickness as he passed. 'Good effort,' Lydia said. 'But you were too hasty to follow.'

The man stopped. 'Excuse me?'

'You've been made,' Lydia said. 'Don't waste my time. Call your boss and tell him I want a word.'

The man feigned confusion very convincingly and if Lydia hadn't been able to catch the faint trace of salted sea air that meant he had been in recent contact with Mr Smith, Lydia might have started to doubt her instincts. 'I still have his number so I can call him. Or I can go to the safe house near his office. I'm giving you the chance to take control of the situation and save a little face. If you're very quick, I might not even tell him I spotted your follow.'

The man glowered and pulled out a phone. He thumbed a text and then walked away.

The Mercedes pulled up silently. Even if Lydia hadn't recognised it as Mr Smith's, she would have guessed 'spy' or 'top-level arms dealer'. The back door opened and she got in.

Mr Smith looked the same. His signature was the same, too, and with mere seconds to prepare for it, Lydia was battling a wave of motion sickness as she settled into the leather seat.

'You look well,' Mr Smith said.

'I thought we were done.' Lydia felt the urge to ask after Charlie and she held her breath until she had it under control.

Mr Smith inclined his head slightly. 'This is something new.'

'I can't help you,' Lydia said. She looked him in the eye. 'I won't help you. So you can stop having me followed. It's a waste of your precious resources.'

'This isn't about you helping me,' Mr Smith said. 'Very much the opposite.'

'Is that right?'

'I'm keeping you under surveillance for your own protection.'

'I doubt that,' Lydia said.

'Wouldn't you like people to know that you didn't kill Alejandro Silver?'

'He's not dead,' Lydia said and enjoyed the look of surprise on Mr Smith's face. It confirmed her suspicion that Alejandro's body hadn't simply been moved elsewhere. 'Something you already knew, of course.'

He smoothed his expression quickly. 'What makes you say that?'

'He isn't in the crypt. And I'm guessing the whole performance is something to do with Operation Bergamot.'

'Ah,' he said, his eyes widening just a small amount at her use of 'Bergamot'. The police database spewed out random words to assign to operations and there was no way she would have been able to guess it or work it out. 'I assume your DCI spilled the beans. Very careless of him. Very unprofessional.'

Lydia ignored the stab of emotion that elicited. Mr Smith wanted her to accept his help, to rely on him, and she would use that to keep him talking. 'I assume the pathologist won't be coming back from his holiday. Unless the trip was part of a bribe? And you must have had a spare body. Swapped in the ambulance? Were the paramedics your employees or was that some more bribery? I saw the corpse in the mortuary and it looked exactly like Alejandro. That's impressive.'

Mr Smith smiled. 'The perks of government work. Ample resources.'

'And he's in hiding now? What from?'

'There was a SOCA operation which was focused on political corruption. Alejandro Silver got swept up in it after his astonishing rise.'

Serious and Organised Crime weren't part of the Met, but they worked together. The fear that Fleet had been keeping information about the Alejandro case from her rose in her throat. 'Swept up how?'

'He had help, obviously, but where the cash came from for that help and who exactly benefited was of interest. Alejandro didn't want a scandal. It would damage his family's reputation, harm their firm, and, besides, he wasn't keen on being dragged through court on the other side of the dock.'

'Can't say I blame him.'

'SOCA offered immunity. Witness protection.'

Lydia snorted. She couldn't imagine Alejandro hiding. What would they do? Set him up with a warehouse job and a little terraced house somewhere up north? Call him Nigel and give him a Ford Focus and a membership to the local leisure centre. No.

'In exchange, he had to gather evidence against the

people who had helped him. That's where I came in.'

Lydia stopped trying to picture Alejandro out of London living a normal life and focused on Mr Smith. 'Why?'

'SOCA was interested in political links to arms dealers and drug barons, very bad people Interpol have been chasing around the globe, and they found Alejandro because of a suspicious death in Greece which was linked to a known assassin.'

'The MP,' Lydia said. 'Nadine Gormley.'

'Exactly so,' Mr Smith said. 'But that turned out to be by-the-by.'

'How so?'

'Alejandro Silver wasn't being bankrolled by someone on Interpol's list. He had been to our old friends JRB for help.'

That brought up several questions, but Lydia settled on, 'How do you know that?'

He glanced down, picked an imaginary piece of lint off his immaculate suit, and offered something else. 'You once said to me that you thought JRB were trying to stir up trouble between the Families.'

'There have always been people who would like to see the Families destroy each other. Either because they fear us or because of the potential reward.'

'A war would have casualties, but it would leave bounty strewn across London, just waiting for somebody else to step in and collect. There have always been those who live from the flotsam of wrecks. I'm interested in the ones that tinker with the lighthouse.'

Lydia followed the metaphor, but wished he would stop talking about the sea. It made her nausea worse. She thought she could hear gulls and the sound of waves crashing. Mr Smith was watching her closely, like he knew she was feeling unwell. It struck Lydia that he may have learned a great deal from Charlie by this point. That he probably knew exactly the effect he was having.

'They don't even need to be destroyed,' he continued. 'Just mistrustful of each other, killing each other one at a time. It makes them vulnerable, open to infiltration and deals from outside agencies.'

Lydia glared at him. 'Something you have already taken advantage of.'

He smiled and Lydia felt her body lurch as if the deck she was standing on had lurched with the roll of a big wave. Not a deck. Not a boat, she reminded herself. She was in a car.

'I am here for you,' he said. 'I have no wish to see you destroyed by Maria Silver.'

'We just established that Alejandro is still alive.'

'And who else believes that? Unless he turns up and does a little dance in Trafalgar Square, you and your Family are chief suspects in his death.'

Lydia didn't reply.

'I can protect you. You are vulnerable and everybody knows it, it's only a matter of time before one of the other Families makes a move on you. Or perhaps the threat will come from within. You just don't have Charlie's killer instinct and everybody knows it. You've seen what my department can do. Let me help you. I don't want to see you harmed.'

'Because you're hoping to use me as an asset in the future.' Lydia couldn't keep the bitterness out of her voice.

'That's part of it, of course,' Mr Smith said. 'My motives aren't really important at this point, though, are they?'

He was right. Lydia had bigger problems and if he was offering to help with one of the biggest, she would be a fool to turn him down. She felt chased down, though. Hemmed in. And that made her cranky. Plus, she had never fancied herself as particularly clever. 'I'll handle Maria Silver on my own. Tell your goons to stop following me. We made a deal and now I'm out. I'm not Alejandro or Charlie and I won't be your puppet.'

CHAPTER NINETEEN

Lydia stood on the pavement and watched the Mercedes peel away. She had the sinking feeling that she had just rejected an offer she couldn't afford to refuse. She turned back to The Fork, trying to stop her thoughts from spiralling downward. She hated that Mr Smith was getting under her skin. He was playing mind games, calling her weak because he wanted her to react, to put her faith in him. Somehow knowing that it was a strategy didn't make it less effective. She was afraid that there was truth to his words. Maybe she couldn't protect her Family, let alone the people of Camberwell?

Refusing to wallow, Lydia paused by the entrance and dialled Ash. She would check in on him. If she could prove she had truly saved Ash, maybe she wasn't a lost cause. And if the Pearls were still watching her, she should show them that she was still keeping an eye on Ash.

It wasn't a promising start. Lydia met Ash at one of the benches on Camberwell Green and he looked just as thin and jumpy as the last time she had seen him. He was clearly still struggling to eat and she would lay money that he was hardly sleeping, either. Jason had been making hot chocolate again, and Lydia had decanted it into two travel mugs. She passed one to Ash and wondered if this was anything close to the way Emma must feel all the time. The worry and responsibility for another human life. The gnawing sense that she should be able to fix him if only she tried harder.

'Thank you for meeting me,' she began, but Ash waved a hand. He was staring at a girl who was running to pick up a fallen soft toy from the path. She had a passing resemblance to the Pearl girl who had been following Lydia, but the similarity was broken when she skipped back to her mum and older brother.

'What do you need?' Ash said, still watching the family.

'I just wanted to check on you. How are you doing?'

Ash twitched. 'I've been in the library. Catching up on the news from the last twenty years. I thought it might distract me.'

'Has it?'

'I still miss them. Have you heard anything? Are you here because they have taken somebody?' He looked at Lydia and his expression was a strange mix of hope and revulsion.

'Not as far as I know. Have you tried to contact them again?'

He shook his head. 'Not really. Only in my dreams.'

Well that was creepy. 'Have you remembered more about your time underground?' She felt bad using Ash for information, but she had to protect her Family and the more she knew about the Pearls the better. Especially since they didn't seem to have forgotten about her. 'Is that okay? I know it might be hard...'

'I don't mind,' Ash said, shrugging. 'I want to talk about them, it feels the most real thing in my life and I can't talk to anybody else about it. Obviously.'

His eyes had lit up and Lydia hoped he was going to manage to stay calm.

'The king suggested they were trapped underground and

I know they use kids as their eyes and ears aboveground. I wondered if that tallied with your experience? Do you remember any of them ever leaving? Did they talk about being trapped?'

Ash had wrapped his hands around the travel mug. 'Time was weird, as you know, but they were always in the court.' His face scrunched in concentration for a moment and then he shook his head. 'No. They never left to my knowledge. The king, anyway, I can't be sure about every single Pearl.'

'That's helpful, thank you,' Lydia said.

Ash was staring into space. 'I don't think they left. They were content. Happy.'

'That's-'

'They didn't talk about mundane matters,' Ash broke in. 'I sort of forgot about all of this, honestly.'

'All of what?'

'The world. London. Normal life.'

LYDIA WALKED WITH ASH, wanting to check that he really was okay after talking about the Pearls. He said that he was heading to an appointment with an acupuncturist, 'mum and dad are getting desperate', but that he was attending the outpatients clinic at the Maudsley every week, too. Lydia was glad he was still getting help, but her heart clenched at the size of the problem.

'I know I'm not stable,' he said, glancing at her. 'I'm not so far gone that I don't know that. I know I can't keep going to the woods. I'm hoping they'll put me back on the antipsychotics. The antidepressants just aren't enough. They don't touch it. The feelings.'

Ash was speaking more quickly, now, and Lydia could see he was getting agitated.

'I can't stop thinking about them. I can't stop missing them. I just feel like I've been hollowed out, you know?'

'I know,' Lydia said, steering him across the main road. 'It'll get better, you've got to give it time.'

They took the cut-through road, Medlar Street, and walked under the railway and past an unwelcoming carpark with rolls of barbed wire. There was a cold wind, reminding Lydia that winter hadn't entirely given way to spring, and she zipped up her jacket. At that moment, Ash stopped speaking and stood stock still. He let out a strangled noise and fell to the ground. The colour fled from his cheeks, leaving him cadaverous and blue-lipped. His eyes were wide open and terrified. He seemed conscious but he clearly wasn't breathing. Kneeling on the cold pavement, Lydia hoisted his upper half onto her lap, cradling his head and calling his name. 'Breathe, Ash,' she said. 'Take a breath.'

She could feel Pearl magic pouring off him and looked around automatically. They were alone and Ash still hadn't taken a breath. How long could you go without oxygen before brain damage set in? First aid training told her to lie him down, tilt his chin back and breathe air into his lungs. Crow training told her that she had to fight the Pearl mojo or no amount of CPR was going to help. 'Ash, you're okay, they can't hurt you. Breathe, Ash.' She kept saying his name, trying to calm his panic. His eyes rolled back, so all she could see was the whites and then they closed.

Lydia leaned down and whispered into his ear. 'Leave him alone.'

She could hear trees rustling, wind blowing through branches and leaves even though there were none nearby. It sounded like laughter. 'Stop it,' she said out loud.

She could see the trees, now. They were twisted and strange-looking, laden with brown-cased fruit and the sweet smell of rot filled her nostrils, obliterating the clean scent of pearls. Lydia closed her eyes and reached out in the darkness. She could hear wings beating, but they were faint and far away. The trees were loud and creaking. Roots were running underneath the earth, below the paving slabs and concrete and the rubble of old buildings. Ancient roots which still connected, roots which still remembered.

Her coin was between her fingers and, following her instincts and with her eyes tightly shut, she felt for Ash's face and forced his mouth open, putting the coin on his tongue. Immediately his head jerked and he took an enormous breath, like a man surfacing from deep water. Lydia's eyes flew open. 'Don't swallow it,' she said, hoping it wasn't too late. Ash's eyelids fluttered and then closed again. He dragged in heaving breaths and on one of the exhales her coin dropped out into her waiting palm.

With her eyes open, Lydia could see the trees, again. They were translucent and ghostly, overlaid on the pavement and buildings and parked cars of the side street and they fanned the flames of panic which were licking at the edges of her mind, clouding her thoughts and making her heart race. She was surrounded by trees. She hadn't walked into the dark forest, but the Pearls had sent the forest to her. She focused on Ash's face, trying to block out the sound of wood creaking and leaves moving. 'We need to move,' she said. 'Now.'

Ash's eyes opened and he looked at her with a strange expression. It was his face, but suddenly looked nothing like Ash. The fine muscles around his eyes and mouth had settled into something unfamiliar. Something mocking. A second before he spoke, Lydia realised who had taken possession of Ash. The Pearl King. The words were definitely not Ash's.

'Do you know where you are, child?'

'I'm in my manor,' Lydia said, staring deep into Ash's eyes. She wanted the creature who was looking back to feel her gaze. 'Camberwell is the Crows' roost and you are not welcome here.'

'This was once an orchard.' Ash's voice sounded different. His vocal cords, the king's intonation and accent. 'Medlar trees as far as the eye could see. Do you know this fruit? The medlar. It is well-named for you, I think. Very appropriate. You are a meddler, Lydia Crow, and we tire of your interference.'

The sound of creaking tree branches, rustling leaves, and buds bursting into blossom was getting louder by the second. Lydia ignored it all and kept her focus on Ash's face. 'Why don't you talk to me in person? This,' she indicated Ash's prone body, 'is beneath your dignity.'

'This boy is my servant and I will use him however I choose, whenever I choose.'

'No need to be tetchy,' Lydia said, trying to annoy the king. If she could annoy the king, she could distract the king and maybe that would give her an opening. At the same time, she was trying to reach out for the sound of wings, a thousand tiny hearts beating, the feel of a warm air current lifting her up. It was difficult while blind terror threatened to engulf her, and Ash's face grew ever-paler, but she tried. She pictured black wings closing over their bodies, shielding them and squeezed her coin in one hand, focusing her energy. There were vibrations in the air and Lydia felt a warmth around her, as if a shelter had cut the cool breeze.

Ash was still white, though, and gasping for breath. His face was still wrong, his expression not his own. Lydia felt a surge of hate for the king and she pushed, trying to usurp the presence that was squatting inside Ash or using him as their own personal puppet. The voice, which was stronger than ought to have been possible from Ash's weakened body, said: 'You were warned. You must not speak of us.'

Ash began to cry and Lydia knew he had returned to himself. The shelter she had pulled over them, formed of invisible wings, was holding back the trees which still reached out twisted branches, but she could sense the roots underneath the ground rising. They had to move. She wasn't going to be able to protect them for much longer.

Lydia forced herself up and pulled Ash to his feet. 'Come on,' she said, towing him for a few paces before he found his feet and began to run with her. They stumbled down the street, dodging the ghostly trees. Lydia tried to keep her balance while holding onto Ash and concentrating to keep the wings closed around them like armour. There was a single stunted trunk growing from a square space in the pavement and it took Lydia a second to realize that it was a real tree and not one of the ghosts brought back by the king. A remnant of the orchard which had once stood here. Lydia paused and closed her eyes, bringing the Crow energy into the front of her mind and then down her arms and into her fingers. She let her anger over Ash's treatment and her fear for him rise up, and then she imagined the king was standing in place of the twisted piece of ancient wood. Her hands were either very hot or very cold, she could not tell. There was a burning sensation which quickly turned to a numbness. She touched the tree, letting the feeling flow out of her fingers. It burst into flames.

The ghost trees vanished in an instant. The rustle of leaves and creaking of branches disappeared and the sounds of the city flooded back. A siren wailed in the distance, like the siren call of home. Lydia and Ash walked out of Medlar Street, breathing hard, and joined the parade of shops and barbers and cafes and the people crowding the pavement. A man was playing steel drums with a hat on the floor and a sign which said, optimistically, 'thank you', and a pit bull on a lead trotted over to sniff at Lydia's leg. Some people might hark to the good old days, when Camberwell was a bucolic idyll with fields stretching as far as the eye could see and orchards thick with sticky fruit, but, on balance, Lydia preferred this version. Still, they needed to get off the streets.

. . .

LUCKILY, The Fork wasn't far and they made it without further incident. Ash's colour was better and he made it up the stairs to the flat in good time, despite seeming to be unable to stop saying 'I'm sorry' in a low monotone.

'Just a bit further,' Lydia said, chivvying him all the way. 'Keep going, almost there.'

Not a natural cheerleader, Lydia felt exhausted from the strain of staying calm. The Pearl King had reached out and manipulated Ash as easily as slipping on a coat. Lydia knew how it felt to have another soul inside herself having given Jason a lift on numerous occasions. It wasn't pleasant. The thought of that soul taking over was unbearable. Lydia was preoccupied with these thoughts and it took her a second to realize that Ash had stopped his quiet chant. She turned in time to see him move suddenly and violently, knocking her to the floor and sitting on her chest, knees pinning her shoulders. His hands wrapped around her throat and his eyes rolled back in his head, showing all white.

The Crow energy was there without her having to think and she used it to throw Ash off, swivelling as he fell to the side and reversing their positions. 'Stop it,' she said, pinning him in place. One arm got free and went straight for her neck in a jabbing blow she only just avoided. 'Stop!'

His body was jerking, straining to throw her. Lydia wasn't sure how long she could hold him in place, even with the Crow power flowing and his emaciated frame. He was being powered by something older and stronger than them both. A connection from far beneath the earth in the Pearl Court. 'Sod it,' Lydia said and punched Ash in the side of the head.

CHAPTER TWENTY

Lydia used duct tape to secure Ash to the chair she usually used for clients. It was a basic upright and her main concern was that he would tip it and break something if he decided to struggle. He was still woozy from the punch to the head and she was getting seriously worried that he had a concussion. How did you know how hard to hit a person? How much was too much? When to stop? Cursing Charlie for not giving her training in the elements that really matter, Lydia held a cold flannel to the back of Ash's neck.

His eyes fluttered open. 'Lydia?'

'I'm sorry I had to hit you,' Lydia said. 'You weren't going to stop.'

'Did I hurt you?' The shadows under Ash's eyes were darker than ever, his skin so pale it was translucent and she could see the veins underneath. His voice was just a quiet croak.

'What the hell is going on?' Jason appeared next to Lydia and she dropped the duct tape. It landed on its edge and rolled underneath the desk.

'Not now,' Lydia said, careful not to look in Jason's direction. Ash seemed pretty out of it but Lydia didn't want to alarm him any further by talking to a ghost.

'What happened to him?' Jason stared at Ash with naked horror. 'He looks half-dead. And are you into kinky stuff, now?'

'I'm going to sort this out,' Lydia said, leaning down and looking into Ash's eyes. 'Everything is going to be okay. I'm sorry I've restrained you. It's for your own protection. Now that we know the king can speak and act through your body, we can't take any chances.' She turned away, glancing at Jason as she moved to check that he had understood.

'Holy shit,' Jason said. 'They can do that? Use a human being like a glove puppet.'

'Apparently,' Lydia said, still not looking properly at Jason. She focused on Ash. 'Can you feel them now?'

Ash closed his eyes, his brow creasing. 'No.'

'Good,' Lydia wiped his face with the flannel. 'You thirsty?'

She moved away to get a glass of water, Jason following. 'What are you going to do?'

'I don't know,' Lydia said quietly, filling the glass. 'He needs to eat and drink and rest. He's exhausted and probably concussed.'

'Where's Fleet?'

'At work. And he doesn't need to know about this until later. I need to get things under control first.'

'He could help. You shouldn't be alone. What if Ash gets free? Tries to hurt you again?'

'Fleet shouldn't be a party to this. He's still police.'

'Lydia,' Jason said. 'Don't be stubborn. You don't have to do everything on your own.'

'I'm not on my own,' she said, smiling at Jason. 'I've got you.'

Back in the office, Ash was as slumped as it was possible for a man to be while firmly taped to an upright chair. She had wound the tape around his chest for extra security and it gave him the unfortunate appearance of Hannibal Lecter strapped to the trolley in a strait jacket.

'Water,' Lydia said. 'Take it slowly.'

Ash lifted his head slowly, as if it physically hurt. His eyes rolled, the whites showing, but then he seemed to focus. Lydia bent down and held the glass to his lips, tilting it so that he could drink. Ash's mouth stretched in a wide smile which looked all wrong. Before Lydia could react, he had bitten down on the glass. It broke and blood spurted from his cut lips. Lydia jerked back as Ash snapped at her, blood flowing. It wasn't Ash looking through the hazel eyes. He crunched the glass, his jaws moving methodically. His Adam's apple bobbed as he swallowed the mouthful of glass.

Lydia's throat had gone dry with fear but she managed to speak. 'If you hurt him, I won't answer your questions.'

Ash grinned, the blood flowing faster as his mouth stretched, opening the wounds. 'What makes you think I have questions for you, child?'

'What else could you want?' Lydia tried to modulate her voice, to sound reasonable. She had to get the king onside before he hurt Ash any further. 'I want a truce. No more watching me, no more intimidation. If you kill me, another Crow will take over and, honestly, I'm the most reasonable one in the Family. Besides, there'll be a whole blood vendetta thing. Eye for an eye and all that. Let's come to a mutually beneficial agreement now.'

'Agreement?' The king spoke in a tone of genuine confusion. Lydia didn't know if that was because they didn't know the word or because they couldn't believe a mere human would dare to use it.

'One leader to another.'

Ash's bloodied lips curled in disgust. 'I do not recognise your authority.'

Okay. Lydia swallowed. Tried a different tack. 'I am aware that I disrespected you and I regret my actions.'

The King, through Ash, laughed and Lydia fought the urge to be sick. The sound was otherworldly and it made every part of Lydia want to curl up in safe space far, far away. 'I imagine that's true.'

'But I can offer you a gift in recompense for my part in the loss of your latest guest.'

'A new toy?' Ash's eyes gleamed.

'Yes. In exchange for a conversation. If we pool our knowledge, it will be mutually advantageous. We have a common enemy, I believe.'

'I find that hard to believe,' the king said. Despite using Ash's vocal cords and mouth, the king's voice was recognisable. At least it was to Lydia, who could feel the Pearl magic flowing with every sound.

'Until recently I was being blackmailed by a government department and I wondered if you or a member of your family might be having a similar problem.'

'These are the concerns of the upper world. They are not mine.'

She tried a different tack. 'Alejandro Silver isn't really dead. He made some sort of deal with JRB, but—'

Ash's face went slack and Lydia thought that king had severed their connection. Then a thin hiss escaped his lips. 'You are unwise to mention that name in my presence.'

'I mean no disrespect, your majesty.' Deference did not come naturally to Lydia, but she was willing to try.

'What is the gift you offer?'

Lydia didn't look at Jason, couldn't bear to see the shock she knew would follow her words. 'Ash. I will bring him to you. Or you can bring him yourself, I guess. But I will smooth his disappearance with the police. I won't come looking.'

Ash's expression changed. It appeared they were thinking, and when Ash spoke it was still with the regal intonation of the Pearl King. 'I believe my small friend told you this once. I like dead things.'

Ash's head twisted and there was a loud crack.

Lydia stumbled back, dimly aware of panicked swearing from a horrified Jason. Lydia forced herself into action and felt for a pulse on Ash's neck. There wasn't one.

'I should call an ambulance,' Lydia said. 'Do CPR.' She began pulling at the tape around his chest. She needed to get Ash onto the floor to do CPR.

'Too late,' Jason said. 'He's gone.'

Lydia knew he was right. Ash was utterly still. And the crack that she had heard, with the unnatural angle of his neck. He was dead. He had been killed. Instantly.

'What are we going to do?'

'You're right. He's gone.'

'But this is our home,' Jason said. 'He's in our home, taped to a chair.' If he needed to breathe, Jason would be hyperventilating. As it was, he was floating a foot above the carpet and vibrating.

'Stay calm,' Lydia grabbed his arm and squeezed, trying to anchor Jason in the room.

'I can't believe how quickly... He was alive just a moment ago. He was talking.'

'Can you see him?' Lydia said as the thought struck her. 'His spirit?'

Jason shook his head. 'He's not here. There's nothing. He's just gone. One moment he was here and the next moment...'

'It's okay,' Lydia said, swallowing her nausea. 'Why don't you put the kettle on.'

'What about the police?'

'I'm going to sort it,' she patted Jason's arm. 'I need a tea. For the shock.'

Jason's vibrating marginally eased as he visibly pulled himself together. 'Of course. Right. I'll do that.'

As soon as Jason moved into the kitchen, she picked up her mobile from her desk.

'Yo, boss.' Aiden answered with his customary enthusiasm.

Lydia was unable to tear her gaze from Ash's lolling head so she turned away. That was worse, it was as if she could feel the dead man looking at her, could imagine his head lifting on its broken neck and the mouth opening. She turned to face the chair again, her eyes pricking with tears at the sight of Ash's lifeless body.

'I've got a small problem.'

AIDEN'S INFORMATION turned out to be very good. Two women wearing pink tabards emblazoned with 'Claire's Cleaning' logos, arrived thirty minutes later. 'You should go out,' one of them said, without preamble.

'I'd rather stay,' Lydia said, not even sure if that was true.

The woman shrugged. 'You're the boss, but the chemicals are very strong.'

Part of Lydia's mind had been trying to work out how they were going to get a body out of her flat without attracting attention. Not to mention manoeuvre a grown man, admittedly a very thin one, when they were about the same height as Lydia. One of the women was built like an Olympic wrestler, but still. Bodies were heavy when they were dead.

Her phone rang. Aiden. 'We should talk. I'm downstairs.'

The women had little wheelie suitcases, matching the pink of their tabards. One of the them unzipped hers and pulled out folded plastic sheeting which they began to lay out on the floor. At once, Lydia decided that delegation was a very important skill. 'I'll leave you to it,' she muttered, backing to the door.

'Three hours,' the first woman said.

LYDIA DIDN'T GO FAR. She felt a strange pull to be nearby while Ash's mortal remains were being handled. She owed him that much. Downstairs in The Fork, she took one of the paperback books from the free shelf and sat at her usual table. Moments later, Angel arrived at the table. Today, her dreads were tied up behind a bright pink scarf and she was only sixty-per-cent managing to conceal her habitual scowl. Since Lydia had taken over in Charlie's place, Angel was clearly trying to be less surly, but old habits died hard. Truth be known, Lydia didn't want her to change. But she couldn't work out how to tell Angel that without losing face. She was pretty sure Angel would lose any respect for her whatsoever if she tried. While it was nice not having to pay for food and coffee and having Angel appear when summoned, Lydia felt an ache at the formality that existed between them now. 'Coffee, please,' Lydia said. She added a sandwich to the order, although she wasn't hungry in the slightest. 'And if anybody asks, I've been here all morning. Spread the word.'

'Is someone going to ask?'

Lydia held her gaze until Angel looked away. 'Coffee coming up. You want that sandwich toasted?'

Alibi in place, Lydia tried to read the book she had picked up. A fat airport thriller with dog-eared pages and a tattered front cover. She sipped her coffee and read the same page several times, picking at the cheese toastie and forcing herself to chew and swallow. Ash's lifeless body, his neck cruelly twisted and his eyes wide and unseeing, kept leapfrogging to the front of her mind. It was an image that wouldn't stay away, no matter how many times she shoved it back into the darkness. Something Charlie had said to her once played in a loop: 'You try to save everyone, you save no one.' She couldn't protect Ash from the Pearls. They felt impunity to reach into her home and kill a man in front of her. She hadn't protected Mark Kendal, a man who ought to be untouchable under the protection of the mighty Crows. Her closest ally, the man who shared her bed, was keeping secrets, and her own family questioned her methods and strategy. Maybe Mr Smith was right. Maybe she was too weak to be the head of the Family.

CHAPTER TWENTY-ONE

That night, Lydia switched off her phone. Fleet had messaged, asking to talk, but she felt physically and emotionally wrecked. The flat was immaculately clean with no sign of the duct tape, any kind of struggle or Ash himself. The air was thick with pine-scented bleach and the synthetic floral of air freshener. Lydia opened the windows and stripped, putting every item of clothing into the washing machine. Then she took a long shower, scrubbing at her skin and underneath her nails. She didn't want to be in the flat but she didn't want to be anywhere else, either. She checked on Jason, who looked as upset as she was. 'How could they do that?' he asked, eyes hollow.

She didn't know if he meant morally or physically or both. 'I don't know. Are you all right?'

Jason shrugged, his outline vibrating slightly. 'Not really. But at least he's at peace, now. He's not here.'

That was something, Lydia supposed. Just not enough.

THE NEXT DAY, Lydia got up early. Her first thought was to start the day with a slug of whisky, something she had been pretty good at not doing for the last few months. With great reluctance, she decided to make another attempt at running, instead. She laced up her trainers and headed out into a damp spring morning. It was a half-hearted effort with Lydia's whole body feeling heavier than usual. She slowed as she approached home, the same dark thoughts swirling. Fleet was waiting for her outside the cafe. She was sweaty, thirsty and not in the mood for more lies. 'We're not open yet.'

'Can we talk?'

He looked wretched and Lydia felt a clutch of empathy. Still. She couldn't shake the fear that she couldn't trust him. He was police. She was the head of the Crows. It was a conflict that couldn't be resolved.

'Please,' Fleet said. 'Can we go upstairs?'

LYDIA WENT into the flat first, making plenty of noise to warn Jason. She downed a glass of water standing at the kitchen sink and refilled it before joining Fleet in the office. He was standing in the middle of the room, looking worried and absolutely exhausted.

Lydia wondered if he had slept at all and then she reminded herself that she didn't care. She leaned against her desk and crossed her arms. 'I've been very slow on the uptake. In my defence, I've always had a blind spot when it comes to you.'

'What are you talking about?'

'Did they offer you a deal?'

'Who?' Fleet looked mystified, but Lydia knew he was a good liar. He was police, after all, and it was part of the training.

'Your boss. Or your boss's boss. Was it for a promotion or more casework or a better salary? I hope it was all three.'

'What Paul said...' Fleet began. 'I only found out that day.

I was going to tell you at the restaurant but he got there first. I swear. He knew more than I did, too. I was only given the bare minimum. You know I'm not flavour of the month with the top brass.'

Lydia wanted to believe Fleet, but she also knew that was part of the problem. She couldn't afford mistakes any more. The stakes were too high to risk trusting the wrong person and, there and then, she realised she would have to go back to her old habit of not trusting anybody at all. That was fine. 'What did they tell you?'

'That there's a task force looking at organised crime. It's been focusing on the Silver Family since last year when Alejandro first started to make a move into politics. I think he made a few bigwigs nervous and they put the pressure on and that filtered down through management. You know how it works.'

'Sure,' Lydia said.

'I didn't know,' Fleet said, again.

'Why did they tell you about it? Are you part of it?'

'Not part of it. They did have questions, though. About Maria Silver. And you.'

'What did you tell them?'

'Only what they already know. Your history with Maria. They have the details from the Yas Bishop case, but I gave them the truth so that they know what she's capable of.'

Maria had killed Yas Bishop, one of the only people linked to JRB, and Lydia had made sure she had been jailed for it. Unfortunately, the conviction hadn't stuck.

'Who is running the operation? Did they believe you?'

Fleet shrugged. 'Kate Harmon. Haven't encountered her before and she wasn't giving anything away.'

'Does that mean you're under suspicion, too?'

'I don't think so,' Fleet said. 'She's just doing her job. We're not really supposed to talk about open cases, not even with other police, unless we're part of the team. You have to put in a request for information through the system.'

'Coppers talk though, right?'

Fleet smiled tightly. 'Right.'

Lydia thought for a moment longer. Fleet reached for her and she stepped away, wanting to keep a clear head.

'You have to believe me,' Fleet said. 'I had no idea until yesterday. I would have told you.'

Lydia looked at him properly. He looked anguished and his eyes telegraphed sincerity. But the doubt remained.

'I chose you,' he was saying. 'I'm on your side first. I swear.' His eyes lit up with an idea. 'Use your power on me.'

'What?'

'I've seen you ask questions. People go all glazed and they answer you. Do that to me. Then you'll know I'm telling the truth.'

Lydia was already shaking her head. 'I wouldn't do that to you. I don't...'

'I want you to do it,' Fleet took her hands, ducking his head to look directly into her eyes. 'I need you to trust me and we're both old enough and experienced enough to know that sometimes trust needs hard proof. I let you down before and I swore to you that I would never do that again. I know that's true, but you don't. I'll prove it to you every day for the rest of my life if you'll let me, but this way is quicker.'

Lydia hesitated for another moment and then nodded her head. She wanted to trust Fleet and he was right, this was a shortcut to that trust. The fact that he was willing for her to use her power on him was almost enough to banish every last scrap of doubt. Almost wasn't going to cut it, though.

She pulled her hands away and produced her coin, making it hover in the air between their bodies. Fleet's eyes widened slightly but he didn't move away. 'Look into my eyes.'

'Is that important?' Fleet said, doing as he was told.

'It's quicker,' Lydia said, wondering why he didn't have the glazed obedience she expected. She pushed a bit of Crow whammy behind her next words. 'Stand on one leg.'

Fleet's lips quirked up at the corners. 'Are you messing with me?'

Well, that *was* odd. The unusual gleam that she had sensed from Fleet when they first met was just part of him, now. Just as familiar and reassuring as his brown eyes and the deep timbre of his voice. Which was probably why it took a moment longer than it ought to have for Lydia to realise that it was getting stronger.

She could hear waves on sand, wind blowing through palm leaves and taste salt on her lips. Lydia blinked, trying to clear her mind.

'What are you doing?'

'Nothing,' Fleet said. 'I'm waiting for you to do your thing.'

Lydia shoved everything she had behind her words. 'Did you know about the operation involving Alejandro Silver before today?'

'No,' Fleet said instantly. She could see that he was trying not to smile.

'This is very weird,' Lydia said, trying harder. 'It doesn't seem to be working—'

In that moment, Fleet let out a strangled sound. His whole body stiffened and his eyes took on the glazed look she was used to seeing in people when she used her Crow magic to gain control.

'Right,' Lydia said out loud, trying not to sound as rattled as she felt. She had pushed hard to get Fleet into a suggestive state and now she wondered whether to pull the throttle back a little. She realised that she had no idea whether this kind of control was damaging for people. If she used too much for too long, would she kill off brain cells?

She had no desire to turn her significant other into a drooling vegetable, but before she could pull back on her power, Fleet lurched violently and almost fell over. He took a jerky step forward to catch his balance and blinked hard. 'What was that?' His voice was normal and slightly pissed-off. 'You didn't say it would hurt.'

'I didn't think it did. No one has ever said so before. I'm sorry,' Lydia reached up and plucked her coin from the air between them, pocketing it quickly before reaching for Fleet. 'Are you okay?'

'Did you get carried away?' His colour was already returning to normal and the tension left his features.

'I might have used more than usual, it didn't seem to be affecting you. You should sit down.'

'I'm fine. It only hurt for a moment.'

'Where? All over, or-'

Fleet took her hand and put it against his chest.

'That's never happened before. I swear I didn't know that would happen.'

'It's okay,' Fleet dipped his head. 'I'm okay.'

Lydia was close enough that she could see a sheen of sweat on his forehead and his skin had an ashy tone. 'Does it still hurt?'

'No. I just feel a bit wiped out. It was like something was clutching my heart. Squeezing it so hard that it stopped beating.'

'Feathers,' Lydia took a step away, but Fleet increased his grip on her hand, keeping in in place.

'It's all right. It's beating again, now. No harm done.'

'We don't know that,' Lydia pulled away successfully this time. 'We should go to hospital, get you checked over.'

Fleet smiled, but Lydia could see it wasn't at full wattage. He wasn't feeling as fine as he pretended. 'Sit down, at least,' she grabbed his hand and pulled him to the bedroom. 'Or lie down.'

'I might need a few minutes,' he said, trying to keep things light.

'Stop it,' Lydia said. 'I'm worried. And you should rest.'

Fleet sat on the bed. 'I really am fine.'

Lydia climbed onto his lap and pressed herself against Fleet. His arms moved around to bring her closer and they kissed. After a moment, Fleet stopped. 'Okay,' he said and Lydia could see the pain on his face. 'Maybe I will rest. Just for a moment. And then you can try again.'

'I don't think so,' Lydia said. 'It didn't work on you.'

Fleet was clearly relieved and just as clearly trying to hide the fact. 'But I want you to know I'm telling the truth about the operation. I really didn't know before.'

'I believe you,' Lydia said. 'The fact that you wanted me to interrogate you and are willing for me to try again. That's enough.'

Fleet's eyes were searching her own. 'Is it?'

Lydia didn't know how else to say 'yes' so she kissed him.

LATER, curled up with Fleet, her back against his chest and his arms around her, Lydia felt the very last of her doubt ebb away. She could feel his gleam and the beating of his heart and every sense, both magical and animal, told her that Fleet was hers. She thought about what Emma had said about isolating herself. She thought about Maria. Furious and alone, surrounded by security she paid to protect her. She twisted around to face Fleet and put a hand on his cheek. 'I'm sorry I didn't tell you about Mark Kendal.'

'I can understand why you didn't,' he said after a moment.

'I'm all in,' Lydia said. 'From now on.'

Fleet's warm smile filled her soul with light. 'Me, too.'

'Which means I've got to tell you something bad.'

'Okay,' Fleet said, looking at her steadily.

'Ash is dead,' Lydia managed to get the words out and then she felt something break inside. 'It's my fault. I thought the king might take him back. He wanted to go back, wasn't coping with normal life. And I thought I could get the king onside. Maybe develop them as an ally. For the good of my Family. The greater good. But he killed him.' She was fully crying by the time she got to end of her confession, the words coming between gasps and hiccups. 'It's my fault.'

Fleet held her and stroked her hair. 'It's not your fault. You didn't kill him. You tried to help him.'

'I was going to give him to the king. I thought better someone who wanted to be with them than an unwilling child.'

'And if the king had taken him, he would be alive. You didn't hurt him, Lyds. You're not a killer.'

Lydia closed her eyes and breathed in the comforting scent of Fleet and allowed herself to be comforted. Just a moment. 'What if that's the problem?'

CHAPTER TWENTY-TWO

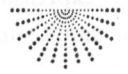

Lydia had fallen asleep in Fleet's arms, waking up with a line of drool connecting her cheek to his chest. 'Sorry,' she said, lifting her head and wiping his skin with her hand.

'I don't mind,' Fleet said, sounding sleepy. 'I told you I was all in.'

'I didn't realise that included dribble. Good to know.'

Lydia kissed him and then untangled herself to get dressed.

Fleet propped himself up on one elbow. 'What's happening?'

'You should meet my parents.'

'Is this another test?' Fleet said, starting to pull on his clothes.

'No. Just something that normal couples do.'

ONCE FULLY DRESSED, Lydia settled into the driving seat and pointed the Audi toward the suburbs. She stabbed at the radio a few times before switching it off.

'Are you nervous?'

'I've never brought anybody home.'

'That can't be true,' Fleet said, but he looked pleased.

The idea of her teenage self rocking up at the parental abode with Paul Fox made her snort with laughter. It was possible that the nerves were getting to her. She felt giddy.

Her mother opened the door with a tea towel over one shoulder and a distracted expression. It cleared to one of pure joy the moment she saw Lydia. 'Hello, love. This is a nice surprise.'

'This is Fleet,' Lydia said. 'My...' She hesitated over the word 'boyfriend'. It just seemed ridiculous.

'Come on in,' her mother said, mercifully glossing over the moment.

Seeing Fleet in her childhood home was something Lydia had been trying to prepare herself for on the drive over. She had expected it to look all wrong. She couldn't picture her London copper in the living room where she had played board games and watched TV after school and gossiped with Emma. Instead, Fleet shook her dad's hand and began chatting about the snooker which was, inevitably, playing in the corner.

Lydia caught up with her mum in the kitchen and helped her bring in mugs of tea and a plate of sliced fruit cake. 'Switch that off,' her mother said, nodding at the television. 'Guests.'

Henry Crow smiled conspiratorially at Fleet and hit the mute button.

'So, you're a detective, Ignatius?' Lydia's mother offered Fleet some cake.

'Call me Fleet,' Fleet said. He chatted with her parents about his work and his upbringing before the conversation moved onto roadworks and urban regeneration, and Henry and Susan's recent discovery of cruises as the ultimate holiday.

'The food was incredible and you're away from everything.'

'Do you want a walk before we head back?' Lydia asked her dad.

Susan Crow looked at the rain-soaked window and took the hint. She kissed Lydia goodbye and hugged Fleet. 'You two must come for dinner next time. I'll do a roast.'

'That would be wonderful, thank you.' Fleet picked up Lydia's jacket and held it out to her.

At the pavement, Fleet said: 'I'll wait in the car. Give you time to catch up with your dad.'

Lydia was going to agree, but she stamped on the instinct. 'Come with us.'

Henry raised his eyebrows but didn't say anything.

'That's all right,' Fleet said, 'you go ahead.' He took the car keys and got into the passenger side to wait.

Walking with Henry Crow through the kind of drizzling rain which didn't seem to be falling from the sky but, nonetheless, soaked through clothes with a tenacious inevitability, Lydia tried to work out where to begin. She started with her topmost worry, the fear that her presence would make him ill again. 'I'm sorry to be here in person. I know we need to be careful, but I wanted to see you.'

Henry shook his head. 'It's a precaution. We don't know anything for sure. It could be that your man has fixed the problem permanently. Besides,' Henry tilted his head. 'You're an adult, now. I don't have to hide. That should make a difference.'

'You're joining the life again?'

'No,' her dad smiled sadly. 'Your mother would kill me. But I've given all this a lot of thought. It's about balance, right? If seeing you powers me up, I just need to make sure I siphon some away every time we meet.' Henry looked around the deserted street and then clapped his hands loudly. When he brought them apart his coin appeared between them, hanging in thin air entirely motionless. He let it hang there for a few seconds and Lydia could see the strain on his face. Then he clapped his hands together again and the coin was gone.

She swallowed hard. 'Is that going to work?'

'I hope so,' Henry said, visibly paler than he had been a minute before. 'What's the alternative? That I never see my only daughter? Just telephone calls for the rest of my life.'

'There are worse fates,' Lydia said and they resumed their sedate pace along the pavement.

'Well, it's my decision. You have nothing to feel guilty about. None of this is your fault.'

'I'm not sure about that,' Lydia said, thinking about Charlie. She still didn't know what her father suspected about that, let alone his opinion.

'I wanted you to have a choice,' Henry said. 'And you did. I was groomed to take over after your grandfather. He was a bastard and liked to pit us kids against each other. Said the competition between me and Charlie would make us stronger. But what I really learned, was the stuff he never said. I learned by watching and I know one thing for sure. You can't lead the family on your own. And you can't let people stew over grudges. You've got to keep everyone together.'

They walked a little further and Lydia tried to formulate a way to tell her father everything that had happened. Charlie. The deal she made with Mr Smith which he didn't seem keen to let drop. Alejandro's faked death. The fact that Maria Silver was still after her blood. Mark Kendal, killed on her watch. Ash.

'Talk to me,' her father said. 'There's one big question in your mind. What is it?'

Lydia spoke without thinking. 'What if I'm not good for the Family? Bringing people together isn't my strong suit.'

'You seem to be working on it,' Henry said. 'Bringing your man around here is a start.'

'You don't disapprove?'

'It doesn't matter what I think. He'll be a tough sell to the rest of the Family, but they'll come round.'

'I'm not so sure,' Lydia said.

'Make them. You're the boss.'

'I'm not sure I ought to be,' Lydia said.

'Don't mistake bad things happening for bad leadership. Bad things happen all the time, especially in our line of business. That's not on you.'

More than anything, Lydia wanted to believe him. 'But two people have died.'

'You think things would have been better under Charlie?'

'No, but-'

'Only take responsibility for what you can control. Unless you pulled the trigger yourself, you didn't kill anyone. Besides,' Henry said. 'Death isn't the worst thing.'

LYDIA SETTLED into the passenger seat, enjoying the new sense of calm that had enveloped her the moment her parents had welcomed Fleet. He had offered to drive back and it was nice to know that she could close her eyes, put her feet up on the dash and enjoy the release of tension. Beckenham was only half an hour's drive, but she hadn't realised how much she had needed to get out of Camberwell, even for a few hours. Maybe her parents were onto something with the cruise idea. 'Maybe not a cruise, but I could consider a holiday,' she said out loud.

Fleet stopped at traffic lights and looked across with a fondness that made Lydia's breath catch in her chest. 'I'll hold you to that.'

At Denmark Hill, Fleet slowed to navigate some roadworks close to Kings College Hospital. He was musing on something Henry had said to him while Lydia had been in the kitchen. 'I think he was quoting poetry. And then he said something about angels.'

'Oh, you know,' Lydia said, delighted that her father had been waxing lyrical on his favourite poet. 'The famous Blake quote from when he had that vision on Peckham Rye?'

'No,' Fleet gestured for a woman on a bicycle to finish crossing in front of the car, before moving off. 'Vision, huh?'

'Yeah, Dad always said it wasn't angels, but Crows. Even though that would be black wings so I couldn't really see it. I mean, Blake says he saw 'bright angelic wings bespangling every bough like stars'. It doesn't track.'

'You don't see much bespangling these days,' Fleet glanced at her, smiling. Then his expression changed and he yanked the steering wheel to the right. In that moment, time seemed to slow. Lydia seemed to have plenty of time to see the side window shatter and then the car was spinning, the street scene outside blurring into something incomprehensible. The tyres were screeching on the wet road and someone was swearing loudly.

A loud crunching sound and then the car wasn't moving any longer. They were facing the wrong way down the road, a people-carrier was stopped so close to them that Lydia could see the woman gripping the steering wheel with shock in her eyes. There was a small child in the front seat, crying. The woman's mouth was opening and closing and Lydia wondered what she was saying. Further away, the sounds of brakes being slammed. It seemed very quiet, suddenly, and Lydia wasn't sure if her hearing had been damaged. Fleet was holding his shoulder, slumped over and eyes closed, blood on his face. For a single, heart-stopping second, Lydia thought he was dead, but then his eyes opened and he looked at her. 'Are you all right?' His voice was groggy and his eyes were trying to shut again.

'I'm not hurt.' Lydia couldn't feel any pain at all, even as she moved to unclip her seatbelt. Probably the adrenaline, but she filed worrying about her own possible injuries to 'later'. Fleet looked bad. She reached across and unclipped his seat belt. 'We need to get out.'

'No,' Fleet said. 'We don't know if they're still out there.' He was more alert, now, and peering through the windscreen.

'Who is out where? We need to get out.' Maybe she had seen too many films, but Lydia had the distinct impression that they needed to vacate the crashed vehicle before it turned into a fiery ball of death.

'Whoever just shot me,' Fleet said, and then he passed out.

CHAPTER TWENTY-THREE

Lydia had never felt a fear like it. She could hear voices, car doors slamming, and feel the rush of air as someone pulled open the passenger side door, but she was focused on Fleet. His breath was coming in shallow gasps, and his eyes fluttered like he was going to pass out. She put her hands on his face. 'Fleet, stay awake.'

He didn't comply. The moment he passed out, his hand fell away from his shoulder and blood gushed out, soaking his shirt and jacket in seconds. Lydia pressed her own hand to it to staunch the flow, but blood was leaking between her fingers. She needed a pad of material. Clean material. And she needed to lie Fleet back so that she could tilt up his chin if he needed resuscitation. She could climb on top of him, maybe hit the recline lever to get the seat back, but what if he had other injuries and she made them worse?

It felt like hours, trying to make simple decisions. Which should she prioritise? Should she go around to the other side of the car and try to drag him out? There could be a shooter waiting for her to do exactly that, waiting for the opportunity to finish the job. And always there, threatening to overwhelm her, was the fear. Don't let him die. Don't let him die. Don't let him die.

A flash of fluorescent yellow through the driver side window and another blast of air, as the door opened. Lydia felt a rush of relief. The professionals had arrived.

LYDIA DIDN'T WANT to leave Fleet's side, but she was persuaded into the adjoining bay in A&E while the trauma surgeon assessed Fleet's shoulder wound. The nurse who accomplished this feat was even shorter than Lydia but she had the kind of authority Lydia could only dream of and she was powerless to resist. 'I need to check you over, hen, and the faster you let me do my job, the sooner you can see your pal.'

Lydia knew when she was beaten and allowed the Scottish powerhouse in navy scrubs to run down a checklist of questions while she palpated Lydia's abdomen, took her blood pressure, shone a light into her eyes and asked her to look left and right. The last bit was the worst and Lydia bit the inside of her mouth to stop herself squeaking with the sudden sharp pains.

The nurse nodded and made a mark on the chart. 'Soft tissue damage in the neck and shoulder, very common in a car accident, I'm afraid.'

'We didn't hit anything,' Lydia said.

'It's the sudden stop. You'll be needing to take it easy for a few days.'

A police officer popped her head around the curtain. 'Sorry. I can come back.'

'I'm done here,' the nurse said. To Lydia she added: 'No alcohol tonight, Ibuprofen for the pain, ice the area if you get any swelling, and come straight back in if you experience any nausea or dizziness.'

Lydia sat up and swung her legs off the examination table.

'I need to ask you some questions,' the officer said. 'If you're up to it.'

'Fire away,' Lydia said and then winced. Poor choice of words. Part of her brain, the tiniest portion which wasn't fully taken up with fear for Fleet, had been running over the incident. She hadn't seen a shooter and, while she was far from an expert, she thought it must have come from somewhere high up.

'This is a firearm incident and is being taken extremely seriously. The Emergency Response Team are conducting a thorough search of the area and I must insist that you do not leave this part of the building without speaking to either myself or another officer.'

'Have you found anything?'

'We are in the very early stages of our investigation, but I want to assure you that your safety is a priority. We believe an individual fired on your car from an upper floor or roof of a building nearby. Can you think of any reason why your vehicle would have been a target?'

Lydia widened her eyes slightly. 'No. Absolutely not.'

FLEET WAS PROPPED up on white pillows, face turned away from the door. His arm was strapped across his chest and covered in bandages. Lydia could see an intravenous line into the back of his hand but nothing else, which she took as a good sign.

He turned his head as she approached.

'Hey you,' Lydia said.

'No grapes?'

Lydia was too tense to attempt a smile. 'What have they said? Shouldn't you be lying down?'

'I'm just waiting for this to be taken out,' he indicated the IV. 'And the discharge paperwork. Can you take me home?'

'Of course,' Lydia said and kissed him lightly on the lips. 'It seems a bit quick.'

'It was barely a graze. Nothing important got damaged.'

'How is the pain?'

He gave her a loopy smile. 'Great right now. But I'm not gonna lie, it's going to suck when the opiates wear off.' He was slurring very slightly and Lydia wondered what they had given him. 'I'm warning you now, I'm going to be pathetic.'

That did make Lydia smile. 'You saved my life. You get to be as feeble as you like.'

Fleet gazed at her fondly. 'I love you.'

At that moment a man with a clipboard appeared, he nodded at Lydia and then told Fleet that he would have to wait for the final sign off, but that he could take his IV out if Fleet wanted.

'I do want,' Fleet said, nodding with the exaggerated care of the slightly high. 'Thank you.'

Lydia took the opportunity to head outside. The police were still very much in evidence, so she changed plan and went to the vending machine in the corridor instead. It was quiet, and once an elderly man being pushed in a wheelchair by an orderly had disappeared around the corner, Lydia used a burner phone to call the number she had for Mr Smith. A woman answered with 'Elias Electrics, how can I help you?' Bloody secret service. 'I need to see Mr Smith urgently. This is Lydia Crow.'

'There is nobody here with that name,' the woman said.

'Just pass on the message,' Lydia said and finished the call. Then she went back inside to collect Fleet.

. . .

Lydia's car had been taken by the police so she called a taxi to get her and Fleet back to The Fork. 'My flat is nicer,' Fleet said, and Lydia was relieved. He must be feeling more like himself if he was complaining about her domestic standards.

'Feel free to go home,' Lydia said. 'But if you want the Lydia Crow nursing experience, you're going to have to deal with my unwashed bedding.'

Fleet raised an eyebrow. 'Nursing, eh? Sounds good.'

'Don't get excited,' Lydia said, paying the driver.

She had just settled Fleet into her bed when her burner phone rang. She closed the bedroom door and moved into the living room to answer it. 'You want a meeting?' Mr Smith asked.

'I want you to come to The Fork and explain yourself,' Lydia said. 'Someone just tried to kill me.'

'I don't think that's such a-'

'Fleet was shot,' Lydia said. 'I'm not leaving him alone.'

A short silence. 'Ten minutes.'

Good as his word, Mr Smith texted the burner phone nine minutes later to say he was outside the cafe. Lydia asked Jason to keep an eye on Fleet, who had already dozed off.

'They wouldn't have let him out if he wasn't okay,' Jason said. 'But of course I'll watch him.'

The sky had darkened in the short time they had been back and the streetlights were illuminated, casting an orange glow on the wet pavement. Mr Smith was standing outside his Mercedes, hands folded. 'I understand DCI Fleet wasn't seriously injured.'

Lydia ignored that. 'What do you know? Is this about

Alejandro and Operation Bergamot? Why am I being targeted?'

'The first part of the operation failed, but the back-up portion yielded promising results. Alejandro offered information on a bill that was coming to Parliament before it was made public. He also offered his vote and a seat on the lucrative advisory position that would open up as a result of that bill being passed. It was intended to gather evidence of corruption by a particular individual and to discover the identity of that individual's managing associate or associates.'

'You can speak in English, you know,' Lydia said, irritated out of silence. 'You got him to dangle something juicy in front of his shady contact and stuck him with a wire.'

Mr Smith inclined his head. 'Quite so.'

Lydia waited for him to elaborate. She didn't want to have to prompt him, but Mr Smith had been being an enigmatic dick for far longer than Lydia. She was never going to win the conversational battle. 'Just tell me,' she said, pushing a little bit of Crow behind her words, just for fun.

Mr Smith's nostrils flared, like he could smell something bad. 'There's no need for that. I'm here to help. Mr Silver's contact was a conduit to a person who conducts business through many aliases and runs their funds through shell corporations.'

'Including our old pals, JRB?'

Mr Smith nodded. 'We didn't get anything useful recorded and Mr Silver made it clear that he would not be testifying in open court. He did discover some details about the contract which had been taken out on Ms Gormley, details we were able to cross-reference to be fairly certain that the job was carried out by the person at the centre of Operation Bergamot.'

'The person? I thought this was about political corruption or terrorism or arms dealing.'

'It's about all of those things, but there is an individual who has been making trouble internationally. Hence the multi-organisation operation and Interpol. I was brought in as an expert on the Families,' he inclined his head slightly, 'but that was only after Alejandro was linked.'

'So, it's not about JRB or the Silvers.' Or the Crows, is what Lydia meant, but didn't say.

'Only tangentially and recently. This Operation has been going on for the last two years. Maybe longer. Even I'm not privy to all of the intel.'

Lydia could see his annoyance at that.

'And when I say 'making trouble' I mean killing key people at inopportune moments around the world.'

'This is about an assassin?' Lydia took a moment to let that settle in. 'Why would they be after me?'

'We don't know that they are,' Mr Smith said. 'I'm inclined to think not. It is more likely that the attempt on your life today was more tangentially linked. Which doesn't mean you shouldn't consider my previous offer. Let me protect you.'

Lydia ignored that. 'You mean, that Maria sent someone to have a pop because she thinks I killed her father? So it wouldn't be happening if it wasn't for your stupid operation. Fleet got shot. Did I mention that?'

'Don't be dramatic. It was just a graze. Not even a through-and-through. He'll be fine. And don't pretend Maria wasn't looking to off you before the operation. You can't blame us for the bad blood between you.'

Lydia forced herself to be quiet, to think. She took a calming breath and squeezed her coin in her palm. 'So what was the back-up part of your grand plan?'

'The public nature of Alejandro's disappearance.'

'The funeral?'

'All of it. Having him die, not disappear. We wanted to see if it would bring the operative to London.'

'Why would it? You had just done their job for them? Saved them a trip?'

'They would have to check he was really dead. And also that it wasn't another operative. Professional pride.'

'That seems far from reliable. Why would they care?'

'Reputation, then. At the level this person is working, there is no margin for error and no room for competition. And, beyond that, there is a chance the assassin may have further targets in the city. If they were commissioned to hit one of the Family heads, it's possible they were commissioned to get them all.'

Lydia went cold. 'So today's attempt could have been your assassin. Make up your mind.'

Mr Smith smiled. 'Anything's possible between heaven and earth.'

Something else snagged Lydia's attention. Which was good because it stopped her from punching him. 'You keep saying 'they'. How much detail do you have on the killer?'

'Very little. We don't have a gender as witness reports are extremely scarce. We have a man in Buenos Aires who swears he saw a beautiful blonde leaving the hotel after a prominent union leader took his own life in his suite. And we have another report of an unknown man with a short beard and brown hair seen driving away from the scene where the head of the Colombian cartel was gunned down as he left his mistress's apartment.'

'Why didn't you tell me this last time we spoke?'

'I work on a need to know basis,' Mr Smith said. 'You know how it is.'

'And getting shot at qualifies me for clearance. I guess it's my lucky day.'

'I'd say so,' Mr Smith said. 'The assassin we are looking for doesn't tend to miss.'

. . .

BACK UPSTAIRS, Lydia held a whispered conversation with Jason in the living room and then went into the bedroom as quietly as possible, not wanting to wake up Fleet. She got into bed with him and lay awake, watching headlights on the ceiling. She knew there was a pressure sensor outside her flat, heavy-duty locks on the building and a watchful ghost in attendance, but her mind wouldn't stop racing.

A couple of hours later, Lydia hadn't slept. She thought she was keeping still and quiet but she felt Fleet stir. 'Can't sleep?'

'How's the pain?' Lydia sat up, reaching for the packet of paracetamol.

'Not too bad,' Fleet said, grunting slightly as he shifted position. 'How about you?'

'I'm fine,' Lydia said. And it was true. Her neck felt a bit stiff and sore, but it paled into insignificance when she thought about how close Fleet had come to being seriously hurt. Or worse. She propped herself up on one elbow to look at him in the dim light filtering through the curtains. Alive and whole. Sleepy-eyed and with a rough scruff of stubble.

'Do you ever wonder about your father?'

'Not really,' Fleet said.

'Not ever?'

Fleet was quiet for a while and Lydia wondered if he was drifting back to sleep. 'Why are you asking?'

'There's something about you,' she began, trying to pick her words carefully. 'Something different.'

'I should hope so,' he said, pulling her down with his good arm and kissing her lips.

After a few pleasant moments of that, Lydia holding her weight off his body for fear of hurting his shoulder, she tried a different tack. 'What do you think makes you such a good copper?'

Fleet frowned. 'Training? Hard work? Ability to not

523

punch people when they're being annoying.' He smiled. 'Most of the time.'

Lydia shook her head gently. 'You have really good instincts.'

'Thank you. I think?' Fleet's frown deepened. 'Why do I feel you are leading up to saying something I don't want to hear?'

'That guy at work. The idiot. He wasn't wrong about your success rate.' She held up her hands. 'Wrong about the reason for it, of course, but I was just thinking… Do you ever get a feeling about something before it happens?'

'Of course, all the time. Everybody does. We've got those evolutionary survival instincts that mean we take in loads of information subconsciously and make decisions quickly before we've consciously noticed. I read a book about it once.'

'Right. But more than that, do you ever have a strong feeling about how something is going to play out. And then everything happens the way you expected?'

'I don't know,' Fleet looked properly wary now. 'Maybe sometimes. But that's experience. I know what's going to happen with some cases because it's happened a hundred times before. Criminals aren't that inventive. They make the same mistakes. They say the same things. I've just been doing this job a long time.'

'And when you're out and about, you sometimes react really quickly. Before even the tiny signs have happened. Like today.'

'That was luck,' Fleet said. 'And I must have seen something. It goes with the job. Coppers are all the same. The good ones, anyway. You develop a sixth sense for trouble.'

Lydia knew he wanted to drop it, but she couldn't. 'I didn't see anything. If you hadn't steered when you did, one of us would have been killed.'

'Unless it was a warning shot,' Fleet said. 'Or we might not have been the targets.'

He was playing devil's advocate, Lydia knew, but she wasn't going to be derailed. 'How did you know to move when you did?'

'The gunshot was a clue,' Fleet said, his voice sleepy now.

'That wasn't how it happened,' Lydia said. 'You wrenched the steering wheel and then the glass shattered. How did you know there was a sniper?'

Lydia stared at his shadowed face, looking for an answer, but Fleet had slipped back to sleep.

"I knew it was a warning shot," Piers said. "Or we might not have been the target."

He was playing the devil's advocate, Lydia knew. But she wasn't going to be deflected. "How did you know to move when you did?"

The gun shot was a tic," Piers said, "but not a sleepy tic. That wasn't how it happened, Lydia said. You wrenched the steering wheel and then the glass shattered. How did you know there was a sniper?"

Lydia stared at his shadowed face, looking for an answer, but Piers had slipped back to sleep.

CHAPTER TWENTY-FOUR

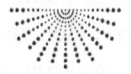

Lydia walked through the downstairs of Charlie's house, closing blinds and lighting candles. She had considered holding the gathering at The Fork, but wanted to make it clear that this was a private family party with a small 'f' on the word 'family'. It was also a gathering of the inner circle of the capital-f Family, too, but it felt important to emphasise the blood ties foremost.

Angel had made two large pans of lasagne and dropped them off earlier with detailed instructions. Even Lydia couldn't mess up reheating them in Charlie's state-of-the-art oven. She had taken a delivery of garlic and rosemary focaccia, six bottles of wine and a raspberry and ricotta cheesecake from the Italian deli. Fleet was in the kitchen, dressing salad leaves in a glass serving bowl. He was only able to use one arm so it was taking longer than it might have done, but Lydia left him to it. Telling her tough-as-nails copper that he wasn't capable of applying olive oil to some vegetation wouldn't be great for his self-esteem.

The guests arrived right on time and there was much kissing and hugging. Daisy and John brought wine and

Aiden staggered under a flower arrangement of unwieldy proportions.

'No gifts necessary,' Lydia said. 'This is just a family meal. Nothing formal.'

She directed the guests to the living room for drinks and then heard the front door open again. She had invited both of her parents, though she hadn't been sure they would come, but there they were. Her mother looked well-rested and surprisingly relaxed, wearing a fitted black dress and her signature red lipstick. Her father was in a suit, something she hadn't seen for a few years and, together, they looked more like heirs to a crime family than she had ever seen. John went pale as Henry Crow walked into the house and greeted everyone and his colour didn't improve when he kissed Lydia and congratulated her on her successful climb of The Shard. It was a public declaration of approval and John would have to be a fool – or sick of life – to challenge her authority now.

After drinks, Lydia led the way to the kitchen where the big table was set.

'What is he doing here?' John said as soon as he caught sight of Fleet, who was chopping peppers, a tea towel over one shoulder.

'We're together. And he's part of the family,' Lydia said.

'Did I miss the wedding?' Daisy said in an acidic tone.

'The man took a bullet for me,' Lydia indicated Fleet's bandaged shoulder. 'And I have just informed you that he is part of this family. Anybody got anything else to say about it?' She looked around, making eye contact. Nobody did.

Lydia told them to sit at the table while she dished up. 'I'll help,' Daisy said, pushing her chair back.

'No, sit down.' Daisy froze halfway out of her seat and Lydia attempted to sound less authoritarian. 'Relax! You can pour the wine.'

In the kitchen, Fleet put a steadying hand on the small of

her back. Lydia leaned against him briefly and then tackled the lasagne, dishing out squares while trying not to think about the weirdness of the atmosphere. This shouldn't be odd. They were family. She had been kept separate from the Family business while growing up, but she had still enjoyed family parties and outings, had still been doted on by uncles and aunts, had played with cousins. A memory of Maddie, dead-eyed in the dim light of her living room with her hands wrapped around Lydia's throat, jumped into her mind. Lydia pushed it away.

'Dig in,' she said brightly, slinging plates in front of people and then carrying across the second pan of lasagne which was still half-full. 'Help yourself to seconds when you're ready.'

Slowly, conversation began to flow. Henry talked to Aiden about snooker and Aiden gazed at him in frank hero worship. John asked Fleet about his shoulder as a way to segue into his own litany of physical complaints; his dodgy ankle, his slipped disc, the time he got shingles. Daisy drank wine steadily and hardly spoke, but you couldn't have everything.

Once plates were cleared and people were sitting back in their chairs making the kind of satisfied noises that indicated a good meal had been devoured, Lydia took a ten-shilling note out of her pocket and put it on the table. Instantly, the conversation stopped, all eyes drawn to the money.

'You all know there is someone taking pot shots at this family.' Lydia looked around the table. 'Someone killed Mark Kendal and I found one of these in his wallet. And this week, someone took a literal pot shot at my car. If Fleet hadn't acted as quickly as he did, I might have been seriously hurt. Maybe even killed.'

Lydia glanced at her mother who hadn't been able to stop a small gasp. She had a hand up to her mouth and her eyes were wide with horror. Henry put an arm around her shoulders, pulling her close. 'It's okay,' Lydia said, taking her mother's hand and giving it a squeeze. 'I'm fine. Thanks to Fleet.' She let that settle in for another moment.

'Thank you,' Susan said to a clearly embarrassed Fleet.

She hated to worry her parents, but any member of the Crow Family who still had a problem with her boyfriend would have to stay very quiet about it indeed. 'I don't know who to blame, yet.'

'Maria Silver would be top of the list,' Aiden said. 'Surely?'

'I'm not jumping to conclusions. Alejandro was mixed up in a government operation and I have it on good authority that there is a rogue assassin currently on the loose. You're right, though,' she nodded to Aiden and he sat up a little straighter, 'Maria Silver is not my biggest fan.'

'What do you want us to do?' Aiden asked.

'I want you to all be on your guard, that's sensible, but I don't want any retribution. No eye for an eye bullshit,' Lydia looked at John as she said the last part. 'But I'm going to sort this out, make sure there is no more unpleasantness.' She tapped the ten-shilling note. 'I'm taking this to Maria, but before I give it to her, I'm going to give her the chance to ally with us. I need you all to understand something very important. Our quarrel is not with the Silvers. Or the Foxes. Or even the Pearls. In fact, if we don't join with the other Families, put aside past problems and learn to work together, we're going to be picked off one by one. There's a government department that would like to use our power, and there is JRB. All I know for sure is that they want us at each other's throats, weak and squabbling like little children. I'm proposing we don't play into their hands.'

'What makes you think she'll even hear you out?' John said. 'Charlie told me what she did to you after you got her arrested.'

'I have some information which is extremely pertinent to the Silver Family. She's going to want to hear what I have to say about her father.'

'What about Alejandro?'

Lydia smiled her shark smile. 'He's not dead.'

AFTER THE FAMILY HAD LEFT, Lydia prepared to head to her meeting with Maria.

'Please don't go,' Fleet's voice was gentle, but very serious. 'I'm asking you.'

'I'm sorry,' Lydia said. 'You heard my rousing speech. Now I've got to follow through.'

What Lydia didn't say was that she couldn't stop seeing Chunni and Heather's frightened faces and Ash's lifeless one. She was head of the Crow Family, but she wasn't Charlie Crow. Or Grandpa Crow. If there was a chance Maria Silver was walking around believing that her own father was dead when he was very much alive, Lydia was going to take her truth. She might be a murderous witch with a cold dead heart, but she was also a human being. And Lydia had seen real grief in her face. She had to tell her the truth.

'Then, I'm coming with you.' Fleet picked his coat up from the chair.

'You don't have to do that.'

'Maybe the presence of the Met will stop it from escalating.'

'And maybe it will do exactly the opposite. If Maria thinks I'm trying something when she told me to come alone...'

'When people say 'come alone' they usually mean you harm.'

'Or they're frightened. Or value their privacy,' Lydia countered. 'Some people find it hard to trust.'

Fleet gave her a long look. 'Tell me honestly, is that what you think is going on in this situation?'

Lydia didn't meet his gaze. 'Maybe.'

'It doesn't matter,' Fleet said. 'I've told you, I'm all in. I'm not a copper first, I'm yours. Whatever that means and wherever it takes me. We're in this together from now on and I'm not going to let you keep me at arm's length.' Fleet was breathing a little harder by the time he'd finished his speech and his eyes were shining a little.

'Well, then,' Lydia said lightly. 'Let's go.'

The meeting was in neutral territory, at least, but Lydia didn't disagree with Fleet's assessment of the plan. It was a clusterfuck. 'At least it's not a multi-storey car park,' Lydia said. 'She can't be planning anything especially bad in a hotel.'

Fleet gave Lydia the look she deserved. Maria Silver had booked the sky bar at one of the nicest hotels in the City but that didn't mean she wasn't planning to stab Lydia over cocktails.

'I'm bringing good news,' Lydia said. 'It could be the making of us. A bright new day.'

Whoever had decorated the hotel had been overly fond of shining black glass and glittering gold decorations. The effect was luxurious but with an undertone of sleaze. Probably not what they were going for, but Lydia would be the first to admit that she might be wrong. Interior décor was not her strong suit, and five-hundred-quid-a-night hotels not her natural environment. Weirdly, Fleet looked perfectly at home. She commented on it as they rode the lift to the top floor. 'You always seem at ease, how do you manage that?'

He flashed her a smile. 'Because I always am.'

A uniformed member of staff stopped them as they

entered the bar. 'This is a private function. There's a bar open on floor seven or the Milanese Restaurant on-'

'We're invited,' Lydia said, and one of Maria's security staff nodded them through.

Maria was standing on the terrace, looking out at the twinkling lights of the city. She turned as they approached. 'You said you have information for me. I'm listening.'

'We should sit down,' Lydia said.

Maria raised an eyebrow but she indicated chairs arranged around a table. Lydia waited for Maria to sit before taking a seat opposite. Fleet remained standing behind Lydia, like a bodyguard. Lydia was glad his jacket hid his bandaged shoulder. She didn't think there was going to be a physical confrontation but, in her experience, it was best not to show any weakness around Maria. With that in mind, Lydia launched straight into her prepared speech.

'I know you don't like me, but I hope you will accept that I am genuinely trying to help. Mainly because it helps me, of course, but also because I think you should know the truth.'

Maria folded her hands in her lap. Her expression didn't change and she didn't speak.

Lydia ploughed on. 'I don't think your father is dead. It definitely isn't his body in the Silver crypt.' She wondered if Maria would be more convinced if she explained that she hadn't been able to sense 'Silver' or whether she would be revealing her secret for no real gain. 'And the Silver cup is a fake, too.'

The only sign that Maria was listening was the very slight tilt of her head. That and the fact that she hadn't smacked Lydia in the face. Yet. 'Can you think of a reason he might have wanted to disappear? It's okay if you don't want to tell me, but I want you to think about it.'

'Why are you bringing this to me?' Maria asked.

'I told you. Whatever has happened between us in the past, I think you ought to know.'

Maria smiled. 'What makes you think I don't already know? How typically egotistical of a Crow to believe she knows more about Silver business than I do.'

Lydia waited a moment, trying to work out if Maria was bluffing. She was incredibly poised if that was the case, but she was the head of the Silver Family. Poise was her birth right. When it became apparent that Maria wasn't going to fill the silence, Lydia said, 'If you know he isn't dead, why have you been putting the word out that I did it? Why send a sniper to kill me?'

A barely perceptible frown creased Maria's brow before she shrugged. 'Opportunity.'

Fleet stepped forward. 'You just admitted to attempted murder, Ms Silver. As you are aware, booking a professional killer is the same as-'

Maria didn't so much as glance at Fleet. Instead, she addressed Lydia. 'You brought your pet policeman. How sweet.'

'And now we're leaving.' Lydia stood up.

'I don't think so,' Maria said. 'We haven't had our drinks, yet.'

'I came to tell you that I believe your father is alive. I was under the mistaken belief that your actions were driven by grief.'

'And you wanted to save your own skin.'

'I have no problem staying alive,' Lydia said. She gestured to herself. 'Look. Here I am. An attempt by a pro and I'm still breathing. I came to deliver the information because I thought it was the right thing to do. Morally. We have our personal differences, but we belong to ancient and respectable Families. I, for one, intend to act like it.'

Maria narrowed her eyes. 'A grubby little Crow trying to get the moral high ground. Have you any idea how ridiculous you appear? I'm the establishment, I'm the law.'

'Very well,' Lydia said. 'If you want to keep it personal, I will behave unprofessionally from now on.'

'Is that supposed to frighten me?'

'That depends. How do you feel about your father's cowardice becoming public knowledge? It's my understanding that he made a deal with the secret service in order to protect himself from JRB. The great Alejandro Silver borrowing money from a company associated with the Pearls. And then, worse for a lawyer, finding out that he had made a deal which made him into a puppet. He had to vote the way JRB demanded, among other less-savoury favours. So to get away from JRB he got into bed with the secret service, and agreed to act as their stooge, instead. In return, they faked his death. He wanted to protect the good name of the Silver Family and the firm, and to keep his daughter from being tarred by the same brush.' Lydia shrugged. 'Wherever your father is, I'm willing to bet he can't come home. A dead man can't be a politician or a lawyer or the head of a Family. It's over for him. The only thing keeping him going is that he kept your reputation clean. You really want to destroy that?'

Maria's lips were in a thin line. 'What do you suggest?'

'That you cancel the hit against me, for starters.'

Maria tilted her head. 'I misspoke earlier. I haven't the faintest idea what you mean.'

Lydia wasn't sure what game Maria was playing and whether or not she believed her. She had the sense Maria had been surprised when she had mentioned the sniper, but then she was a Silver and as twisted as a corkscrew.

'Besides,' Maria said with a chilling smile. 'If I wanted to remove you I wouldn't be so careless as to hire a contractor and leave a trail. I would undertake the matter personally.'

Well *that* had the ring of truth. 'Regardless, you've come for me in the past. And you've made threats. I'm willing to move on, for the sake of both our Families. I'm offering you a free pass just this once, but I will never be so lenient again.'

Maria's mouth snapped shut. Her gaze went to Fleet.

'Don't look at him.' Lydia waited until Maria's eyes were staring into her own and then she drew on the Crow power, the thousands of black feathers and fluttering hearts. She held them lightly, not showing her coin or pushing Maria in any particular direction, just holding the power there so that it filled the room with the sound of beating wings. 'I know that your Family cup has gone. I know that Alejandro is in hiding. Ally with me or I will destroy you.'

CHAPTER TWENTY-FIVE

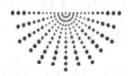

Later that night, Lydia was still wired from the meeting with Maria and felt sure she wasn't going to fall asleep anytime soon. She disentangled from Fleet in order to reach for her phone and checked the news, more by reflex than anything else. She kept expecting to see a story about Ash's disappearance, maybe a tearful plea by his parents, but nothing had appeared, yet. Lydia blinked and turned her phone face down. She thought that she had successfully pushed her feelings about Ash deep inside and then locked them in a box for good measure, but the thought of his parents losing their son all over again made her throat hurt. Fleet turned over in his sleep and Lydia got up and tiptoed out to her office, so as not to wake him up. He was recovering very well, but he needed to rest.

Sitting at her desk, the lamp pooling light on the messy surface, Lydia began looking through the latest batch of correspondence shoved through Charlie's letterbox. She had picked it up during the family meal prep and brought it back and now she needed something mindless to occupy her. Flyers. Insurance renewal. A handwritten thank-you note sent from Australia. Lydia fetched the whisky and treated herself to a slug straight from the bottle. Begging letter for a loan. Catalogue. An offer on a case of wine. Invitation to a charity ball. Wedding invitation. A heavy cream envelope with nothing on the front, not even Charlie's name. Lydia used her pen knife to slit the thick paper. Inside, there was a sheet of Silver and Silver note paper with a typed date, time and address, and the words: 'This is goodbye, old friend.' It was an office building in Canary Wharf, not a place she recognised, and the date was the following day. Lydia looked at her watch. Well, the same day, now.

FLEET WAS NOT happy and not only because Lydia was changing the dressing on his shoulder wound. He hissed a breath between his teeth as Lydia dabbed a little too hard with the antiseptic. 'I don't understand why you think it's Alejandro. Why would he leave a note at Charlie's house? He knows he's gone.'

'But he doesn't know the details,' Lydia argued. 'I've spread the word that he's taken a long holiday. Most assume that means he's dead, but Alejandro might think it means he's also taken a deal with the government. I mean, he might be hoping that Charlie has done the same thing as him. Misery loves company, after all.'

'But...'

'And he might be reaching out to the house on the assumption that Charlie is hiding out there, or checking on it. He might not think there's a high chance of getting in touch with Charlie, but if he doesn't have any options... Or maybe he left notes like this in a hundred other dead drops. Who knows how many little secrets Charlie and Alejandro shared over the years.'

'Fine, but I still don't see why he would get in touch, now. Especially since he's supposed to be dead.'

Lydia stuck the fresh dressing onto the wound and

smoothed down the edges to make sure it was stuck firmly. 'They've been allies for a long time. Alejandro might just want the chance to say goodbye before he gets moved abroad or whatever the leaders of Operation Bergamot have planned for him. Or he might have a plan to get out of his situation.'

'Or he might be hoping to lure you to an isolated location.' Fleet pulled his shirt back on and began to button it.

'Alejandro has always allied with the Crows. He's not going to hurt me. Besides, this invitation is meant for my uncle, not me.'

'Alejandro's not necessarily acting of his own free will. Wasn't he used by the government op to gather evidence?'

'Well, Charlie's not going to turn up, so Charlie can't accidentally give him any incriminating evidence. I'm going to attend, it's the respectful thing to do.'

'Respect, huh?' Fleet tilted his head.

Lydia kissed him lightly. 'That, and the possibility that he might be persuaded to tell us what he found for Operation Bergamot about JRB.'

CANARY WHARF in east London was the second business and financial district after the City. The Mayflower had sailed from the docks nearby, and the East India Quay celebrated trading routes and enterprise. Back in the day, it would have smelled of tobacco and sugar, imported from the newly colonised America, but now it smelled of exhaust fumes and money. Shining skyscrapers housing thousands of offices, concrete-and-glass outdoor seating areas and vast underground carparks. Plus, the ubiquitous ground floor cafes and restaurants, willing and able to feed the stock market monkeys and besuited banking serfs. Plenty of bright young things in sharp suits would be making a killing, Lydia was sure, but many more would be working high-stress positions for a few years before burning out on salaries that seemed good until you factored in London-living, with a precious few at the top of the tree, multiplying their wealth until they were untouchable.

The meeting was set for eight in the evening and the address was on the twelfth floor of a shiny office block with a sculpted concrete concourse with a large lily pond, and a central atrium which was supposed to show off the buildings' 'design forward' sensibilities. At least, that was what the website told Lydia when she scoped it out. It also had at least six floors of offices-to-let, so it seemed that not everybody was lining up to buy.

There was a large reception area and a bank of lifts on the wall beyond. It was deserted, which wasn't a surprise at this time of day. Lydia couldn't see much in the way of security, but Fleet went over to the desk and flashed his badge. 'Floor twelve, need to take a look.'

'It's empty,' the neat young man said. His name badge said 'Mitch' and he had the kind of starter-moustache Lydia associated with fifteen-year-old boys. If he was the guard for the night, they definitely weren't anticipating much trouble.

'That's right, son,' Fleet said. 'And I need to take a quick look at it. Problem?'

The man slid laminated guest passes across the desk. 'Elevator two.'

'Lift,' Fleet muttered as they walked away. 'We're still in bloody London, aren't we?'

They were half an hour early for the meeting to give them time to check out the location beforehand. Plus, you never knew what you might see if you turned up before the party had officially started.

The lift moved smoothly upward and Fleet leaned against the bar against the back wall. Suddenly, he straightened. The lift had stopped and the doors began to slide open but Fleet had already started moving, he lunged in front of Lydia, managing to shove her to the side of the lift and stab the button to close the doors at almost the same time. Lydia didn't have time to process what had happened, let alone ask him what was happening when her head seemed to explode. She threw out an instinctive blast of energy through the gap in the lift doors but her ears were ringing and she had no idea if she hit anybody.

And then the doors were closing again and the lift was moving down. Lydia was about to ask Fleet what had happened, she just needed to wait for the ringing in her ears to stop, when she realised that Fleet was moving in slow motion. No, he was falling in slow motion, his good hand clutching his bad shoulder and an expression of pain on his face.

'Fleet!' Lydia was falling with Fleet, unable to bear his weight, but she hoped that she was cushioning his fall at least.

'I'm okay,' he said grimacing. He moved his jacket aside and Lydia saw a small red stain blooming on his white shirt. He had ripped open his shoulder wound when he had stretched to hit the lift button and push Lydia.

'What the hell was that...' Lydia trailed off as she noticed a dent in lift wall, at chest height. 'Did someone just shoot at us?'

'I need to call it in,' Fleet was saying as the lift descended.

Lydia couldn't take her eyes off the bullet lodged in the metal wall of the lift. It had been so close. If Fleet hadn't moved so quickly one of them would definitely have been hit. She felt weak and fuzzy from the discharge of energy, too. Like three bad hangovers arriving all at once.

The doors opened on the ground floor and it was surreally quiet. The security guard behind the desk still looked far too young for the job and the place was still mercifully empty.

'He might be on his way down,' Fleet was saying. 'This is a public safety issue.'

'I doubt it,' Lydia said. 'He only wants to kill me.'

But Fleet was already moving behind the desk, taking control of the situation in a very Fleet manner. 'There's been an incident on floor twelve, how many people are currently in the building?'

The guard's eyes grew wide as he pushed away from the desk to stand. 'Not many. Ten maybe on floor four, they work late there. Nowhere that high. They're not in use.'

Lydia joined Fleet behind the desk. There were a couple of monitors, the screens showing feeds from the building's cameras. The images changed every few seconds.

'Show me floor twelve,' Fleet said, pointing at the screens.

'I don't know how,' the guard said in a panicky voice. 'They're just on a loop like that and I watch them. I'm not usually on my own—'

'Sit down,' Fleet said, 'put your head between your knees.' He put his hand on the guard's shoulder and pushed him gently back into his chair. 'You're all right. Breathe.'

At that moment, the image on the far-right monitor changed. It showed an empty office floor, deserted apart from a figure lying on the floor. Lydia leaned in, studying the grainy image. It looked like a man, one arm flung out to the side. A very still man.

Fleet had seen it, too. 'Okay.' He had his mobile out and was calling in.

'I'm going up,' Lydia said, already moving. That wild blast of energy. She had hit someone.

'Not a good idea. Back up is on its way. We need to secure the building. Make sure the civilians are safe.'

'Your back up is on the way,' Lydia said. 'I need a look at the guy before they arrive.' What she didn't say but knew

Fleet had observed was this; the man wasn't about to shoot anybody else.

Still, not wanting to be over-confident, Lydia took a different lift to the floor below and then used the stairs to approach the twelfth. And she didn't complain when Fleet insisted on coming with her. She was pretty sure her attacker was dead or unconscious, but there was a chance he was still dangerous.

'I'm guessing this isn't protocol,' Lydia said, getting out at the eleventh floor and taking the stairs.

'No. But you're right. They're unlikely to start attacking random office workers.'

They fell silent as they approached the door to the twelfth floor. The staircase was disturbingly open with lots of glass panels and mood lighting set along each step. Lydia pressed against the wall as she approached the opening to the office floor. She wished there was a nice solid door she could hide behind, maybe with a handy-dandy viewing panel to peek through. Instead, she crept forward, trying to see into the space without showing herself.

Acres of grey industrial carpet broken up with pillars and a few glass boxes which would presumably function as not-at-all-private offices. Even without cubicles and ringing phones, the place was a soul-sucking hellscape.

A hellscape with a dead man on the floor near to the bank of lifts. The way the man was lying and the fallen gun, a foot or so away from his outstretched arm, made it very clear that he was no longer a threat to anybody. Fleet put his good arm in front of Lydia, shaking his head, and making the approach in a wide circle. Once he was close enough, he kicked the gun further away from the body.

'He's dead,' Lydia said quietly. She knew she ought to feel bad, but she was flooded with relief that the man with the gun who had just shot at them was no longer a threat.

Fleet shot her an exasperated look, but she saw his shoulders relax as he got a better look at the body.

Up close, there was no question. Lydia had expected the man to be dead, so it wasn't much of a shock. What did surprise her, however, was that she recognised him.

'Felix,' Lydia said. 'He's a professional.'

Fleet had crossed to the gun he had kicked away and was crouched down, examining it without touching. 'A professional who has been watching too many mob films,' he said. 'He's wrapped the grip with tape.'

'To prevent fingerprints?'

Fleet nodded, still looking. 'That's the idea. Outdated now we've got DNA matching.'

Lydia pulled on nitrile gloves, stepping closer to the body. Then she stopped. Fleet was shaking his head, as if he wanted to deny something, and then he sank to the ground.

She crossed to him, instead. 'What's wrong?'

'I moved before the lift doors opened,' he said. 'I think that precognition thing, that instinct you were talking about. I think it happened again.'

'And thank feathers it did. You saved my life again.'

'I didn't,' Fleet said, looking up at her.

'Don't be modest,' Lydia said. 'You pushed me out of the line of fire. There's a bullet embedded in that lift wall that was meant for-'

'No,' Fleet was shaking his head. 'I saw it happen. That's never happened before. I've had feelings. Hunches. You know the kind of thing. And, yeah, I moved the steering wheel before I'd consciously recognised there was a reason to, but this was different. I saw it happen. When we were in the lift. The doors opened and he was there,' Fleet glanced at Felix. 'He shot me. Here'. Fleet put a hand in the middle of his chest, over his heart. And then the colour drained from his face.

'Put your head between your knees,' Lydia said, but Fleet was way ahead of her.

She spoke to the back of his neck. 'Why would he want to kill you?'

Fleet said something incomprehensible in reply.

She patted down Felix's body until she found his phone. It required a thumb print to unlock and Lydia lifted Felix's lifeless hand and pressed the relevant digit on the button before she could think about it too much. Once unlocked, she navigated to the call history and pressed to redial the last number.

'Yes?' Mr Smith said. 'Is it done?'

CHAPTER TWENTY-SIX

Lydia had left Fleet in the office building before the police turned up. Time was of the essence and she couldn't afford to get stuck. Lydia didn't know how quickly Mr Smith would find out what had happened and she wanted to speak to him while she knew more than he did. He would probably have guessed that something had gone awry, but there was a small window when he, hopefully, didn't have all the details.

'He'll guess that you know he set us up,' Fleet said. 'It's too dangerous.'

'He wants me to run to him,' Lydia said with more certainty than she felt. 'He wants me to make a new deal, to work for him. If I dangle what he most wants, he'll believe me because he *wants* to believe.'

Fleet hadn't looked convinced but he had wished her luck.

Lydia had a tracker in her shoe, the GPS on her phone switched on and exactly zero time to practise her acting skills. She fast walked to Canary Wharf tube station and did a couple of jumping jacks to get herself out of breath before calling Mr Smith. It was testament to the city she loved that nobody so much as broke stride, the pedestrians simply flowing around her as she aerobicized as if it was perfectly normal.

'I need help,' she said as soon as Mr Smith answered. 'It's me. Someone just... Fleet...' Lydia found that it was easier than she had expected to cry. The pent-up feelings about Ash, the fear she had been carrying since Fleet had been shot and then the adrenaline rush of the gunshot in the lift. She had come far too close to losing the man she loved.

'Where are you?'

'Canary Wharf,' Lydia managed. 'I'm going into the station. I need to get away from here fast. I can't see anybody following, but...' She broke off, looking behind her in a panicked way. There was little chance that Mr Smith's resources stretched to commandeering street CCTV in real-time, but it was easier to commit herself entirely to the performance.

'What happened?' Mr Smith asked. 'Are you hurt?'

'No, I'm okay. I think I might have hurt him, though.' She swallowed as a wave of pure fury engulfed her. Mr Smith had set her up, had been threatening her for weeks, trying to intimidate her into needing him. Trying to make her believe that she was too weak to lead the Crows, that she was in danger. When that hadn't worked, he had taken aim at the one she loved. Her voice was shaking with emotion when she spoke and she just hoped that Mr Smith couldn't tell it was anger and not grief. 'He killed Fleet. He just shot him. And I wasn't in control. He was choking on the ground and I ran.'

'Fleet was choking?'

'No, the hitman. He had a gun. I'm guessing it was your assassin.' No need to let Mr Smith know that she had met Felix before and recognised him. She also hoped that he would assume Felix had dialled his number but had been unable to speak. 'I don't know what to do.'

'Get the DLR to Tower Gateway. I'll meet you on the bridge.'

'Just you,' Lydia said. 'If I see anybody else...'

'Of course,' Mr Smith said, his voice soothing.

Lydia cut the connection and followed Mr Smith's instructions, acting terrified and jumpy all the way. It wasn't difficult, as the moment she sat on the scratchy seat of the train and saw her face reflected in the window opposite a truth hit. She had just killed a man. A bad man, for sure, and it had been panicked self-defence, but still. She had thrown out her power with no control and no real grasp of the situation. She began to shake and wrapped her arms around herself. This wasn't the time to break down for real. Still. There were many faces reflected in the train's windows, blurry and indistinct and, for a moment, Felix's dead face was among them.

Emerging from the station, the squat fortification of the Tower of London on her right and a fresh breeze whipping rain directly into her face, Lydia made her way to Tower Bridge. She hoped Mr Smith wouldn't be in his car as she definitely didn't want to get into it with him. She walked to the middle of the bridge, dodging tourists and people heading out on dates and nights in the pub and all the normal things that suddenly seemed so desirable. Fleet isn't dead, she reminded herself.

She forced herself to stop moving and lean against the blue-painted balustrade with its intricate iron trefoil design. It was London twilight and thousands of windows glowing with yellow light shone in the gathering night. The Shard stabbed the purple sky, a futuristic obelisk straight out of a science fiction film. Looking at it in the context of the skyline, Lydia could hardly believe she had climbed halfway up. At least no one would be mad enough to try to get higher.

On the other side of the river, the Gherkin marked the

City. The distinctive dome of St Paul's Cathedral was further away and, just beyond it, the central criminal courts. Lydia wondered whether Alejandro was sad to leave the place. Or whether it was weight lifted from his shoulders.

She felt a rush of motion sickness and heard crashing waves just seconds before Mr Smith said: 'Lydia. Thank God.'

She turned to the man she had made a deal with and who, once upon a time, had honoured his word and healed Henry Crow. She had always known that he had wanted to use her, but she had never suspected that he would go so far. And now she was a killer. She tasted bile in the back of her throat and swallowed. 'Was it your rogue assassin?'

'Possibly,' Mr Smith said, he moved as if he wanted to touch her but then seemed to check himself. 'Did they say anything? Tell me what happened.'

'But why would they target me? What could I have done to get on their radar? I've got nothing to do with international smuggling or toppling governments. Nothing that high level.'

He tilted his head and Lydia could almost see him thinking. He was trying to work out how much to say, how best to keep her afraid and scrambling. Lydia decided to push on with her act, pretending that she believed Felix was an international assassin. 'You. You put them onto me. Why?'

'It's nothing personal,' Mr Smith visibly relaxed. 'We just wanted to ensure they came back to London.'

Back to London. Lydia didn't miss his phrasing. He had relaxed too much and done exactly as Lydia had hoped. Revealed something new. 'So, when you said you didn't know anything about this assassin you were lying. You know exactly who they are.' The final piece fell into place and Lydia resisted the urge to smack herself in the forehead. Instead she stepped back, feeling stupid for not seeing it before. 'They were working for you.'

Mr Smith looked down. 'The service contracted them, yes. But then we lost contact. They've been behaving erratically and we need to bring them in as a matter of some urgency. I didn't want to involve you, but I'm not the only one making decisions. Matters were taken out of my hands.'

'Fleet is dead,' Lydia said.

'And I'm sorry,' Mr Smith reached for Lydia and, if she hadn't known he had ordered it, she might have been taken in. She had to hand it to the secret service, that spook training was top notch. 'But you're in a precarious situation, now. You have to be smart.'

There was no way Felix was the top-level international assassin at the centre of Operation Bergamot, which meant that Mr Smith was acting alone. Lydia felt sure that this was his own personal crusade, building assets for his own, Family-focused department. 'The meeting was for Charlie,' Lydia said, watching Mr Smith's face very carefully. 'I thought it was Alejandro.'

Mr Smith didn't blink. 'Alejandro is far away from London, now. Safe location. New identity. The works. It's the sort of thing we could do for you.'

Lydia nodded as if she was seriously considering his offer.

'Or you could join my department. Help me with my research. It's valuable work. And I can keep you safe. You need people around you, Lydia. You're not safe on your own.'

Lydia made her body sag in defeat. 'Okay,' she said quietly. 'I need to put my affairs in order and then I'll come with you.'

'You shouldn't be alone,' Mr Smith began, but Lydia interrupted him. 'I'll meet you at the old safe house in an hour.'

. . .

It was almost eleven o'clock when Lydia's phone buzzed with a text. She ignored it and the three which followed. She was in the cafe, finishing some much-needed lasagne when she saw a familiar car pull up outside.

Mr Smith got out of the Mercedes. He was irritated but clearly trying to pretend that he wasn't.

'You didn't show. Is there a problem?'

'Have you heard about Felix?' Lydia asked and enjoyed Mr Smith's quick frown. He was so good at controlling his expression that every time he failed felt like a triumph. 'I killed him.'

'I don't know what you think you know…'

'I know you booked a sub-standard contractor to make me feel afraid.'

Mr Smith didn't miss a beat. 'For the greater good. You are in real danger and I just wanted you to understand that.'

'How kind,' Lydia said. 'I believe I will take my chances. No more deals.'

'Let's talk about this. I can see you're upset, now, but when you have time to think things through…'

'You've lost,' Lydia said flatly. 'Any chance you ever had to work with me or study me or use me has gone. It's over.'

Mr Smith straightened very slightly.

Lydia could feel the waves of his unusual signature rolling from him as his temper rose. He might be able to control his expression, but he couldn't control that. There, Lydia knew she was ahead of him. 'You made me into a killer,' she said. 'I crossed a line today and I will never forgive you for your part in that. But there is something else you should know,' she held his gaze and pushed more than a little Crow into her words, 'I became a killer today.'

There was a short silence as Mr Smith seemed to contemplate her words. Then he shifted slightly, rallying. 'You're making a huge mistake. I can be a really good friend to you.'

'I have enough friends,' Lydia said. She turned and indicated The Fork. The cafe lights were blazing and warm light spilled onto the pavement. The figures inside were clearly visible through the windows. Mr Smith's gaze shifted and Lydia enjoyed the change in his expression as he took in Fleet, who was standing next to Maria Silver. Henry Crow was seated at Lydia's favourite table with Aiden and they were laughing about something.

'So be it.' Mr Smith turned away. 'You're making a mistake, but I can see your mind is made up.'

Lydia crossed her arms and watched him leave. He paused, one hand on the handle of his car door and spoke without turning around. 'Check your pocket.'

Lydia waited until the car had moved away down the street, the tail lights disappearing as it turned the corner. Then she waited a little longer, just in case Mr Smith changed his mind and came back around for round two.

When the street remained empty and quiet, she reached into the pocket of her hoodie. There was something papery, folded into a neat square. A ten-shilling note.

CHAPTER TWENTY-SEVEN

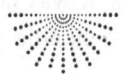

Two days later and Lydia was watching Jason spray a tower of whipped cream onto a mug of hot chocolate. He added marshmallows and then grated a sprinkling of chocolate with the tiny grater Lydia had bought him for the purpose. 'Tell me what you think.'

It would be perfection, like every single mugful he had made this week, but Lydia obediently took a sip. 'Gorgeous,' she said, licking cream from her upper lip. 'I think you've got the ratio just right.'

Jason beamed.

Lydia took another sip. It really was good.

'You know what you need with that?' Jason began opening the cupboards.

'Whisky?'

He shot her a fond look. 'Something to dip. Like a biscuit. We don't have any.'

Lydia could sense this escalating. Before he could start talking about baking, Lydia warned him that Fleet was due home any moment.

'Was he all right to go back to work?' Jason asked. 'Isn't his shoulder still healing?'

'I wasn't sure,' Lydia said. 'But he said he didn't need to be fully fit to sit in meetings.'

'Are you going to tell him about the note?'

Lydia put the mug down, her appetite suddenly gone. 'Yeah. Soon. I will.' She had told Jason about Mr Smith leaving a ten-shilling note in her pocket, but hadn't wanted to worry Fleet. She knew it was falling back into old, bad habits, but the instinct to handle things on her own was strong.

It was probably just a mind game, anyway. Mr Smith had tried to frighten Lydia into joining him and it hadn't worked. The note was just a face-saving exercise. Probably. At least they had the identity of the sniper. The police had raided Felix's flat and found a cornucopia of equipment, including a rifle and long-range scope. Ballistics were checking to see if it had fired the bullet which had hit Fleet, but Lydia was pretty sure it would match. Felix's phone had shown a text from Mr Smith on the day that Fleet was shot, which seemed enough. Lydia had told the investigating team that the number was connected to a member of the secret service, but it was a burner, of course, and she didn't expect to see Mr Smith in handcuffs anytime soon.

FLEET ARRIVED NOT LONG AFTER, his jacket damp from the rain. London in the spring was a damp affair. He kissed her full on the lips, pulling her close in a decidedly rambunctious manner.

'You're happy,' Lydia said.

'Interesting day.' Fleet went to the fridge and pulled out two beers. He looked at the half-finished mug of hot chocolate. 'You want one of these?'

'Yes, please.' They clinked bottles.

'So,' Fleet leaned against the kitchen counter. 'I had a very interesting meeting today.'

'That's not a phrase you use often.'

'It was an unofficial meeting, really. My boss invited me for a coffee out of the building, so I knew it was off the record. She said that Operation Bergamot was being wound up, that it was a budgetary decision for the Met.'

'So the wider operation will continue with all the other agencies?'

Fleet turned his hands palm up. 'Probably. But the rumour is that a key member of the operation here in London was carrying out unapproved actions and the inter-departmental heads want to distance themselves from the London portion.'

'Mr Smith?' Lydia said. 'Sounds like he's in trouble.'

'Good,' Fleet said, raising his bottle.

The last thing Lydia wanted to do was ruin Fleet's mood, but she knew it would get harder to share the longer she waited. She was learning.

'What's that?' Fleet frowned as she pulled the note from her pocket.

'A parting gift from Mr Smith,' Lydia said. 'There was one like it in Mark Kendal's wallet and Aiden told me it was Charlie's old way of letting people know they were in trouble with him.'

'In trouble?' Fleet arched an eyebrow.

'Imminent physical danger,' Lydia clarified. 'Marked.'

'You think he's letting you know he killed Mark Kendal? Why would he do that?'

'I think it's more that he wants me to stay scared. He's told me that his department has access to a high-level assassin. I guess he wants me looking over my shoulder and this is his way of saying I'm still in danger.'

Fleet thought for a moment. 'Why did Mr Smith target Mark Kendal, anyway? Was it just to make you look like a bad leader?'

'I assume so,' Lydia said. 'And to make me likely to lean

on him. He swooped in quick enough to offer help. Besides, he's the only other person who knows about the ten-shilling notes. Apart from my family, I mean.' Lydia didn't want to dwell on how Mr Smith would have got that particular piece of information from Charlie. She had put Charlie and his situation in a locked room of her mind and she had no intention of going inside.

EARLY THE NEXT DAY, Lydia watched Fleet get dressed for work. He had an enthusiasm that had been missing over the last few weeks. 'Getting shot suits you,' she said. 'You're glowing.'

'Bit extreme as far as self-help advice goes,' Fleet said, smiling like the sun. She got out of bed to kiss him goodbye, pressing up against him until he groaned quietly under his breath. 'I'm going to be late, now. You're a bad influence.'

HALF AN HOUR LATER, once Fleet had left, Lydia stretched out in the bed and tried to hold onto the relaxed calm that head-banging morning sex had bestowed. Her phone buzzed with a text and she rolled over to retrieve it from the floor. It was a message from an unknown number.

St Thomas' Hospital. Roof. Come now.

A moment later, another message came through.

Don't make me visit Emma.

LYDIA STARED at the black letters until they became fuzzy, the words dancing in and out of focus as she fought the urge to throw up, to run, to scream. For a suspended moment in time, every muscle in her body flexed. The tension was like a sacred covenant - if she didn't relax a single fibre, then

Emma would not be in danger. Nothing would happen to her, nothing would happen to her children. She would have erased the text message through an act of denial. And then the moment passed and Lydia knew she must move.

Lydia was up and out of the flat without conscious thought. When she found herself in a taxi and on her way to Westminster Bridge she was just relieved to see that she was dressed. The journey seemed interminable. She texted the unknown number to say that she was on her way. Then again to ask the assassin to wait.

It had to be Mr Smith's rogue assassin. He had to have commissioned a hit on Lydia. The ten-shilling note hadn't been an empty threat or a continuation of their dance. Mr Smith had taken his defeat hard and decided to end the game. Lydia couldn't think of any alternative explanation and she was in no state to reason it out.

Getting onto the roof of the hospital was nowhere near as difficult as Lydia had imagined. She had always thought that walking to her own death would feel harder or take longer. As it was, she felt nothing but a calm sense of inevitability. She would not let anybody else get hurt on her account. The idea that her life, her position, her choices, would lead to Emma or her children being harmed in any way was unthinkable. There was no choice to be made. This was what it meant to be the head of the Crow Family. Everything stopped with her.

Coming out of the stairwell and onto the roof, Lydia was slapped in the face by a stiff breeze. At least she wasn't clinging to The Shard, she told herself, while scanning the collection of stone buildings and low walls. She moved around one locked structure with a yellow 'danger of death' notice on the door and the space opened out. Over by the low wall which signalled the edge of the building, there was a slight figure. For a moment, Lydia thought that it was the Pearl King. And then they turned and she realised her mistake.

It was Maddie.

THE END

ACKNOWLEDGMENTS

I am beyond thrilled by the response to this series, and am deeply grateful to my wonderful readers for taking to Lydia Crow and her London with such enthusiasm. Thank you! I will keep doing my very best with the characters and the world.

2020 hasn't been the easiest year in which to write, but I am very lucky to have a wonderful support team. Thank you to my fantastic children, Holly and James, and to family and friends for your love and encouragement. As ever, thank you to my brilliant author pals; Clodagh Murphy, Hannah Ellis, Keris Stainton, Nadine Kirtzinger, and Sally Calder.

Thank you to my editor, cover designer, early readers, and ARC team. You are all wonderful. In particular, thanks to Beth Farrar, Karen Heenan, Judy Grivas, Paula Searle, Ann Martin, Jenni Gudgeon, Stuart Bache, Kerry Barrett, and David Wood.

Finally, my deepest love and gratitude to my husband. I truly couldn't do this without you.

CROW INVESTIGATIONS:
Book Six

The Shadow Wing

SARAH PAINTER

CHAPTER ONE

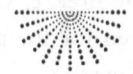

Maddie looked different. Partly because she was wearing a red bobbed wig over her brown hair and heavy-framed glasses with, Lydia assumed, clear lenses, but also because there was a calm stillness that she didn't associate with her cousin. After another second, Lydia realised another reason she felt so alien; there was barely a wisp of Crow. She reached out her senses, giving Maddie a virtual pat-down, but came back empty. There was the smallest taste of feathers and, with concentration, she could feel the warm lift of a thermal current as she lifted and flew...

'Stop it,' Maddie said sharply.

Lydia stopped. She shifted her balance, wondering what sort of weapon Maddie would be carrying and whether she was going to chat before she killed her. She felt strangely calm. In some ways, it would be comforting to die at the hands of somebody familiar, rather than a stranger. Keeping it in the family.

'What's funny?' Maddie said.

Lydia realised she was smiling. 'It's nice to see you. I mean,' she tried again, 'not nice, exactly. It would be. If we weren't on this roof and if you hadn't been sent by Mr Smith to kill me, but still. You look well. I like your glasses.'

Maddie didn't move.

The sky was clear and, behind Maddie, the Houses of Parliament were bathed in morning light. There was warmth from the spring sunshine, which helped to counteract the coolness of the breeze. Up high, the traffic was quiet and, if it hadn't been for the assassin opposite, Lydia would be grateful for the view.

'I didn't know it was you,' Maddie said after a moment of silence.

'You threatened my best friend,' Lydia said, feeling a surge of pure anger.

'It was in the packet.' Maddie waved a hand. 'I was told the target would come running if I sent that message.'

'And here I am,' Lydia said, spreading her hands. 'I thought you weren't taking orders anymore?' At that moment she felt her legs begin to move. She took one step toward Maddie, her body lurching and off balance, and then another. She hadn't told her body to move, it was simply doing so. Which was terrifying. She tried to push back, to regain control of her muscles, but it made no difference. It was as if the connection between her mind and her body had been completely severed.

When she was inches away from Maddie, close enough to wrap her hands around her throat or throw a punch, Maddie said: 'That's better. Now we don't have to shout.'

'How did you do that?' Lydia's mouth flooded with saliva and she thought she might be sick.

'You like my party trick?' Maddie's tone was playful, but her eyes were flat and lifeless. They reminded Lydia of Charlie's shark eyes, but only if the shark had been dead for hundreds of years. And hated other sharks.

'It's incredible,' Lydia forced herself to say. The fear was pounding through her now, and her traitorous legs were liquid. It was one thing to be killed, quickly and neatly by a professional, but to have her body taken over, forced to do things while she was fully awake, that opened a whole chasm of terrible possibility. 'Is this why you're so good at your job?'

Maddie tilted her head. 'You're being very agreeable. Do you think if you flatter me, I'll let you go?'

'I'm just surprised, that's all. You didn't seem the professional type. You were always so...'

'What?'

'Scatty. Undisciplined. Childish.'

Lydia's lungs squeezed and the air whooshed out. She couldn't move her muscles in order to refill them and the panic was instant.

'You're trying to annoy me into finishing this quickly,' Maddie said, her voice even. 'Dangerous tactic.'

Lydia's head was pounding with the lack of oxygen and her panic was beating its wings wildly against the inside of her chest. Just when dark speckles appeared in her vision and she knew she was close to passing out, Maddie released her diaphragm and allowed her to drag in a breath. If she had been in control of her body, she would have slumped down, but she wasn't so she stood, back straight, and pulled in air until her head cleared. After a few breaths, she managed to speak. 'Just making conversation.' Lydia's lungs felt like they were on fire and Maddie was still keeping her spine unnaturally rigid, but she struggled on. 'Do your parents know you're back in town? Do they know you're contracting for the government? I bet they'd be very proud.' In the middle of her last sentence, when she thought Maddie was as distracted as she was going to be, Lydia threw as much of her power as she was able. Maddie took a stumbling step back as it hit, and Lydia felt Maddie's control over her body loosen. She had been ready and threw a punch into the side of Maddie's head, knocking her out.

At least, that was the idea.

Maddie ducked and the blow glanced off her temple. Lydia felt the syrupy sensation of her limbs being taken over, and she fought against it, trying to grapple with Maddie. With a twisting motion, Lydia found herself grasped in front of Maddie, a knife at her throat. Maddie seemed utterly unaffected. 'That was fun,' she said, her breath tickling Lydia's ear. 'Hardly anybody dances with me anymore.'

'We've got all day,' Lydia said, trying to match Maddie's tone.

'Sadly, you do not.' Maddie walked Lydia toward the edge of the roof.

'Why are you working for Mr Smith?' Lydia kept talking to try to mask her fear. If she pretended she wasn't terrified, maybe she could make it so. The breeze seemed stronger here, at the edge of the building, and the traffic noise louder. Lydia could glimpse the street below. Far below.

'I don't know who that is,' Maddie said.

'Government spook. Nice suits. Why are you taking orders at all? You're a Crow.'

Maddie stopped moving.

'How much do you know about the department that gives you orders? I know Mr Smith has been rogue himself or, at least, head of a very hush-hush department. The kind that gives the government full deniability.' Lydia was speaking quickly, trying to find a way in now that Maddie seemed to be listening. 'And I'm the head of the Family, now. You know that, right? Have you asked yourself why they want me dead? I've been working on forming alliances, keeping the old truce from breaking. If I'm murdered, all hell will break loose.' Lydia had no idea if this was accurate. It was entirely possible that Aiden, or even Maddie, would step neatly into her place and Maria Silver would do a dance on her grave.

'The thing is,' Maddie said, after a moment. 'I know I warned you about this. I told you to fly.' And with that, she pushed Lydia so that she was hanging over the edge of the roof. Her body was under the control of Maddie, both physically and magically. Her tiptoes scrabbled for purchase on the stone edge and her mind slowed with the mortal fear. Every single impression, the feel of the wind on her skin, the sounds of the city, the harsh call of a crow. Many crows, in fact, as a group flew into view. A murder of crows, Lydia thought. How appropriate. It was possible that she was being hysterical. Losing her mind. She heard laughing a moment before she realised that it was hers.

'What's funny?' Maddie's voice was almost interested and Lydia could detect a neediness beneath her words. The neediness of a girl who had felt left out. Maybe not the coolest in her gang of friends, maybe marginalised, overlooked. Or maybe Lydia was still grasping at straws.

'I knew they'd played me, but I thought you'd got away. But here we are.'

'I did get away,' Maddie said. 'I make my own choices.'

'Not how it looks,' Lydia said. Then, taking a gamble, 'Charlie's still using you.'

Lydia felt a jerk of movement and closed her eyes. This was it. She was going to plummet to the concrete. She thought of Fleet and felt a deep throb of sadness.

Instead, she landed on her backside on the roof. The jolt sent a spike of pain up from her tailbone through her spine and into her neck, but she wasn't free-falling toward a pavement, so it was a definite win.

'What has Charlie got to do with this?' Maddie was standing over her and she hadn't even broken a sweat. The controlled power of the woman was breath-taking. And terrifying.

Lydia had no idea what Mr Smith had told Maddie, or even if he was her official handler. She tried to weigh up what would most offend Maddie. 'Charlie is working with the government. The spook who has been trying to recruit me teamed up with him last year.'

'Your Mr Smith?'

'Yeah. I named him.'

'Imaginative,' Maddie said. She was poised on the balls of her feet, but was clearly thinking.

For a moment, Lydia allowed herself to imagine a scenario in which she walked away. 'I didn't take Charlie's place just to start taking orders from somebody else.' She tried to keep her voice steady, to match Maddie's strength. It wasn't easy as her whole body hurt and her mind was still a tangle of fear.

Abruptly, the tension in Maddie's body shifted. Lydia tensed. This was it.

'You look tired,' Maddie said. 'You should check your vitamin D level.' And then she turned away.

Lydia twisted to watch her leave. She walked, casual and unhurried, back to the entrance to the stairwell. At the door, Maddie glanced back, and Lydia tried to read her expression. Was she going to change her mind? Come back and finish what she had started? She found herself raising a hand, half goodbye wave and half salute. Maddie smiled and then left. Lydia lowered her hand, unsure whether she had been in control of it.

WALKING from the hospital to Westminster Bridge, Lydia was in a daze. The colours of the day were too saturated, and the morning air felt like tiny needles on her skin. Her legs were wobbly, but she could still feel the adrenaline in her system, the urge to run or fight. Anything, in short, other than walk sedately past the South Bank lion. There was a Nando's next to the statue, and Lydia felt suddenly ravenously hungry. She pictured chicken in a pitta bread with a pile of chips on the side and saliva flooded her mouth. It was before nine in the morning and she didn't even like Nando's very much. It was a reaction, Lydia told herself. Near-death experiences made her hungry, apparently.

She ducked into a chain coffee shop just before Parliament Square and bought a cheese and ham toastie and a pain au chocolat. She was gripped with the realisation that she had never tried an iced coffee. She had always meant to, but hadn't got around to seeing what all the fuss was about. She could have died and then she would never have known. Iced latte in one hand and a fragrant paper bag in the other, Lydia headed for a seat in the square. She passed the statue of Winston Churchill looking, as ever, like a grumpy egg in an overcoat, and perched next to Millicent Fawcett instead.

She ate the toastie without really tasting it. After licking the grease from her fingers, she pulled out her phone and stared at the screen. She wanted to call Fleet. Not just for the comfort of hearing his voice, but because he was the person she wanted to tell. Things seemed both more real and more manageable when shared with him, which was probably what all the love songs and poetry had been bleating on about.

But he was still a copper. If she told Fleet about Maddie, he would call in the cavalry. He would have to. It was probably a public health issue or something. There would be protocol. Guidelines. A handbook of some kind. And if the police started marching around the place, making a fuss, Maddie might take it poorly. And take it out on Lydia. Or Emma. Hell Hawk.

Lydia lifted her drink, surprised by the coldness of the cup. She had forgotten that she had bought an iced coffee in a moment of madness. If she couldn't tell Fleet, what could she do? How could she protect Emma? It was terrible timing. Emma was probably rushing to get the kids ready for school, but she pressed dial anyway.

'Hey hey!' Emma's voice sounded happier than Lydia expected. Lin Manuel Miranda was singing in the background, Archie joining in enthusiastically, if not accurately.

'Shush a minute,' Emma said, and the music dipped in volume. 'Mummy can't hear Lydia. Sorry. You all right?'

'Fine,' Lydia said. 'Is this a bad time?'

'We're in the car,' Emma said. Her voice took on a theatrical tone. 'We're going on an adventure.'

Emma's next words were drowned out by excited cheering.

Lydia felt tears in her eyes as she heard Maisie and Archie and Tom whooping and squealing, Emma dissolving into delighted laughter. 'Sorry, sorry. Tom and I are delirious, we've been up since three so that we could pack in secret. We didn't want to tip them off early.'

'Where are we going?' A chanting had started and Emma shushed them again, without much success.

'We're back on Sunday. Shall I call you then? We can catch up properly.'

'Great,' Lydia said. 'Have a good time.'

After hanging up, a WhatsApp pinged from Emma.

Sorry about the chaos. We're taking the kids to Center Parcs. V excited.

They were heading out of London. That could only be a good thing, even if it was a temporary reprieve. Lydia tapped out a quick reply and then took a slurp of her coffee. It was like milkshake. Not unpleasant, but not coffee. She ate the pain au chocolat and felt a little better. She still wanted to phone Fleet, but the urge was manageable. And now that the fear had subsided a little, clear thoughts were breaking through.

The ten-shilling note that Mr Smith had slipped into her coat was tucked into the inside pocket of her leather jacket.

She unfolded it carefully, feeling the softness of the old paper. This was a method used by Charlie, something he had used to show people they were marked. Mind games and menaces. Typical Charlie, in other words. Still, it was Crow business, twisted and used against her. Now she saw that it was a symbol of the greater betrayal to come. Mr Smith had ordered a Crow to kill her. Her own cousin.

Lydia drained the cup and stood to put her rubbish into the bin. Millicent Fawcett was carrying a banner. It said: Courage calls to courage everywhere. She stared at it for a moment. Was Millicent telling her to call for help? Or to make a stand and inspire others? Or just to remember her courage? That was good. She had courage. And in that moment Lydia realised that she had something else... Fury.

CHAPTER TWO

Lydia wanted to do something. Take immediate and decisive action. Ideally something destructive. Unfortunately, there was nothing physical she could burn down. She had linked Mr Smith to JRB, a corporate entity that had been trying to stir trouble between the Families, and it was entirely possible that he was the man at the top of that particular tree. But the only physical location for JRB was a deserted rented office which was used as a postal address and nothing more. And she knew as much about the organisation and its key players as when she had first heard of them, which was, practically speaking, nothing.

What she did know didn't make her predicament easier or more comfortable. Mr Smith was on the payroll of the British government, running a super-secret shadow department which sat somewhere between MI6 and MI5. She couldn't exactly storm the hulking fortress of MI6 to demand a reckoning. And if his activities went beyond his official capabilities, the service might not even be aware of what he was doing. Worse still, this might be the way the secret service routinely operated. It was secret, after all, and Lydia imagined there were plenty of black-ops-style shenanigans that the powers that be couldn't officially sanction, but for which they, nonetheless, gave tacit approval. Her head hurt with the sheer weight of things she didn't know.

Until she discovered more about Mr Smith's role at JRB and the size of that organisation, and figured out the scope of his department and influence within the secret service, Lydia had to assume that danger could come from any angle. Knowing that she had handed her uncle to a man who was now trying to have her killed spiked her fury. But fury wasn't going to help her, now. She had to *think*.

Lydia wasn't naïve enough to believe that Mr Smith would be working entirely alone. And there was no way she could find out how far his influence within the service went and whether he was taking orders from high up. For now, she had to act as if MI6 were her enemy, too. Which meant no blabbing to Fleet.

If she was being smart, Lydia would run. There was a chance that Maddie would tell Mr Smith that the job had been done and her body had hit the pavement, making a bit of modern art all over the road outside St Thomas's. That would buy her time. And even if Maddie did go running to him to talk about how she'd been thrown by his choice of target and hadn't, on this occasion, fulfilled her brief, he still had no idea of her location at this exact moment. She glanced up as she walked past a bus stop, seeing the camera mounted on the streetlight nearby. He would have quick access to the city's CCTV and she would need to use an ATM to get cash, which would also be traceable, but if she went right now, she could be in Glasgow by the afternoon, and hiking away from a remote station in the highlands by nightfall. Or she could jump on the Eurostar to Paris. Then nick a car and drive to Italy. If it had been an official operation, then he could put an all-ports warning on all transport hubs out of the UK, but if it had been unofficial... Well,

Lydia didn't know exactly what he would do, then. Just send Maddie back after her, she supposed. Or somebody like Maddie. How many killers-for-hire did Mr Smith have in his back pocket?

She hesitated, her mind quickly tracking through the steps to running. The nearest place to buy a rucksack and a pack of underwear, the fact that she needed to destroy her phone, buy a couple of burners. Her passport was back at the flat. Would she be able to go and collect it, or was that too risky? Once she crossed the channel, she could keep driving. Go all the way to Russia. Russia was big. A person could definitely lose themselves there.

Underneath all this, another track was playing. Lydia finding Mr Smith and putting him in a choke hold. Her mum and dad's faces when they were told she had disappeared. Fleet moving on with his life with another, less insane, girlfriend. Maddie, frustrated at her failure, paying a visit to Emma. Her stomach flipped and she turned blindly, going to cross the road and start moving if just for the relief of motion.

A man wearing bulbous headphones and staring at his phone walked right into Lydia, and she almost fell off the kerb and into a black cab. It was a quintessential London moment. The traffic. The idiot pedestrian. The brush with death. She smiled.

She pulled her phone from her jacket and, instead of dropping it and stamping it into oblivion with her DMs, she made a call. She wasn't running. She was Lydia Crow, and London was her home.

LYDIA HADN'T SEEN Paul Fox since he crashed a dinner date with Fleet, intent on stirring trouble. Truth be told, she was nervous. There had been an awkward possible-marriage-proposal a few weeks back, and she wasn't sure where things stood between them. She was pretty sure it had been a business proposition more than a romantic declaration, but still. They had a history.

She had texted her request and he had told her to meet him at a pub in Whitechapel. She was asking a favour, so it was reasonable for him to summon her to his manor, but still, she was on edge as she made her way to the side street off Brick Lane.

It was a traditional boozer, complete with a slightly sticky floor and button-leather and wood furnishings, plus the obligatory old geezers on bar stools engrossed in their pints and the racing paper. Paul was sitting with his back against the wall, watching the door. Thankfully, he was alone. Lydia didn't think she could handle his siblings, too. She was annoyed to find that she still felt off balance and she channelled that, straightening her spine as she approached Paul's table.

'This makes a nice change, Little Bird,' Paul said. 'You coming to me.'

'Don't get used to it,' Lydia countered. She was trying very hard to ignore the animal pull of Paul Fox. No matter how much she prepared herself it still hit her afresh each time she saw him. 'I'll buy you a drink, though. What do you want?'

He tilted his head. 'You want to buy me a drink?'

'Not if you're going to be weird about it.'

He looked at her for a beat. 'You're worrying me. Sit.'

Lydia didn't want to make a habit of obeying Paul Fox, but she was trying to be conciliatory, so she dragged the chair that was opposite Paul to the side of the table and sat. She wasn't going to snuggle up to him on the bench, but this way she didn't have her back to the door.

Moments later, the bar man appeared with two coffees, which he placed on the table with great deference.

'I didn't think this place did table service,' Lydia said.

'They make an exception,' Paul said. 'Coffee all right? I can get us something stronger if you want to kick off a party.'

'Coffee's fine,' she said. It was disgusting, actually, but she pretended to take a sip. It was an excuse to take a beat to collect her thoughts. Now that she was here, Paul watching her with a bright light in his eyes, her plan didn't seem quite as clever. She had to force the images of red fur, dark earth, and the crunch of tiny bones from her mind. She clenched her right hand, feeling her coin appear in her palm. The shape of it was comforting.

'What's different?' He asked finally. 'With you?'

'I don't know what you mean.'

'Suit yourself, Little Bird.' Paul sipped his coffee and pulled a face.

'You remember my cousin? Maddie?'

'I do,' he said cautiously.

'She's back.'

He went still. 'In London?'

Lydia nodded. 'She's working.'

The look of caution increased.

'You know.' The realisation hit. 'You already know. What she does these days.'

Paul touched the edge of his cup with a thumb and forefinger, rotating it once. And then again. Finally, he nodded. 'I have an idea, yeah.'

'And you didn't tell me?'

Paul smiled thinly. 'You rejected my very generous proposal. I don't think I need to apologise for not giving you full access.'

'That's not how this works,' Lydia said. 'This is business, not personal. You are the head of the Foxes, I am the head of the Crows.'

'We don't really have a leader-'

Lydia held up a hand. 'Don't give me that bollocks.

You're the head of your family. Whatever you want to call it, they're not listening to anybody else.'

'Nevertheless,' Paul began.

'No, not nevertheless. And who calls a marriage proposal "generous"? That's some shady shit. No wonder I said no.'

Paul smiled like he had won the lottery. 'I knew you cared.'

She felt a flush creep up her neck. 'I don't care. I just want a bit of respect.'

His smile vanished. 'Don't we all.'

Lydia squeezed her coin and took a deep breath. 'She threatened my friend. Emma.'

'The one with the kids?'

'My friend from school.' Back when she had been a rebellious teen there had been a short, intense fling with Paul. She squashed the memory of pressing up against him, body on fire, mind delirious with hormones and lust. She was older and wiser now. Well, definitely older.

'What are you doing to do about Maddie?'

'Find her. Kill her.' The words were out before Lydia could think. But they made sense. How else could she ensure Emma's safety? She had to stop Maddie for good.

'That's fair. And you want a hand?'

'I was hoping you could keep an eye out for Maddie. Let me know if you hear anything. And something else...' She swallowed. 'Can you spare anybody to watch Emma? She's out of the city for the weekend but will be back on Sunday. I can do some shifts, but I can't cover the whole time. I can pay.'

'Protection?'

Lydia nodded. She waited for Paul to ask her why she wasn't asking Fleet, to take the opportunity to stick the boot in about her copper boyfriend and make some snide comment about him not being able to help her. Instead, he reached for her hand, the one holding her coin, and wrapped both of his around it. Looking straight into her eyes with a sincerity that was unnerving, he promised that his family would keep a personal eye on Emma and her children day and night.

She felt a mix of relief and apprehension. 'You're going to send your brothers?' There was nothing like being given a good kicking to make you wary. But at least she knew they were capable. 'If they hurt her, I will–'

'They're strong,' Paul broke in. 'And fast. Trust me, you want them watching out for your friend. They have good instincts. And they will–'

He broke off, eyes shifting toward the entrance. Lydia hadn't heard the door open, but there was a man walking toward their table. He had a weather-beaten face and a red beard shot through with grey and was carrying a walking stick that looked like a twisted tree branch, worn smooth and shiny with use. He was wearing a tunic and trousers which appeared to be made of pieces of leather and fur. Lydia would have said that he had wandered from a cosplaying event, except that the clothes were extremely well-worn and were giving off a distinctive, authentic aroma. Nobody looked askance, which made Lydia think the man was a regular and perhaps made sense of why Paul had asked to meet her here and not in his hidden den.

He nodded to Paul and changed his trajectory from the bar to their table. She desperately wanted to put a hand over her nose and mouth against the smell, but she sensed this would not be polite.

'Long time,' Paul said. 'Did you do as I asked?'

The man nodded and reached out an open palm. His nails were caked in dirt.

Paul leaned beneath the table and produced a plastic carrier bag. He held it out of reach, his own hand outstretched. There was a curious moment, both men eyeballing each other and neither one speaking or moving.

Then the man dressed like an extra in an extremely low-budget Lord of the Rings, put a folded piece of paper on the table and slid it toward Paul.

After unfolding and reading, his face betraying nothing, Paul handed over the carrier bag.

The man moved away with surprising speed and was out of the door before Lydia had time to gather her thoughts.

'What was that about?' She had thought about not asking, not wanting to give up power by showing her interest, but then had decided that she couldn't be bothered to play games. Besides, if Paul felt a little bit superior, he would be more likely to drop his guard.

Paul pocketed the paper and smiled tightly. 'Just business.'

Lydia nodded. She tried an understanding expression.

'What are you doing?' Paul said, unnerved.

'Empathising,' Lydia said. 'There's always something, isn't there? It's exhausting. Sometimes it almost makes me miss Charlie.'

'It's not the same. I'm not…'

'I know, I know.' Lydia waved a hand. 'No formal hierarchy. Free spirits. I'm not trying to insult your family.'

His mouth twisted. 'Makes a change.'

Lydia pressed a hand to her chest. 'You wound me.'

He smiled then, properly, and Lydia felt it in her gut. And a bit lower down. Bloody Fox magic.

'I had better go,' Lydia said, not moving.

His teeth were white, and she imagined them grazing her skin. His eyes held hers and she couldn't help but notice how black and large the pupils were and, was that her imagination, or were there rings of gold around the light brown irises? They were mesmerising. Alight with a knowing desire. A desire which promised good times in a safe, warm den. She swallowed hard and forced herself upright.

'I'm looking into that firm, JRB.' Paul said, seemingly

oblivious of the effect he was having. 'The place that sent the Russian to mess with my Family. What?' He raised his eyebrows. 'You're not the only one worried about it. If there's a war we'll go to ground, but that doesn't mean we won't suffer. Besides,' Paul smiled a different sort of smile. The sort that promised pain, not pleasure. 'I wish to settle the score.'

CHAPTER THREE

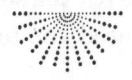

When Lydia walked into The Fork, the scent of fried bacon and toast almost made her cry. She hadn't cried when an assassin had summoned her to die, but the sight of Angel scowling from behind the counter and the familiarity of the cafe with its breakfast-scented air and steamed-up windows almost broke her. That was what she got for drinking a milkshake instead of a proper coffee.

'Feed me,' Lydia said. 'The works.'

Angel raised an eyebrow. 'Rough morning?'

'And tell Aiden I'm waiting for him.'

Angel, sensibly enough, didn't say 'tell him yourself' or 'I'm not your secretary' or any of the other phrases Lydia could see piling up behind her lips. Instead, she caught sight of something in Lydia's face and tone and simply nodded.

Once she was at her favourite table, her back to the wall and with a full English in front of her with both coffee and orange juice on the go, Lydia felt her strength returning. Aiden appeared, pulling his beanie off his head and sitting opposite. Lydia was using a piece of fried bread to mop up the remaining egg yolk. The weight of the food in her stomach was comforting, but she had the feeling she would be ready to eat again in a matter of minutes.

'All right, Boss?' Aiden said, eying her plate enviously.

'How is everything going? Anything on fire?'

Aiden shook his head. 'All cushty.'

Lydia took a sip of her orange juice to cut the grease from the bread. 'I need to tell you something because you've a right to know. And I need you to be on the alert. But it must not go any further.'

Aiden straightened up. He looked so young to Lydia, but she knew she didn't have a choice. He had proved to be reliable and trustworthy so far and he was a Crow. One of her own. Trust didn't come easy, but that didn't mean she shouldn't keep trying. She had already checked that there was nobody sitting near their table, but she glanced around once more before continuing. 'MI5 or MI6 or a department that flits between them has its sights on us. They've been interested for a while and been looking to use us as assets. Or to burn us to the ground, cut out any threat we might pose to national security.'

'That's fucking ridiculous-' Aiden broke in, affronted. 'What have we done to the country? We're not bloody terrorists.'

A man eating a bacon roll on his own a couple of tables over lifted his head and Aiden lowered his voice. 'And how the feathers did we get on their radar?'

Lydia wiped her fingers on a paper napkin and scrunched it up. 'I was in contact with that department. I had hoped it would be mutually beneficial. More for us, than them, obviously,' she smiled and Aiden nodded his understanding. 'But that's off the table. My contact seems to want to end our relationship in a permanent manner.'

'That's okay,' Aiden said, visibly adjusting to the news. 'We don't want anything to do with them, anyway, do we? I mean, we're all right on our own. Always have been.'

'Hopefully,' Lydia said. 'They do seem keen to make a statement, though.' She wasn't sure whether she should tell Aiden the full truth. Hadn't, in fact, been planning to, but the words tumbled out. 'The department took out a hit on me.'

'They what?' Aiden's eyes were wide.

'You heard,' Lydia said, pushing her plate away. She wasn't saying the ridiculous phrase out loud again, once had been enough.

'But you're still here,' Aiden said, admiringly. 'Good job, Boss.'

Once upon a time, Lydia had found Aiden's boyish enthusiasm annoying. Now, she had the awful urge to give him a hug. What was wrong with her? She drained the rest of her coffee. 'I need you to ask around. Discreetly. See if anybody important has made any shady new friends recently. I'm not arrogant enough to think I'm special and if Mr-,' she broke off, stopping the name she had given her spook falling from her lips. A breath. She continued. 'If the secret service were looking to recruit me as an informant, they may have tried their luck with other Crows, too. I'm particularly interested in John and Daisy. I need you to watch them. Covertly. Can you handle that?'

'I mean, I go round there quite a bit. And there's that Easter thing on the weekend.'

Lydia had completely forgotten about the family party. The invite had come via email and she had assumed it was a duty invitation, rather than a sincere one, which had given her the very happy excuse to bow out. She didn't have the closest relationship with Uncle John and Aunt Daisy, John having made it perfectly clear that he didn't think she ought to be Charlie's replacement.

'I won't be there,' Lydia said, 'you can make my apologies.'

'Right,' Aiden said, looking like he wanted to say something else.

Before he could, Lydia barrelled on. 'And I want you to look around for anything out of the ordinary, but don't worry too much. It'll be too busy. I need you to keep an eye on them both. See if there is anyone new in their lives. Any suspicious activity.'

'How will I watch them both? Can I ask my brother to help?'

Lydia shook her head. 'Just do your best. I want this to stay between us for the moment.'

'Why do you think they might be targeted?' There was an element of insult in his voice.

'I don't, really. But an outsider could assume John is senior. And I thought they might be vulnerable to a spot of bribery.'

That slur on John and Daisy mollified Aiden. He nodded sagely. 'Especially since they lost Maddie.'

'Exactly,' Lydia said. 'Just keep your eyes open. And, while you're at it, let me know if anybody in the Family is flashing cash.'

'I just got the new PlayStation,' Aiden said lightly. 'Full disclosure.'

'That's all right,' Lydia said. 'I know you're not stupid enough to cross me.'

UPSTAIRS, Lydia had just sat down behind her desk and was contemplating the drifts of paper and line of dirty mugs, when her phone rang. It was Maria's assistant, and the spurt of annoyance at Maria Silver and everything she stood for felt like a welcome breath of fresh air. The assistant was doing his very best to make an appointment for Lydia at the Silver offices. 'No, thanks,' Lydia said cheerfully, in exactly the same way she had done the last three times he had called. It was nice to have a bit of normality in a very strange day.

'Ms Silver would very much appreciate a meeting at your earliest convenience. If tomorrow isn't suitable, how about Wednesday? Or Thursday? She is in court during the day, but you could come in for eight. A breakfast meeting. Or five-thirty.' There was a note of desperation in his voice.

'You can tell Maria that if she wants to see me, she can make an appointment at my office. I'm not running over to Holborn just because she has clicked her fingers.'

'You don't understand,' the assistant said, sounding utterly miserable. 'That's not how she works.'

'But it's how I work,' Lydia said, enjoying herself far too much. 'You take care, now.'

'Who was that?' Jason spoke near her ear, making her jolt in her chair, her hands coming up in fists.

'Feathers!'

'Sorry,' Jason said, not looking sorry at all. 'You're jumpy.'

'It's been that kind of day.' And, before she could stop herself, the whole story tumbled out.

Jason hovered next to her desk, listening intently. 'So you've got Aiden keeping an eye on John and Daisy?'

'I didn't tell him the real reason, of course,' Lydia said. 'But, yeah. He'll be watching them.'

'I don't understand why you went to the roof in the first place. What the hell were you thinking? Why didn't you call the police? Fleet?'

Speaking to Jason was the closest thing to talking to herself. She trusted him, of course, but since nobody else could see or hear him, it really added a layer of security which helped her to open up. Still, she had to force herself to include the part where Maddie had threatened Emma. It had been bad enough telling Paul. Saying it out loud again made it even more real and she felt her fear spike.

'You could have taken me, at least. I could have helped. Maybe the two of us would have had a chance…'

Jason didn't feel physical things like a normal person, but he still had lots of mannerisms from when he had been alive. Conversely, when he was very upset, he forgot to use them. Now, instead of slumping in shock or sitting down, he went stock still for a full minute, as if someone had pressed 'pause'. Then his outline began to vibrate. His physical form flickered in and out of existence and Lydia had to put her hand on his arm until he settled.

Oddly enough, his reaction made her feel better. He was horrified, and that eased the shock of the situation a little. Lydia supposed that this was what people must be babbling about when they said 'a problem shared was a problem halved'. It was nowhere near that effective, but it was something, and Lydia felt a surge of gratitude.

'What do you think she will do next?'

He meant 'will she change her mind and finish the job?' a thought which had been pinging in and out of Lydia's mind all day. 'I don't know. Mr Smith said that an assassin had gone rogue. Assuming he meant Maddie, that gives us hope that she might decide to ignore this order and disappear again.'

'Unless Smith is rogue,' Jason said. 'And that we can trust anything he told you.'

'Yes,' Lydia agreed, suddenly feeling exhausted. 'Assuming that.'

Relieved that she didn't have plans with Fleet and would have a little bit of time to recover her game face, Lydia had fallen into her bed and slept a deep and profound sleep. She had expected nightmares and insomnia but instead she dreamed of flying. It was so immersive that it took her a while to get properly conscious the next morning. She had dragged herself into the shower and taken her coffee out onto the small roof terrace, letting the morning drizzle and mild spring air rinse away the last dregs of sleep.

The pressure sensor under the carpet in the hallway set off a beeping alarm so that Lydia had prior warning whenever anybody approached her door. Seconds after it sounded, Lydia tasted the clean bright tang of Silver, so she wasn't at all surprised when she opened the door to find Maria Silver glaring at her.

'So this is where you work,' she said, sweeping into the flat.

'Come in,' Lydia said drily, following her into the main room which served as both her living room and office. There had been murmurings in the Family that she ought to move into Charlie's house or, at least, rent an office more befitting of the head of the Crow Family but she had resisted. The main reason for that resistance had, at that very moment, materialised behind Maria Silver's back and was making little bunny ears above her head.

'Tea? Coffee? Valium?'

Maria's frown intensified in confusion.

'Have a seat,' Lydia said, indicating the chair in front of the desk that she used for clients.

Maria was walking around the room, looking at it with an attention that Lydia found unsettling. She was wearing a tight black pencil skirt and a fitted jacket with a red silk blouse peeking from underneath. She looked like money and danger and sex and Lydia pitied the defence lawyers that found themselves opposite her in court.

Jason had moved with Lydia to her side of the desk and was making eye contact, waggling his eyebrows in a questioning manner. Lydia raised hers in reply with the tiniest of shrugs. She had no idea why the head of the Silver Family had decided to grace her office with her presence. They hadn't spoken since Maria had agreed to visit The Fork in a show of solidarity against Mr Smith and his shadowy government department. That had been a week ago and, given that Maria had spent the previous year vowing to kill Lydia, it was a very new, very tenuous truce. Lydia kept her balance light, ready to dive for the floor if Maria produced a weapon.

Jason circled around and got closer to Maria which made Lydia feel a bit better. Jason was a ghost, but he was surprisingly handy in a fight.

'You live here?' Maria inspected the sofa before sinking gracefully to sit. She crossed one exquisite leg over the other and laid her arms across the back of the seat, forming a compelling image. It was calculated, of course, as with everything Maria did. The woman was a master of performance.

Lydia sat in her office chair. She leaned back and put her DMs up onto the desk, crossing one leg over the other in a less elegant motion. 'What can I do for you, Maria?'

'You owe me,' Maria said.

Jason sat next to Maria on the sofa and leaned close. He blew lightly on her neck and Lydia was interested to see Maria shiver.

'We're allies,' Lydia said. 'You want a favour, all you have to do is ask.'

'You did ask,' Maria replied. 'And I delivered. I stood with your family, provided the necessary optics.'

Lydia had wanted to demonstrate to Mr Smith that she had a successful alliance with the Silvers and that further attempts to turn the Families against each other would be futile.

'Not just optics, I hope,' Lydia pushed a little Crow into her words. 'This alliance is only going to work if it's genuine. No more scheming behind my back. The Silvers and the Crows are allied. That means if our fortunes rise, so do those of the Silvers, and vice versa.'

Maria's expression didn't change, although there was the slightest twitch of her left eye. 'Naturally.'

She was lying, but so was Lydia. Alliance meant cooperation while it was mutually beneficial. When stars fell, all bets would be off. 'Good, then. I repeat, what can I do for you?'

'The cup,' Maria said simply.

'What about it?'

'You told me it was fake. Were you lying?'

'I was not.'

'So you will find the real one for me.' It wasn't a request.

Jason pulled a face at Lydia and mimed throttling Maria, both of which she did her best to ignore. 'Why me? You looking to save some cash?'

'Because you know the significance of the piece and because you are properly motivated to carry out a task of this importance. You have incentive that money cannot buy.'

'And what's that?'

Maria smiled. 'My continuing kind wishes.'

CHAPTER FOUR

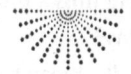

'You're not going to do it, are you?' Jason was frowning as he filled the kettle and hit the switch to turn it on. She was glad to see that he had regained one hundred per cent solidity and was back to looking almost alive. 'Isn't it a good thing Maria doesn't have it?'

'I have to,' Lydia said. 'Gotta keep the alliance in good order.' Lydia knew that her position as the head of the Crows was only as secure as the peace she managed to keep between the Families. She had lost points for winding up the more criminal parts of the Crow empire and knew there were plenty of whispers about her being too weak. She couldn't afford to have anything else slip.

'You don't trust her, though? I mean, do you really think she's on our side?'

'Feathers, no,' Lydia said, smiling at Jason. 'But I have to act as if I do. Believe her, that is.' Lydia had told Maria that the Silver cup, a Silver Family relic which lived in their crypt beneath Temple Church, had been swapped with a fake. She had been in the process of telling her that her supposedly dead father, Alejandro, was not in the crypt either, which had, understandably, been the headline. Lydia hadn't even been sure that Maria had taken in the news about the cup at all as she hadn't reacted and they had soon been back to their usual fare of mortal threats. Lydia ought to have known better. Whatever else she could say about Maria Silver, the woman was sharp. Nothing got past her.

Jason dropped a tea bag into a mug.

'No hot chocolate today?'

He shook his head. 'It doesn't feel like hot chocolate weather anymore.'

'Fair enough,' Lydia said. The sun was streaming through the living room windows, and would be drying the terrace from the night's rain. 'Is it beer weather?'

'Too early,' Jason said. 'And you're working.'

If someone had told Lydia that she would be living with the ghost of a man who had died in the 1980s and that he would treat her with a kind of motherly concern, she wasn't sure which fact would have seemed less likely.

She took her tea and sat behind her desk, feet up. The Silver Family cup had been donated to the British Museum at the time of the truce as a show of goodwill, but had been stolen forty years ago. Lydia had seen the cup in Alejandro's office and knew it was the real deal by her reaction to it. Namely, she had hurled her lunch all over Alejandro's nice carpet. The next time she had seen the cup it had been in the Silver Family crypt and that had most definitely been a replica and not the real thing. Which begged several questions. Did Alejandro place the replica cup in the vault and, if so, did he know it was a fake? If he had been knowingly handling a replica in order to keep the real cup hidden elsewhere, why hadn't he told Maria about it? And, for the grand prize, where the feathers was the real cup?

Lydia sipped her tea and closed her eyes, chasing the threads of her thoughts. Whether Alejandro knew or not, the replica was clearly good enough to fool the rest of the Silvers, which meant exquisite workmanship.

When she had been on the trail of an enchanted statue, Lydia had visited a shop in the silver vaults. Perhaps they could provide details of likely silversmiths.

As for the real cup, the most likely possibility was one which made Lydia shiver. If Alejandro had kept hold of the real cup, placing a replica in the crypt to hide that fact, there was a chance it hadn't disappeared along with him. The government department paying for his relocation package would have bled Alejandro dry and that, logically, would include confiscating any valuable Family relics. They would have argued that it would have endangered his new identity, and explained that it was for his own protection, but the result of that argument made Lydia taste blood and fury. A Family relic sat in a secure room of some shady government department. Worse still, Mr Smith handling the cup, maybe working out some way to harness the power contained within it.

Her tea was cold, and she was gripping the mug so tightly it was in danger of shattering. Lydia pulled herself upright, her DMs thudding onto the floor, and put the mug onto the cluttered surface of her desk. She slid her phone over and tapped a quick message to Emma. She had called to check in on her twice already and knew that if she did so again, she was really going to freak out her friend. After a moment's thought, she constructed a bright and breezy message about avoiding her tax paperwork and then waited, breath held, until the little checkmark indicated that Emma had read the message. Seconds later and a reply appeared. It was heavy on the emojis which meant that Emma was as busy as ever. Alive. Happy. Safe.

. . .

Since Operation Bergamot had been officially wound up and his bosses seemed to have accepted that Fleet's private life had not affected his loyalty to the force, Fleet was no longer out in the cold at work. At least, that was what he said. Lydia didn't know how much he was playing up the positives in an effort to make her feel less guilty. Lydia knew that Fleet's decision to go public with their relationship had caused him no small measure of professional pain.

He texted to ask about dinner plans and Lydia hesitated before replying. She had been spending more and more time at Fleet's comfortable flat. Partly because she was determined to match his commitment to the relationship but mostly, if she was honest, because she didn't feel as comfortable in her own flat since Ash had died in it. The cleaning crew had done an exemplary job, but they hadn't been able to expunge her memory. Not only was a troubled soul snuffed out before his time, in a truly unpleasant manner, but he had been under Lydia's protection. She had failed him. And what was to stop her failing the remaining people in her life?

Jason breezed through the room as she hesitated over the screen. She knew that he preferred her to stay in the flat overnight, and the added responsibility for his wellbeing pulled at her.

'What are you scowling about?' Jason asked, suddenly on high alert.

Lydia shook her head. 'It's nothing. Just thinking.'

'I'll make you some toast,' Jason said. 'Carbs cure everything.'

Lydia didn't bother to argue. Now that he could touch things, Jason found making food and drinks extremely therapeutic. Who was she to disrupt his equilibrium?

The smell of toasting bread floated through the open door to the small kitchen and Jason was singing a Bowie song quietly.

Lydia had never been very good at sitting still. She paced the room until Jason floated through with her food and then wolfed it down. He had been right. Buttery toast made everything better. Not solved. Not okay. But better. 'Thank you,' she said, dabbing her finger in the crumbs.

'I miss eating,' Jason said suddenly.

'Do you?' Lydia was surprised. He had never said as much before.

'It's new,' he said. 'It's been creeping up ever since you came along. Feelings of all kinds.'

Lydia opened her mouth to speak, but Jason rushed on.

'It's good. It's all good. I mean, I like feeling more real. I like being able to touch things and think clearly and care about... Things. It's like being alive.'

It hit Lydia. It was like being alive, but he wasn't alive. It was close but no cigar.

'But there's a cost to wanting things,' Jason continued, sounding forlorn. 'Feeling things. I am aware of what I'm missing. What I can't have. I'm aware that I'm dead and that there are so many things I will never have again.'

Lydia didn't know what to say. It put a lot of things into perspective. She probably ought to have an epiphany about living life to the full while she was breathing, but she just felt an aching sadness for Jason. He didn't deserve to have been cut down prematurely. He didn't deserve this half-life existence.

'But this is better than before,' he said quickly. 'Before you came was way worse.' He was getting upset, Lydia could see his edges vibrating and a sliver of space opened up beneath his feet where he seemed to have forgotten about gravity.

'How so?'

'I was barely here. But I had no control. No peace. I spent a lot of time in that other place, I think.'

Sometimes, without wanting to, Jason disappeared. It

could be for five minutes or five days, but when he came back he was always shaken. He said he couldn't remember where he went or whether it was just like passing out, a blank space, but Lydia didn't know if he was lying. All she knew for sure was that it terrified him. She put a hand on his arm, now, letting the cold seep into her arm until he stopped vibrating and looked solid again. 'What can I do?'

Jason smiled crookedly, looking like himself again. 'Don't leave me.'

'Never,' Lydia said.

Jason still looked as if he wanted to cry, so she added: 'Who would bring me toast?'

DCI FLEET ARRIVED eleven minutes after he had texted to say he was on his way and would be about ten minutes. There were many things Lydia appreciated about her kind, smart, handsome boyfriend, and his reliability was definitely high up the list. Which came as a surprise. As a younger woman, she had never imagined that would be an attribute to set her heart racing. Turned out, she had more than enough unpredictability in the rest of her life.

She kissed him hello in a thorough manner and was pleased to see him looking faintly dazed. Having a steady adult relationship was one thing, but it was good to see that she could still make Fleet temporarily forget his own name.

'I brought food, but it can wait.'

'No it can't,' Lydia said, plucking the paper bag from Fleet's hand. 'It smells amazing and I'm starving.'

'You forgot to eat again?'

That did happen when Lydia was engrossed in work, but today she had still been ravenously hungry. She didn't know if everybody reacted to near-death experiences with hunger, but it appeared that she definitely did. She also really wanted to jump Fleet. All of her appetites had kicked into high gear, which made a kind of sense when viewed as an evolutionary survival instinct. Or she was just twisted.

Once they were ensconced on the sofa with glasses of red wine and forks, Fleet turned serious. 'Any sign today?'

He meant, had she seen Mr Smith covertly or not-so-covertly following her or seen anything out of the ordinary that could indicate his attention. Fleet knew that it wouldn't be anything more than that as Lydia had promised him faithfully that she would call him immediately if Mr Smith approached her.

'Nothing.' Lydia speared a piece of red pepper from the sweet and sour chicken, trying to hide her guilt. 'I think he's moved on.'

'No you don't,' Fleet said shortly.

'Well,' she waved her fork, 'who knows what's going on with him?'

'That's the problem,' Fleet said. 'We know that he was removed from Operation Bergamot, but we don't know what to expect from his department next. He doesn't seem like the type to just stop.'

'I agree,' Lydia said. 'And his pet project has been destabilising the Families. I don't see him dropping that out of the goodness of his heart. I just wish I could be sure he was working alone. If we knew he was the sole operator behind JRB and considered a lone nutter at the service, we would only have one problem to solve.'

'You know I reached out to MI6 to ask for information on his department, but there's still nothing coming back. I'm just a copper and not a very important one. Unless I offer a trade, I don't think we'll get anything.'

'No trade,' Lydia said. The last thing she wanted was more attention from the government.

'I know,' Fleet stuck his fork into the chow mein and reached for his wine. 'And I agree. Mr Smith is clearly personally obsessed with the Families, but we can't be sure there aren't others. Especially with Charlie in custody.'

That was one word for it. Lydia's Uncle Charlie was most likely in a facility deep underground being experimented on to see if Mr Smith could work out the hows and whys of his Crow power. While most of modern London had decided that the legends of the four magical Families were exactly that, just myths and folk tales, fed by exaggeration and repetition, Mr Smith was more clear-eyed. He knew the powers existed and he seemed hell bent on harnessing them. Or, and this seemed increasingly likely now that he had ordered Maddie to kill her, eradicating them. 'Charlie might be dead,' Lydia said.

'I know,' Fleet said quietly and Lydia loved him for not ducking the hard truth and for the steady way he held her gaze.

'Do you think I would feel it?'

Fleet put his wine down and reached for her.

There was a place that made Lydia feel cherished and safe. A place where there was no professional killer stalking the streets with Lydia's name written in her workbook, a place where she hadn't been forced to betray her flesh and blood to save her father's sanity, a place where she wasn't normal but that her difference made her special and strong, a place where she was loved. Settled against Fleet, his arms around her and her cheek resting in the space between his collar bone and chin, the scent of his skin and that sensuous glow which was part delicious warm male and part the intriguing signature of Fleet, Lydia felt like she could breathe.

THE NEXT DAY, Lydia had been awake for over an hour when Fleet turned over in bed and opened his eyes. 'Hey,' she said as she watched him wake up.

Fleet smiled with his soft morning face and Lydia felt the warmth spread through her chest. This unguarded version of Fleet was private and all hers. He threw a warm arm over her body and hauled her close. She closed her eyes, feeling her racing thoughts slow for a few precious seconds.

'Bad night?' Fleet asked.

'Been worse,' Lydia said. He knew that she hadn't been sleeping well, but not the exact reasons why. Every time he brought up Ash or Mr Smith or her family, she deflected him. She couldn't talk to him about those things or how she felt about them, and she definitely couldn't talk to him about the real reason she couldn't sleep. She had no wish to remind the man she loved that he was sleeping with a monster. A murderer.

Over and over, Lydia ran the moment she had panicked and thrown her power through the lift doors. She hadn't even known she could do that. It had been like throwing a ball, if that ball was indescribable and full of pain and fury and dragged out of her own atoms. The man she had killed, Felix, was a professional killer. He murdered people for money. Lydia reminded herself of this fact multiple times a day, but it didn't help. She hadn't meant to kill anybody. She had lost control and a man died. If that had happened once, it could happen again. What if she hurt somebody else? What if she killed an innocent person?

Once they were both up and mainlining coffee, Lydia felt Fleet looking at her. 'What?'

'Nothing. Busy day today?'

'Tracking down a magical item for my sworn enemy,' she said. 'The usual.'

She took another sip of coffee and tried to remember where she had left her keys. Jason often tidied up behind her, so she looked in the top drawer of her desk. Nope.

Fleet ought to have left to make it to work on time, but

he was still by the doorway, coat over one arm. 'You're not looking for the Pearls, are you?'

Lydia closed the drawer and looked at him. 'Why would I do that?'

'Revenge. For Ash.'

Lydia felt stung. The thought hadn't occurred to her. The Pearls were extremely powerful, but they appeared to be trapped in their underground court. While they weren't snatching kids or following Lydia, she was going to leave them well alone. Besides, she had enough on her plate with Maddie. Why go poking the hornets' nest when you're already on fire?

Fleet's eyes were gentle. 'I would understand. If you were.'

Lydia shook her head, unable to speak.

'But you barely got out of there alive. The house was torn up. I've never seen anything like it.'

Lydia was transported back to the court, the Pearl King's unflinching inhuman gaze. She shuddered. 'As long as they stay put, I'm not going to bother them. My job is to prevent a war between the Families, not start one.'

'Good,' Fleet said after a beat. He looked surprised and it hurt.

Was she losing her humanity? Shouldn't she want to avenge Ash? She prodded the thought like it was a sore tooth. 'And I'm more concerned with Mr Smith and JRB.'

'You still think they are one and the same?'

'He's working his own little department at MI6 and we know not everything was official, but we don't know where the lines are drawn. I'm pretty sure he has been trying to destabilise the Families, though, keeping us off balance and apart. He was masquerading as a courier for JRB and said he was undercover, but I think he is JRB. Or, at least, I hope he is as I have no other leads.'

'They certainly seem to have an aligned purpose. How can we prove it?'

'To what end? He's using the company as a shell to funnel money and provide cover, but I'm guessing he has several set up. If we get too close to JRB, what's to stop him winding it up and using the ones we don't know about?'

'You want to go after Mr Smith personally?'

Lydia hadn't told Fleet that Maddie had summoned her to the rooftop by threatening Emma or that she had been contracted by Mr Smith. She knew that she had a bad old habit of keeping things close to her chest, but this instance was different. Fleet would take the information to the police. He *was* the police. And that risked Maddie going after Emma in retribution. Lydia would not risk her friend's life. Police protection would be too little and for too short a time. Maddie had proved that she could kill difficult targets, crime bosses and political leaders and heads of private armies. One mother in Beckenham with the local cops dozing outside in an unmarked vehicle wouldn't even provide a challenge. 'If I can,' Lydia said. 'But not if it's going to come back on the Families. I've got a lot of work to rebuild the trust between the leaders. I need to calm things down or we're going to have another problem. Maria Silver doesn't want her Family cup just for sentimental sake. I've got to assume she's aware of its power and is looking to use it.'

'Do you think she can?'

'No idea,' Lydia said. 'My training didn't cover anything like it and it's not like there is a big book of magic that can give me the answers.'

'Have you spoken to your dad? Henry might know more than he's told you.'

'Undoubtedly,' Lydia said. 'Speaking of fathers. Have you ever thought about finding yours? He might be able to tell you about your heritage.'

Fleet's eyebrows drew down. 'Fine. I take your point.'

'I wasn't making one.' Lydia was bewildered at his sudden hostility. 'It was an honest question.'

'No,' Fleet said shortly. 'I have never been tempted to track him down. He left. And I'm not interested in forcing a relationship with a stranger.'

CHAPTER FIVE

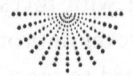

Confronted with questions she couldn't answer and truths she would prefer to forget, Lydia turned to practical matters. She might not be the biggest fan of her current client, but she had a job to do. And it would provide a welcome distraction from her dark thoughts and the dreaded feelings.

The thing about the Silver cup was that it contained power. Whoever had obtained the cup most likely knew that, but it didn't follow that they had the necessary skill to use that power. If they did, that was going to be a bigger problem. What Lydia had, however, was the ability to sense that power. Of course, London was a big city and the cup relatively small. There were a million hiding places and Lydia could hardly go wandering around every part, hoping to pick up its scent.

In the absence of other ideas, Lydia decided to trace its history. She had assumed that it had been stolen back from the British Museum by the Silvers, but perhaps a third party had been involved. If so, had they swooped in and taken it for a second time? Alternatively, maybe the people who had been involved in making the replica of the cup which had been placed by Alejandro below Temple Church had fallen for the real thing? People didn't have to be aware of the Family powers to be affected by them. What if someone had become obsessed and decided to take it for their own personal collection? These thoughts weren't anything close to solid leads or even solid ideas, but Lydia had started with less. That was the thing with investigative work. You just had to start digging, however unpromising the ground.

Roisin Quin had agreed to meet Lydia later that day, on her lunch break from her job in the medieval European and Anglo Saxon department of the British Museum. The sunlight pouring through the arching glass ceiling of the central atrium and bouncing from the white marble was almost blinding and Lydia was relieved when Roisin led her through a wide passage, past the public toilets, and down a spiral flight of stairs to a hallway lined with doors.

The education suite had a number of classrooms and small libraries with study desks and round tables for small groups. One room was filled with excitable primary-age kids, with a pile of brightly coloured backpacks and lunch bags against one wall and a slightly harassed teacher calling for attention. The kids reminded Lydia of Archie and Maisie and she dug her fingernails into her palm to stop herself from pulling out her phone and calling Emma. Maddie had only threatened them as a way to get Lydia to meet her on the roof. She had no reason to hurt them. Apart from anything else, they were valuable leverage for the future. Lydia's guts twisted, and her thoughts ran the now-familiar little maze, like a rat in an experiment looking for the exit, to the inevitable conclusion. There was nothing else she could do to protect them at this moment. She either had to get strong enough to take Maddie out, or she had to do exactly as she asked. Even if she could convince Emma to move her husband and children out of London, Lydia had no idea where would be safe. Maddie had killed highly guarded targets around the globe. And the act of her running might draw her interest, like a tiny mammal scurrying in the earth catching a hawk's eye. Still. Perhaps the Silver cup would offer a well of power that she could somehow harness. Or, she could use it to bargain with Maria for some professional protection. The woman had an impressive security detail and Lydia could hire the same kind of thing for Emma. And her parents. And Fleet. The weight was back on her chest.

Lydia had been distracted by her thoughts and she realised, when Roisin opened the door to a room with a conference table in the middle and an interactive white board on the wall, that she hadn't caught the woman's last few sentences.

Roisin was standing in the doorway, a questioning look on her face. At Lydia's blank expression, she repeated herself. 'We have a study room and a library attached to the department which are accessible to members of the public. If there is a particular item you are interested in, you fill out a study request form and add the objects requested. If possible, they will be collected for your appointment. There are strict handling rules, of course, but all guidance and equipment such as gloves are provided.

'We have over four million items which aren't on display, but there is a database with photographs and so on. Just make sure you fill out all the details correctly for the object request. It's not a simple undertaking to collect the items and nobody will just nip off to swap it for you.' She smiled as if having made a joke and the phrase had the delivery of a well-worn line.

'I understand,' Lydia said. 'I wanted to speak to you about an item that went missing from the collection in the late seventies.'

Roisin frowned. 'Missing? I wouldn't know anything about—'

'According to my research you're the expert on early Modern Europe. I want to find out about a piece which was made at the beginning of the early seventeenth century. It went missing from the museum in the seventies, but I know that a replica was made at some point. I'm not saying it was anything to do with the museum or that it was used to hide the disappearance, just that I have seen a very convincing replica of the item.'

'I do know what you're referring to,' Roisin said reluctantly. 'It's not exactly something we like to shout about. This is a very secure place, even more so these days. The items we care for are in the very best of hands.'

'Doubtless,' Lydia said. 'But this item, an ornate silver cup, was stolen from the collection and, to my knowledge, hasn't been recovered. Made in the early seventeen hundreds by the Silver Family and gifted to the museum as part of a truce in the nineteen forties. I have a personal interest in the truce.' Lydia produced her business card. 'Note the name.'

Roisin glanced at the card but didn't take it. She put her hands on her hips, instead. 'I thought you said you were doing a piece for The Guardian?'

Lydia had forgotten the cover story she had used on the phone to Roisin. Her mind seemed to be jumping from task to task, unable to keep continuity as she spent almost every waking second expecting Maddie, or a new hired assassin, to pop up and kill her. She tried a different tack. 'Look, forget about the cup. I'm not here to make accusations or get anybody into trouble. I assume replicas of very old items are made sometimes? For security. Or educational purposes?'

Roisin frowned. 'The provenance of our collection is well documented, all items are tested for validity before being catalogued. In the rare cases we display replicas, they are clearly marked as such.'

'That's not what I'm... Let me start again.' Lydia's hand itched to produce her coin. It would be so much easier to nudge Roisin with a little burst of Crow. She would go spacey and cooperative and would automatically and truthfully answer every question Lydia put to her. But Roisin wasn't a criminal. As far as Lydia knew. She was a citizen and, as such, Lydia felt she ought to go lightly on the mind control. She was descended from a long line of Crows who had used their abilities to build a criminal empire, but that didn't mean she had to follow in their footsteps. There had to be rules. She hadn't ousted her Uncle Charlie just to morph into him. She tried a smile and saw Roisin get even more discomforted. 'I am not suggesting anything untoward about your collection. But I imagine that occasionally there is need for reconstruction work. Would you be able to point me in the direction of the craftspeople capable of such work?'

Roisin's shoulders went down a notch. 'It's highly specialist.'

Lydia felt her coin appear in her palm and she folded her fingers around it, willing it to retract, to disappear to wherever it went when not in the physical realm.

Roisin stared into the middle distance for a moment, as if captured by a passing vision. Then she blinked. 'The Silver Family cup?'

Roisin looked properly out of it. Lydia had deliberately placed her coin into her jacket pocket and left it there, willing it out of existence at the same time, but some Crow whammy had clearly leaked out regardless. She was definitely stronger. A thought which thrilled and horrified her in equal measure.

Roisin sat down behind the nearest computer, seemingly on autopilot.

'It's not in the online collection,' Lydia said. 'I already checked.'

'Right,' Roisin said. 'I just…'

'You just wanted to make a show of looking in the hope that I would sod off.'

She started. 'No. No, not that. Not at all.'

'If you say something three times, it doesn't make it true,' Lydia said sweetly. 'I think you know exactly what I'm talking about and I want you to show me everything you've got on the Families. Now.'

The photographs showed the cup exactly as she remembered it. Tall and ornate with two handles. Like a trophy. It would be just like the Silvers to award themselves one. In the image, Lydia could see the same aged silver that had been so cleverly replicated in the fake cup currently residing in the Silver Family tomb. What she couldn't see, from the photograph, was the blindingly shiny silver overlay that she had seen from the real thing. The unmistakable sheen of Silver power which had made her throw up in Alejandro's office, just from being near to it. Looking around the busy reading room, the lack of nausea was a blessing, but it would have been handy to confirm for certain that the cup given to the museum had been the real deal.

Whoever had catalogued the cup had been thorough. There were photographs from different angles and one of the base. Four smudges in a row caught Lydia's eye. She magnified the image until the smudges revealed themselves to be stamped markings. One was recognisably the shape of a lion, one a letter L, and one was round and indistinct. The first mark was the most complex and the image too pixelated when magnified for Lydia to make it out.

'The lion is a quality mark, to show it's sterling silver. This is a leopard's head,' Roisin pointed at the round-ish shape. 'It tells you which Assay office tested and hallmarked the cup. Leopard is the symbol for the London office.'

Lydia squinted at the blob. 'I'll take your word for it. What about this one?'

'That's the maker's mark. It was registered with the Assay office and we got the details from them.'

'Their records go back that far?'

Roisin's face was alight with the fervour of a true fan. 'The Assay office began assessing the quality of metal goods in 1300, and the hallmarking office set up in 1478. The records aren't perfect back to that date, of course, but by the sixteen hundreds, they were writing things down. And this piece was important. It was made for the king, after all. See the crown, there. That's to commemorate that it was made for James I. We know the stamp from other royal items. I know it looks like any other crown, but they really are distinctive when you get into it.'

Lydia was studying the maker's mark. 'Is that a G?'

Roisin nodded. 'And that's a "C" on the other side of the hand. Hands have been a common symbol to indicate fine workmanship over the years, but this symbol with the palm facing out can be traced to a French maker.'

'You traced the maker?'

'I found this,' Roisin said, clicking to open a file. It was a photograph of a book page packed with black ink. The script was impossible to read as far as Lydia could see, but Roisin pointed to a line. 'This lists the date and the initials GC. The surname is here, see? It says "Chartes" which certainly ties in with the probable French origin.'

BACK AT THE FORK, Lydia found her old notebook and confirmed what she had thought. She had recognised the name 'Chartes' from an old case. Lydia had been on the trail of a statue of a knight and she had ended up in the silver vaults. A man named Guillaume Chartes had sold the statue to Yas Bishop in her capacity as JRB employee from a shop he ran down in the vaults. A shop which had mysteriously disappeared when she had looked for it a second time.

Yas Bishop was the only other person, apart from Mr Smith, that Lydia had found connected with JRB. And Maria Silver had killed her. The Silvers represented JRB. Mr Smith was high up in JRB. Possibly the sole owner. In fact, Lydia's working hypothesis was that JRB was just a shell corporation, a cover for Mr Smith's pet projects. The ones that didn't fit into his official capacity in his shady department with the British government's secret service. It was all so murky and Lydia had the familiar urge to shine a bright light on the whole lot. Preferably using a flame thrower.

Jason was sitting on the sofa with his feet up, laptop glued in place. He had been ignoring her pacing but finally sighed and looked up from the screen.

'Sorry,' Lydia said, and stopped.

'It's not you,' he said. 'Just someone in the crew is arguing for the sake of it.'

Jason had made a bunch of hacker friends online. If 'friends' was the right term. Colleagues? Cohort? Gang members? 'That's the internet for you.'

'I suppose.' Jason shook his head, clearing the distraction. 'What's on your mind?'

Lydia went over her thoughts, marvelling at how much better it felt to talk the whole thing out. By the end she still didn't have a clue how to find out more about JRB, how to confirm that Mr Smith was a one-man-band, or how to find the cup, or whether she should, but she felt a little better.

'That's a weird coincidence,' Jason mused. 'The name being the same as the guy you met in the vaults. You reckon it's his ancestor? Family firm?'

'Could be. Some families do hold to the same line of work for centuries,' she said, smiling at Jason. 'But it doesn't really help. I'm not sure what I was expecting to find. Looking at the original is a nice history lesson, but it doesn't help me find it now.'

'You're going to find out who made the replica, though, right?'

She nodded. 'That's next. It gives me something to do. Something to tell Maria when she demands an update. And who knows? Maybe it will give me a lead.'

Jason was staring at the wall, thinking. 'That silver statue sent people crazy, didn't it? Could the cup have the same effect? You said it was imbued with Silver power... Maybe that's why it was down in the tomb? To protect people from it?'

Lydia stopped pacing. 'Is that something you could search for? People admitted to hospital with psychosis?'

'I can try,' Jason said. 'Everything is recorded digitally now, but it depends on whether there is a centralised system. If medical records are kept by each individual hospital and institution, it will be harder. What about arrest reports?'

He made a good point. And Fleet would look if she asked.

THAT EVENING, Lydia called into her local deli before heading over to Fleet's flat. She wanted a good bottle of wine and his favourite crisps. She figured she should bring gifts before she hit him with a request. The sign had been flipped to 'closed' but Ciro opened the door when he saw it was her.

'Evening, Ms Lydia,' he ducked his head.

At first it had been strange when men and women old enough to be her grandparents bowed and scraped, their anxiety around her now that she was the head of the Crows palpable, but she had adjusted quickly. That was something she would have to watch, she thought, as she picked up two sharing bags of crisps and waited for Ciro to fill a plastic pot with fat green olives. If she wasn't careful, she would get used to it. Or even start to think she deserved their deference. She had to act the part left by Charlie Crow but she had to be careful she didn't start believing her own hype.

She asked after Ciro's children and grandbabies while he packed two bottles of red into a canvas shopping bag along with the olives and crisps. 'Anything else today?'

'No, that's perfect,' Lydia said. 'You're a lifesaver, thank you for opening for me.'

'Of course, of course.' Ciro ducked from behind the deli counter to open the front door for Lydia.

She didn't try to pay, knowing from experience that this would send Ciro into paroxysms of panicky genuflections and she didn't have time to reassure him. Instead she pushed a little extra warmth into her smile. It wasn't much, but she told herself it was better than nothing.

Fleet hadn't been home long when Lydia arrived. He was still in his suit with his tie loosened and hadn't even got himself a beer.

'Have you eaten?' He asked after kissing her hello.

'No. I brought olives,' Lydia hefted the bag onto the kitchen counter and began unpacking.

Fleet slipped off his jacket and hung it over the back of a chair before getting wine glasses and a bowl for the crisps. 'I've got some Greek salad and flat bread.'

Lydia wasn't big on salad, but she was too tired to think about takeaway, let alone cooking, so she gratefully agreed. She wandered through the flat, telling Fleet about her educational trip to the museum and hearing about his caseload, while music played through the speakers.

Fleet was just about to bring plates over to the sofa when he stood still. 'Can you smell that?'

'What?'

'Something's burning.' He turned to check the stove. 'I've not used the oven. I don't-'

'I can't smell anything.'

'Could be from another flat.' Fleet crossed the room at speed. A moment later, he had the front door open and was in the stairwell.

Lydia trailed after him.

He was turning slowly, frowning in confusion. 'You really can't smell it? It's definitely smoke. Really strong.'

Dutifully, she took a couple of deep snorts. Traces of urine and refuse. Somebody in the building cooking curry. A hint of Fleet. 'No.'

He shook his head and they went back inside.

Lydia retrieved the plates, and they sat on the sofa. She forked up some cucumber and feta cheese and washed it down with a generous gulp of wine.

'It's gone,' Fleet said after getting stuck into his own meal. 'That was weird.'

There was a possibility that Fleet's olfactory hallucination was a result of a head or nose injury, maybe something which hadn't been picked up in A&E after their car crash, as the doctor had been distracted by his gunshot wound. Or, and Lydia decided not to voice this opinion, it was his precognition gleam playing merry havoc with his senses. She glanced at the ceiling. 'Have you tested those recently?'

'The smoke alarms? Yeah. And they have that little light which shows the battery is good.' He looked at her seriously. 'You think it was a sign?'

'I don't know.' She wasn't going to lie to him. 'How have you been? Had any premonitions today?'

Fleet looked down at his salad and speared a piece of tomato. 'Hard to tell.'

Lydia waited.

'I mean... I have thoughts about what might happen all the time. Often I'm right, but that's experience of being an adult in the world. Doesn't make it precognition.'

Lydia put her plate onto the coffee table and drained the rest of her wine. 'Keep an eye on it. Maybe you could start tracking when something comes true? If you have a strong feeling or vision, maybe?'

'Perhaps,' Fleet put his empty plate on top of Lydia's and sat back, rubbing his face. 'I don't want to think about this.'

Lydia climbed onto his lap. 'Lucky for you, I have an excellent alternative.'

He smiled up at her and she felt the kick low in her stomach. 'Is that a fact?'

'It's a promise,' she said, and kissed him.

CHAPTER SIX

Since talking to Fleet about fathers and answers, Lydia had been wishing she could speak to hers. She was still trying to keep away from Henry Crow, in case her presence made him ill again, but she had another idea. The next day was bright and warm and it seemed like as good a time as any to visit the cemetery. With a ghost for a flatmate, the idea of asking her dead relatives for information didn't seem completely pointless. And who knew? Maybe they would answer. If you didn't ask, you didn't get.

The Family tomb was surrounded by bluebells and wild daffodils, ivy ramping across its surface and the old yew tree alive with small birds chattering. As Lydia crested the hill, three crows swooped down and perched on the stone tomb. The small birds took off in fright and the corvids regarded Lydia in an expectant manner. She greeted them politely, as she had been taught to do from an early age, and was rewarded with what might have been an acknowledgement. A slow tilt of their heads, six bright eyes fixed upon her, waiting. Feeling faintly foolish, Lydia faced the tomb and asked the question she had been mulling over on her walk. 'Where did my abilities come from?'

Nothing.

'I mean, I know that I'm a main bloodline Crow and that's why I have Crow power. Like my father and grandfather. But how did we get it in the first place?'

Lydia hadn't expected an answer, but when the crow simply cawed and flew up into the tree, she couldn't help but feel a little snubbed. Then she remembered that she was carrying an offering, and that she was in entirely the wrong place to get answers.

The yew tree had a couple of sturdy limbs which were invitingly low to the ground. Lydia caught one and swung her legs up, trying to imagine her father doing the same when he had been her age. She got herself into a crouch and shuffled along, holding a branch above for balance until she could reach the trunk. She rose slowly, gripping the trunk. Her first thought had been to climb higher but now that she was standing, she felt like she had plenty of height. Her view of the cityscape was obscured by branches and a thick canopy of pale green leaves.

Henry had told her that this was the best way to pay her respects. That her Family had never cared much for churches or carved stones on the ground, that they preferred a perch up high. Somewhere with a view, where you could hear the wind through the leaves and feel the sun on your feathers. Now that she was in the tree, Lydia could see the remains of previous offerings. Small scraps of frayed material, worn to threads by the weather, were tied from upper branches. She had never noticed them from the ground, partly because they were high up and partly because they were black and didn't exactly stand out. Lydia produced her coin and made it stick to the trunk while she tied the piece of black silk around the nearest branch.

'What are you doing?'

The voice startled her and the world tilted sideways for a

sickening second. She gripped the trunk and took a couple of breaths.

Peering down through the foliage, she saw the man she expected. Not just from his familiar voice, but from the strong scent of Fox which had wafted upward, carried on the breeze.

Lydia didn't bother replying to Paul, just saved her concentration for getting back down out of the tree in one piece. Her father might have happily shimmied up and down it in his youth, but Lydia's activities had always been more urbanite. Having never been keen on heights or plants, she wasn't a natural tree climber. Above her, her offering flapped in the breeze, looking uncannily like a wing.

Once she had reached solid ground, she put her hands on her hips and faced the Fox. 'What are you doing here?'

'Charming,' Paul said. 'Thought you would like a status report on the surveillance of your friend.'

Yes. The huge favour Paul and his family were doing. Lydia closed her eyes briefly and called for strength. She forced a pleasant expression onto her face. 'Thank you.'

Paul's lips quirked into an amused smile. 'That must have hurt, Little Bird. Don't strain yourself.'

'Shut up.'

'That's more like it. She's fine. No sign of anyone hanging around. And I've put a tracker on her car so if it goes AWOL we'll be able to find her.'

Lydia ignored the clutch of her chest as she imagined Emma being forced to drive somewhere with Maddie. She could see it so clearly, Maddie in the passenger or rear seat, knife held to Emma or, more likely, just using the threat of violence to Archie and Maisie to gain Emma's compliance. It was unbearable.

'Hey, she's going to be okay.' Paul took an uncertain step forward. 'I swear.'

'You can't know that,' Lydia said, noting that his words seemed sincere. 'But I appreciate you saying it. I do.'

He looked away, embarrassed.

'Now. How did you know to find me here?' She gestured at the tomb.

Paul smiled, the moment of uncertainty erased and swagger firmly back in place. 'I'm keeping an eye on you. We all are. For your own protection, of course.'

Well, that was creepy. But also, weirdly comforting. Next to JRB and Maddie, attention from the Fox Family seemed almost quaint.

'So, what were you doing up there?' Paul lifted his chin, his usual teasing tone and sardonic expression back in place. 'I didn't have you down as a tree hugger.'

'I'm not, as a rule.' She turned and looked back at the yew, the branches stretching over the family tomb. 'I brought something for the grave, but my dad said the Crows didn't care much for the ground. He said it was more respectful to leave offerings in a decent perch.'

'Well it makes a kind of sense. If you believe they're here.'

Lydia rubbed at the tree debris which she had acquired, knocking curls of bark and sap from her jacket and jeans. 'Honestly, I don't. But I'm desperate.'

'Desperate?'

As always, Paul Fox made her instantly wish she had kept her mouth shut. 'Don't get excited,' she said in her most withering tone.

He grinned at her, flashing white teeth.

She was too tired to spar with Paul. The way things stood, their old animosity felt like school playtime. Whether it was sensible or not, he felt like something safe and comforting. Familiar. Lydia had a new benchmark to divide her friends and enemies. Had they attempted to kill her?

She sat cross-legged next to the tomb, resting her back against the cool stone and looked at the vista of London laid out beyond the roll of the hill and the nearby rooftops. Paul sat next to her. Close, but not touching.

They didn't speak for a while and Lydia felt her heart rate calm and her breathing slow down.

'I'm sorry,' Paul said, after a while.

She glanced at his profile. 'What for?'

'About your cousin. It must be hard.'

She watched his face for a beat longer, but there was no malice in his words. No laughter. 'It doesn't feel real. Any of it. I mean, Maddie. I remember her running around and stealing desserts at Uncle John's birthday and making herself sick. She could be a pain, but a contract killer? An assassin? It makes no sense.' Another memory surfaced as Lydia spoke. She and Maddie at another family gathering. Bored of the grownups talking, they had escaped to the garden and were playing underneath the fuchsia bush in the far corner. They had found a dead sparrow and given it a burial. Maddie had cried for half an hour after until Lydia had distracted her with a bag of Skittles. How could that child have grown into a murderer?

Paul shrugged. 'What else does a restless young woman with a flexible moral attitude, an uncanny ability to influence people, move objects with her mind and stop hearts do? If they're not heir to the Crow Family business,' he said, waving a hand at Lydia.

'I am nothing like Maddie,' Lydia said, although she could taste the lie on her tongue.

Paul turned his head to look into her eyes. He smiled gently. 'I can tell you what they're really well suited to, and it's not secretarial work.'

'Charlie wanted to use her as a weapon,' Lydia said. 'He wanted to do the same with me, but we both refused. In our own ways.'

'You can say a lot of things about your Uncle Charlie, but he wasn't a fool.'

Lydia noted Paul's use of the past tense. He believed Charlie to be dead, then. 'But why would Maddie let the government do the exact same thing? She left the Crow Family because Charlie tried to use her.'

'And she hated him for it. I remember,' Paul said.

'So, why let them do it?'

'Maybe they made her a better offer?'

An expression crossed Paul's face that Lydia didn't recognise. 'What?'

'Just… I just thought of what they might have offered Maddie. And it's not good.'

Lydia opened her mouth to ask, but Paul was already speaking.

'Retribution.'

CHAPTER SEVEN

Paul had planted the seed of a very unpleasant idea in Lydia's mind. That Maddie wasn't back in London by accident or even because Smith had contracted her for a job, but instead for her own personal reasons. The assumption was that the rogue assassin Smith had mentioned and Maddie were one and the same, and that certainly seemed to fit. And if the service had lost control of Maddie, that might mean they would be willing to help Lydia to take her out of the picture. A rogue assassin couldn't be a good thing for them, either.

She found Jason in his bedroom, sitting on the floor with his legs stretched out and the laptop open. Knowing him, he hadn't moved all night.

'Can you look for unexplained deaths from the last two years?'

'Where?'

'Worldwide.'

Jason's eyes widened. 'Um… That's…'

'Too many,' Lydia said. 'Feathers. You're right.'

'What are you looking for?' Jason asked.

'A pattern in Maddie's work. Or evidence against her for the jobs she's already done.'

'To take to the police?'

Lydia ran her hands through her hair. It needed a wash, but it was hard to focus on mundane things when she was walking around with a target on her back. 'I'm guessing assassins are considered disposable once they're compromised. Their value lies in the way they move through the population unseen. And Mr Smith, or whoever else has been giving her work, won't want her in custody alive in case she makes a deal in return for information.'

'So, they'll send another assassin to shut her up?'

'Maybe,' Lydia said. 'I really have no idea. But it's what I would do.'

Jason pulled a face. 'No you wouldn't.'

'Okay. Probably not. But it's what I would think I ought to do. If I was being smart.'

'What if I narrowed the search down to unsolved murders?'

'They're likely to not all be marked as murder, though. Like that hit and run in Greece. That was recorded as an accident.' Lydia balled her fists in frustration. She had to do something. Couldn't just wander around waiting for Maddie to decide to fulfil her contract or for Smith to get tired of waiting and send a new assassin. She had to *do* something. 'What about narrowing down by country? Start with the UK or Greece? Her known locations?'

'It would be a start. I can create a program that will comb for certain parameters easily enough, but the problem will be the data generated. There will be a lot.'

'Yeah, I'm sorry.' Lydia knew she was being unreasonable. Demanding the impossible. 'Don't worry...'

Jason had an unfocused look in his eye and he muttered something that sounded like 'script'. Lydia decided to shut up and let him think. She went and put some bread in the toaster and poured an orange juice. A few minutes later, Jason wafted into the kitchen. 'I could ask some of my friends to help. I don't think they're likely to tell anybody, but it's all just screen names. I don't know who they are.'

'Could you give them small parts to do? Not give them the big picture, kind of thing?'

Jason hesitated before nodding. 'That should be safe enough.'

LEAVING Jason to commune with his laptop, Lydia headed to the silver vaults in search of silversmiths. A chatty young man with a passion for the subject, pointed her toward a jewellery company in Mayfair. They had an in-house studio for silver and goldsmithing and they supplied the Gold Cup and the Hunt Cup for Ascot every year, he told her. 'They've got a royal charter and have been around since the seventeenth century.'

'Early seventeenth, do you know?' Lydia was thinking about the cup the Silver Family had made when the king gave the lawyers use of the Temple Church.

The man paused. 'Yes, sixteen ten, I believe.' His mouth twisted into a smile. 'Don't quote me.'

Mayfair was not Lydia's natural environment. The expensive stores went beyond the flashy gilt promise of lesser brands, and spoke of establishment and permanence. Tiffany and Givenchy and Burberry, all housed in buildings which looked like banks. Or temples, which, Lydia realised, were much the same thing.

White columns carved with intricate patterns led to a recessed portico and the entrance to the shop. A shop so swanky it was called a 'house'. The silver vaults contained a glittering array of silver, of course, a cascade of fine items with stories of wealth and privilege, as well as desperation and cunning. This place was something different.

Once admitted, Lydia was surrounded by the hush of true wealth. Recessed lighting provided subtle inducement to look here, or there. To admire this exquisite piece or that. The ambience was a cross between a museum and a high-class brothel. Lydia quashed a snort of laughter. That probably wasn't the vibe they were aiming for, but now that she had thought it she could see it everywhere. The desirables laid out wantonly, batting their expensive gems in the punters' direction. The way they wouldn't glitter quite as much when removed from the expert lighting and velvet display case, moulded to show the necklace or whatever to its finest advantage.

Lydia realised she was light-headed. She wasn't tasting Silver. This was just a vast building filled with ordinary silver and gold. Nothing to trouble her senses. She hadn't drunk any alcohol the day before, so it wasn't a hangover, and Jason had made her a bowl of cereal before she had left home, so it wasn't hunger. She put a hand out to steady herself and felt smooth glass. A subtle gasp to her left indicated that laying fingers on the polished case was a social faux pas. Lydia ignored it and concentrated on sucking in oxygen until the speckles at the edges of her vision receded.

Once she was reasonably sure she wasn't about to keel over, Lydia was able to focus on the man standing close by. He was extremely well groomed and had the glowing skin of a good dermatologist and a comfortable life. As a result, Lydia would have guessed his age at somewhere between thirty and fifty. She also wasn't surprised that he was taking in her general appearance with something close to horror. 'Are you unwell, madam?'

Madam. Lydia would lay money that she was younger than the man, which meant he was being deliberately insulting. Or, perhaps, it was part of his training. Some weird custom among the British upper class. Well, she was a Camberwell girl and wouldn't have the first idea about any of that. She smiled widely and deliberately relaxed her stance. She wasn't going to be subservient in the face of snobbery, but she didn't want to appear threatening, either. This place would be wired up directly to the police and it would be embarrassing for Fleet if she was the cause of an emergency call out. 'I wanted to ask about a job that was done here.'

His face closed. 'We don't give out details about our clients to the press.'

'I'm not a journalist,' Lydia said. 'I work at the British Museum. Research. Roisin Quin,' she held out her hand.

He shook it automatically. 'I don't understand...'

'We're talking ancient history,' Lydia said, smiling again. 'Sometime in the period from the nineteen forties to around nineteen eighty.'

'That's a large stretch of time to check records. Even if we were able to do so. As I say, client confidentiality... It's simply not information we give out.'

'I don't need the client information,' Lydia said. 'I need the name of the person who made the item. You have a studio here, I believe? You must keep staff records.'

Now the man looked thoroughly confused. 'You want the name of the person who made the item? It might be more than one, you know. Pieces are rarely made in isolation. And we don't keep records of individuals.'

'You don't keep staff records? I find that hard to believe.'

The man shifted. 'I mean to say, we might not be able to pinpoint who worked on a particular piece. Besides, we're not about to open up private records to just anybody.'

'Not even for the greater good?' Lydia had her coin in her hand and she squeezed it lightly. 'The historical record of our beloved city.' Well, that was laying it on a bit thick. Lydia was doing her best impression of how an academic historian associated with the museum would speak, trying to emulate Roisin's verbiage. Surprisingly, it seemed to be working. The man was visibly more at ease.

'There's no harm in me taking a peek at your studio, at least?'

The man brightened. Perhaps at the opportunity to offload Lydia onto somebody else. 'No harm at all,' he said.

'Lead the way.'

The studio was in a half basement with a low ceiling, a row of barred windows high up the walls, and wooden desks strewn with chisels, pliers, and other tools. There were tall chests with shallow drawers, spools of wire, tool chests, and a forest of angle-poise lamps.

The air was tinged with the scent of heated metal and something acidic but, Lydia was grateful to note, no Silver tang. The metal she could smell was entirely natural. A woman wearing a heavy work apron and carrying a long metal file looked at Lydia curiously as she took her place back at a desk, but otherwise nobody stopped what they were doing.

'There's a research library next door,' her guide said. 'But you want to speak to Barbara. Barb. She's worked here forever.'

Barb turned out to be a sprightly pixie of a woman, and Lydia would guess her age at around three hundred. If her senses hadn't been telling her otherwise, she would have assumed the woman had Pearl blood. She had some of that ethereal vitality, with eyes that were bright blue and as sharp as a child's and the complexion of a Mediterranean matriarch. Or a woman who had spent the best part of her life under a tanning bed. While her face was entirely creased by wrinkles, like a shrivelled apple, Lydia had the inescapable feeling that Barb would be able to beat her in a fair fight.

'Healthiest substance to work with,' Barb said after the

guide had introduced them and told her that Lydia was interested in the silversmithing side. 'Antibacterial.'

'Right,' Lydia said. She had never thought of silver has anything except potentially lethal.

'I've been here since the sixties. Started at fourteen.'

Hell Hawk. That was commitment. 'Gosh.'

Barb's eyes narrowed. 'You're not interested in silversmithing history, girl. And I've not got time to waste.'

'It's about a replica.'

'This way,' Barb led the way out of the studio and in through the next doorway. The library. Which was a smaller room than the word suggested, but lined with shelves and with a small table in the middle and a couple of chairs. Barb sat down and indicated that Lydia should do the same.

'You're with the police?'

'No, I'm with the British Museum.'

'No you're not,' Barb said, her eyes narrowed. 'But no matter. No skin off my teeth.'

Lydia was finding it difficult to keep her place in the conversation. She decided to take control. She produced her coin and spun it in the air.

Barb's eyes were drawn to it, as Lydia had known they would be. She felt guilty, using her power when she ought to use normal persuasion, but that was like carrying a sharp axe and trying to cut down a tree with a spoon. 'A silver cup went missing from the British Museum in the seventies and at least one replica has been made of it. Probably since it went missing, but I can't discount the possibility that the replica was made before, after the war sometime.'

'What cup?' Barb's voice had the dreamy quality of the hypnotised.

'The Silver Family cup.'

Barb nodded slowly. 'Three.'

'Sorry?'

'We made three here. Expensive job. Especially for that sort of client.'

'What sort of client?' Lydia asked, expecting her to say something disparaging about magic folk or the rumours surrounding the Families.

Barb gave her an imperious look. 'Not royalty.'

'Right.'

'Did you work on the cup yourself?'

'I did,' Barb said. 'Well. I saw it. I was sweeping up shavings from the floor and not much else back then. I was an apprentice, but it was a slow start. I was a girl, after all.'

'But you remember this being made?' Lydia couldn't believe her luck. 'Do you remember if they worked from the original or from photographs?'

'Photographs and drawings, I believe,' Barb said. 'But better than that, we had the original moulds for the body and the handles. There was detail work to be added, of course, but the moulds were key.'

'How was that possible? The original was made over three hundred years earlier. And the British Museum have no records of any such item.'

'There was a man. He didn't work here, but he came in for that job. That's one of the reasons I remember it so well. That has never happened since. Not once. The boss here is very particular about who is allowed in the workshop and especially not to touch anything. It's to do with our reputation. And he doesn't want anybody stealing design ideas, either.'

Lydia felt a tingling. 'And the man brought the mould for the cup?'

'That's right,' Barb said. 'And he supervised.'

'Can you remember his name?'

Barb shook her head. 'Sorry. No.'

Lydia could see she was telling the truth, even without the Crow whammy. She pocketed her coin and made to leave. Finding out where the replica cup had been made wasn't exactly helpful to its current whereabouts, but at least she now knew there were three replicas floating about.

'He had a funny name,' Barb said.

'Sorry?' Lydia turned back to the small woman.

'Foreign, like. French, I think it was.' She smiled dreamily. 'Ooh la la.'

CHAPTER EIGHT

Lydia knew she was dreaming, but the fear was real. She was on the roof and Maddie was smiling like it was Christmas and her birthday rolled into one. She could see her bright lipstick and the hectic light in her eyes, but she couldn't hear anything except the wind rushing in her ears. Lydia knew it was bad. She knew that something awful was about to happen, but her fear was tinged with excitement. The wind was whipping Maddie's hair around her face, giving it a life of its own. Then they were high in a clear blue sky, flying together and she could feel her wings beating and her muscles working in exactly the way they were made to work and there was nothing but pure exhilaration. Freedom.

'It's time,' Maddie said in her ear and they were back on the roof.

Fleet was kneeling in front of her. She couldn't see his face but knew the back of his head, his shoulders, his suit.

'Do it,' Maddie said.

Lydia had a knife and she stepped forward, reaching to draw it across Fleet's neck. His body tumbled forward and she woke up, heart racing and drenched in sweat.

. . .

Once she was up and caffeinated, Lydia knocked on Jason's door. 'Sorry if I disturbed you last night.'

Jason was sitting on the bed with his laptop open. He looked at her over the screen. 'You were shouting in your sleep. Bad dreams?'

Lydia nodded. 'Nothing I can't handle. I'm heading out.'

'Okay,' Jason frowned. Lydia didn't usually inform him of her movements.

She hesitated. 'If I'm not back in a couple of hours, could you... I don't know. Call Fleet? Or message him?'

'What are you doing?'

Lydia gave in. 'Looking for Maddie. I can't just sit around waiting to see what she decides to do.'

'Is there any point in me pointing out this is a bad idea?'

'None at all,' Lydia said, smiling as cheerfully as she could manage. She headed for the door before Jason could talk her out of it. She had to act.

When Maddie had disappeared from her parents' home and Lydia had been charged by Uncle Charlie to bring her back, she had found her hiding out on a canal boat in Little Venice. That had been courtesy of Paul Fox, but when he said he hadn't seen her, she believed him. At least, she thought she did. Lydia couldn't tell if she was just tired of second-guessing everybody or whether it was some Crow-level gut feeling.

Without expecting to find Maddie in such an obvious place, Lydia checked the canal first. The boat Maddie had used before was occupied by a middle-aged couple who seemed as normal as it was possible to be. Lydia had printed some information sheets from the council website on canal bylaws and handed one over as her cover, introducing herself as a council worker on a thankless, box-ticking task.

They were perfectly pleasant, and she got zero Family reading from either one of them.

Next was Uncle John and Aunt Daisy, Maddie's parents. Aiden hadn't noticed any unusual behaviour or heard any useful gossip. Certainly nothing about Maddie being seen around her family home. Still, Lydia felt that she needed to check for herself. It wasn't that she didn't trust Aiden to do a good job, it was just that... She was a control freak who didn't trust anybody.

Uncle John wasn't Lydia's biggest fan. He thought she was too young, too inexperienced and too female to be head of the Family, and he hid it poorly. He let her into his Camberwell house with a palpable reluctance. 'To what do we owe the honour?'

Lydia fixed John with her best shark-stare. She had learned it from Uncle Charlie and, she liked to think, had learned it well.

John dropped his gaze and led the way to the kitchen. 'Daisy's not here. She's at the gym. Or out with the girls. I forget which. It could be shopping.' He shrugged in a faux-apologetic manner. 'I wasn't really listening, I'm afraid.'

'I'll take a coffee, thanks,' Lydia said, taking a seat the large table. 'Do you have any biscuits?'

After a brief session of small talk, which neither of them enjoyed, Lydia cut to the chase. In short order, she ascertained that John hadn't seen or heard from Maddie and, to the best of his knowledge, neither had his wife.

Lydia had never been keen on John and his attitude toward her hadn't warmed her feelings, but she didn't wish him actual bodily harm. Which was why, when he asked why she was asking about Maddie, Lydia didn't lie. At least, not completely. 'Can you keep something between us?'

He nodded.

'Maddie has been seen in central London. I don't know if she is hanging around for a long visit or whether she has already flown away, or if the person who reported seeing her was mistaken, but...'

'When?'

'Last week.'

'I had a feeling,' he said, abruptly. 'When I was in the garden on Friday. You know when you feel like someone is watching you?'

It was Lydia's turn to nod.

'But I couldn't see anyone. And it could have been one of the neighbours looking out of their windows, nothing to worry about. But I felt it on the back of my neck.'

'It might not have been her,' Lydia said, realising that she was suddenly in the strange position of reassuring him. John was clearly unhappy.

'You're right,' he said. 'Why wouldn't she have come in to say "hello" if it had been her? If she had been that close to us, she would have visited.'

Lydia made a non-committal noise.

John walked her to the front door. He probably meant to seem polite, but it felt like she was being seen off the premises.

'Tell me if she gets in touch or if you see her,' Lydia said, not bothering to hide the command in her tone.

At that moment, Daisy opened the front door. She was visibly shocked and alarmed at the sight of Lydia, which set her wondering whether Maddie had, in fact, been around. Or perhaps they were hiding something else. Or they just hated her guts.

'We missed you on Sunday,' Daisy said stiffly, hanging her beige coat on a peg and giving Lydia the lightest of air kisses.

The Easter Sunday garden party. Egg rolling for the little ones and a booze-laden BBQ for everyone else. 'I was working,' Lydia said.

'Of course you were,' Daisy said. 'We all know how

stretched you are. With your little business as well as your Family role. We did wonder if it would be too much for you on your own, didn't we, John?'

He nodded stiffly, eyes wary. John was no fool, and he knew that Daisy was sailing very close to the wind.

Lydia smiled thinly and produced her coin, lazily flipping it over the back of her knuckles. Daisy stopped speaking.

'I appreciate your support,' Lydia said. 'And I know where to come when I need help. It's important to know that family is on side.'

John swallowed and Daisy's eyes widened.

'She meant no disrespect,' John blustered.

Lydia stared him down.

'We meant no disrespect. I mean, neither of us... We respect you.' John seemed unable to stop speaking, while Daisy just stared at Lydia with her mouth open. Frozen.

Lydia let the silence play out for a few seconds longer than was comfortable before flipping her coin into the air and catching it. 'I'll be in touch.'

Now that John and Daisy had joined the growing number of people who knew that Maddie was back in London, the guilt at not telling Fleet was gnawing at Lydia's insides. She was distracted by a fresh source when he called her mobile to ask why she wasn't at his flat. She had forgotten that she had promised to meet Fleet's family, and that they had agreed to go together from his place. 'Sorry, sorry. I'm leaving right now.'

'I'll pick you up,' Fleet said.

Lydia knew her hair was in need of a wash so she pulled it back into a pony tail. She considered getting changed into smarter clothes but then figured that it wasn't likely to make enough of a difference and that she needed all the comfort she could get. A quick look in the mirror revealed an unhealthy complexion, so she added some red lipstick to brighten and distract from the dark circles under her eyes. The face looking back at her was the one she had seen in her nightmare and she hastily rubbed the lipstick off again, erasing Maddie's ghost.

By the time she was outside the cafe, looking out for Fleet's car, she was thoroughly rattled.

After apologising for forgetting and for not having anything to bring his aunt, Lydia slumped back in the passenger seat and tried to calm herself down.

'It's all fine,' Fleet said, not for the first time, as he pulled into a parking space.

The engine ticked as it cooled and Lydia made no move to leave the car. 'Will she like me?'

'Of course,' Fleet said easily. 'She has excellent taste.'

'Will she mind that I'm not...'

Fleet raised an eyebrow. 'What?'

'That I'm a bit paler than you. A lot paler than you.'

Fleet ducked his head to look into her eyes. 'She knows.'

Lydia wanted to tell him that that wasn't a complete answer, but she also knew that she might not want to push him for the whole one. She might not like it.

Fleet's aunt lived in a high rise with open balconies. The buzzer was extremely loud and set off a cacophony of barking from inside the flat. 'I didn't know she had dogs.'

'She doesn't,' Fleet said. 'Too much mess. But my cousin-'

He was cut off by the door opening and a small round woman pulling him into an immediate embrace. She was wearing a red floral-patterned dress which brushed the floor. 'Don't let the dogs out,' she said, her words muffled by Fleet's body.

Two tiny Yorkies were attempting to wriggle through the gaps between her body and the door frame. Lydia stepped up closer and prepared to duck and grab.

Fleet disentangled himself and pulled Lydia by the hand to follow the woman who was retreating into the flat, shooing the dogs as she went. He closed the door and Lydia stooped to unlace her DMs. Fleet had warned her that his aunt had a no shoes rule.

The living room wasn't large and it was filled with bodies. Fleet's aunt was in an aggressively paisley armchair, three young women were squashed onto the too-small sofa, and several small children were on the floor. They leaped up and onto Fleet, shrieking with what Lydia could only assume was delight. Fleet hugged them and twirled them and swung one very small girl high up into the air until she laughed so hard a stream of snot came out of her nose.

The Yorkies were sniffing Lydia's feet. 'Let them sit down,' the aunt said and the three young women jumped up.

'I don't see why…' One of them began and then stopped with a single searing look from Fleet's aunt.

'It's very nice to meet you,' Lydia said, stepping forward, narrowly avoiding standing on a tiny dog. It made a startled little 'yip' sound even though she didn't touch it. Traitor.

'Call me Auntie,' Fleet's aunt said, with a wave of her hand. Lydia caught the three young women making wide eyes at each other.

'Go on and fetch the tea,' Auntie said. 'A body could shrivel up waiting.'

ONCE LYDIA WAS WEDGED on the sofa next to Fleet, had drunk two dainty china cups of tea and eaten a slice of lime cake which was sticky with syrup, she was beginning to think she might just survive this exposure to Fleet's family.

'Your daddy is Henry Crow.'

It was a statement, not a question, but Lydia nodded anyway. 'Yes, Auntie.'

'He ought to be with your family. Leading.'

Well that was a slap in the face.

'Not that you're not capable, child,' she waved a hand. 'But he shouldn't have left his responsibility.'

'Auntie...' Fleet cut in and received a blistering look from Auntie in return.

'You stay out of it, child,' Auntie said, heaving herself upright. 'And you. Come along with me.'

Lydia followed Auntie down the narrow hallway. Behind one of the flimsy doors was a small room. It was the kind of size which got called 'a lovely space for a baby' because you couldn't fit anything larger than a cot into it. There was a chest of drawers, the surface crowded with framed pictures, melted wax and the stubs of half-burned candles. It had the look of an altar.

'That's my sister,' Auntie said, pointing at a picture of a smartly dressed woman with a gangly looking boy. 'And Ignatius.'

Lydia scanned the other pictures. She saw one of Auntie when she was younger, shoulder to shoulder with Fleet's mother. Two pretty unsmiling women in flowery dresses. There were a couple of men flanking them. 'Is that...'

Her lips pursed. 'His daddy? No. No pictures.'

Auntie clearly wanted to say something else and Lydia waited.

'I saw something,' she said eventually. She patted her chest. 'In here.'

Lydia nodded to show she understood, but didn't speak.

'That boy in there.' Auntie jerked her head in the direction of the living room. 'He's very precious.'

Lydia was embarrassed to find her eyes welling with tears. 'I know that.'

'Then you should do the right thing.'

There was a prickling sensation along Lydia's skin and she consciously unclenched her fists. 'And what's that?'

Auntie gave her a long, assessing stare. 'Do you know

what you're doing to him?'

Lydia wasn't sure if Auntie could somehow sense her Crow power and the way she powered up those around her, or whether Fleet had confided in her about his increasing clairvoyance and she was putting the blame on Lydia regardless. Or, and this was very possible, that she was talking about something else entirely. The fact that Lydia was as white as her Scandinavian ancestors, perhaps? Or the fact that she was a private investigator and not good wife material. Or, maybe Auntie simply disliked the thought of Fleet attaching to anybody. She was clearly protective of her nephew. 'I won't hurt him,' Lydia said. She wanted to add that she loved Fleet, but her throat had closed up and she didn't trust herself to get the words out without seeming unhinged. Once upon a time, she had prided herself on her toughness. These days, she seemed to have lost the barrier she had kept between herself and other people. It was exhausting.

Auntie's expression didn't soften. 'I'm not saying you'll mean to hurt him, but he'll be hurt just the same.'

The door swung inward and Fleet appeared, looking deeply unhappy. He shot Auntie a look which could have stripped paint from a car. 'We've got to get going. Are you ready, Lyds?'

'Sure am,' Lydia said and escaped in front of Fleet.

OUT IN THE CAR, Fleet turned in the seat. 'I'm sorry about that.'

'How much did you hear?'

'Nothing. But it's not a good sign when Auntie takes a guest away on their own. I can guess enough to know that you are probably really freaked out. I'm sorry.'

'It's fine,' Lydia said, cupping his cheek. She was surprised to find she was telling the truth. There was some-

643

thing to be said for having a professional hit hovering over her head, it really put 'scary' into perspective. 'Bring it on.'

He kissed her before starting the engine. 'Are you sure you're okay?'

'Your aunt is protective of you. It's nice. And I'm not keen to start comparing family drama.'

Pulling into the traffic, Fleet nodded. 'Fair enough.'

BACK AT HER FLAT, once she had eaten a restorative plate of pasta and they had shared a bottle of wine, Lydia checked in on Emma. She had to be careful not to alarm Emma with her increased contact, but the only alternative was to ask Paul and that held its own set of problems. After a moment, she did it anyway and got a fast text message back telling her that there was no cause for alarm. Well, as Paul put it, 'her dull life is singularly unenlivened'. He added a suggestion that they meet for a drink to 'discuss all the boring details' which Lydia ignored.

Curled up and preparing to sleep, Fleet breathing evenly beside her, Lydia pushed thoughts of her nightmare out of her mind. She had no intention of having a bad dream again and she told her subconscious so in firm tones. In the safety of the dark, she could admit to herself that the visit with Fleet's family had been a little unsettling. But, she reasoned, the fact that she had dreamed about hurting Fleet before Auntie had said she would do so, was comforting. Perhaps Fleet's aunt had a bit of the gleam that she sensed in Fleet. If she had heightened perception, then perhaps she had sensed the psychic imprint left by Lydia's nightmare. Perhaps Lydia's deep fears that she would cause harm to Fleet had leaked out in the presence of a highly sensitive individual. It made sense. And, as it was based on dreams and fears, it didn't mean anything. She was in control of her actions and she would never hurt Fleet. So she could go to sleep.

CHAPTER NINE

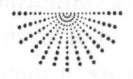

The next morning, Lydia was woken by her landline ringing in the next room. She ignored it and was successfully staying asleep when her mobile rang. A shot of adrenaline and one clear thought – Emma – brought her to sudden consciousness and she grabbed the device from its place on the floor. It was a terse message from Maria's assistant, requesting a progress report. The entire purpose was to remind Lydia that she was working for Maria and to rub it in as much as possible.

Fleet was awake by this point and she updated him on her progress on finding the silver cup. It didn't take long.

'What are you going to do if you find it? Give it to Maria?' Fleet asked once she had finished.

'I don't know,' Lydia said, sitting up against the pillows. 'I told her I would find it, I was very careful not to say what I would do with it after.'

'Sneaky,' Fleet said.

'It's her fault for not pinning down the wording of our agreement. It's not like she didn't know who she was dealing with.'

'And she's got legal training. She knows about contracts.'

'Exactly,' Lydia said, refusing to feel bad. She might have called a truce with Maria and the Silver Family, but that didn't mean she liked or trusted them. And it didn't erase the past.

Fleet was silent for a moment. 'You know there's a good chance Alejandro took the cup with him when he left?'

Lydia shifted to a more comfortable position. 'Or he gave it to the government as part of his immunity deal. I know.'

'And if that isn't the case, it might be better if you don't find it.'

'What do you mean?'

'Wouldn't it better for it to stay lost? Collecting dust in someone's trophy cabinet rather than... Well, whatever Maria wants it for. What does she want it for?'

'Pride, I think,' Lydia said. She could imagine Maria displaying it in her office to remind people of her heritage. The ultimate status symbol. 'Although it is chockful of Silver power. Maybe she could use that somehow. I honestly don't know enough about their potential.' The Family lore said that the Silvers used to be able to convince a person to do anything they wanted, just with the power of speech. They could make a person stroll off a building, thinking they could fly. They could suggest someone didn't need their property, car or cash, and they would just hand it all over with a smile. If Maria was brought up on those bedtime stories, maybe she thinks the cup is the key back to glory.

'Have you got any leads?'

'Not yet. I've spoken to the expert at the British Museum and seen the pictures and description from before it went missing. Not surprising, she was pretty cagey about how it got nicked. Doesn't look very good for the museum security.'

'I can look up the report, if you like?'

'I don't want to waste your time. I know where it ended up, after all. I need to know who has it now, not who took it back in the day.' Lydia sat up and began pulling on her clothes. All this chat had just reminded her of how little progress she had made. She had to get going. 'There is something I hoped you could look into for me.'

Fleet had sat up behind her and he dropped a kiss onto her bare shoulder. 'What's it worth?'

She shot him a look. He held up his hands. 'Joking. What do you need?'

'You remember the effect that the silver statue had on Robert Sharp and Yas Bishop? I was wondering whether whoever picked up the Silver cup might have suffered the same problems.'

'You want me to search arrest reports for mention of a cup?'

'If someone is cognitively compromised, they might be babbling about it. That would get recorded in the report, wouldn't it?'

'Should be. I could look for reports that had contacting mental health services listed as an action. There will be quite a few.'

'I saw the cup with Alejandro last year in the summer. That gives us a time frame, at least.'

'It's still going to throw up a lot of results,' Fleet said. 'Just to warn you.'

'That's okay. And thank you.' She turned back to kiss him and he cupped her cheek with one hand.

She could be a little late.

AFTER FLEET HAD GONE to work, Lydia forced herself up and into a hot shower. Padding through the flat with still-damp hair, clean skin and a hoodie for comfort, she felt ready to face the rest of her day. Strong enough to make coffee, at any rate.

Lydia was sipping from a novelty cupcake-shaped mug,

the only clean one left, and contemplating the prospect of returning Maria Silver's phone call, when Jason mercifully appeared from his room to distract her.

'You know you asked me to look for Maddie's handiwork? I've got something,' Jason was carrying his laptop. He didn't need to sleep so didn't look any different to usual, even though Lydia knew he had been working non-stop since she asked him to trace Maddie's movements.

'In Albania. Just over the Greek border.'

'What makes you think it's Maddie?'

'Location, partly, this was just two weeks after the hit and run in Greece. But also because of this,' Jason spun the laptop around so that Lydia could see the screen.

An image was open and, for a moment, Lydia thought it showed a gigantic black bird. She blinked and the picture became clear. It was a man hanging from a tree, arms spread wide. He was wearing a long black coat which was open, the material mimicking wings. Lydia squinted at the scenery. The tree had a thick trunk with peeling white bark and the sky was blue.

'It's an oriental plane,' Jason said. 'I looked it up. And in the next image you can see some olive trees. And a bit of old blockwork. The man was found in the Butrint national park, there's an amphitheatre and all sorts. Looks very nice.'

'Apart from the man in the tree,' Lydia said.

'Yeah. Apart from him.'

Lydia flicked her attention back to the figure and forced herself to focus on every aspect. She used the technique her old boss had taught her of breaking the image into a grid of one centimetre squares and examining them in order. You had to look at the image overall, too, but breaking it up was important for the detail. And for not allowing emotion to cloud your vision. She realised that the long coat wasn't just opened, the material had been cut up the back and the two long flaps folded up and attached at the wrists. The man's arms were straight out, unnaturally so, with something cylindrical poking out of the cuff of the coat. Maybe the handle of a broom, threaded through the coat sleeves.

The material looked dry. The man was somewhere in his forties or, at a push, fifties. Slim and in good shape. He was wearing black trousers which had an expensive cut and seemed to fit well and black socks. His shirt was also black, buttoned right up to the neck, but it looked loose on his frame.

'Are there more?'

'A couple,' Jason flicked through the images. One was taken from closer to the body and at a high angle. It showed a slice of ground beneath the figure and there was something brown at the edge of the shot.

'What's that?'

'The report of the scene described a pair of shoes near the trunk of the tree. Could be those?'

'Makes sense,' Lydia said, looking at the flash of brown.

'What about this makes sense?'

'Brown shoes. That's why she took them off. They didn't match the aesthetic.'

'You're sure it's Maddie, then?'

Lydia nodded. 'I mean, look. She's dressed him up as a crow.'

'He might have just liked wearing black.'

'Not with brown shoes. And I don't think he was wearing the shirt or the coat when he turned up to meet Maddie. The shirt doesn't fit him properly. She guessed on the size.'

'It's not bad,' Jason said, squinting at the picture. 'Could have been something he bought himself.'

'She guessed well,' Lydia said.

'So who is he?'

'Sergio Bastos. The report doesn't give much detail and he's got a severely minimal online presence. Jobs listed as a stint in the SAS and "analyst" for GCHQ and then he drops off the net. And there's a note on the report which indicates the file was closed almost as soon as it was opened.'

'What does that mean?'

'I think it means he was Maddie's handler.'

Lydia leaned back in her chair. 'You are amazing. How hard was it to break into the Albanian police database?'

Jason looked embarrassed. If he was alive, he probably would have blushed, but instead he began hovering slightly above the ground. 'I only hacked the staff database to get some contact details. Then I bribed an officer for the report.'

'All via email?'

Jason smiled paternally, like she was a toddler. 'It's a little bit more complicated than that.'

'Right. Well. Well done.' How likely was she to go to prison in the event of Jason being prosecuted for bribing an officer of the law? I mean, she could hardly say that a ghost did it. Then another thought struck her. 'Where did you get the cash?'

'I invested in bitcoin last year. Been doing a bit of trading in crypto ever since.'

LYDIA HAD BEEN CHECKING in on Emma every day via WhatsApp, keeping it light and breezy. Still, Emma had picked up on the increased contact and invited Lydia round to the house.

Maisie and Archie were in the living room watching CBeebies. Emma had put the kettle on and was making tea. 'I've got wine if you want, but I can't join you.' She pulled a face. 'Spring fair at the school tonight.'

'I would have thought that meant alcohol was even more necessary.'

'Tom is working and I have to drive. I'm in charge of the tombola and I'm not lugging all those tins on foot.'

Lydia rummaged in her bag and brought out two large bags of chocolate. 'I bought these for the kids but I wanted to check with you first. I didn't know if they are allowed it or...'

'Oh, yes,' Emma said. 'All my sugar-free ideas went out the window as soon as they started school. Sometimes I pay Archie to do his homework with Dairy Milk.'

Lydia laughed to show she got the joke, although she wasn't sure how serious Emma was being. She was trying to be normal, but her face felt like she was wearing a mask and she was sure Emma would notice. She was her oldest friend. Her only friend, in fact, until she had met Jason, and nobody knew her better. At least, nobody had known her better. But she tried very hard to keep her Crow Family weirdness away from Emma and her safe, normal life. Maddie's text flashed across her mind and she felt the roil of fury and fear in her stomach. Her own cousin, threatening Emma.

Emma put her elbows on the table and cradled her mug with both hands, regarding Lydia over the rim. 'What's up?'

'Nothing,' Lydia said, looking at her tea. There were little bubbles on the surface and the milk hadn't quite dissipated, yet. Her stomach turned over again.

'You're very pale,' Emma said, reaching out a hand to her forehead.

It made Lydia feel about five years old, but she was alarmed to discover she didn't mind. 'I'm fine.'

'That's what you always say.' Emma took a sip of tea. 'And you're usually lying. Let's face it, you're here. That means something is definitely wrong.'

Lydia opened her mouth to say that wasn't fair, but then she closed it. Emma had a point. And, besides, the words hadn't been said sharply or with a single drop of malice. Emma gazed at her steadily. Accepting. Knowing. And somehow still her friend.

'I love you,' Lydia said, her eyes prickling with unexpected tears.

'Oh Jesus,' Emma said in alarm. 'What's wrong?'

Lydia smiled and shook her head. 'I'm fine, honestly.'

'Don't say that when it's clearly not true,' Emma said. 'Are you ill? Just tell me.'

'Nothing like that.' Lydia couldn't tell Emma about Maddie. She couldn't run away or hide successfully and would only live in fear. 'I've just been feeling a bit off recently.' As she spoke, she realised it was the truth.

'Are you pregnant?'

'No!'

Emma gave her a long look. 'Are you sure?'

'Stop it, yes.'

At that moment an unearthly howling started up. 'I'll just...' Emma headed to the living room to deal with whatever crisis had befallen her children, and Lydia sipped her tea and catalogued her symptoms. She had been feeling tired. And there had been a couple of almost-fainting episodes. On the other hand, her Crow abilities seemed more powerful than ever. Just that one thought and she could feel her coin in her hand. She slipped it into her pocket and tried to clear her mind, but there was a humming at the edges. A vibration in her body and mind which felt like a prelude. A tuning up. A warning.

'They're tired,' Emma said when she returned. 'Don't know how they're going to cope with the excitement of the fair.'

Lydia wasn't sure if she was being sarcastic or not. Perhaps a school fair was exciting when you were a small child. Lydia couldn't remember.

'So, are you working too hard? I know you've got a lot on your plate. I mean, you're the big boss, now, right? That's got to be stressful.'

When Lydia had first taken over from Charlie it had

been extremely stressful. Now she had settled into a good routine. She had impressed upon the Family that there was a new order and that certain old practices were no longer acceptable. Now that had filtered through, Aiden took care of the day-to-day. She still had to speak to him regularly, though. And, worst of all, be 'seen' in Camberwell. Once every fortnight she sat in The Fork and people came and aired their grievances, begged favours, and offered deals. Plus, she was still trying to keep her investigation firm going, not to mention be a half-decent partner to Fleet. She shrugged. 'It's not so bad.'

'Do you miss him?'

For a second Ash's face flashed in front of Lydia and her guts twisted. 'Who?'

'Your uncle,' Emma said.

'No.' And she really didn't. Things were tangled and tricky and Mr Smith had turned out to be very bad news indeed, but at least that was a clear kind of hatred. It was easier. Her guts twisted, again, as if to call her a liar. And then they cramped and she rose hastily.

'Tummy bug?' Emma's face was the picture of concern.

'Or something,' Lydia said as she rushed from the room.

CHAPTER TEN

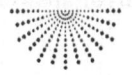

Lydia was in the training room at Charlie's house. It had a wall of mirrors which gave her a perfect view of the coins she was spinning all around the room. She made them spin and then stop, swoop together like a flock of starlings and then disappear, leaving only her true coin. When she felt warmed up, the vibrations humming through her mind and body and the sound of wings filling her ears, she threw a bundle of energy at Charlie's punchbag. She had hoped to knock its stand over, maybe even cause some damage to the bag itself. What she hadn't expected was for the metal stand and weighty bag to fly back into the mirrored wall with such impact that a large starburst crack appeared.

She bent over, breathing heavily, but she didn't feel light-headed. For a few moments, she felt clear headed and strong, like an unexpected pause in a hangover, but then the fog and sickness crept back. She sat on the floor cross-legged and looked at her fractured reflection in the broken mirror. Her power definitely seemed to refill. It wasn't something that got used up and that was good. The problem was, she hadn't meant to hit the punchbag with that amount of force. It was like the burst of energy she had thrown through the lift doors killing the hitman, Felix. And if the punchbag had been a person, they would also be dead. The point of training was to stop that from happening, not to repeat it.

'What do I do?' She asked out loud, but none of the multiple Lydias in the mirror answered.

LYDIA HAD INTENDED to do another hour of training, but the cracked mirror was mocking her so she trailed downstairs to make some coffee instead. She switched on the machine and downed a glass of water while it warmed up. What she really wanted was a proper drink. The last few months of laying off the whisky hadn't left her feeling any healthier. If anything, she felt worse. Although her power seemed much stronger. Either she was an alcoholic in withdrawal or the whisky had been dampening her power to a manageable level and now she was suffering as it grew. The unanswered questions made her head hurt, so she helped herself to a swig of Charlie's single malt. The burn in her stomach and the smoky aftertaste was soothing, so she took another swig. And another.

'Day drinking,' a voice said from behind her, making her jump. 'Not a good sign.'

Maddie was lounging in the entrance to the hall. She wasn't wearing a wig this time, but she still looked different to the girl Lydia remembered. Her brown hair was expertly highlighted and fell in shiny curls below her shoulders and there was a hardness in her face.

Lydia gripped the bottle tightly. 'It's nice that you care.' She was making a quick inventory of her chances. She had no gun, the knives were held on a magnetic strip next to the cooker, too far away for comfort, and she was still feeling exhausted and odd after her training session. She was facing an experienced killer with nothing but a glass bottle. She relaxed her hold on the neck, letting her arm fall to her side, as if this might make Maddie forget she was holding it.

'So,' Maddie moved into the room and looked around. 'You really have taken over.'

'Aiden's on his way,' Lydia said, 'we have meetings here.'

Maddie shook her head. 'Gotta hope that isn't true. For Aiden's sake.'

There was a block of ice in Lydia's stomach, the cold radiating along her limbs and creeping into her chest. It was dread. She instinctively knew that dread would paralyse her. Root her feet to the floor and leave her helpless. She reached instead for bright hot fear. That she could work with.

'Don't look so tense,' Maddie said. 'I'm not here to kill you.'

'Change of orders?'

Anger flashed across her face and Lydia mentally kicked herself. This wasn't the time to annoy the woman. Old habits died hard, though.

'I told you,' Maddie had opened the fridge and was gazing inside. 'I don't follow orders.'

'You've been working for the government, though. Their top international assassin by all accounts.' Maybe flattery would get her off guard.

She closed the fridge door and prowled to the large glass doors overlooking the garden. 'I hated it here.'

'Me, too,' Lydia said. 'I still do.'

Maddie was turned away, gazing out into the garden, and Lydia took an experimental step back toward the hall. An image of Sergio Bastos's dead eyes flashed into her mind and she pushed it away.

'Why do you come here?'

'Duty.' Another step back. 'And the training room is handy.'

'I only did the jobs because they coincided with my own

plans. It suited me. When it didn't suit me anymore I stopped.'

The entrance to the hall was close. Then it was a short run past the stairs and the living room. She couldn't remember if she had locked the front door. 'They're not too happy about that,' Lydia said. 'You make them nervous.'

Maddie shrugged, still looking out to the garden. 'They know what I can do.'

Lydia was calculating whether she could get out of the front door and down the street ahead of Maddie. How much of a head start she would need to get somewhere busy and safe. Or safer. Perhaps Maddie would happily shoot her in a crowd.

'I can see you in the glass,' Maddie's voice was conversational. 'It's rude to leave the party early. Especially without saying goodbye.'

Lydia stopped moving. She wondered whether Sergio had known Maddie was going to kill him before she did, or whether it was a surprise. That split second when he saw the clothes she had brought, perhaps. 'What do you want?'

'Answers.'

Maddie turned away from the window and Lydia was struck by how much older she looked. There was nothing physical, no fine lines on her skin, but there was a new knowledge in her eyes. Perhaps it was because Lydia knew what she had been doing for the last year or so, and that coloured her view, but she didn't think so. Looking into Maddie's eyes was like staring into the entrance to a long dark tunnel.

'Why are you on a hit list?' Maddie tilted her head very slightly. There was a cleaver in her right hand and Lydia had no idea when it had appeared. Or from where.

'I told you,' Lydia said, swallowing. There was no point in lying. 'I wouldn't join Mr Smith so he opted to take me out, instead. I refused to be his weapon, and he obviously decided he didn't want me to be a threat.'

'That's it?' Maddie held the cleaver up and carved strokes through the air. 'This is a well-balanced blade. Charlie splashed out.'

Lydia licked her lips. They were as dry as her mouth. 'I've been looking into a company called JRB. They seemed to be behind a number of attacks on the Families. I assumed they were trying to destabilise us, disrupt alliances and maybe start a war. I found out that Smith is part of that company. High up. Maybe he even is the company. I'm still looking.'

'Why?'

'Why am I looking into it?'

'No. Why is this company interested in messing with the Families?'

Lydia shrugged. She told herself that this was just a normal conversation. That Maddie wasn't, at this moment, admiring her reflection in the surface of the Sabatier meat cleaver. 'I don't know. There's probably money to be made. Or it might be fear. Of what we could do as a combined force.'

Maddie snorted. 'Yeah, I don't see that happening.'

Lydia thought of the Pearls and the Foxes and the Silvers and the Crows all standing shoulder to shoulder on the field of war, a common purpose, and felt herself smile. Which was wrong, of course. She shouldn't be smiling. Was it part of Maddie's power that she had used some sort of mind control? It occurred to her that she could be like an animal walking into the slaughterhouse, being calmed with a soothing word from her handler. She squeezed her coin in her hand and tried to focus. 'Agreed. But I guess not everyone knows that. From the outside, it must feel threatening.'

'Good,' Maddie said and smiled.

For a second, Lydia saw her cousin as she had been. In that moment they could have been back at a family party, sneaking away together to eat cake and avoid the grownups.

'I know you've been looking for me,' Maddie said, and the illusion disappeared.

'I'm scared of you,' Lydia said. 'When I'm scared of something I like to know where it is.'

'I'm not an it.'

Lydia wanted to say 'prove it' but she didn't want to goad Maddie.

'You need to stop,' Maddie said.

'Okay.'

Maddie shook her head. 'I mean it. You're going to get yourself hurt.'

Lydia had a wild urge to laugh. Safety tips from the knife-wielding assassin. She still couldn't get a read on Maddie, couldn't feel Crow from her at all. It was creepy. Her mind expected it and the absence made her feel off balance. She wondered if Maddie knew. Before she could phrase the question, Maddie had turned back to the glass doors and was sliding them open. 'I'm taking this,' she raised the cleaver.

Lydia didn't know what to say to that, so she kept her mouth shut.

Maddie slipped through the gap in the doors and didn't look back.

FLEET HAD BEEN at the gym and was shower-fresh and relaxed when he arrived at the flat. The bullet wound in his shoulder was healing well and his work seemed to be at least fifty per cent less annoying than it had been, which made Lydia happy for him. There was a very small part of her that wished he was still being driven mad by management bullshit so that he would stop being a copper entirely, but it was a very selfish part and she liked to pretend it didn't exist. Besides, there were times when Fleet's badge came in handy. This, however, was not one of them.

'So, there's this thing,' Lydia began.

'Okay,' Fleet said, looking guarded. 'Why do I feel as if I should be worried?'

'You know Mr Smith said that he was trying to find an assassin?'

'The one who shot me?'

Lydia appreciated that he didn't say 'the one you killed'.

'No, not Felix. He's a local contractor. Was a local contractor.' Lydia found small glasses in the kitchen and brought them through. She poured a couple of generous measures of whisky and handed one to Fleet. 'Mr Smith was talking about someone who had been working for the service. Someone who had gone rogue. They thought she had something to do with the death of the MP in Greece. The one who paved the way for Alejandro's political rise.'

'She?'

He was quick. Lydia took a slug of her drink and willed Fleet to do the same. He didn't. Just looked at her steadily.

'How do you know it's a woman?'

'I've met her,' Lydia said in a rush. 'It's Maddie.'

For a second or two, Fleet didn't move. Then he nodded. 'Okay. Tell me.'

Lydia finished her glass of whisky and told him about Maddie summoning her to the roof of the hospital. About how strong she was. How she had an order to kill her and had been going to make it look like Lydia had taken a swan dive. How she had changed her mind.

'When was this?'

'Couple of weeks ago,' Lydia said.

The tension in Fleet's face went up a notch. His warm brown eyes had gone flat and unreadable. Lydia wasn't sure if it was concern or fury. Probably both.

'And you're telling me now,' Fleet said in an extremely careful way. 'Interesting.'

Lydia fetched the whisky and poured another shot into her glass. She held up the bottle but Fleet put his hand over his glass.

'She threatened Emma. If she got the idea that the police knew, she might have... I don't know.' Lydia wasn't going to say the words out loud.

'Is Emma all right?' He asked immediately and Lydia felt a rush of love and gratitude.

Lydia nodded. 'Paul put his brothers onto her.' She wished she could grab the words out of the air.

Fleet had definitely flipped to anger, now. 'You told Fox?'

Lydia skipped over that tricky detail to the main event. 'Tonight, I was at Charlie's, training, and she turned up.'

'Wait... What? You saw her today?' He took a step closer, raking her body with his eyes. 'Are you hurt?'

'No fighting,' Lydia said. 'She didn't even threaten to chuck me off a roof.'

Fleet did not seem ready to joke about it. His hands were bunched into fists and there was a muscle jumping in his jaw. Lydia watched him take a deep breath and let it out slowly. 'What did she want?'

'I don't know. Maybe just to chat?'

'Jesus Christ, Lyds. I can't... You can't keep being so... Flippant. This is serious. You could have been hurt. You could have been killed. She could have...'

'I am aware,' Lydia said, draining her glass.

'You should have told me,' Fleet said.

'I'm telling you now.' She should be being conciliatory. Apologetic. Part of Lydia knew this, but it wasn't a large enough or loud enough part to override the idiotic rest of her brain. 'Did you want to order takeaway? Or we could raid the cafe kitchen.'

'I'm not hungry,' Fleet said. 'I'm going to head home.'

'Don't be like that. Let's talk about it.'

'So now you want to talk?' Fleet shook his head. 'Ignore me. I'm just... I need to process.'

'Okay,' Lydia said. She understood that impulse. He wanted to go and sort his head out. Then he would come back and they would talk it through properly and everything would be fine. Everything had to be fine.

AN HOUR LATER, the pressure sensor outside the flat told Lydia she had a visitor. She recognised Fleet's shape through the obscured glass and got a hit of his particular signature, a bonfire on a beach, a warm salt-tinged breeze ruffling through palm leaves.

'I'm sorry,' he said as soon as she opened the door.

Lydia stepped into his arms. 'Me too.'

After a moment, Fleet pulled back slightly. 'I'm ready to talk.'

'We should make up properly first,' Lydia said. Mostly out of the need to be naked with Fleet but also, partly, to put off the talking part.

Jason was on the sofa, the laptop sitting innocently next to him, waiting for them to pass through before picking it up again.

Lydia was towing Fleet by the hand, but he stopped and stared at Jason and, for a moment, Lydia thought he could see him. He had glimpsed him once but hadn't mentioned seeing him again.

'New laptop?'

'That's my old one,' Lydia said.

He stood for a few seconds longer, frowning in Jason's direction.

Lydia watched Fleet staring and then she squeezed his hand. 'You see him, don't you? Jason.'

'Jason?' Fleet glanced at her quickly and then back at the

ghost.

'Hi,' Jason said, waving in an exaggerated way.

'Did he...' Fleet swallowed, grey showing under his skin. 'Did he just wave at me?'

'Yep,' Lydia said. 'If you're going to pass out, please get on the floor. I don't want you to knock yourself out.'

'I'm not going to faint,' Fleet said, but he didn't sound sure.

At that moment Jason flickered and disappeared.

'So,' Lydia said. 'That's my flatmate. His name is Jason. He makes a mean hot chocolate. And he died in the nineteen eighties.' Murdered on his wedding day. By Charlie. But Lydia decided not to say that bit out loud. She didn't know where Jason went when he disappeared or whether he became invisible and could still hear her. She had decided long ago that was a hornets' nest she would prefer not to kick. It was easier to live with a ghost if she decided that he couldn't become invisible and hang about without her knowledge.

'You know its name.'

'Not it. He. Jason. He's my friend.' Lydia was going to explain that Jason was also her partner and that he was extremely handy when it came to internet research requiring hacking, but she thought that might be a revelation too far. Fleet still looked a bit queasy.

He looked at her for a moment. 'I thought it was more a... I don't know, casual haunting thing. One of your... Side effects. Of being...'

'A Crow? Seeing Jason is a side effect, I guess. And I have made him stronger. He wasn't able to touch things before, and he disappeared a lot, but now he can make me coffee.'

'That's...' Fleet ran out of words and the pause stretched on.

'Weird? Handy? Amazing?'

He nodded, a trademark sunshine smile appearing. 'All of the above.'

LYDIA POURED them both a stiff drink and waited for Fleet to take the conversational lead. She was still wary of how much he was able to process in one lump. She was a lot. She had always been a lot and her life just kept getting stranger.

Finally, Fleet drained the last of his whisky and spoke. 'So. We need to leave London.'

'She's been working as an international assassin, I don't think it would make a difference.'

'Witness protection. New identity. You know the drill.'

'I'm not leaving,' Lydia said.

'This is serious, Lyds. You've got no choice. I would come with you,' Fleet said. A beat. 'If you want me, that is.'

'I'm not leaving,' she repeated. She was not having this conversation.

'She is going to kill you,' Fleet said starkly. His expression bleak. 'I can't stop her. You can't stop her. You need to hide.'

Lydia met his gaze. 'She was there to do a job. When she discovered it was me, she chose not to do it. I don't think we should be so quick to assume she is going to top me.'

'What if Mr Smith ups her fee? Offers her something she really wants? And that's assuming she's in her right mind. She's not normal, Lyds, we have no idea what she's going to do.'

'I'm not normal, either. Does that make me an unpredictable psycho?'

He frowned. 'That's not...' He stopped. 'We're not talking about you.'

'I'm not hiding,' Lydia said. 'So we need a new plan.'

. . .

OUT ON THE TERRACE, whisky bottle and glasses on the table and the fairy lights on, it could have been a normal social occasion. The three crows which were perched on the railing watching them were a little unusual perhaps, as were the house sparrows which were sat along the roof line. A magpie flew down and stood on the table, eyeballing Lydia like it was trying to tell her something. 'I know,' Lydia said to it. 'I'm an idiot. Warning received.'

The magpie tilted its head and half-flew half-hopped over to the railing to join the crows.

'At least the birds agree with me,' Fleet said easily, pouring them generous measures.

'Hey,' Lydia complained without conviction. She was just glad he was here. No amount of crazy seemed to be too much for Fleet and the small part of her that had been waiting for the other shoe to drop, for Fleet to realise that Lydia wasn't alluringly mysterious, that she was just strange, broke free.

'Here's the thing,' Fleet said. 'I know you don't want to trade with MI6, but I don't think we have a choice. We need to find out what is going on with Mr Smith's department. We need to know if there is an official kill order out on you or whether that was off the books.'

'Are there official kill orders? I thought all of that was clandestine.'

'There are books and then there are *books*,' Fleet said. 'Someone will know something.'

'How will it help, though? To know if it's just Mr Smith or goes further?'

'So that we know who to trade with to get it rescinded. The only way to stop Mr Smith going after you is to make you more valuable alive.'

Lydia put her glass down so quickly she was surprised it didn't smash. 'I'm not working for him. That's the whole point...'

'Not for him, but what about for MI6?'

'No,' Lydia said flatly.

'Okay, not working for, but what about working with? Helping with enquiries? Being a useful contractor from time to time? Isn't that worth your life?'

Lydia was about to say 'no'. She was nobody's weapon. Nobody's tool to be taken out of the box and used, but Fleet wasn't finished.

'Isn't that worth Emma's safety? Her life?'

Lydia glared at Fleet but it didn't make him any less right. *Hell Hawk*.

CHAPTER ELEVEN

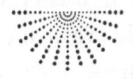

The sun was out and the sky was blue, and Lydia felt a darkness in her heart which made her want to set fire to things.

'You've got nothing to worry about,' Fleet was saying as they approached the columned exterior of the Tate Britain. 'You don't have to agree to anything. Let's just see what we can get without promising anything. She wants to cultivate a source as much as we do.'

Lydia clenched her teeth and squeezed her coin in her fist. She didn't want to be a source. She didn't want to be anywhere near another bloody spook. When she thought of Mr Smith the rage rolled over in a hot wave of fire. She knew this was unhelpful, but she couldn't help it. It wasn't that he had proved to be untrustworthy, it was the extent and breadth of that untrustworthiness which burned. She had misread the situation, the relationship, the man, and that had shaken her more than she would ever admit.

Inside the gallery, there was the usual hushed air of people appreciating art. The walls were pastel tones and the ornate white cornice was a foot deep. Two women stood in front of a bronze sculpture of a man grappling with a python. The figure had extremely impressive musculature and Lydia didn't blame them for their intense interest.

Fleet was walking slowly, looking at the art as if he were any other visitor. Lydia emulated him as best she could, but her mind wouldn't stop racing. She was in partial fight-or-flight mode and had been since meeting Maddie on the hospital roof. She knew it wasn't sustainable, this level of hypervigilance. She would crash and burn.

'See the brushwork, here,' Fleet said, pausing in front of another dark and dreary oil painting. He took her hand and squeezed it and she felt the message. Be calm. Unclench your jaw. At least standing still meant she could stop counting her strides. Her footsteps were audible on the parquet flooring, despite the sturdy soles of her DMs and it had become an obsession since they had walked into the large room. Lydia forced herself to look at the painting.

Her heart stuttered. The painting showed a terrified horse, brought to the ground with its head twisted back to stare, wide-eyed and panting at the lion biting its back. The lion looked faintly comical, but the horse's fear was palpable.

'George Stubbs.' A woman with salt-and-pepper hair and red-rimmed glasses had stopped next to Lydia, her gaze focused on the canvas. 'He was obsessed with the subject for over thirty years. Created at least seventeen works which depicted horses being frightened or attacked by lions.'

Fleet nodded. 'Ms Sinclair. I know you wanted to meet Lydia.'

Lydia had now met two members of the secret service to her sure and certain knowledge. Mr Smith had first appeared at her gym and later as a courier, looking completely at home in both guises. It was only once she knew his role that she saw him in a suit. Ms Sinclair, on the other hand, was wearing a complicated amount of grey-toned, layered separates and she looked like an art critic or a professor of something vaguely trendy. Scandinavian studies, perhaps. Or film.

'Very pleased to make your acquaintance,' Sinclair said, glancing at Lydia before resuming her study of the art. 'Apologies for not bringing you into the office. It's easier this way.'

'I wouldn't have come,' Lydia said, and Fleet squeezed her hand. Warning her to play nice, no doubt.

'I always wonder what started it,' Sinclair mused, her eyes roving over the painting. 'After all, lions aren't exactly common in England.'

'Maybe that's what attracted him,' Fleet said. 'The lure of the exotic.'

Sinclair looked at Fleet approvingly. 'Exactly so. People fear what they don't understand, but they adore the novel.'

'Is that what I am?' Lydia was already fed up with this covert shit. Why wouldn't spooks just get to the point? 'A novelty?'

'Hardly,' Sinclair said. 'Crows have been of interest since the service was first created.'

'What is it you want?' Lydia said. 'In return for the information I require.'

She looked at Lydia properly, then. 'You grossly misunderstand the nature of this meeting. I am merely considering an exchange, we are a long way from discussing terms. Didn't your uncle teach you the art of negotiation? First the introductions, then you give me something to create good faith, then you sweeten the pot and then, maybe then, I will consent to a mutually beneficial deal.'

Lydia produced her coin and flipped it into the air where it hung, motionless just in front of Sinclair's face. 'Didn't your boss teach you not to piss off a Crow?'

'Lyds,' Fleet said. 'There's no need...'

'There's every need,' Lydia said. 'I'm not in the habit of wasting time. Especially when dealing with death threats.'

'I told you,' Sinclair was addressing Fleet, now. 'I don't know anything about that.'

'Well, what is the point of this, then?' Lydia cut in. 'If you have nothing for me, I'll be heading off. I hear there's a van over the road which does insane falafel wraps. Hard to believe, I know, but I'm willing to give it a try.' She made as if to leave.

'You're making a mistake,' Sinclair said. 'DCI Fleet, you need to make her understand.'

Fleet shrugged. 'I can't make Lydia do anything. I don't believe anybody can.'

OUTSIDE THE GALLERY, Lydia crossed to the river and stared at the moving water until she was fairly sure she wasn't going to punch anything. She knew it wasn't smart to piss off a valuable contact, and that Fleet had no doubt put his professional reputation on the line in order to set up the meeting in which she had just acted like a furious child, but she couldn't stop the swirl of panic and mistrust. Her whole life, she had trusted herself and had felt that she had pretty decent instincts. She had made mistakes, of course, like dating Paul Fox, but she had known full well they were mistakes at the time. She just hadn't cared. When she began training as an investigator with her old boss and mentor, it had been like coming home. This job had been perfect for her with the weird hours, the working alone and the need to assess people accurately. Immediately, she had excelled and Karen had said it was like she was born for it. Now, she was second-guessing her every impression and interaction. It was exhausting and disabling.

Fleet arrived, quietly standing next to her for a few minutes before speaking. 'Well, that could have gone better.'

'I don't trust her.'

'You don't have to. You just have to use her.'

'That's what I thought about Mr Smith,' Lydia said. 'Look where that got me. You were shot. You could have been killed.'

'Just a graze,' Fleet said, trying for levity.

'I don't know what to do. Everything I've tried with JRB and Mr Smith has made things worse.'

'That's not true.'

'Tell that to Ash,' Lydia said and then wished she could take the words back.

Fleet put his arm around her shoulder and pulled her close. 'I know. I'm sorry.'

Lydia let herself lean against him and she closed her eyes. With the sounds of her city and the river flowing past and Fleet's signature glowing around them, she felt a moment of calm. Broken by her mobile buzzing.

It wasn't a number Lydia recognised, but she answered. 'This is Miles Bunyan,' the caller said, mercifully preventing Lydia from having to admit that she didn't recognise his voice. 'You found my daughter.'

Lucy Bunyan. Taken by the Pearls and retrieved by Lydia. Much to the annoyance of the Pearl Court. Best not to think about that.

'Yes, Mr Bunyan, of course. How are you?'

'Lucy set fire to her bed last night. Luckily nobody was hurt. I keep an extinguisher in the kitchen and I managed to put it out, but I'm worried. Of course. That's not normal. And it could have been so much worse. I've told her, if she does anything like it again we'll have to call the fire brigade. The police will have to be involved. She could be convicted.'

'Slow down, Miles,' Lydia said. 'Is everybody all right? Was Lucy hurt at all?'

'No. Smoke inhalation and an overnight in the hospital but I'm allowed to pick her up this afternoon. That's why I wanted to speak to you first. What do I do to help her?'

Lydia thought of Ash, unable to function in the real

world after decades in the Pearl Court. Lucy had been with them for a relatively short time and had seemed unscathed. She had talked of being at a fun party. Apparently, she wasn't as unaffected as she had appeared.

After promising that she could call round that evening, she finished the call and filled Fleet in.

'Poor kid,' Fleet said. 'There's a chance it's unrelated. I mean, she's the age for acting out.'

Lydia appreciated his attempt to ease her guilt, but she wasn't buying it. Lucy was another casualty of the magical Families of London. It wasn't enough to be the head of the Crows or to keep the peace or to look after Camberwell. London was her city and she had to do more to get her house in order.

CHAPTER TWELVE

Miles Bunyan opened the door. 'She's upstairs. Asleep.' He had purple rings under his eyes and when he turned around Lydia could see that his hair was in need of a wash and was sticking up in the back where he had missed with the comb.

'You want tea?'

'Thank you,' Lydia said. She always accepted drinks when offered. It was investigator training basics. People found it easier to talk when they were busy doing something and the normality of it helped to build intimacy, which increased the likelihood of trust and honesty and openness. At least, that was the theory.

Back in Miles' house, Lydia was reminded of her initial impressions of him. A good dad, for sure, but there was something she didn't trust. Or, more accurately, didn't like. He was talking about Lucy, describing her changeable mood, deteriorating behaviour, the way she had become more withdrawn. 'All since… Well. You know.'

Lydia did know. She accepted the mug of tea and sat with Miles at the kitchen table. 'You know that contract you told me about? With your father's old company? May I see it?'

'I burned it,' Miles said, surprised. 'You told me to.'

It was typical, of course, that the one time a client had decided to actually obey Lydia was the time she would have wished he hadn't. Ever since Miles had rung, she had been nursing a small hope that the contract would provide a clue or confirmation about the business structure of JRB. Or another contact name for her to follow up. Another crumb of information. Instead, it was another dead end. And, looking at the beaten and exhausted Miles, sipping tea while his disturbed daughter slept upstairs, another damaged family that Lydia had let down, she thought that maybe she should step down as the head of the Crows. Perhaps Maddie would do a better job.

Back in her office, Lydia planned to do some work or, at the least, think of some new ways to tackle the problem of the missing cup. She couldn't settle and her mind kept jumping from problem to problem. Outside on the terrace, she stood in the London drizzle and listened to the sounds of the city, traffic, sirens, a distant voice shouting obscenities. The urban symphony usually calmed her mind and helped her to think, but all she could see was the shape of a man hanging from a tree, strung up to look like one of the crows that was currently strutting across the paving. She went back inside and paced the room instead. Movement had always helped her think, but today not even the well-worn track around her office was working. And she felt odd. The nausea was back and her hearing felt as if she was at the bottom of a swimming pool. Then the room tilted, and she felt herself fall.

Lydia came round on the floor of her office. She saw a slice of her desk, the patchy paintwork of the ceiling and Fleet's concerned face. The back of her head hurt. She must have cracked it when she had fallen and she was extremely glad there was carpet, however thin and functional. Her thoughts came back in bits, the pieces sliding together until she was fully conscious. She realised that Fleet was speaking, he repeated her name.

'I'm okay,' she managed. 'Just fainted.'

'Can you sit up?'

'Yeah,' Lydia said and then felt the room swoop and had to lie back down. 'No.' Her body was tingling and her mind was a tunnel, the black edges threatening to send her back under. 'Lift my legs.'

Fleet did so, and she felt the blood returning to her head and the faintness and nausea retreat.

'What made you pass out?' Fleet was frowning down from what seemed like a very great height.

Lydia closed her eyes and tried to remember what she had been doing. She had been struggling to focus, pacing the room to calm her mind.

'Have you eaten today?'

And there was the problem in a nutshell. She had eaten. She had been feeling fine. It had just happened.

'Were you working?'

'I was stretching my legs.' Lydia tried not to sound defensive, but she was embarrassed. And worried. She was already at a severe disadvantage facing Maddie. If she was going to start keeling over at random moments, too, her chances of survival were diminished further.

'You need to get checked out,' Fleet said. 'Could be anaemia.'

She sat up without passing out again. Progress. 'I'm fine.'

Fleet didn't say anything else, but she could see he wasn't happy.

'I'll call tomorrow,' Lydia said, to appease him. Although they won't be able to help, she added silently.

. . .

HAVING BEEN POKED and prodded by her GP to no avail, Lydia was sure that her first hunch was correct. Whatever was off and causing her system to misfire was related to being a Crow. Unable to see any other option, she called home and confirmed that her dad was at his usual afternoon haunt, The Elm Tree in Beckenham, just a few streets from her childhood home.

Henry was sitting alone with an open newspaper and a half-drunk pint.

'Hello, love,' he stood when he saw her approach and they hugged. 'This is a nice surprise.'

It still felt miraculous that her dad recognised her and that she could speak to him without confusion. Whatever else had happened, she would always be grateful to Mr Smith for reversing the cognitive degeneration which had taken Henry Crow prematurely from the world.

Henry was frowning lightly. 'Did your mother send you? Did I forget you were visiting?'

'No, no. I haven't been home. I just came to see you.'

'Right.' He was clearly relieved. The ghost of his previous confusion was still a powerful spectre. 'What would you like to drink? Are you hungry? They do a decent Ploughman's here. Or the steak pie is good.'

'I'm fine.' Lydia sat opposite her dad, keen to get to the point. Just because Mr Smith had cured her dad and that he was no longer denying his Crow nature in the same way, didn't mean that she didn't act like a battery on him, still. By amplifying his Crow power, she was giving him more to siphon off. And they were working on the theory that this would keep him from getting ill again. It was by no means a certainty. For the first time, Lydia could see the point in Mr Smith's department doing actual scientific research on the Families and their abilities. It would be nice to have some hard data. Guidelines to follow to keep them all safe and healthy.

But for now, she didn't have a choice. She needed to know more and there wasn't anybody else to ask. She didn't know if she had truly expected her ancestors to answer her questions after she had visited the cemetery, but she hadn't had so much as a vivid dream. 'I need to know more.' She glanced around to make sure that nobody was listening. She knew her father wouldn't appreciate her being indiscreet. 'About our Family. My Crow power.'

'Why?'

'So that I can control it.' *So that I don't murder anybody else by accident. Or pass out when I'm fighting for my life.*

'I'm out, you know that,' Henry said, his voice gentle but with an undercurrent of steel.

'But you can tell me what you know, whatever Grandpa Crow told you?'

A shadow passed across Henry's face. 'I have no wish to pass on my father's lessons.'

'There's something else,' Lydia said, gripping her coin for strength. 'I've been feeling unwell.'

Henry stiffened. 'How so?'

'A bit off, I guess. Faint at times.'

'Have you told your mother?'

'No,' Lydia said. 'But I've been to the doc and been checked over. Physically, I'm fine. But we know that our power can have adverse effects.'

'That was different,' Henry said, clearly hating every second of the conversation. 'You're using yours. It's not... building up or whatever was happening with me.'

It was time. She couldn't tell her father that she had killed a man. Accident or not, he would see her differently and she couldn't stand it. Instead, she went with the other pressing reason she needed help. 'Maddie is really strong,' Lydia said.

'Maddie?' Henry frowned. 'Your cousin Maddie? Didn't she leave London? John said something-'

'The very same. Well, she can control a person's body, move them against their will.'

Henry narrowed his eyes. 'You know this how?'

'I know this,' Lydia said, putting emphasis on the words. She didn't want to worry her dad but, right now, she needed him to be Henry Crow, not her father. 'Now I need to know how to beat her.'

Henry shook his head. 'No you don't. Feathers, Lydia, you don't know what you're asking.'

'Tell me, then. Explain. Because if I can't match Maddie...' She left the sentence unfinished, unable to say the words out loud. She didn't want to make it real.

Henry took a sip of his pint, thinking.

Lydia had just decided he wasn't going to answer when he began speaking. 'Back in the day, I was next in line and doing my duty, toeing the line for your grandfather because, well, because there wasn't a lot of choice. My heart wasn't really in it, though, even before I met your mum.' Henry smiled a little sadly. 'I fell for her, Lydia, one look and I was a goner, but it's also true to say that she looked like a lifeline to me. A way out. She was this whole other...' He waved his hand, at a temporary loss. 'She represented something different. A whole way of being, of living, and I wanted it almost as much as I wanted her.'

Lydia kept quiet, not wanting to interrupt the flow of reminiscences.

'But Charlie. He was always hungry. He wanted it all. And when it came to it, it seemed like the perfect solution. We would both get what we wanted. Your grandpa wasn't too happy, of course, but I stood up to him.' Henry paused, looking uncertainly at Lydia. 'Are you sure you want to hear this?'

'I really do.'

'Right,' he looked down at the table before continuing.

'I've told you before that I wanted out, but I don't think I told you why. Not really.'

Lydia had assumed it was the whole slightly dodgy business thing. Wanting a less criminal life for his wife and daughter.

'Charlie was stepping up to me. It wasn't anything personal, but he was ambitious and I was… Well, I was in his way. He was doing anything and everything to get an edge. He would scheme, he would work all the hours, he would take any job from our father and never ask questions, but most of all, he would train. Hours and hours he spent working on his speed, his strength, his fighting skills. And he tried to work his Crow angle, too. He always wanted me to show him anything I could do, to see if he could learn it. Any bit of power from anyone, Crow or Silver or whoever, he was drawn to them. It wasn't healthy. He had a hunger for it.'

Lydia found it hard to imagine Charlie as a young man, everything laid bare for her father to see. The man she knew was closed and controlled and moved through the world like he was cutting it to pieces.

'Your grandpa encouraged it. He liked us at each other's throats. Called it healthy competition. Luckily, Charlie hated the old man as much as I did, and we didn't let him break our bond. We were close. We liked each other.'

'What happened?'

'Our father told Charlie that the only way to increase his power was to take it.' Henry paused. 'From me.'

'Is that even possible?'

Henry looked down for a moment. He seemed to be deciding whether to continue or not, but Lydia hadn't come to Beckenham to be sent away with an intriguing silence. She needed her family to start being straight with her. Feathers. She was the head of the Family. She was, she realised with a rush of embarrassment, her father's superior. 'Tell me,' she said.

Something moved behind Henry's eyes and he straightened in his chair. 'I don't know if it was true, but dear old dad told Charlie that he could take a person's power by killing them. And since I would need to be out of the way if he was to become the head of the family, anyway, it was a done deal.'

Lydia stared at her father. 'You're not serious. He can't have been serious. He can't have meant...'

'Yeah. He did.'

'That makes no sense,' Lydia said. 'Putting emotion and morality aside, why would he want to lose a member of the Family? A trusted part of the business? What had you done?' She winced with how cold that sounded, but still. The point stood. Why would Grandpa Crow deliberately reduce the ranks of main bloodline Crows?

'He thought I would kill Charlie.' Henry said flatly. 'In his mind, it was a neat solution to the problem.'

'What problem?'

'The Charlie problem. Grandpa Crow was a complete bastard, don't know if you've gathered that by now,' Henry smiled wryly, 'but he was a good leader. And he wasn't crazy. He saw something in Charlie which concerned him.'

'If you're concerned about your son, you get them counselling. You don't set him against your other son in the hope that the favourite kills the younger one. You don't do that.' Lydia had always known her Family was half myth, but that was ridiculous. 'There had to be another reason. Or you both misunderstood his meaning.'

Henry smiled sadly. 'This was why I kept you away. This is why I'm out. There is poison in this Family.'

'No,' Lydia said. 'I don't believe that. There are people. And some of them are awful, but that doesn't make the

Crows cursed. It's not poison. Or predestination. That's the easy way out.' Lydia was aware that her voice had got faster and was in danger of cracking. She would not be cursed. She was her own woman. She made her own choices.

'You have to be careful,' Henry said, tapping the back of her hand. 'Promise me. Don't kill in anger.'

Lydia noticed he didn't say 'don't kill' full stop. Not for the first time, it struck her that her life was weird. Pushing down the sudden urge to laugh, she nodded her agreement. 'Fine,' she said. 'Now will you promise to tell me how to get better control? Maddie's nearly killed me two times already. I need to prepare for the third.'

To his credit, her father didn't even blink. 'You have to practise.'

'Fine. What else?'

Her dad looked uncomfortable. 'You have to really practise. You need to practise killing.'

'How?'

'Animals. Birds.'

'No.' Lydia said flatly.

Henry shrugged. 'That's what I was told. I wasn't any good at it either, but Charlie was. And, let's be honest, Maddie is, too. If you want to win, you have to be able to play the game.'

'No,' Lydia said again. 'What else can I do?'

'I don't know.' Henry looked as miserable as Lydia felt. 'Maybe put yourself under pressure? See if you can maintain focus even while other things are going on. Or when you're in danger. It's not very easy to artificially create those kinds of situations. Not safely, anyway.'

'And if they're safe, they're not really putting me in danger.'

'Yeah,' her dad said. 'That's the issue. Sorry.'

'It's not your fault.' Lydia touched his hand.

'Be careful, won't you?'

'Of course,' Lydia said and ignored the taste of feathers on her tongue.

CHAPTER THIRTEEN

It was almost midnight and Lydia was still wide awake. She knew she wasn't even close to sleep, so she got out of bed as quietly as possible. There was a shaft of orange light coming through a gap in the curtains and Lydia thought she would be able to get her clothes without putting on a light.

'What's wrong?' Fleet's voice drifted from the humped-up duvet.

'Nothing. Go back to sleep.'

The sound of the covers shifting and then Fleet was propped up on one elbow. 'Can't sleep?'

'No,' she said. 'I'm just going to sit up for a bit. Watch Netflix.'

'I don't think so,' Fleet said. 'You're going out.'

'Maybe,' Lydia conceded. 'If the TV doesn't work.'

'I'll come with,' Fleet was already reaching for his clothes.

'You don't have to,' she said. 'Go back to sleep.'

His eyes gleamed in the darkness. 'Can't. Got a bad feeling.'

Lydia paused, the door handle smooth under her palm.

Fleet had always had a particular signature, a special something that wasn't Crow or Silver, Pearl or Fox, but was definitely not nothing. Most non-Family people were just that. Nothing. They smelled of aftershave or perfume or sweat, they might seem dodgy or give out a good, kind vibe, but that was it. With Fleet – and Mr Smith – Lydia got the same hit of impressions that she got with the Families, only she didn't have a convenient label for it. Fleet's was just Fleet. When she had met him, she would have laid money that there had been something a bit magical way back in his family. Now, after so much time in close proximity to Lydia, that power had intensified and sharpened. Its edges more defined. The impressions quick and clear. And now, when Fleet said he had a 'bad feeling' it was perfectly possible that he was getting a premonition. 'You saw something.'

She saw his head nod.

'And you want me to come back to bed?'

Another nod.

'It's bad?'

'Yeah.'

'Right.' Lydia's mind flashed with images of Maddie out there in the dark. Black against black, stepping out of the shadows with a length of wire or a sharp blade. She stepped away from the door, dropping her clothes on the floor. She got back into the warmth of the bed and Fleet's arms encircled her, pulling her close.

'Thank you,' he breathed into her hair.

LYDIA WOKE up still feeling antsy. She contacted Paul for a meeting and agreed to meet him halfway between their territories. 'Potters Field will be busy,' Paul said, and suggested a park a little further from the river. It was technically closer to Camberwell, which gave Lydia the advantage, so she agreed. Less than an hour later, she arrived at the meeting. She had decided to walk in the hopes it would calm her jangling nerves. No such luck.

Paul Fox was sitting on a bench in Leathermarket Gardens, his face tilted to the sun. He spoke without moving and she wondered whether he had excellent peripheral vision or similar senses to hers. Or whether he would have greeted anybody the same way, just for the chance of appearing superhuman. 'Hello, Little Bird.'

'I just wanted an update on the surveillance,' Lydia said after sitting next to him on the bench. She hoped that keeping it all business and her language professional, it would keep the Fox from getting any other ideas.

'I love the spring,' he said, eyes still closed.

Lydia waited to see if he was going to say anything else, studying his face without the disturbance of him looking at her. He didn't, just kept his eyes shut like he was too busy enjoying the warm spring sun to bother himself with anything else. Lydia didn't have time for games so she spoke again. 'On Emma. Any sign of my cousin?'

'All quiet,' Paul said, finally opening his eyes and looking at her.

Lydia appreciated that he had dropped his habitual teasing tone.

'There's been no indication of Maddie approaching your friend,' Paul added and Lydia realised she must be frowning.

'Thank you,' she said.

'No sighting of her at all, in fact. And I've got everyone on the alert.'

Lydia wondered how large a number 'everyone' included. She had been around town, alerting the sources she had been cultivating, like the lads running the food booths along the embankment by Westminster Pier, but it felt like a drop in the ocean. Especially when looking for a professional ghost. 'It's scary,' Lydia said. 'She could walk past our people. Hell Hawk, she could probably walk past us, and we wouldn't have a clue.'

Paul looked surprised. 'Wouldn't you do your,' he waggled his fingers. 'You know, sensing thing?'

Lydia hesitated. Then she realised that he was helping her and looking out for Emma and that, after everything that had happened with Maddie and the Pearl King and the Silvers, the Foxes were probably the closest she was going to get to a real alliance. 'About that... There's nothing from her. I don't know how she's done it or what has happened, but she doesn't feel like a Crow anymore. It's disturbing.'

Paul was quiet for a moment. 'I've never heard of anything like that. I mean, people will say "they're not acting like a Fox" or they're not a "real" one if they want to insult someone, put them in their place, but it's not literal.'

'I know.' She leaned back and closed her eyes. It felt like she was dealing with too many questions. Too much was at stake and she didn't know what she was doing about any of it.

'Is it possible that it's you?'

Her eyes snapped open. 'What do you mean?'

'Could your power be on the fritz? You look a bit knackered, could be that. Or was it the adrenaline?' He held up his hands. 'No shade intended. She's scary.'

'It's not me,' Lydia said. 'I'm firing on all cylinders. You, for example, are giving off an unbearable amount of Fox.'

'Unbearable, is it?' Paul said in a low voice.

Lydia felt her whole traitorous body respond. 'Stop it.'

He grinned. White teeth flashing. She could see red fur, feel a warm body moving against her in the dark, smell good earth and fresh rain.

'I'm serious,' Lydia said, producing her coin and squeezing it in her fist.

He raised his hands in mock surrender. 'Okay, okay.'

Lydia took a few deep breaths. She could feel the Crow

power rising through her, the urge to spread her wings and take flight, the thousand tiny hearts beating an urgent tattoo. A warning call. A swell of support. Both. She could feel the urge to tear into flesh with her sharp beak. The world was tilting, and she caught herself before she fell.

Her head was between her knees and she was aware of a firm hand on the back of her neck. Paul's thumb was rubbing small circles on the skin at the top of her spine and that wasn't helping to clear her head. Or perhaps it was. She was definitely anchored into the seat and the ground and the reality of the closeness of the Fox. She was no longer soaring high on a warm thermal or pecking at a carcass.

When she straightened up, the first words which came out of her mouth were 'I need a drink.'

Paul removed a flask from his inside jacket pocket and passed it over. The fine smoky whisky moved over the tongue and throat and, seconds later, she felt a welcome calm. This was the problem, she realised, she had cut down on alcohol and it had put her out of balance. Maybe the whisky had been keeping the Crow power damped down to a manageable level. Of course, the problem with going back to that coping method, was that she wouldn't be getting stronger. She needed the strength, needed the full power in case she had to face Maddie, but she also needed to be able to control it. And to not faint.

Of course, Lydia thought, in a moment of optimism, there was every chance that Maddie had headed off of her own accord. Paul hadn't seen her in Beckenham and neither Uncle John nor Aiden had sounded the alarm. Maybe she was on the other side of the world, back in the MI6 fold and merrily killing for the government.

CHAPTER FOURTEEN

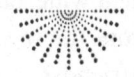

Back at The Fork, Lydia was thinking about raiding Angel's fridge before heading upstairs and was preoccupied by thoughts of food. It took her a couple of seconds longer than it should have done for her to notice that the closed cafe wasn't empty.

There was something in the air. Vibrations, perhaps. Or her Crow senses setting off the alarm. She felt her shoulders raise and her coin was in her hand as she scanned the dim room. It wasn't dark outside but the overhead lights were off. A green light blinked on the coffee machine.

'Angel?'

A figure rose from behind the counter.

'Ta-da!' Maddie was wearing a wavy blonde wig today and her lips were the colour of fresh blood. 'Pleased to see me?'

'Not exactly,' Lydia said.

'Now, now. That's no way to greet your own flesh and blood.'

'I thought you didn't want me to look for you.'

Maddie pulled an expression of faux sympathy. 'Oh, Lyds, I'm sorry. I didn't mean to hurt your feelings. Just because I don't want you tracking my every move, sticking your beak into my business, doesn't mean I don't want us to be friends.'

Lydia scanned the room for her nearest escape route, while trying to pretend she was doing nothing of the sort. Her heart was hammering, and she felt the itch in her arms. She wanted to spread them wide, take off for the clear blue sky. Get far, far away from the woman leaning against the counter. 'You want to be friends?'

'I told you, I didn't know it was you on the roof. And I blew off the job. That's got to show affection.'

'I'm very grateful,' Lydia said, trying not to sound like a sarcastic witch.

Maddie's mouth twisted, so she wasn't sure she had succeeded. 'And that's not my first peace offering. I've been on your side for months.'

'You have?'

Maddie blew out a sigh. 'Who do you think took care of that Kendal problem? And what thanks have I received?'

'Kendal?' The name fell into place. Mark Kendal. 'The guy who ran the phone shop on Southampton Way?' It took Lydia another beat to realise what Maddie meant. 'You killed him?'

Maddie smiled. 'Of course.'

'Why?' She was mystified. Kendal wasn't exactly the preserve of high-level assassins and he had nothing to do with Mr Smith, as far as Lydia knew.

'To get your attention, silly.'

'But you didn't sign your work. How was that getting my attention?' As she spoke, Lydia remembered the ten-shilling note she had found in Kendal's wallet. She had assumed it had been Mr Smith, but perhaps it had been Maddie's idea of a calling card.

'I know you like a puzzle,' Maddie said. 'Besides, I have my standards. Ghosts never leave a trace.'

Lydia had the sudden, inappropriate urge to laugh. She could picture a line of cereal bowls and mugs of tea on her kitchen counter, Jason making yet another hot chocolate. She made herself nod thoughtfully instead.

Maddie had moved from behind the counter and Lydia didn't like it one little bit. She tried to think of a way to distract her. If she could just get outside or upstairs and behind the locked door of her flat. Somewhere she could phone for help.

'You said you were helping me. I don't understand...'

'Hell Hawk, Lyds. Where is your head?' Maddie twisted a strand of blonde hair with a finger, her head tilted as she contemplated Lydia. 'Kendall was moving product on a massive scale. Quite impressive ambition, really. But it looked bad for you. Made you look weak. People were whispering that you had no idea, that you were asleep at the wheel. Seems they were right.'

'He came to me for help,' Lydia said, hating the confusion evident in her voice. 'Wanted me to stop the hairdresser over the road from selling phone cases.'

'No,' Maddie shook her head. 'He wanted you to pay them a little visit. And if you didn't take lethal action, he could arrange a cleansing fire and solve his problem with you in the frame as the arsonist. Everyone would know that the big bad Crow had paid them a warning visit.'

'Why did he want them dead? If he was moving drugs, why would he care about phone cases?'

'Oh, Lyds,' Maddie said. 'You really are lost in the clouds, aren't you? Keep up, babes.'

Lydia was distracted from her fear by embarrassed fury. She had believed the little twerp. He had played her. Or tried to play her. She would kill him. Lydia remembered a second later that he was already dead.

'The woman who runs the salon. She offers extras in the back room, cash payments only, but that's beside the point.

She didn't like Kendall or the police attention he was risking with his activities. Perhaps if Charlie was still in charge, she would have been worried about Crow attention, too.'

Lydia ignored the barb. 'And?'

With exaggerated patience, Maddie explained. 'She made the mistake of confronting our man Kendal, asking him to keep things quiet. He decided to make sure she was going to keep quiet, instead. You know how important the flow of information is, how you've got to mark out your territory and make sure that everybody in it knows that you're in charge?' Maddie let the insult dangle before continuing. 'Well that applies all the way along the chain. Even the rats in the gutter have an order to maintain. But I wasn't going to have Kendal disrespect you like that. It really didn't look good. So I dealt with it.'

Lydia tried to come up with a response but her mind was unhelpfully blank.

'You're welcome,' Maddie said, a note of irritation creeping in. 'No charge. This time.'

By this point, Lydia had recovered enough to reply: 'There's always a charge.'

Maddie nodded approvingly. 'Quite right.'

'I'll pay it,' Lydia said, 'of course. But no more unsolicited help. I'm handling things.'

'Is that what you truly believe?' Maddie asked, looking genuinely interested.

'Why? Do you want the job?'

Maddie's laugh made all the hairs on the back of Lydia's neck stand up. 'I hadn't thought of that.'

Well, that had the ring of a lie.

'But it's not my style. I'm more a moves-in-the-shadows type. I could be the power behind the throne, though. Your trusted advisor. Right-hand woman.'

It was the old offer and Lydia had been half-expecting it

since discovering that Maddie was back in town. 'Isn't it time to get a new tune?'

Lydia didn't see her intention or her movement but there was Maddie toe to toe, holding an extremely sharp knife to her throat. She felt the sting as it nicked her skin. 'Don't be rude, Lyds,' Maddie said and her eyes were dead.

Lydia didn't answer, just returned Maddie's gaze as best she could.

After a moment, a spark returned to Maddie's eyes and they widened ever so slightly. She moved away, the knife stowed as quickly as it had appeared. 'I'll leave you to think on it.' She made a show of checking the time on her phone. 'Oh my days, is it two already? Got to motor, babes. hope you don't mind. You know how it is? Places to be, throats to slit.'

Lydia stiffened as Maddie swooped forward, but she just kissed Lydia on each cheek. 'Ciao, bella.'

AFTER MADDIE HAD SAUNTERED out through the front door, Lydia's first urge was to be sick. Instead, she locked the door and pulled the deadbolt. Upstairs in the flat, she found Jason pouring the last of the cereal into a bowl. More accurately, he was pouring the last of the cereal onto the counter next to the bowl and Lydia guessed he was deep in thought. She hated to be the bearer of bad news, but if Maddie was going to start showing up at The Fork, she had to tell Jason. He was almost certainly safe from her, but she could still give him a fright.

Jason didn't go pale in the way that a living person did, but his outline shimmered and he became more translucent. Sometimes he disappeared altogether. Right now, Lydia would say he was about seventy per cent solid. 'What does she want?'

Before her cousin had found her professional calling,

Maddie had tried to throttle her and had then offered a partnership. To say she was dangerously unpredictable would be quite the understatement. Now she was a loose cannon and seemed to want to taunt Lydia. Or help her. It was very hard to tell. 'Your guess is as good as mine,' Lydia said.

'She might be playing with you. Like a cat with a mouse,' Jason said, pushing at the folded cuffs of his baggy eighties suit jacket. 'Sorry.'

'I think that's likely.' It wasn't as if it hadn't crossed her own mind. She smiled robustly, still trying to reassure Jason. 'Lucky I've got you.' The first time Maddie had attempted to kill Lydia, Jason had saved her life.

'I'm not with you all the time,' Jason said.

Lydia pressed down a flare of annoyance. He was just being concerned, and she knew her anger wasn't with Jason. It was with Maddie for making her frightened. 'I'm a lot stronger, now. And it won't exactly be unexpected. I'll be ready.'

'I'm not sure that's true,' Jason said. 'She's nuts.'

'We don't say that anymore,' Lydia said, trying to lighten the mood and ease Jason's anxiety. 'It's mental health issues.'

'She's a fucking psycho. Is that better?'

'Maybe,' Lydia smiled at him. 'It's a specific diagnosis, at least.' And accurate.

'I'm being serious,' Jason said, still looking dangerously transparent.

'I know,' Lydia said and touched his arm.

AFTER CALMING JASON DOWN, Lydia called Fleet and asked him to meet her at Charlie's for some training. She couldn't face updating him on the phone and she needed to expel some of the terror-induced energy with some exercise.

At the training room in Charlie's house, Lydia kicked the

join between the crash mats she had bought and lugged up to the room so that they lay together neatly. Then she went through her stretches and some strength training, ignoring the distracting sight of Fleet doing the same. Feathers, the man looked good.

When she was ready, she got into the middle of the mat. 'I want you to come at me.'

Fleet hadn't been fully on board with Lydia's new training plan when she had first described it and the intervening days didn't seem to have improved matters. He made a half-hearted feint and went to grab her, circling his arms around her waist in an easy-to-duck manoeuvre.

'Not like that,' Lydia said. 'Come. At. Me.' Practising spinning coins was all very well when she was on her own in the studio, but she wanted to see if she could maintain focus while under stress.

'I don't want to hurt you,' Fleet said. He held up his hands. 'I know you're perfectly capable of defending yourself, but-'

'Then you've nothing to worry about.'

Fleet rolled his shoulders. 'Fine.' His attack came quickly and without warning. Lydia was on her back on the mat, her whole spine vibrating with the impact. When she could draw air into her lungs again and her mind was unscrambled enough to form words, she said 'good' and got herself upright. 'Again.'

AFTER AN HOUR of being flung to the mat by Fleet, Lydia was sweaty and exhausted. She followed Fleet down to Charlie's kitchen to make a post-workout coffee using Charlie's excellent machine.

She tried not think about Maddie standing in the same room and how much she didn't want to tell Fleet that she had visited her again. Once they were leaning against the cabinets, sipping coffee, Fleet ran through the rest of his week. He checked on which nights they were going to stay at his flat and which ones they would be at The Fork. After a while she realised that he was no longer speaking. 'Sorry? I zoned out there for a moment. I need another coffee.'

'That is never true of you,' Fleet said. 'You are ninety-eight per cent caffeine at this point.'

'That takes work,' Lydia said, switching on the machine.

'I was saying that I have some work to catch up on and I need a shower, but I could come over later. Are you around for dinner?'

'Maybe. Can I let you know?'

'Sure.'

She could see that Fleet wanted to say something else. 'What is it?'

'What was that about? Just now.'

'I have to get stronger,' Lydia said. 'I told you.'

'You're already strong.'

'More focused, then. I can't lose control. People will get hurt.'

Fleet watched her for another moment. 'It wasn't your fault. It was self-defence.'

There was a sudden lump in her throat and she swallowed hard. This was the moment when she should tell Fleet about Maddie's continuing interest. She knew that, but she couldn't. He would want to fix it. He would urge her to tell the police. However much he had embraced her weird life and her magical Family, he still believed in the system.

'It wasn't your fault,' Fleet said again and wrapped his arms around her. She could smell the clean sweat from the workout and the indefinable odour that was 'Fleet'. With her head on his chest, she could hear waves rolling on a distant shore and feel fine white sand between her bare toes.

CHAPTER FIFTEEN

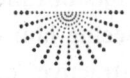

When Lydia woke up, Fleet's arm was heavy across her body, as if he had been anchoring her in place even while unconscious. She turned over to wrap herself around him.

'What's on the agenda today?' Fleet asked a little while later, stretching his arms above his head in a distracting manner. Lydia was out of bed and pulling on her clothes but she paused to reconsider. She could be ten minutes late.

'Meeting mum for lunch,' she said, dropping her jeans and climbing back into bed.

Fleet kissed her before asking about the time. 'You have to get up, then,' he said, sitting up. 'Come on. I'm not going to make you late for Susan Crow.'

'You could come with,' Lydia said impulsively. 'If you want.'

Fleet's smile was like sunshine. 'Thank you.'

The restaurant was an authentic and, considering its central location, refreshingly unpretentious Italian. Susan Crow had always been excellent at finding good places to eat and Lydia made a mental note to suggest that she and Fleet come back as soon as possible.

She ploughed through a plate of fried courgette flowers and a perfect tomato, basil and mozzarella salad, while Fleet held the conversational fort. She had never realised how charming Fleet could be. It wasn't like they had lots of mutual friends or spent lots of time in purely social situations. She was used to seeing him in copper mode, which she found alarmingly attractive, or in his private mode, which was just for her, but this was entirely different. He made her mum laugh, encouraged her to have a second glass of Sauvignon Blanc, and discussed, with all evidence of genuine interest, the merits of planting geraniums next to green beans as a natural pest deterrent.

When he had gone to the bathroom and, Lydia had a hunch, to settle the bill before anybody could argue with him, she fully expected her mum to compliment Lydia on her excellent choice of man.

Instead, Susan Crow leaned forward and took hold of Lydia's hand. 'Please don't ask your father about that stuff again.'

The warm glow snuffed out. She didn't need to clarify what 'stuff' her mum was talking about. 'Who else am I supposed to ask?'

'I know it's not fair. I'm sorry.'

'It's not fairness I'm concerned about,' Lydia said, hating that she sounded petulant. She wanted to explain to her mum that she had to find out more about her Crow power and the legacy of being the head of the Family, that she was likely to be fighting for her life, quite literally, and that she needed to be ready. What was a bit of upset compared to that?

'He can't do it,' her mother said. 'He just can't. Please trust me. It will kill him.'

Lydia let the words sink in. Susan Crow wasn't given to

hyperbole. And she loved Lydia. That was one thing Lydia had never questioned, not even for a single second, not even when she was at her teenage worst. If the woman opposite her was saying she couldn't do something, then she couldn't do it. If she said it would kill her father, then it probably would. Still. Lydia couldn't help the way her stomach plunged to the floor. She had wanted some firm ground to stand on. She had hoped Henry would be able to reach out a hand and lead her where she needed to go.

Her mother looked like she wanted to say something else, but Fleet arrived back at the table, and Lydia watched her expression alter. She favoured Fleet with a warm smile. 'That was delicious. We should do this more often.'

ON THE WAY HOME, Lydia was quiet and, after a while, Fleet ran out of conversational openers. Once they were parked, he said. 'I thought that went well.'

She put a hand on his leg. 'It went extremely well. I think she likes you more than she likes me.' The words came out more seriously than she intended and she felt stupid tears in her traitorous eyes and had to swipe at them unobtrusively. Unfortunately for her, Fleet was a sharp copper and he didn't miss a trick. Instantly, his arms were around her. 'What's wrong?'

Lydia started with the fact that her mother had warned her off asking her father for help with her power and ended with Maddie's most recent visit. He didn't take it well. 'We need to meet with Sinclair. And you need to make a deal. I'm serious, Lyds. You are in real danger.'

'No deal,' Lydia said. She couldn't explain it to Fleet, but the business with Mr Smith had made her feel like she was losing pieces of her soul. She would not do it again.

'She's showing signs of obsession. With you. This is really bad and you can't handle it alone.'

'I'm not alone,' Lydia said. 'I've got you.'

'You do, but I'm not with you all the time.'

It was an echo of Jason's concern. And it just made her feel worse. Like something fragile to be protected. She was the head of the Crow Family, not a damsel in distress. 'I'll figure it out. We don't need Sinclair. I promise.'

'It's escalating, her behaviour, I don't know why you can't see that.'

'Please, can you just drop it? Let's go upstairs. Work off lunch.'

Fleet looked through the windscreen, his hands tensing on the steering wheel. He was clearly struggling to hold his temper and Lydia wanted to tell him not to bother, to just let it out. To stop being so bloody careful around her. 'I've got a load of paperwork to catch up on,' he said eventually. 'I should go home.'

'I'll come with you,' Lydia said. 'I don't want to fight.'

'We're not fighting,' Fleet said tightly. 'I'm just worried.'

'I know. I'm sorry.'

He blew out a sigh. 'Don't be sorry.'

Fleet insisted on escorting Lydia to the flat, as if he thought Maddie might be waiting to jump out at her. Once he had checked the place through, examined her door and window locks and generally acted like she was a victim, which made her want to kick him in his soft parts, he accepted a coffee.

Before leaving, Fleet made a call, pacing the roof terrace while he spoke. 'I've posted a couple of officers to keep an eye tonight. Don't give them a hard time.'

'I won't. Thank you.' Lydia refrained from pointing out that if Maddie wanted to kill Lydia, then a couple of coppers sitting in an unmarked car along the street weren't going to stop her. She could see that Fleet needed the illusion of control. And, in the privacy of her own mind, she could admit that it was comforting to have them there.

. . .

WITHOUT FLEET'S calming presence and the knowledge that Maddie was most definitely in London and seemed keen to progress some kind of relationship with Lydia, sleep did not come easily.

When she had finally dropped off, it seemed like no time at all had passed before her phone woke her. The ringing was muffled by the duvet on Fleet's side of the bed and she realised that she had fallen asleep with it under her pillow, just in case he had rung.

'No news,' Lydia said, expecting Maria's assistant.

'That's disappointing,' Maria's voice was cold. 'It is difficult not to take your lack of progress as a sign of your disinterest.'

'That's not...'

'And disinterest in my case is disrespectful. Disrespectful to me. And to the Silver Family as a whole.'

'I'm not disinterested,' Lydia said, gritting her teeth. A thought which had been lapping at the edges of Lydia's mind for some time burst into technicolour. Of all the people who would be likely to know about the whereabouts of the silver cup, Maria would have been top of her list. Surely Alejandro would have left it for his daughter? Or at the very least told her about the replica. Perhaps she was sending Lydia on a wild goose chase? An impossible mission that she was destined to fail, either keeping her busy and distracted from something that Maria was planning and didn't want attention drawn to, or forcing her to let Maria down and provide an excuse to break their shaky alliance.

'Let me prove it,' Lydia said. 'I'll come in and see you today. You are right, I do have something to share.'

Maria sounded thrown, which added to Lydia's paranoia that Maria was playing her. She recovered to say, 'I can fit you in at eleven. For ten minutes, anyway.'

. . .

IT WAS a relief to have a clear mission and, after dressing in her usual uniform of jeans, black T-shirt and leather jacket, Lydia forced herself to eat some toast before spending time on her roof terrace. She tilted her face to the sky and tried to calm her thoughts. She didn't have high hopes for a zen state of mind, but she was willing to try anything to get better control of her power. Even meditation.

The Silver offices on Chancery Lane were bustling with suited people with shiny hair and serious briefcases. It was a very nice building, but it was filled with the sound of telephones, eye-scorching lighting and an undeniable atmosphere of stress. It gladdened Lydia's heart and reminded her that, in some ways at least, she was living life right.

Maria's assistant greeted her politely and offered a choice of beverages. 'I'm fine, thanks,' Lydia said. 'I'll go right in.'

Not waiting for an answer, Lydia strolled into Maria's office. The bright taste of Silver intensifying as soon as she stepped into the room.

Maria was standing in front of the floor-to-ceiling windows with her back to Lydia, speaking on the phone.

Lydia sat in an uncomfortable chair facing Maria's giant desk and waited while Maria took her time in wrapping up her conversation. The room looked the same as the last time she had seen it, when Alejandro had been in situ, down to the treadmill and the modern wood panelling.

Maria looked as groomed and terrifying as always. She was dressed entirely in black, in the kind of tailoring that brooked no argument from the mortal flesh beneath. Her waist was drawn in so tightly that she resembled a wasp and the red soles of her high heels flashed as she crossed the room and sat in the large leather chair opposite Lydia.

'Sorry about that,' she said with absolutely zero sincerity. 'I believe you have news for me?'

'What can you tell me about the cup?'

Maria's brow didn't crease but her eyes flashed with displeasure. 'Is this a joke?'

'No joke,' Lydia said. 'The more I know about it, the better. Maybe a detail will help me find it.'

'I don't see how. This is clearly a waste of time. I had hoped that you had grown out of this sort of game-playing, but clearly not.' Maria stood, motioning for Lydia to leave.

She stayed put and flipped open her notebook. 'You commissioned me to do a job. This is how I work. What did Alejandro tell you about it?'

Maria sighed and sat back down. 'Not much. It's the Family cup. It's solid silver and very old.'

'Made in the early sixteen hundreds as part of the agreement for the use of Temple Church.'

Maria's eyes narrowed. 'You've done your homework.'

'It's my job,' Lydia said evenly. 'And I like to be thorough. You sent Yas Bishop to purchase a silver statue to use as a bribe for Robert Sharp.'

Maria didn't flinch. 'Did I?'

Lydia didn't bother to elaborate. Both Robert Sharp and Yas Bishop had suffered a personality change and Lydia had suspected that the statue had been enchanted in some way that caused psychosis. 'The shop you sent Yas to was in the silver vaults on Chancery Lane. I wish to speak to the proprietor of the shop, Guillaume Chartes.'

'Well go and see him,' Maria waved a hand. 'Sounds like part of your job.'

'The shop is no longer there.' It had disappeared without a trace, the people either side of the unit claiming to have never heard of the man or the shop.

'If it was easy to find the thing, I wouldn't have bothered

commissioning you,' Maria said. 'What do you want from me?'

'I think you know how to contact him,' Lydia said. 'And the fact that you are avoiding telling me is curious.'

Maria's eyes slid left.

'Okay. Let's leave that. Now that we're in alliance, all cosy like, I need some information on one of your clients.'

'That's not possible,' Maria said smoothly. 'Client confidentiality, blah, blah.'

'JRB.'

Maria's expression didn't so much as flicker. 'What about JRB?'

'They are your clients. I am now pretty sure that Mr Smith, a government spook who arranged to have Fleet shot among many other transgressions, is JRB. That JRB is a shell corporation held by said spook and other spook or spooks as yet unknown.' Lydia did not like being honest with Maria. It went against all her instincts, but she hoped that being transparent would encourage the same in return.

Maria didn't seem impressed. Her lips remained a tight little line.

'I need every detail you have on them. Who was your contact? Apart from Yas Bishop.'

'No one,' Maria said. 'Yas Bishop was our sole contact.'

Which was convenient, since Maria had killed her in cold blood to cover tracks. Maria probably had her filed under 'cost of doing business' in some neat ledger tucked in the back of her mind.

Lydia balled her fists and then released them. She wasn't going to waste anger on Maria Silver. And she couldn't afford to lose control. She forced a political smile. 'Well, I appreciate your time. If you remember anything else which might be useful, you'll let me know?'

'Certainly,' Maria said. 'I thought you would be coming with news for me.'

'Not yet,' Lydia said, standing up. 'But I'm working on it.'

Leaving the office, Lydia turned and raised a hand in goodbye. Maria was sitting behind her gigantic shiny desk looking like exactly what she was, a deadly insect, but Lydia hadn't been waving to her. Just to her left, shimmering and translucent in the sunlight pouring through the copious glass, Jason raised his hand in return.

Now, yes, Lydia was nodding up. But, I'm working on it.

Leaving the office, Lydia turned and talked a hand in ponder. Maria was sitting behind her nighttime thing desk, looking like exactly what she was, a deadly piece, but Lydia hadn't been waving to her. Just to her left, shimmering and translucent in the sunlight pouring through the curtains past Jason raised his hand in return.

CHAPTER SIXTEEN

Getting back into the offices to collect Jason was always going to be the tricky part of the equation. Lydia had thought about leaving her jacket or a hat or something that she could collect, but she was concerned that it would put Maria on her guard. The woman wasn't a fool and Lydia wasn't in the habit of getting comfy in her office.

Then it occurred to her that all she needed to do was lie.

She called Maria at six that evening expecting her to still be in the office. She was not disappointed. 'Twice in one day, what a treat,' she said. 'This had better be good.'

'It is,' Lydia said. 'But I'd rather discuss it in person.'

'If you insist.'

MARIA WAS WORKING at her desk. There were piles of documents and, although still immaculately made up and with lipstick that looked as fresh as it had in the morning, there was tiredness around Maria's eyes. Lawyers might have been backed by the devil, but they weren't enjoying a free ride.

'Have you heard from Alejandro?'

Maria held her gaze. 'What kind of question is that?'

'Just interested. And I'm showing sympathy. Asking after your old dad.'

'You are being obnoxious. Deliberately so. Why?'

Lydia shrugged. 'Old habits.'

'You said you had something important to share.'

Maria's irritation was palpable and Lydia calculated she had exactly zero seconds before she called some of her private security and ejected Lydia from the building. Painfully. 'There were three replicas made. You've got one in the crypt so that leaves another two floating around.'

Maria placed the top back onto the fountain pen she had been using and placed it neatly beside the pile of documents. 'I see.'

Lydia had glanced around the office casually when she had arrived and hadn't spotted Jason. Since then she hadn't been able to look away from Maria without it being obvious. She felt a coolness on the back of her neck and hoped, fervently, that it was Jason appearing behind her.

'It's not in your interests to tell me this. If I didn't know there were further replicas, you might be able to give me one and keep the real cup for yourself.'

'I've agreed to find the cup for you,' Lydia said, not clarifying that she never agreed to give the cup to Maria. 'If this alliance is going to work, we need to trust each other's word.'

'That's true,' Maria nodded. 'I don't, I must be honest, but perhaps in time.'

'It's a starting place.' Her neck was freezing, now, and the urge to look around was almost unbearable. 'I'll let you get on. Looks like you've got a lot of work. No rest for the wicked.'

Maria made a little shooing motion with her hand, dismissing Lydia in a practised manner.

Lydia stood and, as she turned, caught a glimpse of Jason,

flimsy and almost entirely see-through in the bright office lighting. A second later and he was flowing into her body, lodging a block of ice in her stomach and seizing her lungs for a terrifying few moments. She couldn't speak to say 'goodbye' so left Maria's office in silence.

BACK AT THE FORK, Lydia sat with Jason while he recovered his equilibrium. She was tense with anticipation, but didn't want to rush him. There was no earthly reason for Jason to help her out, after all. Most ghosts would be enjoying a gentle retirement, maybe with a little light poltergeist action just for fun, not hacking into national databases and running around London playing spy.

'Okay,' he said, once his outline had stopped shaking and his body had solidified again with Lydia's touch.

He still didn't look quite right and Lydia could see that the excursion had cost him. 'Take your time.'

He rolled his shoulders, the movement jerky like he had forgotten how to move naturally. 'After you left, she made a call.'

Lydia waited, letting Jason marshal his thoughts. 'She thinks you have it.'

'The cup?'

'Yeah. There was a break-in at her father's house, just after he "died".' Jason made bunny ears on the last word. 'At the time she didn't think anything had gone missing, but when you told her the cup in the crypt was a fake, she realised that the real cup might have been the target of the robbery.'

'Why didn't she tell me this?' Lydia wondered if she had been right and that Maria was setting her a deliberately difficult task, withholding information so that she would fail.

'Because she thinks you took it. Or a Crow, at any rate.

That's what she said to the person on the phone. She commissioned you to find it because she thinks you have it and it's an opportunity for you to return it without losing face.' He shrugged. 'Although she didn't put it quite like that.'

'Who was it? On the phone?'

'I don't know,' Jason said. 'She didn't say their name. And she stayed in the room after, working for ages. By the time she went to a meeting, I was too weak to press the buttons on the phone and I couldn't access the dialling record. Sorry.'

'No, no. Don't be. You did a brilliant job. This really helps.' Somebody had broken into Alejandro's home and, most likely, taken the cup. If it hadn't been the target, other items would have been taken. So whoever was responsible knew about the cup. 'Who knew about the cup? Mr Smith, I guess. Although I would have thought he would have pressured Alejandro to hand over the cup as part of his immunity deal and wouldn't have needed to nick it.'

'What if it was just a random burglary? A thief could have just seen an expensive looking antique and taken it?'

'I bet Alejandro had a lot of other expensive stuff lying around. Seems unlikely that it would be the only thing taken. I'm guessing the Silvers didn't file a police report? They wouldn't want any evidence of weakness getting out.'

Jason nodded. 'True. So, apart from us, the Silvers, and Smith, who else knows about the cup?'

'The person who made the replicas. We need to find Guillaume Chartes.'

'There's another possibility,' Jason said.

'What's that?'

'The other Families. I mean, you all put items into the museum for the truce, right? That means the Pearls and the Foxes also know about the cup.'

. . .

Lydia didn't see the Pearls sneaking into Alejandro's house in order to steal a silver cup. Apart from anything else, they were trapped in their underground realm. It was a strange liminal space which didn't obey the normal rules of time and one they didn't seem able to leave. They had descendants all around London, of course, people with varying amounts of Pearl blood and residual magic, but they hadn't shown any indication of having formed a meaningful hierarchy or purpose. The Pearl Court underground were the powerhouse, and they used children as their emissaries above ground, running errands, luring new playthings like Lucy Bunyan for the pleasure of the king, and, occasionally, following Lydia.

It was early evening and Lydia hadn't contacted Fleet during the day. She figured he needed a bit of time to process the latest news about Maddie. And to calm down from his annoyance that she hadn't told him about it straight away. She would go round, now, and update him immediately on her progress with the cup. She could even tell him about using Jason as a listening device.

Fleet buzzed her into the flat and then went back to what he was doing. Which was folding a shirt and putting it into a suitcase.

'You're leaving?' Lydia's body went cold. This was it. The other shoe. Dropping like a stone.

'Only for a little while.'

'How long?' Lydia had wanted him to stop treating her like a fragile thing that needed constant monitoring, but she hadn't meant for him to leave her altogether.

'Not sure,' Fleet was concentrating on packing the case, didn't look at her. 'A couple of days. Might be longer, but I hope not.'

Lydia pressed her lips together to stop herself from saying 'stay'. Or 'why now?'.

Fleet finally turned to look at her. 'It's important. I wouldn't go if it wasn't.'

'Is it work?'

'Sort of. It might help, but I don't want to get your hopes up.'

'I'd rather know,' Lydia said. 'Aren't you always telling me that communication is key?'

He smiled gently. 'That's definitely something we need to work on. But right now it's better if I don't tell you.'

'That makes no sense,' Lydia said.

'You know you can trust me. Remember that.'

At the door the panic was sudden and overwhelming. They were hugging, and she pulled away to look at his face. Afraid of what she might find there, but needing the truth. 'Is this because I didn't tell you about Maddie?' She wanted to ask if it was because she had told Paul Fox first, but couldn't make herself say the words. It would be like conjuring a curse.

'No,' Fleet said, but his eyes flicked away.

'Go then,' Lydia said, stepping back. If he didn't go, now, she was going to start crying, and that wasn't going to improve matters.

He looked anguished. 'You must understand-'

'I don't,' Lydia said. All she could feel was the abandonment. This was why you shouldn't trust other people, *rely* on them. They only let you down in the end. What had Jason said about 'everybody leaving?'. Turned out, some left earlier than others.

'This isn't about us,' Fleet tried again. 'I swear I'm not running out on you.'

'But you are leaving.' She refused to make it a question. She couldn't stand the hope.

'Yes. But it's just temporary.'

Lydia wanted to believe him. She reminded herself of all the ways in which Fleet had proved himself to her, proved to be a reliable, loving partner. He had always been on her side. She knew that. She forced a weak smile. 'Okay. Stay safe.'

He kissed her, again, and left.

Lydia closed the door and felt unshed tears hot behind her eyes. Fleet had always had her back. The man had taken a bullet for her. So why was he leaving now?

CHAPTER SEVENTEEN

Lydia went for a walk and called Paul Fox on the way. The sky was a uniform grey and a one-eyed pigeon followed her as if hoping for crumbs. She wanted to tell it not to bother. That it ought to look after itself because those it trusted would fly off on a secret mission leaving it to peck for crumbs alone but she was aware she might have been projecting. Just a bit.

Paul answered. 'Hello, Little Bird. Always a pleasure.'

'Someone broke into Alejandro's house and stole the Silver Cup. I think it was a Fox.'

Paul was quiet for a few beats. 'Just when I think we're making progress, you make a baseless accusation like that…'

'I'm not accusing you of anything,' Lydia side-stepped an abandoned Styrofoam kebab container. 'I'm trying to help.'

'You've lost me,' Paul said, his voice dangerously even.

'I'm worried about whoever has the cup. Maria is looking for it. She's commissioned me, but I'm betting I'm not the only one she has put on the case. She had deep pockets and, as you know, she's utterly ruthless. If it's someone in your den, I thought you would want to know. So that you can protect them.'

'She hasn't got any leads,' Paul said. 'Unless you're running to her with your tall tales.'

'I am not,' Lydia said. 'I have no wish to be your enemy. I hope you know that by now.'

'There you go, then,' Paul said.

'It might have a psychological effect. On whoever is holding it. I've encountered enchanted objects before and they made a man go off the deep end. This is a friendly warning to be careful with it.'

'I told you, I don't run the family. We don't have an official hierarchy or anything like it. But I will ask around. See if some young cub decided to take a trophy.'

'Like I said, it's just a friendly warning.'

LYDIA DIDN'T HAVE high hopes that her offering to her ancestors in Camberwell Cemetery would have resulted in some kind of answer, but she headed to the family tomb anyway. The sky was bright blue and she didn't need her jacket on the walk through the graves. It was peaceful in the cemetery with wide paths and benches and not many people. A man was sitting on a bench with a box of sandwiches and a Thermos and a couple were standing in front of a fresh-looking plot, holding hands in silence, while their small girls ran around the nearby stones shrieking.

The English weren't great with death, Lydia thought. Everybody pretended it wasn't going to happen and, when it did, spoke in hushed tones and anodyne euphemisms. Like it was something unseemly. Or a curse that you could summon by naming it.

The air at the rise of the hill was thick with the scent of bluebells, which seemed even more rampant than her last visit. Lydia went to the yew tree and peered up through the branches, trying to locate the scrap of black silk she tied there. She couldn't see it and didn't feel inclined to climb the tree, again. Once had been enough. A crow landed on the stone surface of the tomb and tilted its head.

'I've come for my answer,' Lydia said, after bobbing her head in greeting. 'I need to know how to control my power. I wanted to be strong enough to beat Maddie, but now I seem to be misfiring. I keep fainting or being sick. I don't know if it's because I have too much power or that I'm not using it right...' Lydia sank down among the flowers and leaned her back against the trunk of the tree. 'And I'm so desperate I'm talking to myself.'

She closed her eyes, feeling her head swim. *Not now.* She produced her coin and spun it in the air. With her head tipped back against the tree, she watched her coin and let the branches and sky in the background of her vision blur. She focused on the flash of gold as the coin revolved. The image of the crow was in flight and then standing and then in flight, and then the wings seemed to be moving, flapping in time with her heartbeat.

A black wing was flapping in the tree. Or was it the black silk? Lydia blinked. It was a fledgling taking flight from a nest in the tree. It was no more than a couple of metres from the nest to the top of the tomb where it sat for a moment and then, with an encouraging caw from the waiting adult, fluffed its stubby feathers and made it back up to the tree.

'Is that my answer?' Lydia asked. 'Because I don't get it.'

That's when she became aware of something moving in the grass to her right. In the shade of the spreading branches, another fledgling was twitching its wings. It fixed Lydia with one bright and frightened eye and made a clumsy hopping movement. One wing wasn't opening the way it should, and Lydia realised that it was probably broken. It had fallen when it had tried its first flight. Or the parents had realised it was sick and had shoved it out of the nest to conserve resources for the successful offspring. If *this* was the answer, then she wished she hadn't bothered coming back.

Her heart tugged with sympathy as the young bird tried to spread its wings, the damaged one clinging uselessly at its side. The more she looked, the more clearly Lydia saw. The bird had a wet-looking head and its feathers were dull and patchy. It settled down low in the grass, its small chest heaving. Henry had told her that she should never touch a fledgling. Even when they were on the ground and seemed to be alone, their parents were probably nearby and she would do more harm than good by scooping it up. He had also told her that if one was injured or sick, it was kinder to finish them off with a rock. Not that she ever had.

The adult crow was still on the tomb and Lydia could swear it was waiting for her to make a move. 'I'm not going to do your dirty work for you,' Lydia said. 'I can't.'

The fledgling was close to death, she could feel it now. Its tiny heart was beating so loud that the sound was filling her ears. Henry had told her that the only way to get strong enough to beat Maddie was to practise. That she had to kill. She had rejected the idea that she had to take from another life in order to save her own, but her own father had told her that her Grandpa Crow had expected Henry to kill Charlie. To become the strongest version of himself. She hadn't wanted to believe that was the way, but the spirits of her ancestors seemed to be telling her the same thing. Unless she had completely lost her marbles and it was a perfectly ordinary crow waiting for her to leave so it could feed its fledgling.

Lydia got up to leave. Either way, she knew one thing was certain. She didn't have what it took, and she wasn't willing to kill to get it. Which, possible insanity aside, meant there was one essential truth – she was going to die.

CHAPTER EIGHTEEN

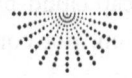

Guillaume Chartes' shop in the silver vaults had disappeared, seemingly overnight. With a professional crew of movers and the ability to glamour – or pay – the surrounding businesses to say they had never heard of you, it was perfectly possible. But only with at least one of two things: money or power.

Lydia searched for him online and asked Jason to do the same. She also forced herself to practise producing coins and trying to move her mug around her desk without touching it while she searched, figuring that every second she wasn't training was a wasted second.

With the realisation that she couldn't beat Maddie came the knowledge that it was only a matter of time before Maddie killed her. And it turned out that knowing death was imminent was extremely motivating. She was determined to get as much done as possible. She was going to lose to Maddie, but she would do everything she could to protect those she was leaving. Which also meant doing her very best to take Maddie with her.

There was a Guillaume Chartes listed by the London Assay Office, but no way to contact him. Lydia called the office number and pretended to be calling from the British Museum. No dice. The man she spoke to was either genuinely unable to give her an address for Guillaume, or unwilling.

Jason, however, had no problem in nosing around in the Assay Office's database. 'It's not exactly high security,' he said. 'They're using a cheap cloud-based system and they've only got native encryption, not continuous.' He shook his head fondly. 'The muppets.'

'Did you find him?'

'Oh, yes. All entries for Guillaume Chartes as a registered maker. Same name, different dates going back a couple of hundred years. Either there is one hell of a naming tradition in that family, or it's the same guy.'

'That's impossible,' Lydia said automatically.

'Said the magical PI to the ghost.'

THE ASSAY OFFICE didn't hold home address details, but they did have relevant places of business for the makers. These were mostly galleries, shops, and smithing studios. The database still showed Guillaume's shop in the silver vaults, so it needed updating, but there was an additional piece of information in the 'biographical notes' section. Lydia read it three times to be sure, before calling to make an appointment.

Lydia couldn't help feeling, somewhat superstitiously, that the man would manage to remove his current location from existence before she managed to speak to him. Of course, that would be quite some conjuring trick, Lydia mused as she tramped through Kensington Gardens at the edge of Hyde Park and approached the palace. It was a modest palace, as these things go, but still pretty tricky to erase. People would notice for one thing.

Once she gave her name and confirmed that she was

here to see the 'Surveyor of the Queen's Silverware', Lydia was waved through security. A woman who was definitely carrying a concealed weapon patted her down and led her deeper into the palace. She tried to make conversation, but the woman answered with two word 'yes, ma'am' or 'no, ma'am' responses until Lydia gave up and let silence prevail.

GUILLAUME CHARTES LOOKED EXACTLY as Lydia remembered. Like a lizard in a suit only somehow less appealing. He was sitting behind a polished hexagonal table which was laid with a delicate china tea set and was holding a pair of silver tongs. 'Tea? Or I can call for coffee…'

'No,' Lydia said, the word coming out fast and instinctive. She added a 'thank you' and forced herself to approach.

'I won't pretend I'm pleased to see you again, Ms Crow,' Guillaume said, dropping a cube of sugar into his tea and replacing the tongs. He picked up an ornate spoon and stirred, not looking at Lydia.

'That's good,' Lydia replied. 'I won't either.'

'In what way do you believe I can help you?'

After parsing the sentence, Lydia took the information she had printed from the London Assay Office. 'This is your mark, yes?'

Guillaume didn't even glance at the paper. 'I'm but a humble conduit. I buy and sell silver. Very nice pieces, if I may be so bold, and I have a modicum of historical knowledge which is useful in the assessing of pieces, but still that is the extent of my skill.'

'Why are you lying?' Lydia raised the paper slightly. 'This is your maker's mark.'

He smiled and Lydia's skin prickled in horror. 'I believe you are mistaken.'

'Your mark is on the base of a cup that was made for the

Silver Family. They wanted a suitable gift for the king. James I to be precise.'

Guillaume had lifted the teacup to his lips and now he took a delicate sip before replacing it on the saucer with the faintest of sounds. 'I think you must realise that is an impossible accusation. James I was on the throne in the early seventeenth century.' He gave her a slimy smile. 'That's a long time ago, Ms Crow.'

'I'm in the business of the impossible,' Lydia said. She produced her coin and flipped it, slowing its spin and moving it through the air so that it danced between them, curving lazy arcs and dips.

His eyes widened a fraction and his tongue darted out, moistening his lips. It wasn't much of a tell, but it was something. She leaned forward a little, pressing. 'Could you do it again?'

Chartes seemed to relax. 'You want to commission me?'

'Yes.' An idea had been forming in the back of Lydia's mind. She didn't trust this man, naturally, but if she could imbue an object with Crow power, just as the cup was imbued with Silver magic, then maybe it would work to keep Jason powered up when she was gone. Like a battery. It wouldn't last forever, of course, but it would give Jason more time and maybe let him decide when he was ready to go rather than have consciousness ripped away. 'Can you work with gold?'

'Easily,' Chartes said. 'But you can't afford me.'

'Don't be so sure,' Lydia said.

He produced a card and fountain pen from inside his jacket and wrote down a number.

Lydia glanced at it, keeping her features immobile. 'What if I offered a favour? In return for a steep discount. As well as my discretion regarding your unnaturally long life. How do you do that, by the way? You're not the first I've met, but you don't smell like a Pearl.'

'Silver is an extremely healthy substance,' Guillaume said.

'So, I've heard. Doesn't quite cut it as an explanation, though, does it?'

'I jog,' Guillaume said, producing that slimy smile again. 'I eat a healthy diet. Don't get involved with dangerous people.'

'Now I know you're lying. You enchanted that cup for the Silvers, for starters. Was it a surprise or did you know you could do it? Did someone teach you?'

Guillaume's tongue darted out, again, licking his lips. 'It would have to be a very large favour.'

Lydia spread her hands wide and fixed Guillaume with her shark smile. 'A favour from the head of the Crows. What could be bigger?'

He stared back at her, impassive, but considering.

IN THE END, the worst part had been shaking on the deal. Guillaume's hand wasn't damp, but cold and dry with a subtle waxiness. Lydia had never handled a snake, but she imagined it would feel the same.

There were smithing studios for hire around the city, and several in the Hatton Garden area. 'You don't have your own workshop?'

Guillaume had given her a pitying look at that. Of course he wasn't going to let her into his private domain. 'Safer to be in public, I believe.'

Too late, Lydia realised the truth. He was wary of her, too. Lydia had always been scrappy, but true strength was such a new thing, she kept forgetting she had it. The studio was on the middle floor of an old industrial building off Greville Street. There was a pub on the ground floor and an advertising agency above.

As directed, Lydia had hired a bench for a day. She

wasn't entirely certain Guillaume would show up, but there he was, on time and carrying a battered leather bag. Inside the studio, there were three other people, spaced out around the large room. Two were chatting, takeaway coffees in hand, while the third was sketching on paper, head down. All of them ignored Lydia and Guillaume, which was a relief. Lydia's stomach was in knots and the idea of making small talk seemed even more impossible than usual.

Guillaume opened his bag and began laying out tools on the bench. Lydia recognised the hammer and pliers, but couldn't name the others. They all looked extremely old and well-used, the wooden handles worn smooth and ashy. He pulled out a blackened canvas apron which reached right down to his ankles and a pair of leather safety goggles.

Lydia had settled on a simple curved bracelet made from a single band of gold. She wanted to spend as little time with Guillaume as possible. Besides, it wasn't as if Jason would be too fussy. She wanted it to be a wearable item, in case it turned out that he needed constant contact for it to work.

Guillaume had a lump of raw gold which he placed into a crucible. Fitting his safety goggles over his head, he told Lydia she should do the same. There were some hanging up on a rack with stringy rubber straps. She put a pair on, knotting the straps to make them stay in place. Guillaume pulled on heat resistant gauntlets and used a blow torch to heat the block. Using long-handled tongs, he brought it to a hand-powered machine with iron wheels. It looked a bit like a mangle and, as it turned out, acted similarly, too. The heated gold went in one side and came out the other in a flattened lozenge.

'This is it,' Guillaume said, clipping the edges with a cutting tool and picking up a small hammer.

Lydia produced her coin and focused her attention while Guillaume tapped the surface of the band, creating dimples in the surface. He worked steadily and without hurry, looking to Lydia before each tap. Lydia imagined her Crow power flowing from her and into the hammer so that with the blow, the power would transfer to the gold. She wasn't sure if it was working, but she kept picturing it and pushing.

The warmed gold was dull in colour, but after a few taps it had darkened to an ochre. Just as Lydia was going to ask Guillaume if they should start again, that it didn't feel as if anything was happening, he hit the metal and left a spot of shiny black. Black like a shadow. Black like a crow's wing. The kind of black that Lydia saw in her dreams, that made her want to spread her arms and take off into the sky. She almost lost her wits and stopped concentrating, and Guillaume tutted. The next blow was the same and the area of shiny black extended. Lydia pushed more Crow to the hammer, focusing everything she had on that one point. The place where the metal head of the hammer was meeting the band of gold.

Once the tapping finished, Guillaume picked up pliers and a thick wooden pin. He laid the band over the wooden cylinder and smoothed it down with his gloved hands, like he was moulding plasticine. Lydia didn't know if that was usual, but she was light-headed from concentrating and the fumes and the flow of power which had left her body, and couldn't spare much brainpower to question it. Once the band was shaped into a circle, Guillaume flattened the ends with the hammer and slid it off the wooden cylinder. He removed his gloves and used a file on the hammered edge. The band tapered at each end and the filing made this more pronounced until two points emerged. They looked sharp, like they might cut into the wrist of the wearer if they weren't extremely careful.

'It's done,' Guillaume said, dropping the piece onto the bench as if it was still hot. 'Anything else would be purely decorative.'

'Why did you file it like that?' Lydia said, reaching out and touching one of the points. It was as sharp as it looked.

'I don't know. It felt right.' He gave her a look. 'Things like this? They become the shape they're meant to be.'

The black colour which had begun halfway through the process, seemed to have set. Guillaume had a cloth and was polishing the band's surface. Half was now a shining warm gold and then other half the strange black. A black that looked like no material Lydia had ever seen before. The bracelet was heavy in her hand. 'Do you have something to wrap it in?'

Guillaume took a clean rag from his bag and passed it over. 'No extra charge.'

CHAPTER NINETEEN

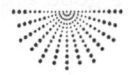

Lydia parked around the corner from The Fork and scoped the cars lining the side streets as she walked home. She spotted the undercover officers with zero trouble, which meant that Maddie would be able to do the same. She hoped they were armed and experienced. She also restrained herself from tapping on the roof as she passed and saying 'boo'. Fleet would be proud. A thought that was instantly followed by the gut punch of missing him. Where the hell had he gone?

Angel had already left for the night and the cafe was dark. Lydia raided the kitchen for some lasagne and took the plate upstairs to nuke it in her microwave. Despite the surveillance reminding her that Maddie was a clear and present threat, and the absence of Fleet that made her chest ache, Lydia realised that she was humming as she waited for her dinner to ding. She also didn't feel queasy or faint. She took the bracelet out of the cloth bag and ran her fingers over the strange black surface. The crow power was there, vibrating beneath the surface of the metal like a tuning fork. She tucked it away and ate her lasagne sitting on the sofa. Perhaps making the bracelet had siphoned off some of her power and that was why she felt better? Had Guillaume shown her a way to keep on top of her abilities without having to kill?

She was almost asleep when her phone rang. It was Paul and he didn't sound happy.

'Do you know what time it is?' Lydia rubbed her face, fighting the feeling that a good night's sleep had just been snatched away.

'I need your help.'

That woke her up. Paul Fox rarely spoke so plainly. 'What's happened? Are you all right?'

'I put the word out about that robbery. Turns out one of my lads did knock over Alejandro's. Said he nicked the cup and was going to bring it to me. Not that I believe the little shit.'

'Was going to?' Lydia latched onto the past tense.

'Yeah. He sold it on sharpish. Said it gave him a funny feeling.'

'Smart little shit.'

'Foxes ain't stupid,' Paul said. Then a pause. 'Not as a rule, anyway.'

'Did he tell you who he sold it to?'

'Eventually.' Paul's voice was grim and it sent a shiver down Lydia's spine. 'I'm going to buy it back and I want you to come with.'

Lydia was just about to ask why, when Paul answered her question.

'You said the one under the church was a fake. I want to know if this one is real before I pay for it.'

Lydia was privately surprised that Paul was planning to offer cash. She would have assumed he would take a more violent approach, but she also wanted to be invited along so she didn't say so out loud.

. . .

The buyer lived in Knightsbridge which seemed like the kind of place someone would be shopping in Harrods for solid gold spoons, not plundering the dark web for stolen silverware. 'Your boy sold it to this guy online, right?' Lydia asked Paul.

'Apparently. Kids today, eh?'

Paul looked as out of place as she did. Two black-clad chancers walking among the social climbers and upper middle class of London. Lydia had convinced Paul to go for an early morning visit the next day. He had been hell bent on going straight round after their chat in the middle of the night, but Lydia had pointed out that there was a high chance of things going pear-shaped with a midnight visit. People were just generally more wary of folk who showed up under cover of darkness and asked to do a deal. If he wanted this to be all nice and professional with a neat exchange of cash, it would be better not to act like crazy gangsters.

The street was tucked behind Cadogan Square and filled with smart brick terraces. Number eighteen had steps leading up to an arched entrance with stonework balustrades and ornate black iron railings. The door was freshly painted and there was a keypad entry lock with a row of buzzers. 'Flat four doesn't have a name,' Lydia said. 'Hope your info is solid.'

Paul shot her a look.

Lydia pressed the buzzer for flat three. When it crackled into life she said, 'Parcel for flat four, can you buzz me in?'. She hadn't even finished speaking when the door unlocked.

The shared stairs were extremely clean, the white walls lined with tasteful framed photographs, and the air smelled of polish and expensive perfume. It was, in other words, a far cry from any rental place she had ever lived.

Lydia was hoping the buyer was home and this could remain a legal and friendly exchange. She had come prepared for plan B, though, with her pick set in her pocket, and Paul was carrying a duffel bag with some power tools, but they didn't need either. The flat door was already ajar and the place where the lock had been a splintered mess.

They exchanged a silent look and Lydia put her ear to the gap and listened. A muffled thump came from inside. Lydia stopped thinking and pushed through the door.

It opened into a short entrance hall with doors leading off. There was a shoe rack overflowing with trainers and an expensive looking bicycle leaning against the wall. The place might have looked fancy, but the buyer clearly still didn't want to risk leaving his bike in the communal area.

'Wait,' Paul whispered. He seemed as confident as he always did, but there was a wariness to his gaze as he looked around. There was another sound from the end of the hall. The door was half-open and Lydia moved toward it. She was aware, in her peripheral vision, of family and travel photographs lovingly framed and displayed on the walls, and of Paul walking behind her. She glanced at him, eyebrows raised and he nodded. She pushed the door open, muscles tensed, hoping and praying that the room was empty and that whoever had broken the front door was long gone.

The room was not empty.

'I told you to stop following me,' Maddie said, straightening up from a figure lying in the middle of the carpet. She was covered in blood up to her elbows. Bright, wet, red. Very recent.

'I wasn't,' Lydia said, her gaze skipping over the dead man on the floor. He looked young, but it was hard to tell at this point. His clothes looked young at any rate. 'I'm looking for that,' Lydia pointed to the cup, which was in the dead man's hand. He was still clutching it by one handle, which can't have been easy during the attack. 'For a job.'

'Finders keepers.' Maddie tilted her chin. 'Long time no see, Paul. How's tricks?'

Lydia was trying very hard not to stare at the blood. She glanced at the man on the floor. He really was a mess. Her stomach flipped over and bile rose. She swallowed it down. She couldn't see the weapon Maddie must have used. Her hands were empty but that didn't make her any less deadly.

'Not so bad,' Paul was replying to Maddie and his tone was impressively even. 'I can see you've been keeping busy.'

'I was very clear,' Maddie said, flicking her gaze back to Lydia. 'You can't be showing up at my work. You want to see me, you call. Okay?'

'Maria Silver commissioned me to find that cup,' Lydia said, pleased with how steady her voice sounded. 'I swear. I didn't know you would be here.'

Something fluttered behind Maddie's flat eyes. 'You're helping the Silvers?'

'Not helping. Doing a job. A return favour.'

'Charlie was in Alejandro's pocket, but I never thought you would be the same...' Maddie looked disgusted. 'And what's our old squeeze doing here? Looking for a threesome?'

Lydia didn't look at Paul and she didn't give him time to respond, either. 'I'm not in Maria's pocket. Just trying to keep the peace. That's all I want.'

At once, Maddie was toe to toe with Lydia, her face unnervingly close. Lydia had blinked and missed her moving. Her speed was breath-taking. And terrifying. Her breath was warm on Lydia's skin and she could smell her perfume, fighting against the metallic tang of the blood. Still no Crow, though. Not even the tiniest taste of feather. What had her cousin done? 'Don't you get bored of peace?'

Lydia swallowed, feeling every part of the movement. 'No.'

Maddie's eyes were searching her own. Looking for what, Lydia hadn't the faintest idea.

'Liar,' she said, eventually, stepping back. She picked up the cup and Lydia winced.

'What?' Maddie had caught Lydia's reaction.

'I don't know how you can touch it so easily,' Lydia said. She had no idea if being honest with Maddie was sensible, but with the waves of Silver coming from the cup and the man slumped in a pool of blood and the terror of being this close to Maddie, Lydia had no room for strategic thinking. 'It makes me feel ill. The Silver.'

'The silver?' Maddie frowned. 'I didn't know you were allergic to silver.'

'Not the metal,' Lydia said. 'It's full of Silver power. I can feel it. It's enchanted.'

Maddie laughed, disbelieving. Lydia understood how she felt. She had had the same reaction initially. 'An enchanted cup? This isn't a fairy story.'

'I am aware,' Lydia said drily. 'Nonetheless.'

'And you don't like it?'

'Not particularly. It's giving out a bright silver flavour. And a light. It makes my head hurt.'

'That's your thing?'

'That's her thing,' Paul chimed in. 'Lame, right?' He had put a hand on the small of Lydia's back and she felt his warning. *Don't be so interesting. Don't engage the crazy killing machine.*

'Yeah,' Lydia said. 'I sense Family power. It can be useful, but it's not very exciting.'

Maddie shifted. 'Oh, come now. Don't be so modest. I know what you're doing.'

'I'm not doing-'

'You think that if you play possum, I'll think you're dead already. It won't work,' Maddie nudged the dead man's leg with her foot. 'Just ask this guy.'

Sirens sounded, suddenly, approaching.

'That's my cue,' Maddie said, stepping away. She paused. 'You could come with.'

'No, thank you.' Lydia was still struggling to hold on to consciousness.

'Suit yourself,' Maddie said. 'I won't keep asking nicely, though.'

At least, Lydia thought she heard Maddie say those words, but the darkness had crowded in from the edges of her vision until it filled her mind completely. Her stomach lurched as she fell and then there was nothing.

WHEN SHE CAME ROUND, the room was filled with police and there was no sign of Paul. A woman Lydia knew was senior from her commanding tone, was issuing orders and a paramedic was crouched next to her, fiddling with the straps on a back board.

'I'm fine,' Lydia said, starting to sit up.

'Stay down,' the paramedic said, placing hands on her shoulders. 'Don't move. We're going to lift you onto the board. Okay? One, two, three.'

'I don't need-'

'It's all right, we've got you. You're fine.'

Lydia wanted to say 'I know I'm fine, that what I'm telling you' but she decided to save her breath. The woman was clearly on a mission and Lydia was already being lifted onto the board. She closed her eyes and concentrated on taking slow breaths through her nose. The swaying motion of being carried, along with the natural terror of being strapped down, was making her feel sick. 'Let me up,' she said, eyes open and pulse racing. Something was wrong. Someone was there. Danger, her brain was saying. Get up. Get out. Fly.

'Shit,' she heard a muffled stream of swearing as her body lurched down.

'It's okay,' a familiar voice. Fleet came into view above her. 'Are you hurt?'

'I'm fine,' Lydia managed, suffused with sudden relief. He was back. Fleet was back. 'They won't listen.'

'Let her up,' Fleet said.

The straps were undone and Lydia sat up, rubbing her arms, and then got herself upright. The world tilted and she had to swallow hard to stop herself throwing up. She squeezed her coin for strength and waved the paramedic away. 'Thank you. I'm okay.'

'This is against my official advice,' the woman said, giving Fleet an extra frown.

He nodded, calm and unflappable. 'Noted.' He ducked his head to look into Lydia's eyes. 'Are you all right? Did you hit your head?'

'You're back,' Lydia drank in the sight of Fleet. Tall, dark and beautiful. Here.

'I'm back. Now, answer the question. Did you hit your head? Black out?'

'I'm fine. She was here.'

'It could be a concussion. Let me take you to A&E to get you checked out.'

She scanned the room. The dead man was on the ground, three SOC officers were securing the scene and the silver cup had disappeared along with Maddie. 'Hell Hawk.'

'You want to tell me what happened?'

'Of course, Officer,' Lydia said, letting Fleet know that she was going to give him the official version.

He nodded very slightly, indicating his understanding, and Lydia proceeded to give him a sanitised version of events, light on the details and even lighter on the truth.

. . .

BACK AT THE FORK, after making Lydia sit on the sofa and drink a cup of sweet tea even though she had asked for coffee, Fleet undid his tie and slumped next to her. He looked exhausted.

'It was Maddie.'

He took it pretty well. Just raising his eyes to the ceiling for a brief moment.

'She has the cup.'

Fleet nodded. 'At least that makes sense.'

'You're being very calm.'

'You spoke to Maddie?'

'Briefly, yeah.'

'And you're still breathing and in one piece. That's cause for celebration.' His lips quirked into a smile.

'She took the cup. I'm guessing that's the real reason she's in London.'

Frustration broke through Fleet's calm exterior. 'I don't care about the bloody cup.'

Lydia paused in acknowledgement of his outburst. She took one of his hands in hers and squeezed gently. 'It's important. If I don't bring it back to Maria, she might break our truce. It's pretty shaky.'

'Wasn't the deal that you find it? You found it.'

Lydia smiled. 'That's definitely my planned argument, but I don't think it will fly. Do you?'

He breathed in deeply through his nose and passed a hand over his face. 'No.'

'So that means I need to get it back.'

'How are you so calm?'

Because I know I'm going to die.

She couldn't say that, so she made up something else about having a plan. About not giving up. Luckily, Fleet was used to her pig-headed determination, and he didn't bat an eyelid.

. . .

THAT NIGHT they slept wrapped around each other and Lydia needed every centimetre of contact. His scent, his presence, and the Fleet signature of waves on a beach, salted air and a fire crackling in the dark. She needed all of it. Felt like she could finally breathe. The stubborn part of her had wanted to be angry over the last week, to rail at him for leaving her at this time of crisis, but it had been a token effort. She had just been worried. And missing him. And wanting him back, safe and whole and hers. If there was anything important, he would tell her. She knew it. And, although she fully expected to dream of Maddie drenched in blood and smiling like a kid with an ice cream, she fell into a peaceful blackness, feather soft and mercifully quiet.

CHAPTER TWENTY

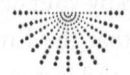

Early the next morning, Lydia woke with the realisation that Fleet was already awake. He had his arms crossed behind his head and was staring at the ceiling, deep in thought. She propped up on one elbow to kiss him good morning. He still looked exhausted, grey shadows under his eyes.

'Couldn't you sleep?'

'I'm all right.'

That wasn't an answer, but Lydia didn't press him. She knew very well what it was like to have bad dreams and, sometimes, you just didn't want to talk about them. Didn't want to bring them into the day with you.

Once they were up and eating toast on the sofa, Lydia's legs over his, he rubbed a hand over his face and gave her a serious look. 'If I tell you something, you have to promise not to do anything stupid.'

'You know me,' Lydia said.

'I do,' Fleet said. 'So I need you to promise.'

'Define stupid,' Lydia said, aiming for a little levity.

Fleet raised his eyebrows in response.

'Fine,' Lydia said. 'I promise. Spill it.'

'I made a deal with Sinclair to get information.'

'I told you, no more deals...'

'I made the deal, not you,' Fleet said. 'You aren't a part of it, I promise. We needed information and this was the only way to get it. I did it for you.'

Lydia forced herself to shut up and listen.

'The project being run by your agent has been wound up. Nobody really believed that the Families were any kind of threat. Bedtime stories and some good PR. They didn't think it was a good use of the budget, and I can believe that. Everything in my work has to be justified with finance allocation docs, they would have had a hard time funding research into magic.'

'So it's definitely just Mr Smith?'

Fleet shrugged. 'I mean, he might have some acolytes, fellow believers, but from an official point of view, yes. Mr Smith was a one-man crusade within the service and the Families his pet project. With global terrorism and fears over Russian interference in politics taking the headlines, it's not such a surprise. Organised crime on our home turf is important, of course, but it's left to the NCA.'

The National Crime Agency definitely had a dossier on the Crows. Organised crime was their area and back in the bad old days, the Crows kept them sweet with well-placed bribes. At least, that was what Lydia assumed. It was all ancient history, as far as she was concerned. 'What about the NCA? I don't think we've been doing anything serious enough to pull their attention. Charlie wasn't squeaky clean but it was small time, really.' A thought hit her. 'Unless they were interested in the rumours. The power stuff. That might have drawn them to Mr Smith. Could they have been working with Mr Smith's department? His project?'

'Not as far as anyone knows,' Fleet said. 'According to Sinclair, your man Smith has a personal obsession. She showed me some of his departmental files and they were really something.'

'Don't tell me he had a Crow shrine with pictures of me with the eyes cut out.'

'Don't joke,' Fleet said. 'He's been collecting for years. The company, JRB, you know he took it over in 2001 when it went from being a family firm to the corporation we know and love. There was a copy of the contract in the file, the agreement with the Pearls? It seems it was the closest he could get to owning them. And he's been searching for the Silver cup. He's got Charlie, and he wanted you to add to the collection. Plus, he has a few other artifacts in storage. A coat that belonged to the Foxes back in the eighteen hundreds and some pearls that may or may not be connected with the Pearl Family. His notes recorded some uncertainty.'

'I bet he wanted me to take a look, see if they were the real deal.'

'Probably,' Fleet agreed. 'But the main thing is that his department at the service really does just boil down to him. It doesn't go further in any meaningful way, which means we just need to neutralise one man.'

'So he bought JRB in order to acquire the contract with the Pearls? And he's the sole director, now?'

Fleet passed his phone over and Lydia swiped through the images until she found the articles of incorporation for JRB. Lots of legal language and a name which rang a faint bell. Oliver Gale.

Fleet was looking over her shoulder. 'That's your man Smith's real name. Sinclair confirmed it.'

'If you trust Sinclair. What would stop her from lying or only showing you some of the file and not the whole picture? She could be working with Mr Smith. She could be part of his department.' Lydia knew she sounded paranoid, but she felt like it was more than warranted.

Fleet shook his head.

'You really trust her?'

Fleet held her gaze. 'I do.'

Lydia wanted to just believe him. Fleet was an excellent judge of character, a talented copper with a nose for bullshit and a gleam which had been giving him an edge of precognition his whole life. Still. It was too important. And Lydia couldn't take anything at face value, it just wasn't the way she was wired. 'Why are you so sure she isn't stringing you along? Why would she give you the goods?'

Fleet touched her arm. 'Because I traded.'

'I don't...'

'If the information doesn't pan out, she doesn't get my offering and, trust me, she really wants it.'

'What is it?'

Fleet grimaced very briefly. A quick expression which Lydia almost missed. Almost. She felt cold. 'What? What did you offer to give Sinclair?'

'Don't worry about it.'

Lydia waited a beat. 'You're not going to tell me?'

'Best not,' he said, looking away.

'Yeah, that's not going to work this time.'

Fleet closed his eyes. 'I went to see my father.'

Lydia kept her mouth shut, waiting.

'Well, I went to find my father. Wasn't sure I would manage... It's been a while.'

The silence stretched on and Lydia reached for his hand. 'Did you find him?'

He nodded slightly, eyes still closed.

'What did he give you that Sinclair wanted?'

Fleet opened his eyes and looked at Lydia with clear anguish. 'I can't talk about this. I'm sorry. I just can't.'

Lydia couldn't stand the pain in his eyes. She put her arms around him and rested her head on his shoulder. 'It's okay.' If there was one thing she understood, it was not wanting to verbalise something difficult.

'There's something else,' he pulled back to look into her eyes. 'Sinclair showed me Maddie's file, too. She's a stone-cold psycho.'

'Tell me something I don't know,' Lydia said.

'I'm serious,' Fleet said. 'You need to stay away from her. You have no idea what she is capable of.'

'I'm not exactly looking to braid her hair,' Lydia said. 'But she's on my patch.'

'I have a friend, a psychologist I know through work. Will you speak to her?'

'You want me to see a shrink?'

'No. I thought it would be useful to know more about Maddie. Maybe it would help to predict her behaviour.'

LYDIA MESSAGED EMMA and watched for the blue ticks which showed she had read it. A reply came back quickly that all was well. Next, Lydia rang Paul. 'All quiet,' he said. 'Nobody sniffing around.'

'Thank you,' Lydia said. 'But I wanted to check on you after yesterday. Did you get away all right?'

'Little Bird,' Paul said, his voice shooting unwanted feelings through her body. Damn Fox. 'Are we becoming best friends?'

'In your dreams,' Lydia said. 'But you are doing me a favour. And I don't wish Maddie on my worst enemy.'

His voice went serious. 'She's changed.'

'You felt it, too?'

'I could see it. Something is broken in that woman. And the way she was looking at you... You need to be careful.'

'I am,' Lydia said. 'I'm not an idiot.'

'I didn't leave until she had, wasn't sure what she would do once you were taking a nap.'

'Thank you,' Lydia said with genuine gratitude. 'But I know my cousin. I know how to handle her.'

'You were out cold, you didn't see her face. She looked hungry.'

Lydia felt a frisson of pleasure. It was nice to be wanted.

'And she kissed you on her way out.'

'What?'

'On the forehead. She didn't even look at me.'

In usual circumstances Lydia would have said something arch like 'jealous?' but Paul had watched over her until the psycho had left the flat so she kept her lip buttoned.

'You need to stay away from her. She is way too interested, and it's only going to end one way.'

'I know,' Lydia said. She didn't want to talk about Maddie anymore. 'I've got something for you. You know that company, JRB? It turns out there's one main driver behind their activities. A spook with a hard-on for us all.'

'That sounds uncomfortable.'

Lydia had regretted her choice of words the moment they left her mouth. She felt the traitorous blush creep over her face and thanked feathers he couldn't see her. 'He's been gathering information for years and he tried to recruit me. You know him as the guy who orchestrated the trouble between us. And got the Crows killed in Wandsworth. I call him Mr Smith.'

'He wants a war? Messy.'

'He wants us at each other's throats. If we tear each other apart, we're not a threat. Plus, we're more likely to work for him, give up power or information.' Lydia didn't mention the Silver Cup. She owed Paul Fox, but she didn't trust him. Not completely. 'He's vulnerable, though. He's been working outside his remit at MI6. They are looking to clean up his projects and won't be too sad if he disappears.'

'And how do you know that?'

Lydia wasn't going to mention Fleet, it would only

provoke some macho posturing. 'I've gone to some lengths to make sure it's good information. I can't guarantee that someone else won't pick up his research in the future, but for now they've got bigger fish to fry.'

'It's not going to be easy to get to him. JRB is just a shell.'

'The Pearls.'

'What about them?' Paul's tone was dismissive. 'Bunch of grocers.'

'You've only met the descendants,' Lydia said. 'I've met the original family and, trust me, they're not to be fucked with. They're more powerful than you, me, Henry Crow, Maria Silver and Maddie put together.'

'Is that a fact?' Paul still sounded unimpressed.

'But they've been trapped. Bit of tricky contract work. Some agreement with the original incarnation of JRB.'

'A written contract? If they're so powerful, how did that work?'

'I have no idea,' Lydia said. 'Maybe back in the day, all kinds of things got imbued with power?' She was thinking of the power in the Silver Cup, power that had been contained in ordinary metal. Maybe power had been contained in the ink and paper of the contract, or in the pen they used to sign. Maybe the Pearls just believed in the power of language to such an extent that it worked its own kind of magic on them. It didn't matter. 'What matters is that I've got a bargaining chip. I'm going to deliver Mr Smith to the Pearls. He's the sole owner of JRB and I bet they can make him renegotiate. They want to be free.' This last part was the bit which made Lydia sweaty with nausea. If this worked and the Pearls broke their contract, what would their freedom mean? Would they stay to their underground realm out of choice? Or would they rise up into the city? All she could do was hope they would be feeling magnanimous toward the Crows.

'And what will they do with Mr Smith? The embodiment

of the contract which has kept them trapped all of these years?'

Lydia shrugged, even though Paul couldn't see her. 'Not my problem.'

LYDIA DIDN'T THINK that a clinical psychologist was going to be any help in predicting Maddie's behaviour, but she couldn't get over the image of Maddie leaning over her unconscious body and planting a kiss on her forehead. It was somehow more disturbing than the times she had threatened to kill her. Uncharted territory.

Fleet was pleased when Lydia agreed to the meeting, too, which was a bonus. She could see the tension radiating from him and wanted to ease his concern.

The psychologist worked part time for the prison service and part time in private practice, and she agreed to see Lydia at the end of the following day. 'I can fit you in at five.'

Fleet was still at work at that time. 'Sorry,' he said, sounding distracted. Somebody else was clearly still talking to him in the background and a phone was ringing. 'I was going to come with you.'

Lydia reassured him that it was fine and made her way to the psychologist's office. It was north of Camberwell Green in a converted Victorian house and former bakery. The inside had been gutted and remodelled to house several rental offices and a reception area.

'DCI Fleet's friend,' the doctor greeted her. 'I'm Emi Hase. Come in. How can I help?'

Lydia wasn't sure what she had expected from the label 'forensic psychologist' but it wasn't this small smiley woman in a floral dress that looked like it had been bought in the children's department.

'I'm not here to talk about me.'

'You'd be surprised how many people think that.' The

doctor had her hands neatly folded in her lap and was unnaturally still. She had shiny black hair in a neat bob, held back from her face with a red Alice band.

'No, really. I'm an investigator and I'm here in my professional capacity. I want to ask about my client. Well, not really my client.'

'We can talk about whatever you want.'

'It's my cousin. She is disturbed and I want your professional opinion on her behaviour, her perspective.'

'You think your cousin has a problem?'

Lydia flipped open her notebook. There was something unsettling about the office with its calming pictures on the walls and the box of tissues on the low table. Something in the vibrations of the air which made her feel on alert. Like the woman opposite her had x-ray vision and could see straight into her heart. 'I know my cousin is a psychopath. I want to know how best to handle her.'

'Psychopathology is rare.' A pause. 'And it's not what you see in the movies. They're not all serial killers.'

Lydia quashed the urge to smile. The head doctor didn't look as if she would appreciate that. She would probably interpret it as a sign of Lydia's mental illness. 'What if I am talking about a serial killer? But the professional sort.'

The doctor paused. 'Military?'

'Let's say "yes". How do I get her to do what I want?'

'I can't talk specifics without meeting the person. And I would also be extremely wary of diagnosing them as psychopathic without a formal evaluation. Plus,' the doctor gave the smallest of smiles, 'I'm not in the business of teaching manipulation techniques.'

'I'm not a patient or asking about a clinically vulnerable individual. I need to know how to handle a person who I believe to be psychopathic. Or, if that's too difficult, then just some general pointers on what it means to be psychopathic. For example, if I had made a deal with a psychopath, what are the odds of them sticking to it? Are they more or less unreliable than the general population?'

'A clinical diagnosis is not a predictor of behaviour.'

Lydia stamped on the urge to sigh loudly. 'I am aware. But what can you tell me? Are they likely to stick to a prearranged deal or plan?'

'Unlikely,' Emi said. 'Psychopaths are impulsive. They don't see consequences in the same way as neurotypical people.'

'But they can be very effective. What about a high functioning psychopath?'

Emi leaned back in her chair slightly, settling in as if to give a lecture. 'I didn't mean they couldn't see the consequences, that was poorly phrased, what I mean is that they may well comprehend all the possible consequences of their actions, but they just don't care.'

'Right...' Lydia was lining up her next question, but the doc hadn't finished.

'No. You don't understand. The most important thing for you to know is that your cousin won't have the range of emotions that you or I experience. She won't feel fear or excitement or love or sympathy or anything. Psychopaths describe everything as monotone. They can tell they are experiencing physical reactions to danger, such as increased heart rate, but that doesn't translate to fear.'

'That sounds quite handy.'

'It can be,' Emi said. 'But it can lead them to harm themselves. Because they just don't care. About pain, about hardship, about dying. None of it. That can lead to extremely risky behaviours. Like most people with a mental health condition, psychopaths are more of a danger to themselves than they are to others.'

Lydia thanked the doctor for her help and made to leave.

Emi hesitated before speaking. 'Do you really think your cousin is a psychopath?'

'Yes. Without a doubt.'

'And they are trained to kill?' Em had gone pale, but with a prurient interest lighting her eyes. 'You know that they have killed someone?'

'Many people. She's good at it and she likes doing things she's good at. We all do, I suppose, but with her... It's like she doesn't have anything else.' As soon as she spoke the words out loud, Lydia realised that they applied to her. Or they had done. When she had started Crow Investigations it had been a revelation. She had been completely obsessed, so happy to have found something that she was good at after years of flailing and failing. It suited her and it made her feel useful. And, yes, powerful.

'May I be direct with you?' The doctor didn't wait for an answer. 'I'm concerned this may be the result of projection on your part. This is nothing to be ashamed of, but it does indicate the need for ongoing professional support. Is that something you would consider? If so, I would suggest you don't delay. I can provide you with the details of some highly recommended specialists in this area...'

Lydia was already on her feet. This had been a waste of time.

'However,' the doctor held up a finger. 'On the small chance I am wrong in that assessment and your cousin does exist in the manner you have described, I would advise that you do not approach them or attempt to engage with them. And to notify the police.'

'Your advice is noted,' Lydia said. How wonderful to hand the responsibility for Maddie onto the authorities or to another person. Anyone. But she couldn't. Maddie was a Crow and she was Lydia's problem to sort.

CHAPTER TWENTY-ONE

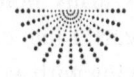

Knowing that she couldn't win was curiously freeing. After leaving the psychologist's office, Lydia had walked to Camberwell Cemetery and sat among the bluebells next to her family's tomb and thought through all of her options. There wasn't a better one as far as she could see and, as long as she managed to take Maddie with her, she felt like it wouldn't be so bad to die. Of course, given the choice she would prefer to live, but she knew now that Maddie wasn't going to stop.

Back at The Fork, she ran over her idea with Jason. He was horrified. 'I don't care about Smith. He's bad news. But isn't there a chance that they will break the contract?'

'I expect they will.' This was a problem and not one Lydia had been able to solve.

'But won't that free them?'

'I can't fix everything,' Lydia said, frustrated that she was close to tears. 'If JRB is no more, then there's no Mr Smith trying to fuck with the Families, killing Crows to start a war. If the Pearls get free and decide to cause hell once they are, then everyone will have to deal with it. Hopefully they'll abide by the treaty. And feel some gratitude to us, at least, for passing on the contract.'

Jason opened his mouth to argue.

'Besides,' Lydia said, cutting him off. 'It's not like they're exactly harmless at the moment.' They both looked into the middle of the room, where Ash had been tied to a chair for his own protection, his arms bound to stop him from hurting himself. The Pearl King controlling his body as effortlessly as a child playing with a doll.

'What aren't you telling me?' Jason said after a moment.

'I've got you something,' Lydia said, trying to keep her voice steady. She produced the package from her bag and unwrapped the cloth. The bangle looked as peculiar as it had in the studio. It pulled at her. Touching the black surface with one tentative finger made her stomach swoop as if her whole body had just lifted into the air. She felt wings spreading wide, shoulder muscles tensing, and the sharp stab of beak against skin and bone.

'What is it?'

'It's for you to wear. If you want. It will power you up. The way that I do.'

Jason was frowning, his expression between hope and consternation. 'Will that work?'

'I believe so,' Lydia said. She hoped so.

He reached out and touched it, a smile breaking out. 'Bloody hell, I think it might work. I felt something then.' He looked at her with wonder. 'Where did you get it?'

'I made it,' Lydia said. 'With help.'

'That's amazing,' Jason said. Then his expression fell. 'Why?'

'We should sit down,' Lydia said.

'I don't need to sit down,' Jason said. 'What's going on?'

'I might have to go away for a bit,' Lydia said, chickening out of the truth. She couldn't say it. The finality of it.

'Where?'

Then it hit her, the ridiculousness of avoiding death talk with the ghost. He wasn't just a ghost, either, he was her friend. Her close friend. Hell Hawk. 'Maddie. She's not going to stop. I have to stop her.'

Jason caught on immediately. 'You're not a killer.'

'Technically I am,' Lydia said. 'And I've got to try. She has a twisted idea that we're meant to be something together. Either running the Family or running around the world killing people, I don't know which. But sooner or later she is going to snap. She's going to get tired of waiting or I'm going to do something she doesn't like. She'll want to hurt me and that will mean hurting those I love. I can't have that happen. I can't.'

'What are you doing to do?'

'I can't beat her,' Lydia said. 'I'm not strong enough. I'm not ruthless enough. She's a trained killer and a psychopath, I can't win. So, I'm going to give her what she wants.'

HAVING MADE the decision to go down swinging, Lydia felt a sense of peace. It might not be a good plan, but at least she had one. And she had always preferred action to waiting for the sky to fall. Her phone rang with Paul's number and she answered it straight away.

'She's here.'

Her stomach sank. 'Where?'

'Beckenham. Couple of streets from your folks place.'

'That's close to Emma's, too.' Lydia hadn't intended to produce her coin, but it was there in her hand nonetheless. She squeezed it.

'I know,' Paul said. 'She's just sitting there. Plain sight.'

'Where?'

'Bumble Bee Cafe on Bromley Road. She's been at one of the outside tables for the last hour.'

'I'm on my way.'

The traffic was mercifully light and Lydia made it to Bromley Road in record time. She parked at the more residential end and speed-walked toward the parade of shops, cafes and pubs. Paul was waiting outside the dry cleaners. 'She's still there,' he said. 'I don't know what she's doing. Well, she's eaten a toastie and an ice-cream sundae, but I mean...'

'I know,' Lydia put a hand on his arm. 'Thank you for contacting me. And for watching Emma all this time. I won't forget it.'

Paul looked sideways at her. 'That plan you mentioned... What aren't you telling me?'

'Nothing,' Lydia said brightly. 'Can you go to Emma's? I'm going to try to redirect her attention, but if I fail...'

Paul nodded, his face serious. 'I'm the back up. I won't let her near Emma.'

'I will pay you back,' Lydia said. She was looking down the street, trying to see if she could see evidence of the psycho up ahead.

'I know you will,' Paul said, which wasn't entirely reassuring. And then he loped away, taking a side street in the direction of Emma's house.

THE BUMBLE BEE Cafe was as nauseatingly cutesie as Lydia remembered, with cartoon bees decorating the windows and tablecloths. Maddie was pouring tea from a hive-shaped teapot and the juxtaposition was enough to make Lydia's head spin.

'Let's take a walk,' Lydia said. 'You've had enough tea.'

Maddie tilted her head and gazed up at Lydia from behind enormous sunglasses. 'And how would you know a thing like that?'

'My boyfriend's a copper. It has its perks.' Lydia wasn't going to throw Paul under the bus. 'You are being watched.'

'Please,' Maddie said, standing up. 'Don't pretend the Met has the resources. They're not interested in little old me.'

'You'd be surprised,' Lydia said, moving away from the cafe. 'Aren't you going to pay?'

Maddie pushed her sunglasses onto the top of her head. 'When are you going to stop pretending to be normal? You're the head of the Crows. You should act like it.'

Lydia didn't answer.

'And I don't know why you're pretending things are all cosy with your policeman. I know you haven't been seeing him much lately. Has he lost interest?'

'He had to go away for work,' Lydia said, trying not to panic that Maddie seemed to know so much about her day-to-day life.

'That's men for you,' Maddie said, watching Lydia with bright eyes. 'Unreliable.'

Lydia didn't take the bait.

They were walking down the street toward Lydia's car and away from the busy parade. It was safer for the general public but probably not Lydia's smartest move. Her mind was racing at Maddie's proximity to Emma and her family, not to mention her own parents. She knew she had to refocus Maddie, but the chat with the forensic psychologist hadn't exactly buoyed her confidence.

They reached Lydia's car within minutes.

Maddie nodded at a bus stop over the road. 'This has been fun, but I'm going in another direction. You should think about what I said. You can't rely on your policeman.'

'I hope you're wrong,' Lydia said, trying to keep her tone friendly and non-confrontational. 'I've moved my stuff into his flat. It's what he has wanted and I said "yes". This is the last of my stuff.' She patted the roof of the car. Inside there were boxes, a duffel bag, a rucksack and a couple of bin bags of clothes. She had filled the car after

Paul had called, figuring that she would need to sell the story.

Maddie went still. 'I don't believe you.'

Lydia forced a shrug. 'I don't want to lose him. And things have to change or we're just stuck. He's right. It's the next move for us. Anyway, I can't live at The Fork forever.'

'That's what I've been telling you. You need to spread your wings.'

'You understand then.'

'No,' Maddie looked stricken. 'This is the opposite of what I meant. Spreading your wings does not mean moving into a pokey little flat with your tame copper.'

'It's actually a really nice flat...'

Maddie had already gone. She was crossing the road just in front of the approaching bus.

Lydia stood and watched Maddie board, wondering if she would raise her hand in a 'goodbye'. If she waved then maybe she hadn't just set her off on an anger-fuelled rampage. She lifted her own hand ready as Maddie took her seat by a window, but she didn't turn and look at Lydia as the bus pulled away. Lydia put her hand down and took a couple of deep breaths. Mission accomplished, she told herself. Maddie was definitely now more interested in Fleet which should keep her away from Beckenham. Lydia got into the car and called Fleet to warn him.

CHAPTER TWENTY-TWO

She had a plan. Jason thought it was a terrible idea, the psychologist thought she should stay far away from her cousin, and even Paul Fox was dubious about it. Still, it was a plan. And her disturbing dreams had stopped. It was as if her subconscious had given up on her. She woke up early from a dead sleep and realised that Fleet was the one having a bad dream. He was sweating and muttering in his sleep. She woke him as gently as she could and made soothing noises until his eyes focused on her.

'Sorry,' he said, embarrassed. 'Nightmare.'

'Want to talk about it?'

He leaned over and took a swig of water from the pint glass on his side of the bed. 'Not really. I don't know.'

Lydia wrapped herself around him and waited, stroking the hair at the base of his skull.

'I couldn't see who it was, but I thought it was you. I was at my flat and I was just sitting on the sofa, waiting. Everything was normal and then it wasn't. There was a woman in a hoodie, but I couldn't see her face. I thought it was you but she had a knife and then I felt really scared. I couldn't move, you know, classic nightmare stuff. My body was completely paralysed, and I knew I was going to die.'

'That's horrible, I'm sorry,' Lydia put her forehead against his. 'It was just a dream, though, right?'

'I think so,' Fleet whispered. 'I mean I get lots of visions. Things that are going to happen, but then they don't. The only ones which have come true have happened immediately after the vision. If they are too far in the future, I think there are too many variables. Chaos theory. Or free will. Or that thing about how you change the future as soon as you look at it. Is that a physics thing? Atoms behave differently when observed? I can't remember.'

Lydia stayed quiet and let Fleet talk it out. She knew that feeling. Half-asleep terror being eased by action of talking. When he had gone quiet, she asked if he wanted to try to go back to sleep.

'I don't think so,' he said. 'You can if you want. Sorry I woke you.'

'It's fine. How about just lying down?'

Lydia had just fitted herself into the hollow of his body when he said something she didn't quite catch.

'There was a fire. The woman in the hoodie was laughing and I couldn't move and my flat was on fire. I could feel my body burning, taste the smoke. Smell it. It was so real.'

ONCE LYDIA WAS UP and dressed, she went onto the terrace for a little privacy. Ever since she had taken Charlie's place at the head of the family, the crows gathered on the roof and along the railing of the terrace. She took the time to greet them all and then set to work. Producing her own coin was as natural and easy as breathing and, now that she had practised, she could create a room full of duplicates and have them dance in any way she wanted.

She wasn't after anything showy this morning, though.

Just control. Ever since making the bracelet with Guillaume Chartes she had felt steadier. The nausea hadn't returned and, although she had passed out in the presence of Maddie and the Silver cup, she put that down to heightened circumstances. Circumstances she was planning to repeat, but still. She would be prepared this time.

There was a light drizzle falling but Lydia barely noticed her clothes slowly saturating as she stared into the middle distance and focused on the idea of her coin. She could feel her power humming in the background and hear the thousands of hearts beating, the crows that lived in the space that wasn't physical but that she somehow could access. She called to mind the feeling of her power running into the bracelet as Guillaume had twisted the metal and, now that she knew the shape of that feeling, found she could repeat it. She felt her power focusing and channelling and when she stopped she saw a single coin, larger than hers and jet black, hanging in the air. She clapped her hands together and it disappeared, but the feeling of calm remained.

Fleet was inside, working on his tablet. He looked up when she came in. 'You're soaked.'

'I've got a plan.' Lydia licked her lips. 'But you're not going to like it.'

He closed the laptop. 'I will support you whatever, you know that. I'm on your side.'

'I'm going to turn over Mr Smith to the Pearl court and let them deal with him. They hate JRB with a cold passion and I think they will deal with him.'

'Okay.'

To his credit, Fleet was hearing her out. It was a plan involving kidnapping and cold-blooded murder, but all he was doing was waiting patiently for her to elaborate. Probably for the part where she explained that it was a bait and switch and she wasn't really going to deliver a man to his almost-certain death. 'And I'm going to use Maddie to help me do it.'

Fleet remained calm. 'What makes you think she will help you?'

'She hates him as much as I do. And I will tell her that I'm going to work with her. She wants a partnership so I think she'll do this to prove to me that she's serious about that. That I can trust her.'

'I don't think she cares about being a good partner,' Fleet said.

Lydia knew there was truth in that, but she was pretty sure she knew that there was something else. 'She's lonely. She's sick of being alone. She wants a companion.'

'What makes you think she wants you?'

'She thinks we're the same. She's too narcissistic to want to be with anybody except her own reflection. She seems to think I'm close enough.'

'But you're not.'

Lydia shrugged. She wasn't sure whether she agreed with Fleet. They were both Crows, they were both killers. Maddie was insane, but she wasn't stupid. There were similarities. Instead of voicing this to Fleet, she said, 'I can act the part for long enough to get her on board.'

'Then what? Maddie is the problem, not Smith. She's not listening to his orders anymore. If your plan works and you get rid of Smith, you've still got Maddie to deal with.'

This was the tricky bit. She couldn't have Fleet guess her plan or he would try to stop her. 'I think there's a good chance it will give her closure. And then she'll leave and go back to her contract work. It's not like the service won't be happy to keep her on the books. She's certainly effective.'

He looked doubtful. 'She went rogue. She killed her handler and then, if this plan works, an MI6 agent.'

'Sinclair says Mr Smith is on his own and out of favour. They might be happy for a quick solution. And from what I have gathered, talented assassins don't grow on trees.' She winced as the image of Sergio Bastos swinging from one jumped into her mind. 'I mean, I think they would be willing to keep her in work. She's a valuable asset to the service.'

He nodded. 'That's true. It's a bit of a gamble, though.'

'You traded with them, what do you think they'll do?'

Fleet's brow furrowed as he considered the question. 'I think they'll close the files on your Family and roll Smith's department into an existing one.'

Lydia nodded. 'It's settled then.'

AUNTIE'S FLAT was quiet when she knocked and Lydia hoped there wouldn't be visitors and dogs this time. She wanted to speak to Fleet's aunt in private.

Lydia was just about to press the bell for a second time, when the door swung inward. Auntie looked unsurprised but not especially happy to see her. 'I brought alcohol.' Lydia raised the carrier bag in her hand.

'I don't drink,' Auntie said, but she stepped back and motioned for Lydia to enter the flat.

'It's for me,' Lydia said, toeing off her trainers.

'You had better come through.'

If the last visit had been a formal affair with teacups and comfy seating, this time Auntie was all business. She led the way to the small kitchen and got two small glasses down from a cupboard. She put them on the cream Formica drop-leaf table and sat down on the matching chair. Lydia unscrewed the bottle and poured them both a generous measure before sitting in the other chair. The room was dominated by an old-fashioned dresser, overflowing with mismatched china, and the open shelving above the sink was lined with handmade-looking pottery and houseplants. If she reached out an arm she could almost touch the sink, and she wondered how Auntie managed to work in the room without knocking things over.

'Is this a goodbye?' Auntie said taking the offered glass of single malt.

Lydia felt her eyes prickle with sudden tears. There was a gleam about the woman, just like Fleet's, and she had to struggle to keep her emotions in check. She realised that she wanted to lean into this prickly and unwelcoming woman and have her hold her and stroke her hair, tell her everything was going to be all right. Although it wasn't. Not for her. She raised her glass. 'Yes.'

Auntie raised her glass in answer and drained it in one.

Lydia followed suit and then refilled both glasses. 'I thought you didn't drink.'

'That was before I saw your purpose,' Auntie said. 'Occasions like this, they demand it. And you brought the good stuff.'

She wondered how much of Fleet's gift Auntie shared and how much she knew. Or had guessed.

'You're doing the right thing, child.'

Lydia blinked several times to stop herself from crying and drained her glass. The whisky burned her throat and warmed her chest and, most importantly, reminded her that she wasn't the type to dissolve in a stranger's kitchen. No matter what the circumstances.

She squared her shoulders. 'I want you to pass a message to Fleet for me. Ignatius.'

Auntie nodded. 'You're not coming back.'

'No. I don't think so.' Lydia had tried to write a letter for Fleet, something to explain to him what she had done and why she had done it. She had tried to find the words, but it had been too hard. Now, sitting opposite Auntie she wondered why she had thought giving a verbal message would be easier.

'What do you want him to know?'

Lydia swallowed. 'That I didn't have a choice. This was the safest way. The way to make sure he was safe. And Emma. And my parents. I had to be sure.'

Auntie nodded. 'Anything else?'

'Just that I love him. And I'm sorry I couldn't think of a better way.'

CHAPTER TWENTY-THREE

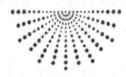

Finding Maddie turned out to be the easiest part of the plan as she responded to Lydia's first overture. Lydia had sent a message to what she hoped was still her phone, promising something of 'mutual benefit'. A text message invited her to 'come and play' with an address. And a random Bill Murray gif.

Lydia made her way to the address in Belgravia which turned out to be a five-star hotel with a smoked glass frontage and an abundance of planters overflowing with lush greenery. Maddie messaged as she approached the front steps with the words 'garden terrace'. Lydia wondered if Maddie was watching from a balcony using her sniper scope. She felt her skin prickling. Here she was again walking toward Maddie when she ought to be flying away.

Maddie was sitting on a low sofa in the corner of the terrace, surrounded with flowers and lush trellises. The retractable roof was pulled back to reveal the blue sky and spring sunshine and the air was scented with jasmine. She was sipping from a pale pink cocktail, which had a matching partner on the table.

'Drink up.'

Lydia eyed the cocktail. It had probably cost more than she spent on food in a week, but might also have a nasty surprise. She tried to see if there were visible crystals in the bottom of the glass or powder on the rim.

'Oh, give me strength.' Maddie swiped the glass and took a long drink from it, wiping away the lipstick mark after. 'There. Now stop hovering. You're making the staff nervous.'

Lydia sat on a padded velvet chair opposite Maddie. It left her with her back to the entrance but she figured her biggest threat was on the other side of the table. 'Cheers,' Lydia said, toasting Maddie before taking a sip of the pink drink. It was sharp and delicious.

'I was glad you got in touch,' Maddie said. 'I was beginning to feel like I was doing all the running in this relationship.'

Lydia decided not to tackle the use of the 'r' word. She was pretty sure Maddie wouldn't kill her in broad daylight in a busy hotel restaurant, but not certain enough to push her luck. Lydia kept her face neutral. 'I wanted to talk. To find out what you want.'

Maddie fluttered her eyelashes. 'You care about me. I knew it.'

'I just want to know if there is anything I can do to speed up your London visit.'

'I might settle down. London is my home, after all. Maybe I'm tired of living such a reckless life. I look at you and your friend, what's her name, Emma? And that handsome boyfriend. You've built a nice steady life. Makes me wonder what that's like.'

Lydia felt sick. Just hearing Emma's name in Maddie's voice set every nerve jangling. She had to keep Maddie distracted and away from Emma and her family. She said the first thing which popped into her mind. A corpse swinging from a tree. 'It was pretty reckless, killing your handler.'

Maddie frowned. 'Sergio? Trust me, nobody is grieving that sack of shit.'

'Was it your idea? Or an off-the-books commission?'

'Everything I do is off the books,' Maddie leaned back and prodded the crushed ice of her cocktail with the stirrer. 'And I'm very happy with that. They love my work and they pay me well for it.'

She was lying, Lydia realised. She wanted something else. Recognition? 'You killed your handler, I would have thought even secret ops aren't keen on that kind of thing.'

Maddie shrugged. 'I've not heard any complaints.'

'That's because they haven't found you, yet. When they do…'

Maddie smiled. 'I'm not losing sleep over it. And I never liked him. He was rude.'

Lydia wanted to say that it didn't seem like enough to warrant being murdered and hung from a tree, but there was a fervent glow in Maddie's eyes.

'Fine. You want the truth?'

Lydia resisted the urge to say 'this will be good' and just nodded.

'I fancied a change.'

'Of handler?'

'No, I wanted out. I thought it was going to be so different, but it was just like being back here. Some old man telling me what to do. But it's not that easy to stop working for them, you know? You understand. You had to do the same thing with Charlie. You have to do something definitive, it's the only thing people like that understand. They weren't just going to rip up my contract and wish me a happy retirement. I had to make a statement.'

Lydia was pretty sure that the order to kill her had come

from Mr Smith but she didn't know if Maddie knew that. If she had a handler before, filtering the information, she might not have known the difference between on-the-books orders from MI6 and Mr Smith's pet project. 'But then they sent you,' Lydia caught herself before she said 'orders'. 'Information direct? Didn't you think that was odd? After you'd made it clear you weren't working for them anymore?'

Maddie shrugged. 'I told you, already. I'm too valuable to them. I got a text. It was a job and I was in London already so I went to do it. I had made my point, but that didn't mean I wasn't open to renegotiating terms.'

'But it was me.' Lydia stopped herself before she did something truly stupid, like pointing out that by failing to kill her, Maddie was blotting her own copybook, again.

'But it was you,' Maddie raised her glass in salute, her expression suddenly grim.

Ice poured down her spine. 'Are you going to kill me?'

Maddie stared for a long moment, unsmiling. Then she took a sip of her cocktail. 'Not today.'

Lydia worked hard on keeping her breathing even, keeping hold of the fear that was lapping at the edges of her mind. She forced herself to take a sip of her own drink, to mirror Maddie's movements in the hopes it would build some kind of rapport. 'So, what's next for you?'

'I go freelance. No handler.'

'Don't you need contacts for that?'

'What makes you think I don't have contacts?'

'Nothing,' Lydia said quickly. Everything about Maddie was a performance, but the flash of anger was real. Maddie definitely wanted to be seen as smart and capable and in control. Then it hit Lydia... Maddie wanted her to be impressed. She tried to think about what Maddie wanted to hear. But that she wouldn't see through immediately. 'It's just I struggled with that... When I started my business. I didn't know anybody, and it was hard to build a client list.'

'Is that why you took the job from Uncle Charlie?'

'Partly,' Lydia said, truthfully enough. 'I did need the work.'

'I suppose I can forgive that,' Maddie said. 'Besides. It's in the past. I'm not hanging onto the old ways, I'm looking to the future. I've had my chakras aligned and I'm ready for the new me.'

Lydia didn't know how to respond to that.

Maddie's laugh made her skin prickle. 'Not really. The old me was perfect.'

'I KNOW a way for you to resign permanently. To make it stick.'

'Do tell.' Maddie was smiling so widely her mouth was like a red slash across her face.

'I can get you access to Mr Smith.'

'I can get to him any time I like.'

'Fair enough,' Lydia said and made to leave.

'Just like that? Finish your drink at least.'

'Look, I want him gone,' Lydia said. 'He is running a personal mission and has the Families in his sights. It's unacceptable.'

'I don't disagree,' Maddie said. 'He's overstepped. I could teach you to shoot. Get him from a distance with a sniper rifle, it's the safest way. Especially for a beginner.'

'I don't need a gun,' Lydia said, trying to distract Maddie.

'What are you going to do?' Maddie didn't change position. 'Investigate him to death? Sooner or later you're going to have to toughen up. I didn't like Charlie, but he had that bit right at least.'

'You don't know what I'm capable of,' Lydia said. 'I don't need a gun, because he's already a dead man.'

That made Maddie cheer up. 'He looked pretty perky last time I saw him.'

'I was thinking we could work together. For a common purpose.' Lydia outlined her plan while Maddie finished her drink.

The waiter appeared and Maddie ordered champagne which Lydia hoped was a good sign.

Once the business with the ice bucket and the glasses and the popping of the cork had been dealt with, Maddie picked up the long-stemmed glass and raised it in a toast. 'To us.'

'To us,' Lydia echoed, hoping that she hadn't just made a huge mistake.

CHAPTER TWENTY-FOUR

Lydia pulled up in Emma's suburban street. She had chocolates for the kids and a bottle of wine and was feeling strangely calm. She had weighed up the possibilities and decided that Emma was the most vulnerable. Fleet was prepared and she had warned her parents. They had left London for an impromptu package holiday and hadn't told anybody, not even Lydia, where they had gone. And, as she reminded herself repeatedly, Henry Crow was no longer helpless.

The car door shut with a reassuring thunk and she could hear birds in the trees which lined the road. Children were playing in a nearby garden and their young voices tugged something painful inside Lydia. She wasn't going to worry Emma, she reminded herself. She would just sit and have dinner and make conversation and play with Archie and Maisie. Be a good friend.

In Emma's warm kitchen-diner, the evening sun pouring through the large windows, Lydia tried to breathe normally. She had thought she would feel better once she was here, but instead she felt like a bad omen. She had brought the darkness with her. She wondered what Fleet was doing and whether he had sensed anything when she had said goodbye. It was good that she was with Emma. If she spent her last night with him, she wouldn't trust herself to walk to her fate in the morning.

Emma had poured three large glasses of wine and Tom was stirring something on the stove. He had a tea towel draped over one shoulder and was telling Lydia about his recipe for... something. She realised that she had zoned out and took a large sip of wine to avoid answering his question about coriander. She couldn't summon an opinion.

Emma had clearly noticed her distraction. 'Shall we sit outside?' She put a hand on Tom's arm. 'Is that okay, babe?'

THEY SAT on the small patio in foldable deck chairs which Emma had hauled out of the shed. The garden was filled with plastic ride-on toys, a small climbing frame and slide, and a couple of abandoned bikes, one of which didn't have any pedals. It looked like an entire football team had been playing, not just two small children.

Although they weren't quite as small as they had been. Dispensing hugs and chocolate when she arrived, Lydia had been hit with the changes. Maisie was taller and her vocabulary had doubled. Archie had lost a tooth and it gave him a rakish look. Like a tiny pirate.

'I can't believe how big Maisie has got,' Lydia said. It was the kind of thing she had heard other people saying, proper grown-up people. Finding the words leaving her own mouth was odd, but not unpleasant. It made her feel responsible and capable. Which made a nice change.

Maisie and Archie were upstairs having something which Emma called 'special time'. She pulled a face. 'We decided that they could have a slightly later bedtime on weekends, but we've dressed it up as special time. If they have earned all their stars during the week, they can have an extra twenty minutes playing in their rooms before bedtime.'

'Cunning,' Lydia said. The secret service had nothing on parents for making loaded deals.

'So,' Emma regarded Lydia over the rim of her wine glass. 'What's going on?'

'I'm visiting. For dinner.'

'And you're staying the night?'

'If that's still all right?' Lydia raised her glass. 'Then I can have a couple of these.'

'Bollocks.'

'I'd prefer wine.'

Emma ignored the pathetic attempt at humour. She gave Lydia a serious look. 'You know what I mean. Tell me what's going on.'

Lydia briefly thought about playing the 'can't a girl visit her best mate' card, but she could see that Emma wasn't in the mood. 'You know my MI6 guy?'

'The one who wanted information on your family?'

'Yeah. I told him to take a hike, that I wasn't going to work for him anymore.'

'Hadn't you made an agreement?'

Emma wasn't accusing Lydia of anything, but she felt it like a blow, anyway. Her word should be her bond. That was the kind of code she had been raised to hold. 'He forced one on me. And I considered it fulfilled.'

'But he had other ideas?'

'He wanted me to join his department. Doing what, I'm not exactly sure. Using my Crow abilities in some way.' Lydia looked away as she spoke, finding it hard to look squarely at Emma when she referred to magic. The ways in which she was so different. So *weird*. 'He took it poorly when I refused.'

Emma was sitting very still. She was no dummy and knew something bad was coming. Lydia was glad they were outside as it wasn't the sort of thing that belonged in Emma's safe and normal house. She said it quickly, like that would make it easier.

Emma didn't react for a moment. She had always been calmer than Lydia, more able to take a breath and process things before acting. When boys started pinging their bra straps in class, Lydia had turned around and smacked the perpetrator without hesitating. Which meant she had ended up in front of the headteacher for violence. Emma had taken a moment to think, then bawled the guy out, and then been to see the head of year to demand immediate action. In short, Emma was smart. And had been a proper grown-up ever since Lydia had known her.

'Isn't that illegal?' She said now, calm and collected, like Lydia had just told her that Mr Smith had had her car towed, not sent an assassin to murder her.

'Very much so,' Lydia said. 'But I think the secret service get special dispensation from the police. Or they do it without getting caught. Honestly, I'm a bit hazy on how it all works.'

'I'm guessing the secret service don't advertise their methods. They probably don't produce handy pamphlets, either.'

Lydia slugged her wine, relaxing a notch. She was relieved that Emma was still able to make jokes, but more relieved still that she hadn't immediately sent her packing.

'You're worried about me, aren't you?'

'Maddie got me on the roof by threatening you,' Lydia said. 'And it worked. Which means you're perfectly safe.'

'How so?'

'Because the threat of hurting you worked to control me. No one would throw away that kind of weapon. You're too useful.'

'Well, that's good to know.' Emma drained half her glass in one long swallow. After a few moments of thought, she asked the question Lydia really didn't want to answer. 'So, why are you worried enough for a sleepover tonight?'

Lydia had rehearsed this. She wasn't going to tell Emma the truth. Not all of it, anyway. It was too much to tell her friend that this was, most likely, her last night and that she wanted to spend it in her normal, happy house, with Maisie and Archie and all their life and promise and energy. That she wanted to laugh with her best friend and go to sleep hearing the faint murmur of her voice, the timbre of it so familiar and comforting. So she went with the other part of the reason. 'I'm teaming up with Maddie to take Mr Smith out. It turns out he is a rogue element in the service and if he disappears, my problems with MI6 should disappear.'

'Just like that?'

'Well, hopefully disappear. There's no guarantee, but he's definitely the one with the Crow obsession.'

'And Maddie wants him gone, too?'

'Our goals temporarily align, so we're going to work together.'

'What aren't you telling me?'

Lydia widened her eyes. 'Nothing. Just that I don't trust her and I wanted to be here tonight on the off-chance she decided to pay you a visit.'

Emma frowned. 'Why would she...? Oh.'

'I don't think she will,' Lydia said quickly. 'She's got no reason to threaten you, now, I'm doing what she wants.' She had stumbled over the words 'hurt you' when she had practised, so had changed it to 'threaten'.

'We've been in danger for weeks,' Emma said, cutting to the truth of the matter with her usual clear-eyed efficiency. 'Why are you here tonight?'

Lydia couldn't look her square in the face. 'I just wanted to see you.'

. . .

THANKFULLY, Emma let it drop. They had dinner and Tom made them laugh with his descriptions of his new line manager. The food was good and the conversation flowed. Emma played along that it was a normal evening and Lydia was grateful.

Lydia was rearranging the sofa cushions when Emma walked in with an armful of duvet and pillows. 'Are you still with Fleet?'

'We're all good.'

'Aren't you worried about him, too?'

Lydia didn't want to admit that she had deliberately played up her relationship with Fleet to further distract Maddie from Emma. It was the truth, but it sounded cold. 'Fleet's got police protection.' It wasn't entirely a lie. Fleet was police. And he was protecting himself. It felt rude to tell Emma that Fleet could look after himself, like she was accusing Emma of being weak for just being a normal human being, for not being trained for violence and threat.

Lydia didn't expect to sleep, but she had brought a book to read. She dozed a little in the early hours, but started drinking coffee at five. Maisie and Archie were up just after six and Emma sent them downstairs to play with 'Auntie Lydia'.

Lydia was engrossed in building a complicated vehicle from random Lego bricks when Emma told her to check her phone. 'Local news.'

In the Camberwell and Peckham section of the BBC news site, there was a report of a fire in a flat. The building had been evacuated and fire fighters were on the scene. The amateur photo illustrating the article showed Fleet's block. There was a red block headline which said 'breaking news' and a video alongside the article. Lydia clicked it.

A reporter was standing in the street along from Fleet's flat. The carpark for the building was, presumably, filled with fire engines and police, but his position still gave a clear view of the smoke-filled sky and the damaged building. Lydia didn't need time to work out that the source was on Fleet's floor and side of the building. She could see it instantly.

The reporter was speaking to camera, his face serious. 'London Ambulance Service treated three people on the scene and one has been taken to hospital for smoke inhalation. There is one confirmed fatality. The identity of this individual is not being revealed at this time, although their next of kin have been contacted. We have information that it is believed to be a Metropolitan police officer and there is an appeal for witnesses to what may not be a tragic accident, but a targeted attack.'

CHAPTER TWENTY-FIVE

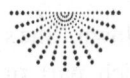

'Oh my god,' Emma had been watching over Lydia's shoulder and she wrapped her arms around her. 'Lydia...'

'It's okay,' Lydia said, her voice muffled by Emma's arms. 'It's not Fleet.'

'What?'

Lydia extricated herself from Emma's embrace and turned to face her. 'It's okay. I promise, he's fine. He wasn't in his flat.' She showed Emma the text message on her burner phone that had just pinged through. 'See. He's all good.'

'What's wrong?' Archie's little face was crumpled with concern.

'Nothing's wrong,' Lydia said quickly. 'There was a fire but nobody was hurt.'

'Fire?' Maisie said. 'Get engine.' She disappeared below the edge of the coffee table and reappeared carrying a Lego fire engine.

'Why don't you two go and make sure Daddy's up. You can tickle his feet if he isn't out of bed.' She waited until the small people had thundered out of the room and up the stairs, before turning back to Lydia.

'Sorry... I hope I didn't worry Archie.'

'Was that-?'

'Maddie. Yes. I told her I was moving into his flat. I thought it would keep her focused on Fleet and away from you.'

'Oh God,' Emma sat down. 'She's properly psychotic.'

Lydia wondered which part of 'contract killer' hadn't given her the tip off, but she restrained herself from saying so. Her world had always been hard to comprehend. Especially in the cosy and comforting living room with cushions and lovingly tended pot plants and toys in the corner. It was completely fair that Emma was leaning forward, head between her knees and dragging in lungfuls of air like she was trying not to hurl. Lydia patted her shoulder and murmured comforting words. After a while, Emma straightened up and managed a watery smile. 'Sorry. I think I just hadn't taken you seriously before. About her, I mean. Your cousin.'

'That's okay. Best way to function.'

'How do you do it?'

Emma looked sympathetic and Lydia couldn't stand it. 'Practise. And denial.'

'And alcohol?'

Lydia grabbed her for a quick hug and then Emma left to hustle the kids to get ready for school.

LYDIA TOOK the opportunity to wash her face and brush her teeth, then she called Fleet, needing the reassurance of his voice more than she cared to admit. As arranged, he had rung his gaffer and had a false report fed to the press. Male police officer found dead at the scene.

'Sinclair came through on that one,' Fleet said. 'The gaffer wasn't going to say no with her backing me.'

'I'm sorry about your flat.'

'Nobody was badly hurt, that's the main thing. And hopefully it will sell the deal to Maddie.'

'She'll believe me,' Lydia said, injecting certainty into her voice. Now that she knew Fleet was safe, she couldn't let herself speak to him for too long.

'Call me as soon as you can.'

She was grateful that he didn't question her further. She felt like glass, as if the slightest thing could make her resolve falter. And if that happened, she would fall and shatter on the floor.

LYDIA WENT to the safe house in Vauxhall, the place where she had met with Mr Smith when he had blackmailed her into sharing information. She waved at the cameras she knew were hidden in the reception area and held up a piece of paper with some handwriting in block capitals, then sat on the pavement outside to wait. She could have used the phone number that she still had for him, but she wanted to speak to him in person and she was pretty sure he wouldn't be able to resist.

The black car pulled up, tinted windows obscuring the interior. The back door nearest Lydia swung open and Mr Smith, sharp suit and patrician smile in place, inclined his head.

She hesitated. This was probably a very bad idea. The man wanted her dead.

'In or out?'

She got in.

. . .

THE CAR PULLED AWAY and soon they were passing the hulking geometric mess of MI6 and crossing Vauxhall Bridge. 'Fleet knows I'm here,' Lydia said. 'As does your boss.'

'Which boss would that be?'

'Sinclair,' Lydia said, watching his face carefully.

He didn't so much as twitch. 'You're getting more cautious. That's undoubtedly wise.'

Swallowing down the urge to tell Mr Smith she didn't need his advice or his approval, she looked at the man in the front passenger seat. He was large and wearing a suit. The man driving looked identical except his haircut was, if anything, even shorter and neater.

She had been prepared for Mr Smith's signature but, having not seen him for a while, it still made her feel nauseous. She could hear planks of wood creaking, hear the slap of sails in the wind, and taste gold on her tongue. Salt air and brine and sunlight catching the surface of the waves, shattering the water into a thousand painful white diamonds. She had been practising on accessing her well of Crow power without having to move physically and she used it, now. Imagining turning down the volume on his signature until it was barely detectable.

Mr Smith was watching her carefully. 'I take it you want to trade?'

'I wanted to warn you,' Lydia said, pausing before she used his real name, 'Gale.'

His lips stretched into a thin smile. 'Sinclair?'

She nodded. 'I still think of you as Mr Smith, though. For old times' sake.'

'Warn me?'

'Maddie is very unhappy.'

'I am aware.'

'Yes, poor Sergio Bastos.'

This time she thought she did detect the tiniest flicker

around his eyes. It felt like winning. 'And you know she is still in London.'

He inclined his head.

'You also know that she is no longer taking your calls. Does that make you nervous?'

'Not particularly.'

Lydia gave him a long look. 'It should.'

The car was moving smoothly through traffic along the embankment. This being London, they still weren't moving particularly fast and Lydia could see the large plane trees, benches, and statues which lined the route. She watched the scenery and waited. Back when she was playing this game with Mr Smith before, she had no idea how far he was playing her. Now, she still wasn't entirely certain, but she felt more prepared. And, ultimately, compared to the raw terror of Maddie, he no longer felt like a threat. The goons in the front were no doubt highly trained killers and carrying firearms, but Lydia felt her Crow power around her like a cloak. Next to Mr Smith, she felt invincible. She wondered if this was how Maddie felt all the time.

'Why don't you tell me what you want?'

'What did you do to Maddie? I know she went through training, but I think there was more.'

'She is very talented. It was more a case of honing what was already there.'

'There is something wrong with her, now. Something is missing.'

'I didn't do anything,' Mr Smith said, his voice dripping with faux concern. 'I think there was always something missing. That kind of asset, they're all the same. Damaged. It makes them mouldable. You take the broken pieces and you put them together however you want.'

Lydia felt a flare of anger. It was a strange, almost protective, feeling. Not that Maddie needed her defence. She squeezed her coin.

He smiled at her, clearly aware that he had hit a nerve. 'Don't be offended. She's a good one. Most of the assets aren't too bright. Doesn't matter what the films would have you believe most hired killers don't need that much spark. Up here.' He tapped his temple. 'They just need to be able to pull a trigger.'

'Plenty of military types can do that. And you must know hundreds in your line of work.'

'Killing from a distance. Or in self-defence. Or in service of an ideal. Protection of a country or leader. Something. It's actually harder than you think to find someone who will stab a stranger for money. More than once, anyway.'

'I would say I'm sorry for your inconvenience.'

'But that would be a lie.'

Lydia didn't reply. Then, after the thoughts kept swirling, she did. What did it matter, now? Mr Smith wasn't getting out of his alive. And she wasn't, either. 'Maddie wasn't entirely all right, I can accept that, but she wasn't broken. She used to be a Crow.'

'She's still got that dubious honour.'

'I'm not so sure,' Lydia said. 'I can tell what Family people are from, and whether they are packing any power. She has lost that signature. If I wasn't looking right at her, I wouldn't know she was a Crow.'

'They say that you lose a part of your soul every time you take a life.'

'That's it? That's your answer?'

He shrugged. 'She's taken a lot of lives.'

LYDIA DIRECTED THEM TO HIGHGATE. It was the only entrance to the Pearls' domain that she knew of, although no doubt there were many more.

Once the car was parked in the road between Highgate

and Queenswood, Mr Smith turned slightly in his seat. 'Tell me why I would go with you?'

'I'm unarmed,' Lydia said. 'And your large friends can come with us. You'll be perfectly safe.'

'I'm not concerned for my safety,' Mr Smith said. 'But I'm a busy man. You made it abundantly clear that you are not interested in working with me so, I ask again, why would I go anywhere with you?'

'I'm meeting Maddie. Thought you might want to tag along. You two can catch up.'

He went still. Well, more still. It was subtle but the tension in the car increased sharply. 'You are hoping I will kill her?'

'Before she kills me. Yes.'

'And if I fail, she'll probably kill me.'

Lydia nodded cheerfully. 'That's about the size of it. It seemed like a neat solution.'

'Why are you telling me?' Mr Smith sounded genuinely curious, and it was nice to have surprised him.

'I'm not a killer. If you come with me, I want you to know what you're getting into. It's your choice.'

'Well, then,' Mr Smith settled back in the soft leather. 'I choose not.'

'Fair enough,' Lydia said, and grabbed the door handle. She had barely made it out of the car when doors opened behind her and she found herself being forcibly detained by one of the large men, while the other gave her a professional and thorough pat-down.

'She's clean,' the man that Lydia privately named 'Handsy' called to Smith.

He emerged from the car, shooting his cuffs.

The other man, the one who had grabbed her, and who was still gripping her shoulders with meaty hands, suddenly let her go. Lydia stumbled forward but regained her balance before she did anything too embarrassing.

'Uhhh,' Meat Hands was saying. It wasn't coherent, but it got the gist across. Something unexpected and unpleasant had just happened.

'Let's go for a little walk,' Maddie's voice. Bright and chirpy like a talk-show host, emanated from behind Meat Hands.

'We...' Meat Hands began, in a triumph of hope over experience, before finishing with another involuntary noise as Maddie punched him in the kidneys. 'Uhung.'

'No talking, please, children,' Maddie said.

'What makes you think I'm going to come with you?' Mr Smith asked, not unreasonably. The plan had been for Lydia to lead Mr Smith into the woods to meet Maddie and for her to ambush them under cover of the trees.

'You still want them, don't you?' Maddie said and winked at him.

'Wait,' Lydia said. 'What?'

Maddie cocked her head. 'I made a little deal with our mutual friend Gale, here. Amnesty from the service and maybe a few contacts. Just a little retirement package that will help me set up on my own.'

'And in return?'

'The Silver cup,' Maddie said, still hidden behind the massive bulk of Meat Hands.

'And me,' Lydia said, the truth dropping like a stone.

'And you. Sorry, cuz.'

CHAPTER TWENTY-SIX

Maddie did not sound sorry. Lydia wasn't exactly surprised that Maddie was double-crossing her, but she was weirdly disappointed. She had known it was a possibility, but Maddie's attention had felt like affection in some way and that had clouded her view. And it had all seemed different, then. She had been running terrifying scenarios in her mind as a theoretical exercise. Now one of those terrifying scenarios was actually happening, Lydia wanted to go back in time and deliver a swift kick to her past self. 'So, why would I come with you, now?'

'Because I'm asking nicely.' Mr Smith had produced a gun while they had been speaking. The sight of it made Lydia's insides go liquid. She wasn't experienced with firearms and wasn't used to seeing them anywhere except the TV screen. 'We'll all go in a happy little party. Once I've got the cup, I'll transfer the money and the contacts and we'll be done.'

'That's the deal,' Maddie said.

The liquid fear was tinged with anger. Lydia focused on the anger, using it to keep herself together. 'You duplicitous little...'

'Careful, now,' Maddie peered around Meat Hands to wink at Lydia. 'Don't say anything you'll regret.'

WALKING through Highgate Woods had never been Lydia's favourite activity and doing so with a gun held against the base of her spine did nothing to improve the experience. She concentrated on watching her feet and making sure she didn't trip over a stray root. It wouldn't do to get shot by Mr Smith just for falling over.

As they moved further from the main path and the trees got closer together, Lydia could taste the Pearl magic. It was dark green leaves, buds bursting on the branch and youth and beauty reflected in a thousand shining surfaces. Not exactly a chatty party to begin with, the group had gone utterly silent. Something pale slipped through the trees to their right, keeping pace. It was a small figure and Lydia assumed it would be the girl the Pearls used as one of their emissaries in the aboveground world.

'Why did you stash it out here?' Mr Smith said, his voice slightly strained.

Maddie was walking behind them, covering Meat Hands and Handsy with her own gun. 'I needed somewhere you weren't going to wander past. Coincidences do happen, but I knew you avoided this place.'

'What makes you say that?'

'Don't be coy,' Maddie said. 'It really doesn't suit you.'

Mr Smith shook his head. 'I don't know what you mean.'

'So, you're not shaking like a tiny little leaf?' Maddie's tone was teasing.

'Shut up.'

That surprised Lydia. Mr Smith had never been anything other than coldly superior with her, except when he had been laying on the false concern. Hearing him snap made her like him a great deal more than she had and guilt stabbed her in the stomach. He prodded the gun a little harder into her back and she stopped feeling bad.

'What's that?' Meat Hands stopped walking. He was looking around at the trees which had been groaning for a while.

'Nearly there,' Maddie said. 'Keep moving.'

'Do as she says,' Mr Smith said.

Lydia couldn't remember the route through the woods very well, but she knew they were almost at the entrance. She could taste it. And the trees were leaning down, branches twisting and writhing. The inky sky was no longer visible, replaced with an impossibly thick canopy of green leaves. It was how the forest must have looked to Londoners hundreds of years ago, back before the roads and pollution and city sprawl had got in on the act. The Pearls probably considered the change a travesty. If Lydia had her way, the whole lot would have been bulldozed to make way for a nice cheerful shopping centre. Maybe a Nando's.

The small girl with the long dirty blonde hair stepped out from the undergrowth. 'Shiny?'

'Not today, kiddo,' Lydia said. 'Sorry.'

'I brought you something pretty,' Maddie said, showing her teeth in what she probably thought was a friendly smile. 'It's over there.'

The girl was no idiot, and she hesitated.

'It's really pretty,' Maddie said.

The girl tilted her head, considering. 'Is there glitter? I like glitter.'

'So much glitter,' Maddie said. She was visibly confused at the child's total lack of fear.

'They aren't expecting you.' The girl pulled at a thick strand of her tangled hair and began winding it around her fingers.

'That's all right,' Maddie said. 'Help yourself to your gift, anyway.'

The girl stepped over to a hillock of moss and stones. A red leather purse on a braided cord had joined the variety of rainbow plastic beads hanging around her neck and it swung forward as she leaned down to peer under the leaves and stones.

'Where is it?' Mr Smith said. He sounded agitated and Lydia hoped he didn't slip and shoot her accidentally. How much field time did Smith have? She was used to seeing him on the other side of a table or leaning back against the leather seats of his car.

'Don't worry, it's here,' Lydia said, as the Silver tang hit her nostrils and the back of her throat. It was bright and clean and cold and it cut through the choking taste of foliage.

'Bring it to me–' Mr Smith was saying, his voice urgent with need, when he was interrupted.

The sound of the gun was so loud and sudden that Lydia let out an involuntary noise. One she wasn't proud of making. On the plus side, she managed not to wet herself. Small mercies.

Meat Hands toppled like a tree.

Handsy had spun around at the sound, his own weapon rising to fire, but Maddie was too quick. Faster than a blink, she was behind the man and drawing a knife across his throat. He fell to his knees, blood flowing. His expression was so surprised it was almost comical. Almost.

'There was no need for that,' Mr Smith said and wrapped an arm around Lydia, pulling her up against his front. He was surprisingly strong and Lydia found she was up on tiptoe. She tried to move and couldn't.

With his signature mixing with the Pearl magic and the Silver rolling off the hidden cup, Lydia was finding it difficult to stay conscious. She was glad she had spent so much time training and she used that focus, now, finding the quiet space in the centre of it all and drawing her wings around her like a shield.

'Time to go.' Lydia could dimly hear Maddie's voice but it seemed to be coming from a great distance. 'You give me Lydia and the contact list and my new friend here will bring you the cup.'

'That's not what we agreed. I get Lydia and the cup.'

'Deals change. Just ask your friends.' She waved at the bodies on the ground. 'The cup is fair payment for the contact list. And Lydia will be more trouble than she's worth.'

'Maybe you're right. Maybe I'll just kill your cousin here, leave her body for the birds.'

Don't try to bluff the psychopath, Lydia thought, wondering how he could possibly still be underestimating Maddie.

'You want the cup and I want the contact list.' Maddie's gun was steady in her hand and she looked relaxed. She could have been discussing the purchase of a loaf of bread. 'All we have to do is swap. Don't make this more complicated than it has to be.'

Lydia felt Mr Smith's body relax slightly, even though his grip on her remained firm.

She was still concentrating on staying conscious, but it was much easier. She could feel strong wings wrapped tightly and taste soft feathers. Whether it was the training under stress or the siphoning of her power into the bracelet or a combination of the two, Lydia definitely felt more in control. She could still sense the bright Silver from the cup but it was no longer blinding.

She blinked and focused on the scene. Maddie was holding the little girl who was holding the silver cup and looking pissed off. The trees seemed even closer than before. The small clearing they had been standing in was now a tangled mass of roots and trunks and foliage. A branch the thickness of a body builder's thigh was snaking down behind Maddie's head. It had a cruel intent, like it was sentient, and it made Lydia's stomach flip over.

'Watch out!' Lydia shouted.

Maddie ducked, narrowly missing the sudden swipe. The branch plunged into the ground with a sickening crack and leaves rained down. The other trees had awoken, too, and there were more branches moving in unnatural ways. There was one to Lydia's left that she would have sworn was staring at her.

'We need to go if we're still going,' Lydia said, speaking to Maddie, and trying to stay calm.

'You're not going anywhere,' Mr Smith said and then he was maybe going to say something else but Lydia would never know because the next sound out of his mouth was a kind of 'mnumph' and he let her go.

Lydia knew that Maddie was back on plan and was now controlling Mr Smith. She glanced back at him, stock still and with his eyes bulging. His jaw was working but his lips were clamped shut. Even though it was something she had signed off on, it was still a freaky sight. She turned away and climbed over the tree roots to get closer to the girl. She crouched down as best she could and looked into her pale blue eyes. 'We humbly request an audience with the King. We bring a gift of great value.'

The girl sucked on the end of a piece of hair and regarded Lydia balefully.

'You can keep the shiny cup, kid,' Maddie said.

The girl brightened and hugged it closer.

And then the ground opened up.

CHAPTER TWENTY-SEVEN

The last time Lydia had entered the Pearl court, there had been a black door covered in a mosaic of mother-of-pearl hidden in the basement of a ten-million-pound house. This time, it was an archway of twisted tree roots lifted to reveal steps roughly cut from black earth.

The girl twisted away from Maddie and skipped down, her blonde hair a beacon in the dark.

'You first,' Maddie said, pushing Lydia in the shoulder. 'Then you,' she added to Mr Smith.

Lydia was concentrating on the steps and heard the sounds of Mr Smith stumbling over the uneven ground. He was making a low moaning sound which made the hairs on her neck stand up. She knew what it was like to have your body controlled by Maddie and she could empathise with the sound effects.

The air was dank and cold and the earth seemed to press in from both sides. Stray roots poked through the packed soil walls. They were a stark reminder that this wasn't a carefully engineered structure and Lydia could feel her heartrate kicking up. She wasn't a fan of going underground at the best of times and at this moment it was extremely hard not to picture the metres of heavy earth and rock above her head.

Finally the steps ended and a short passage led to a door. Lydia recognised it as the same kind she had seen in the mansion. Shiny black lacquer which seemed to be catching the light, even though there wasn't any. No candles. No lightbulbs. No torches. Trying not to think too hard about how little sense it made, Lydia put her hand to the door. The blonde girl had no doubt already gone through and she had left the door ajar.

The court was as Lydia remembered. The magic was thick in the air as a group of beautiful young things danced to a pounding bass rhythm. Music which clearly should have been audible in the passageway they had just walked along. Lydia swallowed down the urge to be sick. That was the problem when things didn't obey the laws of physics, the human brain rebelled and that made a person mighty queasy. No wonder most people just decided they weren't seeing what they were seeing or hearing what they were hearing. It was easier on the gut.

Lydia's stomach turned over again, and she summoned her coin. Squeezing it hard in her right fist helped a little, and seeing that Maddie had gone a greenish shade helped a lot.

Poor Mr Smith had clearly lost the battle with the urge to vomit and he kept lurching over and his face was pale and sweaty. His throat was moving convulsively as he, presumably, swallowed back the bile. Maddie seemed oblivious and Lydia decided not to request that she unseal his lips. She told herself that it was because she wasn't sure Maddie wouldn't see it as a challenge to do something worse but the truth of the matter was that his comfort was not high up her priority list.

The girl had disappeared and the Silver cup with her. Lydia didn't have time to worry about that, though, as the crowd had parted to reveal the Pearl King sitting on their throne and it was as if the whole cavernous space went instantly silent. Maybe it did, Lydia could no longer tell what was real, what was imagery cast by the Pearls and what was the white noise of her fear. The King was just as beautiful as Lydia remembered, but easily twice as angry. Their face remained immobile and fixed, but when they spoke the tone was truly terrible. 'You are not invited.'

The figures nearest the throne shrank back and Lydia thought, when the monsters are afraid it's time to run. Instead, she stepped forward. 'We come to pay our respects to the Pearl King and to offer a valuable gift, a token of our esteem in the hope of a new peace between our Families.'

The King inclined their head. 'The King will grant you audience.'

She had warned Maddie of the archaic way the King spoke and the need to lay on the courtly obsequiousness, but Lydia could see she still wanted to dive over and punch them in the face. Quickly, she tugged on the bound figure, pulling Mr Smith into the King's view. A murmuring chatter began among the crowd of Pearls.

The King's face flickered. For a split second their habitually blank and bored expression became avid, and they leaned forward a fraction. It was the equivalent of most people falling over in surprise.

Clearly fed up of obeying the 'let me do the talking' portion of their plan, Maddie stepped directly in front of the King, dragging Mr Smith with her. 'After the truce between our Families you made another deal. Not an honest handshake one, like our truce, but a tricky one, written on paper.'

'We have not invited this one to speak.' The King looked at Maddie like she was something foul on the bottom of their shoe.

'You discovered after the document was signed that you

had made a deal with a company, not an individual and that it didn't just die with that person. It held strong as long as the company existed, no matter how many times the directors changed or the company was sold.' Maddie wagged a red-nailed finger. 'That was very silly.'

The crowd surged as if ready to crush Maddie, but the King held up a hand. Their voice was flat and utterly devoid of emotion, which made their words more chilling. 'You will die screaming.'

Maddie stiffened and Lydia knew the King was probably taking control of her body. Or trying to, at least.

'Your Majesty,' Lydia said. 'My cousin means no offence. Just to underline the immensity of our gift. We have found the sole owner of the corporation trading as JRB. He holds the ability to release you from your bond. He can dissolve the contract between your family and JRB.'

The King's gaze moved back to Lydia. 'You should not lie.'

It wasn't a question, but she answered it, anyway. 'This man owns JRB.'

Mr Smith was sweating profusely. Lydia felt bad for him, but she also knew she didn't have a choice. He had come for her, he had used Emma as leverage, he had tried to have Fleet killed. 'You did this to yourself,' she said, not meaning to speak the words out loud.

Smith's eyes rolled to look in her direction, the whites showing. She couldn't tell what he was trying to communicate, but it didn't matter. She couldn't trust a single word from his mouth.

'Is this true?' The King asked.

Mr Smith made a muffled sound but his lips didn't move.

'Why does he not answer the King?' A member of the court stepped forward.

'He can't,' Maddie said, clearly struggling to speak. 'I have... Him. Locked.'

The King waved a hand and Mr Smith's mouth popped open, a stream of vomit-tinged saliva immediately flowing out and over his chin. The muffled moaning became, abruptly, a loud gurgling cry.

'Enough.'

The cry stopped and his shoulders heaved as he fought to get control of himself.

'Are you the owner?'

Mr Smith nodded.

'Do you have sole authority to break the contract signed on the twelfth day of the twelfth month in the aboveground year two thousand and one?'

He straightened his spine and nodded. 'I do.'

His voice was raspy and the front of his shirt was flecked with vomit, but Lydia had to hand it to Mr Smith. He had regained his composure remarkably quickly.

'So do it, already,' Maddie said. 'But in return I want my cup. Where's the girl gone?'

Her mouth snapped shut, her teeth making an audible sound as they clashed together.

'Lydia Crow,' the King beckoned. 'Do you make a demand in return for this gift?'

'No,' Lydia said. 'It's a gift.'

'Safe passage out,' Maddie said over her, somehow managing to fight the King's control and continue to have the use of her lips, tongue and vocal chords.

Lydia had thought about this and she figured that if the King decided to kill her, he would kill them all. Being struck down by the King wasn't a pleasant thought, of course, but the result was all that mattered. Her friends and family would be safe from Maddie and Mr Smith. She closed her eyes and hoped it would be quick.

'I can break the contract here and now,' Mr Smith said. 'But what do I get in return? Apart from safe passage?' He nodded at Maddie. 'You can do what you like with her.'

The King smiled thinly. 'How quickly you turn on your friends.'

'They are not my friends,' Mr Smith said, 'they are my subjects.' Lydia realised instantly what he was doing. He was shooting for comradeship with the King, trying to position himself on a similar level. There was probably a seminar on it at MI6. 'Making Friends With Despots for Fun and Finance.'

'There you are wrong. They are the closest thing you have in this place. But you have shown your lack of loyalty. It has been noted.'

'It's simple,' Mr Smith began. 'I break the contract between your Family and my company and we both walk away free men.'

'I am not a man,' the Pearl King said.

'It's a figure of speech, I meant no-'

Whatever Mr Smith meant was lost as his head rotated a hundred and eighty degrees with a sickening crunch and he fell to the ground. Lydia stared at his body lying on the packed earth, his dead eyes gazing from their unnatural angle.

'Why did you do that?' Maddie sounded mildly irritated.

Lydia managed a step backward. She didn't think she could make it to the exit before the King snapped her neck, too, but she could try.

'No living entity owns the company,' the King said, their voice quavering very slightly with the tiniest betrayal of emotion. 'We are free.'

And this was the part that had always been hazy for Lydia. In her plan, she would die, that was almost a hundred per cent certain, and she had hoped that Maddie would be executed alongside her, but the question of what the Pearl Court would do with their new freedom was the big unknown. Would they be free to roam above ground? And, if so, what did that mean for London?

She realised that the ground was shaking. Then a thick root burst through to her left, narrowly missing Mr Smith's lifeless body.

Maddie was advancing on the throne and Lydia had a spark of hope that the King and the courtiers would be distracted enough for her to make it out. She couldn't back out, keeping her eyes on the King and Maddie, not with roots bursting through the ground and the unpredictability of the courtiers. She turned and moved over the pulsating, shaking ground toward the exit, pulling her jumper up and over her mouth and nose to try to filter out the dusty earth which was now whipped up through the air.

'It's over,' she heard a courtier say in wonderment.

'Free,' another said. The word was running around the cavern like fire. Free. Free. Free.

The place had already been thick with Pearl magic, but when Lydia was hit in the back with a solid blow and knocked to the hard ground, she had no doubt what it was. Pearl magic unleashed. All that potential, all that rage, all that power. The cork had been popped. Feeling too vulnerable on her front, tiny shoots and roots pushing up through the packed earth on either side of her face, Lydia flipped over as quickly as she could. She was just in time to see the Pearl King rise from their throne, face shining with terrible power and purpose.

They were unleashed. They were uncontained. They were...

Lydia blinked soil from her eyes. The Pearl nearest to her, a girl with beautiful high cheekbones dusted with shining glitter, was screaming. Lydia had heard it as a whoop of joy, but looking at her face she could now see it was a cry of panic and pain. Her face was twisted, her large eyes suddenly grotesque, and she wasn't the only one. Around the cavern, through the swirling earth and plant debris, faces were twisting, lithe bodies convulsing.

Maddie had moved away from the King and Lydia could no longer see her. The King was staring wide-eyed, their beautiful features utterly impassive. Something was moving under their skin and it took Lydia a horrified second to realise what was happening. Their flesh was rippling and changing, becoming wrinkled and shrivelled. The King's shoulders rounded and slumped as their spine curved, their eyes clouded and lips thinned to the point of vanishing.

Lydia had glimpsed the true age of the Pearl Court once. A single split-second image which showed the wizened figures of humans long past their natural lifespan. Now those images were developing all around, as if emerging in a photographer's dark room. The Pearls were withering and dying in a matter of seconds, like a gothic stop motion film or one of those speeded-up nature documentaries. The strong and the beautiful crumbled to desiccated figures which fell and began to decompose. The contract which had kept them contained in these liminal underground spaces and had prevented them from roaming London, had also kept them in a time capsule of sorts. Sealed from the world and sealed from the passage of time. It looked as if time was rushing back in and was eager to get to work.

As the Pearls died, their hold on the earth and rock crumbled. The whole space was shaking violently, the ground and walls and chunks of compacted earth and stray rocks were falling from the ceiling. There was going to be a cave-in any moment and Lydia turned and pushed her way toward the exit, praying it was still open. Her mind raced, trying to remember the advice for being caught in an avalanche. Her old boss at the investigation firm in Aberdeen had sent her on an outdoor skills weekend. Part of preparing her for some of the surveillance jobs which might take her into the Scottish countryside. She had, quite rightly, sized Lydia up as a southern softie who had never knowingly been further than ten metres from a Starbucks. That experience was mostly an unpleasant blur of stinging rain pelting her face and hiking for endless hours, while a barking ex-Forces man encouraged the group through the means of sweary shouting and telling stories of the hardships he had encountered while serving and comparing the group, unfavourably, with his old unit. Which, while perfectly fair, got a little bit old. Things like, 'if we were in Libya right now, you'd already be dead.'

The air was filled with the thunderous sound of the ground shaking and breaking and Lydia could no longer see the dead Pearls nearest to her, let alone the opening which led to the steps out. Finally, she recalled the outdoor survival instructor. His voice spoke loud and angry inside her head. 'In an avalanche, oxygen is your priority. You can live with broken bones but you cannae fuckin' last without air.'

Helpful. Thanks, pal. Lydia knew she was panicking, now. Speaking to a phantom of her memory and one she hadn't particularly liked, was surely the first sign of madness. She couldn't see and her eyes were burning. She wondered if a mains pipe had been ripped open and that there was poisonous gas filling the cave. That wasn't a calming thought.

She gripped her coin until she could get a hold of her racing thoughts. She told herself it was just the earth and grit making her eyes burn and that she was breathing good clean oxygen and that she was going to survive. She just needed to think. The pep talk didn't exactly help, but her autopilot must have kicked in as she had already pivoted around and begun working her way back into the middle of the cavern. She realised, seconds behind her deepest survival instinct, that she was looking for the throne. The King might have aged rapidly, their body decomposing somewhere on the floor ahead, but the throne was carved wood and inlaid precious metals and stones. It hadn't dissolved in a puff of smoke. It was the largest intact structure in the place. Her arms were out, but she kicked it before finding it with her hands.

The roof was coming down in chunks and a boulder landed to her right, narrowly missing spreading her brains across the dirt.

She felt for the back of the throne and tugged to pull it over. It didn't move. A moment of despair. There was no light, and the air was chokingly thick with earth and the sounds of moaning. She was going to be buried alive under Highgate Woods. She would have been better off being knocked out. She tugged again, leaning back with all her weight and trying to get the oversized chair to budge. And then it did. It rocked up onto the edges of its legs. With what felt like the last of her strength, she hauled hard and felt the throne go past the centre of gravity and fall. With the long back of the chair resting on the churning ground, it formed a slanted roof. She scrambled into the space created and put both arms in front of her face, trying to form an air pocket. Even though the air was choked and foul, she inflated her lungs as deeply as possible, knowing that every centilitre of air could mean another minute of survival, another minute for the rescue crew to find her and pull her out.

THE SHAKING earth and roaring sound of ripping, crunching, falling, eventually slowed and then stopped. It became strangely peaceful. Lydia could no longer see anything at all. There was no Pearl magic creating light in an enchanted subterranean playground, just dirt and rock and tree roots, churned up and thrown back, ready to start the organic process of rebuilding itself. Worms and beetles would tunnel through, seeds would grow, ripped roots would mulch down and new ones would be sent out from the trees. The ground would heal and it would be as if nothing had ever happened here. Except, Lydia supposed, the ground would be extra rich from all the human remains. Her body and Mr Smith's and, she fervently hoped, Maddie's. That was the tiny splinter she held onto in the dark. She had lost sight of Maddie and there was a small chance she had slipped away, making it back up the steps before the cave-in. If that had happened, Lydia had to stay alive. She had never realised what it felt to truly hate a person, but now she knew. She hated Maddie with an intensity which burned from inside and made her skin feel on fire. That might have been referred pain from her tissue compressing and slowly dying of oxygen deprivation, but she preferred to think of it as hatred. Bright, clear, burning, energetic hatred. She would survive so that she could check that Maddie was dead. Lydia couldn't grip her coin, her fingers didn't seem to be working. The space she had created with her arms was impossibly small. Who knew how many minutes of air she had left? The panic surged and she forced herself to ignore it. If she panicked she would gasp in air, use up her precious oxygen and die more quickly. The fallen earth was pressing against her folded arms, but she could lift her head a small amount. There was a pocket of space between her head and the back of the throne. It was a couple of inches at most, but it meant more air. She had enough, she told herself. More than enough. And Fleet would be coming.

IT WAS GETTING COLDER in the dark. Lydia had no idea how long she had been crouched beneath the fallen throne, but the intense pain from her cramped muscles told her that she couldn't take much more. Give Lydia something to hit, something to puzzle out, something to run from. Those she could do. Curled up here in the freezing darkness, lungs choked and a terrible silence blanketing her ears, unable to move, and she thought she might rather die.

CHAPTER TWENTY-EIGHT

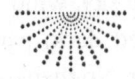

Lydia had been dozing. She had been dreaming, at least. She couldn't feel her coin in her hand anymore, but she could picture it there. And she had imagined other things, too. An arch of blue sky. Stretching her aching arms out wide. Straightening her back and breathing deeply, her lungs expanding with sweet clean air. The pain was almost gone. No. That wasn't true. At all. But it seemed further away somehow. Like it was happening outside The Fork on the street while she was sitting cosy in her favourite seat, a plate of buttered toast and a coffee on the table.

She wasn't an idiot. She knew this new comfort was not good news. It meant she was dying. Friendly brain chemicals and, maybe her Crow ancestors, were easing her passage to the great beyond. She would be the wind in the branches of the tree which shaded the Family tomb in Camberwell Cemetery. That didn't seem too bad.

There was a rumbling coming from above or maybe the side. Lydia had no sense of direction in the pitch black. Her eyes were tightly shut against the grit and she could no longer tell if she was still crouched underneath the tipped throne or whether she – or it – had been tumbled into a different position. Her arms were still folded in front of her face and she couldn't move.

The rumbling was sending vibrations through the earth and Lydia's first emotion was irritation. She was floating away in the dark and the vibrations were bringing her back to her body. A body which was flooded with pain and fear. Soaring in the wide blue sky, wind ruffling her feathers or crouched in the cramped dark, pain searing every nerve, every muscle. No contest. No thank you.

A thunderous ripping was accompanied by a draught of air. She sucked it in. Automatically and unthinkingly first and then, gradually, with new awareness. There was a strange sound, muffled and distant but getting closer. Voices. Calling her name. One voice in particular set her pulse racing and brought her thudding back to full consciousness. Fleet.

Blinding light against her closed eyelids. Instinctively, she kept them shut, even though she wanted to see what was happening. There was new air, that was clear, but there was a pattering of earth all around. Then a shout. 'I've got something.'

'That's it,' Fleet's voice. Unmistakable. 'Careful. She's underneath.'

More digging. More shouts and more air.

'Hang on, Lydia,' Fleet was saying from somewhere above.

And then there was a release of pressure from around her arms and torso. A voice she didn't recognise told her to keep her eyes shut, and that they were going to cover them to be sure. 'Too much light too quickly can damage your retinas.'

Her eyes were stinging, so Lydia could easily believe that. It was nothing, however, to the pain which was flooding through her body.

'Careful. Careful. Okay, Lydia, stay put, okay? We're

going to dig around you some more before we move you. Just hang in there, you're doing great.'

The rest of the rescue was a little hazy. Now that Lydia was back in her body, feeling the pain of her cramped muscles and the burning in her chest and throat, it was taking all of her concentration to hold still and not cry.

After what seemed like hours, but was later explained to be mere minutes, she was hauled out from underneath the throne.

Her face was rinsed with water and soft material bound over her eyes to stop her from opening them too quickly. Fleet's signature grew stronger and then she felt his hand taking hers and squeezing gently. 'We're going to the hospital to get you checked over.'

'Do it here,' Lydia said, her voice nothing more than a cracked whisper. She coughed violently and tried again.

'No can do,' the voice of the paramedic was closer than Lydia expected. Her blindness made her feel vulnerable.

'You need to be checked. And hydrated.'

Lydia wanted to argue but her throat hurt too much to speak. She shook her head, but could feel a deeper darkness encroaching.

When Lydia woke up, she knew instantly that she had lost the battle. She was in hospital. The institutional smell was unmistakable, along with the squeaking sound of footsteps on rubber flooring, and rings rattling on a rail as a curtain was pulled somewhere in the room.

Her tongue felt swollen, stuck to the roof of her mouth. She tried to produce some saliva, but her mouth felt desiccated. And her throat was raw. She peeled her lips open. 'Water.'

There was a rustle of movement.

'I'm here,' Fleet's voice was reassuringly close. 'Watch out, straw incoming.'

The water was possibly the best thing she had ever tasted. It beat the finest malt hands down. Although, now she had thought of whisky, she really wanted a nip. That would take the edge off the discomfort.

Besides, she'd had one hell of a day. She deserved a drink.

There was still something over her eyes. She opened them and saw the darkness of the material blindfold. Pinpricks of light exploded, and she waited for them to calm down before pulling the material.

'They said you have to keep... Never mind.'

Her eyes hurt, were streaming in the light, but Lydia blinked lots and the stinging gradually eased. Her vision returned, and the blurry shapes resolved into a bed with NHS blanket. A pale green chair pulled up close holding a worried-looking DCI.

'Hey,' Fleet said. 'That's gotta hurt.'

'Worth it,' Lydia said, drinking in the sight. 'You're okay?'

'I'm fine.' Fleet's mouth turned up at the corners. 'And I think I'm the one who should be asking that.'

'I'm sorry about your flat.'

'It's just stuff,' Fleet said.

'I'm sorry I pointed Maddie at you. The fire's my fault. I just couldn't have her go anywhere near Emma. Her kids...'

Lydia's eyes were stinging and she blinked furiously.

'It was the right call,' Fleet said, taking her hand. 'I'm just glad it worked.'

'Thank Feathers you were staying at The Fork,' Lydia said, smiling a little. 'What were the chances?'

Fleet's tentative smile matched her own. 'Yeah. Lucky that. Precognition paranoia for the win.'

'And listening to your very wise girlfriend.'

'That, too.' He squeezed her hand.

. . .

THE DOCTOR EXPLAINED that Lydia was extremely lucky. She didn't have crush syndrome or any of the other nasty-sounding hazards of being in a cave-in. She had been dehydrated, but they'd run fluid through an IV and her vitals were all looking good. 'Your blood oxygen is normal, which is excellent news, and there is no sign of organ or tissue damage.'

'Did they find the others?'

'Gale's body was recovered, but nobody else so far.' He squeezed her hand gently.

Lydia hoped the Pearl girl had made it out. She wasn't a member of the court and moved above ground so she assumed she wouldn't have crumbled like the old ones. She might have been a Pearl and an emissary of the court, but she was still just a kid.

'Maddie?'

Fleet shook his head. 'No sign. Yet.'

Lydia let her head fall back on the pillows. Hell Hawk. Of course she had escaped. It would be too much to ask that Maddie would have conveniently laid down and accepted death under the ground. She was too determined and too strong to let a little thing like being buried alive stop her.

A nurse wheeling a blood pressure monitor arrived to check on Lydia. 'Visiting hours finish at four,' he said to Fleet.

Fleet presented his warrant card, and the nurse rolled his eyes. 'Suit yourself. But don't blame me if one of the others yell at you. It's for infection control, you know.'

'It's fine,' Lydia said. 'You can go and check on your place. Maybe it's not as bad as we think. You might be able to salvage some of your stuff.'

'I'm not leaving.'

'Really, it's fine. I'm going to take a nap before dinner.'

The blood pressure cuff was inflating automatically, and the nurse was washing his hands and pretending not to listen. She lowered her voice. 'If you wanted to come back in later with some takeaway, I wouldn't complain. I'm not excited at the prospect of hospital food.' She glanced at the nurse. 'No offence.'

'None taken, treasure.' He released her from the cuff and Lydia rubbed her arm to get the feeling back. 'Especially if you want to bring in a little extra for me.' He winked at Fleet and moved to the next bed. There were four in the room, but only one other was currently occupied. Lydia assumed that wouldn't last and, if she had any intention of staying put, she would be worried about being able to sleep surrounded by strangers.

As soon as Fleet had left, Lydia got up and sussed out her exit route. Luckily, the staff were swamped with duties and the corridor outside the ward was deserted. There was a door open at the end which revealed a small office. She was in her rights to sign herself out, but it would be quicker and easier just to leave. She was still plugged into an IV, but after a couple of deep breaths, she pulled that out and held the puncture site until it stopped bleeding.

Clothes next. The locker next to the bed contained the bag that Fleet had brought and, thank feathers, it revealed clean jeans, underwear and a loose T-shirt. The curtains were closed around the other occupied bed so nobody had to witness the humiliating sight of Lydia getting winded after putting on her jeans and having to sit on the bed for a few moments until the room stopped spinning.

It occurred to her that it was a sign she should be resting in bed, but she couldn't stay still. Maddie's body hadn't been found. That meant she was out there somewhere. Maybe she was hurt and lying low to recover. Maybe she was still trapped underground. Or maybe she had got out before Lydia, discovered that Fleet hadn't really been in his flat when the fire took hold and was, at this very moment, following him with a gun.

No. Maddie wasn't superhuman. Lydia did up the laces on her Docs while she calmed herself down. If Maddie had escaped from the cave-in, she wouldn't have been completely unscathed. She would check hospitals. Just because the crew hadn't pulled her out didn't mean she hadn't been hurt. If she needed help, she would have given a false name, or maybe she collapsed on her way out of Highgate and was picked up. She could be lying in a bed in this very building, about to wake up any moment. What would she do then?

Docs on, T-shirt over head and jeans done up, Lydia was ready to move. The drawn curtains seemed to grow larger in her vision. They were hiding the bed. What were the chances? Suddenly, she was seized by a sense of dread. What if Maddie was lying in the bed next to her, hidden by those anonymous blank curtains? Her mind flashed through the images. Maddie found unconscious or delirious with concussion, rushed into the emergency department, treated and then shunted up here to this room. Maddie lying awake and fully alert, listening to Lydia speaking to Fleet. Fury that her plan to get rid of him had failed. Was that a shadow behind the curtain? A figure standing just the other side of the pale material, gathering strength to attack?

She had no weapon. There was a plastic jug and a cup on the table and nothing else. Not even a pen or pencil. She didn't know if she would be able to stab Maddie with a pen, but it would be nice to feel she had the option.

She produced her coin and squeezed it. Whether it was the adrenaline spike or her Crow magic, strength seemed to flow through her body. She stood, every sense on alert. She could hear Maddie breathing, but there were no other sounds from behind the curtain. Maddie was standing very still. Waiting.

Lydia knew she had to act fast. If she failed, Maddie would kill her. And if they attracted attention, she might hurt the staff or other patients, too. She launched herself across the gap between her bed and the curtains, aiming for the middle of the shadow, hoping to wind Maddie with her first blow.

Lydia stumbled forward, almost falling. She had empty fabric gathered in her fists and forward momentum carried her onward, her feet hitting the edge of the bed. She released the curtains and fell through, palms out to catch herself.

A woman with grey curled hair and a pale pink nightdress was standing on the other side of the bed, a cup of orange squash in her hand. She looked at Lydia with undisguised disgust. 'What the fuck are you playing at?'

Lydia apologised. 'Tripped.'

'Aye, right,' the woman said, calming a little. 'Mebbe stick to your side, eh?'

Lydia apologised again. Her heart was hammering, and she wiped her palms on her jeans.

It was official. She was going mad.

She had just poured a glass of room temperature water from the plastic jug and was chugging it down, when her phone buzzed with a text. It was Maddie.

Roof. Now.

CHAPTER TWENTY-NINE

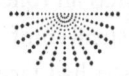

There was no choice. If Lydia didn't obey Maddie and meet her on the roof of the hospital, she would come looking for her. At this moment, there was a chance that Maddie believed Fleet to be dead. If she came to the ward, she might be there when Fleet came back with dinner.

Besides. This had to end.

At least she had seen Fleet one last time, Lydia thought as she got into the lift. At the top floor, she had to leave the lift and take the last flight of stairs to the roof. Her muscles seemed to be obeying her and she could breathe steadily, which was a relief. Still, getting trapped underground for a few hours wasn't the best preparation for tackling a trained killer in combat. She squeezed her coin and imagined strength and power flowing from it. She wasn't sure whether she could feel anything, but the shape and weight of the coin in her palm was comforting.

The sky was black and there was a little rain falling when Lydia pushed through the door to the roof. The drops struck her face, stinging her raw skin. She hadn't looked in a mirror since waking up in hospital and it crossed her mind that she might be horribly disfigured. Another great reason to end it all today.

Maddie was standing near to the low metal fence which edged the roof. She turned as Lydia approached and smiled like she had won the lottery. It reminded Lydia of her recurrent nightmare. Maddie on the roof looking like it was her birthday, wedding and Christmas all rolled together. At least Fleet wasn't here. That was the small comfort. She had kept him safe. He would be angry that she had faced Maddie alone and the message she had left with Auntie wouldn't help much, but he would be alive to be angry with her. That was what mattered.

'You made it,' Maddie said.

'I didn't have much choice,' Lydia said, stopping a couple of feet from Maddie. 'Are you going to threaten to kill me, again, because that's getting old.'

Maddie's smile dimmed. 'You should show me more respect.'

'I'm here, aren't I?' Lydia had walked slowly and with a slight limp. Now, she shifted as if in pain, and made sure to keep her posture slightly bowed. Beaten. In pain. Weak. 'Speaking of which, how did you get out unscathed?'

In truth, Maddie wasn't looking too clever. Her face and arms were smudged with dirt and blood, and her hair was matted, sticking out wildly on one side. When she had turned, Lydia had seen her holding her side, as if injured, although she had dropped her hands, now. They hung, open and ready for action. 'That was wild,' Maddie said. 'You weren't lying about the Pearls.'

'So, what's next for you?'

'That depends.'

'You've got the cup. You've killed your handler. And now your handler's handler is dead, too. What is keeping you here?'

'I think you know the answer to that.'

'I don't.'

'I'm proud of you,' Maddie said, and it sounded strangely sincere. 'You killed him. I knew you could do it.'

'That was the king. I didn't…'

'You walked Gale into that place knowing he wouldn't come out. Same thing as pulling the trigger.'

Lydia shook her head, ignoring the throb of pain in her temples. 'It really isn't.'

'It's okay,' Maddie took a step closer. 'We're not like other people, you and me, we're special.'

Lydia wanted to say that she wasn't anything like Maddie, but her mouth was full of feathers, choking back the lie.

'I know you see it, now. We should be together. That's why I sent a warning to your pet policeman.' She pulled a mock-sorrowful face, bottom lip out. 'I hope you're not too cross about that. I gave him a fighting chance, at least.'

'You arranged the fire.'

'Like I said, he had a chance to get out. But he didn't, did he? I saw the news.'

'You murdered him.' Lydia didn't think she was a wonderful actress, but found she didn't need to dig very deeply to sound outraged and devastated.

'I set you free,' Maddie said. 'He was always going to hold you back.'

'You want me to come with you?'

Maddie laughed and shook her head. 'I think I should stay here. We could run the Family together. I can take it from you, but I would rather we teamed up. I'm tired of being alone.'

'It's hard to get enthusiastic after seeing your last business partner. I don't fancy ending up hanging from a tree.'

Maddie waved a hand, dismissing Sergio Bastos. 'He wasn't my partner. It would be completely different for us.'

'For a while,' Lydia said. 'Until you get bored. Or I piss you off.'

'You already piss me off,' Maddie snapped. 'I've never known anybody to be as annoyingly stubborn as you. Except me.' She smiled again, showing the impeccable orthodontic work that had no doubt set back Uncle John a fair whack. 'That's the point. We're made for each other.'

'Is that why you wanted Fleet out of my life?'

'Of course. I need space in your heart. I'm very needy. You know that.'

Lydia could feel Maddie's power plucking at her. She forced herself to relax, to let it happen. She had to let Maddie feel safe and in control. 'I can't do it. You killed Fleet. You killed Sergio. You're basically a monster.'

Anger and disappointment flashed across Maddie's face before her features smoothed. 'I guess I was wrong about you. You don't understand, after all. Oh well.'

Lydia felt her legs pulled by Maddie's power. In her mind, she welded her feet to the ground. In reality, she stumbled toward the edge of the roof, powerless to stop her legs from moving. She didn't have to pretend to show sudden terror. 'So, this is it? Bit unimaginative. Thought you might mix it up.'

Maddie laughed, and the sound cut through Lydia. She was so far gone, she barely seemed human. Whatever was left of the girl Lydia remembered from her childhood, it was surely burned away by her actions. That was something her mother had said when Lydia was very young. People weren't good or bad, they did good or bad things. It didn't matter what you thought, it mattered what you did.

'I will find everyone you have ever cared for, you know.'

The wind was blowing straight into Lydia's face, making her eyes water. She blinked to clear her vision and felt the salt water cold on her cheeks.

'Fleet was just the start.'

'They haven't done anything to you,' Lydia said, hating the wobble in her voice even though she knew it was a good thing. The weaker and more defeated Maddie thought she was, the more chance Lydia had of catching her off guard.

'You know that's not true,' Maddie said.

Hating herself as she did so, Lydia made a last attempt to protect Emma and her parents. If this plan didn't work and Maddie survived, she had to put her off the scent. Of course, that meant putting somebody else in danger, but Lydia had never claimed to be a good person. 'It's Paul. He's the reason I can't leave.'

'Fox?'

'You remember we had a thing? Back in the day? Well, it started again. I love him.'

'Nice try,' Maddie was smiling, but there was the smallest hint of uncertainty.

Lydia clutched that uncertainty to her heart, squeezed it close and prayed it would be enough to stop Maddie from hurting Emma. If this didn't work. But it had to work.

She was at the edge, now. If Maddie just nudged her over, using her mind, then Lydia would die for nothing. She had to get Maddie closer.

'Wait!'

'Last words? I don't think so.'

'You can't kill me.'

She felt her body lurch and for a sickening moment her feet lost purchase on the ground and she was hanging over the edge, all centre of balance off and only Maddie's will stopping her from freewheeling into the air. 'Wait! You don't want to do this!'

'I do,' Maddie said, eerily calm. 'I really do.'

'I left insurance.'

And her feet were making full contact on the concrete, her body tilted back and away from the edge of the roof. She felt the control release a little and she stumbled back.

Maddie had taken a step closer. Still not in arm's reach, but closer. 'I'm listening.'

Lydia was gasping for breath, tears still streaming down her face, so it wasn't much of a stretch to struggle to speak. She exaggerated a little, playing for time, and Maddie folded her arms, waiting.

Lydia had played this moment over and over in her mind. The confident part of her wanted to take Maddie on, to straighten up and throw her Crow power and see if she could beat her one-on-one.

But, as always, her mind ran through the possibilities. If she failed, Maddie would kill her instantly. And then she would hurt Emma. And Fleet. And, now, possibly Paul Fox. And maybe her parents, and anybody who had ever meant anything to her. It was too big a risk. Lydia had to make sure.

Maddie's hold over her was like bands of steel wrapping around her body, but also like having Jason on board, the sense of something inside stretching its limbs within hers and inhabiting her every organ and blood vessel and nerve. She wanted to test it, to see if she could break the bond, but didn't want to alert Maddie to her power. She hoped she was strong enough to overcome Maddie's control for a few seconds and, if she managed to catch her by surprise, that would be all she needed. If she tested it and failed, though, Maddie would be on alert and that could be all the edge she would need to keep Lydia's body under control. She was itching with the desire to flex and push back and it was taking every ounce of self-control she had to hold herself in check. All the while acting desperate and terrified and as if she was struggling. She hung her head down, doubled over as far as she could with Maddie holding her in place, and forced her words out in a strangled whisper.

'What?' Maddie took another step closer.

'Charlie,' Lydia said, using the only name she knew had ever frightened Maddie.

'What about Charlie?'

Another garbled whisper. She could feel the cold annoyance radiating from Maddie. Either her frustration would snap and she would shove Lydia over the edge of the building or, perhaps, pull out a knife and stab her to get it over with. Or, and this was crucial, she might take another step and bring herself close enough for Lydia to make her move.

She took another step.

Like a bird taking flight, Lydia unfurled her wings and threw everything she had outwards. Maddie's control over her body snapped in an instant and she was propelled forward. Before she could react, Lydia had wrapped her arms around Maddie and was pulling her over to the edge of the roof.

Maddie's split second of surprise had passed and she was fighting back with everything she had, both physically and with her controlling power. Lydia could feel the attack, trying to stop her muscles from behaving, trying to pull her away from the edge.

She was grateful for the hours she had spent being flipped and grappled on the mat, otherwise she wouldn't have lasted a single second with Maddie. She was throwing her Crow whammy at Maddie, too, blocking her and attacking with the same motion, feeling the thousands of tiny hearts, beating in time, wings sweeping the air and feathers filling her mouth.

Another step and she half-fell, half-jumped, dragging Maddie along with her.

CHAPTER THIRTY

The wind rushed past Lydia as she fell. She couldn't see as her eyes had filled with tears from the cold air and the world was a blurry mess in shades of grey and brown. She couldn't blink to clear her vision, couldn't think past the sharp terror, which was like a single high note screaming in her ears. She had been falling for a second and also forever.

The air finally whipped away the water from her eyes, enough that she could see the ground below. Her arms were spread wide, desperately trying to slow her descent and a tiny part of her brain, the oldest part, told her to flap her arms to give herself a little uplift to catch a thermal. But she wasn't a bird, she was a human. She knew she couldn't fly.

Another second and the ground was very close. There wasn't time. Lydia knew she was falling to her death and that there wasn't time to be thinking this much. It simply wasn't possible. Which meant she was probably already dead. Lying on the concrete with her wings smashed, and these were the last random firings of her neurons before the lights went out for good.

Her heartbeat was in her ears, pounding in panic, but the sound was like an orchestra. A thousand small hearts beating with hers, but much faster, filling in the gaps in her pulse so that it was a constant noise. Not overwhelming, but uplifting. The taste of feathers in the back of her throat and the sharp scrape of talons on stone. At once, she felt it. A draught of air from beneath, lifting her up and slowing her fall. She saw the blockwork of the building, a window, and then another. Separate and distinct impressions which were like slow motion after the blur of before. There was something underneath her, cradling her body. She felt her shoulders straighten and her arms lengthen, her wings spreading wide.

Then she hit the pavement.

Her arms were slightly outstretched and took the force of the fall along with her knees. She felt her forearm snap, and the pain whooshed like fire up to her shoulder. She lay on the concrete as if at the bottom of a pool. The noise of the city was muffled and her ears were still pounding with the drumming heartbeats. Slowly they faded and Lydia began to make sense of what she was seeing.

Maddie was lying a few feet away, on her back. Her head was turned toward Lydia and her eyes were open and fixed. Quite dead.

The pain in Lydia's arm was vying for attention with a very bad feeling in her face. Her nose was broken for sure, and possibly some other small bones too. She didn't want to move her legs to test her knees for fear of what fresh pain she would unleash. Instead she rested her cheek on the cold ground and dragged lungfuls of air in through her chapped lips.

She shifted and felt her arm complain, but in that moment she knew she would heal. Maddie had hit the ground first which meant that whatever Lydia had felt had not been a hallucination brought on by mortal danger. She had slowed her descent enough to survive. A pool of blood was spreading out from beneath Maddie's head. A demonstration of what ought to have happened to Lydia, too.

She dragged another breath as the sound of sirens in the distance brought her more fully into the present. She couldn't smell the exhaust and blocked drains and dropped takeaway containers which made up the London bouquet, but she knew they were there. She had fallen and her city had caught her.

Lying in her double bed with freshly changed sheets, a cup of coffee laced with a secret splash of whisky that Emma had provided, and Fleet in the kitchen making a late breakfast of scrambled eggs and crispy bacon, Lydia though that plunging several floors off a building had its advantages. She shifted and felt a bolt of pain from her broken left arm and sprained shoulder and thought that maybe it wasn't something that she ought to do on a regular basis.

She picked up her phone and checked her messages. Her mum had replied that they were having a lovely holiday and Maria had sent a terse email demanding an update on the whereabouts of the silver cup. She dialled her number, feeling magnanimous in her lovely alive-ness. 'This isn't the service I'm used to,' Maria said. 'I hope you have good news for me.'

'I found the cup,' Lydia said. 'But I don't have it. Best guess, it's buried in Highgate Woods.'

'Is that a joke?'

'Nope,' Lydia said, wincing as she shifted. 'I know you think I stole it, but I didn't. And neither did any Crow. When I say your best chance of finding it is to excavate the recent cave-in in Highgate Woods, I'm telling you the truth. And that's the end of my favour. We're even.'

'I don't think so,' Maria began, 'this is hardly-'

'I am the head of the Crow Family and I located a highly

important Silver relic as a personal favour. My advice is that you take better care of your things in future.'

Hanging up on Maria was always enjoyable and Lydia leaned back, closed her eyes, and savoured the moment. There would be fall out, of course, but that was for another day.

When she opened her eyes, she found Jason hovering at the end of her bed. He was staying out of the kitchen because Fleet was using it, but she knew it was taking an enormous amount of self-control. 'He won't be much longer,' she said.

'It's not that,' Jason said, pushing the sleeves of his suit jacket up even further. 'There's something I wanted to ask you.'

'Fire away,' Lydia said. Her stomach dipped at the nervousness in Jason's voice.

'You know the bracelet. It's not that I'm not grateful...'

His form was shimmering and Lydia patted the bed in an invitation for him to come closer. 'What is it?'

'I don't think I want to stay. After you... Go.'

'After I die?'

'Yeah. Or if you move to Fleet's place. Or somewhere else. I don't want you to feel responsible for me. And I don't think I want to be like this forever. I mean, it's good, now. I'm kind of happy. I like living with you and I like helping out but, you know, everything ends.'

'You don't have to feel guilty,' Lydia began. 'I like living with you, too. You're not a responsibility, you're my friend.'

His face brightened. 'I know. And I feel the same. I mean, you're my friend.'

Lydia felt a sudden lump in her throat. 'Well, I'm glad that's settled.'

They looked awkwardly at each other for a beat longer. Lydia tried to lighten the moment. 'I should jump off a building more often.'

Jason smiled sadly. 'Everything ends,' he said again. 'Or it should.'

Fleet pushed the door open and Jason slipped past him before Lydia could say anything else. 'Your grill pan is a disgrace.' Fleet had found a tray from somewhere, possibly one he had brought from his flat as Lydia was pretty damn certain she didn't own such a thing, and he placed it on her lap. 'Were you talking to yourself just now?'

'Jason,' Lydia said and watched Fleet straighten and look around the room.

'He's not here. You can relax.'

Fleet sat next to her on the bed, stealing a piece of bacon. 'What do you think John is going to do?'

'Can you just relax, woman? You did it. You don't have to worry about Smith or Maddie. It's over.'

Lydia dug into the eggs and bacon, trying to relax.

'No bad feelings,' Fleet tapped his temple. 'No premonitions, bad dreams... nothing.'

After she had finished her breakfast Lydia relaxed back against the pillows. Her eyes wanted to drift shut and, after a few minutes of battling, she let them. Fleet was right. She had won. Maddie was dead. Smith was dead. She was free. Fleet was safe. Emma was safe. She still had to deal with John and Daisy. And no doubt Aiden was hovering somewhere outside the building, kept at bay by Fleet for the time being, but waiting to march into her office with a line of complaints and concerns and new jobs. Being head of the Crow Family as well as running Crow Investigations was a crazy idea. Two full-time jobs squished into one life, but it was her life. Her choice. She was drifting off, now, could feel sleep tugging at her sleeve. Her stomach swooped as her centre of gravity altered. She was rising up into the air, wings stretched wide. The sky wasn't blue, it was a multitude of tones from pale grey to purple to a bright cerulean. The air currents were shifting within it, whirlpools and vortexes forming and disappearing, and a warm draught lifting her higher. She wasn't alone, there were crows flying with her. Hundreds of black shapes matching her every move. Lydia knew she was asleep, now, so she wasn't frightened when one of the crows came very close and its beak opened to greet her. Maybe it was her grandfather. Or great-great grandmother. Or maybe it was Maddie, finally arrived home to the flock.

One thing Lydia knew for certain, dream or not, was that she couldn't really fly. Not in the real waking world. But she also knew she no longer had a fear of heights.

She was no longer afraid of falling.

THE END

ACKNOWLEDGMENTS

I am deeply grateful to you, dear reader, for embracing the Crow Investigations series. I am having so much fun writing about Lydia, Fleet and the Families, and can't believe I get to call it my job!

Thank you to my friends and family for their love and support, and to my brilliant publishing team. Especially my wonderful early readers, editor and designer.

In particular, thanks to Beth Farrar, Karen Heenan, Jenni Gudgeon, Caroline Nicklin, Paula Searle, Judy Grivas, Deborah Forrester, and David Wood.

Thank you to my lovely writer friends, especially Clodagh Murphy, Hannah Ellis, Keris Stainton, Nadine Kirtzinger, and Sally Calder. Our group chats and Zoom sessions in lockdown have kept me halfway sane - thank you! And I can't wait to see you all in Real Life.

As always, special thanks to my patient, clever, loving husband. You are the best. And I'm not just saying that because you do all the accounts.

LOVE URBAN FANTASY?

The Lost Girls

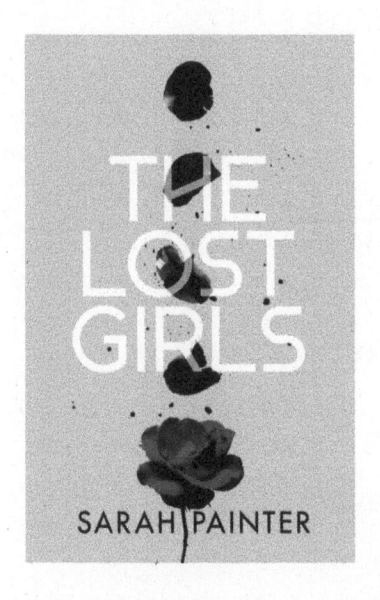

A 'dark and twisty' standalone urban fantasy set in Edinburgh, from bestselling author Sarah Painter.

Around the world girls are being hunted...

Rose must solve the puzzle of her impossible life – before it's too late.

AVAILABLE NOW!

ABOUT THE AUTHOR

Before writing books, Sarah Painter worked as a freelance magazine journalist, blogger and editor, combining this 'career' with amateur child-wrangling (AKA motherhood).

Sarah lives in rural Scotland with her children and husband. She drinks too much tea, loves the work of Joss Whedon, and is the proud owner of a writing shed.

Visit the web address below to sign-up to the Sarah Painter readers' club. It's quick and easy to join, and you'll get book release news, giveaways and exclusive FREE stuff!

geni.us/Club

facebook.com/SarahPainterBooks
twitter.com/sarahrpainter
instagram.com/sarahpainterbooks